The Inheritance:

A Chapman Family Mystery

D1555529

© 2021, Andrew P. Shafe

ISBN: 9798599818472

Cornish Morning

Hedgerows waking,
pasties baking,
salt-sea smells,
ocean swells,

grey gulls calling,
bright boats trawling,
buoys bobbing,
sea pinks nodding,

tussocked moors,
rocky shores,
breakers beaching,
seaweed reaching,

harbor sights,
grassy heights,
cliff-trail pleasures,
tide pool treasures,

hidden coves,
tidal troves,
secret stairs,
smugglers' lairs,

sunlight glistening,
headlands listening,
blue day dawning,
Cornish morning.

A good man leaves an inheritance to his children's children…
Proverbs 13:22 (ESV)

The boundary lines have fallen for me in pleasant places;
surely I have a delightful inheritance.
Psalm 16:6 (NIV)

With heartfelt thanks to Martyn and John for encouraging me in writing,
Hillebrand for paving the way and giving excellent feedback, and Ethan
and Dwain for their tireless editing.

And of course love and thanks to my dearest Cathy for patience and
encouragement, and Holly, Hannah, Ethan and JJ for being the real
Chapman family, following your mother and me on our own amazing
adventures by God's grace.

In memory of my great, great grandfather, Captain George Tolman Ralls,
master of the 'City of Auckland,' and his amazing wife, Adelaide, whose
courage and strength ensured the continuation of our family tree.

Above all, I dedicate this to my Savior Jesus, for His glory.
Surely, I have a delightful inheritance in Him.

Contents

Prologue

He lurched upwards—tripping, stumbling, his heart pounding in his chest. With one arm he desperately clutched the precious package; with the other he vainly attempted to ward off the clutching branches of the wind-twisted pines, their bony fingers snatching at him across the path. His shirt was soaked with sweat despite the chill night air, and a terribly sharp pain under his ribs caused him to gasp as he forced himself onward. A quick glance over his shoulder showed that the village below was already shrouded in sea mist, but a few roving points of light betrayed the presence of his pursuers.

He turned back and struggled on, his thoughts a confused jumble. He had known for some days that he was being watched—the hostile glances and whispered accusations were becoming more frequent—and he knew that it was only a matter of time before he was publicly accused and even arrested. He had started sleeping fully dressed, never sure of when the crisis might come, but even so, the actual confrontation that night had come as a brutal surprise—the sudden pounding on the door, the harsh cries of "heretic!" wrenching him from sleep into a confusion of thought and action.

He had planned an escape route several days before, and that had enabled him to will his body forward, even as his mind struggled to clear. Shaken but resolute, he had snatched up the heavy leather pouch beside the bed and flung himself through the open window onto the low roof of the scullery. Rolling off he had landed heavily in the garden, then clambered awkwardly over the low fence into the dark lane behind the house, surprising a scavenging dog that shied away in alarm before unleashing a torrent of barks after the shadowy fugitive.

Turning right at the forge, across the packhorse bridge, and then up the narrow track behind the crofters' cottages, he had willed himself to run, run, run his very fastest.

He stumbled on, gripping his cherished package even tighter. Yes, it would have been safer kept permanently hidden away, but that would have defeated its purpose—the reason for its being. Instead for months now he had carried it secretly with him to the nearby villages, sharing its blessing with the dedicated few who, like him, would risk life itself for a share in its treasure.

Risk life itself. That was clear—it must not be found, whatever the cost. He had to make it to the hiding place he had prepared, secure from those...those *rabid wolves* that lusted for its destruction. Even if he himself were taken, he could be assured that it would be safe, and his successor could retrieve it when the crisis had passed.

Risking another glance backwards, he saw with a shock that the searching lights were much closer, following his path, scenting their quarry was at hand. Turning back, his foot caught on an unseen root and he found himself falling, tumbling off the path into space, his flailing arms flinging out in a vain attempt to save himself, his precious package flying out of his grasp into the darkness. With a jolt that knocked the breath from his body, he hit the ground and rolled into a thorny bush by the side of the path.

For a moment he lay there, stunned. His mind, unable to immediately process what had happened, grew slowly aware of multiple sensations: the dampness of the grassy verge seeping into his breeches, a sudden gust of wind chilling his sweat-soaked back, the sharp pain and trickle of blood from a cut on his knee. A great weariness descended on him. Surely it would be easier to just lie there—to let them have him. He was so tired, and death for him was not to be feared.

But then an inner voice swept over his confused thoughts, bringing a sudden clarity. It was not just about him. His treasure was the important thing. They wanted it. They feared it. They hated it because it had power—yes, power to *dethrone* them.

With a sudden panic he realized he had lost the bag as he fell.

"Lord, Thy strength…please," he gasped.

Then, as if in immediate answer to his prayer, his searching hand found the leather bag, wet with dew, and grasping it, he felt an unseen force lifting him to his feet and pushing him on up the path.

A yell from behind told him that he had been spotted, but *praise God* it was not much further now. Right at the fork, up the stone steps, through the lych-gate, and the gray bulk of the chapel loomed up suddenly from the gathering mist.

Ignoring the main entrance, he skirted the stone walls to the right, ducking under the branches of a twisted yew tree, and snatched up the iron key from its hiding place near the chancel door. His blood pounding in his ears, he fumbled with the lock, murmuring another prayer for help, then falling into the darkened chapel as the key turned suddenly beneath his shaking hands.

There was not a moment to lose. Lurching forward he directed his weary legs towards a point on the far side of the nave, not even noticing the pain as he struck his shin against the end of a wooden pew. His practiced hands located the iron support in the semi-darkness, and his firm jerks down and across were rewarded with a slight grating noise as a stone block slid sideways several inches.

"There'll be no sanctuary for you here, filthy lollard!"

The cruel yell came from the other side of the oaken doors and a terrific pounding and crashing showed he had only a few seconds left. Heaving the package into the hiding place, he pushed the support back up, securing it from sight.

"Thank you, Father," he breathed. "Protect thine own."

The burden he had borne lifted suddenly from His heart, as if he was already assured of the answer to his prayer. His own safety meant nothing now, now that *it* was safe.

Ignoring the violent sounds from the other end of the aisle, he moved up to the altar steps, and falling on his knees, spread his arms out to heaven under the stained glass image of Christ on the cross. As the wooden doors gave in suddenly with a jarring crash, he closed his eyes.

"I am thine, Jesus. Thy will be done."

Chapter 1 - Are We There Yet?

Emily sighed, her arm propped against the window and her eyes following the monotonous passage of hedgerows and trees as the minivan sped along the motorway. Slowly sliding trails of raindrops gave testimony to the frequent showers that had fallen from the low gray sky since that morning.

"What's up, sweetheart?" Her father, his eyes on the road ahead, had noticed the slight sound, even with the impressive level of noise a family of six could produce when squeezed into an enclosed space.

"I thought the English countryside was supposed to be a little more interesting—you know, rolling hills, church towers, castles…" Emily tapped on the window as they passed several huge container trucks, stranded at the side of the wet road like beached whales. A line of scrubby hedges behind obscured any possible view of the landscape. The Chapman family was on the move again and, not liking change very much, sixteen-year-old Emily was feeling decidedly unsettled—a feeling not helped by the moodiness of the weather.

"Well, this isn't the most interesting stretch of road I've ever driven on," her father admitted, frowning a little as the driver of the old yellow sports car ahead seemed to be paying more attention to his map than the road. "It does seem to be brightening up, though. What's everyone else up to?"

Craning her neck, Emily took a quick appraisal of the rest of the family, squeezed among a confusion of pillows, books, toys and water bottles. "Rachel's looking at a horse magazine and listening to music which is a little *loud.*" She frowned at her sister whose mp3 player was audible even with her headphones in. "Danny's reading his chess book and tapping on it," Emily continued, trying unsuccessfully to hide her annoyance, "and Stevie's being noisy as well and…er, what are you doing Stevie?"

Her seven year-old brother sitting next to her popped his head up from where it had been buried somewhere down around his feet. He paused in the loud

9

humming which he always seemed to produce when he was concentrating. "I dropped my thing."

"Your what?"

His freckled face gave a sudden grin. "My string thing--under mommy's seat!"

"Hold on, I'll get it for you—whatever it is." With another sigh, Emily reached under the seat in front of her and patted around.

"That's dangerous, you know," warned Danny looking up from his book. "You remember when we found that old taco all smushed up under the seat when we were cleaning out the car that time?" A redheaded ten year-old, Danny was an expert on all things weird and wonderful.

Emily hurriedly pulled her hand back and displayed her finds to her little brother, wrinkling her nose.

"Oh, boy, all kinds of stuff!" he exclaimed, poking at a cracked marble, a gold foil candy wrapper, a piece of Lego, a length of thick, black cord, and a toy soldier with a pretzel around its neck.

"So which one is your thing?"

"This," said Stevie in triumph, grabbing the black cord. "It's my slingshot."

"Er, that's Mommy's sunglasses strap—the one she's been missing," informed fourteen-year old Rachel matter-of-factly from the back, popping out her ear-bud headphones.

"That's okay," the children's mother volunteered absently from her cramped position in the front seat.

Their father glanced beside him with a wry smile. No matter how carefully he packed, there was always a whole slew of last minute odds and ends that had to fit somewhere in the car, and invariably they ended up wedged around his wife, Kathie. She was twisted sideways now, one foot resting on the dash, the other slotted into a ridiculously small space on the floor between two water bottles, a backpack, the camera case, a box of Kleenex and a Ziploc bag of chocolate chip cookies—rather crushed and crumbly now, but still available for emergencies. And in the midst of the jumble, his wife was absorbed in an intricate cross-stitch, bordered by primroses. How she could manage to pinpoint a millimeter square while bouncing along at seventy miles per hour he just couldn't imagine.

"You know, dear, this has been a long stretch." She looked up briefly from her work. "When's the next rest area?"

"Aha, I just saw the sign—there's one coming up in about five minutes, I think. My schedule says we can take a good 20-minute break."

His wife glanced at him with a raised eyebrow. Dave Chapman was big on schedules—at least when driving. He had printed out directions from the web, complete with projected times for arriving at each major town, time for breaks, and the all-important final time of arrival, highlighted in green. She didn't want to feel rushed on an already fairly stressful day, but decided she wouldn't say anything for now. God's in control, she reminded herself.

Dad raised his voice. "Are you ready for a break, kids—and maybe we could rustle up an ice cream somewhere?" Loud cheers accompanied this statement, and four eager faces started scanning the road ahead for the coming exit.

10

Now that he'd mentioned it out loud, Dad realized that he couldn't wait to take a break himself. The car journey had been a decidedly long one already, and he was finding it increasingly difficult to adjust his body into a position that didn't protest back.

This job assignment had certainly meant a new life in so many different ways, not the least of it all the travelling--first uprooting the whole clan from their comfortable existence back in Oregon and flying goodness knows how many miles over to Europe, then the last two months tooling all over the Savoy region of France researching the history of Protestant persecution in the area. And there were still three months left to go. Writing articles and stories for a Christian history magazine sure fit well with his love of the past, but he was used to being in one spot to do it. *Could he even make the transition to this new sort of work successfully?* He still wasn't sure. And what about Kathie and the kids? He and his wife had prayerfully decided to home school their four children this term and take this trip as a family, hoping both to mold them all together more, and give them the rare chance of learning firsthand about other places and cultures. In fact, that had been a large motivating factor in taking the assignment in the first place, but it hadn't been all fun and games, *no sir*. It had been a huge transition, and everyone was still adjusting to the new lifestyle.

He changed his grip on the wheel and slid his rear sideways half an inch, wincing a little at the resulting pain. The English weather was living up to its reputation for sogginess, and the wet roads did nothing to help him relax. Since they had crossed on the ferry from Calais that morning it had been nothing but gray skies and slick conditions—and that after a long drive through France the day before. No wonder he was tired.

"I see the sign!" shouted Danny suddenly, interrupting Dad's musings.

The children strained to look out the front of the van, eager for a sight of their goal.

"Hmm, they seem a little excited," grunted Dad.

Mom extracted herself stiffly from her nest, searching for her sandals in the confusion at her feet. "No wonder!" she exclaimed. "They've been drinking all morning. Shoes on everyone! Emily, help Stevie find his, please. You know how they tend to worm their way into some dark corner."

There was a sudden burst of activity in the back seats and by the time the van turned into the parking area, everyone was pretty much ready to go, peering out at the rest area facilities which were in a long, low building of glass and metal tubing, looking like some kind of alien mother ship that had touched down in the clearing. It evidently housed not only toilets, but a small café, coffee bar and gift shop.

"There's a spot, by the doors," indicated Mom who was chief parking-space finder.

"Perfect," said her husband. "We can...whoa!" Another car had appeared out of nowhere and muscled its way into the space, barely missing their front fender. Dad had to slam on the brakes. "Where on earth did *he* spring from!" he exclaimed, recognizing with surprise the same yellow sports car he had seen earlier.

"That wasn't very nice," frowned Rachel.

"Well, it was rather rude," her father admitted, trying not to say what he was really thinking. "He must be in some sort of hurry."

"Maybe he's been drinking all morning, too," suggested Stevie.

"Maybe," laughed Mom. Even Dad had to smile.

They found another parking space under a dripping oak tree not too far away from the entry, and after a tangle of arms being thrust into coat sleeves and the chasing down of a rogue water bottle that had bounced out and under the van, they were ready, enjoying the clean, damp freshness of the outside air.

Mom beckoned to the girls and started off at a trot. She called back over her shoulder. "Will you take the boys, and we'll meet you at the café? We girls are in rather a hurry here!"

◈❧◈

Ten minutes later the family was seated around a glass table by a window, the children and Mom enjoying their ice creams and poring over the worn road atlas in front of them while Dad stretched out his legs, making a mental effort to relax and not look at his watch. The sudden appearance of the sun outside sent diagonal shafts of light across the table before them, and Dad inhaled a deep, satisfying sniff of his favorite smell in the entire world—fragrant creamy coffee. He took a careful sip from his steaming cup and nodded his head, impressed. This was actually one of the best white chocolate mochas he'd ever tasted. Not the sort of thing that should be rushed.

He glanced down at his schedule. Maybe they could stretch their break to twenty-five minutes. They could make it up somewhere, couldn't they? He would just try not to worry about it right now. "Ah, thank you God for a place to take a break!" he said out loud, trying to reinforce that conviction.

"Where are we, Daddy?" inquired Danny peering at the map sideways while trying to catch a drip of mint chocolate chip that had almost made its way clear to his elbow.

His father leaned forward. He loved maps, and this was a great way to occupy his mind. "Well, here's where we got off the ferry this morning, at Dover, and then we took this motorway across here, below London, and now we're here, near Basingstoke."

"And where's Cromwell?" piped in Stevie. His mother smiled at his mistake, and the perfect mustache and beard of melted chocolate that gave him a look like some sort of junior musketeer.

"Cornwall. It's this whole part here—with lots of rocky coves and beaches. We're planning to stay in this little village--Penrithen." She pointed at a tiny black dot about midway up the western coastline.

"When will we get there?"

Ah, the age-old question, and probably not the last time it would be asked that day. "According to my schedule, about five-thirty this evening," Dad interjected.

"But that's in God's hands, right, dear?" reminded his wife, not wanting to catch his worry bug today.

"That's ages of time to go!" Stevie's face looked very glum.

"And still such a long way," said Rachel with a sigh.

"Don't worry. The scenery will get much more interesting as soon as we leave the motorway," assured her mother.

"And I've got a great game to play," put in her dad, coming up with the idea suddenly. "It's called 'Pub Cricket'."

This brought a chorus of questions from the sticky faces surrounding him.

He held up his hand. "Listen, it's simple. You know how in baseball the goal is to score runs. Well, cricket is an English game with the same goal."

"You said I can't throw a ball in the car after what happened last time," said Stevie seriously.

"That's right," said his dad, considering.

"Do we play it on the car roof? Cause if we do we'll need suction cups on our shoes and a great big net." Danny always liked to come up with wacky ideas. He gave a sideways glance at his dad while he sucked the ice cream out of the bottom of his cone.

"Okay weirdoes," smiled Dad. "Listen up. There are lots of inns or public houses in England—people here call them 'pubs.' They are all named something and usually have a painted sign hanging outside with the name and a matching picture. The first person who is up to bat—that means it's their turn—gets a run for every leg in the inn's name."

"Every leg?" Emily was puzzled.

"Yes. Suppose we pass one called "The Jolly Farmer." A farmer would have two legs so you'd get two runs. If the next is called 'The Racehorse' you'd get four runs—four legs, see? If there are no legs, like 'The Royal Oak', the person is out and the next is up to bat."

"What if the Jolly Farmer only has one leg?" inquired Danny mischievously.

"Then he probably wouldn't be very jolly," replied Rachel. "But either way, you'd only get one run!"

"Can I play?" asked Stevie. "Maybe I'll get 'The Centipede'!"

They all laughed. Dad glanced at his watch. "Okay, we need to get going. Let's finish up and hit the road again."

৵৯৫

Twenty-nine minutes and thirty seconds. His schedule wasn't *that* flexible.

They were waiting for Danny to come back from washing his hands, and by the amount of time he was taking, Dad wondered if the boy had decided to brush his teeth and wash his hair as well.

A sudden commotion over by the café counter caused them all to turn their attention that way. A tall, intimidating-looking man was arguing with the cashier about something, thumping his fist on the counter as his face beneath his untidy mop of gray hair grew red with anger. Obviously not pleased with her responses, the man yelled something that they couldn't quite understand, shook his fist in the surprised lady's face, and stormed off towards the exit. Unfortunately, Danny chose just that moment to appear from the restroom door, stepping right into the man's path. The man had to leap aside to avoid a collision. He stooped over the alarmed boy and fairly shouted in his face. "Watch where you're going!"

Danny stood frozen in his tracks, his face a mask of fear. The man snorted in disgust, threw his rain jacket angrily over his broad shoulders and strode out of the building. Too surprised to react, the rest of the family watched through the windows as he headed over to his car—the same yellow sports car that had almost hit them as they arrived.

"Are you okay, son?" Dad shook himself and hurried over, Mom just behind.

"I, I think so," stammered Danny, still in shock and his eyes beginning to water.

"Let's pray," said Mom, giving him a squeeze.

"And pray for that man," put in Emily. "I think he needs it."

"Well, maybe…" said Dad, unenthusiastically. Or maybe they could save a few minutes of his precious schedule by skipping praying for the guy, especially when he would rather go give him what for.

"That's a good idea," agreed his mother, firmly. "Let's do it right now before we forget."

⊰⊱

It wasn't long after they resumed their journey that they left the motorway and turned onto a two-lane road. "We're now on the A43," announced Danny, his nose buried in the road atlas. Dad had given it to him to try to get the boy's mind off of his recent shock. "There should be some towns coming up pretty soon," he added, looking up.

"Don't forget to keep your eyes peeled for those signs," reminded his mother. "Who's up to bat first?"

"Can I be first," begged Stevie, who was always worried about getting left out.

"May I please," said Dad.

"May I please be first?"

"Okay. I'll let you know when we're getting near to a town." Dad was feeling like a new man after the break and had found a comfortable groove in his seat. He had tried to consciously put aside his worries and concentrate on where they were headed: *Cornwall*, the county on the southwestern peninsular of England, and the home of rocky coves, tussocked moors and secretive fishing villages, not to mention the historical haunt of smugglers, wreckers and pirates—at least that was how he had described it to the four enthralled children. After immigrating to the United States when he was a teenager, he had so missed the Cornish coast where he had spent so many summers as a boy. It was a chance for the family to have a nice two-week vacation before the continuation of his assignment on this side of the Channel, and maybe they'd even get some sunshine. Cornwall was supposed to get some of the best weather in the British Isles, though it was still only late spring.

As if in answer to his hopes, the sky had indeed brightened up considerably, and the sudden appearance of the sun had given a vibrant glow to the rain-soaked fields lying in sodden waves off of both sides of the road. Emily noticed with satisfaction that she could now clearly see her missing rolling hills with dark patches of trees nestled comfortably in the nooks and crannies of the landscape, solid square church towers here and there in the distance betraying the location of hidden villages. The whole atmosphere in the car had also brightened, and the children kept their eyes peeled for inns as the van cruised on towards their goal.

❖❖

The sleepy hamlet lay nestled in a wooded hollow about three miles off the main road, strung along the shady bend of a pebbled river. It was that lazy part of a day when time itself seemed to stand still, the only sounds being the light splashing of the water, the muffled clucking of contented hens in a cobbled yard, and the distant whirring of some sort of farm machinery several fields away. The rain had passed and the sun was caressing the land with warming rays, lifting a trail of steaming wisps along the country road. A bored tabby, paws curled under its chest, surveyed the empty street disinterestedly from its perch on a mossy garden wall.

The drowsy atmosphere was shattered by the roar of a powerful engine as a yellow sports car swept around a curve and into the constricted passage between the low stone walls , the driver down-shifting frantically as he realized he had underestimated both the tightness of the turn and the sudden narrowing down to one lane. The noise sent the cat shooting across the lawn like a furry firework, disappearing under a hawthorn hedge at the far side.

Cursing under his breath, the driver swerved to avoid an errant garbage can and braked again as he suddenly remembered that many of these places had speed cameras to catch unwary folks like himself. That would be just what he needed!

"Shortcut?" he snorted out loud. "If I'm too late…" He left the threat hanging.

Satisfied that he had made it through without being caught on radar, he floored the accelerator again and shot out the far end of the village, steering rather precariously with one hand while taking quick glances at a crumpled map in the other. *Why on earth hadn't he stuck to the main road?*

Snorting again in disgust, he tossed the map down onto the passenger seat where it lay on top of a disheveled newspaper and several crumpled cigarette packets. The map showed an untidily penned line across southern England leading to a town listed in small type on the western coast—a town that was firmly circled twice in red: *Penrithen.*

❖❖

"Okay, my turn!" said Rachel, looking up from her horse magazine.

After a lot of success in several large towns, the inn signs were proving rather few and far between on this stretch, so Dad had interspersed the sightings with one of his favorite pursuits—*trivia time.* It was his way of trying to pass on a love of learning as well as testing the kids on their schooling, and they seemed to enjoy it as far as he could tell. He took a quick glance in his rear-view mirror. "We're still on Bible characters. Ready, Danny?"

"My turn? Okay!" exclaimed Danny sitting up a little straighter, causing a small cascade of felt-tips pens into the black hole at his feet.

15

"Right, who sold his birthright for a bowl of soup?"

Danny paused for a moment staring off into the distance, then yelled "Lord Nelson!"

There were a few barely suppressed snorts from his siblings. "Er, I don't think he sold his birthright for a bowl of soup, Danny," said Emily.

"No, outside! We passed an inn called the Lord Nelson. That's two more runs for me!"

"No, only one run. Nelson only had one leg didn't he?" frowned Emily.

"Nuh-uh," put in Stevie. "That was Long-John Silver."

"Nelson had two legs, but only one arm, right?" said Rachel.

"We seem to have some disagreement," smiled Dad. "So, what's the correct answer?"

"One!"

"Two!"

"Two and a half!" Danny grinned.

"You know it, so why don't you tell them?" said Mom, looking up from her cross-stitch.

"Okay. Nelson had two legs…"

"See," said Rachel triumphantly.

"But only one arm and one eye. War wounds."

"Oh, the poor man," said Emily. She had a tender heart.

"Esau," put in Danny, suddenly.

"Esau, yes, but not very well," said Dad, giving a sideways glance at his wife. Contrary to other's opinions in the marriage, he saw a pun as the highest form of humor.

Emily groaned. Mom shook her head but chose not to say anything.

"What?" said a puzzled Danny. "Not Nelson. Esau! Sold his birthright for soup."

"What a mix-up!" laughed Mom suddenly. "Are you sure you're all having fun?"

Loud, affirmative cries reassured her. She breathed a silent thanks to God again for His shepherding of the family despite their current rather scattered lifestyle, and a prayer that He would somehow use this time to bind them together as a family.

"Okay, so who's ahead in cricket?" she added out loud.

"If Nelson really had two legs then Danny's in the lead with nine. Then me with seven. Then Stevie with six and Emily with only three." Said Rachel matter-of-factly. She looked sideways at her sister, with a mischievous smile.

"Just you wait!" said Emily with a determined look on her face. "I'm going to get 'The Centipede'! It's out there somewhere!"

✥

The park was a large green oasis hemmed in by an irregular border of brick houses with gray slate roofs, their back gardens displaying a rich assortment of flapping laundry braving the still unsettled weather. A winding gravel path led across the grass to where a few majestic horse chestnut trees stood sentinel near some play equipment on the far side.

After leaving the van near the imposing iron gates, the family had set up at a picnic table dotted with left-over raindrops, just a few feet from the unhurried stream that formed one edge of the park. Several towering weeping willows dipped and swirled in the dark water, their net of spindly branches masking a variety of moorhen, coot and mallard ducks.

"Can we go play?" begged Stevie, gesturing towards the play equipment.

"Okay, but just while we get lunch together." The words had barely left Mom's mouth before all four children were sprinting across the grass, their stampede causing a sudden panic in a flock of grazing starlings, and a reproachful cawing from an offended crow.

"Are you doing alright," asked Dad, noticing her wistful gaze towards the disappearing kids. She was playing with her favorite lock of hair—a sign that she was thinking hard.

"Yes, I guess so. I was just wondering about how they're all doing. I mean, this has been such a change for them—all this travel…home schooling…" her voice trailed off.

One of the things Dad appreciated about his wife was the way she kept her finger on the emotional and spiritual pulse of the family—something he often struggled to do.

He thought for a second. "Remember how we prayed so much, though, for God to lead us as a family. He's got them in his hands. We *know* we're supposed to be doing this." He took her hand and gave it a quick squeeze.

"I know. I just want to really keep close tabs on them, and I need you to help me. I so want their faith in God to be more than head knowledge—to really express itself in love. It's so easy for us to be just caught up in our own worlds—to be selfish."

Dad was trying to catch up with all her thoughts. His focus had honestly been elsewhere for this vacation time. "Well, honey, you're right. It's a struggle for us all."

Mom was still looking towards the kids. "I'm praying that God would use this time to really do something in us and through us as a family."

❧❧

Responding to their father's shrill whistle, the kids raced back towards the picnic table which was now set out in a jumble of Tupperware, potato chip bags, paper plates and plastic cups. The grinning, glowing faces looked like they could tackle the feast with no problem.

"Hand sanitizer first," reminded Emily, digging in her purse. She was waging a personal war against germs after some recent, startling discoveries in her science textbook, and considered herself the protector of the family's health in that regard.

"Watch your plates," warned Mom, "or they'll be sailing off to join the ducks!"

A mischievous breeze had already snatched a few items off the table, but the family was grateful for the fresh, clean air and pleasant outdoorsy smell. After a hearty prayer of thanks for a safe journey so far and a peaceful place to eat, the six of them dug in.

"Dad, why did you choose the village of Penrithen for our vacation?" Emily asked, wiping up some errant salad dressing that had dripped off her carrot stick onto her knee.

"Well, I wanted to stay near where we used to go when I was a boy," her father explained, "and I looked on the Internet for somewhere we could afford. There's a place there called the 'Squire Inn' that fits the budget, and they gave a discount for staying two weeks, plus it's not the British holiday season yet so prices are lower anyway. I've never been to Penrithen, but the pictures online looked really neat."

"Why, what's there?" wondered Danny indistinctly, his mouth rather full. "Is there a ruined castle, or a pirate's cave or something?"

"I want to find a secret passage," added Rachel, reaching for some more chips. Stevie's eyes grew as big as his paper plate.

"You've been reading too many 'Famous Five' books," smiled Mom, referring to the adventure series that her husband had so enjoyed as a boy. Rachel had found some copies in the attic several years ago.

"I can't promise anything like that," said Dad, "but it did look like a really interesting village, right on the coast with a small harbor and lots of narrow streets."

"And," put in Mom with excitement, "it's really close to some wonderful beaches, and some other really neat places."

"Like Tintagel—said to be the ancient home of King Arthur," said Dad dramatically.

"Hey! Wasn't he the one who pulled the sword from the stone?" Danny asked excitedly, demonstrating with his carrot stick and a roll. Stevie was suitably impressed.

"And Treyarnon—a beach with a tide pool big enough to swim in." added their father with a faraway look in his eyes. "I loved those holidays when I was a boy. I can't wait!"

The children looked at each other with joy. *This all sounded great!*

"Dad, where will we be going after our holiday?" wondered Emily. She always wanted the security of knowing exactly what was coming up and in what order.

Mom glanced at Dad. This was a sore spot, and one of her main worries. "Well, we have a place reserved in the town of Birmingham, further north. Someone associated with Dad's magazine has an office there with an apartment in the same building, right above it."

"In the industrial part of the city so not quite so much fun," admitted Dad, "but I needed to find somewhere as a base for my research that wasn't too expensive. Anyway, you'll be back schooling again, until we leave in November." He looked apologetic and Emily realized that they should probably try and make the best of the time they had in Cornwall. The future beyond didn't look too bright at all.

"The 'Coach and Horses!" exclaimed Danny. "How many points do I get?"

The game of pub cricket had been going on all day, with each child out in front at various times. Stevie was ahead at the moment, to his unbounded delight, but Danny was a close second.

"If it doesn't state the number, you assume two, so you get eight runs for your two horses," said Dad.

"That's seventeen then! I'm in the lead!" Danny couldn't help glancing triumphantly at Stevie, who looked less than pleased. Being the youngest was a constant thorn in his flesh.

"Don't brag, though," warned his mother. "It's important to be a good winner as well as a good loser. We're just playing to have fun, right?" She shot a meaningful glance at Stevie, who colored slightly and looked away. "Plenty of opportunity for character building," she added.

No matter the game, there was always lots of parental supervision required it seemed, but at least for the last hour nobody had asked *are we there yet?*

Miles ahead, a contented group of Friesian cows, placidly chewing their cud under a spreading oak tree, were mildly surprised by a yellow blur that passed across their vision. Navigating the narrow country road at high speed, it slowed down only long enough to careen around the tight bend beyond the field, disappearing towards the setting sun. The driver, gripping the wheel and muttering to himself, was suddenly startled by a strident ringing, coming from somewhere in the passenger seat. Without slowing down he switched his grip and started rummaging through the mess next to him, tossing wrappers and papers aside in a one-handed frenzy.

"Yeah, yeah, what it is?" he snarled, shooting quick glances right and left for hidden police cars while trying to steer with his other hand. "Have you seen if she's made any steps towards getting the inheritance? Okay. Good that she's not getting around much...I was afraid she'd have it already. Well...keep an eye on her. We need to know what it is and when she'll try to get it." A pause. "Well, I don't know. Figure it out. But be discrete. Yes, I'll be there tonight. Uh-huh, it's called Chypons. Cornish name—you must know it—house by the bridge, right? They said it was the last one on the row—should be just a couple of houses up from hers. Don't worry, it'll be a cinch."

He threw the phone back down, and focused back on the road ahead allowing himself a thin smile. He wasn't in quite such a rush now. Maybe this really could work after all.

The later the day, the weirder they get, no doubt about it. Dad glanced over at his wife and gestured with his head back towards the back seats. She rolled her eyes. It was early evening and the four children were doing their own version of trivia time, but it was getting decidedly wacky.

"*The Sound of Music*. What were the names of the children?" It was Emily's turn to ask.

"Friedrich!" yelled Rachel.

"Gretel!" put in Stevie.

"Beetle!" offered Danny with a huge grin. The others fell about laughing. "Myrtle, Weasel, Sneezy!"

"Okay, okay," said Dad, breaking in. "Your trivia's getting a bit derailed."

His kids had distracted him momentarily, but his concerns snapped back into focus. To his consternation, they were running way behind schedule. His hoped-for six o'clock arrival time had long since passed, and it was already getting close to dusk. An unexpected traffic jam and a slow farm truck that had been impossible to pass had run roughshod over the website's estimations. Trying to make up some time they had even just grabbed a selection of pre-made sandwiches from a service station as dinner, which even Mom had agreed had to be eaten on the go, but it still hadn't gained them much. Straining to read road signs in the dark, with the whole family tired—not on his list of fun ways to end the day.

"I think it's time for some quiet music. It's getting dark outside and it's been a long day," suggested Mom sensing Dad's stress. She uncoiled herself from her uncomfortable position and tried to wiggle her feet down through the mess to the floor.

"Are we there yet?" wondered Stevie for the umpteenth time, bouncing in his seat.

"If we were there, we wouldn't still be going." Rachel was getting rather fed up herself.

"But are we getting any closer?"

"We've been getting closer since we left this morning," said Danny, unhelpfully.

"We'd better be getting close now," said Dad, glancing disgustedly at his schedule again propped against the hand brake. His two attempted phone calls to the inn had been unsuccessful. What if they arrived after hours for goodness sake? Would their hosts be in bed? What a thought! *Please, no. This was supposed to be a restful break!*

"We'll get there. God has taken us this far, right dear?" said Mom looking meaningfully at Dad, who felt suddenly ashamed. She could always read him like a book.

She popped in a cassette of instrumental praise music, and squinted at the directions. "We just passed the sign to Millpool didn't we? Well, we need to look for Bodmin next and take the A389," she said, trying to sound positive.

"Roger." Dad made a concerted effort to do the same. "We'll keep our eyes peeled."

✌🏾

The driver of the yellow sports car was going way too fast for this type of country lane, careening wildly around the corners, then pushing it to the limit on the short straight stretches. Forget about no need to hurry, he was absolutely fed up--fed up with the trip, fed up with the endless narrow roads, fed up with tooling along behind vacationers pulling bulging trailers with excruciating slowness. Even worse, he was completely out of cigarettes.

The lowering sun was almost dead ahead, hitting him right in the eyes, and he angrily snapped down the sun visor. At least he was finally getting close. He had actually seen Penrithen's name appear on a signpost, so it couldn't be that far, could it? It had been years since the last time he was here. He glanced over, fumbling for the map that had slipped off the passenger seat onto the floor.

What was that? He swerved, the car slewing violently across the road, just missing some sort of fleeing animal. A large sign appeared right ahead and the corner of the car collided with the wooden post sending it flying into the road behind him, the sign smashing into pieces. He finally got the car under control as the road dipped down towards a stone bridge, the sudden panorama of a village harbor opening out in front of him. With shaking hands he pulled over and stopped, his chest heaving and his heart pounding loudly in his ears.

As the dusk deepened, the van sped on, the cassette finished, and a kind of melancholy mist settled over the family as each member retreated into their own little world of thoughts.

Dad had to consciously restrain his tendency to speed. *They were so late!* He was trying to trust God, wasn't he?—but still way too stressed. And speaking of stress, these articles of his were turning out more difficult than he had thought. All that research in France had been fine to a point, but he was still missing something. *Could he really even pull this off?*

Mom glanced back at the kids. *How were they doing really?* The years were flying by, and it wouldn't be long before Emily would be on her own. Could they do better in raising them? They didn't want the children to just fit in to the world— they wanted them to make a difference. *Please Lord,* she prayed. *Give them a heart that loves you and wants to serve others.*

Emily was staring out the window, thinking about the coming weeks. Wasn't the break going to just fly by like all the other good times, and then she'd be back to school again? Dad hadn't sounded too thrilled about their next spot. And what about after that? She didn't want to even *think* about leaving the family in a few years and going to college. She curled up as much as she could in her seat. *Jesus, why am I so scared? Help me trust you.*

Rachel tugged absently at one of her earrings and stared into space. She was tired of this endless journey. She loved adventure, and was excited for the coming weeks, but right now she just wanted to be out of this car! *Why was it taking so long? Couldn't they just be there?*

Danny peered out into the gloom, pretending they were driving through enemy territory on a mission to find the hilltop fortress where the General was prisoner. For some reason the the enemy commander had taken on the features of the angry man at the café. Danny glanced out the back window. No-one was following them, but boy, was it black out there! He gave a sudden shiver. Sometimes his own imagination could run away with him. He focused back on his immediate surroundings. *Now where was his pocket flashlight?*

The sole exception to the sea of moody thoughts was Stevie, mesmerized by the relentless passage of white lines lit up by the headlights in the road ahead, his snoozy mind like so much spaghetti. *Beach, sand, castles, secret passages...* He couldn't wait.

❧☙

"There are some really strange town names," piped up Danny, peering at the map with his flashlight. "Broadwoodwidger, Pipers Pool, and look at this! Felldownhead. Ouch!"

"Shhh dear," said Mom absently, intent on the view out the windshield. "We're getting really close, and Daddy's trying to find the sign."

Her husband was bent over the wheel, his nose seeming to touch the glass in front of him as he strained to see down the gloomy narrow two-lane road. The infrequent gaps in the eternal towering hedgerows were too well hidden to be discerned much in advance. There was supposed to be a sign, but he hadn't seen anything. The owner had said it was impossible to miss, but only in the daylight, evidently. *But what was that?* It looked like a splintered post. *Was that all that was left of the signpost to the inn, for goodness sake?*

"I think I saw it!" Dad sat straight up. "Just back there. We'll have to turn around."

"Thank you, Jesus!" His wife turned with a smile to the sleepy nest in the back, noting a few pairs of open eyes. "Girls, shoes on please! You too, Danny. Don't wake Stevie. I'll carry him in."

Emily and Rachel both looked up expectantly and stretched as the van made a bouncing U-turn—the headlights swinging wildly across the hedgerows. An open metal gate, half hidden in the bushes, loomed into view, and as they turned into the dark gap, a curving driveway unfolded before them ending in a small parking area ringed by white-painted stones. The large, somber house beyond looked imposing to the kids—even a little scary—its ancient granite walls thrown into relief by the glare of the headlights. A faded sign swung carelessly over the shadowed entrance, and the girls caught a glimpse of other dark buildings off to the left and the dim outlines of what appeared to be a line of bean poles to the right as the van pulled to a stop. A small patch of lawn beside them gleamed with dew in the chill evening air. The girls gave a shiver. Danny refused to look out, but concentrated instead on the squished granola bar peeking out of the seat pocket in front of him. For some reason he had half expected the yellow sports car to be parked off in the shadows, the scary driver peering out of one of the empty windows.

"Why is it so dark?" wondered Rachel. "Is anyone at home?"

"Don't worry, they're expecting us," assured her father, but sounding much more confident than he felt. *Had the owners gone to bed?* His worst fears might be realized. It was almost nine forty-five, and they had hoped to arrive about four hours ago. He had really prayed that this wouldn't happen! This was one of those times when he fervently wished someone else would take charge, but it was up to him, no question about it.

"Wait here, I'll check it out," he informed the expectant group behind him.

"Are we here? Did I win?" Stevie suddenly popped bolt upright.

"Shhh. We're here. And yes, you won, buddy," whispered Mom. "Twenty-one runs. But just rest easy. Daddy'll be right back." Stevie slumped back, contented.

Dad got out stiffly, and reluctantly approached the front door, praying under his breath while trying to shake out the wrinkles in his trousers. This was just about his least favorite situation—inconveniencing someone else, and being mortally embarrassed to boot.

The door was set at the back of a solid, covered stone entryway. Short benches set into each side held a variety of small gardening tools, plus several pairs of muddy rubber boots. His feet crunched on a scattering of seeds, spilled from a collection of open packets. The door itself looked like surplus from the Tower of London with its solid oak construction and black metal hinges. He peeked surreptitiously through the small, mullioned window and could just make out a wide, paneled hall, with a small ribbon of light at the base of a dark door to the right. His heart lifted a bit. *Could there be someone up after all?* He grasped the iron knocker and gave a few timid taps, then peered again. No response. *A little firmer then.* He knocked, then waited. Nothing. *Okay*, he thought, *here goes...*

Abandoning all caution he gave a succession of loud raps, then pulled his face back quickly as light suddenly flooded the hallway. An elderly woman of impressive circumference appeared, walking with a slightly rolling limp. She was dressed in a long, flowered nightgown modestly topped by a tired, blue quilted bed jacket. Her gray hair was pulled back rather severely in a bun, but the effect was softened by an untidy pink ribbon. As her face appeared in the window, he noticed that her features seemed friendly enough, with a grandmotherly kindness that put him a little more at ease.

The door groaned open, and the woman studied him with puzzled interest. "Well, now. Good evening to you." She had a wonderfully unique Cornish accent, gentle and slow. "Can I help you?"

"Er...We're here to stay in the inn. We have a reservation?" Suddenly he didn't feel so sure. "I'm so sorry we're so late. A nasty traffic jam, and then we got a little lost in the dark. I hope you didn't have to stay up waiting for us." Dad realized he was beginning to babble.

"Well, now. That's right. Mr. Waterman, right? I'm Mrs. Tremannon. No reason to fret, dear. We always stay up late of an evening, watching the box. Now we've retired from the farm, it's a real luxury. Come in an' meet my husband, and then I'll show you your room."

"Thank you, but actually I'm Mr. Chapman. With my family. They're in the car..." His voice trailed off into uncertainty. This whole interaction was becoming rather surreal. *Were they even at the right inn?*

"Oh, yes, yes, so sorry. I remember now. Mr. Chapman and family. We're expecting you. Come in. Come in." She beckoned to him, and then paused. "You know, it's a good thing you were late."

"Er, a good thing?" Dad stopped in his tracks.

"Oh aye." Mrs. Tremannon looked suddenly very serious. "Because of the accident."

"Accident?"

"Yes, yes. Terrible, terrible. Well, not actually terrible, but it could have been terrible."

"I'm sorry, I don't quite understand."

Mrs. Tremannon shook her head and clucked her tongue. "Well, it was Mr. Perry—who owns the pottery place in town. He was on his way back from visiting his mother out in Scunthorpe...or was it Skegness? Anyway, he was coming back after being gone and he was driving in this evening in his van—the white one with the pots on the side—and coming down the lane near the inn, and him speeding a bit being late for the council meeting and all, and then he hit it. He must not have seen it." She seemed to consider for a moment, then shook her head. "I don't think he would have hit it on purpose"

"Hit what?" Dad glanced back at the family watching expectantly in the car and motioned them to wait. Hopefully it would be only a moment. The lady seemed to have trouble getting to the point.

"The sign—the inn sign. Our inn sign."

"Aha." Finally the answer. *So that's why it was so hard to find the place.* "So he knocked it down."

"Oh, no."

"No?" Dad's head was beginning to spin.

"It was already down. Smashed all over the road."

"Smashed?"

"By someone—someone else who didn't have the decency to let us know. Anyway, poor Mr. Perry hit it. And then hit our hedge." The lady shook her head sadly. "There was an ambulance—all the way from Padstow—and P.C. Monroe and that new fellow that's helping him out—whatever his name is."

"Was everything okay?" Dad was finally beginning to understand.

"With the hedge? Yes, and with Mr. Perry too. Nothing serious broken for either. So that's why it was good you were late an all. It might have been you." The old lady nodded in satisfaction, then turned back towards the doorway through which she had appeared.

"Yes, I see," said Dad wonderingly. He motioned to the others to wait just a bit more.

So it was a good thing they were late, he mused. That was a revolutionary thought after all the worrying he had done. He couldn't quite process that right now.

He followed Mrs. Tremannon into the dim sitting room, the only light coming from a flickering television set, its volume apparently all the way down. It was perched in a place of honor before a plush, patterned sofa that seemed to fill the rest of the room. Mr. Tremannon had been sitting with his legs outstretched, but he slowly pushed himself up as they entered and extended his hand, his tanned, weathered face breaking into a wrinkled smile. Two bright china-blue eyes twinkled from beneath a pair of the bushiest gray caterpillar eyebrows Dad had ever seen, though there was no more hair to be found anywhere on his head. He was dressed in shapeless gray trousers hung by suspenders over a rumpled checked shirt, and though tall and very thin, he had a sturdiness about him that bespoke of years of hard work.

"Mr. Tremannon? Dave Chapman. It's a pleasure to meet you." Dad found his hand engulfed in an iron grip which left him slightly pop-eyed after a fervent shaking.

"Pleasure," echoed the old man, in a slow, resonant voice.

"I am so sorry we're late. I tried to call you a couple of times, but there was no answer."

Mrs. Tremannon gave a reassuring smile. "That's right, we heard the phone go, but I couldn't find it, wouldn't you know. My son bought us one of those wireless things, but we keep losing it. These new-fangled whatsits. And then my husband thought he'd found it and pressed the answer button, but it turned out to be the TV remote, and now we've lost the sound."

Dad couldn't help smiling. "Well, I think I can help you get the sound back."

"That's alright. We like it better this way, to be honest. There's not much worth hearing nowadays." Mrs. Tremannon smiled. "Anyway, let's go show you your rooms. You must be all done in."

"We are. Thank you so much. I'll just go get the family."

Dad darted back out the front door and gave a thumb's up sign. He could still hardly believe it. Everything was going to be alright.

Not too far away in a little cottage overlooking the harbor, an elderly hand slowly turned the pages of a cracked photo album, the faded black and white images passing one by one in silence as the dusk deepened outside the windows. The hand paused at the picture of a young girl, snuggled in the lap of a pleasant-faced man with a distinctive mustache who was reading to her from a large book. The album seemed to tremble for a moment and a single tear fell onto the page, rolling slowly down to form a glistening line between the two faces.

Just up the road, the last house in the row was completely dark. The man from the motorway café stood alone in the front room. He took a deep draw from his cigarette and slowly blew out the smoke, pondering the faint outline of the harbor through the window in front of him. A few scattered lights revealed the cluster of houses and shops along the steep road on the far side.

He shook his head. *What a day.* Rushing halfway across England, and then barely making it here at the end of it. He was mighty lucky he hadn't killed himself. *Well, what if he had?* It would have solved his problems pretty effectively, wouldn't it? He gave a cynical smile.

But that wasn't what he really wanted, was it? All his life he had been waiting for this sort of opportunity. This was the sort of thing that could wipe out all his mistakes in the past and set him up for the future. It would also be a revenge of sorts, and that sounded pretty sweet.

Was it possible to pull it off? He really didn't think it would be too hard getting his hands on the inheritance, once he knew what and where it was. But that was the problem; he had to get a look at that will, and in his current frame of mind he was ready to do pretty much anything to get it.

Dad sat on the edge of the huge bed. He swayed slightly as he peeled off a sock, convinced he could almost see his foot expand at its release from prison. *How could he be so tired when all he'd done was sit all day?* Well, yes, he had just made five trips up and down the old staircase, wondering whether it was the stairs or his back that creaked impressively with each step.

He looked around at the room while massaging his foot, amused at the odd assortment of furniture—the stained dressing table with its collection of antique-store refugees, the Victorian floral basin and pitcher in the corner... A huge dark wardrobe lurked against one wall, its mirrored door refusing to stay shut without the aid of two of Stevie's socks jammed in at the bottom. It made the hulking monster look as if it was in the process of swallowing a small child. The whole was illuminated by a light fixture that appeared to have once graced the lobby of the Moulin Rouge, its dark red glass shades festooned with a dangling fringe, suffusing the room with a rosy ambience that only served to emphasize his sleepiness. And was it his imagination, or did the whole floor slope slightly towards the window? This place had character, no doubt about it.

"The kids are ready for goodnights," informed his wife, yawning widely in the doorway.

He could see her eying the bed, ready to take a running jump and disappear under the comforter. *It would take an Olympic leap for her to make it up and over the edge,* he mused. This thing was built for Mr. and Mrs. Goliath. *But inviting? It was positively magnetic.*

"You'd better hurry, dear. They're almost out."

Me, too, he thought, but pushed himself up without complaint. This bedtime custom of prayers, snuggles and a goodnight song was one of the family rituals that was critical in maintaining a sense of security in the midst of so much change—an anchor for the day that the kids looked forward to with sleepy eagerness. He was back within ten minutes, but his wife had already tumbled into contented oblivion. This would be one of the rare occasions when they didn't end the day praying together, "so it's up to me, Lord," he murmured, crawling under the covers. He lay there in the dark, his hands behind his head. *So it was good that they were late. It was actually good that they had been late.*

He thought back over the day—the speeding, the agonizing traffic jam, the worrying... *Had God really made them late to save them from an accident?* And what about his wife's concerns for the family? This vacation wasn't panning out to be restful at all!

He closed his eyes. "Lord, here I am again. Thank you for your protection and for getting us here. Your timing was perfect. Forgive me again for not trusting you, and being grumpy. And Lord, please help me to learn this lesson. Something's got to change. Please use these two weeks to do something special in us and through us." He paused as an enormous yawn overcame him. "You are so good to us," he murmured. "Use our time here for your glory. Guide us…help us…'" and he was asleep.

Chapter 2 - The Lay of the Land

Danny stirred slightly, turned over and popped an eye open, annoyed by the unwelcome intrusion of light sneaking around the edges of the heavy red curtains next to his bed. Lying back with a yawn, he stared up at the ceiling and stretched. This place actually didn't seem creepy at all in the daylight. A faint scent of roses gave a pleasant aroma to the room.

The house seemed quiet as a tomb, the only sound being some deep breathing to his left. A quick glance confirmed that Stevie was still far from consciousness, his head back and mouth wide open. For just a second Danny imagined popping something into his brother's mouth, but, squashing the desire, he turned back and reached for his Bible. He had been given the book as a prize in Sunday School and was extremely pleased and proud to have his very own copy now.

He decided to read the book of Joshua, who was supposed to be a pretty fearless guy. Maybe that would help him with his own fears. He pulled the book open but then paused. He had almost forgotten to pray first. But who could he pray for? *His family?* He sometimes struggled with his brother and sisters. *Yes, that would be a good idea.* And who else was he struggling with? *Oh, yes,* that scary man at the motorway café. Jesus did say to pray for your enemies. But that guy wasn't really his enemy, was he? He fervently hoped not. He hoped he would never see him again. Maybe he would just skip praying for him after all.

Fifteen minutes later, dressed in shorts and a wrinkled soccer shirt he had extracted from his suitcase without troubling to open the zipper all the way, Danny was ready for the day to begin. No-one else seemed up, though. Could he dare go exploring by himself? Maybe if he pretended he was someone brave it would help. Maybe he could be a secret agent now, infiltrating the enemies' headquarters.

Peeking out of the doorway, he surveyed the hallway. To his immediate right it terminated in another door, this one closed, with a brass number five hanging a little askew from a bent nail. *Mom and Dad's room*, he thought. *Dead end.* He looked at his own door. It had a number four.

Trying to project a seriousness equal to his mission, he padded stealthily down the hallway, taking note of the faded prints lining both sides. They seemed to be mainly pictures of the countryside and each hung a little crookedly. In fact, the whole corridor was a little crooked. It sloped slightly sideways and downwards ahead of him to where it took a sharp right turn, a floor to ceiling tapestry of some sort of old hunting scene covering the whole wall at the end. Next to it on the left, a small window let in a cascade of unrestrained sunlight across the faded carpet runner.

He sneaked down to the window, taking care to stay on the carpet so as not to alert any possible guards. Peering stealthily out on tip-toe he glimpsed a cobbled yard surrounded by low grey-roofed buildings before snatching his head back. He had spied a tall man carrying a bucket of something, emerging from a shed by the rear wall. *Obviously an enemy agent.*

Now what to do? Could he go down the stairs? All was quiet below, so with exaggerated stealth he glided silently down to the first landing where an open door led to the cramped bathroom he remembered from last night. The door to his sisters' room was right next to it. He noted that their room was number two. *Hmm. That was a little strange.* He filed that away for future reference.

Screwing up his courage, he slowly descended the final set of stairs, his heart pounding. Here he was confronted with a choice of three doors. One looked like another guest room but the door was shut. The next just led to a small sitting room with a cheery gathering of plump flowered furniture, a large pair of French doors at the end. The last one proved much more interesting. It led to a long room, darkly paneled, with a huge wooden table down the middle. Three large, heavily-curtained, mullion windows shed a diffuse light across the antique furnishings under a low-beamed ceiling that seemed to be sagging slightly with age. The whole effect reminded him of the great hall of a castle he had once seen in a library book. He sniffed a pleasant, slightly musty smell of old books and furniture polish. This room was much more remarkable and mysterious than anything he had yet encountered, and he wasn't too sure about venturing through the doorway. He had a very vague memory of the place from last night, but he had been barely conscious then. Now he wanted to take it all in and make sure it was safe.

A long, dark sideboard festooned with old framed photos anchored the wall to his left. He took a cautious step in, his curiosity overcoming his fear. There were more photos on the walls—the kind of photos full of men with walrus mustaches and women in constricting black dresses, all stiff and unsmiling.

Next to them was a large framed picture--some sort of family tree. *Hadn't he seen something like this in his history book? English Kings and Queens or Dukes or whatever?* There were lots of names written on gold-edged cards, with lines joining them together. He scanned the names: *William Lonsdale, Kenwyn Penrow*... No, he didn't recognize any of them.

Turning slightly he got quite the shock. In the corner was an ancient suit of armor leaning slightly askew. He took a step back in alarm. *There wouldn't be anyone inside, would there, like that scary man?* He was wrestling with that thought when a voice at his ear caused him to leap like a startled hare.

"Good morning, Tiger! Doing a little exploration?" His dad gave a big grin, which dropped on seeing Danny's wide-staring eyes. "Whoops. I didn't mean to scare you!"

"Ah, oh, wow Daddy." Two big shocks in a row had lost him the ability to form sentences. He took a deep breath. "I was pretending I was an agent in the enemy headquarters."

"Ah, in that case, you are under arrest for trespassing." Dad paused a moment as if to consider. "But all will be forgiven if you give me a good-morning hug."

Glad for an easy way out, the chastened agent gave his Dad a squeeze.

His father smiled. "Why don't we take a look around together? This place is really ancient." Blast if he didn't love exploring as much as his son. He led Danny over to the nearest corner where a glass display case held a menagerie of stuffed birds.

"They're real, right?" questioned Danny, impressed, taking them in one at a time.

"Uh-huh. If I'm not mistaken, these are all birds found around the coasts here." Dad read the name cards aloud. "*Kittiwake, Skua, Tern, Gannet, Storm Petrel, Puffin, Chough.* That big one is a Peregrine Falcon."

"Cool names," said Danny. *But who would want a bunch of dead, stuffed birds in their house?* "Do you think we'll see any of them?" he added, glancing out the window. Through the puffy white clouds, a swath of blue hinted at the possibility of a fine day.

"Maybe so. God is really creative, isn't He? We'll keep our eyes peeled. These stuffed ones are pretty cool themselves. They might even be quite valuable."

"No, no, not at all valuable, I'm afraid." The sudden voice behind them caused Dad to jump this time. It was Mrs. Tremannon who, with her slippered feet, had entered the room without a sound. Dad turned around sheepishly, noticing Danny's big grin.

"Ah, good morning, Mrs. Tremannon. We were, er, admiring all the interesting things you have here. And what an interesting house!" He gestured vaguely around him.

"Good morning to you, Mr. Redman." The old lady gave a wrinkled smile, and patted Danny on the cheek with a hand evidently still wet and soapy from dish washing.

"Er, it's Chapman," corrected Dad, puzzled.

"That's right...Chapman. Aye, it's a funny old place. Hundreds of years old, if it's a day. Used to be a manor house—*the* manor house, you know—home to Squire Penrow and his family." A wistful expression seemed to pass over the old lady's face, and she ran a work-worn hand along the top of the display case.

"So, when did you move here?" wondered Dad.

"Oh, not long after the Squire had to move out. Let me see, that was five or six years ago now, or was it longer? He couldn't take care of himself any more. Well, he'd had to have help here for a while, but in the end he had to go to a nursing home. He lived there until he passed away, just last month in fact, God rest his soul." Mrs. Tremannon glanced briefly but reverently upwards. "A strange man in some respects 'e was, but a heart of gold. You see, our old farm was getting too much for me and the mister, and my son, David—he's a strapping lad with a fine family of his own, you know—well he offered to take it over and the Squire, you know, before he got really bad, well he helped us out by letting us come to here to, er, watch over the place you could say, and we've been here since."

"And you decided to turn it into a Bed and Breakfast."

"That's right, that's what we did—with the Squire's permission of course. Got to keep active, and it's never too late to try something new—besides…" She winked at Danny. "These old bones would seize up pretty quick if I didn't keep 'em moving. And speaking of moving, I need to move these old bones into the kitchen and get your breakfast on the table. I forgot to set a time with you last night. Would half past eight be alright today? That'll give you a bit of time to get yourselves together."

"Er, that should be fine." Dad tried to mentally estimate the time it would take to get everyone down, especially if some were still in the Land of Nod. "I'll go get them."

He looked at his watch. *Oh my, it was eight o'clock already.* That gave them only thirty minutes! He rushed upstairs, his junior agent at his heels.

Exactly thirty-three minutes later, the whole family was grinning at each other around one end of the huge table, a little rumpled, but ready for the day—and especially breakfast, which, by the intoxicating smells coming from the hallway, promised to be beyond their expectations. Fortunately, only Stevie had actually still been asleep, but he was pretty low-maintenance. A quick slick of the hair and some reasonably fresh clothes and he looked his usual mischievous self.

Dad was just finishing thanking Jesus for a safe trip, a good sleep and the coming meal, when Mrs. Tremannon appeared in the doorway carrying a loaded tray. She set a huge bowl of steaming oatmeal in the center, and proceeded to frame it with a selection of toppings: raisins, sugar, strawberries, bananas, and a tall blue-and-white striped jug of creamy milk.

"So, the whole Chipford family here together," she said with a smile.

Dad quieted the surprised looks of his family with a subtle finger to the lips.

"That'll get you started, and I'll be back in a mo' with the rest." She ambled back to the kitchen as Mom proceeded to dole out the oatmeal to the eager group.

"Chipford?" whispered Rachel questioningly, pushing the sugar bowl over to her sister.

"She's had a little trouble with our name. No problem. At least we're here safe and sound," smiled Dad, passing her the raisins. "Whoa, go easy on the goods, dear!" His wife seemed intent on making Mount St. Oatmeal in front of him. "If I remember Cornish breakfasts, this is just the beginning!"

Sure enough, the elderly lady soon appeared with another loaded tray, from which she deposited a huge platter holding fried eggs, fried bread, farm sausages, crispy bacon, baked beans, grilled mushrooms, and an assemblage of grilled tomatoes to top it all off. The hearty fragrance about sent their taste buds into orbit.

A rack of toast, a collection of jams and marmalade, and a pot of tea took up the rest of the space, and Mum looked at Dad, who looked at the kids. By all accounts some regular exercise better be high on the list of priorities or they'd all be blowing up like blimps.

❧ ❧

"Well, Hon, what do you want to do today?" Dad didn't have a printed list for the day, but he still thrived on having things well planned out in advance. "I know the kids are excited to see the sea, but we also need to get settled a bit and get some food for lunches. Mrs. Tremannon showed me a fridge we can use."

"Well, that's fine, but you know dear, I'm not ready to go rushing off anywhere. We just had a whole day traveling, and I for one haven't had any time with the Lord yet today."

Her husband noticed the almost desperate look she gave, and hastily adjusted his thoughts. "Tell you what. Why don't I take the kids and go check out the lay of the land. We'll get some stuff for lunch and meet you back here with a full report. That way you can have a quiet morning."

Aha! By the grateful look he received he knew he had scored a bullseye.

❧ ❧

It wasn't long before the four kids were assembled in the entryway, chattering excitedly, while their father sat on a small bench, knotting his shoelaces, and going over his mental checklist of what they needed: water bottles, shopping list, some cash, Kleenex, and a credit card just in case. *Yup. Got it all.* He marveled again at how easy it was to go places, now that the kids could get themselves ready. But there was one thing still…

"Stevie. Have you used the bathroom?"

"No, but I don't need to go." It was always the same response, and it was usually pretty accurate. He was like a camel. Still, better to be safe than sorry.

"I want you to try. We don't know if we'll be able to find a place in town."

Stevie trailed back off through the big room and Dad sat back and idly picked up the newspaper by his side—the *Penrithen Times* apparently. *Definitely a small town publication,* he thought, as he quickly scanned the headlines, smiling at the big news items: *Local Cows Annoy Motorists* and *Lady Inherits Mystery.* He flipped the paper over as Mrs. Tremannon appeared from the kitchen, wiping her hands on a rough checked cloth.

"Off for a walk now, are we? You've got some nice weather for it. It should a fine day."

"Yes. We're going to take a stroll around the village. Can you recommend a place that sells groceries—like things for lunch?" Dad set the paper aside and patted his pockets one more time to make sure he had his wallet. Stevie reappeared and ran to his side.

"Oh, you'll be wanting Peterson's Grocers—that's where you'll want to go. Down the hill, across the bridge and follow the road up to your left. You won't miss it."

"Great, and what time would you like us for dinner?"

"Six o'clock is the time, but I can make it later. There's no-one else staying here."

"Six o'clock would be perfect. Thank you, Mrs. Tremannon. We'll see you later."

"Cheerio now dears." She waved her cloth and ambled back to the kitchen.

Dad heaved open the front door and they stepped out into the fresh morning light.

"No, we're not taking the car," Dad announced as the kids raced to the van. "We're walking! We did more than enough driving yesterday, and we've got a mighty big breakfast to work off."

Ignoring their grumbles, he crunched off across the gravel, delighting in the scent of cut grass and wildflowers chased across the fields by a brisk wind. Sometimes it took a bit of persuasion to get them up and out, but it never failed that the outdoors worked its magic on his kids. Sure enough, it wasn't long before they had forgotten their complaints and, to their dad's secret amusement, were skipping alongside and around him. There was something about the air here that caused each of them to get an extra thrill of excitement. Was it because it was seasoned with salt from the sea, still hidden somewhere behind the hedgerows, or was it the promise of adventure, stirring up suddenly inside them? Whatever it was they felt light and free.

✥✥✥

Mom gathered her Bible, journal and favorite travel mug from the bedroom and made her way slowly downstairs, enjoying the peaceful sense of the old inn settling around her. When was the last time she had been alone in a house? She honestly couldn't remember. Such was this new life of a home schooling mom, and it made these rare occasions even more precious.

She stopped by the little kitchen alcove to fill her mug from the thermos conveniently left there by Mrs. Tremannon and pondered where to go next. She was still feeling rather unsettled and wanted to find a special place where she could meet with the Lord and sort out her thoughts. *But outside or in?*

A quick scalding sip told her the mix was just right, so she pressed the lid firmly down, grabbed her books and stepped into the entryway. A bold ray of sunshine poured through the small window in the front door, illuminating a slanted patch of faded carpet at her feet and unmasking a floating fairyland of dust particles. She felt suddenly drawn to step out into the sunny brightness. Why waste such a day indoors? Finding herself humming a worship song she'd heard on one of the kids' CDs yesterday, she heaved open the heavy front door and stepped out into the open air.

⊷❧

The Squire Inn was comfortably situated in a small grove of trees on the lower slopes of Tregarth Watch—the grassy headland on the south side of Penrithen. A steep curving road bordered by tall hawthorn hedges led from the main gates down to the village, and Dad and the four children clumped down it chattering excitedly, each eager to be the first to glimpse the sea.

It was only about a five-minute walk, and as they rounded the last bend, they all stopped in delight at the view laid out before them. Rachel felt like she had stepped into a living painting, as the family seemed suddenly to be surrounded by light and color.

The road at their feet descended sharply to a stone bridge whose graceful arch spanned a cheerful stream, running between low granite walls. The water bounced down its pebbled channel, under the bridge and wound across a narrow patch of sand into the lapping waters of a small, picturesque harbor, dotted with quaint, painted fishing boats. Shimmering sunlight danced along the stream and sparkled across the waters of the inlet.

"I can see the sea!" sang out Danny, pointing excitedly to the stretch of cobalt blue visible between the cliffs that marked the harbor entrance. Stevie frowned, annoyed that he hadn't been the first to say it.

As they left the protection of the hedgerows, the full force of the wind met them squarely, sending the girls' long hair whipping across their faces. The unmistakable harbor mix of fish, seaweed and salt air smells swept over them. Stevie forgot his annoyance and closed his eyes, inhaling deeply with a silly grin on his face. He absolutely loved the sea.

Emily couldn't believe all the flowers. They seemed to be everywhere— peeking from around fence posts and telephone poles, spilling over walls, and cascading in a profusion of violets, pinks, reds, blues and yellows from window boxes and stone planters. "Beautiful," she murmured, enthralled.

The village itself shone like a jewel in its little valley under a sky of cornflower-blue, the sun reflecting off its white-washed walls and brightly-painted doors. It straddled both sides of the harbor, with the bulk of its buildings lying across the bridge and along the steep road that backed the inlet and ascended the low hill behind. Several of the houses and shops actually overhung the waters of the harbor, and the rest seemed to be jostling each other for the best view. The girls looked at each other with joy. This place looked great—so many things to discover!

Danny nudged Stevie and pointed across the harbor to where several narrow paths and steep flights of steps led between the buildings and across the cliffs.

"Hey, look at that. Those are secret paths—probably for smugglers."

"Pirates!" Stevie could picture it too.

"Spies!"

"Secret agents!"

34

"Visigoths!" Danny remembered that word from his history lesson, and it sounded cool.

The boys gave each other a knowing look. What an awesome place to explore!

As they continued down the hill, a seagull perched on a nearby chimney rose up in annoyance at their appearance, its raucous call rising and falling on the wind like a siren. That sound, above all the other sensations of the moment, swept Dad back to his childhood, and the joy he had felt at the prospect of seemingly endless days of sun and sand stretching ahead, with school nothing but a misty memory.

He looked around at the smiling faces. *What a blessing.* Maybe this would be a really good break for the family. "Okay, gang, where to first?"

"Can we go down to the water?" Stevie was jumping up and down.

"May we please?"

"May we please go down to the water?"

Boys and water—one of the strongest attractions found in nature--except at bath time, of course. Dad raised his eyebrows and looked at the others, receiving nods of confirmation all round.

"Righty-ho. We can go for a bit, and then we'll go and find that store."

"Well, Jesus, where shall it be?" Mom murmured, mentally sorting out the choices before her as she looked out from the stone porch. To her left a sunken curve of paving stones beckoned along the edge of the vegetable garden and around the side of the house. Now that looked definitely inviting. She stepped carefully along the path, enjoying the nearness of the old house's granite walls, bathed in sunlight.

Behind the building, a well-tended shadowed lawn sloped upwards to a long laurel hedge. In the far corner, almost hidden under the drooping branches of a straggling wild cherry, a white clematis-covered arbor formed an opening through the leafy barrier and she sensed a nudge to head that way. She ducked under the untidy frame of flowers, keeping a sharp eye out for spiders' webs, and stopped suddenly in surprise and delight. She had found her very own secret garden.

The room-sized sanctuary was completely hemmed in by a barrier of green— high enough to afford privacy but low enough to still allow plenty of light. The morning sunshine was already sneaking through the leaves and, blocked from the wind, the heady scent of flowers embraced her. Mom gazed around, trying to take it all in. A queenly perennial border framed the area with layers of showy blooms, from leggy Cosmos and stately Lupine, to vibrant clumps of Dianthus and Penstemmon. As she stepped further in, her feet crunched on a carpet of old leaves, almost completely obscuring the colored flagstones beneath.

She smiled to herself. Though evidently somewhat neglected, there was still a quiet elegance to the setting. It was at once a peaceful and somewhat mysterious place, and she wondered how long ago it was since someone had tended it.

Nestled in one corner was a wrought-iron garden seat, a straggling honeysuckle pushing brazenly through the wooden slats at the back. At its side stood a small round table, its stone top inlaid with a mosaic of smooth, colored glass. A plaque was set into the surface, and Mom bent over to read the inscription: *In Memory of my dearest Rosie, March 23rd, 1957*. Perhaps whoever had placed the inscription had found some sort of solace here. To some degree, that's what she was seeking too.

She set her mug down, plopped onto the bench and stretched out her legs. Yes, this would be perfect—an answer to prayer—a place where she could meet with the Lord, praise Him and gain His perspective on the needs of the family. She opened her Bible, closed her eyes, and smiled.

Fickle—that was the word he was looking for.

Dad was viewing the sights while perched on the harbor wall, but he wasn't especially enjoying the moment. He had found himself thinking of his assignment again, and suddenly noted how his thoughts could be so untrustworthy at times— yes, definitely fickle. Here he was, in a beautiful place, with nothing on his mind except the scent of the sea, when all of a sudden his worries came barging in at the door, without even knocking. *These articles of his on the Protestant persecution seemed to be going nowhere. Talk about writer's block! He needed some inspiration. Should he even have taken this assignment?* And something his wife said yesterday came back to him. She had said there was something missing. Boy, if he couldn't figure out what he was missing, how could he lead the family?

"Help, Jesus!" he managed to say, trying to wrestle back control. What was that great verse in 2nd Corinthians—*take every thought captive*. Stop worrying and take it to the Lord. *Show me somehow what to do with these articles, Lord, and please help me trust that you have the future in your hands.*

He remembered how God had handled them being late last night, and a measure of calm broke in again. *What was the time anyway?* He glanced at his watch. They really should be starting for the store. He looked over to where the kids, shoes and socks off and jean legs rolled up, were wading along slowly and peering into the dark water as if for a hopeful glimpse of something interesting.

He heaved himself off the wall, and brushed some traces of dried seaweed from his jeans. It was time to get going and if they kept busy, the less time he'd have to think about those articles.

Far above them on the hill, a pair of binoculars swept the scene below, past a group of fisherman stacking lobster pots on the pier and a young mother in curlers and a bright pink headscarf straining to push a pram up the slope from the bridge, and then pausing to focus on the family gathering their shoes and socks by the water's edge. Next they swung over to the row of cottages on the near side of the harbor, freezing as the back door of the second one swung open and an elderly lady emerged to throw some crusts out onto the lawn. As she disappeared again inside, the binoculars relaxed their gaze, and a waiting crowd of sparrows and starlings swooped down to fight over the unexpected feast.

Elton Buckley, the Penrithen postman prided himself on the fact that he did most of his route on foot. Yes, he had a mail van, but he only used it as a base to hold parcels and such. He liked to challenge himself and see if he could park it by the war memorial and only return to it now and then to replenish his goods for the next set of deliveries.

Today, however, though he was loathe to admit it, he was tempted to just go ahead and drive. He had a particularly heavy box to deliver as well as the sack of mail slung over his shoulder, and Slade's Hill stretched up before him with its intimidating grade seemingly more ominous than usual.

Well, the package was for the *Mole Hole*, only about halfway up, and how could he even think of driving when there went Mrs. Robinson pushing her pram with her chubby toddler going up the far side? His pride couldn't take that sort of hit.

He adjusted the sack on his shoulder, took a firmer grip of the box and started up.

Instead of taking the apparently boring route along the road, Rachel convinced Dad to go for a more interesting option. It involved clambering up some steps onto the harbor wall and following it as it ran along the base of the cliff towards the open sea. The water to their left rapidly deepened, the color passing from a luminescent emerald to a green so dark it was almost black.

Dad had insisted on holding Stevie's hand, much to the lad's disgust. They carefully skirted several large rusting iron bollards circled by thick, rough ropes that swung downwards to the assortment of swaying fishing boats moored along the edge. About ten yards ahead, the pier angled back out into the sea to form a rounded breakwater. Rachel's attention was drawn by the black flag with a white cross dancing at the top of a tall pole right at the end of the pier. Looking back she noticed that, just at the angle, several trails led up the cliff. One gradually climbed along the side of the harbor to disappear around the edge of the inlet; the other, a narrow series of uneven steps cut into the rocky wall, ascended upwards across the face of the cliff to the line of buildings on top.

Rachel looked over her shoulder. "Which way, Daddy?"

Dad gestured up the cliff. "Up there. We're heading to the shops."

Danny liked the look of this option. He shared a knowing grin with Stevie. Hadn't he seen a picture of a path like this in one of his adventure books about smugglers? It was a secret staircase, probably used only at night. *Maybe smugglers or pirates had used this very path!* He hurried on after Rachel.

He couldn't believe it. The *Mole Hole* was closed. *Why was it closed at this time of the morning?*

Elton the Postman carefully slid the box down his side and onto the pavement, grimacing in pain. *Mercy, it was heavy.* He shielded his eyes and peered through the shop window. It looked dark inside. He turned to ring the doorbell but stopped short as he saw the notice taped to the door. Closed until Thursday.

Thursday! He just couldn't believe it. Jennings had never done anything like that before.

He was about to give full vent to his frustration when he noticed Mrs. Robinson and her pram crossing the road in his direction. He swallowed down his words, manhandled the package back onto his arm and swung the sack back on up to his shoulder. Then grumbling under his breath, he turned and stumbled back down the hill to his waiting van.

After several minutes of hard climbing, the twisting trail took a sudden sharp turn, and then ascended straight up between narrow walls of grey rock. Danny sighed with disappointment. They were almost at the top and it looked like it was just a staircase up a cliff. There hadn't been any hidden passages, secret caves or anything else out of the ordinary. Maybe they should have taken the other way after all.

The path continued to a short alleyway between two gardens backing on to the cliff edge. Danny, who was still second in line behind Rachel, paused to look back at the view, causing the rest of family to bump into each other like skittles. He caught a brief, airy panorama of the harbor below and noted what looked like a low yellow car pulling up in front of the farthest of the group of cottages directly across the inlet. He stared at it hard. *No, it couldn't be, could it?*

A chorus of complaints from the pack behind interrupted his thoughts and, forgetting his concern, he turned and scurried up into the alley, the others close at his heels. They passed into the chilly shadows between the two old stone buildings, and emerged back into the welcome sun at the narrow road that led up from the bridge, directly across from a short row of shops.

Dad had to pause to catch his breath. "Okay. Wow. That was some climb! Eh, what's up, Stevie?" The boy was bouncing up and down and plucking at his sleeve.

"Is that a bakery, Daddy?" He pointed across the road. "We could get a chocolate treat for Mommy!"

Dad raised a suspicious eyebrow. This sudden concern for Mom's sweet tooth was unusual. "And…"

"Well…and maybe we could get a treat too?"

Aha. He thought there might be an ulterior motive. He glanced down at Stevie who was trying his best to look cute and hopeful, and realized he couldn't resist that freckled grin. Evidently, he was getting to be easily swayed in his old age.

"The Crusty Muffin." He read the sign over the window. "Okay, we'll have a look."

Who was he kidding, though? As if anyone went into a bakery just to have a look.

The shop bell jangled merrily as the family crowded in from the breezy outdoors, enjoying the sudden transition to the warm, fragrant interior. The bakery was actually combined with a tea room café with a group of cheerily decorated tables by the window, each set out with cups, saucers and a vase of flowers.

Hmmm, a possible place for a date, Dad thought, always on the lookout for places to take his wife.

The lady behind the counter looked up at them from the display case where she was setting out a tray of currant scones. With her plump figure, greying hair, and pleasant expression, she reminded Dad of one of his favorite English aunts—the one who had run a florists shop for years somewhere up near Leeds. She was certainly quite a splash of color, he mused, with rouge spots on her cheeks like two jam tarts and a flowery dress almost completely obscured by a bright orange apron that proclaimed '*Born to Bake.*'

The girls smiled at her earrings shaped like iced pink cupcakes. She looked a little like a cupcake herself.

"Well, well, what a crowd! Good morning to you all!" She smiled at their rosy cheeks and eager faces. "You look like you've been enjoying the wind! How can I help you?" She patted down her hair, leave a trace dusting of flour among the errant strands.

"Well, this is our first time here, and we thought we might take a little look at what you have, if that's alright." Dad looked at his kids who were eying the range of goodies with eager faces. This is where he needed to step in quickly or they'd want something like this every day. There would go all the fine talk about getting exercise!

"Just something simple to add to our lunch, gang. We've got plenty of days here, and I'm sure we'll be back." Dad scanned the shelves for something on the lighter side, but without much success. Cream horns, Bakewell tarts… *Talk about tempting.*

"Are you here on holiday?" The lady shifted several chocolate éclairs to the front of their tray as if to further advertise their presence. *Rather unnecessary*, thought Dad.

"Yes, we are," answered Rachel. She was never afraid to enter into a conversation, and liked the look of the cheery faced proprietor. "We're staying at the Squire Inn."

"Oh, yes, with the Tremannons. What a lovely couple they are. That manor house now. It's one of the oldest buildings around. Are you liking it there?"

"Yes!" put in Emily. It's a really neat place."

"It's got a special feel, doesn't it? The old owner was a real lover of antiques. He was quite a collector and the place was full of them, but most were sold off when he moved out." The lady seemed well disposed to chat, and Dad wondered if that was typical of the pace of life in the village.

"The dear old Squire really loved that home," she continued. "It broke his heart to leave, but he just couldn't take care of it by himself. He was slowing down, you know."

"Happens to the best of us," nodded Dad.

The shop keeper laughed heartily. "Right, right, I'm not so spry myself." She wiped a floury hand on her apron and extended it over the counter. "I'm Flora Cribbins. My husband and I own the shop, though I'm the one you'll see up front—he's usually in the back putting together some culinary masterpiece. But if you ask me," and she winked at the kids, "I think he's happier with his mixing bowls and leaving the chatterboxing to me!"

"Well, I'm David Chapman, and this is Emily, Rachel, Danny and Stevie. My wife, Kathie, is back at the Inn, having a slower morning. We only got in last night."

"Well, then, welcome, welcome. So what do you think of our little village?"

"We love it!" said Rachel, her eyes shining. "It's really exciting—with the harbor and cliffs, and all the trails leading every which way. It's just like a mystery story I read once."

Mrs. Cribbins laughed again. "I don't mean to disappoint you, but nothing much happens here in the way of excitement." She paused for a second. "Though I take that back. Funnily enough we do have our own little mystery right now."

"Really, what is it?" Rachel wondered. Danny and Stevie listened, wide-eyed, and even Emily stopped peering at a tray of strawberry tarts and looked up.

"You should read this week's paper. It's got a good story on it, with all the details. Hang on a minute, I've got one here." She disappeared into the rear of the shop, only to emerge a few moments later shaking her head. "It's not there, and who knows where it's gone. Harry probably used it to wipe his boots off! His brain's in his baking most mornings, with no time for anything else." Her mock disgust was accompanied by a twinkle in the eye, assuring Emily that she really was very fond of her husband.

The other kids looked disappointed, however. Dad patted Stevie on the shoulder. "No problem. There's a paper back at the inn. Thanks for looking Mrs. Cribbins!"

"Oh, call me Flo, please! Mrs. Cribbins sounds stuffy-enough to plug your nose. You can call me Auntie Flo," she added to the kids with a smile.

"Got it!" said Dad. "And now, what can you recommend for lunch? We'll probably do sandwiches if you had some bread or rolls that would work…"

"Well, I've got both, but how about trying some of our specialty breads? We've garlic-cheese, parmesan-herb, sesame-onion, and one with ham and cheddar." Flo gestured to a warming rack, the glass front steaming up from the dozen or so golden round loaves inside. "Crusty on the outside, and soft on the inside. Try some! Here you go, kids!"

She extracted a loaf and broke off some generous portions, doling them out to the eagerly waiting hands. By the expressions on their faces, it didn't take long for the kids to be sold. As he chewed thoughtfully, Dad had to concur. He'd better be careful here. Flora Cribbins was a skilled saleswoman, and he already had a weakness for this stuff.

"Okay, Mrs. er, Flo. It looks like you've made a sale. We'll take a ham and cheddar and a garlic-cheese. No doubt we'll be back to try some more another day." *Now, what was that?* Aha. Stevie was plucking at his sleeve again.

"Don't forget a treat, Daddy, and you know Mommy likes chocolate."

Oh, yes. There was that, too. Dad hesitated, not wanting to spend too much, but realizing he had promised something along that line.

Flo noticed the exchange, and evidently read his mind. "As first-time customers, I want to give you a little something as a way to say welcome to the shop, and Penrithen village." She selected six squares of something dark and chocolately-looking from a tray behind her and popped them in a paper bag. "Chocolate-Toffee Brownie Cake—guaranteed to bring a smile to the face and joy to the stomach. A gift for you all and the missus. I know they're good…I had four of them for breakfast!" She exploded again into a hearty laugh.

"Well, now, thank you, but I couldn't…" Dad stopped as he noticed his kids were performing some sort of bouncing dance with big smiles on their faces.

"Yes, you can! No arguments please." Flo thrust the bag into his hand with a meaningful look in her eye, as if daring him to challenge it.

His mind had apparently been made up for him. "Well, okay then. They do look fantastic, and I know Kathie will be delighted. We do appreciate your generosity very much."

Flo looked pleased and rang up their total, while Rachel took the bag with the bread.

"Do come by again! Cheerio, now!" she smiled.

The children all waved as they exited the shop with a chorus of thank-yous.

"She was so nice, wasn't she," said Rachel. The others nodded.

"Yes," agreed Dad, zipping up his jacket again against the brisk wind. "She was definitely nice. I'm sure we'll talk to her some more soon." Though how he would survive this vacation without having to extend his belt a few notches, he had no idea. *Auntie Flo and her Chocolate-Toffee Brownie Cake indeed.* Friendly bakers could be dangerous to the waistline!

�

They had no trouble at all finding Peterson's Grocers a few hops further up the road from the Crusty Muffin. *"Excellence in Victuals since 1913"* the sign on the door had boasted, and Mr. Peterson himself, a lanky grizzled specimen who glared at them through small owlish spectacles, looked like he might have been in on it from the beginning. He stooped, vulture-like over the checkout counter, drumming his fingers with apparent impatience. Emily and Rachel nervously emptied the shopping basket in front of him, while Dad tried to come up with some light conversation but was defeated by the shop-keeper's taciturn manner. Dad's attempt to pay with a credit card resulted in almost palpable waves of disapproval from the other side of the counter, and he had to delve deep in his pockets to come up with enough money to pay the bill. They ended up fleeing the premises as soon as they were handed their bags, feeling like they'd escaped from a suffocating prison.

"Whew!" Dad shook his head wonderingly. "He wasn't exactly a bubbly personality. He and Auntie Flo need to hang out together more."

"Perhaps he doesn't like strangers. You know, some people might not like tourists and such. This *is* a small town." Emily was always kind. It affected her tremendously when she encountered someone less than pleasant, and she made a personal goal to both pray for Mr. Peterson, and see if somehow, someday she could get him to smile.

There was a tiny art gallery, a small bank, a woolen shop, and an intriguing little place called the 'Mole Hole' that Emily and Rachel both agreed was definitely worth visiting, the sooner the better. At the bottom of the hill was what the British called a newsagents—a small store selling newspapers and candy, with racks of postcards and a bright assortment of beach toys crowding the sidewalk outside.

"Those look interesting." Emily pointed to where several narrow streets led off of the mini roundabout just beyond the store.

Dad glanced at his watch. "We'll have to explore those later. It's time to head back."

On their right they passed a large stone building overlooking the harbor— some sort of village hall apparently, with a sign proclaiming a Bingo tournament every Thursday evening at seven—come one, come all. Just beyond was what looked like a small Fish and Chips shop. Dad took special note. *Fish and Chips!* My, my! Not inexpensive these days, no sir, but worth at least one visit during their stay.

"Do you think we can go up above the inn and check out that field?" Rachel pointed up to the hill in front of them as they crested the little bridge. "I think I saw some horses!"

God must have had young girls in mind when He created horses, thought Dad. *Talk about magnetic attractions again.* "I think we could manage it," he said out loud, "but after lunch though. Mummy will probably want to get out and stretch her legs then."

Kathie Chapman had grown up with horses herself, and wouldn't take much persuading to go on a horse hunt, that was for sure.

⊰⊱

The lane up to the inn had grown at least twice as long since this morning— at least that's what Stevie thought. Danny noticed his lagging pace, and dropped back to his side.

"Hey, Stevie! Remember what that baker lady—Auntie Flo—said about a mystery? It's in the newspaper, and Daddy was looking at one at the inn when he was tying his shoes."

He and Stevie were on the same wavelength, and his words had a magical effect.

"Right! Let's go!" Stevie shot off up the hill, Danny breathlessly trying to keep up.

Dad and the girls looked on in amusement. Evidence again of how one's state of mind affected one's physical energy. Stevie was proof in person.

As they rounded the corner into the driveway, however, the boys stopped in alarm, sending a spray of gravel around the feet of a giant figure silhouetted against the sun. Mr. Tremannon calmly looked up from where he was trimming the hedge by the gate with a pair of long-handled shears, acting as if it were a normal occurrence to have small boys drop out of thin air.

"Morning," he said, drawing out the word in his rich, warm accent. He didn't exactly smile, but his eyes softened slightly at the sight of the wide-eyed pair beneath his gaze. The others nearly bumped into them as they came around the hedge. Dad took in the situation in a moment and came to the boys' rescue.

"Hello, Mr. Tremannon! Fine day for a little trimming."

"Aye."

"We were just enjoying a stroll through the village. It's a lovely place."

"Right," the elderly man agreed with a slight nod.

"We met Mrs. Cribbins." Dad really had a hard time calling her Flo.

"Aye."

"That's quite a bakery she has there."

"Right."

Hmm, this conversation doesn't seem to be going anywhere fast. Time to come up with an exit line. "Well, we'll leave you to carry on. Have a good day!" With a smile that was feeling a little fixed, Dad turned and ushered his brood on up the driveway. That friendly baker must truly be the exception to the rule in terms of chattiness in this place, he decided.

Mr. Tremannon looked after them for a moment and then resumed his measured clipping.

∽◌∾

"Where's the newspaper?" Stevie was bent almost double looking under the bench where Dad had been reading earlier. "I can't see it."

"I left it right there on the bench." Dad was trying to determine whether it would be better to put the mayo in the fridge or on the shelf, seeing as it hadn't been opened yet.

"It's not there!"

Dad looked up briefly. "Ask the others to help. I'm trying to put away the groceries!"

Stevie peered into the big dining room, and spied Danny examining the stuffed birds in the case. The girls were nowhere to be seen.

"Danny! We were going to look for the newspaper, remember? For the mystery!"

Finally a sympathetic ear. Danny abandoned his scrutinizing and trotted over eagerly.

"We'll be like Sherlock Holmes, the detective," said Danny, seriously. "He always finds a clue." Stevie nodded at him, impressed.

The two of them searched around the entryway, and even into the dining room, but to no avail. They couldn't believe it. Mr. Holmes would have been sure to find something.

"It's not here!" yelled Stevie again, poking his head into the entryway. His Dad was just about to respond, when Mrs. Tremannon bustled in from the kitchen.

"What's not here, love?"

Stevie found himself suddenly tongue-tied. Fortunately Danny came through.

"We're looking for the newspaper my Daddy was reading. It was on the bench."

43

"Oh yes, I saw it in the kitchen. Hang on a sec." She disappeared for a moment, and returned holding the paper rather gingerly by its corner. "I'm afraid one of the dogs must have drooled on it, but there you go. I'll set it on the bench and you can look at it when it dries." Content with this, Mrs. Tremannon disappeared back into the kitchen, leaving Danny and Stevie looking at each other.

Dog drool? Did Sherlock Holmes ever have to deal with dog drool?

Chapter 3 - An Unexpected Encounter

The wind chime hanging from the eaves rang a rich yet uneven melody as the family munched their sandwiches, enjoying their view across the lawn and through the trees to where the headland sloped up to meet the sky. They had found an ornate metal table and chairs on the small stone terrace near the back door, and were putting it to good use. The children had been doing more talking than eating though, spilling out all the adventures of the morning to their mother who was almost always a patient and interested listener. She was good at encouraging conversation—asking questions, smiling or exclaiming at all the right spots—and each child tried to outdo each other recounting the trivia of the morning.

"Well," she said at a momentary lull in the conversation. "You *have* had quite a morning! Thank you for all the details of the town and all the interesting people you saw."

Dad winked at her surreptitiously. Perhaps a few more details than necessary in his opinion. The fine art of summarizing was a wee bit of a challenge for his kids.

"How was your morning, Mommy?" asked Emily politely. "Did you find a quiet spot?"

"Oh, yes…but it's a secret." His wife had a faraway look in her eyes. "Oh, I'll show you sometime," she added, noting Stevie's disappointed look.

"Mommy, would you like to go for a walk up the hill? I think I saw some horses." Rachel gestured over the trees with her sandwich.

"And we could stroll up to the top of the headland. There's sure to be quite a view," added Emily.

Danny glanced at Stevie. That sounded fun, but what about the newspaper? Wouldn't it be dry by now? Stevie chewed thoughtfully, pondering the same dilemma.

"I'd love to go. I'm ready to stretch my legs!" Their mother poured herself a glass of lemonade. "But first the girls still need to put away their clothes."

"What about the boys?" questioned Dad.

"Theirs are already done, but actually I need to do a tiny bit of school grading."

Dad nodded, agreeably. "No problem! I'll gather stuff for our walk."

Stevie looked at Danny, who raised his eyebrows. *Maybe they would have some time after all.*

⸙

"It took a few minutes to find the paper again. Someone had moved it off of the bench and onto the sideboard in the dining room. The boys stood looking at it, both excited to delve into a potential mystery, but neither one really wanting to risk getting drooly hands.

"Hey, boys, have you seen my sunglasses?" Dad had apparently appeared out of nowhere and had put his hands on the boys' shoulders, causing them both to leap in shock. He studied their scared countenances and the newspaper in front of them. There was something up here, for sure.

"I'm really sorry for scaring you, but what are you two up to?"

"We found the newspaper about the mystery." Danny tried to calm himself down.

"Aha. That makes sense. So why are you standing there staring at it?"

Danny wrinkled his nose. "Mrs. Tremannon said a dog had drooled on it."

"But it's probably dry by now," added Stevie brightly, hoping Dad might take the hint.

Dad smiled and picked it up. "Hmm, well, it's a bit damp but not too bad." He checked his watch. They still had a few minutes so, to the boys' delight, he led them over to one of the window seats and plunked down. Shaking the paper open, he found the article.

"Well, boys, I'm afraid the dog did have a bit of a drool problem." Dad indicated the stained area where the dog must have gripped the newspaper. "At least I can read *some* of the article. Let's see. 'Something *woman inherits mystery.*' If I remember, I think it said "local" but it's a bit goopy there. I can't read her name, but then it says '*has received an inheritance, but it remains a mystery as to what that inheritance is. Mrs.*'—unfortunately I can't read the last name——'*is the sole inheritor of the estate of*—rats, I can't read a whole chunk here. It may say something like '*collecting antiques*' but the rest is too blurred. Okay, here it says '*and his late wife, Rosemary who had no*'—something. Then it's all blurry again, but I can make out a word or two. Let's see—maybe '*Wormly*'—that must be a name I suppose—then '*envelope addressed to*' and then the last bit, '*this month, but declined to elaborate on the details, citing client confidentiality.*'"

The boys slumped in disappointment. This didn't seem to tell them much at all!

"I didn't really get it." Stevie pored over the somewhat soggy article.

"Well, a lady inherited something, but it looks like no-one knows what it is. Inherited means that she received something that a relative wrote down in a will—that's a special kind of document that says what people want done with their things when they die."

"And what about the envelope and that last legal something," Danny wanted to know.

"Well, the will could be in an envelope, or maybe the envelope contains what she's inheriting, like a check or something." Dad got up from the seat. "And her lawyer doesn't want to reveal the details. He doesn't have to, you see. Now, go use the bathroom."

Stevie started to say something, but Danny interrupted him. "Yes, Daddy, we'll go."

He whispered to Stevie. "Don't give up. Maybe we can find out some more stuff somewhere! We're detectives now, and we're on a case!"

Galloping across the green fields on a beautiful chestnut mare, the blue of the sea in the distance and the scent of wildflowers on the wind—Rachel was daydreaming as she rested her arms on the top of the old iron gate. She could almost feel the contours of the land rising and falling beneath the pounding hooves. The sound of her Mom taking a snapshot of her brought her back to reality.

"Oh, Mom, my hair is probably all over the place!" Rachel tried to subdue the waving strands.

"Don't worry, you look lovely." Her mother smiled. "I know what you were thinking about!" She gestured into the sloping field where five or six horses were contentedly feeding, their tails swishing against the flies. "Can I come with you?"

"Sure, let's go! We can be back by dinner." They both laughed. As her daughters were rapidly growing up and experiencing all the blessings and challenges of the teen years, it was a special treasure for Mom to find those moments when she could really connect emotionally with them.

Dad looked over at them from where he and Emily were examining the flowers along the hedgerow. "If you ladies are done with your ride, we should probably get going again."

Mom looked at her watch. "You're right. The afternoon's getting on, and I don't want to have to rush back for dinner."

Stevie took a look up the lane, which disappeared around a leafy curve a little way ahead. The church might still be miles away for all he knew. "I don't think I can make it. I'm so tired." He slumped over and stumbled forward a few paces.

Mom looked at Dad and winked. Dad raised his eyebrows, then caught her idea and whispered something to Danny.

"Hey, Stevie. Race you to the top! Last one there is a rotten egg!" Danny took off at top speed.

"What? Hey, wait! No fair!" The young lad tore off after his brother with an amazing burst of energy. You could almost see the smoke coming from his shoes.

Emily looked after his retreating back, and gave a little laugh. "Well, well, well."

⋙⋘

The little chapel slumbered peacefully in the hazy sunshine, protected from the wind as it crouched in its hollow near the top of the headland. The grey granite walls, spotted with yellowish lichen, were crumbling in places, while the stained slate roof seemed to be sagging with the weight of the years, giving an impression of both age and gradual neglect. Even the steeple seemed to be leaning a little, as if tired from its long service.

The timbered lych-gate led through a low wall and up some stone steps into the yard, where a sea of unkempt grass scattered with daisies and dandelions lapped against the weathered gravestones. It had obviously been a while since anyone had taken care of the grounds, and a mass of brambles had engulfed the whole back side of the churchyard—threatening to swallow up the building itself. Runaway branches intertwined with a straggling climbing rose that curled in tangled arches around the door, ready to snag the hair of any unwary visitor.

The winding lane up the hill had gradually narrowed until it came to a dead end at the gate, from where a narrow footpath curved up to the church. A few stunted pines traced the line of the trail, their reaching branches leaning away from the wind. The boys considered whether to go on, but decided to stop at the gate and wait for the rest of the family. Stevie was just about to say that he was sure he had touched the gate first, when Danny raised his hand.

"Hey, do you see that?"

"What?"

"There was someone there."

"Where?" Stevie didn't like the way Danny's voice sounded.

"Over there, in the graveyard. He was looking right at us, but then he disappeared around the back."

"Well, it was probably just someone else seeing the church." Stevie had no desire to think about spooky things this close to a bunch of graves. "Why don't you go ahead first? You're the oldest." This was one time when Stevie didn't mind being last in line.

Danny hesitated, not sure how to best come up with an excuse. He looked back to see where the rest of the family were. *Oh, thank goodness!* There was Dad's head bobbing along the top of the hedgerow.

"We'd better wait," he said. He picked up a few loose stones and tossed them idly into the bushes. "We don't want the others to get lost."

⋙⋘

"Here, kitty, kitty." Rachel was crouched down, her hand outstretched to a prim-looking plump grey tabby sitting upright beside the church door, its purple collar accentuating its rather regal appearance.

"Oh, how cute!" Mom came over from where she had been trying to help the boys decipher an ancient memorial stone. "Don't run, boys—you'll scare it."

48

But the cat didn't seem at all disturbed by the sudden crowd. It lifted its chin to Rachel's attentive scratching, closing its eyes in bliss until, unable to resist any longer, it collapsed onto its side, stretching in ecstasy, a loud purring emanating from its body like a mini motorbike warming up.

"Be careful," warned Dad as Rachel started to scratch its stomach. "Not many cats like being touched there." He'd had a few memorable experiences himself to that effect, with the cat transforming in a split second from friendly and relaxed to a ball of claws and teeth wrapped tightly around his arm. This one, however, seemed to relish the attention, stretching even more to a seemingly impossible length.

"It's really friendly. I wonder whose it is," said Emily, impressed.

Danny and Stevie looked at each other. *They* knew. That guy! Was he inside?

"Probably someone visiting the church," suggested Dad, indicating the cat's purple leash that was looped around a metal post at the roots of the climbing rose.

"And loves taking their kitty for walks," smiled Mom. "Come on, let's go on in."

Dad pointed to a sign attached to the huge oak door with a bright orange thumbtack: *This church is a place for quiet reflection and prayer. Please respect its sanctity.* "Okay, boys. Hats off now, and remember to keep your voices down."

Even though it had seemed quiet enough in the open air, the inside of the chapel had a rich, heavy silence that they noticed at once. The little foyer had a distinguished if rather cluttered appearance with an uneven stack of old hymn books in the corner, several cardboard boxes by the far wall and an assortment of cleaning supplies, brooms and mops behind the door. A notice board held nothing but three or four brass tacks and a faded card announcing a wedding being held on January 16th, 1978. Stevie took a long sniff, kind of liking the smell of beeswax furniture polish with a suggestion of musty dampness somewhere in the background.

A set of dark doors stood slightly open to the right, and Rachel peered around them into the nave. A short aisle led between six or seven straggling rows of oak pews to the small chancel, separated from the nave by a low lattice screen. The musty odor was stronger here, but actually didn't seem all that unpleasant in the surroundings. Judging by the dark stains she noticed along the top of the walls, there had been some problems with the roof leaking. Maybe that was what caused the smell.

At the end of the nave a few steps led up to the altar, above which a bright stained glass window showered colored light onto the faded silk altar cloth.

"I think it's empty," whispered Rachel. She beckoned to the others and they tiptoed in.

Stevie wasn't sure what to think. It was so quiet in there. The building almost seemed to be listening to them. But to the others there was something indefinably special about this little chapel, neglected as it seemed. There was a coolness from the old walls and flagstones that was refreshing somehow, and a coziness in the low arched ceiling and cramped confines that hinted at an intimacy with God. Judging by the disorderly arrangement of the pews though, the place hadn't been used for a long time. *Why did it seem so abandoned now?*

Stevie took a careful look around. Thankfully there didn't seem to be any sign of the mysterious man. He plumped himself down on a pew and looked up at the stained glass window above the altar. It was a picture of Jesus on the cross. He gazed at it, swinging his legs back and forth. It was pretty clever, he thought, the way it was done with all those different pieces of glass.

Emily took a seat next to him after carefully dusting off the faded wood. There was something about this old church that had a calming effect on her soul. Not that she had really been stressed today, but that lurking uncertainty about the future was never far away. She looked at the set of arched windows set deep into the old stone walls on each side of the nave. There were four on one side and three on the other, each with a beautiful scene from the Bible formed in a mosaic of glass. Those on the west side of the church were illuminated by the afternoon sunlight, a kaleidoscope of scarlets, magentas, and emerald greens spilling across the floor and giving a richness to the otherwise rather drab surroundings.

Mom looked over to where Dad, Rachel and Danny were examining a huge stone font lurking in the corner which seemed to hold nothing but an assortment of tarnished candle sticks. She was wondering how long it had been since anyone last used the building when she heard a slight noise from somewhere at the head of the nave. Curious, she walked quietly up the aisle to where a short transept led to the base of the steeple. A few benches had been left there, apparently for use if the congregation had been uncommonly large, and on the farthest one, out of sight from the rest of the family, a lady was sitting, her head bowed and hands clasped together, a large blue envelope on her lap. She couldn't see the person's face, hidden under a dark red headscarf, but she was obviously elderly and seemed to be crying softly. As Mom paused, unsure of what to do, the lady looked up. Her face, framed in white curls, was pleasant enough, but care worn, Mom thought, like someone who had had more than their share of sorrow.

The lady stood up, grabbing onto the back of a bench to steady herself, the envelope sliding to the floor. She reached down quickly, grabbed it up and stuffed it in her handbag.

"Oh, I'm terribly sorry. I was just going," she stammered as she hurried past Mom to the side door facing the transept. In her fumbling haste to open the door, she dropped her bag, which spilled its contents across the floor. The rest of the family, amazed as this sudden demonstration, watched open-mouthed as Mom leapt to her aid. She got on her hands and knees and helped gather the various items from where they were scattered under the pews.

As she handed them back, her eyes met the lady's for just a moment and Mom smiled in compassion. In that split second something unexpected happened— something quite extraordinary according to Mom as she struggled to describe it later. It was like something passed between them—there was a connection of some sort. It felt almost like she had been given a portion of this elderly lady's sorrow to share.

As their gaze lingered, the woman's worried look was replaced by one of puzzlement. Then she pulled herself together and stood up rather stiffly. Muttering some thanks, she hurried out the side door.

❧❦❧

Stevie was having trouble concentrating. The family had decided they would pray for the mysterious lady, and were gathered on the pew next to the font. Stevie, nearest the aisle, could see something by the leg of the pew on the other side near the front, and was trying to figure out what it was. *Now if he only had a long stretchy neck, he could stretch it way over there and check it out.* And then he could stretch it up and check out the inside of the steeple. Maybe there was a hole or something his head would fit through, unless there were bats or something up there. *Whoops,* he remembered. *They were praying.* Feeling guilty, he abandoned his musings and tuned back in.

"And please give her your peace," prayed Emily.

"And show us how to be a blessing to her if our paths cross again," added Mom.

"And, Jesus, please help us to find her so we can give her back her thing."

Dad and Mom both popped their eyes open. Where had *that* comment come from?

"Amen," said Dad and turned to address the lad. "What thing, Stevie?"

The whole family looked puzzled, which made the young lad feel kind of special. He knew something important!

"I think there's something over there that fell out of her bag—you know, when it spilled everywhere." Stevie nodded to himself seriously. "I'll get it!" He scampered over and grabbed it up.

"It looks like some sort of locket," said Rachel, examining what her brother retrieved.

"Yes, but missing the chain." Her mother took it carefully and turned it over in her hands. It appeared to be made of silver, slightly tarnished, and with an intricate filigree front. There was a tiny catch on the side, and she had to use her fingernail to open it. Inside was a cracked grey photo of a smiling white-haired man with a big walrus moustache and round reading glasses perched on the end of his prominent nose. Even across the years Mom could tell that he must have been a merry old gentleman—there was something in his eyes and maybe the way he was smiling that gave him an almost mischievous look. She held it up for the others to see.

"Is that a picture of Saint Nicholas?" wondered Stevie. He knew the true story of Santa Claus, and this did seem to match a lot of the pictures he'd seen around Christmas time.

"Stevie! Saint Nicholas had a beard! Right, Daddy?" Danny was sure of it.

"Well, we don't really know, but he did live long before cameras, so I don't think it's his photo." Dad looked again at the faded image. "He looks like a really pleasant fellow, doesn't he?"

51

"But how are we going to find the lady and get it back to her?" Stevie felt personally responsible since it was his discovery.

Mom patted his shoulder. "I'm not sure, dear, but if it's meant to happen, God will make a way." She looked thoughtful for a moment. For some reason, she felt sure of it.

Dad stood at the crest of the hill just above the church, looking out to sea. His wife moved over and stood next to him and he put his arm around her waist. "Beautiful, isn't it," he murmured.

From their breezy, lofty eyrie they could see a long way up and down the coast. To the north, lodged comfortably in its little valley, the village lay like a perfect model, and on its near side they could just make out the chimneys of the inn peeking above the trees. Beyond the town, a string of coves and headlands melted into the haze. To the south, the coast swung outwards forming a series of precipitous cliffs, looking like the walls of an imposing fortress trying to resist the assaults of the pounding surf. Every now and then they could hear the dull thump as a huge breaker exploded on to one of the sharp rocks at their base, sending up a plume of water and spray. Above the cliffs loomed a lofty point about a half mile away, its pale green sides crisscrossed by the thread of a narrow trail leading to a large stone column at the top. The sky beyond was a pale eggshell blue, darkening to a deep cobalt hue overhead where frail wisps of cirrus cloud fanned delicately across the expanse.

Mr. Chapman looked across at his wife, curious that she hadn't responded to his comment. To his surprise her face was serious with a faraway look in her eyes. She was playing with that lock of hair again, twisting it tightly between her fingers like she was tugging thoughts through her mind.

He put his hand on her shoulder. "Honey, what are you thinking about?"

"Hmm?" She stopped her twirling and looked at him. "Oh, I was just thinking about that lady. Something was really up with her. I don't know..." She trailed off.

"Oh, I see." *Not exactly the most intelligent response,* he thought.

His wife's train of thought was broken though, and she glanced down at her watch, her eyes widening. It was later than she thought.

"Come on, kids. It's time!" Mom looked across to where the girls were reluctantly stirring from where they had been stretched out on their backs, making chains out of the daisies scattered across the grass. *And where were the boys?* She spotted them peering around to the back of the church. *What were they up to, anyway?* They looked like they were being pretty sneaky. Maybe they were still looking for the lady, but when they'd left the church she had seemingly vanished from sight, along with her cat. Mom looked down the hill to the village. The compassion she had felt earlier welled up again. Somehow, somewhere she hoped they were going to run into her again.

Danny was getting desperate. He was hopping from one foot to the other, trying not to think about how much he needed to go. Apart from the bathroom off the landing, the only other facility was off his parent's bedroom, and both places were unfortunately currently occupied. The family had got back to the inn about ten minutes ago to a wonderful aroma drifting from the kitchen. The smell was not as fully appreciated as it might have been, however, with the more pressing business at hand. Danny, distracted for a moment, had lost his opportunity for leading the dash for the stairs.

Mom and Dad's room lay along the front side of the inn, and the late afternoon sunlight poured in through the large window. The peaceful scene didn't match the lad's mood, however. Stevie was humming something from the other side of the bathroom door, and Danny fervently wished that he himself could be so relaxed.

"Hurry up!" he yelled impatiently. The humming stopped for a moment as if in consideration, then resumed unconcernedly.

Okay, he really needed to occupy his mind somehow. He focused his attention on a framed picture, hanging below a brass candle holder. It was a painting of a house on a cliff—a large white house with big chimneys. *Now who might have lived there? A sailor, and captain even? Or how about a family of smugglers?* It was really too hard to think about anything right now. Maybe he would have been better off waiting at the other bathroom door.

He decided to try looking out the window. Pushing aside the sheers, he took in the view across the gravel parking area to the vegetable garden beyond as he bobbed up and down. It looked like Mr. Tremannon had finished with his trimming, and was now pruning something or other. Danny could just make out the elderly man's body beneath the inn sign which almost blocked his view, hanging just to the left of the window sill.

He had never really looked at the sign before—he had just a vague impression that it had a picture of some old guy on it—but it was actually rather interesting. His eyes suddenly widened. In fact, it was *very* interesting. Above the inn's name written in ornate gold strokes was a painting of an elderly man playing chess at a table, with a globe on a stand and a bright stained glass picture of a ship hanging in the window behind him. But it was the gentleman's face that made Danny stare in astonishment. The white hair, the round glasses and above all the amazing walrus moustache—it was the same person in that locket they'd found at the church! No way! He couldn't wait to tell someone!

"Stevie, I found him! I found the guy!" He yelled through the door and then tore out of the room, completely forgetting about his other predicament.

There was a sudden silence from the bathroom—then a plaintive wail followed by the sound of hurried flushing. "Wait, Danny, wait, I'm coming! Wait for me! No fair!"

Dad was waiting for his chance. The family was seated around the dining table, the remains of their meal spread across its broad expanse. The evening's fare had consisted of the most exquisite chicken pie they had ever tasted, its flaky crust and succulent filling jostling for culinary preeminence with enough crispy roast potatoes, steaming vegetables and home-made gravy to—according to Dad— *sink the Bismarck.* Eating dessert after all that seemed rather superfluous, but that didn't diminish their anticipation of Mrs. Tremannon's next masterpiece. She was a singular cook, no doubt about it.

Despite all that, however, there was something even more pressing on their minds. They were all bursting with suspense at knowing more about the mysterious gentleman on the inn sign. Was he the squire that their hostess had mentioned—the namesake of the inn? Unfortunately, they hadn't had a moment yet to ask her. She was a bustler—that was for sure. She bustled in and bustled out again, chatting away while moving at a surprising speed despite her limp. She was even more talkative than usual this evening, and there hadn't been a second to get a word in edgewise. They could hear her coming now, and a moment later she ambled in through the doorway balancing a tray that could have doubled as a Viking shield, loaded down with six glass dishes full of something pink and frothy, a pot of decaf coffee with fixings, and several large mugs.

"Now then, dearies, let me just set my tray down here and I'll get rid of the rest of the dishes. Here's something light to finish off with. It's called strawberry fool and there's whipped cream in the bowl. Coffee's hot and so's the milk in the jug. I didn't make any tea, 'cause I thought you'd prefer the coffee, but I can make you some tea if you like."

Dad leaned forward, his mouth open to speak and his face stuck in a kind of expectant look, much to the amusement of the children, but Mrs. Tremannon wasn't done yet.

"I've got cheese and crackers, too, if you want. I've found some right good cheddar, and some Edam, and even some of that smelly French cheese with the blue bits in it if you're fond of that sort of thing. Not that you have to have any cheese. I've just read that all the posh places serve cheese and crackers at the end of the meal."

She was setting out the contents of the tray as she spoke, and the children looked from her back to their Dad, wondering how he might break in to the constant stream of chatter.

"There now, I hope you enjoy it. I made some of that dessert for a family a few weeks ago and they just loved it—wanted me to make it every night! Not to say that you'll feel the same, though." She started stacking the dirty dinner plates without pausing. Dad raised his hand slightly, causing Stevie to have to stuff his napkin in his mouth to keep from snorting with laughter.

"They were from Scotland, or was it Wales? But everyone's different, aren't they? Now, I knew a family from Bogna Regis who wouldn't eat dessert at all. At least the parents wouldn't let the kids have any. Maybe they belonged to one of those groups who don't eat certain things for religious reasons, or I suppose the father might have been a dentist."

Mrs. Tremannon was done stacking the dishes and was headed for the door again. Dad made a sudden decision and leaped out of his chair, accidentally knocking it over backwards with a loud crash. Rachel and Mom had to look away to keep from laughing uncontrollably. Mrs. Tremannon paused, looking back in concern. "Are you alright?"

Dad hurriedly set his chair back in place. "So, sorry. I just had a quick question."

"Well of course. How can I help you?" She set the tray down on the corner of the table.

The kids all sat up a little straighter. *This was it! Way to go, Dad!*

"The squire you were telling me about the other day—the one who used to live here." Dad didn't want to lose his captive audience and tried to cram all his questions in together. "He's the one on the inn sign isn't he? Did he have any relatives? And didn't you say he died rather recently?"

"That's right, the squire—Squire Penrow."

Danny stiffened slightly. Penrow—he knew he's seen that name, but where?

But Mrs. Tremannon was continuing. "That's him on the sign sure enough—playing chess. A local artist painted that–a kind of tribute, you could say. The Squire loved chess, almost as much as he loved collecting old things. He had some really old chess sets, but I think he sold them all off. This place used to be full of antiques—real treasures you know. He was a collector he was—really knew his stuff. Very smart, and yet one of the nicest men you'd ever want to meet. Always doing nice things for folks—helping them out."

She had a faraway look in her eyes again, and Dad saw his opportunity and jumped in.

"You said that his wife passed away. Was that a long time before he died?"

"Dear me, yes. She died in…let me see. It was back in the sixties I think, or was it the fifties? I remember her funeral was right after cousin Daphne married Percy the fishmonger. Now when was that?"

"Nineteen fifty-seven, wasn't it?" Mom leaned forward. "His wife's name was Rosie."

For a full five seconds Mrs. Tremannon was speechless. The rest of the family turned and looked at Mom with admiration. This was better than a play!

"Well I never! That's right. But how did you know…?"

"In the flower garden out back…I saw a plaque. I just remembered."

"That's right. Of course, the garden! I haven't been back there for ages. It probably needs a trim now, doesn't it? The Squire used to spend a lot of time in that spot, thinking or praying. There were some right pretty flowers there. Nineteen fifty-seven!" She chuckled reflectively. "You gave me quite a stir! A lot happened that year, didn't it? And Daphne only seventeen years old and her father weren't too keen on Percy the fishmonger." Mrs. Tremannon shook herself back to the present. "But there, now, the dishes are waiting."

She rescued her loaded tray and turned to go. Dad flashed a concerned look at the kids. This was interesting information, all right, but he still didn't have all the answers.

"So did the Squire have any children?" he called in desperation after the woman's retreating back.

Mrs. Tremannon stopped in the doorway without turning around.

"No, he didn't. Well, sort of." She paused. "Little Ruthie." Her shoulders drooped slightly as if the name itself bore some weight of sorrow. Then she seemingly pulled herself together and disappeared around the corner.

The family looked at each other. Rachel raised her eyebrows. Stevie wrinkled his brow in confusion. So far this mystery was like trying to work on a jigsaw puzzle where the picture was all sky, and half the pieces were missing!

∽᠗᠗ᢌ

"So, what do we have so far?" Rachel wanted to know, taking a flopping leap onto Mom and Dad's barn-sized bed. She was hoping to delay bedtime a little, their mother having announced they should get another good night's sleep after the day's activities.

Emily and Danny appeared at the doorway, toothbrushes in hand. Stevie popped up from the other side of the bed where he was looking for a toy car. Mom paused in her rummaging through the chest of drawers. This was one thing she didn't mind interrupting the proceedings for. That old lady was still on her heart. She nodded at Dad with a smile.

"Well, let's see," said Dad, pleased to have the chance to reconstruct the evidence of the day. "This house used to be the home of Squire Penrow, who just recently died—I think about a month or so ago, Mrs. Tremannon said. What else do we know about him?" This was a family affair and he wanted everyone involved in the process.

"He loved collecting antiques," said Emily.

"This house was full of them, but they were sold off," added Rachel proudly. "Flo the baker said so."

"Not all of them!" put in Danny, indistinctly, his mouth full of toothpaste. "There's still a suit of armor downstairs."

"And those stuffed, dead birds," said Stevie, excitedly, glad to be able to add something important to the discussion. Rachel and Emily looked a little confused. There was silence for a moment. A gust of wind ruffled the curtains, and Mom reached over and pulled the window shut.

"And the Squire loved chess—hence the inn sign with a painting of him playing," realized Dad.

"And," said Mom, raising her finger, "the sad lady at the church had a picture of the Squire in the locket in her purse."

"So is she the Squire's wife?" wondered Danny returning from spitting in the sink, a perfect ring of toothpaste around his mouth.

"No, no, his wife died a long time ago." Rachel was sure of it.

"And her name was Rosie," finished off Mom. "So, we still don't know who the lady is, and why she was crying, and what connection she has to the Squire."

"This is hard," said Stevie.

"No it's not," frowned Rachel. "We've found out a lot."

"Why don't we pray?" suggested Emily suddenly, not liking any sign of conflict.

Mom looked at her in surprise. It didn't seem often that the kids suggested praying. "Great idea. Will you do the honors?"

Emily bowed her head and the others followed suit. She took a deep breath. "Dear Jesus. If you want us to help that lady, please show us how to find her, what she needs and what you want us to do. Please comfort her and show yourself to her. In Jesus name."

"Amen" the family intoned together, all except Rachel who was staring into space.

"Little Ruthie," she said, her voice barely above a whisper.

"What did you say?" Her mother looked at her, intrigued.

"Mrs. Tremannon said the Squire had a sort of daughter. Could that be the lady?"

"Oh, I don't think so, do you Daddy?" Emily considered. "Why would she call her 'Little Ruthie' when the lady is old now?"

"Well, I just don't know," shrugged Dad. "Mrs. Tremannon didn't exactly say they had a child, remember, but honestly that was a bit unclear. The thick plottens" he added, using one of his favorite mixed-up expressions. The others giggled.

"Let's sleep on it," suggested Mom.

"And, that, dear children, is your mother's subtle way of saying it's TIME FOR BED!" Dad grinned. "We'll be in to pray and snuggle in a min. The court is adjourned!"

⚛⚛

Kennedy lay back on his pillow, his arms behind his head. It had felt so good to rest up these past few days--life had been intensely stressful and he was getting more and more concerned about the effect on his blood pressure. Though he hated having to depend on someone else, there was a selfish comfort in knowing it wasn't him up there on the hill, dealing with the boredom and the biting cold breezes that seemed to sweep in, even on sunny days.

There was that gnawing worry in his gut, though. Every day that passed was a day lost—a day closer to when the old lady might locate her inheritance and all hope would be gone. He gritted his teeth. Something had better happen tomorrow, or else...

57

Chapter 4 - Disappointing News

Rachel scampered along the hallway, a fleet-footed fairy in a pale green bathrobe. She had popped awake a few minutes ago and—wouldn't you know it—needed to make a hurried trip to the bathroom. Now she wanted nothing more than to dive headfirst back under the covers before she woke up too much. *What was the time, anyway?* It was light outside, but of course it was almost summer. Well, maybe she didn't want to know. She would just assume she could afford some more sleep. After all, ignorance was bliss.

As she jumped back into bed, she saw her sister stir. *Now that was a bad sign.* Emily never woke up early. Rachel reluctantly reached for her watch, accidentally knocking over the cup of water on her nightstand. Emily's eyes popped wide open, and Rachel sighed. This wasn't working at all.

"What time is it?" wondered Emily, a little grumpily.

"Seven-thirty." Rachel found herself deriving a guilty sense of satisfaction from her sister's dismayed expression. *Misery loved company, didn't it?* And she could use a little companionship in her suffering. This enforced 8:30 am breakfast time wasn't cause for much rejoicing, no matter how good the food. This was vacation and that meant sleeping in, right? *Sleeping in and then fun, fun, fun.*

Rachel threw herself back on her pillow which swallowed her head with a loud poof, sending a couple of stray feathers dancing into the air. She glared up at the ceiling—there was no way she would be able to get back to sleep now. She wondered what they would be doing today. Yes, it was only day two of a two-week break, but every day was precious and it seemed like the resumption of school was already looming like a greedy monster, eagerly devouring the vacation days.

She glanced across at her Bible perched on the window sill. She could feel the struggle between what she knew she should be doing and her desire to pretend the day hadn't started yet. She heard Emily unzipping the cover of her own Bible, and felt a distinct prick in her conscience. Emily always seemed to do what was right. *Okay, that did it.* She flung back the covers, grabbed her Bible and plumped herself down in the armchair by the bed.

Mom was enjoying the seclusion and peace of her secret garden, broken only by a committee of sparrows, arguing feistily in the nearby cherry tree. It was a bit chilly this morning and she pulled her jacket more tightly around her and took a welcome sip of her coffee. Yes, she still loved this spot and she decided to start by telling the Lord thank you for it. In her recent Bible readings, she had been struck by how often she ran into the command to be thankful, and right now was a perfect time to write some of those things down. It wasn't hard when she considered all God had done. Safety on the journey, a lovely place to stay, the fact that they were together as a family—there were many ways she could see His goodness, and she listed them all.

She thought for a minute about all her concerns and wrote those down too, determined to pray through each one. She prayed for her husband, that he would sense God's peace and have wisdom in his continuing work. She prayed for each of her children by name, that God would give them hearts that would desire to love, follow and serve Him above all else, and have a passion for His Word. She prayed for herself, for a spirit sensitive to God's leading, to be a godly wife and mother, to be content in all circumstances, and to trust her Heavenly Father for the family's future. Oh, yes, and above all to be thankful.

Then she pulled out the locket and looked at it tenderly, touched by the kindly features of the man, and the obvious tenderness held for him by the mysterious old lady.

And Lord," she added. "About this dear lady, who you love. We don't know how we can possibly help her, so please do more than we can ask or imagine…"

Dad was having a harder time being thankful. Yes, he was enjoying staying at the Inn, but it seemed like any time he stopped moving long enough to have a good think, those wretched articles crowded in again, front and center. He was perched in an armchair with his Bible, mechanically flipping through the pages, a parade of disconcerting questions blocking whatever concentration he might have achieved in his semi-awake state.

What was he going to do? He had no real idea where to start on his research here, but his editor would be expecting something meaty by next month. Two weeks off sounded heavenly at first, but could he really afford the time? He hadn't heard back yet about the first draft he had sent from France. What if it didn't go over well? He had a sneaking suspicion that it wasn't up to snuff. *Jesus, help!*

This wasn't a quiet time, he realized suddenly. It was a battle!

Amusements in Mathematics by Henry Ernest Dudeney. You have got to be kidding!

Rachel was thumbing through the selections in the bookcase in the dining room. She had been first to finish her breakfast and was looking for something light to read, but without much success. There didn't seem to be anything here newer than the Stone Age. She read the titles to herself in disgust.

"*Litchfield's Illustrated History of Furniture* and what's this? *Diseases of the Horse's Foot* by Harry Caulkin Reeks." She sniffed the musty tome. "And it certainly does!"

She was still struggling with guilt feelings about her Bible time this morning. Sometimes it seemed so easy to see it as just a chore, especially on vacation. This was the time to put aside things that felt like school work, and concentrate on relaxation and recreation—not that there was any other reading material here that was relaxing!

She suddenly pricked up her ears. Her parents were talking about what to do today. She sidled over to where they were sitting at the table, the remains of another impressive breakfast spread out before them. Mrs. Tremannon seemed to be mortally afraid lest they waste away of hunger during their stay.

"Well, we'll need to go shopping again today, I'm afraid." Mom took a tentative sip of her tea, which was still scalding hot.

Dad crunched a few times and swallowed a bite of toast and marmalade. "That's fine. That grocery store was really well stocked. We can try and get enough for quite a few days so we don't have to worry about lunches for a while."

"And then can we go to the beach!" Rachel grabbed her Dad's hand.

Mom smiled at her enthusiasm. She knew her daughter well. "You know, I would like that, even for part of the day. Mrs. Tremannon might know a place we can explore nearby."

"But I do need to see if I can rustle up an Internet connection somewhere." Dad suddenly remembered his battle from this morning. "I really need to email the editor, plus it would be good to check our mail." *Better to find out the bad news right away, hey?* he mused.

"An internet connection here?" Mom wasn't so sure such technical innovations had reached this corner of the Cornish coast.

Just then Mrs. Tremannon appeared with her tray, and Dad jumped in before she had a chance to speak. "Thank you for a wonderful breakfast. It was absolutely delicious." He switched gears without stopping. "I was wondering though if you could help us out. We need to check our email and wanted to know if there's an Internet café nearby." He realized he was in trouble even as the words left his mouth.

"A what-net café? Oh, dear—I'm not sure. Is that a place that serves fish?" Mrs. Tremannon was obviously way out of her depth. Mom shook her head, but Dad didn't want to give up so easily and ploughed on.

"No, no, a Cyber café, where you can get online and check your email—on the web."

Mom could almost sense the puzzling visions of spiders passing through the woman's mind. The old lady obviously had no idea what to say.

Mom came to her rescue. "Well, never mind, but we were also wondering if you know of a nice beach near here—somewhere we could go this afternoon." She glanced out the window. It did seem like there was another nice day in the making.

Mrs. Tremannon relaxed visibly. This was familiar territory again. She set her tray down, and adjusted her apron. "Well, you know, there are lots of lovely beaches near here. There's Treyarnon with that lovely rock swimming pool, and Polzeath—well it's so big and open and I've heard that it's great for surfing, not that I've ever done that, but I've heard it is—and Daymer Bay is pretty, and really good for families I think…and let me see, there's Harlyn Bay—that's not so far off too. You'll have to drive of course, but not more than half an hour or so, probably."

"I remember some of those beaches from when I came here as a boy," said Dad, excitedly. They sounded great to Rachel, too, whose face broke into a broad grin.

"Well, isn't that nice, and if you want something closer there are quite a few sandy coves near here, too," Mrs. Tremannon started to stack up a few dishes. "There's Dubbock's Scoop just a bit down the coast, and we actually have our own little beach just over and around the point. It doesn't have a name marked there as far as I know, but we call it Wolf cove, after the rocks nearby. You just go straight instead of turning on to the bridge and up past the fishermen's cottages and up and over the steps to the left. You could even walk there if you like—it's not far. "

"Really," said Mom. "Is it nice?" She motioned to Rachel to help clear the table.

"Well, dear, I don't know what you'd call nice or not, but there's some sand, and some tide pools, and a cave, and lots of shells."

"That sounds nice to me!" gushed Rachel as she stacked some plates. "Can we go there?" It definitely seemed the best option so far to ensure they did something today. She could just imagine getting their chores done and not having any time left to go anywhere.

Mom looked after Mrs. Tremannon's retreating back as she limped off with her loaded tray. "Well, we'll see. First things first. Get your sister to help you get the table cleared for Mrs. Tremannon, and I'll see about making a list."

"And I'll ask Mr. Tremannon about a cyber café," added Dad, seriously. Mom and Rachel both looked at him in surprise.

"Just kidding!" he grinned. "I'll just have to ask someone in town."

The man leaned over the fence and peered down along the row of cottages. He could just spy the front garden of number two—the old lady's place. The sky was clear, the salt air felt fresh and clean and the muffled roar of the surf could just be heard from the nearby cove, but the man wasn't the kind of person to notice such trivial things. His attention was fixed solely on the problem at hand.

What were the facts? The old lady had received the letter from the lawyers, but there was obviously some confusion about what she had inherited. That it was something valuable, he had no doubt. He knew the Squire's canniness for acquiring antique treasures. Whatever it was, though, it apparently wasn't something he just wanted to drop in the lady's lap. *Why was that?* This was where he had to move from fact to conjecture. Did the Squire want her to learn something about it first—perhaps the value of it so she could convert it into the most cash possible? Maybe he was trying to find a way around the notorious British inheritance tax. The lady wasn't related to the Squire, so why was she inheriting anything anyway? She'd seemingly materialized out of thin air.

The man lit a cigarette and rested an arm on the top of the fence, narrowing his eyes. He remembered clearly what he had overheard at the estate sale. As far as he knew, nothing had surfaced since then on the market that matched what they had spoken of—so it had to be the inheritance. That meant it was stored or hidden somewhere, waiting for whatever conditions were spelled out in the will. *The will.* He just had to see that letter. But that was exactly why he had to be patient. Jennings was keeping an eye on things and he would let him know the moment there was an opportunity to get it.

He chuckled to himself. *Jennings.* That simpleton. If he played his cards right Jennings would be the one taking the risks and he himself would be the one taking the prize.

✧❧✧

"You know, we forgot to ask Mrs. Tremannon about little Ruthie." Emily adjusted her sun hat to protect the back of her neck. It wasn't so breezy today, and even though there were a few clouds, there weren't enough to make much difference.

The family were strolling up the steep road from the bridge towards the supermarket, but Dad's mind was still on his quest to find some sort of Internet connection. He was scanning the side streets to see if he'd missed something on their last trip.

"What's that you said?"

"Little Ruthie. We wanted to find out more about her. I've been praying for that lady at the church."

Dad suddenly felt a little guilty. Emily was following in his wife's footsteps alright, with a spiritual sensitivity that he envied. He gave his daughter's hand a squeeze.

"I'm glad you're praying. Will you help me remember to ask Mrs. T at dinner?"

Behind them, Stevie and Danny were having a serious conversation of their own.

"Hey, if you could have an extra arm or an extra leg or an extra eye, what would you choose?" Stevie wanted to know.

Danny considered thoughtfully as he walked, kicking a stray rock in front of him.

"I think an extra eye would be great, unless it was on the back of my head 'cause then it would be under my hair and I couldn't see anything."

Stevie nodded seriously. "I know. Maybe it would be best to have one on the end of a tentacle or something so you could look around corners without being seen."

Rachel and Mom, coming along behind them gave each other a look. The mind of a young boy—who could plumb its extraordinary depths?

As they drew near to the Crusty Muffin, Dad suddenly had an idea.

"Hey, I could pop in and ask Mrs. Cribbins if she knows of any place to get online. She seemed like someone who knows what's what around here. Do you want anything?"

"No, I think we'll just stick with the grocers. I'll go and get started shopping. Who wants to come with me?" Mom looked around for volunteers.

Emily hesitated. She wasn't too keen on seeing that cranky Mr. Peterson again, but she had been praying for him. She silently asked Jesus again for strength to be nice to him. "I'll go," she said out loud.

"We'll come, too," said Stevie, nudging Danny. "Maybe we can pick out some candy or something," he whispered to his brother. "How about you, Rachel?" he added out loud.

Rachel, however, was thinking of the fantastic smells in the bakery, plus she had a funny desire to see Auntie Flo again, and maybe meet the mysterious Harry, her husband. "I'll go with Daddy," she said.

Ten minutes later, Dad found himself outside the bakery with a set of directions in one hand, a bag of Bakewell tarts in the other and a daughter who was grinning from ear to ear.

So much for just popping in to get directions, he thought. Flo—as she insisted on being called—had obviously had other ideas. Just a quick taste of a tart, still warm from the oven and meltingly delicious—that's all she wanted him to take. *Ha!* She was as cunning as a fox, and definitely didn't play fair, no sir. He'd do better next time though, yes he would. *But how was he going to explain this to his wife?*

Take a left at the memorial. Bear to the right up the cobbled street and take the first right after the Lawyers Office of Scrub, Wormly and Clink. Quite the names, thought Dad checking his scribbled directions. *But now where had he heard that name Wormly recently?*

He shook the thought out of his mind. They didn't have tons of time. Down the lane and second house on the right, after Mrs. Shribbley's Sewing Shop. *Now that was a tongue twister!*

"Here we are," announced Rachel as they halted in front of the narrow building.

Dad stuffed the directions back in his pocket. The place looked like it was straight out of a Dickens novel, a little crooked and with an upper story that overhung the entrance like it was leaning forward to peer down the street. Sure enough, the sign across the front announced Captain Jack's Coffee House, while the placard near the narrow green door proclaimed Internet Available, with a small WIFI symbol.

The door opened with a protesting squeak, a little bell announcing their arrival. As they stepped in, father and daughter both stopped and inhaled deeply. They looked at each other and laughed, both knowing what the other was thinking. *Now this was a real find!* They had stepped into the long narrow front room of what was evidently a remodeled house—all dark wood and greens and purples—where the rich smell of coffee hung around them like a comforting blanket. A mismatched selection of wing-backed armchairs and small wooden tables were grouped here and there in a companionable fashion like Baptists chatting in a church foyer, while the soft yellow glow of the various antique lamps created a warm, intimate atmosphere. A spidery wrought iron staircase spiraled into the ceiling at the far end of the room beyond a huge stone fireplace. Antiques and old pictures dotted the walls.

Just about perfect, thought Dad. *Cozy was the word, but not cramped.* It looked like an ideal place to relax, chat, and sip something hot. There were even some interesting books and magazines available for perusing—a definite addition to the date place list. He almost couldn't wait for a drizzly day—this would be just the spot to take refuge.

The long, curved wooden serving-counter at the back held stacks of assorted cups and mugs and a rack of exotic tea blends, with just enough room to stand and give your order. Momentarily forgetting her impatience, Rachel examined the list of available drinks on the chalkboard behind the counter, while Dad poked around unsuccessfully for a computer. *How could he have forgotten his laptop?* Well, they needed some assistance it was apparent. Where was the owner?

He pushed smartly on the small bell on the counter. The door behind the counter was just ajar, offering a glimpse of a metal shelf stacked with cups and bowls, and from somewhere beyond a voice called out. "Just a sec—I'll be right there."

A few moments later, a lanky, curly-haired man appeared from the back room sporting a dark green apron and struggling to carry four stainless steel thermal carafes. He was in his thirties, and wore small round glasses that made him look rather studious, Rachel thought, but also kind of trendy. He had one of those remarkable wisps of a goatee that Dad figured were favored by folk singers and young men studying Shakespeare at liberal arts universities.

"Hello, there." The man plunked the carafes down by the tea display, and ran his fingers through his hair, obviously not caring what it looked like when he was done.

"Sorry there wasn't anyone up front," he continued. "We just opened and there's not usually anyone beating down the door at this time of the morning." He straightened the tea display with one hand while sweeping a dusting of sugar granules off the counter and into his apron pocket with the other.

Dad liked the look of the friendly-faced proprietor. "No problem. We were just looking to see if we can use your Internet. We've been on the road, and I need to check my email."

"Oh, are you here on holiday? It's a good time to come 'cause the British schools aren't out for the summer yet." The man tossed his cloth expertly through the open door and skirted the counter. "Follow me. The PCs are upstairs, unless you have a laptop with you. We've got wireless set up down here."

"I actually forgot my laptop," said Dad sheepishly, "but I can view my web mail."

Dad beckoned to Rachel who was still trying to decide what she would order if she ever had the chance. The man was already climbing the stairs two at a time, and they had to hurry to catch up. The staircase deposited them in a tiny room with a low slanted ceiling lit by a dormer window. Several computers were arranged around the room, looking a little incongruous in the rustic surroundings. It was rather warm and stuffy, and Dad quickly unzipped his jacket. He had what he called a notoriously sensitive temperature regulation system, and considered himself the only person in the world able to break a sweat just watching a National Geographic special on the Sahara.

The man was quick to apologize. "We've been working on more air in here, but the fan doesn't seem up to the job. He tugged regretfully at his goatee. "Do you need much time?"

Dad made up his mind that he didn't. "No, no, just a few minutes. Well, maybe ten or so." After all, it had been a while since he'd last checked his mail. "Do I pay by the hour…?"

"It's two pounds an hour for the PCs, but I'll prorate it if you're only here for a bit."

"Sounds great! Thanks a lot."

"Just yell if you need anything." The man disappeared downstairs before he finished his sentence.

"Busy guy," said Dad, sitting down at one of the PCs. "Well, great. Let's get started."

⊰⊱

Emily shifted the box of Weetabix to the left a little so she could peek over the shelf. Mr. Peterson was at the till, scanning a long ribbon of register tape and scowling. She looked over her shoulder to where her mother was bent over the apple display, apparently trying to choose between Granny Smiths and Red Delicious. Her brothers were further down the aisle, having a somewhat loud discussion on the merits of sour cream and onion versus barbeque potato chips. It sure would be a lot easier to just join them and avoid her present predicament. *Why did this have to be so hard?* A sensitive conscience often seemed more like a curse than a blessing.

"Jesus, I just want to try to be nice," she muttered desperately.

She sidled around the end cap display of discounted suntan lotion and tried to appear nonchalant as she worked her way towards the front. She had rehearsed a few pleasant comments to see if she could break through the man's tough exterior. They had flowed easily enough when she had practiced in front of the mirror this morning, but now she wasn't sure if she could force the words out. *He was so intimidating in person!*

She had just made up her mind to go ahead and boldly step forward when a loud ringing interrupted her resolution. Mr. Peterson threw the register tape aside and, after a few moments of rather frantic searching, retrieved a phone from somewhere under the counter.

"Peterson's grocers. Peterson speaking." His voice had a squeaky sound to it, like he was inhaling a kazoo. And he really did remind her of a vulture with his sharp nose and round-shouldered posture. The man listened intently, his forehead creased into a frown.

"Yes, yes, at Chypons. I can do it. Deliveries are from twelve to one, and five til six."

A pause, during which his face reddened noticeably. Was it Emily's imagination or could she actually hear a voice yelling on the other end of the phone.

"I'll take care of it when I can!" No doubt about it, Mr. Peterson was angry now. It wouldn't be too hard to picture smoke rising from his ears.

"I'll be there! Good day!" He snapped off the phone and for a moment Emily thought he might fling it across the room. She could see his mouth moving, evidently expressing his sentiments under his breath. She tried to make herself as inconspicuous as possible behind a rack of newspapers. All her resolve had vanished, and how she only wanted to escape. *What if he turned on her, next?*

Fortunately, Mr. Peterson had apparently decided to take his frustrations out in other ways. He grabbed a mop from a bucket in the corner and started slapping it back and forth across the floor with rather unnecessary vigor, muttering to himself. Emily took advantage of his concentration and fled to where her mother was comparing prices of boxed juice in the far corner of the shop.

She would try again next time, yes she would. *But not today.* She shuddered a little. *No, not today.*

⇛⇝

Dad slumped back in his chair, digesting the news. There had been forty-three messages in his inbox, but most had been advertisements from an online computer supply store. *How on earth had he got on their mailing list?* But that wasn't his main concern. He had pounced immediately on the one email that he was expecting *and* fearing—the one from his editor, Brian Stearns. It was fairly brief and to the point. *'Thanks for the articles you submitted'*...blah, blah, blah. *'They were very interesting. However, while of some historical value, we feel they are missing something to grab the reader's attention and draw them into the emotions of the times. You've talked about persecution in a general way, but we need something more intimate—more real-life stories. Please consider this in your current research. We are confident you will be able to accommodate our wishes and provide work that is satisfactory for publication.'*

Blow, blow, blow. He knew it. Those articles were just not quality. Mr. Stearns had called them "interesting"—and that seemed a singular choice of word. You could use 'interesting' to describe a neighbor who liked dressing her fifteen cats in dolls clothes, or a smell you discovered in the basement--a polite way of saying *weird, boring* or *not the quality we expected.*

And how about that last sentence? *Ouch*. The bottom line was, his current stuff wasn't satisfactory for publication. This was just what he'd feared.

"Daddy, are you okay? Are you done?"

His daughter's voice broke into his dark thoughts. He glanced up at her face. She sure had a dazzling smile. He sighed, trying to break out of the gloom. No, he didn't want to explain all his feelings right now. He didn't think he could conjure up anything positive to say, so best leave it be.

"Oh, I'm okay." He tried to sound convincing. "Let's go and find the others."

He logged off and they trooped back downstairs. Several customers had come in and the owner was busy behind the counter. Dad waited for the steaming roar of the espresso machine to subside before trying to talk.

"We're all done. So how much do we owe you?"

The man glanced at the clock on the wall behind him. It was shaped like a cup of coffee with a spoon in the top swinging to and fro like a pendulum.

"Well, now, that's about fifteen minutes so why don't we say fifty pence. Here, pop it in the slot. I'm trying to see how much business we get with the it to see if it's worth it."

He offered Dad a tin shaped like an English phone box with a slot in the top.

"How about a pound?" said Dad, dropping a pound coin in the slot. "Fifty pence seems a bit too low."

"Well, thanks," said the owner, pleased.

"So, did you just open recently?" Dad wondered.

"A couple of months ago. Folks are still discovering the place, but I hope that things will really pick up with the tourist season."

"Well, I'm sure we'll be back often—either to check our mail or for coffee. My wife'll love this place. Great atmosphere." Dad gestured around him. "Great job with the decorating. My name's Dave Chapman, by the way. This is my daughter Rachel." He extended his hand across the counter.

The man gave it a vigorous shake. "Geoff Ketchum. Glad you like the décor. We got a lot of antiquey stuff from an auction up at the Manor house a number of years ago. The squire who used to live there had all kinds of things stashed away. We were just saving it up until this place was ready to go."

"No kidding!" *It seemed that you couldn't hold a conversation in this town without the Squire's name coming up*, thought Dad. *Must have been an interesting guy.*

"Daddy, we better get going." Rachel was keeping a mental eye on the time of day, and was getting a might frustrated again.

"Okay. Thanks again." Dad grabbed a business card off the counter. "Does this have your hours and everything?" He wasn't feeling so hurried, savoring the ambience wrapped in that wonderful smell. Maybe they could do a date tonight—and take his mind off that dratted article.

"It's all there. Hope to see you around again." The man called over his shoulder as he disappeared into the back room.

"Busy guy," noted Dad again. "Okay, okay," he directed at Rachel as he found himself being ushered to the door. "We're going!"

Aha. Perfect timing. There were the others coming down the street. Rachel waved and the boys came running over, each swinging a bulging plastic grocery sack.

"Hi honey, how did it go?" Mom came up hefting a couple more bags which Dad promptly took. Emily had a couple as well. Dad raised his eyebrows. My word—that lot should keep them in lunches for the rest of their lives!

"Fine." Dad decided not to mention the email yet. He needed to digest it some more. "The coffee place was wonderful. We've got to go sometime!"

"I'm so hungry," interrupted Stevie suddenly, giving a soulful look and clutching his stomach as if he were in the last throes of existence. "What's in your bag, Daddy?"

Dad eyed him suspiciously. Quite the little actor. He should be on the stage.

"Yes, what *do* you have?"

Uh-oh. Now his wife was giving him her prosecuting attorney look.

"Just a little something from Auntie Flo." He gave an apologetic shrug and smiled.

"Hmm. Just asking for directions..." Mom winked at the kids. "I think *I'll* go next time."

Rachel cleared her throat. "Er, um, excuse me, but we should get going." She was glancing at the sun. *Wasn't it already past noon? And they still had to make lunch before hitting the beach!* "Come on!" She grabbed a bag from Emily and set off towards the bridge.

Mom and Dad looked at each other. *Action Woman* was off again. The rest of family took her cue though and followed along. All except Stevie, Dad noted with narrowed eyes, who seemed to be barely moving at all—dragging along at the pace of someone trying to wade through a swamp in swim flippers.

Stevie couldn't believe the interesting bakery bag hadn't been examined. He moaned again. "Is there anything to eat?"

"You poor deprived child." Dad wasn't big on moaning. "How will you survive?"

"Actually dear," whispered Mom, eyeing the fish and chip shop by the bridge. "We could get some fries or something couldn't we? If we're going to eat on the beach it will be a while before lunch, and I'd rather have something remotely like food to snack on than candy or sweets."

Dad considered it for a moment as they walked along. A bunch of French Fries didn't seem to him to be more like food than a Bakewell tart, but he found himself surprisingly open to the suggestion. He could use a little pick-me-up after that email, and there *was* an intoxicating smell coming from the shop—kind of like a wispy hand that beckoned him to follow, floating along, nose first. "Well, okay," he said out loud. "Let's do it."

❧☙

Chippy Twiston was having a slow day and was none too happy about it. On a sudden impulse he had decided to start opening his fish and chip shop for lunches, but was now kicking himself for being too hasty. The dinner trade was pretty steady all year long, even in a town as small as Penrithen, but outside of summer there wasn't much interest in Fish and Chips for lunch, more's the pity.

He retrieved the spoon he'd dropped in the batter and tossed it in the sink, absentmindedly rubbing his nose with his knuckle and leaving a streak of white. He leaned his tall skinny frame against the freezer to ponder his fate, chewing on the string of his apron. No, this wasn't like the tourist season. Nothing like the holidays to bring a pack of lunchtime visitors pouring through the door, hungry as hunters, and ready for something hot and crispy. *Then old Max worked overtime, that's for sure.* He gave the big, stainless-steel fryer a friendly kick.

Speaking of Max though, he fervently hoped the fryer had a few more years in it. He hadn't budgeted for a new one—there was always something else more pressing. His savings held the grand total of a mere £43.50 and that was only because he had recently sold his coveted Star Trek VHS collection to his cousin Derek in Boscastle.

He stood back up straight with a sigh, his hands still covered in batter, and glanced over at the goldfish bowl perched on an old metal shelf by the window, the bright orange occupant watching him languidly from behind a feather of plastic fern.

"So what do you think, Ahab?"

The fish made no response. Chippy poked at the glass, leaving a perfect circular smudge of batter. "I agree. It looks like I'll have to raise prices again this year."

Yes, though he hated to do it. Never mind about whether he was making much of a profit or not, the locals considered any change almost scandalous— like a personal affront. As if he could just keep on charging the same prices as their grandparents used to pay, what with the costs of fish going through the roof! Yes, that was the problem. He'd tried to move his lunch opening up a few weeks to squeeze out a little more potential profit. Hadn't he seen a bunch of out-of-towners the past week, and that coach-load that went through last Tuesday? But now it was quiet as a tomb again. Bother it all.

He smacked his hand down in frustration on the pile of Penrithen Times that he used for wrapping the orders. His hand stuck to the paper and he had to shake it loose. What a mess. *Wait a minute, though. Was that someone coming up the walkway? Was it? Yes, yes, yes!*

Standing on tip toes to look over the menu in the window, he did a quick count. Six people. Well, yes, some were kids, but still—six fish and chips could be a nice addition to the day's earnings.

He hurriedly wiped his hands on his apron, and then looked down at the mess he'd created. Whipping his apron over his head, he flung it under the sink as the door opened, squeaking on its hinges.

❧ ❧

Mrs. Chapman peered without enthusiasm through the grease-stained glass at the piles of crispy cod on the warming racks. Fish was absolutely last on her list of preferred foods, but fortunately they weren't there to get any. She looked up to where the tall, freckle-faced proprietor was bobbing up and down behind the counter, his boyish face smiling ingratiatingly as he cracked his knuckles in anticipation. Dad stepped forward and raised his eyebrows questioningly at his wife, who nodded back.

"Three orders of fries, er, chips, please." Dad remembered the British word just in time.

Chippy Twiston stopped bobbing. His smile became rather fixed.

"Three chips," he repeated slowly. "And how many portions of fish with that?"

"Oh, no fish right now, thank you—just the chips." Dad smiled apologetically.

Chippy struggled rather unsuccessfully to keep the disappointment from his face as his potential profits took flight out the window. He racked his brain for a plan.

"Well fine, but there's, er, a smashing special today. Er, two lovely large pieces of cod for...£6.50."

"That's great, but we're just getting chips for now." Dad smiled again.

"Well, how about three for £6.50?"

Mr. Chapman raised an eyebrow and glanced over at this wife, who gave a slight shake of her head. He tried to sound as resolved as possible. "No, thanks. We're fine with chips."

"Two pounds a piece?" Chippy appeared to have lost all modesty now.

Dad leaned forward and looked kindly but firmly into his eyes. "Just the chips. That is alright, isn't it? You can order just chips?"

"Yes, yes, absolutely." Chippy became suddenly brisk. "Three orders of chips, coming up."

He grabbed some grease-proof paper and his tongs off the hook by the fryer and started making up three bulging parcels, wrapping them all expertly in several sheets of newspaper from the pile and plopping them in a plastic bag.

"Is that a goldfish?" said Danny suddenly, noticing the occupant of the fish tank.

"Er, yes." Chippy paused, seeming a bit derailed by the interruption. "That's...er...Ahab."

"Ahab?" Danny looked at the goldfish in curiosity.

"Named after the white whale in that book, like the village pub here. That, er, famous book." The title escaped him at the moment.

The family looked at each other in puzzlement. Chippy mistook their confusion. "It's a really famous book, but maybe you haven't read it. I thought it would be a good name, even though he isn't white." He paused. "Or a whale."

"You mean the book *Moby Dick*?" said Dad.

"Yes, yes, that's the one."

"But Moby Dick was the name of the whale. Ahab was the captain—the one who wanted to kill it."

Chippy's smile froze. He looked distraught for a few seconds, then slowly resumed his wrapping.

Dad paid the total and the family all shuffled out again, vying for who got to carry the aromatic offering. Chippy watched them for a minute through the window, his shoulders slumping slightly. He glanced over at the fishbowl.

"Hey!" he exclaimed, with an injured air. "Don't look at me like that, Ahab. It's still a great name. And they'll be back, I tell you. They'll be back!"

The Chapmans had polished off the fries, quickly gathered all they needed and headed back out down the lane. Following Mrs. Tremannon's directions, they crossed the bridge and puffed up the steep road on the near side of the harbor towards the line of cottages they had seen from a distance the day before. Dad was already regretting they hadn't taken the car, though Mrs. Tremannon had insisted it was only a short walk. A short walk if unencumbered for sure, but the six of them were carrying enough supplies for the whole British Eighth Army. He glanced over his shoulder. Amazingly, the boys weren't complaining. Trailing along at the rear, Danny and Stevie, hefting an assortment of beach toys and towels, were deep in conversation.

"Don't forget, we're supposed to be detectives." Danny adjusted the plastic bag of toy cars that was slung over his shoulder and beginning to wear a groove in his flesh.

"I haven't," said Stevie, offended. "I'm looking for clues. There just haven't been any."

"Well, they mayn't be easy to spot. In the Hardy Boys books, they're always on the lookout."

"Well, what are we looking out for?"

Good question. Danny had to think for a minute, and almost tripped over his towel that had unrolled and was trailing beside him.

"Well, the newspaper article. We never found the whole thing." He tried to flip the end of the towel over his arm, but only succeeded in getting it dustier.

Stevie stopped suddenly and stared off into space, mouth hanging open. A newspaper. *The Penrithen Times.* Now where had he just seen a copy of the Penrithen Times? The Hardy Boys would never forget where they saw a copy of the Penrithen Times.

"What is it?" Danny asked, puzzled.

But Stevie wasn't going to admit his shortcomings, no way. Not when he was trying to prove he was every bit the sleuth as his older brother.

"Er, nothing." He tried to sound unconcerned. "Just thinking. Come on, let's catch up!"

Rachel took a glance over at the line of cottages they were passing, strung together along the steep road—anything to help take her mind off the fact that her arm was feeling like it was about to rip off. She and Emily had the lunch cooler slung between them, and what with it banging her shin every few paces and about dislocating her shoulder, she was tempted to drop it entirely. They could eat right then and there by the side of the road for all she cared. She had

71

been keeping a nervous eye on the sun, and had more than once wished she could just beam the family to the beach before they lost the day altogether.

The cottages all looked rather old, from the irregular grey slate roofs to the way the window frames seemed to be slumping like drowsy eyelids. They were cute, though, she had to admit. There were five of them, each freshly whitewashed with a brightly painted door, tiny yard and colorful window boxes. The second one along was especially pretty, with cheerful patterned curtains and a climbing rose dominating the whole front with its leafy tendrils and scarlet blooms. She thought she could even spy the outline of a large cat watching her through the sheers.

Switching her grip with some difficulty, Rachel looked ahead to where the road flattened out and came to an abrupt end by a large, gabled house, perched right by the edge of the cliff. Its windows were boarded up and its front garden unkempt, but despite its neglected appearance, its stately presence still seemed to be guarding the entrance to the harbor. To her left, the hill sloped up steeply and a jagged curve showed where the cove must lie, just on the other side of a ridge of rock behind the house. She looked over her shoulder at the boys, a good way back.

"Come on, boys!" she yelled. Her Mom and Dad up ahead glanced back her way, and she tried to soften her voice somewhat. "Do you need help?" There, that sounded like she was thinking of them, rather than being annoyed.

But Danny wasn't listening. As he reached the end of the row of houses he had glanced to his left. Now he was pointing, wide-eyed. She turned to follow his gaze. Why did he look so scared?

Chapter 5 - A Mysterious Inheritance

Beach Access, the faded sign read, its small arrow pointing to the rough set of stone steps that lead over the ridge and presumably down to the cove itself. The family clustered next to it, the girls grateful for a chance to drop their burden—even for a minute.

"Well, it does look like the same type." Dad looked back over the sleek old yellow sports car, parked slightly askew at the end of the row of houses, right against the cliff. "But honestly Danny, there's almost no chance it's the exact same one."

"I think it is," stated Stevie with the authority of Sherlock Holmes himself. He didn't mind the sports car—he just didn't like the creepy look of the boarded up house. He would rather it wasn't there at all.

"Well, what if it is the same car?" Rachel wanted to get this unnecessary conversation over quickly.

But Danny didn't want to answer. He was feeling decidedly embarrassed now that all the attention was focused on him, and was regretting reacting so strongly. For the hundredth time he wished his imagination wasn't so vivid.

"Do you think it belongs to the end house here? C-H-Y-P-O-N-S—Chypons," Emily read aloud, squinting back at the name plate on the wall of the last house in the row. "Are you worried about seeing that man at the café?"

"Well, I, er," Danny stammered, quite at a loss for what to say.

His mother swooped in to the rescue. "It's alright, dear. We can talk about it later. Grab your things, everyone. Dave, go ahead and lead the way. I'm not sure how steep it is."

She waited until the others had started up the steps, then gave Danny a quick hug. "Were you worried about seeing that man again?"

Danny nodded.

"Don't worry, dear. I'm sure it couldn't be his car—we're miles and miles away now, and anyway, you're working on not worrying, aren't you? Remember: God is in control, and He loves you dearly. So try and rest in that truth." She sent a quick prayer heavenwards that this fact really would move from his head to his heart. "Now," she added, "let's get down to the beach!"

Danny felt a bit better, but as he followed the others up the stairs, he couldn't help glancing back. Could it be the same car? *Please, God*, he prayed. *Let it be somebody else's.*

❦❦

Far above them on the hillside, at the base of the old churchyard, a bearded figure in an old brown raincoat and tweed cap shifted uncomfortably in his crouched position at the foot of a stunted, twisted yew tree. A battered thermos, a brown satchel and a variety of food wrappers littered the ground around his feet. He sniffed once or twice and dug unsuccessfully in his pocket for a handkerchief. Not finding one, he gingerly dabbed his nose with the back of his coat sleeve and looked around him disconsolately. Too bad he couldn't get up and stretch his legs a bit, but he was nervous about being spotted up here by some random hikers, like that family that popped out of nowhere the day before.

Setting his binoculars down beside him, he vigorously rubbed his right calf muscle, groaning at the dull ache. He couldn't believe he had to be up here. Couldn't he just watch from the *Mole Hole*? He could see the lady's house from there. But no, Kennedy had insisted it was possible to see the whole village from this spot and tell if she was really going to be gone for a while.

He started rubbing the other leg, shaking his head in disgust at his predicament. Why on earth had he let himself be talked into this ridiculous spying thing? Like he was some sort of idiotic secret agent or something. *Well, he actually did know why, didn't he?* It was because he didn't have the guts to say 'no.' And more importantly, he didn't have a choice. To put it plainly, he was being blackmailed.

How had it come to this? He sighed in resignation and dug for the pipe in his satchel. He was just patting his pockets for his matches when the phone at his feet burst into life, blaring out a rendition of the 1812 Overture that made him almost leap up in sheer surprise. He needed to adjust that ring volume. Hurriedly setting the pipe aside he flipped open the phone, abruptly cutting off the music.

He glanced furtively around. "Yes, this is Jennings," he whispered. "What is it?"

He listened for a moment, becoming not appreciating what he was hearing.

"No, she hasn't left the house since I got here...well except to go feed some birds out back. Please listen for a moment. I've been up here all yesterday and today. I'm stiff as a board, and all out of Salt and Vinegars." He kicked at the empty potato chip bag at his feet. "What's the rush to get this thing?"

He listened some more, plucking agitatedly at some tufts of grass.

"Alright—so it's important. Good thing I saw she had it in her hand on the way up here yesterday." *It would have been dumb going through her house for nothing,* he added in his mind.

He listened again, trying to gather his courage. He hated conflict.

"But I don't get why it's got to be me watching. You're the one practically next door."

He flung the bits of grass away from him and leaned back on his elbows, switching the phone to his other hand. "Well, I suppose so. But please make this the last day! I can't keep the Mole Hole closed forever. It really must be in her house!" A pause. "Alright, alright, I'll call you the second she leaves. Just remember all this when you get the goods! It will make us all square, right?"

The reply caused him to furrow his brow. He snapped the phone shut and looked off into space.

"This is absolutely crazy," he muttered under his breath. He had always prided himself that he never lost his temper, but these days he was in serious danger of doing just that—just one more reason to blame Kennedy for all this mess.

Grabbing his binoculars in one hand he peered down the hill again, fumbling for his pipe with the other. "Come on, old lady," he said out loud with a hint of desperation. "Time to go shopping…please."

❧❦❧

'*Caution. Slippery when Wet*' the sign at the top had read, and they had dutifully taken note. As they had carefully negotiated the metal stairway, they had a bird's eye view of the cove laid out below them. It was as if a giant hand had taken a scoop out of the headland leaving crescent walls of chiseled rock enclosing a small, sandy beach—a line of partially submerged rocks protecting it from the thunderous surf just outside the cove. The far side of the cliff sharpened into a ship's prow carving the open ocean, with a tumbled rocky mass at its base harboring numerous glistening pools. A curved shadow lay obliquely across the sand, the sun just emerging from behind the mass of headland looming above them.

"Don't go in very far!" Mom yelled after the four kids who had torn off their shoes and socks and were dashing towards the water with wild, raucous cries like a gang of bandit monkeys. She shook her head in disbelief. "Well, I guess they weren't hungry for lunch yet after all."

"I'll set up the stuff—you go and enjoy yourself," volunteered her husband, gratefully heaving the last of their belongings down onto the sand. "We can eat in a bit."

She considered for a moment, then tore off her socks and shoes and ran down after them, yelling like an eight-year-old. Dad smiled. His adventurous wife could always be depended on to join in the fun.

It didn't take him long to arrange things, and then he threw himself down on the beach blanket. *Now what should I do?* he wondered. It was so tempting to just lie there on the sand like a slug and abandon himself to snoozy thoughts. His mind began to drift back over the day—that great breakfast, the walk to town, the bakery, the internet café, that email… He sat up straight with a start. Not that email again. He wasn't going to think about *that* again!

"Help me, God," he said out loud, heaving himself to his feet. Hopping on one foot as he unlaced his shoe, he yelled down to the others. "I'm coming! You'd better look out!"

It was Mom's turn to drop onto the sand, panting and laughing. The sun completely filled the cove now, highlighting the rocks with a palette of warm late-afternoon colors. They had taken a break to enjoy a relatively sand-free picnic lunch and then returned to play in the waves until they were plum worn out. The others had decided to take a long breather now and explore the cove, but she had other ideas. She was ready for some sun time. She shook out a beach towel and flopped over onto her stomach, taking a quick inventory of the rest of the family. Rachel and Emily were hazily silhouetted against a backdrop of sparkling light, perched on the edge of a rocky tide pool, their toes just dipping into its mirrored waters. Mom smiled at the beautiful scene, like a living painting.

Now, where were the others? Oh, yes. Dad and the boys were over at the base of the cliff, examining the dark entrance to a cave just visible behind a protruding slab of rock. Officially considering herself off duty, Mom sighed with contentment and laid her head down, abandoning herself to the warming rays.

Stevie was a wee bit out of his comfort zone. The cave was cold and smelled like old damp seaweed or slugs or something. No matter that they could maybe see a hint of daylight at the other end—it still seemed really creepy. His small hand crept into his Dad's big one.

"Doing okay, tiger?" Dad wondered.

"Uh-huh." Stevie replied unconvincingly. "Why does this cave smell funny?"

"'Cause it's not a cave. It's the throat of a gigantic sea serpent!" Danny grinned over his shoulder.

Dad glared warningly at him. "It's a tunnel through the cliff, Stevie. It just curves so we can't see the other end. I think the smell is from the old seaweed. We don't have to go any further if you don't want."

Stevie paused to consider. The sand beneath his bare feet felt chilled and slimy, and the smell was really yucky. He looked back to the sunny brightness of the cove, framed by the cave's jagged entrance. He wanted to be back there, in the real world, but he still felt kind of torn. *Wasn't he supposed to be a detective now? They were brave. They wouldn't be afraid of a stinky cave or tunnel or whatever it was.*

He swallowed and looked up at his Dad. "No, it's okay. We can go just a bit more."

Danny actually felt a bit disappointed at Stevie's response. Despite his brave front, he had secretly hoped his brother didn't want to go any further. It really was rather unpleasant, and his own allusion to a gigantic throat seemed nearer the truth than he cared to admit. He couldn't back down now, but maybe he would wait for his Dad to get right next to him.

"Okay, we'll go on just a bit." Dad wasn't too thrilled either. For some reason his toes always rebelled against being cold, and right now on this damp sand they felt like they might just snap off one by one like pretzel sticks. But exploring was one of those guy things that was good for the boys, wasn't it?

The rocky passage went straight on for a few yards before curving slightly to the left, its low ceiling causing Dad to have to stoop somewhat. A strange muffled sound seemed to be coming from up ahead. He suddenly wondered if this was such a good idea. He had no clue if the tide might be coming in. As he peered ahead he could now see the other opening with a glimpse of blue sky and ocean. *And what was that coming towards them?*

"Whoa! Stevie, come here!" Dad grabbed the boy and hoisted him up onto a ledge of rock. He pulled Danny to him and held him pressed against his legs as a swooshing wave of water swept around the corner and surged about them sloshing up to Danny's waist.

Danny gasped at the shock of cold while Stevie scrabbled to find a hold on the slimy walls. His searching fingers found what felt like a large rough metal ring above him and he grabbed on to it as Dad tried to scoot him up higher with a hand under the seat of his pants. The swell of water swirled past them and broke with a foaming roar at the cave's entrance, then sucked itself back past them and around the corner to disappear as quickly as it came.

"Ah, oh, wow" Dad had received quite a soaking. "Sneaker wave! Are you okay, guys?"

Danny nodded, his teeth chattering. Stevie had mostly escaped the wet but had had enough of this cave now, no question. "I want to go back," he whimpered. "Can you carry me?" He let go of the ring and allowed himself to drop into his Dad's arms.

Dad heartily agreed, berating himself for being careless. He led them sloshing back out the way they came. As they broke into the sunshine, Danny glanced back over his shoulder, his natural good humor returning as quickly as the warmth and light.

"Well, if that was a sea-serpent, I think it just spat us back out."

❧☙

"And it smelled like really old seaweed soup." Stevie's voice sounded muffled as his mother toweled him off rather vigorously.

"Well, we can thank God that He was watching over you." Mom glanced up at Dad who was looking a little sheepish.

Stevie's head broke free of the towel, his spiky hair shooting in all different directions. "Yeah. It must have been him that put that ring there."

"What ring?" Danny was rummaging for a dry shirt in the bag of extra clothes.

"There was some kind of ring—maybe metal or something—up on the cave wall. I grabbed it to hang on. It swung around a bit and it turned my hand brown." He displayed his palm where there was a streak of color.

Dad examined it. "Looks like rust. It must have been some kind of old mooring ring, though why it was in a cave is anyone's guess."

"What time is dinner, dear," interrupted Mom suddenly. She had just remembered that they had completely cleaned out the lunch cooler and there was nothing like a close shave to give boys a sudden appetite. Any second now and they would realize it.

"We told Mrs. T around six today."

"Okay, well it's almost five now, so we'd better head back." She tossed Stevie his T-shirt and shorts. "Put these on quickly, please. We need to start packing up."

⁂

In the second cottage along, the elderly occupant sat quietly in a tapestried armchair, reading from a pale blue sheet of paper with an official-looking letterhead. She adjusted her glasses—they always seemed to want to slide to a point midway down her nose—and sighed deeply. The large tabby at her feet arched itself up and rubbed against her knee, purring richly—almost as if it had sensed her distress and was doing its best to comfort her. She reached down absently and massaged its chin, causing the purring to double in volume.

"Thank you, dear Pickwick," she murmured.

Putting the letter back in its light-blue envelope, she set it on the arm of the chair and stood carefully to her feet. It always took her a few moments to unstiffen after sitting in one place for a while. The cat left her side and paced primly across the carpet and into the kitchen. He knew his mistress's habits well, but just to make sure he paused in the doorway and gave a loud mew over his shoulder.

"Yes, yes, I'm coming."

She had felt so overwhelmed lately—so much sorrow, mixed with a distressing sense of guilt—and now the confusion of the document she had just set down, not to mention that article in the newspaper. She so regretted agreeing to an interview. The only thing in which she had found some slight consolation was the solace of a hot cup of tea—that and the company of her dear friends, of course. She smiled slightly at the sight of her cat in the kitchen, waiting for her to fill the kettle—always the first step in her little ritual. But first she paused by the ornate bird cage in the corner and tapped lightly on the bars.

"And how are you, sweetie? I can tell you're doing better than I am, aren't you?"

The blue budgerigar hopped down onto a perch near the front of the cage and cocked his head on one side as if listening. A sudden mew from the next room announced that someone there was getting impatient.

"Okay, I really am coming." She gave the bird's head a little stroke through the bars. "I'll talk to you later, dear."

Quickly filling the kettle, she put it on the stove to boil, then pulled the tin tea caddy off of the shelf above the bread bin. She pried off the lid, and reacted in surprise.

"Oh, my. We're out of tea. How can that be?" She was sure she had filled the caddy a few days ago. *Or had she?* Her mind was so muddled, she just couldn't be sure. And could she make it all the way to the shop? Well, she just had to. There was no getting through the rest of the day without tea.

78

She addressed the cat who was prowling around at her feet, wondering what the delay was. "Well, my dear, I think I'm going to have to go out."

As she reached to retrieve her purse from the kitchen table she heard the kettle whistle behind her. She had forgotten to turn it off. She shook her head in resignation, turned off the burner and moved the kettle to one side. Then she grabbed up her purse and checked that her keys were inside. In her current frame of mind, she was likely to lock herself out.

"Finally." She addressed the cat again. "I won't be long."

As she moved to the closet to get her coat, the cat watched her closely, then bounded over to where a long purple leash hung from a hook by the front door jam. Reaching up, it batted the end, making the metal clip clink loudly against the door hinge.

The lady couldn't help but smile. "You silly old thing. You want to come, don't you? Alright. I suppose I could use the company."

Fastening the leash to the cat's collar, she set her purse by the door and took her coat off of its hanger in the little closet. As she slowly put it on, she glanced over at the envelope on the chair. A sudden cloud passed over her thoughts again. *What did it all mean? Why had he done this to her?* It was almost as if she was being punished. If only she had made the effort and seen him before it was too late. If only...well, there was a lifetime of regrets piled one upon another right now. So many "if onlys."

She tried to focus back, desperately trying to clear her mind. Now what was she doing? *Oh, yes, tea.* "Come on, then." The cat trotting in front, she pushed the front door shut behind her and stepped out onto the little path, completely forgetting that she had left the door unlocked and her purse on the floor.

Inside the house, the swoosh of air caused by the slamming door sent the envelope dancing up into the air, flipping over and over to eventually settle in the corner behind the chair—quite out of sight.

❧❧❧

Stevie slowly picked up his T-shirt, his mind full of dismal thoughts. He was really hungry and now they had to walk all that way back. *What if he couldn't make it until dinner?* It seemed ages since lunch and an absolute eternity since those French fries.

He was in the process of struggling reluctantly into his shirt when he froze, one arm straight up in the air and his shirt collar just under his eyes like some sort of headless Statue of Liberty. *A newspaper! Their snack of French fries or chips or whatever they were called—it had been wrapped in newspaper!* The sudden realization drove all other thoughts from his head. The newspaper was the Penrithen Times, he was sure of it. He started jumping up and down, his shirt suddenly snapping down into place.

"Oh, oh, oh, wow!" It was all he could manage to squeeze out in his excitement.

"What's the matter, Buddy?" Dad spoke for the rest of the family who were looking on in amusement.

"The missing newspaper with the article. The fries were wrapped in it, I know it."

"Aha." Now Dad understood. "But we threw it away."

"Oh, no," cried Stevie. "It's in the trash at the Inn. We need to go!" He started grabbing up towels.

Dad looked at Mom, both thinking the same thing—boys and the continuing mysteries of their motivation.

"Come on you guys." Stevie glared at his siblings. "Let's go! Hurry!"

⋙⋘

Up on the hill, the man in the raincoat set down his binoculars with an air of finality. He paused, then squared his shoulders and reached for his phone. Dialing the number, he sat up straight, waiting for the call to be picked up.

"Yes, it's Jennings. Listen, it's gone five and I want to pack it up for the day. There's no way she's going out now. Old people don't go out this late."

He waited for the inevitable angry response and then took a deep breath again.

"I get it, but we need to come up with some other idea. I'll come over and we can talk this thing out." *Maybe he could figure a way to get out of the whole deal altogether.*

He paused again to listen. What he heard shocked him, but it gave him a courage to speak with a forcefulness he didn't expect. "Well, what are you doing way over there? What if she left right now? You couldn't make it over in time?"

There was obviously some yelling going on at the other end of the line. Jennings felt a knot in his stomach. If only he could be free of this guy—if only he wasn't so afraid of the consequences.

"But I never agreed to that. I'm not going to... Wait!" He flung the phone aside and snatched up the binoculars. A quick look down the hill and he grabbed the phone again.

"No, wait, listen! She's gone out. You've got to get over there now!" He listened incredulously.

"No way!" He racked his brain for an excuse. "I've got all my stuff up here." He looked around at his scattered belongings, then took another frantic glance through the binoculars. The voice was yelling so loudly he didn't even have to hold the phone up to his ear.

With a sudden decision he leaped to his feet and started charging down the steep hill, trying to keep his balance while still shouting into the phone.

"Alright, alright, okay, I'm going in. Just make sure she doesn't run into you. Who knows where she's off to! Yes, yes, I've got the kit."

The slope was steeper than he thought and he had a couple of close calls, finally breaking his momentum just in time as he reached the bottom. He stepped as nonchalantly as possible into the road, a furtive glance around convincing him that the coast was clear. Forcing himself to breath more slowly, he tried to smooth out his clothes as he walked along, pulling out a few bits of twig he had picked up on the descent. He tried to push down the fears that welled up within him. *How had this happened? What if he were caught?*

Looking to his right, he noted that the lady and her cat were already halfway across the bridge. "Keep going please. Don't look back. Time to take a walk...a nice long walk..."

Dad looked around at the procession behind him, like a general marshaling his troops. "All ready then? Shoulder arms and let's go."

Buckets were hoisted, towels were slung over shoulders and the cooler was lugged into position. With a few glances of concern at the steep stairs ahead of them, and not a few regrets that they hadn't brought the van, the family started on their expedition back.

The man checked again that no-one was in sight, then knocked loudly at the door, just to make sure there was no-one else home. He realized his heart was pounding in his ears. It was definitely the first time he'd done something like this, and hopefully it would be the last. He checked his watch, then looked around again, feeling apprehensive and foolish at the same time. The coast was still clear—no sign of her or her cat. He pulled a black zippered case from his inside coat pocket and took out a small bent wire tool. Inserting it in the keyhole, he turned it back and forth, prodding and twisting like he'd been shown, then tried the doorknob. It wouldn't budge. A trickle of sweat ran down his cheek, and he swiped it away with the back of his sleeve. He realized he hadn't paid as much attention as he should of. He really hadn't believed that he'd ever have to do this sort of dirty work.

Taking a deep breath he started again with another round of poking and turning. Still no movement. In frustration he smacked his hand on the door, almost falling onto his face as it swung wide open.

The elderly woman made her way slowly up the road from the bridge, her cat padding along beside her. The going was a bit steep here, and she paused for a moment to catch her breath. That walk up to the chapel the other day had been quite an achievement, and she was still feeling the effects. Now, what she really fancied was a little something to suck on. Didn't she have some butterscotch sweets in her purse?

Wait a minute, where was her purse? She looked down at her empty hand in disbelief, then at the one holding the cat's leash. *No purse.* She turned and looked back the way she had come. No, it wasn't lying in the road. Could she have actually left it back at the house? She was so absentminded these days. Yes, it was possible—it was certainly possible, and there was her key, in her pocket instead of in her purse. At least she hadn't forgotten that.

With a long sigh she looked down at the tabby waiting patiently at her feet. It noted her gaze and scrunched up its eyes in what almost seemed a smile. She shook her head in resignation. "Well, Pickwick. We're going to have to go back.

Inside the house, the man took stock of his bearings. *Now where would an old lady keep an important letter?* He scanned the room for likely places. A large dresser stood imposingly on the opposite wall, its shelves lined with patterned plates. It was as good a place as any to start. He yanked open the drawers and rifled through them. Knitting needles, stamps, scissors, old greeting cards—there was no end to the junk—but no letters. He slammed them back in and looked around. There was a small table with a drawer in it over by the armchair. A quick scan of its contents and he slammed that one closed, too. Nothing but a pair of eyeglasses, some pills and a couple of pens.

Aha, there was a purse by the door. *That must be it!* He rifled through the contents, then flung it disgustedly down again. *Nothing.* He felt a stabbing anxiety. Where would the old lady hide something like this? He definitely didn't have all day.

⋙⋘

As the rest of the family gathered at the top of the steps they could hear Dad still on his way up, grunting and groaning as he came. He had somewhat gallantly declared he could handle the cooler by himself, but was now having second thoughts. He had a water bottle dangling at his side and the strap kept slipping off his shoulder to hang around his wrist causing him to almost trip up.

This was crazy. It didn't take much imagination to picture himself hurtling to the bottom.

"Honey," he called up.

His wife's anxious face appeared at the top. "Are you okay?"

"Sort of. Can you help?"

⋙⋘

The man was getting more and more desperate. He'd checked the kitchen, in-between all those books in the bookcase in the hall, both the bedrooms, and even the lavatory. Nothing but junk. He'd even lowered himself to checking under the disgusting newspapers in the bottom of the bird cage. The clock on the mantelpiece struck the half hour and a wave of frustration swept over him. *Why did he agree to this mad scheme?* Here he was, practically burgling someone's house and…*wait a minute.* What was that by the wall?

He pushed aside the armchair and grabbed at the envelope like a drowning man grasping for a lifeline. He scanned the return address. Yes! *Scrub, Wormly and Clink.* A quick inspection of the papers inside and he knew he had got all he needed. Now for a picture.

He was spreading them out on the table when a sound at the door made him freeze. It was a key turning in the lock, a silhouette outlined through the net curtain. Grabbing up the papers, he looked around frantically for a place to hide.

⋙⋘

"Now stay here, Pickwick. I'm just getting my purse."

With an effort the old lady pushed open the door and stepped in. *Now that was strange.* Was she imagining things, or did her house look a bit untidy? Steadying herself with one hand on the back of the sofa, she looked around.

A few drawers looked like they hadn't been closed properly, the lace doily on the table was slid to one side, and one of her purple plaid cushions was on the floor by the lamp. Oh, dear! What was happening to her? Was she just getting too old to take care of these things anymore, or was it just her present anxiety that was causing her to have all these issues? First the tea, then her purse, then the door being left unlocked and now this disheveled look to her things. Perhaps she ought to go see a doctor?

She just didn't have the energy to think of that now. Tea was what she wanted most at this moment. *Now, where had she left her purse?*

The man crouched at the back of the coat closet, the blood pounding loudly in his ears. He'd only just made it in time, but he couldn't close the door from the inside. His frantic scrabbling at the edge had just enabled him to pull it to. Would she see the open door? What would he do? He pictured himself jumping out and yelling like a banshee in her face—then dashing out the door to freedom. *Would that work? Did he have the gumption to do it?* With a lurch in his stomach he realized he didn't even have a picture of the letters yet.

He shifted his position, trying to worm his way silently behind the row of coats and cardigans. Some boxes at his feet made it so he had to lean backwards and it was no easy feat maintaining his balance. His knees weren't used to this. A trickle of sweat ran down his back. *How long could he keep this up?*

The yellow sports car was gone! Danny didn't know whether to feel relieved that it had disappeared or worried that it might turn up again somewhere else. He would keep his thoughts to himself this time, though.

As soon as Dad reached the top, puffing and panting, the family reformed their procession and trudged back down the line of cottages, Stevie in the lead and urging the others to hurry up. The others didn't feel like hurrying, though. They were tired from their afternoon in the sun and wind, not to mention the climb up from the cove. Mom murmured a prayer of thanks for the light sea breeze that played over their backs, cooling them off as it ushered them down the hill.

Below to their left, the harbor was aglow with color, every white-washed building radiating the late afternoon sunlight. The tide was a long way out and the collection of fishing boats leaned at odd angles on the wet sand, straining for the sea at the end of their long mooring chains. As she looked around, Rachel forgot her tiredness, delighting in the surroundings and a sense that they had really done something today. She just couldn't stand a day that flitted away without anything significant happening. She started to skip a little, swinging her side of the cooler back and forth.

Emily was about to complain, when she noticed something that quite drove the thought from her mind. The next cottage had a very small, neat front yard, and sitting quietly at the end of the path by the front door was a large cat. It appeared to be on a leash that was tied loosely to a metal hook. Emily was struck with the thought that she had seen the cat before, but where? *Where had she recently seen a grey tabby with a purple collar?*

"Rachel, do you recognize that cat?" She gestured with her free hand.

Rachel stopped her skipping and exclaimed in delight. "It's the kitty from the church yesterday! Hey, Mom! Look, I think that's the old lady's cat!"

The rest of the family crowded in front of the low stone wall. All except Stevie. He had a mission in mind and nothing could deter him right now.

Dad had a mission in mind, too. He wanted to make it back to the inn in time for dinner. He couldn't imagine being late for that—that would be too embarrassing.

"Well, it could be," he said, "but we need to keep going. We're going to be late."

"But wait a minute, dear, what if it is the right place." Mom hadn't forgotten the lady's grief, and that moment when their eyes had met. "This could be an answer to prayer."

Dad sighed inwardly. He guiltily realized that he wasn't interested in answers to prayer at this moment—he had his own agenda in mind. And what if this wasn't the house? It would be up to him to go and knock and be potentially embarrassed. *What should he do?*

He looked at his wife's expectant face. There really wasn't a question, was there? He should go ahead and knock.

There was her purse, right by the door! *What a silly thing to do.* It looked like she had just thrown it down there in a hurry. The old lady shook her head at her own absentmindedness, trying to make light of one more distressing symptom of forgetfulness. With an effort she retrieved her purse and put her wrist through the strap. Now if she could just muster the energy she needed to be off to the shop again, But first would it make sense to change her cardigan for a light jacket? It was getting late, and the sea breeze could be a little chilly. She took a step towards the coat closet.

Well, look at that, now—another thing that she'd forgotten to do. She'd forgotten to shut the closet door all the way.

Mustering his courage, Dad strode up the path. This was the second time in a few days he had found himself in front of a door feeling foolish. By God's grace the last time had worked out okay though, hadn't it? Why hadn't he asked Him for help this time?

"Jesus," he muttered. "Help me not to worry about being late, and please let this all work out." With a bit more optimism, he reached up and rang the doorbell.

The lady was just about to open the closet door when a ring at the doorbell stopped her in her tracks.

Now who could that be at this time of day? She really didn't have the energy to deal with anyone right now. Turning, she saw a large silhouette outlined through the sheers. It was rather unsettling. She knew almost no-one in the village—just the Tremannons, but she had successfully avoided running into them so far.

For a moment she thought about ignoring whoever it was, but then her basic sense of good manners got the better of her. For all she knew, it could be someone nice. Shuffling to the door, she looped the security chain through its little hole, just to be safe. She wasn't tall enough to look through the window, so she cracked the door open just enough to peek through. It was a tall man with a pleasant face and he looked sort of familiar. She relaxed a little at his apologetic smile.

"Er, excuse me madam, I'm really sorry to bother you. We weren't sure if this was the right house and whether it was you or not, but we thought we recognized the cat."

The lady tried to make sense of all this. Her confusion must have been quite apparent, for the man took a deep breath and started again a little slower.

"I'm so sorry. Let me explain better. I'm David Chapman. My family and I saw you up at the church yesterday. You must have dropped your locket, and my son found it under one of the pews. We were pretty concerned. We weren't sure how to get in touch with you, but then we thought we recognized your cat outside." He smiled, gesturing down to where her cat was patiently waiting at his feet.

Her locket! Oh dear oh dear. Had she lost that too? She wanted to burst into tears, but she couldn't—no, not in front this nice man, and anyway didn't he say he had found it? It would be one of the first things that had gone right all day.

She had a sudden memory of the lady's face—it must have been the man's wife—and the eyes smiling into her own tear-stained ones. She remembered the stab of joy she had felt—that perhaps, just for a moment, someone had cared about her pain. Making a sudden decision, she unlatched the chain and swung the door wide open.

My, that was a whole crowd behind him, she thought. *It must be his family.* They all looked very nice, though. She smiled, feeling much more at ease now. "Oh, yes, I remember you now, Mr. Chapman. Thank you, thank you. Please, do come in." She gestured inside.

Dad looked apologetic again. "You know, I'm really sorry but we're in a bit of a hurry—we just wanted to make sure this was the right place, and we actually don't have the locket with us. Could we possibly drop it by tomorrow morning?" He glanced back at his wife, who gave a confirming nod.

The old lady looked at their smiling faces. She felt that queer little sensation of joy again. She wanted to grab onto that feeling and not let go. Something about this family... She made a sudden decision. "Would you...could you come over for tea and biscuits tomorrow? The whole family—perhaps around eleven? I would love to have you." She hoped she didn't sound like she was pleading.

Dad glanced again at Mom. This time she was smiling really big and nodding hard.

He turned back. "Yes, we'd love to. Tomorrow at eleven, then. And we'll have the locket for you. Goodbye 'til then Mrs...er, Ms..."

"Renton. Mrs. Ruth Renton. I'll be looking forward to it."

Yes she would, she convinced herself. She would indeed.

Scream—he was going to scream. If he had to stay in this closet one more minute he was going to lose control, he knew it. He had been in this painful crouched position for a quarter of an hour, and his muscles were crying out in pain. All through the seemingly interminable visit with whoever it was at the front door he had crouched there, drips of sweat running down his back.

And then he heard it—the sweetest sound possible on earth at that moment. He heard the front door close and a key turn in the lock. He burst forth from his prison gasping for air, threw his phone and the letter onto the armchair and collapsed onto the carpet, frantically rubbing his legs to restore their circulation. It was a good five minutes before he was able to stand again, and now there wasn't a second to lose. Who knew if she would be back again in a moment?

Shuffling stiffly over to the table, he spread out the letters and tried to smooth out the creases. He took several photos with his phone camera, quickly checked they were legible, and then carefully folded the papers back into the envelope, placing it back on the floor behind the chair where he'd found it.

He shook his head in disbelief. *What a fiasco.* For a moment he pictured giving a certain someone a piece of his mind, but it was a ridiculous fantasy. He knew he didn't have the guts to do it.

A quick scan of the room assured him he hadn't left anything behind. He pushed the closet door closed and took a careful peek through the curtain sheers. It looked like the coast was clear. Fortunately the front door could be opened from the inside but still stay locked. He stepped carefully into the little front yard and closed the door firmly behind him, testing to see it was shut good and tight.

There was the lady and her cat again, on the other side of the bridge heading up to the shops. He shook his head again and, muttering to himself, limped as quickly as he could back to the path up the hill.

"It's not here!" Stevie's despairing wail came out of the garbage can by the front gate. He was standing on his tiptoes with his head and shoulders leaning over the opening, scanning the contents and wrinkling his nose at some rather unpleasant smells wafting up.

The others had gone on ahead to change, but Dad had gallantly promised to help Stevie look for the newspaper, as long as he was quick. It was weird though, going through someone's garbage. Dad had put himself on sentry duty while Stevie was doing the digging.

The boy had actually not done much digging as it turned out. The thought of moving some of those indefinable smelly objects in front of him—well, he thought he could just look really well and not touch.

Dad was about to respond to the boy's disappointment when he caught some movement out of the corner of his eye. There was a tall figure carrying a box and what looked like a rake, rounding the house and apparently heading their way. *Mr. Tremannon!*

"Quick, Stevie, let me look." Dad lifted the boy out of the way and, with a conscious effort to ignore what he was touching, started rummaging through the contents of the can. Thank goodness it only took him a minute to find the paper under a pile of carrot peelings. He shook it off and showed it to his son.

"Got it! Now let's get back to the house and get ready for dinner." He looked up the driveway again. *Rats!* Mr. Tremannon was coming right towards them. He must have something to put in the can. *Oh, great. One more embarrassing situation for the day.*

He squared his shoulders, grabbed Stevie's hand and walked as nonchalantly as possible towards the approaching figure. Should he just smile or should he say something? Well, he might as well just go ahead and try to explain.

"Hello, Mr. Tremannon. You're probably wondering what we're doing." He gave a light laugh.

"Afternoon." The old man greeted them. He did have a questioning look.

"We accidentally threw away this newspaper, and really needed it, and then my son remembered it was there." He held up their precious find to illustrate. Oh, brother, there were still a few peelings stuck to it. *Wonderful, just wonderful.*

"Aha," said Mr. Tremannon.

Dad was looking for an exit strategy. He waved the paper, causing the peelings to fall at the old man's feet. "Well, er, thank you very much." *Thank you for what—for letting me look through your garbage can? Boy oh boy, that was inspired.*

"Right." Mr. Tremannon was a man of few words—that was for sure.

"Well…see you later." Dad's cheeks were burning. Should he pick up the bits of carrot? No, it was time to abandon ship. He started for the house, almost dragging Stevie along. He didn't dare look back.

Mr. Tremannon watched them leave with a slight frown on his face. Then he shook his head, picked up the carrot peelings and continued on down the drive.

It took Stevie two tries to jump up on his parent's barge-like bed. Dad had called a family meeting after dinner, and everyone was jostling to find a place, chattering excitedly. The girls had picked up on the boys' excitement and were eager to read the newspaper article. It had almost driven Stevie mad with anticipation, but Dad had insisted on waiting until now to look at it. It had been worth the wait, though. This was serious business, and he was proud of his sleuthing. Just because he was the littlest, didn't mean he couldn't be an ace detective.

"Okay, family," announced Dad. "God really helped us today. Thanks to Him giving Stevie a great memory"—the boy blushed with pride—"and helping us find the newspaper, we can find out a bit more about this mystery. He also helped us find the lady with the locket. I'll read the article, and then we can spend a few minutes thanking God for all He did today." He saw his wife smiling at him from where she was propped up against a couple of pillows at the head of the bed.

"But," he continued, "because it was Stevie who remembered where the newspaper was, I want him to do the honor of reading it. Here you go, buddy." Dad handed over the paper, and Stevie grinned widely at this unexpected privilege, then thought about it for a moment and handed it back.

"Um, Daddy, can you read it? There are lots of big words and it would go faster."

Dad smiled. "Sure! Okay, let's see. Er, *local woman inherits mystery. Mrs. Ruth Renton...*"

"Wait a minute!" interrupted Rachel, bouncing up and down. "The lady today said her name was Ruth Renton! She's the one! She's the one!"

This revelation caused quite a stir. Everyone suddenly was talking at once and Dad had to raise his voice to be heard. "Okay, everyone, okay. I know this is really exciting, but let me finish and then we can talk about it." He shifted his position and continued on. "*Mrs. Ruth Renton has received an inheritance, but it remains a mystery as to what that inheritance is. Mrs. Renton is the sole inheritor of the estate of Mister Kenwyn Penrow who passed away on the seventeenth of May this year. Mr. Penrow, known locally as 'The Squire' was well known for his acts of generosity to those in need and also for his habit of collecting antique curiosities*—you know, like funny old things that are maybe valuable," Dad explained.

He continued reading. "*Mrs. Renton, who moved to Penrithen shortly after Mr. Penrow's death, was the estranged ward of the Squire and his late wife, Rosemary, who had no biological children. Though Squire Penrow had auctioned off his extensive collection when he moved out of his long-time home at the Manor, it was rumored that his most valuable piece had not been sold—an item that remains a mystery. Family solicitor Mr. Fenton Scrub, of the law firm Scrub, Wormly and Clink, confirmed that Penrow's will accompanied by an envelope addressed to Mrs. Renton was presented to her this month, but declined to elaborate on the details, citing client confidentiality.*"

The family looked at each other with amazement and delight. This was an absolute gold mine of information. They all started to talk at once.

Dad whistled loudly and the chattering died away as if by magic. "Okay people, one at a time. How about you, dear?" He looked at his wife.

"Well," said Mom, pleased to be able to go first, "I'm just amazed what God has done. When I looked at the lady--Mrs. Renton--up at the church, I could tell she was really distressed, and then Stevie finding the locket and us seeing her today, and now we find that she's the woman with the mystery inheritance—well, it's all pretty amazing."

"Emily?" Dad smiled at his daughter who was nodding her head eagerly.

"And Mrs. Renton lived with the Squire who we've been hearing so much about. A ward means that they were responsible for her, right? Maybe she used to live in this house."

"Right," nodded Dad. "Rachel?"

"Do you remember Mrs. Tremannon mentioning 'Little Ruthie'—when we asked if the Squire had any children? And she seemed really sad when she said it, like there had been a problem or something."

"You're right, I'd forgotten about that."

"So 'Little Ruthie' must be Mrs. Ruth Renton!" Rachel concluded with satisfaction.

"My turn now," put in Danny. His father nodded.

"So the man on the Inn sign and in the locket is the Squire and the lady's kind of adopted dad. And when he died recently, he left her something in his will, right?"

Everyone nodded. This was pretty cool, how everything was adding up. The only disappointed one was Stevie, who was thinking there was nothing left for him to say. He racked his brain for something, and then waved his hand frantically.

"Oh, oh, and the Squire really liked collecting weird old things and maybe he's left a fantastic treasure for the lady. Maybe a chest of gold or some pirate stuff or something!"

The other children giggled, but Dad nodded seriously.

"You know, Stevie, you're right. The article did mention that he could have left something valuable. He did collect all kinds of things. It's possible he left the most valuable one to this special lady."

This revelation caused the kids to look at each other in wonder. *This was exciting!*

"It's kind of like a real mystery adventure story," said Rachel with shining eyes.

"Yes, but there's one more thing," put in her mother. "The lady, Mrs. Renton, seems really upset. Yes, I know she must be grieving the Squire's death, but I just feel that there's more to it. Mrs. Tremannon seems to think there's something sad about her and the Squire—like there's some story there in the past that's affecting her deeply right now."

This made them all think. What could it be?

"Can we stop and thank God for what He's done," added Mom, remembering her goal.

"Of course," said Dad, feeling suddenly inspired. "For safety, for the beauty we've seen…"

"For saving us in the cave," put in Stevie.

"Yes," continued Dad, "and for helping us find the lady. Let's praise Him for His goodness and then would you mind, Kathie, praying for our meeting with the lady tomorrow—that God would direct it?"

"I'd love to," smiled Mom. "Let's follow Him step by step, and see where this little adventure leads."

❧ ❧

Through the curtains, the muted glow of the street lamp outside gave a soft radiance to the bedroom. She could just see the outline of her cat's warmly purring form at her feet.

As she lay there Mrs. Ruth Renton realized that for the first time in days—or was it weeks?—she wasn't overcome with worry. Somewhere inside a tiny bud of hope had sprouted and she wanted to nourish it with all her heart. Though she hardly dared admit it, in the midst of her confusion and grief she had actually for

89

a moment felt loved again. She couldn't understand it, but she wanted to embrace it. Yes, she would have this family over and she would serve them something really nice and maybe, just maybe—if she could pluck up the courage—she might share a little bit of what had been troubling her.

Chapter 6 - A Painful Memory

Mom had installed herself in the corner of the huge dining room, next to the stuffed bird display where there was a good light from the window. The weather was definitely on the change, and the threat of rain had made her think it was wisest to stay indoors this morning, instead of retreating to her secret garden spot. A tantalizing smell of frying bacon wafted into the room, or was it sausages? Breakfast was definitely in progress, and she needed to focus. She really wanted to pray for each member of the family, but it was hard not to keep wondering about the meeting today with the elderly lady. How would it go? Could they offer to help her in any way? She seemed so needy.

But surely God was leading in all this, Mom mused. She just needed to leave it in His capable hands and quit worrying. She was still noting in her journal what she called her 'thankful list'—thinking through all the things God had done or was doing—and it was amazing how many things there were. It was helping her realize how much God was in control, both with the old lady and her family's needs. She just needed to remember it.

Now where was she? Mrs. Tremannon could be coming in at any moment. Oh, yes, she wanted to pray for Dave. She could tell he was stressed, no matter how he tried to hide it.

"And dear Jesus, please help Dave to be able to relax and enjoy this break. Help him not to worry about his assignment, and please give him inspiration for what to write about. You know he wants to serve you and do what's right, and help people understand how you have carried your people through persecution in the past. Remind him of the promises in Your Word, and please help me to be a blessing to him today. For your glory. Amen."

Dad pulled the van to a stop in front of the cottage and rested his arms on the steering wheel. It was just a short trip, but the threat of rain had made it seem preferable to drive.

It was Sunday, and they had gathered in the sitting room that morning for family church time, singing some favorite praise songs before watching a sermon on Dad's laptop. He had saved a selection of their church pastor's teachings and the one they watched today on loving one's neighbor had seemed particularly pertinent, bringing to mind their suddenly conflicting thoughts about helping the old lady.

Dad craned his neck around and looked at the family. They were unnaturally quiet. *What was up?*

Emily tried to avoid his eyes. She was feeling a guilty mix of both compassion for this lady and worry about how she was going to relate to her. She wasn't very used to older people. She would just die if she said the wrong thing.

Rachel was looking glumly out at the house, wrestling with a grumpy feeling again. Her top-ten list of fun things to do on vacation didn't include sitting and listening to adults talk. Yes, she was sort of interested in learning more about their little mystery, but she'd rather have the synopsis at the end and not the long running commentary. Her request to explore the village or go to the cove again while the others talked had seemed perfectly reasonable. Unfortunately, Mom and Dad didn't share her enthusiasm for the idea.

If Rachel was a little grumpy, then Danny and Stevie were decidedly down in the dumps. They too wanted to find out more, but this wasn't the kind of glamorous sleuthing they had in mind. They had firmly decided that it was going to be an interminable visit of hanging out in a boring house, perched on uncomfortable chairs with boring conversation droning on around them—a veritable prison sentence.

Mom was wondering again about what it was the lady was struggling with. Why had she been crying up at the church? Would the lady feel comfortable enough to open up to them? Maybe they should have left the kids back at the Inn. The girls could have watched them well enough. She really didn't want to overwhelm the lady. She had to voice her concerns.

"Dear, do you think it's really okay, all of us being here? It's not too much for Mrs. Renton?"

Dad considered. "Well, she did say she wanted the whole family. Anyway kids, you'll remember to be quiet and good, right? We can put into practice loving our neighbor."

He got some rather unenthusiastic nods in reply. *Oh, boy.* He hoped this visit didn't turn out to be one big train wreck—bored kids, sputtering conversation…

"Let's pray again, right dear?" His wife must have read his mind like always.

"Yes—okay everyone. Dear Jesus, please guide this time. Lead us step by step and help us to be a blessing. If you want us to be a help to this lady, please use us. Help us all to behave." He paused a little to let that sink in. "And please fill us with your Spirit. Amen."

He looked around. Not many smiles yet. He didn't really feel like smiling himself. Well, it was up to him anyway. "Come on, gang. This isn't the dentist's. Let's go."

∽⚬∾

"Come in, come in." The lady seemed genuinely glad to see them all, amazing as it seemed. The family crowded into the front room, a little unsure of what to do next. Should they all sit down? There was only one armchair and a really little couch, and they didn't want to look silly and jam themselves all in there like a can of pilchards.

The old lady herself seemed momentarily at a loss. Then she pulled herself together, remembering what she had planned the night before.

"Now then, why don't you two sit right down there?" She smiled at Mom and Dad and gestured to the couch. "Children, follow me. I want to introduce you to my friends." She shuffled over towards the kitchen door.

Was there someone else here? The kids looked at each other in surprise for a moment—then followed docilely behind. Mrs. Renton paused by the bird cage, and tapped lightly on the bars, making a sort of kissing noise with her lips. She turned to the kids with a smile.

"This is my dear budgie, Sweedlepipe."

The kids' eyebrows rose in surprise. Had they heard right?

Even Dad was intrigued. "Er, did you say Sweedlepipe? That's, er, an interesting name."

"Oh, yes. Have you never read anything by Charles Dickens, the Victorian author?"

Dad shook his head. "I know who he is, I just never got around to reading any of his books."

"You watched 'A Muppet Christmas Carol' with us that one time," reminded Rachel.

"That's…not quite the same thing, honey."

"The book Martin Chuzzlewit?" Mrs. Renton didn't seem to have noticed the interchange. "The barber with all the birds in his house—Paul Sweedlepipe? I thought it rather fitting."

"Well, why not?" Dad nodded in agreement. "So you're a Dickens fan?"

"Oh my goodness, yes—ever since I was a girl. I have nearly all of his works right over there." The family could just see the set of shelves in the hallway by the stairs. It was crammed full with an assortment of old-looking volumes, like an escapee from an antique bookshop.

"And we already met your kitty," put in Rachel. "Does it have an unusual name, too?"

The tabby was weaving itself in and out of the chair legs under the kitchen table, as if waiting to bestow its royal presence on an adoring public. Mrs. Renton patted her knee and the cat immediately padded primly over to her feet, purring like a motorboat, its tail swishing back and forth. *Like a windshield wiper*, thought Emily. She and her sister couldn't resist cats and went to work at once, petting the tabby all over, scratching its chin, stroking its back and rubbing its ears. The cat responded by abandoning all pretense of decorum and collapsing unresistingly onto its side again, the enraptured purring reaching an astonishing volume.

Mrs. Renton looked pleased at this display of affection. "And this is Mr. Pickwick, though I just call him Pickwick to save time."

"Another Dickens character?" wondered Rachel. The old lady nodded. Rachel gave the cat a little extra scratching around its whiskers. "He is such a dear, isn't he Emily? And look, he's smiling!"

It did indeed look like the cat was grinning, its eyes closed in bliss, its legs stretched out.

"Better be careful girls, or you're going to have just a puddle of melted puss in a minute," called Dad from the couch.

Mrs. Renton put her hands on Danny and Stevie's shoulders. She had thought of an idea for them last night, and really hoped it would work. She paused for a second, and took a deep breath. Why did this seem to be such a difficult undertaking? Well, it was true that this was the first time ever she'd entertained a family. She steadied her voice.

"Now, young men, I need your help with something in the kitchen."

Stevie groaned inwardly. Probably help with the dishes or something boring like that.

But the old lady was still talking. "Now sit yourself at the table and I'll get my tin."

The boys obeyed a little reluctantly, and she pulled a large container off a nearby shelf and set it in front of them. It looked like an old biscuit tin, embossed with the image of a schooner under full sail.

"I've been meaning to sort these out for ages, and just never got around to it." It took her a few tries, but she managed to pry off the lid and display the contents. It was full of old postage stamps, all neatly cut off their envelopes and squeezed in together.

The boys sat up straighter. This looked interesting!

"Can you sort them in piles for me? I want them put in groups by country— all the British ones in one pile, all the French ones in another and so on. I've got stamps from all over the world. Now that I think of it, you'll need some little plastic bags. What's your name, dearie?" She looked at Stevie.

"I'm—I mean, my name's Stephen." He thought it appropriate to use his full name for some reason.

"But we call him Stevie to save time too," put in his brother.

"Well good, Master Stevie. In that drawer over there you'll find two magnifying glasses—a small one and a big one. I'll get you some little bags. And you can keep twenty stamps each—whatever are your favorites."

"Wow, thanks!" Stevie ran to retrieve the glasses and the two boys started pawing through the stamps in delight. There were all kinds of interesting ones— birds, trains, landscapes, ships and a whole slew of people, from sour-faced royalty to suavely-smiling movie stars.

Mom and Dad glanced at each other, impressed. That would keep them entertained! They heaved a sigh of relief.

"And now, you two young ladies follow me." Mrs. Renton pottered over to the cupboard by the back door and retrieved a couple of smaller tins and a quilted sewing basket which she set on the table near the boys. She wasn't half as nervous now that she saw that the boys were doing well.

First she opened the tin decorated with the Victorian winter street scene. It was full to the brim with a potpourri of buttons. Next came the tin marked "Cornish Clotted-Cream Fudge" with a photo of a sandy beach under a cobalt sky. This one was filled with a treasure-trove of beads and little pewter charms. The girls oohed and aahed appreciatively.

"There now. You'll find string, wire, ribbon and such in the basket. I think there may be some earring hooks, too. Perhaps you could find a way to make some pretty things." She leaned in closer. "Is your mother's birthday coming up?"

"In a couple of months," whispered back Emily. She suddenly realized she didn't feel nervous at all!

"Well, there you are. See what you can make her." Mrs. Renton patted her on the shoulder and gave the girls a conspiratorial wink.

There, the children were taken care of and she was on familiar ground again. She knew very well how to make tea. She already had the cups and plates out-- she just needed to put the water on to boil and get the cream and jam from the fridge. So far she hadn't forgotten anything, thank goodness, but the hardest part was coming up. *Should she, could she share what was troubling her?* She still wasn't sure.

❧❦

Wreathed in a cloud of cigarette smoke, the grey-haired man leaned back in his chair and studied the second of the two copies he had just printed out. The picture resolution wasn't fantastic—Jennings' phone didn't have a great camera— but at least it was legible. *But what did this first part mean?* Grabbing his phone off the table, he hit the speed dial.

"Jennings? Yeah, it's Kennedy. Okay, I got your email and printed out the pics. The one from the lawyers isn't worth anything, but the other one's just what we need, I think." He listened for a moment.

"Yeah, well, you did alright," he admitted grudgingly. "Though you almost blew it all, getting stuck in that closet. Anyway, we've got to get this first part figured out. It looks like some sort of book, but I've no clue where. And flightless birds... Any ideas?"

He took another drag of his cigarette and switched the phone to his other ear so he could tap off some of the ash. "Well, maybe. She did live in the manor house with them. It's as good a place to start as any."

He shook his head. "No way—you know I can't risk her seeing me! You've got to do it!" He threw the empty cigarette packet at the basket by the wall, and rolled his eyes in exasperation as it missed by a good two feet. The voice at the other end seemed to have a lot to say at his last comment.

"Wednesday? But it can't wait that long. We need to act as soon as possible!" he interrupted.

This produced another long speech and Kennedy rolled his eyes. He couldn't stand whining. He heaved a frustrated sigh. This was too important to foul up now they had the contents of the will in hand.

"Listen to me. I'll go myself, alright? But it's not going to be easy. I'm pretty sure the old couple don't remember me, but I've still got to be careful going over there. I'll have to come up with some excuse."

❦❧

Scones with clotted cream and strawberry jam! In Dad's opinion clotted cream was one of God's greatest gastronomic gifts. Rich and thick, yellow and sweet and as firm as butter--the temptation was to scoop it on like so much ice-cream-on-a-pie. He glanced over at his wife, who was resisting the temptation to over-indulge. He needed to follow her lead, and he definitely didn't want to end up with cream and jam oozing onto his lap. Mrs. Renton had just got some napkins from the bureau drawer, obviously expecting the worse. As he tried to assemble his scone he could feel both ladies watching him. It was clearly time to come up with something to divert all this attention.

"Well Mrs. Renton. Thank you so much for having us. Yes, I'd love some tea." The lady was pouring a cup and giving him a questioning look. "A spot of milk and one lump please," he added. He'd always had his tea the English way with milk and sugar.

He took the cup, set it on the small table beside him and pretended to examine his scone for a second. He needed to think. Should they just try to make small talk as they munched and sipped, or dive right in to a big discussion? His wife wasn't any more thrilled than he was to direct a conversation. *Was it up to him to decide, then?* Being at the dentists' was actually sounding pretty good right now.

There was an uncomfortable silence, broken only by the animated conversation coming from the kitchen. The kids had evidently finished their scones and were back enjoying their little projects. He'd rather be in there going through stamps himself. He risked a peek at the others and his toes curled suddenly in embarrassment. They were both looking right at him. There was nowhere to hide.

But wait a minute! Of course! He couldn't believe he'd forgotten... "Mrs. Renton...we wanted to return your locket."

With an almost imperceptible sigh of relief, his wife took the cue and retrieved it from her purse. She handed it across and the old lady took it and clasped it to her heart. A few tears came into her eyes.

"I really don't know how to thank you," she murmured, dabbing her eyes with a hanky.

Mom felt a surge of compassion again that overcame her shyness. She leaned a little closer and put her hand on the lady's, noticing how cold and frail it felt.

"It's our pleasure. I can see that it means a lot to you. I'm so glad we could find it." She paused. "You seem distressed about something, and we…" She looked at Dad who smiled reassuringly. "We don't want to pry in any way, but if there's anything we can do to help…"

Mrs. Renton glanced up at them both, took in their smiling yet concerned looks and suddenly couldn't contain her emotions anymore. She began to sob.

Dad felt his insides jump a little. He had been just a mite concerned things might go this direction. He really didn't do well when there were emotions overflowing all over creation. Not that he didn't care about people's feelings—he just wasn't sure how exactly to help right in the midst of the crisis. He'd blown it not a few times trying to fix things there and then, when his wife just needed someone to listen.

He threw a despairing glance over at her.

The man named Kennedy lay back in his chair, studying the ceiling as if trying to find an answer among the old wooden beams. With a sudden thought he jumped up and strode over to the bay window. He could just see down the lane to the old lady's house. There was some sort of minivan parked outside. That was interesting. He didn't think she had any friends. Well, anyway, she was probably occupied, so this would be a good time. He looked down again at the paper in his hand. *Flightless birds.* There was something about that that stirred in his memory. *Could it be?*

He made a quick phone call. "Listen, I think I've got an idea. I'm going to head over to the inn right away. I'll call you if I find anything. I'm not too worried. We've just got to stay ahead of her, and believe me; she's not going to figure this out any time soon. Penrow was an idiot—all this mystery nonsense. Anyway, it works to our advantage. I'll call you as soon as I get it. Later."

He snapped the phone shut and stood there for a moment, running his fingers through his untidy mop of hair. Then snatching his keys off the sideboard, he headed to find his coat and shoes.

Mom was holding Mrs. Renton's hands across the coffee table. Dad marveled at how wonderfully she was handling the situation. "Thank you, Jesus, for my wife," he prayed silently. He didn't feel like he was contributing much to the conversation, but perhaps that was better anyway.

"To have to leave your parents and be so far away," Mom continued. "I've heard about all the children sent away from London during the war, but I admit I never really thought about it,".

Mrs. Renton nodded. "I was actually one of the older ones. I left two weeks before my twelfth birthday. I didn't know anyone else on the train—just the lady in charge who my parents introduced me to at the station." She sniffed, and Mom let go of her hands so she could dab her eyes.

A babble of conversation came from the kitchen. Mom thought about what it must have been like leaving her own children—not knowing if they would ever see each other again. The thought brought tears to her eyes too.

Dad could understand that it must have been traumatic, but was that really the thing that was troubling this lady right now, around sixty years later?

Mrs. Renton must have been reading his thoughts. "That's not the reason I wanted to share with you today—but it's a part of my story that's important. I don't want to take too much of your time." She looked at the Chapman's with concern.

Mom patted her arm. "Please don't worry. We're fine. Go ahead."

The old lady looked like she was going to cry again, but with an effort managed to master it. She gave a small, apologetic smile. "Life is full of hard times, and that was an especially difficult one, but there was worse to come. I came to Penrithen in March of 1942, just at the beginning of the Blitz—that's what they called it when the Germans started bombing London."

Dad nodded. He knew all about the Second World War, having studied it with schoolboy relish in his younger years.

"It was the Penrows who took me in. They really did their best to help me—I was so lonely and scared. I missed my parents terribly, but I did actually start to adjust to living here—the Penrows were so kind and loving. I thought of them as my aunt and uncle—like family, you know. I called them Auntie Rosie and Uncle Kenwyn, and they called me little Ruthie. We lived at the manor house—where you're staying now—and went to church up at the chapel on the hill where you found me."

Though they hadn't noticed it, the room had gradually darkened, and a sudden patter of rain dashed itself against the window. Mrs. Renton reached over and turned on the lamp. Dad's mind was suddenly wandering again. He couldn't help but feel a little satisfaction that it had been worth it after all, bringing the van. He was wondering whether he had rolled up all the windows, when he realized that the old lady was speaking again.

"And then…" She paused, unsure if she could say it out loud. "That horrible day."

Dad felt suddenly guilty for thinking about the car and gave her his full attention. Mom prayed silently. "Oh, Jesus, please help her."

Mrs. Renton closed her eyes. "I was out playing with my rabbits. Uncle Kenwyn had built a hutch for them next to the old tool shed behind the house. I remember him coming with Auntie Rosie, coming across the lawn—they were holding hands—and Uncle had a letter—a telegram."

She looked up. Her voice became suddenly brisk and business-like—as if she had decided the only way to deal with the pain was to try and stay detached emotionally. "My parents were dead…killed in an air-raid. Most people had gone to the underground station where a shelter had been set up, but Mother and Father were both in the Red Cross. They were at an aid station down the road. I found out all this later from a neighbor. They thought they were obeying God by helping people, but he obviously didn't care to protect them. And it wasn't even a bomb. A German plane had been hit by anti-aircraft fire and crash-landed right on the building. What were the chances of that?"

Suddenly her voice broke, and the façade crumbled. "I couldn't believe it when Uncle told me. I was numb. I remember stroking my little white bunny and not even looking up. Uncle and Auntie tried their best to comfort me, but it was like something had died in me that day. The only real consolation I had felt in being so far from my parents was that one day we would be reunited—but now that hope was gone."

Now Mom and Dad both had tears in their eyes.

"I stuffed the hurt deep down inside. Uncle and Auntie tried to help—they tried to pray with me…to convince me that God was in control, but I thought, if God was in control, that plane would have crashed thirty yards behind the building in the town park and Mummy and Daddy would still be alive.

"I didn't have any other relatives—I had nowhere else to go, but Uncle and Auntie told me I could stay with them after the war. I realize now how much they loved me—and I wasn't lovable back. They must have seen something in me, I don't know. They just chose to love me, even when I misbehaved, even when I rebelled. I wouldn't read the Bible or go to church with them anymore—I was so angry at God—but they didn't force me. They just kept on loving me."

The old lady gave a deep shuddering sigh, then reached over and picked up the locket again. She gazed at the photo in it for a second—then passed it to Mom.

The face of the Squire smiled back at Mom across the years. Was she imagining it, or did she now see just a hint of sadness in his face too?

"Mrs. Renton," Mom took her hand again. "This must be so hard on you. Are you sure you want to go on?"

The lady clutched at Mom's hand with a surprisingly firm grip. "Yes, yes I must. If I stop now I'll never get it all out." Even as she said it she thought to herself what a—*dare she say it?* Yes, what a miracle that she was sharing all this with perfect strangers. But she didn't want to think about that too much or she'd lose her nerve. No, she must go on quickly.

"Things came to a head when I was sixteen, soon after my birthday. Uncle and Auntie had given me a party with a birthday cake. They gave me my own Bible, with my name embossed in silver on the cover. They were so excited to give it, but I don't even remember saying 'thank you.' It wasn't what I wanted. Uncle Kenwyn gave me some little speech about how the book held the path to hope and peace for me, but I didn't believe it. I never once opened it. For some reason, though, they still kept on being kind to me. Several weeks later Uncle Kenwyn took me into his study and told me that he had some good news. I remember standing there, waiting. I had what I would call an 'attitude.' I was trying to be—how do you say it? What is the word they use nowadays? *Cool?* Yes, I was trying to act cool." She gave a sad laugh.

"Anyway, Uncle Kenwyn told me that they had finally got the permission to adopt me. He said that they both considered me their daughter anyway, but now it could all be legal. I could be their real daughter. He paused to let it sink in. I could tell he was really happy. I suddenly knew that I was at a turning point. It was like right then and there I was being given an opportunity to choose a new path. I could start all over, finally putting to rest my anger at my parents' deaths, and be part of a new loving family. I could be a daughter again, and have a Mother and Father once more."

Mom and Dad felt a sudden dread. They could sense in their spirits what her choice had been that day, and now they understood the source of the old lady's pain.

"But I wouldn't do it. It was like all my anger of the past boiled over suddenly and I said things—things I know now I didn't really mean. I told Uncle Kenwyn that I didn't want to be his daughter—that I never wanted to be his daughter. That I hated God, I hated the Bible and I hated them for trying to make me accept His will. I left in tears and I ran—I ran out the back door, and across the fields 'til I found a spot under some trees and I flung myself down and cried and cried until I had nothing left."

⊰⊱

The rain squall had passed, but the weather was still unsettled. Down on the quay, old Jack Carrick wasn't in the best of moods. The grizzled fisherman in his trademark peaked cap and blue sweater plunked himself down on an upturned bucket and hefted up the lobster pot at his side. After a fruitless morning out on Jasper's boat there wasn't much else to do other than patching up some of his old stuff. Not that there was ever much going on here anyway. Most of the pilchard fishing was over on this stretch of the coast and who could compete with those bigger fishing operations down south?

He rubbed his three day-old stubble and looked around the harbor. This used to be a hive of activity, with the days' catches coming in, the fish for sale on the quay or being packed up for delivery, the harbor crammed with fishing boats. Now it was only a few souls like himself, struggling to make a living, and the town going to pot with all the homes being bought by out-of-towners.

A violent banging came from the *Seagull*, moored over against the quay. Jack gave a knowing grimace. Jasper must be working on the engine again; in fact, it sounded like he was taking all his frustrations out on it. The old girl had been pretty temperamental lately. On days like this, Jack thought he'd like to take a turn with the hammer himself.

Grumbling under his breath, he was fumbling for his penknife when he was startled by a sudden roar behind him. A yellow sports car was shooting down the lane towards the bridge at a decidedly unsafe speed, just missing someone's van parked in front of the cottages. At the bottom of the hill it swerved to the right and ground its gears as it started the steep climb back up towards the Inn.

The fisherman shook his head in disgust. This just confirmed his petulant thoughts. Those *fyslek havysi*—he preferred using the Cornish terms when he was mad—yes, those *annoying tourists* thought they owned the place!

⊰⊱

"So after you ran away, did you ever see the Penrows again?" Mom's heart was heavy, both with a compassion for the lady mixed with a searing pain for this couple she would never meet.

Mrs. Renton shook her head sadly. "If you can believe it, I never did. They found my new address somehow and continued to write to me faithfully over the years, but I didn't reply. At first I didn't want to, and then later, when I grew to realize how bad I'd been, I was too prideful and too ashamed to write back. When Auntie Rose died of cancer in '57, I didn't even go to the funeral." She dabbed her eyes again.

"I actually think I may have gone if I'd known, but I was in Europe for several years with my job and they didn't have my forwarding address. I didn't find out until I got back, and then once again I was too ashamed to contact Uncle. I know it's hard to believe this isn't it? How can a person get so hard—so resistant to someone's love? Sometimes it can happen bit by bit, with little daily choices that all add up over time, but for me I think my shock and anger at my parent's deaths—well it just created a deep wound that never healed." She stopped and thought for a moment.

"But you know, I can't blame it on that. No, it was my choice." She glanced up and met their eyes with an almost pleading look. "No matter what happens in life, we always have a choice as to how to respond. In the five years I lived with them, they chose to love me and treat me like a daughter, no matter how I treated them, and that love—that choice to love—continued until the day Uncle Kenwyn died. And now it's too late."

Dad sat back in his chair. What a testimony to the power of unconditional love, and what a picture of God's love. He was humbled just thinking about it.

Mom silently prayed, *O Father, show Mrs. Renton that it was your love for her all those years, and that you love her now. It seems impossible, but please do more than we can ask or imagine.*

"And that brings me to this." Mrs. Renton sighed and pulled several sheets of paper out of the envelope at her side. She held the top one up.

"You can imagine my shock when I received this from the lawyers. It seems Uncle Kenwyn left something incredible for me. His love—their love—seems to follow me even beyond the grave."

Dad could read the letterhead from where he was sitting. So there were those funny names again—*Scrub, Wormly and Clink*. Offices at number three, Mizzen Lane, Penrithen.

"So when did you move back here to Penrithen?" he wondered.

Mrs. Renton poured another cup of tea. "Well, I had completely lost contact with Uncle by then. It seems he had a stroke about ten years ago. It left him bedridden. Someone in the village here looked after him, but he never really recovered. Then he apparently went downhill very quickly a month or so ago, and passed away. Somehow the Tremannons managed to get word to me about Uncle's funeral, and I decided to come. I felt so guilty, but I had to do it.

There were so many people there—he was so loved in this community—but I honestly didn't want anyone to see me. I crept in and sat at the back. As I heard people sharing about what he meant to them, I realized clearly for the first time what I had thrown away. If there was a God, I felt like I was being punished for my wrongdoing. The minister spoke about hope—not wishful thinking, you understand, but a reality. He said that Uncle was in heaven with Jesus and reunited with his wife. He said we could have joy, even on this sad occasion because we knew for sure where Uncle was. I hadn't had hope or joy for years and years." Her voice trailed off.

"But do you have hope now?" said Mom, earnestly.

Mrs. Renton seemed surprised, even a little flustered at the directness of the question. "Well, I'm…I mean, I, well, I'm not sure." She took a sip of tea as she tried to search her jumbled thoughts and feelings. "After the funeral, I was so distraught. It was so strange being back here, but I couldn't bear the thought of leaving again. Somehow I had to find what I was missing—you know, to satisfy this aching in my heart. I thought perhaps the answer could be found here. And then I got the confusing letter from the lawyers, but as for hope… Well, all I can say is that, for some reason…" She looked a little embarrassed. "Well, after seeing you at the church, I was touched by something—something I couldn't quite understand. It's like I knew that I needed to talk to you, that somehow you were…well, this is so hard to put into words." She thought again for a moment.

"It's like I felt again that same love, and yes, I suppose I did experience—well not exactly hope, but perhaps the smallest possibility that there may be hope in the future. I don't know why I would think that. It's too late, isn't it?" She had a pleading look.

Mom looked at her directly in the eyes. "With God, all things are possible, and while we live, it's never too late."

The lady looked flustered again. She lowered her eyes and took a quick, nervous sip from her cup. Mom sensed it was time to change the subject a little.

"So was there something in the will that is troubling you?" Mom's gentle smile seemed to put the lady at ease again.

"That's where I'm so puzzled. I honestly didn't expect anything at all—in fact, I thought Uncle had given everything away to charity when he had to move out of the manor."

"The manor? Oh, do you mean the inn where we're staying?" Dad wondered.

The lady nodded. "I've heard there are a few things still there, but apparently all the valuable items were sold off at auction and the proceeds given to the Children's Hospital in Newquay, down the coast. It was really strange what the lawyers wrote." She passed him the letter. "Please read it. I'm so confused."

Maybe this was some way they could help the lady in a practical way. Dad scanned the first paragraph, and his eyes widened slightly. "But the lawyers say that you have been left something very valuable. Do you know what it is?"

He passed the paper to his wife who was trying to read it upside down.

"It mentions a letter from the Squire," said Mom, reading further down. "Did you receive one?"

"Well, I received this with the will, but it's really strange." Mrs. Renton passed them the second sheet of paper and they looked at it together. It was a section of handwritten verse, in a flowing, even script.

"Is this it?" Dad turned it over, but the other side was blank.

"Yes, that's all. I read it through, but none of it makes much sense to me." The old lady set her cup down on the table and ran her hand over her eyes. "It's not as if I even want anything—not anything valuable, you understand. I know I

102

don't deserve that, but part of me is hoping that there is still a chance..." She paused, looking into the distance for a moment. "Well, that there would be something that would give me hope..."

There was that word again, thought Mom. "Hope?" she gently prodded.

"Yes, hope that they had forgiven me. That this awful wound in my heart could be healed."

Mom nodded, understanding.

Dad read the verse out loud. *"'Neath Flightless birds, a book of verse,*
The way begins, a trail diverse.'"

He shook his head. It was a bit like one of those mystery stories that the kids liked so much, and he himself had enjoyed as a boy. Missing treasures, cryptic clues... *But why would the Squire do this, especially as he probably knew the lady would have trouble figuring it all out?* It was beyond him. "Well, it's definitely a puzzle," he said out loud.

The clock on the mantel struck three. He looked at his wife. There was a decision to be made, and he wasn't sure he wanted to make it. Weren't they supposed to be on vacation? He sighed inwardly. He had really wanted a break— a fun, relaxing time. Did they really want to get more involved with this? It would be much easier to just say they'd pray for the lady and step out of her life again.

Yet even as he thought this, he felt the conviction of the Holy Spirit—that inner nudge that he couldn't ignore. Yes, it was always easier to avoid difficulties, but was that really the road God had marked out for them? Was that the purpose of life? Wasn't it more about learning to trust him? He so didn't want to have to learn that lesson the hard way, but it seemed that trust was only necessary when he was in a situation where he couldn't figure a way out.

Mom raised her eyes and looked in his. No matter how much he still struggled to read his wife with some degree of clarity, there was no question this time what she wanted to do. *Okay, time to take the lead*, he thought. *Just don't think about the consequences. God will have to take care of us.*

"Mrs. Renton." He paused, and she looked up at him expectantly. "We don't feel like it's an accident that we met you up at the church."

Well now, wasn't that just like always? It didn't matter how blue the sky might be when she checked out the window or how sure it seemed that there was finally a break in the rain--as soon as she tried to put washing on the line a whole sky full of pesky dark clouds would sneak up from nowhere. It was afternoon already, and this was the third time today she'd had tried to put the washing out.

Mrs. Tremannon was attempting to hang up a pair of her husband's trousers when a sudden gust almost tore them out of her hands, the last clothespin springing from her grip to disappear into the jungle of crabgrass at the base of the washing line post. The line of wet clothes danced wildly about, and she took a thoughtful look at the darkening sky over towards the sea. Out of the corner of her eye she noticed the top of a ladder bobbing along the roofline of the shed. Her husband was obviously giving up on fixing the broken gutter, and he wasn't one to postpone a job unnecessarily. *Oh well.*

With a phlegmatic shrug of her shoulders, she started back along the line, unpegging the assorted clothing one by one and dropping them into the basket at her feet.

જેન્જી

Now how was he going to do this without being seen? No, he hadn't really thought this through, had he. Well it was too late now to think of parking back down the lane.

With a crunch of gravel, Kennedy pulled the yellow sports car up in front of the old house and checked his watch. Five past three. It was just possible the old couple might be working outside, but with the look of those clouds, it wouldn't be for long. Scanning around for some inspiration, he spotted the Inn sign swinging lightly in the fresh breeze. *Now that was a thought.* Yes, he could just be inquiring about a room. That would work.

જેન્જી

"Oh, and don't forget Daddy that you were going to write down the clue!" Stevie was so excited. *This was becoming a real mystery!* Mom and Dad had filled the kids in on the strange clue and Mrs. Renton's dilemma, and they had listened open-mouthed.

"I didn't forget. I took a picture of it." Dad patted the camera hanging from his shoulder. "And I've got your phone number." He smiled at Mrs. Renton.

The family was gathered at the door, the girls giving the cat a generous scratching and stroking in way of a goodbye. Mom and Dad had shared their decision to help the old lady with the family, and they had all taken it pretty well, even Rachel. After all, she had considered, mysteries were fun, and surely it wouldn't interfere too much with the holiday, would it? She fervently hoped not.

જેન્જી

Kennedy stood at the front door for a moment, debating what to do. Then he squared his shoulders and gave a firm knock. He drummed his fingers impatiently on the door post while mischievous gusts of wind swirled into the cluttered porch, scattering more seeds from the spilled packets around his feet.

He knocked harder, sneaking a peak through the little window. There was no sign of anyone. Now what should he do? Should he risk going in and perhaps being discovered, or come back later? No, he wanted to get this thing over with.

He tried the door. It was unlocked. Wincing a little at the squeaking hinges, he stepped carefully into the hall and closed the door behind him. He peered into the large front room, dark and quiet with just some filtered daylight coming through the windows. *Oh yes, he remembered this place.*

There was still no sign of anyone. Maybe he wouldn't need his alibi after all, but even so he still needed to move quickly. Now was it still here? Yes, there, in the far corner. *Perfect.*

જેન્જી

Mrs. Tremannon heaved the heavy laundry basket back in through the kitchen door and plunked it down by the stove. She would just have to keep checking the weather throughout the day. It wasn't the first time this had happened, and it wouldn't be the last. A lifetime of hard work had given her a practical outlook on life. There was always something else to do, and experience had taught her that it was no use getting all wound up about little delays.

She limped over to the fridge. It was a newer model and looked rather out of place in the old kitchen, standing at attention in the corner like some sort of robot servant waiting for orders. Her to-do list was stuck to the side with a butterfly magnet, and she perused the items, squinting a little as she struggled to decipher her own writing. Her reading glasses had wandered off again somewhere.

Vacuum the upstairs hallway. Well, that did need doing, but she would have to get her husband to carry the vacuum up the stairs so it would have to wait.

Washing. Yes, of course, that's what she had planned on doing before the rain!

Dust the dining room. Well now, that was something. She had noticed it needed doing yesterday evening when the sun revealed her neglect along the surface of the sideboard. It was no good having folks stay if they were going to drown in dust. It all needed a good cleaning. Now where was her duster?

She stuck the list back on the fridge and started a patient sorting through all the cleaning supplies leaning behind the back door. Brooms, mops, a plunger, and yes, there at the back was her bucket with several clean dusters draped over the side. Now if she could just reach it through the web of wooden handles… *Whoops!* There went the whole caboodle.

With a clattering of sticks, the stack of implements fell around her, one of the handles neatly flipping a tray of silverware off the counter and on to the floor with a resounding metallic crash.

Mrs. Tremannon surveyed the scene. Now that wouldn't do at all. It was no use trying to clean up one mess and creating another!

The sudden cacophony of sound caused Kennedy to freeze in alarm. *Someone was in the house!* He was going to be caught red-handed, and this would be hard to explain. The blasted cabinet was locked and the key was missing. He might have forced the lock, but there wasn't time now. His plans were unraveling. *Time to get out.*

He made a desperate, split second decision. Darting out of the doorway nearby, he dashed into the sitting room. Yes, he had remembered the layout of the house correctly. The big French doors might provide a way of escape, if only they were unlocked. He tried the handle, and it turned easily. *Yes!*

Closing the door carefully behind him, he sprinted across the lawn to his car. He jumped in, started the engine and backed out, thinking hard. He must come up with another plan. And the sooner the better.

As the van approached the turning to the Inn, Dad glanced in the rear-view mirror. His family all had goofy grins on their faces. Boy, did he ever love those guys! They were all excited about this little mystery, probably thinking they were in their very own adventure story. Yes, they had better—*woah! What on earth?*

He had looked forward just in time. A yellow car was coming out of the gate just as he was about to turn in. He slammed on the brakes, swerving as he did so. There was a violent lurch and the van bumped to a stop with its right side against the hedge.

❧❧

Kennedy cursed loudly. *That idiot! Why couldn't he look where he was going?*

As he pulled out into the lane again, he glanced over to where the offending vehicle sat unmoving on the shoulder. There seemed to be a bunch of people inside and some animated discussion going on. He could see one face looking right at him with wide eyes—some kid with red hair.

❧❧

"It was him. I know it was him!" Danny was pointing frantically out the back window.

The rest of the family looked at one another, confused. It couldn't really have been that same guy from the café. That would be too weird.

Dad started the engine again and eased carefully back out onto the road and in through the gate. He glanced across at his wife who gave him a meaningful look. *Right.*

"Let's park then we'll pray. God knows if it was the guy or not, and he's in control."

❧❧

Kennedy drove up the hill towards his lodgings, thinking hard. No, this wasn't going to be as easy as he'd thought. It was no use just waltzing on ahead without really thinking this through. The stakes were too high. He glanced over as he passed the old lady's house. *What was she thinking?* Surely she wasn't in danger of figuring all this out—not all by herself?

A thought suddenly hit him. *Who had been at her house earlier today?* There had been a van parked outside, though it wasn't there now. And that van, now. There was something significant about it. *Yes—that van he'd just almost hit.* They were both silver, with roof racks. Could it possibly be the same one?

He pulled to a stop by the big white house and sat there with his arms resting on the steering wheel. *Hmm…* he hadn't banked on the possibility that she knew someone who might help her. This would bear some thinking—some serious thinking indeed.

106

Chapter 7 - A Sudden Inspiration

Lunch was cleared away and Dad had retrieved his laptop from upstairs and was searching for a place to plug it in. There didn't seem to be an overabundance of outlets in the room. *Well, that did seem to fit with the medieval motif,* he mused. No matter—he should have enough battery left.

It was normally pretty dim in the dining room anyway, but with the darkened sky outside they had definitely needed some extra light as they ate. For some reason the funny candelabra above the big table wasn't working, so they'd had to turn on an assortment of lamps giving the meal a sort of mysterious aura that the children secretly delighted in. It seemed a fitting setting for a mysterious clue.

Dad set the laptop at the end of the table, hooked up the camera and started downloading photos.

"Hey, give me a second here!" It was a little annoying that opening his laptop seemed to exert some sort of irresistible magnetic force that attracted kids from all over the planet. Stevie's face had miraculously appeared almost under his arm, with Danny peering over on the other side.

"Give your father some room," said Mom, scooting them back with a wave of her hand, but then pausing herself and looking over his shoulder.

Dad had to smile at that, but chose not to say anything. He scanned the list of thumbnails—some shots at a pretty rest stop in France, lots of photos of the family on the ferry deck, hair blowing every which way and with some truly bizarre expressions on the faces of the boys, the little hams. *Ah, finally.* At the very end was the picture he had taken of the strange verse in the will. He double-clicked to zoom it up and checked it out critically. Good, it was clear enough to read, and he could copy it onto his notebook without any trouble. What did it all mean though? Why had the Squire made it such a puzzle? And what about '*the way begins?*' That didn't sound like a quick and easy solution.

Mrs. Tremannon appeared suddenly at the far end of the room, accompanied by her husband who was brandishing a huge screwdriver in one hand and lugging a positively enormous rusted tool box with the other. They noticed the group gathered at the table, illuminated in the glow from the screen.

"Well, now, how are you all today? Did you have a nice morning? I wondered if you went for a drive or maybe down to the cove?" Mrs. Tremannon was full of questions but didn't seem overly concerned about the responses. "It was probably a bit brisk there today, what with the wind and all. I suppose you probably didn't stay long if you did go." She glanced up at the candelabra. "I'm sorry the light's out again. My husband's going to see to it right away. Oh, you have one of those little TVs don't you."

The elderly lady ambled over to where they were grouped around the screen. "It's funny how some folks just love to watch the telly all day. I had a nephew who loved it so much that he had one in every room—all on at the same time. When we went to visit him I kept thinking he had a crowd of folks hidden in his flat, chattering away." She looked at her husband who was unscrewing the light switch plate on the far wall. "Isn't that right, dear?"

"Right." Mr. Tremannon nodded without turning round. The kids giggled.

"Well, it's not exactly a TV. It's a portable computer." Dad turned it slightly so she could see the image.

"Portable computer? Well, now, that's something different. But who'd want to take a computer around with them? These new-fangled whatsits. I don't suppose it'll catch on."

"Perhaps not," said Dad, seriously.

"And did you find that net-shop the other day?" Mrs. Tremannon felt quite proud of herself for remembering the technical name.

"Yes, the internet café. It was called Captain Jack's Coffee House."

"Oh, yes, that place. We know the owners well. Lovely couple. They only recently opened, didn't they? I didn't know they served fish *and* coffee, though."

Dad tried not to smile. "No, just coffee actually, but they have a way to connect a computer to the Internet. It's a…er…way to look up information."

"Oh, like a dictionary."

"Well, sort of." Dad thought he'd better leave the explanation at that.

"We were looking at the mystery verse that the Squire wrote," piped up Stevie. Mr. Tremannon suddenly paused in his work and turned his gaze on the family, a strange look on his face. Emily shot a glance of surprise and concern at Rachel, and Danny poked Stevie hard with his elbow.

"Shhh," he whispered fiercely.

"Hey!" Stevie didn't appreciate that at all.

Dad came to the rescue. "So Mrs. Tremannon, could you tell us more about what the Squire was like? Did he like—oh, puzzles and such?" *Kind of a weird question, but hey, why not try?*

Mr. Tremannon turned back to his work. The old lady looked a little surprised but then considered the question seriously. She put her hands on her ample hips and looked off into space with a slight smile.

"Well, yes, he was right fond of crossword puzzles. Is that what you mean? Those complicated ones that would take most folks half their life to finish—he was always doing them, and he could finish them in nothing flat. Course, he was such a clever man, always reading some complicated book or another. He had such a brain, he did. And you take chess, for instance. Now, I've never figured out how folks get so interested in all those fiddly pieces, but he just loved to play." She shook her head in admiration.

Dad raised an eyebrow with a sideways glance at his wife. This was all interesting stuff.

But Mrs. Tremannon wasn't done yet. "And he loved history. He was president of the local historical society and knew all there was to know about our little village—fixed up loads of old places, he did. He even wrote a book about it. You know, one of his ancestors really used to be the squire of this place. Mr. Penrow's great-great-great—well, I don't know how many greats—but some grandfather way back. Anyway, Mr. Penrow carried on that tradition of caring for this place, looking after folks, helping out wherever he could."

Mrs. Tremannon paused, then fumbled for a handkerchief in her apron pocket to dab her eyes. "He was a right good man with a heart big enough for the whole village and everyone in it." She sniffed a couple of times, but then became suddenly brisk.

"But there now, I must be back to work. Looks like I may have a moments break in the weather to get my wash back out." She bustled out again.

Mr. Tremannon straightened up and flicked the switch, flooding the room with light. The candelabra was back in action. He nodded in satisfaction.

"There." He grabbed his tool box and strode out of the room.

Dad smiled at the family. "Well, it looks like Mrs. T could be a big help—she's a veritable fount of information."

He felt a gentle hand on his arm. "But I think we need to be a bit careful in asking her about the Squire. We don't want to badger her too much. She must really still miss him."

Dad's enthusiasm suddenly evaporated.

"But how can we find out about this poem thing," he blurted out, gesturing at the screen. As he said it, his eyes met his wife's and he suddenly knew what the answer was. *Rats and double rats again.* It should have been his first thought.

"You're right." He grabbed Mom's hand. "We don't want to do this on our own strength. If this is God's plan then He's the one who's going to help. Let's ask Him for wisdom."

❦

The colors of the village looked muted under the ragged grey sky. It was a little cooler than they had anticipated, and Mom and Dad and the boys descended the lane at a brisk trot, the boys a little brisker than perhaps necessary.

"Wait for us!" yelled Mom.

The consensus had been to take advantage of the rest of the afternoon and get outside, much to Rachel's satisfaction. They were all a bit stumped on what the poem meant anyway, and maybe God would even give them some inspiration when they were out and about. The girls were going for a short walk up to the horse field, all giggly with anticipation. Dad and Mom had agreed that they were old enough now to do something on their own, and they were relishing this opportunity for a little independence. On their part, the boys were excited about using some of their birthday money for some sort of pirate souvenir or something while Mom looked for postcards.

As they reached the end of the lane, Mom glanced over at the harbor. The tide was in right now, and the assortment of fishing boats rose and fell languidly with the slight swell.

She looked over at her husband. "You are okay about helping the lady, aren't you?"

"Yes, I think I am. I feel sure that it was God who brought us together. I think it'll be fun for the kids as well as good for them to serve someone else, and we can still have a great vacation." Though he spoke with conviction, he did have a twinge of concern. Could they still have a great vacation?

As they crossed the bridge, Danny took a quick, furtive glance up the hill past the old lady's cottage. No, he couldn't see the parking area by the house on the cliff from where he was, which also meant he couldn't see if the car was there. That was fine with him.

A gust of wind swept across the harbor. Down on the quay, an old fisherman in a peaked cap looked up from his lobster pots and seemed to be scanning the sky. The weather was certainly looking rather iffy.

Well, even if it started to rain it wouldn't be too bad, Dad reasoned. They could take refuge in the bakery. Well, maybe not the bakery. He was supposed to be avoiding Auntie Flo and her Chocolate Toffee whatevers, but maybe that coffee place instead. Yes, that could be a plan—as long as it didn't bring on his worries again about the discouraging email from his editor. Somehow he had to deal with that struggle—the tendency to focus on his fears instead of believing God would help him. He didn't want to ruin his whole vacation.

"Let's get the postcards." He gestured at the shops ahead. "That newsagents has some in front."

As they approached the fish and chip shop, both boys stopped suddenly, lifted their noses and sniffed. "Can we stop and get some French fries?" said Stevie. Danny already had his hand on the gate.

"We just had scones! And what about lunch? If you had eaten more fruit, you wouldn't be hungry right now." Mom was incredulous.

Dad wasn't so sure. Boys had at least several stomachs it seemed. One tiny one for fruits and vegetables that filled up amazingly quickly, another one for the main dish, and at least one other auxiliary one that could always be relied upon to be empty if French fries or dessert was being offered. This wasn't the time to debate it, however.

"Come on, boys. Your Mom's right. Let's stick with the mission." He waved his hand towards the shop. "We'll come back some other time."

"And this was the episode when Kirk and Spock went back in time with Dr. McCoy." Chippy held the Sci-Fi magazine up to the tank where the goldfish appraised it with a baleful eye. "Definitely one of my favorites."

He froze suddenly, his gaze fixed through the window to where the road led up from the bridge. A small group was right outside the gate and looking at his fish shop.

"Customers, Ahab!" he cried, flinging aside the magazine and grabbing his white paper hat which he jammed down on his stringy hair. *This was it! Proof that staying open this late would pay off after all.*

He watched breathlessly as the family seemed to discuss something right there, and then to his horror turn and cross the street towards the Newsagents. His mouth dropped open. *No, no, no, no, no!*

Kennedy jumped to his feet, almost upsetting the bottle of beer at his side. That did it! He just had to find out if that family was meddling with the inheritance.

He had been sitting, staring into space, trying to figure out a way to get another look at the display case, but he just hadn't been able to concentrate. Like the persistent, nagging buzzing of a fly trapped in a light fixture, the image of that family's van wouldn't quit irritating his thoughts. Everything had seemed straightforward—him and Jennings pitted against the old lady—two against one, if he could count that idiot Jennings as a whole point. But now did they have competition? That family must be staying at the inn. *If they really were helping her, odds were they'd find the inheritance before he did.*

Overwhelmed by a sudden wave of anxiety, he grabbed up his coat and shot out the door.

Rachel and Emily stood on the second rung of the rickety gate, learning as far over as they could. They could just see the horses, huddled together against the far hedge to the right, frankly looking rather miserable.

Rachel blew the air out of her cheeks. "Well, this isn't much fun. Do you think we could see them better further up?" She gestured to where the lane climbed up the hill.

Emily followed her sister's gaze. She could just see the top of the church steeple, standing up like a sentinel above the hedge line. The clouds seemed much lower now, almost touching the top of the headland. She didn't really want to go up towards the church. Not that she was scared—not exactly. It was just the thought of being up there, by themselves, with all those gravestones...

"Well, okay I guess," she said, with more than a little reluctance in her voice.

Rachel reached for her hand. "Just for a minute. Then we'll head back."

She started up the lane, half-pulling her sister along beside her.

"So I found out that the Penrithen Times only comes out once a week." Dad fished for a tissue in his pocket. This change in weather was making his nose run like a racehorse.

The family was clustered in front of the newsagents, zipping up jackets and adjusting hats. The breeze had freshened and a few of the more violent gusts whipped a salty spray into their faces.

"We found out they don't have any piratey stuff." Danny pulled up the hood of his raincoat. "Just plastic soldiers and jacks and things."

"Well, I did get plenty of postcards." Mom showed them the bag. "Where to next?"

Dad blew his nose again. "I've been mulling over the poem, but I haven't had any inspiration about what *'flightless birds'* means. Penguins?"

Stevie looked hopeful for a moment before realizing his Dad was only joking. A sudden chilly gust swept around them, the old shop awning rattling in its supports.

Mom was having second thoughts about a longer excursion. She looked around at the sky. "It's getting cold, and look at those clouds!"

As she spoke another huge gust almost rocked them on their feet. The door of the newsagents slammed, and they turned to see the shopkeeper grabbing a rack of postcards and muscling it inside.

"Honey, I think he knows something. Do you think the girls are okay?"

Dad glanced up the hill towards where the horse pasture lay below the churchyard. It looked like the leaden clouds were almost touching the top of the steeple. He frowned. His girls were up there, all by themselves. He made a quick decision.

"You know, I think we need to head back. If we hurry, we might be able to beat the rain. When we get to the road up the hill I'll head up to find the girls. Will you keep on with the boys to the inn, honey? Hopefully we won't be much farther behind."

Mom looked visibly relieved. "Alright, that sounds good. Boys, we need to head back right now."

Danny nodded. Stevie was about to protest when he saw the look in Dad's eye. Not a wise move, he decided. He shut his mouth and grabbed his Mom's outstretched hand.

❧❧❧

Kennedy had tried jogging down the lane, but quickly abandoned the idea. It was his first attempt at exercise in about forever and his lungs were just not cooperating. He had to settle for a stumbling speed walk, his mind full of concern. The van wasn't parked at the lady's place, but he had no idea if that was good news or not. They might be even now searching at the inn, and he was sure it wouldn't be long before they figured out the clue.

A sharp gust of wind struck his back, pushing him forward, and he took note of his surroundings for the first time. Talk about a threatening sky—it was like a leaden shroud, hovering menacingly over him. He had a sudden thought that his thin coat wouldn't be much protection if the heaven's opened, but thrust that revelation out of his mind. He couldn't worry about that right now. He had to keep moving.

ؘؙ

Rachel was standing on tip-toe, trying to see over the hedge, and getting rather frustrated in the process. She could hear the horses stamping about, but she couldn't see them.

Emily's mind was elsewhere. She had been mulling over the strange poem from the will. Flightless birds? She could only think of ostriches and emus, and that didn't seem to be possible here in Cornwall. And then something about a *way beginning* and a *diverse trail.* That sounded complicated.

A sudden chilling gust swept across the headland, through the trees and around her neck, causing her to shiver and she looked nervously over her shoulder.

"Can we go? I'm getting cold." She tugged at her sister's coat.

"Not yet. Just a minute, okay? What's the big hurry?"

"Look, it's going to pour any second."

That got Rachel's attention. "What d'you mean? She looked around her, suddenly noticing how dark it was getting and how close the menacing clouds really were now. There was another gust, but this one brought a rush of rain that got steadily harder.

They looked at each other for a second, then grabbed each other's hand and tore down the hill.

ؘؙ

"Here it comes!" Dad gripped Stevie's hand.

Danny frantically tried to close the zipper on his raincoat as it whipped and snapped in the wind. They could actually see the line of rain sweeping in from the sea, churning the harbor into a frothing mass. As they hurried down the hill to the bridge, the downpour suddenly engulfed them, drenching them in seconds. They were passing the Fish and Chip shop, and Dad shot a desperate glance over at the doorway. Should they make for shelter and wait this thing out? No, the girls were out in this, too. They just needed to keep going.

As they squelched on, he took another glance backward at the shop. Was it his imagination, or was someone watching them through the window? Someone with a dejected look on his face.

ؘؙ

Kennedy staggered forward, his arms flung across his face. Driving sheets of rain swept around him, soaking him to the skin and leaving him disorientated in the violence of their passage. He wiped his eyes desperately with his sodden sleeve.

But what was that? He screeched to a halt and peered into the deluge. There were three, no four people running across the bridge just ahead. Two adults and two kids and they were turning up the lane towards the inn. *It must be that family.* With a sudden, distressing revelation he realized there was no way on earth he could make it up there himself and get to the display case unnoticed.

113

He stood there for a moment in misery, a despairing drowned rat buffeted by the tempest. Then shielding his face again with his arms, he turned into the gale and staggered back up the streaming road.

❧ ❧

The girls were soaked to the skin, trying to maintain their balance as they slipped and slid down the lane, a river of rainwater running ahead and around them. The trees and hedgerows were thrashing wildly about--shaken by some sort of vengeful beast intent on flinging twigs, leaves and bucketfuls of water into the girls' faces. The lane seemed so much longer than they remembered, and they were beginning to lose heart. They finally skidded around the corner and onto the main road, almost running smack into the rest of the family who were in a soggy dash for the driveway. Dad had just let go of Stevie's hand and was preparing for a sprint up the hill after the girls. He was immensely relieved to be spared that ordeal.

"All okay?" he yelled over the wind as they struggled on together through the gate, heads bowed against the driving rain. They nodded, too tired to say anything.

In a huddled mass, they pushed on up the gravel driveway. The lamp-lit windows of the dining room beckoned—a haven of warmth and comfort that gave them just the encouragement they needed. Dad had to carry Stevie the last twenty or so yards, but they finally made it to the house and everyone crowded into the entryway. They stood there for a moment, catching their breath and looking at each other's streaming faces, glowing red in the porch light. Then everyone burst into laughter.

"Wowee, what a washout," chuckled Dad. "Let's get inside and get dried out."

"I think hot baths are in order. We've got time before dinner," added Mom, firmly. She didn't want the whole family coming down with bronchitis.

There were a few suppressed groans at that, but Dad put up his hand.

"No complaints, please. It's a good idea. Let's get warmed up, and then we can eat in peace."

❧ ❧

Kennedy stared at himself in the mirror, a grimly determined expression on his face that surprised even him. A hot shower and mug of black coffee had done wonders for his outlook and his mind was thinking clearly again. He had only one option. The only way to safely search for the inheritance and keep an eye on that family was to get a room at the inn himself.

❧ ❧

Mom leaned back in her chair in tired satisfaction. What a meal! And just what they needed after that drenching—steaming bowls of potato-leek soup with warm, buttery farm-fresh bread, followed by an enormous creamy trifle fit for the Queen herself. Two cups of decaf coffee had finished the job, sending delicious tendrils of warmth worming themselves all the way to her toes.

The amazing meal had driven away all memory of their soggy misery, the kids setting to with marked enthusiasm. Mom was still slowly savoring her trifle, bite by bite, but the rest of family was scraping up every last bit as if their lives depended on it.

Dad looked around at them in astonishment. "Hey, leave the pattern on the plates!"

Emily got the message right away. Setting her spoon aside, she started stacking plates, feeling a sudden inner compunction to help Mrs. Tremannon with at least that part of the cleaning up. The other kids chose to ignore her, assuming a post-dessert stupor.

"Kids, please help Emily stack things." Mom realized that the table did rather resemble a battlefield.

The boys nodded somewhat reluctantly, both secretly blaming their sister for bringing about this sudden chore. They looked across at Rachel, who didn't seem to have heard Mom's request.

"Rachel, Mom said to help clear the table." As always, Stevie wanted to be sure that everyone did their share, even if it meant not getting going himself.

Dad glanced over. This was familiar parenting territory. "Stevie, you just concentrate on obeying. Don't worry about what the others are doing."

He was curious, though. Rachel was just sitting, staring towards the corner of the room, her brow kind of furrowed. *Zone city.* "Hey, Rachel!"

Rachel gave a start. "What? Oh, sorry." Her voice got excited. "But Daddy, look in the corner—the display case with all the birds. Do you think that's what the poem meant?"

That got everyone's attention. Even Mom stopped with a bite of trifle halfway to her mouth. The boys almost threw the plates down in their eagerness to be the first over to the cabinet.

"Hey, hey! Hold it right there. We didn't say you could stop cleaning up." Dad frowned at the boys, who skidded to a sudden halt. "This was Rachel's idea. Let her check it out."

The boys grudgingly returned to the table, but couldn't resist watching as Rachel examined the cabinet. She took a good look. The cabinet had several glass shelves, with the birds arranged on various bits of stick or rock. The bottommost shelf was of wood, and the narrow space under it was empty except for one thing...

"I can see something! It's a book!" she squeaked. "Hang on." She squatted down to better squint through the glass. "I can't read the title. It's just the wrong angle."

Dad came over to check it out. The cabinet had a single large glass door and he gave its handle a tug. "It's locked. There's a keyhole, but no key," he reported.

"Oh, no! Now we won't be able to find the clue!" Danny looked dismayed.

"Now wait a minute. We don't know that." Dad ran his hand through his hair. "We could maybe ask Mrs. Tremannon where the key is." His voice trailed off.

Mom shook her head. "She would be curious as to why, and then we'd have to explain all about Mrs. Renton and the will. I'm not sure we should do that without getting permission. She might not want the Tremannons knowing about that right now."

At that very moment Mrs. Tremannon came bustling into the room with her huge tray, accompanied by her husband with his tool box again. Rachel jumped up quickly, and Mr. Tremannon looked over at her in curiosity. Dad noticed the look. Time for an emergency change of subject.

"Thank you so much for fixing the light. And thank you, Mrs. Tremannon, for a fantastic dinner."

Mr. Tremannon nodded and his wife smiled round at the group. "You're right welcome. Did you have enough? I've got some crackers and cheese, and some sticky buns I made this morning."

"No thank you. We're fine." Dad nodded at the kids who got the message and started stacking plates on the tray. *Well, sort of fine*, he mused, but it was somewhat distressing that helping the old lady was already proving to be much harder than they had thought.

Emily studied the pictures on the staircase rather critically as she brushed her teeth. The bathroom was rather crowded with flossers and brushers and she had wandered out to the stairs to get some breathing room.

The family had just finished a raucous round of card playing in the sitting room downstairs which had helped them put aside their disappointment with the locked cabinet. They had gathered there initially to pray for wisdom about how to solve this problem, and then Rachel had suggested a few games of "Nerts" to get their minds on something else. The games had been hotly contested, but it had definitely been Rachel's night. She had won four games out of five.

Emily left her art appraisal and stepped carefully down to the ground floor, still brushing vigorously. Being concerned about all forms of hygiene, she wasn't going to skimp on minutes, no matter what her siblings thought. Stevie, for one, believed brushing teeth to be an almost agonizing torture and to be avoided where possible at all costs.

She wandered into the dining room. The light was still on, and she glanced around, enjoying its antique atmosphere. She pictured it as the great hall of a castle. Perhaps there was going to be a ball, and she would be dressed in a flowing gown with flowers in her hair. She closed her eyes and began to dance, twirling an imaginary train, toothbrush in hand. The room was filled with light and laughter, with beautiful ladies and handsome knights and...*oof*. She bumped up against the corner of the table and popped her eyes open, feeling rather foolish and glad that no-one had seen her. *But wait a second—what was that?* She had stopped just in front of the cabinet, and there was something on the floor at her feet.

It was a key.

"But I don't understand!" said Rachel looking at the key. It certainly fit the lock, but she was absolutely sure there was nothing on the ground when she had examined the cabinet at dinner time.

"You must not have seen it." Stevie was convinced.

"Now, now, none of us saw it. I think we just need to say it's an answer to prayer," said Dad. He beckoned to Emily and then waved his hand with a flourish. "You can do the honors, madam, since you were the discoverer."

Emily smiled gratefully, feeling a little thrill of excitement. As the family jostled for a good viewing position, she turned the key. There was a little click and the door swung open. Reaching down, she drew out the book and turned it so she could read the title.

"*Collected Works of John Betjeman*," she read aloud. "Is it a poetry book?"

"Yes," said Dad excitedly. "Betjeman was a famous English poet. My Grandad gave me a book of his when I was a boy. 'Betjeman's Cornwall' or something like that."

"So it's the 'book of verse' from the clue," put in Mom before Dad could start quoting his favorite Betjeman poems. "At least, I suppose so. What was the next part?"

"Something about a way beginning. Hey!" As Emily spoke she was thumbing through the pages and something fluttered to the ground.

Stevie made a grab for it. "It's a letter, look!" Now this was definitely exciting.

"Be careful, Stevie. Here, let me have it." Dad didn't trust little paws.

It was a fairly standard-looking small white envelope. Dad held it so they could all see. The name *Ruth Renton* was written in a neat flowing script on the front, and a partial address in the top-left corner: *190 Cratchit Road*. There was no stamp, and the envelope hadn't been sealed. Dad peeked inside and saw a folded sheet of paper.

"Open it, Daddy! Read it!" Stevie could hardly contain himself.

Mom laid a hand on Dad's arm. "This isn't for us, though. It's for Mrs. Renton."

"You're right," Dad agreed, much to the children's audible disappointment. "Hey, kids. I know this is interesting, but it's still a private matter. We need to give this to Mrs. Renton, for her to read. We're just trying to help her a bit."

"Can we go right now?" said Stevie. "I'll get my shoes."

Mom smiled. "I think it's going to have to wait 'til tomorrow."

A few groans escaped the group.

"Do you think this envelope is the treasure?" said Rachel. She had a keen feeling of disappointment. This mystery wasn't turning out as exciting as she had hoped.

"I don't know. We've got tons of questions, but they need to wait. It's really time to head for bed."

"But..."

"No 'buts', Stevie."

"But..."

"Still no buts, Danny. To bed!"

Dad held the drapes aside at the window, looking past his own shadowed reflection to the darkness beyond. The curtain of night had been drawn across the little valley, only a few winking lights visible in the distance. He glanced at his watch. Almost ten. It had been quite a day, hadn't it? But now it was done.

"Honey…"

Well, maybe not. There was a mission coming, he could sense it.

His wife appeared in the bathroom doorway. "I can't find my lip balm, and my lips are really chapped from yesterday. I think I left it in the dining room.. Would you mind…?"

Aha. He was no dummy. It was just a wee bit too much of an adventure for her to go looking downstairs on her own at night, and she needed her husband to do it for her. He squared his shoulders and saluted.

"No problem, ma'am. Be back in a jiffy."

Dad stepped into the darkened dining room, the vague scent of dinner still lingering in the air. Now where was the light switch?

He found it finally in the corner by the suit of armor. Dad shook his head. This place just oozed character. He searched unsuccessfully on and under the table and was just about to step through into the entry when it suddenly flooded with light, Mrs. Tremannon popping into view like a pantomime genie. She was talking earnestly into the cordless telephone, and judging by her volume level either the person on the other end was hard of hearing, or they soon would be.

"That's better," she fairly shouted. "I couldn't hear you with the telly on in the other room. Now what was it you wanted?"

There was a pause as she listened, her back turned away from Dad, and he took the opportunity to have a quick check on and under the bench in the entryway.

"Well, I do have one room left. It's number one. The Chapfords are in the other ones."

Dad wasn't trying to eavesdrop, it was just impossible not to hear, and he couldn't help smiling at the lady's mistake again. Maybe they should wear name tags.

"No, I'm sorry, we do have other guests…no, they're not leaving for a couple of weeks." Mrs. Tremannon seemed a little out of sorts.

Well, he had struck out here. Maybe he should ask Mrs. Tremannon. Should he wait until she was done? Who was on the phone, anyway? And why did they care if anyone else was here? Maybe they just wanted some peace and quiet. *That must be it.*

"No, I'm sorry. It just can't be done. Will you take room one?" Mrs. Tremannon's voice was uncharacteristically clipped. She listened, frowning for a moment. "Alright. It's £30 a night, and it will be available after four p.m. tomorrow…no, not any earlier. I need some time to get it ready, and, hello? Hello? Well, I never!" She looked at the phone in disbelief for a few moments, slowly slumped her shoulders and limped back into the TV lounge without even noticing Dad by the far door. She was gone before he thought to stop her.

Well, that was quite a little interlude on the phone! he thought. Feeling a mite guilty for having overheard, Dad turned back and immediately spotted the lip balm under an armchair. *Mission accomplished*, he thought smugly, putting all thoughts of the weird phone call out of his mind. *The mighty hunter successfully traps his quarry. Thank you, Jesus, and now to bed!*

Chapter 8 – A Puzzling Letter

Rachel was trying to concentrate, but it just wasn't working. She had installed herself in one of the big, flowery chairs in the sitting room and was having her morning Bible and prayer time. At least, that had been the goal, but her mind wasn't cooperating. She had started thinking about the old lady and the letter, and then her thoughts had jumped over to the prospect of today and whatever plans might unfold. Would they, should they go see the lady and give her the letter? How much time might that take? Would another day sneak by without getting much done? Maybe the mystery was already solved. Maybe the letter said what the treasure was—if it even *was* a treasure.

She had real mixed feelings over that—relief that perhaps they could get on with the vacation now, and disappointment that it had all been so easy after all. What if it could have been a bit more exciting, with hidden passages, secret signs, and all the other things that seemed to accompany the mysteries she'd read about? That would have made it all worthwhile. What other cryptic clues might they have had? What other cool places might they have found to explore? And what was in that glossy magazine on the coffee table in front of her? 'Excursions in Cornwall'. It looked much more interesting than her Bible.

No, no, no, she was going to read her Bible. Emily had set the example again that morning, and she wasn't going to be outdone by her sister, even if her example seemed rather annoying at the moment.

Rachel normally wanted to spend time in the Bible, so why was it such a struggle today? She looked again at the passage she had been reading in Deuteronomy. It wasn't exactly easy to understand. Her mind wasn't awake enough for this. She needed something simpler, like that magazine.

She squashed down her guilt feelings, reached over and grabbed it. After all, she was only going to leaf through it quickly and then get back to reading and praying. *Right?*

"The best thing would be to give her a call," said Mom, rummaging around for her lip balm again. She had used it just last night, hadn't she? But now it had disappeared into the black hole of her purse. Dad had joked many times that Mom's purse held everything possible for any emergency, up to and including nuclear war. Useful, yes, but it did make it hard to find things.

Dad had the road atlas open on their bed. They had discussed a possible beach trip at breakfast, and he was checking out the route. He looked up, considering the suggestion. "Yes, I guess so."

He really wasn't at all sure how to manage this vacation, now that it seemed to have two mutually exclusive goals—helping the lady, and making sure the family had some fun. It was the sort of stress he tried to avoid at all costs.

He checked his watch. "It's already nine o'clock. It'll take us about 45 minutes to get to the beach at Treyarnon. We could drop the book and letter by Mrs. Renton's on the way out. It needn't take long."

"Perhaps..." Mom looked doubtful.

Dad grabbed his phone off the night stand, excited to have found a potential solution to his dilemma. "Let's find out."

Mrs. Renton had just settled down with the copy of "*The Pickwick Papers*" she had found at a jumble sale, a cup of Tetley at her elbow, and her cat at her feet. *Dickens and tea.* This was as close to relaxed as she felt these days, though it was a temporary relief at best from the troubling thoughts that plagued her. She looked down at the cat, patiently poised and waiting for the opportune moment to spring into her lap as soon as she was settled.

"Yes, I'm reading your book, Pickwick. And yes, you can join me in a second."

She settled into a comfortable position, adjusted the cushion at her back, and at that very moment the phone rang. She sighed in frustration. Who could that be, and right at her morning tea time?

She suddenly checked herself. Who else had her phone number except the Chapman family? They couldn't possibly have found out something, could they?

Dad and Mom perched on the edge of the sofa, waiting while Mrs. Renton carefully poured three cups of tea from her big brown teapot with the knitted cozy.

So here we are again, Dad thought. *Back here having tea and feeling apprehensive.*

"Here you are." Mrs. Renton offered him a cup, interrupting his ponderings. "And won't you try one of these?" she continued. "I'm sorry I didn't have enough time to bake anything fresh, but I bought these at the bakery on the high street yesterday." She pointed to a plate stacked with a dozen or so familiar-looking goodies. "I think the bakery lady called them 'Chocolate-Toffee Brownie Cakes.'"

Dad froze for a second. The long arm of Auntie Flo had somehow found him again. Was it impossible to escape her culinary clutches? He pondered that for a moment. It *would* be impolite to decline, wouldn't it? He reached over and took one.

Mrs. Renton noticed the kids hovering in the background. The girls had, with permission, been examining the Dickens collection in the bookcase down the hallway, along with a fine collection of books on birds that Mrs. Renton had explained she had amassed over the years as an avid bird-watcher. The boys had been quietly and unsuccessfully trying to teach Sweedlepipe the budgie to say its name while keeping several ears open for mysterious revelations coming from the living room. The advent of the brownie cakes, however, had changed all that. The old lady smiled and called to them.

"Children, there's some goodies in the kitchen and some orange squash. Please help yourselves."

The kids didn't need much prompting, even if they had no idea what orange squash was.

"And here's what we found, Mrs. Renton." Dad didn't want to waste any more time and handed the envelope over to the old lady. "I hope it's what you needed."

He settled back with his tea and cake, munching in anticipation. What would the letter reveal? And would it reveal it quickly enough that he wouldn't have a mutiny on his hands? Rachel at least would be watching the clock.

Mrs. Renton took a sip of tea, then carefully held up the envelope and adjusted her glasses. Mom smiled encouragingly, fervently praying inside that whatever was in the letter would provide some much-needed hope to the old lady.

"Well, I suppose I should open it, shouldn't I?" Mrs. Renton gave a faint smile, trying to mask a sudden twinge of fear. What if, after all these years, the Squire had some harsh words for her—finally taking her to task for all the hurt she'd caused him?

Mom could sense the lady's concern and thought she might understand the reason. "May I—can I pray for you? I know this must be very difficult."

Mrs. Renton thought for a moment and then nodded silently, a tad embarrassed and unsure of what else to say. It couldn't really hurt though, could it?

"Dear Heavenly Father," began Mom. "You understand Mrs. Renton and her needs. You understand her concerns. I know You love her. Please help her right now. I pray for strength for her, and that whatever news this letter brings, You would use it for good in her life, and to bring her hope. I pray this for Your glory. Amen."

"Amen," echoed Dad.

The old lady looked up with a certain mistiness in her eyes. She hadn't realized it until that moment, but it had been ages since she'd heard someone praying for her—not since Uncle Kenwyn and Aunt Rosie used to pray for her at bedtime—and how many years ago was that? And was it possibly true what Mrs. Chapman had prayed—that God loved her? How could He when she had rejected him for so long? She was so jumbled up inside.

She looked down at the envelope and sighed. Did she have the strength to find out what was inside? She couldn't go on as she had been, though—that was certain.

With the Chapmans smiling encouragingly, and both of them praying under their breath, she reached in and pulled out the letter. She scanned it for a second. "It's from Uncle Kenwyn," she confirmed. She put her hand over her heart, as if to protect it from whatever the contents of the note might be.

Mom and Dad leaned forward, watching as she absorbed what was written, the old lady's eyes showing a mix of surprise and puzzlement.

"Oh, my," was all she managed to say. She handed the note to Mom and reached for her hanky.

Mom was about to read it when she noticed something out of the corner of her eye. The kids' heads were popping around the doorway to the living room like so many prairie dogs from their burrows.

Mrs. Renton dabbed her eyes, then beckoned to them. "It's alright, dears. You can come in." She turned to Mom. "You can read it out loud. I feel that you've all been a part of helping me find this, so you should share it, too."

Mom nodded, and the kids quickly trooped in and arranged themselves on the floor at her feet, grinning at this sudden opportunity.

"Okay, kids," said Mom. "This is from the Squire to Mrs. Renton. It's dated January 18th, 1988."

"My birthday!" squeaked Stevie.

"You weren't born in 1988," contradicted Danny.

"But my birthday IS January 18th!"

"Shhh, you two," said Dad, with a warning look. "Go on dear."

"And there's an address here: 190 Cratchit Road, Penrithen—the same as on the envelope. Is that where he was living? I thought he lived at the inn."

Mrs. Renton shrugged. "As far as I know he always lived in the manor house, yes."

"Well, it may not mean anything," said Dad. "What's next?"

"*Dear Ruthie,*" went on Mom. "*So you made it past the first clue! Congratulations! You remember, of course, that I love puzzles, but I am sure you are still wondering why all the mystery. Well, first of all, I want you to know that I love you very much, and my intent is not to cause you any grief. I cannot say that I don't want to cause you any trouble, because in some ways I do, in fact! I want to lead you on a quest—on a trail I should say. The goal of any journey is, of course, to arrive somewhere, and I'm praying that that somewhere is a place that you will be overjoyed to discover. But you must know that the journey itself is important. Each step will be revealing, and will bring you to a deeper appreciation and understanding of what lies at the end. I have saved my greatest treasure for you.*

Proverbs 20, verse 21 says "An inheritance quickly gained at the beginning will not be blessed at the end." I want you to be blessed, so we're going to take our time!

Your Aunt and I always loved you, Ruthie. Even though I don't even know where you are as I write this, my thoughts and prayers are always with you. And now, I suppose, as you have this note in your possession, it means that I have gone to join my dear wife in the presence of my

Savior. If it's true that we can see events on Earth from Heaven, then know that we are cheering you on from somewhere beyond the blue."

Mom paused, blew her nose, cleared her throat and continued. *"Don't give up. Help will find you along the way. I have prayed and planned for it! And now the way begins. Follow this to start on the journey:*

A father's love, a sacrifice, A flight in fear, will faith suffice?
A haven home, A mantel's tile, A photo's clue, a life worthwhile.
With all my love, your Uncle Kenwyn."

Dad raised his eyebrows. Mom sat back and looked around at the others. The kids weren't sure what to think. Hadn't the mystery been solved then? Danny and Stevie got a sudden thrill of excitement. Perhaps this was just the beginning. This was shaping up to be a real adventure!

Rachel frowned a little in concentration, trying to understand the implications for their vacation. Emily looked over at Mrs. Renton—like her Mom, concerned about how the lady was handling all this.

Mom handed the paper back. She wasn't quite sure what to say, but she felt like she should say something. "Er, this must be quite a surprise to you," she said hesitatingly. "Are you...alright?"

Mrs. Renton's face still looked concerned and confused. She shook her head, wonderingly, but then gave the merest smile. "Uncle Kenwyn...you know, this is so like him. I shouldn't be surprised at all. It looks like it's not going to be very easy to learn what my inheritance is." She looked down at the note again and her smile faded.

"He said that he loves you. Did you find some encouragement in that?" said Mom carefully. She knew that the lady's emotions were very tender right now.

"He did, he did..." the old lady's voice trailed off.

"But you don't believe him?"

"It's just hard to really accept it after all this time. I mean, I'm still the same person, still the guilty one." She gave another deep sigh. "And do you remember what he said—that he wanted to cause me some trouble? Well, I guess I deserve it, though it's hard to hear."

Mom was feeling just a tad bit bolder now. "But look at the context of where and how he said it. The whole letter seems full of love."

The old lady set her cup back on the table and looked down at her lap, nervously smoothing out her skirt. "I just don't know..."

Dad suddenly noticed a slight disturbance at his feet. Stevie was starting to wiggle. Either he was getting bored, or he had something he wanted to say.

"What's the matter, son?"

"Um, are we going to try to figure out the clue? It might tell where the treasure is."

Dad had to explain to the lady. "Sorry, Mrs. Renton. You see, the whole family is kind of excited about solving this mystery."

Well, as long as we can still have a vacation, thought Rachel, glancing at the clock.

"But we're not trying to rush you. We just want you to know we're willing to help if you want us to."

The old lady looked up and seemed to be examining their faces. What she saw must have reassured her, because she seemed to visibly relax.

"You have already been a real blessing, but you know..." She hesitated and then took off on a different tack. "The Squire—Uncle Kenwyn—I think he must have meant me to have this a long time ago. He first got sick back in the late eighties, and perhaps he thought his time was drawing near so he put this plan together. But I was a lot spryer in my 50s than I am now. I have a feeling it will be a bit of a challenge for me doing this. If you're really willing..." She didn't want to add out loud that she felt she couldn't show her face at the Inn. The Tremannon's must think terribly of her, she was sure.

Dad looked around at the family, getting encouraging nods from almost everyone as far as he could tell. His stomach gave a lurch. It looked like another step down the road of commitment—a much greater step than before, now that this quest thing was a bigger beast than he'd previously thought. He'd really have to manage this balancing act somehow. It was possible he could do it, as long as everyone was on board with the idea, but could he commit to it out loud?

"We're willing," said Mom firmly, a little concerned about Dad's seeming hesitation, and hoping that the lady knew they really meant it.

"Yes, yes," added Dad, realizing he needed to sound decided, no matter his misgivings.

Mrs. Renton leaned back in her chair, and smiled, realizing as she did so that perhaps it was the first real smile she had produced in years—not just pasted on or making the best of the circumstances. She didn't have to do this alone. And now she knew she was sensing for real that elusive feeling—the one she never thought she'd have again. She was really, actually experiencing a tiny ray of hope.

❧❧

The country lanes were impossibly narrow with room for only one lane of traffic, if that. There were occasional wider spots where two vehicles could pass each other, but the towering hedgerows and twisting lanes had made it blind corners and heart attacks all the way. They had already had one close call with a painter's truck hurtling towards them with an apparent complete disregard for the possibility of oncoming traffic.

The crazy driving conditions weren't the only thing on Dad's mind. When all was said and done he felt really unsettled about their visit that morning. The letter had left them with more questions than answers. What was all this about? Was this Uncle Kenwyn for real? I mean, who would turn a will into some sort of bizarre mystery thing? It was like some sort of crazy children's story. After a bit of fruitless discussion about the clue they had finally had to excuse themselves, take a photo of the letter and leave with a promise to contact the lady as soon as they had any further ideas. It had all seemed very hurried, leaving him with a slightly guilty feeling. And now there was all this unexpected stress trying to get to the beach. *This was supposed to be a vacation wasn't it?* He was beginning to wonder if it was doing his nerves any good at all. And where was that turning? Their destination of Treyarnon Bay, a particularly fond memory of his childhood holidays, seemed to him about as elusive as...as what? As finding ketchup in a

125

French restaurant. The trouble was, none of these crazy lanes headed straight in any direction for any time at all.

"Look, look!" squealed Rachel suddenly. "Treyarnon Holiday Park and Campground, three hundred yards ahead on the right. Do you see the sign? The beach must be that way."

"Great job, sweetheart," said Dad, relaxing a little. "Tough place to find."

The signpost Rachel had spotted was almost hidden by tall grass and a clump of foxgloves. Dad turned carefully onto the road, paused while another car scraped past on the right, and then cautiously continued on. The lane wound slightly downhill to where the hedgerows suddenly dropped away on either side, an expansive view of the sea appearing before them. The long, narrow cove ahead was bordered by low cliffs, their grassy tops sprinkled with an assortment of white-washed holiday homes.

"Wow! Look at the sea!" Stevie was straining in his seatbelt to look over his Dad's shoulder.

"We're finally here," murmured Dad as he pulled into the grassy field which served as a car park. He noted the time. Twelve-thirty already. Was there enough time left in this day to still meet both of their apparently conflicting goals—that of helping the lady and having a relaxing vacation?

Well, that just remained to be seen.

❧❦❧

Rachel gingerly poked a toe into the water at her feet. *Oh my goodness.* It was freezing! Should she, could she just go ahead and take the plunge? She didn't really want to wait for the others who seemed to be taking their own sweet time changing into swimsuits. She had congratulated herself on having thought ahead and worn hers underneath her clothes not wanting to waste a moment, but she would lose all that advantage if she couldn't get up the nerve to jump in.

She was perched on the edge of the biggest tide pool she had ever seen, easily as big and deep as a good-sized backyard swimming pool. It lay to the right side of the beach, up on a ledge of rocks protruding from the low cliffs below the parking area. The family had all noted it with excitement as they trooped down to the sand, tripping over the paraphernalia of bags, toys, beach umbrellas, towels, and body boards they were lugging along with them. The tide was way out, and the rocky pool had been the natural choice for the first dip, but she hadn't banked on this sub-arctic temperature.

A breeze rippled the azure water in front of her as she pondered her dilemma, soft green fronds of seaweed waving just below the surface. She thought back to the morning. It had been just as she had feared. The visit with the lady had turned out much longer than expected. And then her Mom and Dad had reconfirmed their desire to help her out—not that anyone had any clue of what to do next of course. *There went the rest of the vacation.*

She grabbed a limpet shell and chucked it into the pool. Lazy circles spread out in front of her and she watched them morosely, her grumpy feelings gradually being replaced by a nagging sense of guilt. She was being kind of selfish, wasn't she? God probably wanted them to help the lady—her Mom and Dad had really stressed the need of serving others as a way of showing love to Jesus. And what was it they always said? *Trials build character.*

But she didn't want any more character. She wanted fun. She smacked the rock with her hand, wincing a little as she struck a colony of barnacles. It just wasn't fair. This was their one break from schooling, and now it was being jeopardized. Couldn't they prove their character during the school term? Then the interruption wouldn't be a problem at all!

She looked out to where the sea shimmered in a silvery haze dappled with scattered pearls of sunlight, crowded with silhouettes of people swimming, splashing and surfing in on the foaming waves. Even from this far away she could tell *they* were having fun.

Okay, that did it. She wasn't going to waste another minute. And here came the boys at a run. It was time to just go for it.

She stood up and with one final glance over to where the boys were starting to scramble up the rocks, she screwed up her eyes and jumped into space.

For just a moment all she felt was the smack of her body hitting the water and then the cold struck her like a wall of nails. Her foot felt the rocky bottom and she pushed desperately upwards until her head broke the surface again, gasping and spluttering. It felt like someone had put a freezing clamp around her body and was tightening it remorselessly. She frantically shook her head and blinked her eyes in an effort to clear her vision until she could just make out the boys, peering over at her from the edge.

"How is it?" called Danny anxiously.

How was it? She was swimming in glacial melt water. Her body was turning into a block of ice.

"Fine," she stammered, swirling her arms and kicking her legs in an effort to keep her head out of the water. "I just went ahead and jumped in. What are you waiting for?"

Danny looked at Stevie. Stevie looked at Danny. Danny raised an eyebrow.

They weren't buying it.

❧❧

Leaving Rachel to her shivering, the boys had ambled back, a little at a loss for what to do until Danny had suggested that they make a sandcastle. Stevie had been reluctant to take on this seemingly significant project, but Emily and Dad had joined in with a will, and Stevie had warmed to the idea.

Mom, however, had been content to wait for the finished result. *After all*, she reasoned, *the builders needed someone to impress—someone to ooh and aah over the results.* She did wish Rachel would join them, though. According to the boys, Rachel wanted to keep on swimming by herself for a bit, but Mom had wondered at that. She glanced at her watch. It had been over forty minutes. She was suddenly a might concerned about how her daughter was doing.

She looked over her shoulder and spied her husband strolling down from the little beach store at the edge of the car park. And there was Rachel at last. She had evidently given up on her solo swim and was heading to intercept her dad about halfway back.

Mom watched her daughter for a moment. She could sense something was up—and not just today. Something had been brewing for a few days. It was disconcerting and just added to her sense that the family just wasn't doing well.

Lord, she prayed. *Please show us what's up with Rachel. Help us know how to lead her, and help Dave even right now know what to say to her. And please give us wisdom with the family.*

She opened her eyes again and checked on their progress. They had met up and she could see that Dave was deep in conversation with his daughter. Good. Perhaps it was something significant that would help Rachel with whatever was troubling her.

"Do you know, I used to get this same set of sandcastle flags when I was a boy! I can't believe they still sell it!" Dad excitedly showed off the little package of brightly colored paper flags.

Rachel glanced up. "It's nice," she muttered without much enthusiasm, wrapping herself even closer in her towel.

"Look, here's the Welsh flag." Dad waved it in front of her nose. Rachel and Emily really liked Celtic things. "It's got a red dragon."

"Right."

She didn't sound too thrilled. Dad gave her a sideways glance. No, she didn't look her usual peppy self. In fact, she looked downright grumpy.

"What's up old chum?" He gave her a playful nudge. Rachel looked away.

"Sweetheart. Hey, Mrs. Grumpy Pants." Aha, he caught a slight smile, though she was trying hard to hide it. "Look, I really do mean it. What's the matter?"

"Nothing really."

"Okay, I'm not buying that." Dad stopped, put his hand on her shoulder and looked in her eyes. "Come on, sweetheart, what's up?"

"I don't know." Rachel had trouble looking right at her Dad, but she could tell she wasn't going to get away with not saying anything. She sighed. "I guess this vacation isn't turning out like I thought—you know, like with the old lady. It's taking a lot more time than I thought it would."

"Aha." Dad nodded. "And you're worried you'll lose out on some fun."

"I guess it sounds kind of selfish doesn't it?"

"Well, actually, to tell you the truth…" He scratched the end of his nose. "I'm struggling with it too."

"Really?" Rachel looked at him in surprise.

Dad grinned. "Even when you make a choice to do the right thing, it doesn't miraculously make it easy. I've been wrestling with how much time it's going to take same as you. It's not easy keeping everyone happy." He ruffled her hair. "But even so I do really think we're doing the right thing."

Rachel looked down at her feet. "Yeah, I guess so."

"Hey, I think I have a Bible verse that might help." Dad felt a sudden wave of inspiration.

"Uh huh." She wasn't really in the mood for a Bible verse.

"Well it's funny, but I think there's something there for you. It's one of my memory verses: Psalm thirty-seven, verses three and four. *'Trust in the Lord and do good, dwell in the land and enjoy safe pasture. Delight yourself in the Lord and He will give you the desires of your heart.'*"

"I don't really understand."

"Here, let's keep walking. You look cold." Dad ushered her on again. "Okay, so what are your desires right now?"

That was easy. "To have a really fun vacation. To be outdoors as much as possible. To have some adventure. To…"

"Whoa," Dad interrupted. "Okay, I get it. Right. Now in this verse God promises to give you the desires of your heart, but there are some conditions."

Rachel's face fell. She knew it. It couldn't be that easy.

"But," Dad continued, "they're not that complicated." His thoughts were tumbling out as he counted off on his fingers. "*Trust in the Lord.* He knows you and knows what you need and what you want. *Do good.* Even when you're frustrated and wondering what He's doing, continue to do what is good. *Dwell in the land and enjoy safe pasture.* I think for us that means be content where we are without always wishing things were different. Last of all, *delight yourself in Him.* Talk to Him, spend time with Him, thank Him, put your hope in Him, not circumstances." A sudden guilty thought occurred to him. He definitely wasn't practicing what he was preaching.. "And I'll try to do the same," he added quickly.

Rachel felt especially guilty about delighting in the Lord. She knew she hadn't been entirely honest with her morning prayer time. And she rarely even thought about God during the day at all. All of this seemed too difficult—too out of reach in her present mood.

Dad could see the struggle on her face. They were almost up to the others, and he thought he'd better finish up quickly. He'd have to chat with her some more later. "So sweetheart, talk to Jesus, tell Him your concerns and trust that He'll work things out. He knows what's best, and He can change your desires to be in line with His will." He hoped that didn't sound too trite. He had sure just dumped a lot of info on her.

Rachel considered what her dad had said. *So God might make me not desire a fun vacation any more. That's not what I want.*

"Okay," she said out loud, glad that it looked like the conversation was over. This was just a wee bit embarrassing, and she didn't want Mom to get involved too. She needed to get the attention off of herself and on to something else.

"Wow. That's quite a sandcastle," she volunteered, trying to sound as upbeat as possible.

As she looked it over, she realized that it was indeed the truth. There were actually two castles on nicely smoothed islands of sand connected by a driftwood bridge that Stevie had found in a nearby tangle of seaweed. A moat surrounded both islands and the boys had dug a trench over from the stream so that water flowed around the whole thing. The two mounds were topped by imposing—if a little lopsided—towers carefully made with their plastic castle bucket, which gave them crenellated tops and neatly formed doors and windows. There was a winding road down from one tower, across the bridge and up to the other into a little tunnel that Emily had carefully scooped out with an old plastic spoon. She had lined the edges of the roads with shells, and then she and her dad had topped the whole thing off with a veritable forest of drip-trees, made from dripping wet sand into what looked like realistic-looking fir trees. Rachel suddenly wished she could shrink to mouse-size and explore the whole thing.

"I've got the flags!" announced Dad, proudly. "Hey, boys!"

Stevie and Danny looked up from their work and Dad beckoned them over.

"Check it out, hon. They still sell the very same sandcastle flags that I bought as a boy." He spread them out so that Mom could see. Mom nodded, impressed, though she couldn't help feeling it was pretty funny how excited Dad was about it.

Rachel was actually interested in them now, despite herself. "They're nice. What flags are they?"

"Uh-oh, trivia time," said Mom rolling over and sitting up.

"Right, let's see how much you can remember. You know this one, right?" Dad waved a familiar-looking red, white and blue flag.

"Oh, oh, I know!" Stevie wanted to make sure he got to answer first. "It's the British flag—the onion something."

Dad's raised an eyebrow. "Er, right! The Union Jack—the flag of the United Kingdom. And the United Kingdom is…" He looked at the others.

"England, Scotland, Wales and Northern Island." Rachel knew that. She'd had to memorize it in his geography lesson last term.

"Good job. And how about this one." He selected a bright yellow flag with a red lion. "Do you remember what they call a lion like this?"

"A red lion," said Stevie, proudly, so glad he had something to offer again.

Danny started to laugh, but Mom stopped him with a warning glance.

"Well, that's right, but I meant a lion on its hind legs with its fore paws raised." The kids looked at each other with raised eyebrows. No idea.

"A lion rampant. From heraldry. There were all sorts of different names for the various poses of animals on family crests and coat-of-arms." Dad smiled. He loved this stuff.

"Wow," said Emily. "They have a word for everything!"

Mom rolled her eyes. She sometimes had to question the practical side of these trivia times. She glanced at her watch.

"I think heraldry is cool," put in Danny. "Do we have a coat of arms?"

Dad nodded. "I looked it up once on the Internet, but I can't remember what it is now."

"Probably a lion rampant holding a cup of coffee and a brownie," said Mom with a straight face.

"Ha ha ha." Dad gave her a look.

"But seriously, dear, if we're thinking of going swimming, we should go now. Time's getting on." Mom gestured to where they could see the water's edge, much closer to them now with the advancing tide. This trivia time didn't seem to be winding down at all yet. She clambered to her feet.

"Well, okay." But Dad couldn't abandon it just like that. "So quickly, to finish off, the blue one with the yellow harp is…?"

"Ireland?" guessed Rachel throwing down her towel and grabbing a surf board.

"Right. The ancient kingdom of Ireland. And what does the harp have to do with Ireland?"

"We're not sure, dear. Okay, camera, keys and wallet hidden? Food out of reach of seagulls?" said Mom, trying to nip things in the bud. She got nods in reply. "Okay, let's go!" She took off suddenly at a run. The kids looked at each other for a moment in surprise, and then dashed off after her, yelling.

"And do you know what these ancient kingdom flags of Ireland, England and Scotland make up when they're arranged together?" called Dad after their retreating backs.

There was no answer. Evidently they were already too far away to hear.

"The Royal Standard of the UK. It flies wherever the Queen is in residence!" he yelled, waving the last flag.

"I guess trivia time is over," he said to himself with keen regret. He looked down at the flags in his hand. He'd have to explain about the Royal Standard later. Shading his eyes with his other hand, he scanned the beach until he spied the family almost at the water's edge. Then with a sudden resolve he jammed the flags in the tops of the castle towers and dashed off in pursuit.

≼∞≽

Kennedy pursed his lips and looked critically around the front room. It looked like he had everything packed up, even the stuff he had accidently kicked under the bed and the pile of dirty laundry behind the bathroom door. The smell of it still lingered, even though he'd jammed it all into his suitcase.

He had paid for two weeks in advance, but there was no chance of getting any of that back. That was frustrating as he was getting a bit short of cash. He hadn't planned on having to change lodgings. Well, he was banking on a big payoff here sometime soon. That was the whole point.

He wandered over to the window again and looked back along the lane. There was no van parked in front of the old lady's house now, but it had sure been there quite a while this morning. He pondered the implications. There was a distinct possibility the family were staying at the inn. The worst thing would be if they were staying there *and* involved in helping the old lady. Could they even possibly figure out the clue and find the inheritance?

He looked at his watch, shaking his head in frustration. *What a pain!* He couldn't move over there until four, and for all he knew, they could be solving the mystery right now.

He groped for his cigarettes, quickly lit one and took a deep drag, exhaling slowly through clenched teeth. This was way too important to lose now. Ever since he had been at the auction and learned that the Squire's rarest item wasn't up for bid he had thought about how he could somehow get his hands on it. There had been some amazing treasures in that collection of antiques the old guy had managed to acquire, so he knew this thing must be really special—maybe even worth hundreds of thousands of pounds.

Hundreds of thousands of pounds. Yes, he was banking on it—literally. His business had been really struggling lately and his debts were mounting. Rich folk just hadn't been dying fast enough—that and those investments of his that had suddenly gone sour. He had needed some lucky break, and then he'd received the notice of the inheritance and realized he still had a chance. Suddenly there was a real possibility of a solution. Yet now to be so close, only to feel it slipping through his fingers…

He smacked his hand against the wall. That was no way to think. He had to remain positive. He would go over there as soon as he could and look for the book. If it was gone, well, he'd just have to find out where it was and get it back.

Emily had had enough sea-time for a while. What with all the running, jumping, splashing and surfing both before and after lunch she was content to have a breather. Besides, with only two surf boards being shared among six people, the others wouldn't grudge her a break. She plopped down on the damp sand at the edge of the surf and stretched out her legs.

As she sat there wiggling her toes and enjoying the warmth of the sun on her back, she had a sudden realization that she had been feeling completely happy playing there with the rest of the family. She had forgotten all about her concerns for the future—what she was going to do after high school, where she would live. Now with a shock she realized that she was thinking about them all over again. Quick, what could she turn her attention to?

What about that weird clue this morning—something about a mantel's tile? Wasn't a mantel above a fireplace? She didn't remember the inn having a fireplace—or did it? That funny old inn—too bad they couldn't stay there longer. Yes, soon they would have to be moving on—going to Birmingham for a while. That didn't sound too much fun. And then back to the U.S. in November to finish up the school year. But what after that? She suddenly realized her thoughts had come full circle again to her concerns. Could she ever escape them? She must try to think of something else.

She noticed a movement to her right. The beach patrol's white pickup truck had driven down almost to the water's edge and the lifeguard guy was heading to move back one of the large red and yellow flags that marked the safe swimming area. Its metal stand was half submerged in the incoming tide. She looked across to her left. He had already moved the other one back up the beach some fifty yards or so.

Her dad had explained the flag system earlier. Red and yellow flags marked the safe swimming area. Black and white checkered flags marked the surfing zone—not for body boards but stand-up surfboards. And then of course there was the solid red flag warning where it wasn't safe to go all.

She watched as the lifeguard deposited the flag quite a way up the beach and then zoomed off again in the pickup. A quick check assured her that the family was still well within the safe area.

A sudden thought struck her. In a way, wasn't that what was troubling her? She wanted her whole life to be clearly marked out, like the safe area in the sea. She wanted that feeling of security—to know that both where she was and what she would be doing were completely safe—no surprises, no difficulties, no struggles. And yet it seemed that God had a different idea of where the flags should be set. He was creating a situation where she had to step outside of her own safety zone and trust that He knew what was really best for her in the future. That was scary. She didn't want to be challenged; she didn't want to be tested. Why did life have to have trials and trusting God have to be so hard? Was there any way she could stop worrying about the future?

With a sudden decision she clambered to her feet and sprinted back towards the sea. She would ignore her weariness and keep playing hard. Anything was better than just sitting there worrying.

As the van bumped over the grass back to the road, Mom shot a quick glance back at Rachel, remembering her earlier concerns. How *was* Rachel really doing? Had she guessed right that she was struggling with something? She snapped the mirror back into place and craned her neck around. "Did you have fun today, Rachel?"

Rachel wasn't quite ready for that question. She did a quick evaluation of her thoughts. It *had* been a fun afternoon, but in a sense it only whetted her appetite for what the rest of the vacation could be, if they didn't have to spend too much more time sitting and talking in the lady's front room. Well, she didn't want to have a discussion about that right now—best to sound as cheery as possible. "Yes, it was great!"

Mom looked across at Emily, who made a show of nodding vigorously as well. She turned back again, frowning to herself a little. Her motherly instinct told her something was up with both the girls, but she didn't have the energy to pursue it for now. She'd have to follow it up later, after she'd had a shower.

Chapter 9 - An Unwelcome Visitor

Kennedy muscled his suitcase into the corner and then flung his heavy duffle bag onto the bed, which groaned loudly in protest. He took a quick look around at the room, shaking his head at the slanted ceiling and what he considered to be cheap antique furnishings. Not exactly the Savoy Hotel, and nothing to change his lousy mood. Those *had* to be the flightless birds in the clue, and he was sure he had seen a book there on the lower shelf the other day, but it obviously wasn't there now. Even though he'd only had a moment as Mrs. Tremannon led the way through the dining room to the staircase, he had been able to clearly see that the shelf was empty now. *So where would it be? Could someone else have taken it? To read perhaps? Maybe one of that family?*

Kennedy narrowed his eyes. *Could they have taken it on purpose?* But Mrs. Tremannon had said they were on holiday--they'd never been to Penrithen before. How could they know about the treasure, or even the old lady? *And yet, and yet...* He was sure he had seen their van parked at the lady's house.

Well, whether it was them or not, he'd rather not face them at dinner tonight. He wasn't prepared for any awkward questions. No he'd best skip the dinner, even though it was included in the price. In fact, he needed to get going. Thankfully they were still out, but they could be back any time. He'd best find somewhere else to eat, and do it quickly.

Danny suddenly stiffened in his seat. He recognized that last turn—the one with the sign for the tea shop next to the old stone bench. They were getting close to the inn. For some reason he had another surge of anxiety about that man from the café—the one with the yellow car. He was sure he had seen him when they had that near miss that morning. Might he have been going to the inn? What if his car was there when they turned in? He tried to remember a Bible verse about trusting in God, but he was too anxious to think straight. All he could manage was an emergency prayer. *Please God, don't let the man be there.*

As the van turned in through the gate, Danny held his breath, and then let it all out suddenly in relief. The parking area was empty.

Mom sat on the edge of their barge-sized bed, her head bent over her cross-stitch. She had enjoyed a refreshing shower and could hear her husband taking his. She had noticed some little signs of reluctance in him regarding helping the lady with her inheritance, and it concerned her a bit. It made her wonder again—was this the right thing to do? It would have an impact on the vacation—that was for sure. And on the whole family. Was she just being selfish—wanting to help the lady so she could feel good about herself? It was honestly hard to discern her own motives sometimes.

She frowned a little, poking at her cross-stitch without really seeing it. She thought back to their meeting in the church, and then how they had found the lady again on the way back from the cove. She remembered the joy on the older woman's face as they had committed to help her. No, it must be alright—it had to be the right thing to do. God had done this, and He would take care of the consequences wouldn't He? And that included Rachel.

Yes, Rachel. Rachel must be struggling with all this. She really must talk with her. And it wasn't just Rachel—Emily had looked a little strained too. And that wasn't all. There was the travel, the lifestyle, and home-schooling in this crazy way. *As if they even had a home right now*, she thought wryly

Mom laid her cross-stitch carefully down. She needed to share all this with her husband—they needed to have a talk to make sure they were on the same page with all this, and the sooner the better.

The main room in the 'White Whale' pub was a babble of noise. The regulars were sitting or lounging around at the many tables, enjoying amber pints and swapping improbable stories, punctuated by the clink of glass. A few of them had ordered Cornish pasty and chips or some other sort of pub fare, but most of them were just having a drink before heading home. A hotly contested game of darts near the crowded bar added to the clamor.

Kennedy had tried to find a quiet nook where he could eat his dinner and think hard. A quiet nook was evidently out of the question, but at least he had sniffed out a spot away from the general hubbub. His table was against the wall in a corner, his general view of the room blocked by one of the pillars supporting the room's low beamed ceiling. An ancient framed print of a whaleboat braving a fearsome-looking sea hung crookedly by his head, and he gazed at it morosely, trying to sort out his thoughts.

He was interrupted by the arrival of a server, plunking down a plate in front of him—a slice of meat pie and a pile of chips. He poked at the meat suspiciously with his fork

"Hey, what is this anyway?"

The server, a tall tattooed college-aged lad with pony-tailed hair and a harried expression, paused as he turned to leave. "Eh, what? It's steak. Steak and kidney...what you ordered." He waited for a response. Apparently there wasn't going to be one—and not so much as a thank you either. After waiting a good five seconds he turned to go, his mind full of less than savory thoughts about the guy in the corner.

Kennedy continued poking. "Steak from what sort of animal?" he sniffed. But the man was already too far away to hear.

Kennedy gave a frustrated sigh. No battered haddock for him, nor cod neither. He couldn't afford it. So he was stuck with this. Paying for the inn had just about wiped him out. He just had to get his hands on that whatever it was. So, how could he find out if the book had been taken? He didn't want to ask the Tremannon's, that was for sure, and not the parents either. That left the kids.

The kids...hmm. Yes, he was sure he could get it out of one of them.

"A *father's love*. A *photo's clue*. What on earth is it all about?"

Dad addressed his reflection as he shaved in front of the mirror, trying to remember the words of the clue. He was in vacation mode regarding facial hair, and a shave once every couple days was par for the course. He paused and tapped out the razor, rinsing the hair down the sink. *And wasn't there a haven home mentioned? Was that the inn?*

Dad stopped shaving and looked at himself in the mirror. "So, how can we figure this all out?" he demanded of his reflection, gesturing with the razor. There was no answer forthcoming. He shrugged his shoulders.

Was this how it was going to be? Day after day of trying to decipher cryptic clues while trying to wrangle some sort of vacation time as well? And then there were those articles. He'd forgotten all about them. They were still lurking, unfinished, in the background of his life, wanting to rob him of whatever joy he might get from this break. He looked into his eyes in the mirror, noticing their suddenly strained look. He had to shake his head. Seeing his reflection shaking back at him seemed to emphasize his sorry condition.

"Okay, God," he said out loud. "I'm doing it again. I need your peace." He closed his eyes. "And will you please help me balance all this? If you want us to help this lady please give me some wisdom."

A thought came immediately to mind. He should take Kathie out on a date tonight—to that coffee place. He paused and opened his eyes, a little unsure of what to think. Was the thought just a random one, or was it perhaps an answer to his prayer? Was it just a coffee thought, or did God put it on his mind?

"God, do you want me to do that?" he prayed and waited. There wasn't an audible answer, but he did feel a sense of peace that wasn't there a moment before.

Well, why not? It would be a fun way to get his mind off of his troubles, and a great excuse to have a good cup of coffee in that cozy atmosphere. Yes, it was sounding better and better.

"Honey, are you almost done?" His wife's voice interrupted him from the other side of the door. "I know Mrs. T was expecting us a little later for dinner, but it's going on six-thirty now."

He snatched his shirt off the rack. "Yes, I'm all done. You can come in."

She popped her head around the door. "Can I have my hairbrush?"

"Here." He handed it to her. "By the way, sweetheart, I think we should go out tonight after dinner, just the two of us." He gave what he hoped was a winning smile. Could he convince her to go? "It'll be great. It's been a while since we've been out alone. The kids'll be fine here."

But Mom actually didn't need convincing at all. "Yes, that'll be great, if the kids feel okay about it."

"Oh, I'm sure they'll be fine," assured Dad. "They can play a game or watch a movie on the laptop. I think they'd enjoy that. Anyway, this is a pretty snoozy place. It's not like they'd have any trouble, right?"

✁✃

Kennedy pushed his plate away and dug into his pocket. The meal hadn't been that bad actually, but he wasn't going to admit it. He carefully counted out the exact change for the bill and stuck it under his empty glass. There was no way he was going to leave a tip.

He checked his watch. He had delayed as long as he could and he was more than ready to get out of this rowdy place. Dinner must be over at the inn by now and hopefully he could slip in to his room without a lot of explanations. He grabbed his coat and headed out to the street.

✁✃

Dad held the door open for Mom and they went in, both relishing the transition from the rather cool outdoors to the richly-scented warmth inside. It had made sense to walk to the coffee place rather than use the van. They enjoyed walking together anyway, and there was something romantic in the leisurely stroll down the hill and across the bridge, the early summer sun sinking in the western sky and a chilliness riding in on the evening sea breeze.

The village had seemed mostly deserted, and Captain Jack's Coffee House was fairly bustling by comparison. They felt quite fortunate to find a couple of free armchairs in a corner by the window, and dropped their coats on them to reserve the spot. The owner was busy behind the counter, crouched behind the espresso machine which was emanating a steaming roar like some sort of agitated dragon, almost drowning out the happy chatter of the evening crowd.

For a new place, it didn't look like it had taken long to get popular—quite amazing in a town that had looked pretty much battened down for the evening, and it wasn't even tourist season yet. Dad was impressed. The owner had obviously been augmenting the décor, and the walls now had some vintage travel posters and framed antique maps along with all the assorted antiques—just the kind of thing he himself would have put up. There was even some light jazz playing in the background. *Could he buy shares in this place?*

He led the way, threading through the tables to the counter. The roaring suddenly died away and the proprietor handed a large cup to a waiting lady, gave a quick apologetic wave in their direction and disappeared through the kitchen door.

"Still a busy guy," murmured Dad. "There's the list," he said out loud, nodding at the chalk board.

Mom didn't take very long to make up her mind. "I'll have the 'Captain Jack Chocolate.' Would you mind getting it? I want to go sit down."

"No problem. I still need a bit of time." This was a special occasion and Dad wasn't sure how many more times they'd get to come. He wanted to make an unhurried decision.

So what was a *Captain Jack Chocolate*? Hot chocolate with a touch of orange, topped with whipped-cream, chocolate shavings and a chocolate syrup swirl. *Aha.* Chocolate was mentioned three times in the description—as good as ringing bells and neon signs for his wife.

He scanned the rest of the choices. They had a White Chocolate Mocha, his old standby, but should he branch out a bit and try something new? He didn't want to be stuck in the same old rut. So…a caramel macchiato? A chai latte? Maybe he could ask the owner—what was his name? —for a recommendation. Rats, that's right. He had forgotten the guy's name. *What on earth was it? Jim? Jerry? Jack?* No, that was the name of the café: Captain Jack's. But could it be named after the guy? He was awful at remembering names. He was quite capable of forgetting them as they were in the process of being spoken to him—unless there was some extraordinary circumstance, like Auntie Flo and her association with that sneaky, ubiquitous brownie dessert thing.

Wait a minute! Bingo! Dad snatched up one of the business cards from the rack on the counter. Captain Jack's Coffee House, Geoff and Maggie Ketchum, owners. *Brilliant, brilliant, brilliant!*

At that very second the kitchen door opened and the owner pushed his way out, manhandling two gallons of milk. He smiled in recognition. "Hello there again. Dave wasn't it?" He set his burden down and shook Dad's hand.

"That's right. And you're Geoff, right? Geoff Ketchum." Dad couldn't resist feeling a little smug. He'd been able to deliver a first *and* last name. "My wife's over there. We came to have a date night."

"Hey, I like that idea. Just don't say it too loud." He put a finger to his lips. "My wife and I have been too busy to have a date night for weeks, what with getting this place going, and the project she's been working on." He grinned. "Now, what'll it be?"

Dad froze for a second. He'd forgotten all about making a decision.

"Well, my wife would like the Captain Jack Chocolate and I'll have a…" He had to look at the list again. Mocha, macchiato, chai, the house coffee…oh, hang it all, he couldn't decide under pressure. "Er…I'll have a…a…White Chocolate Mocha. Decaf."

Yup, the old standby again. Feeling a bit disgusted with himself, Dad fished in his pocket for his money and paid the total.

Geoff noted down the order. "I'll bring it over to you in a minute, if that's okay. I have to get some more whipped cream from the back. Do you want some on your mocha?"

Does a cow go moo? thought Dad. "Yes, thanks!" He added out loud, but the man had already disappeared into the back. Dad shook his head. *Busy, busy, busy.*

The kids were sprawled on their parent's park-sized bed, their attention focused on Dad's laptop in its position of honor at the head, propped up on Mom's make-up bag. They were watching an old favorite—an animated classic that they could all quote the lines from by heart, but still enjoyed immensely. Rachel shifted her position slightly to get a better view. This was one of her favorite parts.

All of a sudden Stevie reached over and tapped the space-bar, causing the screen to freeze.

"Hey!" Rachel glared. "What are you doing?"

"I've got to go to the bathroom."

"No way! You never have to go!"

Stevie shrugged.

Emily tried to bring some order. "It's okay—we could all use a break. Go on Stevie—be quick."

Stevie rolled off the bed and scurried into the bathroom. Rachel got up rather more leisurely and moved towards the door into the hallway.

"Where are you going?" wondered Danny.

"I'll be back in a minute," replied his sister over her shoulder.

"Bathroom," said Danny, with a knowing grin.

Emily set her feet on the floor and stretched. She glanced over at her parent's alarm clock. There was still a while before Mom and Dad were due back. She didn't want to get to bed too late, though—not if they were going to get going early tomorrow. She assumed they had plans to go somewhere, unless they were going to visit the lady again. But why would they do that if they hadn't solved the mantel clue?

The mantel clue. She shot up straight suddenly. *A mantel. The sitting room. Of course!*

Dad was ready now—coffee in hand and feeling relaxed. Time to stretch out his legs and give full attention to the issues at hand. It was frankly just a little too difficult to connect with his wife during the routine of the day. They had to get away to a conducive environment and this one fit the bill perfectly. Mom took another sip of her hot chocolate and closed her magazine. It looked like she was ready, too.

"So…Rachel," Dad began. "I did get a chance to talk to her a bit, though I admit it wasn't an especially fruitful conversation."

"Did she say anything?"

"Yup. She said she was struggling with some disappointment. You know, she thinks our vacation is going to be all taken up with helping Mrs. Renton—or at least, a chunk of it will. She was looking forward to the break, and now I think she's expecting the worse." *Kind of like me*, he thought.

Mom looked off into space, absentmindedly giving her hot chocolate a stir. "Hmm, yes, I thought that might be the problem."

It struck a dissonant chord with her, however. She had been concerned about whether the rest of the family would be on board with helping out. After all, it was her idea—it was her initial impression that this was God's will. As she considered it, she had another twinge of doubt.

"I do wonder…" She left the thought hanging.

Dad was thinking fast. He could see the struggle in his wife's face and tried to guess the reason. He took her hand. "Are you still concerned that we're doing the right thing—that this really is God's will?"

She nodded silently.

Bingo. He'd nailed it for once—maybe because he himself was wondering the same thing. *Yet was that really the issue?* All of a sudden Dad realized that it wasn't the question of God's will that he was struggling with after all. Yes, it was all becoming clear now.

"Honey, when we looked over the circumstances of our meeting and how much it meant to the lady, we were sure we were doing the right thing. The only thing that's making us question it now is that we're struggling with contentment— the kids' contentment and our own. I confess I've been worried myself about how much time it's all going to take, and whether we'll have any vacation at the end of it."

Mom nodded. She understood completely.

"I really do think this is the right thing to do, though." Dad leaned forward in emphasis, feeling more certain himself even as he said it. "I'm going to try to rally the troops and lead us together."

His wife looked into his eyes. Her face relaxed and she gave him a lovely smile. "Thank you, dear. I needed to hear that."

"And you know," put in Dad, getting excited. "If this is God's will then He's got a plan for our family. He promises He'll work out all things together for good for us—each one of us, Rachel included."

"I think we should talk to her about that," agreed Mom.

Dad thought for a moment. "You know, I did try a bit, but I think I came on a little too strong." He shook his head ruefully. "On the beach, when we were walking together. I had this sudden inspiration that a verse I had recently memorized really applied to her."

"And?"

"And I realize now I kind of crammed it down her throat."

Mom frowned.

"Well, maybe that sounds more dramatic than it really was, but I kind of gave her a mini sermon without really listening to her." Dad looked off into space and then gave a wry smile. "But you know, that verse really did seem appropriate for the situation. It could have been written just for her."

Mom took another sip, considering. "Well, maybe you could talk to her again when there's a bit less pressure. I think it's better coming from you. I want her to know you're in agreement with me."

Dad nodded. "Okay, I'll do it." He shifted in his seat, still a little sore from his surfing adventures that afternoon.

"I think it would actually be good to talk to all the kids again," Mom went on. "Emily looked a bit stressed today too."

Dad nodded again, but with just a twinge of concern this time. He really did believe that God was leading in this, but there was still the question of how this would pan out on a day by day basis. There was that *haven home* clue floating out there still, and they hadn't decided how they were going to spend the day tomorrow. He didn't like all these things hanging unsettled in the air. Could he trust God that it would all get worked out? It was a bit hard leading his family if he was struggling too.

⋖⋗

Danny sat on the edge of the bed, bumping his legs against the side and wondering what everybody was up to. He heard a car door slam outside. *That must be Mom and Dad*, he realized with a sudden shock. He checked the time on the laptop. Only eight forty-three—they must be back early. Maybe they wouldn't let them finish the movie. *Oh no!* He jumped off the bed. He needed to find Emily. Emily would be able to convince Mom and Dad to let them finish.

He was about to run out the door when he remembered something. A quick search in the depths of his pocket revealed his mini-LED flashlight. Feeling a bit more confident, he scampered down the hallway, checking the other bedrooms as he went, but without success. He stopped at the top of the stairs. *Could he go down all by himself?* He had done it in the daylight, but this was something way different. It was true that at least the lights were on in the hallway below, but what if Emily wasn't there?

He considered for a moment. His Mom and Dad would be down there any moment, and that was the whole point of rushing—to get to Emily before they saw him. He screwed up his courage and crept down, feeling his heart pounding in his chest. *Could he do this? And where should he look? He wasn't ready to have to go searching in any scary dark places.*

Rats. The drawstring on his pajama pants was coming undone. That was all he needed. He set his flashlight down on the bottom stair so he could use both hands to fix the knot. The doors to the dining room were open and he snuck a peek around as he bent over. The lights were off but the entryway glowed brightly beyond.

Who was that? He snatched his head back as someone came in through the front door.

At that very moment Emily stepped back out of the sitting room. Her search had proved fruitless. It was a wooden mantel with no tiles anywhere near that she could see. After a good five minutes of searching she had given up and decided to rejoin the others. She stopped short as she saw Danny.

141

"What are you doing?" she questioned, surprised at seeing him there looking strangely furtive.

"Shhh," whispered Danny fiercely. He risked another quick peek. Whoever it had been had disappeared for the moment. He beckoned Emily over with a frantic gesture.

"What's the matter?" Emily felt a little annoyed at all this excessive drama.

"I think Mom and Dad are home. I want to get back to the movie before they come upstairs. Otherwise they might want us to stop."

"Why would they want that? It's not very late."

"I don't know, I'm just worried they might. Come on!" Danny started up the stairs holding his pants up with one hand.

Emily shrugged her shoulders. *Whatever*, she thought, still frustrated at the results of her search.

She followed him up.

⊰⊱

The doorbell jingled as another couple sought refuge from the evening chill. Dad slurped the last of his coffee and reluctantly set the mug back on the table. That had been really, really good, but over way too soon. He stuffed down his concerns and smiled across at his wife. "I'll try to chat with all the kids tomorrow. I think we should pray together as a family, too— so we can really be united in this."

Mom nodded. She was definitely feeling some relief now. She took the last sip of her drink and leaned back in her chair.

"Now if only we could figure out this next clue," Dad added with a slight frown.

"I've been praying off and on all day about it."

"Me too." Dad looked at her empty cup. "Hey, do you want something more to drink?"

"Maybe some water, if you don't mind."

"Okay, I'll be right back."

Mom watched him thread his way back over to the counter. The place was almost full, but everyone had their own little nook with all those high-backed wing chairs. And she liked the idea that it was a converted house. Some of the coffee places in the U.S. looked more like fast-food restaurants—not the sort of place that invited lingering.

Her eyes ran over the pictures on the wall to her left. There was an old framed map of the Cornish peninsular, what appeared to be a vintage travel poster encouraging a train trip to Cornwall, and a small painting of a ship under full sail. She wondered if Dave had seen it. He loved sailing ships.

She looked over to where Dave was chatting with the owner guy. The espresso machine was roaring out again. A young couple were standing over by the fireplace, the man gesturing like he was telling some sort of funny story. He had to put his coffee down on the mantelpiece so he could use both hands. *That was quite the mantel,* she mused. *It was huge.* Mom furrowed her brow suddenly. *A mantel...that was in the clue wasn't it? A mantel's tile.* She looked again at the

142

mantelpiece. It was made of stone, but there did appear to be something set right in the middle. Wasn't it a single tile?

Mom shook her head. That was silly. Why would the clue be hidden right here, and in a coffee place, for goodness sake? *It hadn't always been a coffee place, had it though?*

Her husband sauntered back over and handed her a glass of water. "Sorry, no ice," he smiled apologetically. "Hey, I had a chat with the owner. It was actually really interesting."

"That's nice," replied Mom, distractedly. "But I want to ask you something."

"Okay," said Dad, puzzled.

Mom leaned forward, excited in spite of herself. She nodded over towards the fireplace. "Do you think that the mantel's tile in the clue might be referring to the one here?"

Dad followed her gaze. A mantel's tile? There did seem to be something embedded in the center. It was a bit hard to see with those people in the way.

"Maybe," he said doubtfully. "Why here, though?"

Mom laid a hand on his arm. "What was the address on the envelope?"

Dad had to rack his brains a bit for that piece of information. "Er, I think it was Cratchit Street or Lane or something."

"Do you know the name of this street?"

"No, I don't remember looking."

"Could you ask the guy?" She smiled her most winning smile.

"Well…" That sounded a bit embarrassing to him. "Wait a minute though…" He dug excitedly into his pocket. "I've got his business card here somewhere. Here it is--Captain Jack's blah blah blah, 190, Cratchit Road!"

"The same place!" Mom's eyes were shining. "I remember the street number now."

Dad was trying to sort all this out. "So, this was where the Squire wrote the note from?"

"The haven home perhaps," murmured Mom. She looked around with a fresh interest, trying to picture the place as it might have been. "A haven from what, I wonder?"

Dad was still puzzled. "So I need to check out that tile I guess. Want to come?"

Mom considered for a moment. "I think it would look kind of weird if we both went."

"I think it'll look weird anyway. What am I going to do? Take a rubbing of it? And I don't even have the camera. Not that I want anyone seeing me taking a picture of the mantel anyway. Weird city."

"Well, I guess try and memorize what it looks like. I'll find something to write on."

"Okay," sighed Dad, pushing back his chair again. He looked over to the fireplace. The couple was still hanging out by it. What was he going to do?

Mom gave him an encouraging smile, then settled back to watch the show.

Dad sauntered over, frantically trying to come up with a good reason to stop and peer at the mantel. Nothing came to mind. He abandoned the idea of pausing and kept going, taking a hurried glance over as he passed. It was a tile alright, with some sort of coat of arms, but that was all he had time to see. He carried on towards the counter. Maybe he could appear like he was checking out the menu again. No, wait, he could get another glass of water.

Pleased to have found an excuse, he went over and poured a glass from the jug on the counter, then turned and looked back. He could see his wife grinning over in the corner. Yup, she was having a great time for sure. Her husband—*Mr. Entertainment himself.* Now the obvious route back was a general straight line, but that wouldn't take him close enough. *Oh well.* He hoped no-one was taking notes.

He headed towards the fireplace, trying to look like he was going slowly to avoid spilling his glass. As he got near to the couple again they paused in their chatting and looked his way. Yes, they were probably thinking *didn't we just see this guy? Is he selling something?*

Dad felt himself turning red. He avoided their gaze and shot a glance at the tile. It was a coat of arms, black on a white background. He tried to commit it to memory and then made a bee-line for their table in the corner. It seemed like an eternity before he was safely back in his seat, breathing heavily.

"Did you get it?" Mom pushed a napkin towards him. "Can you draw it?"

"Yes, I think so, but next time I'm sending you!" Dad slumped back in his chair.

"I'm sorry it was tough—really I am. *I am!*" she insisted, noticing her husband's skeptical look. "Thanks so much for going."

Dad shook his head in mock frustration. He really wasn't upset. It was just humbling knowing that he had probably looked like an idiot. He sat up straight again. "Okay, I'd better try to draw it before I forget. Do you have a pen?"

"Don't you have one? You always seem to."

"No, I checked. Surely there's one in your bottomless purse."

"Okay, okay, I'll look. Maybe I have something." Mom dug down deep—then dumped on the table her finds: three black pens, two blue ones, a green highlighter and box of crayons.

Dad gave her a look. "Are you sure you don't have Mrs. Renton's inheritance in there, too? It would save us some time."

"Ha ha ha. Go ahead and draw before you forget."

He grabbed a pen and started scribbling, giving a running commentary as he went.

"Okay, there was a shield, of course, and divided into four. Top left was two crowns I think, and three in the bottom right." He sketched them in.

"What about the other spaces?"

"Hang on." Dad took a quick glance back at the fireplace to refresh his memory. "Oh, yeah, a kind of star, and a ship, like this." He pushed the napkin back at his wife.

"Okay," said Mom, a little puzzled. "So how do we find a clue in all that?"

"Well, do you remember the next part? It said *a photo's clue,* then *a life worthwhile.* So I think the clue is in the photo."

"And the *life worthwhile?*"

"No idea."

"Well I guess the photo's what we need, though I still don't understand about the tile." She looked around the room. "Are there any photos on the wall?"

"Maybe. Is there one above the mantel?" Dad craned his head around again. "Nope."

"How about a photo with something in it like the coat of arms on the tile?"

"Aha, now you're talking."

"Yes, but I don't see any photos," Mom frowned. "Maybe upstairs...?" She gestured to the spiral staircase.

Dad followed her gaze. "I was up there the other day. I don't remember seeing any photos."

"But are you sure?"

Dad slumped a little in his chair again. No he wasn't. And guess who was going to be the one to have to go up there and check.

⊷❦⊶

The ending credits began to roll and Emily reached over and clicked the stop button.

"Hey," protested Stevie. "I like that song."

"Sorry buddy, but Mommy and Daddy could be home any minute."

"But I thought you said they were already back."

Danny got up stiffly. "We thought they were. It must have been Mr. Tremannon or someone."

"I wish you'd checked," grumbled Rachel getting up herself.

"Yeah, no fair getting us all worried," agreed Stevie. "I kept thinking they'd be in here any second."

"Well they weren't," retorted Emily, sounding rather grumpy herself. She was supposed to be in charge and didn't relish dealing with all this dissension. To make matters worse, she had realized that no-one had brushed their teeth yet, and that was supposed to have been done before the movie.

"I want to watch the credits," insisted Stevie, making as if to start up the player again.

"No, it's time to brush your teeth." Emily snapped the lid of the laptop shut in emphasis.

"Hey!"

"I want to watch them too," added Rachel, flopping back down on the bed. Danny followed her.

Emily had a sudden feeling of panic. She was losing control. *Where were Mom and Dad?*

"Oh no!" exclaimed Danny suddenly.

"What?" Emily snapped.

"My flashlight. I left it downstairs."

"So go and get it."

"But I don't have my flashlight to see."

"Turn on the lights." Emily's compassionate nature was being tested right now.

145

"The light switch for the downstairs is downstairs."

"Look, we'll be right up here, brushing our teeth, right?" She glared over at the others.

Rachel and Stevie both suddenly decided that brushing their teeth would be much better than having to accompany Danny downstairs. They scooted off the bed and made a beeline for the bathroom. Emily gave Danny a look and followed them. The lad was suddenly all alone with his thoughts.

Could he do it? What if there was something scary down there? What about that suit of armor? He rubbed his forehead. He had to get his flashlight. What if he woke up in the night and worst yet, had to go to the bathroom? He gave a heavy sigh and slid reluctantly off the bed. *Okay.* He had to go, but he was going to go like Superman, at lightning speed. He pulled his pajama pants up an inch or so, took a deep breath, and tore out the door.

✌️👏

Kennedy stumped through the dining room and back into the entryway. He glanced around. The only sign of life was the muffled sound of a T.V. from behind the closed door to his right. The family's car had been in the driveway, so they were evidently here but thankfully they must have gone to bed already. He wanted to deal with them as little as possible. He really, really didn't want to have to eat meals with them. He'd decided he'd have to have a talk with Mrs. Whatsername.

He knocked firmly on the door and tapped his foot impatiently, nervously checking over his shoulder every few seconds. He was in no mood to run into anyone else.

He knocked again—this time a bit louder. The door suddenly flew open and there stood Mrs. Tremannon in her bathrobe. Her expectant smile disappeared. She folded her arms and appraised him somewhat coolly.

"So you're back then Mr. Kettridge. Did you forget which room you're in? It's number 1, through the dining room and turn right. Not upstairs now. Just around the corner."

"I know, you showed me already," replied Kennedy through clenched teeth. "And it's Kennedy."

What an annoying woman. She couldn't even get his name right, let alone remember what she'd done a few hours ago.

"What about having my meals in my room? I'd prefer not having to mix with the other guests." He tried to give what he hoped was a firm look. There was something about this oversized old lady that he found intimidating.

Mrs. Tremannon's mouth fairly dropped open. She put her hands on her hips, bursting with indignation and prepared to tell him exactly what she thought, but Kennedy, his confidence evaporating, wasn't sticking around to listen. He spun on his heels, grabbed his bags and leapt into the dining room, away from her offended presence.

The room was pretty dark, but as he scampered around the table, he took a quick squint over at the bird display in the corner to see if there was any change and skidded to a halt in amazement. There was a book there after all. *How had he*

146

missed it? A quick glance back confirmed that the old lady had disappeared again. He wrenched around the key but as he snatched up the book, a sudden clamor from the direction of the stairs caused him to look up in alarm. Someone was coming, and evidently at top speed. *What could he do?*

He was still hesitating when, with a thump, a young red-headed boy appeared out of thin air. He must have jumped down the last few stairs, landing right in the doorway. Kennedy gave a start of surprise. The two stared at each other for several seconds, the boy's eyes widening in shock.

Kennedy tried to think of something to say. The boy looked familiar, but he just couldn't place him. Anyway, Kennedy was in no mood for conversation, especially with the book in his possession. He glared at the boy, trying to assume his fiercest expression, his bushy eyebrows almost meeting in the middle. Evidently it worked. The boy gave a startled yelp and tore back up the way he'd come.

Kennedy sat back on his heels. He narrowed his eyes and tried to think. *Where had he seen that boy? He was sure he had seen him somewhere.* He had a sudden recollection. It was the same kid who had stared at him from the mini-van, when they had almost collided. That made sense. He must be a member of the family. But no, there was something else. Now that he had seen the boy up close, he knew he had run into him before somewhere else—somewhere where he had seen him right up close as well--but where? Well, wherever it was, it had to wait. Someone else could come by any minute.

Kennedy clambered to his feet and quickly locked the cabinet. Jamming the book under his arm he hurried around the corner, flung open the door of his room and jumped inside.

Mom and Dad tiptoed up the stairs. The hallway light was on, but it looked like the bedrooms were dark. Could the kids really be in bed? That would be a first, though it was almost ten. Mom couldn't help feeling relieved though. They had seen the yellow sports car in the driveway as they walked up to the inn, and they had immediately thought of Danny. Hopefully he hadn't seen it yet, and they could deal with it tomorrow when they had a bit more energy. It seemed like an amazing coincidence that the car was parked right there, but they agreed it was probably best in the long run. Now they could explain to Danny again that whoever owned the car—and was now apparently visiting the inn—could not possibly be the same person as the man in the café.

They peeked in on the girls. By the sound of regular breathing and a little light snoring they could tell they were already asleep. But what was that sound coming from the other room?

They both went in. Stevie was sprawled across his bed in his usual random fashion, one arm above his head. Danny, however, was lying curled up in ball, facing away from them. It sounded like he was sniffing. Had he been crying?

Dad stared up at the ceiling. What a bizarre day. First the time with the lady and the mysterious clue, not to mention the realization that this was a bigger fish than he had bargained for. Then the beach—yes, it had been pretty fun and all, but he hadn't been able to completely relax, what with those nagging thoughts about how to balance their time and his rather unsuccessful attempt to talk to Rachel. Then there was that award-winning dinner, followed by their outing to Captain Jack's and the remarkable discovery of the tile, dampened by their subsequent fruitless photo search. And to top it all off, Danny's startling story. It had taken a lot of talking and praying to get him calmed down enough that he could fall into a restless sleep. Dad plumped up his pillow a bit and then lay back with his arms behind his head. The luminous hands of the clock indicated it was getting close to eleven-thirty. Would he ever get to sleep?

A muffled murmur came from beside him. "Honey?"

"Uh-huh?" Evidently he wasn't the only one having trouble sleeping.

"Are you sure it can't be the man from the café?"

He closed his eyes. He didn't really want to go over all this again.

"Yes, I am. I mean, think about it. We've come about 150 miles since we saw that guy, and not just in a straight line. We've wound our way to this tiny village—one of thousands in this country. There's just no way. And how many yellow sports cars are there in Britain? Hundreds? Thousands?"

His wife sighed and snuggled down a little deeper under the covers. "I guess you're probably right."

"I really think I am, but either way, God's in control. We don't have to worry." Dad felt a little guilty though, even as he said it. He was actually a bit worried himself. What if it was the same guy, as unlikely as it seemed? What would they tell Danny?

Chapter 10 - The Mystery Deepens

Kennedy sat alone at one end of the massive table, trying to plough through a huge bowl of oatmeal while casting a furtive glance over his shoulder every few seconds. The oatmeal wasn't the sort of breakfast to be inhaled at lightning speed, and he was considering abandoning the effort, even at the cost of some serious hunger pains later on. The priority was to be out of there before the family showed up. At some personal cost to his pride he had coerced Mrs. Tremannon into bringing his food out early, but now he could sense he was running out of time.

And there it was—the sound of voices coming from the stairs. Time to make an immediate exit. He paused for a second, looking down at the stodgy mound remaining. Then with a sudden decision he grabbed up the bowl and hurried out to the entryway.

❧❧

Mom checked her watch. It was time. Hopefully her husband had been able to get a hold of Mrs. Renton on the phone. They really needed to tell the kids their decision before breakfast. She picked up her Bible and notebook, brushed a few stray petals off her jeans and headed back out under the arbor. She had spent a good hour in her secret spot, talking to God about the events of the past few days and was feeling more settled now about helping with the inheritance. That episode with Danny last night, however, had brought on some fresh concerns. The boy seemed almost obsessed with the idea that the sports car guy had followed them all the way here. That brief encounter in the cafe must have left a deep impression. She knew Danny struggled with fear, but this was especially troubling. She had tried to leave it in God's hands, but it was still hard not to worry.

Well, she supposed they would meet this mystery man at the breakfast table. It would be pretty strange now, with someone else sharing the inn—it had been nice having it all to themselves. It wouldn't do to be selfish though, would it? And anyway, now they could prove to Danny that it wasn't the man from the cafe. He had admitted he had only seen him for a moment.

As she passed the open kitchen window, she caught a fragrant whiff of frying bacon—a wonderful reminder that breakfast was on its way. Her stomach growled in response and she quickened her pace. As she rounded the corner of the house, she heard the front door open and close. She quickly tried to smooth down her hair, which had been at the mercy of the morning breeze. It must be one of the Tremannons.

But it wasn't. Someone else appeared from the front porch—someone she recognized, but had no wish to see at all. She stopped dead in her tracks, finding herself face to face with a tall, mean-faced, grey-haired man—*the* man—the man from the motorway cafe. Danny had been right after all.

Her initial amazement was quickly replaced by a wave of indignation. *This was the man who had scared her son!* She opened her mouth to speak but suddenly couldn't think of what to say.

Kennedy had no recollection of Mrs. Chapman at all, but had been thinking over what he should say if he ever had to talk to a member of the family. The only way to figure out if they were involved with the inheritance was to be on some sort of speaking terms with them. Startled at this sudden appearance, he tried to put on his most charming manner—something he hadn't practiced much lately.

"Oh, I'm most terribly sorry for startling you. I'm late for an appointment...er...for my job...and I'm in a bit of a hurry." He looked down at the bowl of oatmeal clutched in his right hand, then quickly switched it over and held out his free hand to shake. "I'm, I mean my name's Kennedy. Michael Kennedy."

Mom was taken aback. She had intended to express at least some level of outrage at his treatment of her son, but the man's friendly attitude had all but disarmed her. She looked at his outstretched hand. Her natural good manners couldn't just ignore it. She reached over and shook it, managing a slight smile.

"I'm Kathie Chapman. My husband and I are staying with our family here at the Inn." She paused for a second. Should she say something? Yes, she felt she should. "I think we may have met before."

"Really?" That caught Kennedy completely off guard. He started racking his brains.

"Yes. A few days ago—at the motorway cafe. You got a little annoyed at my son."

Kennedy's mouth dropped open. Now he remembered. That red-headed kid who had got in his way—it was the same one he had run into last night. *What miserable misfortune!* His mind started whirring. He had to fix this somehow if he wanted to be able to figure out what this family was doing. This was going to be difficult. He couldn't remember the last time he'd apologized for anything

"I'm really, really...sorry about that." He pushed the words out of his mouth. "It was quite wrong of me. I was upset about something. Yes, I had just come from the hospital. My brother was seriously ill. I'm afraid I wasn't myself."

Mom wasn't quite sure what to think now. There was something in this man's manner that didn't ring true. And why on earth did he have a bowl of oatmeal in his hand? Was he stealing the thing? Or maybe he really was in a hurry. Maybe he was telling the truth. She supposed she had no good reason not to believe him.

"Well, Mr. Kennedy, I'm sorry to hear about your brother. It was unfortunate that my son got in your way when your mind was so pre-occupied. Perhaps when you see him here you could explain. He's been rather afraid of seeing you. He struggles with fear a bit you see."

Kennedy tried to give what he hoped looked like a humble nod, but filed that interesting piece of information away. "I am really sorry. Of course I will be sure to apologize and put him at ease. And now I must be off, if you will excuse me. Like I said, I have a pressing appointment at work."

"Yes, certainly," said Mom, moving aside. She had a sudden thought. "Well, I hope you get a chance to finish your breakfast. What line of work did you say you were in?"

Kennedy was already halfway to his car. He stopped, cursing under his breath, and turned slowly. "I'm a...I sell...insurance." He quickly turned back and hurried on.

Selling insurance. *That was inspired*, he thought bitterly, but it was the only thing he could produce in that instant that wasn't close to the truth. He climbed into his car and plunked the bowl onto the seat next to him, muttering to himself.

Mom stood there looking after him, not sure what to think. Then she shrugged her shoulders and headed inside.

❧❧❧

Dad was still struggling to believe it was actually the guy from the café, but Mom was evidently quite positive. This was going to take some processing—and some really careful handling of Danny's emotions. Dad wasn't ready for either—all he could do was fling up a quick prayer for help. He already had enough on his mind with this family meeting he'd just called, which possibly wasn't going to be about a popular topic. Emily, Danny and Stevie were already there, looking a bit glum, and here came Rachel, looking like she was in line to have her blood drawn. *Great, just great.*

They were in the downstairs sitting room. Rachel plopped into an armchair, trying not to look at the others. To her, a family meeting meant only one thing that she could figure: *bye-bye vacation.*

Dad tried to push aside his concerns. He and Mom had talked and prayed about this, and they were sure they were doing the right thing. Time to take charge.

"Okay, gang. I just wanted to let you know what we decided about today." He looked over at Mom, who gave him an encouraging smile.

The kids looked up expectantly, Rachel trying not to let her apprehensions show too much.

"Well, you know we mentioned yesterday about going to Tintagel." The kids nodded, their faces immediately falling. They knew what was coming. A change of plans.

Dad saw the looks, and hastened to explain. "We're still going. I think you're going to have a blast."

Now the kids had quizzical expressions. Where was he going with this?

"Your Mom and I talked, and prayed, and we feel that it would be a real blessing to bring Mrs. Renton along with us today. She's an older lady, and doesn't get out as much as she should. We think she's pretty lonely, too." He looked over at his wife, who shrugged her shoulders. "Well, she's pretty sad about something, and we feel that God wants us to bless her."

So that was it. The kids looked at each other. Danny and Stevie couldn't see any problem with that, as long as they could still do all they wanted to. Could Mrs. Renton play okay in a castle? Maybe.

Emily smiled and nodded slowly. This meshed well with her desire to bless the lady somehow. Rachel was a bit taken aback, however. What did that really mean for the day?

Dad decided to just plough on. "We've been helping her with the mystery inheritance, and we really feel that this is God's will for us right now." He let his gaze linger on Rachel, who colored slightly.

"With that in mind," added Mom, wanting to give some support to Dad, "we're going to try and see if we can find the next clue for her. Dad and I have discovered something!" She paused for effect.

"What is it," said Stevie, bouncing up and down. Even Rachel felt an unexpected thrill.

"We found the mantel's tile!"

❧❧

Kennedy pulled into the cliff-top parking area and chose a spot facing the sea. He gazed morosely out the windshield. Gusts of wind shook the car's antennae and tore the tops of the whitecaps surging towards the shore below. So much for a walk. He needed to clear his head and think this thing through, but he didn't relish getting blown to bits--he could feel a nasty cold coming on.

As if to emphasize the fact, he gave a sudden, massive sneeze. He wiped his nose and allowed himself a huge sigh. What he really needed to do was talk this over, and his only option was that prized idiot Jennings, who couldn't even do something simple like stealing a paper from an old lady without almost getting caught in a closet. He hated having to depend on that whining softie. He had passed Jennings's shop on the way up Slades Hill, but of course it was still closed at this hour—he didn't even open until ten. In fact, the lazy brute was probably still in bed. He knew from bitter experience that it was no use knocking. He'd have to call him on the phone, and it gave him a certain satisfaction to think that he might catch him still asleep. It would serve him right.

He reached in his inside coat pocket for his phone. It wasn't there. He rummaged unsuccessfully through his other pockets—then scanned the car. *Nothing. No way!* Kennedy couldn't believe his foul luck. He'd left his phone back at the inn. And now that family was probably eating breakfast. There was no way he wanted to deal with them until he'd talked things over. He glanced at his watch. He'd give them about forty-five minutes to finish and take off for the day. He adjusted his seat back a bit, gave another heavy sigh, lit a cigarette, and settled down to wait.

Danny and Stevie dashed up the stairs, elbowing and shushing each other and trying not to laugh, Dad following along behind at a more leisurely pace, glad that Danny seemed to have momentarily forgotten his distress with a welcome distraction. Figuring the photo in the clue was likely at the inn, the family had split into two groups to search--and it was a contest between the boys and girls as to who could find it first.

"I know there are some photos in the hallway," said Dad as they reached the top. "Let's check them."

"Er, I don't think it's here." Danny was remembering the morning he had pretended to be a secret agent. "I don't remember anything like that."

"Well, it could be pretty small—just something in the background," said Dad, examining a faded photo of an old stone cross in a clearing.

Stevie ran to the next picture. He really wanted to be the one to find the clue. "I'll look at this one."

"Wait a minute," said Danny. "There were some pictures on the stairs. I'll check them out."

"Wait! I'll go look." Stevie did an about face and made a dash for the stairs.

Dad grabbed him as he tore by. "Whoa, hang on old chum. Let Danny look."

"But he might find it!"

"Now wait just a minute. What's with all this? It doesn't matter who finds it, right?" Dad looked Stevie right in the eyes. "Right?"

The boy averted his gaze. "Um, well..."

Dad suddenly thought he understood. "Are you thinking that the big kids are going to solve everything and since you're the smallest you might get left out?"

Stevie hung his head but didn't say anything.

Dad smiled to himself. "Hey, buddy, you're a smart guy and I think you're just as likely as the others to find a clue. God can use you, but you need to have a good attitude."

Stevie didn't look too convinced.

❧❧❧

Mom and the girls were systematically searching the dining room, examining every one of the numerous old photos on the walls. It was an interesting collection, full of dated shots of the village, views of the coastline, or miscellaneous gatherings of stiff, unsmiling individuals looking like they'd been coerced at musket-point into having their photograph taken.

Rachel was getting antsy again. If the old clock on the bureau was right, it was getting on for nine. She glanced through the door into the entry way. There were more pictures there, too. At this rate their search could go on all morning. Well, she could at least do a quick look and check that place off the list. She ducked around the corner and started scanning the wall on the near side by the front door. *Five photos, and all landscape shots. Okay.* Across the hallway there were two more. One was a picture of the church they had visited up on the cliff top. The other was some sort of monument on a hill.

Rachel looked around to see if she'd missed anything. *Oh, yes.* Over by the kitchen door there were two framed photos, one above the other. She trotted over and took them in at a glance. The top one was a picture of an old man with glasses and a walrus moustache, standing by a window with a stained glass picture of a ship. *She'd seen that guy before! It was the Squire, she was sure of it!* No mantel's tile though. *How frustrating.* She bent over a little and looked at the photo below. It was another black and white one in a thick, carved wooden frame. There were two couples standing in front of a fireplace, one on one side and one on the other. Between them was clearly visible the center of the mantelpiece, the younger man's hand resting right above the coat of arms that Dad had described. With a shock Rachel realized the coat of arms was carved into the picture frame too. She gave a squeal. She'd done it! *Now they could get on with the day!* She raced back into the dining room, waving her arms in the air.

"Mom, Emily, it's here. I found it! I found it!"

Kennedy rolled his window down a crack, pushed the stub of his cigarette through the opening and then started the car. It was nine o'clock. The family must be out of the inn by now, he reasoned. Time to go get the phone and then figure out what to do next.

The whole family gathered in front of the photo, the kids jostling each other to get a good view.

"It's the one, isn't it?" said Rachel excitedly. "We've got the clue, and it didn't take too long."

"I'm not sure it's the one," said Stevie, trying to sound like a wise detective. He was frustrated that he hadn't been the one to find it and didn't want to give Rachel any credit.

"It sure looks like the correct one to me," said Dad. "And there's the coat of arms on the frame!"

Stevie frowned.

"But what does it all mean?" wondered Emily. "I mean, it's just an old photo."

"Is there anything on the back?" suggested Mom.

"I guess it's okay to take a look." Dad carefully lifted the frame off its nail and turned it over.

"Wow, jackpot!" said Danny peering under Dad's arm. "What's it say?"

On the back of the frame, beneath a line of twisted wire, was taped a padded brown envelope with something written across it in a neat flowing script.

"*For Ruthie,*" read Dad. "Amazing!"

"Can we open it?" cried Stevie, jumping up and down and forgetting his annoyance.

"Well, I think...wait!" Dad held up his hand. A door slammed in the kitchen, and they all clearly heard Mr. Tremannon's tuneless whistling.

Dad put his finger to his lips, then whispered. "Quick, let's go to the sitting room."

❧❧

As Kennedy turned up the driveway, his heart plummeted. The van was still there. Now what was he going to do? Maybe they weren't going to go out today at all. He pulled over to the right side of the parking area and turned off the car. He'd have to go in anyway. Maybe he could just be careful and he wouldn't have to do any talking.

He opened and closed the car door as quietly as he could and walked carefully over to the entry. A quick glance through the little window assured him that there was no-one in the hallway. He snuck inside and peered into the shadowy dining room. It was empty. Maybe this would work after all. He trotted across the room, but then pulled up short on the far side. He had heard muffled voices. *Where were they coming from?* He took a moment to listen carefully. Apparently from the sitting room just through the door and to the left. Well, that was okay, as long as they stayed there.

He was about to tiptoe past when he heard something that made him pause. *What were they talking about in there?*

❧❧

Rachel squirmed in her seat. The family had hurried back to the sitting room and distributed themselves across the couch and armchairs with Dad standing in the middle. This wasn't what she had expected. Couldn't they go now that they had found the clue?

Dad caught her eye, and gave the merest shake of his head. He knew what she was thinking. He took a glance at his watch and then cleared his throat. The rest of the family looked up at him expectantly.

"Okay, first of all, I don't think we should open the envelope. It's for Mrs. Renton."

There were a few groans.

"Do you think it might be the inheritance, though?" wondered Emily.

"In the envelope?" said Stevie incredulously. "What about the jewels and stuff?"

"It could be," said Dad. "It could tell her exactly what the inheritance is."

"Won't she be surprised," said Emily. She could picture the old lady's smile.

"Yes, she will," agreed Mom, "but I hope it's a nice surprise. Whatever the Squire intended for her with these clues, it seems like it might be a bit of painful journey for her."

"What do you mean?" said Emily, suddenly concerned.

"I'm not sure exactly. She's struggling with her past and her relationship to the Squire and his wife. I'm praying that she will find healing in the process."

"Is there anything we can do right now?" said Stevie, disappointment written all over his face.

"Well, let's at least look at the photo." Dad bent down and held it so they could all see.

"Is that the Squire?" said Danny, pointing at the older man in the picture.

"I don't know?" said Mom. "It doesn't really look like him. Nor does the other man."

"I wonder..." Dad had a sudden thought. He examined the back of the frame. "I think I can open it." There was a little catch and he turned it carefully and lifted off the back, the envelope still attached in the center. "Look here, there's some writing on the photo itself. Here, Rachel." He beckoned her over. "Why don't you read it? You found the photo. Give her some room, please."

Rachel looked at him, surprised. She gave a sudden smile. "Okay, thanks!"

The others moved back a little reluctantly and Rachel scooted forward in her chair and peered over to look. The writing was cursive and a bit hard to read. She turned her head this way and that, trying to puzzle it out. "I think it's some names—probably the people in the photo—and a date."

"Well, what are the names?" said Danny impatiently.

"Hold on. I think it says 'William and Muriel Penrow.' Those are the older couple on the left. And then the others are Elaine and...and Jowan I guess. Penrow, too. 1903."

"They must be the Squire's relatives then," said Emily.

"I think you're right," said Mom, studying the photo. "Maybe the younger couple are his parents, and the others his grandparents."

"But what's that got to do with anything?" said Danny.

"We don't know, but that's why we need Mrs. Renton to read the letter," said Rachel.

Dad looked at her in with a raised eyebrow. Rachel saw his look and guessed its meaning. "I mean, I hope it doesn't take too long. Maybe we're close to being done now." Yes, she didn't like to admit it, but she was getting kind of intrigued in spite of herself.

Outside the door, Kennedy was having trouble hearing. He moved closer. It was a risk, especially as he kept having to sniff to keep his nose from running, but he had to hear more.

"And the picture was taken at the coffee place where we went," continued Dad, smiling to himself at Rachel's interest.

"Do you think that's important for the inheritance?" wondered Danny, his mind conjuring up images of trapdoors and hidden rooms. "Maybe it's buried there."

"Perhaps we'll find out from the letter," said Mom.

"But we can't open it!" howled Stevie.

"Shhh! We're trying to be quiet," reminded Dad.

"We can ask Mrs. Renton," said Rachel. "We're going to see her right now aren't we?"

"I guess that's your way of saying it's time to go," smiled Mom.

"Well, yes," said Rachel, feeling a little embarrassed. She did want to hurry things up, but that wasn't the only reason she'd said it. She had realized now that she really did want to find out what was in the letter. Maybe this whole quest thing for the inheritance could be interesting after all.

"We do need to get going," said Dad. "I need to put the photo back before someone comes out of the kitchen and misses it. You guys go grab your stuff, use the restroom and we'll meet down at the van in ten minutes."

"Can I just have another look at the photo before you do?" said Mom, leaning over.

Outside the door, Kennedy couldn't believe his ears. The family knew about the clue and it sounded like they had solved it—something to do with a photo and a letter. *Could that be the inheritance?* They were going right now to see Renton. What was he going to do?

At that critical moment he was seized by a sudden panic. He could feel a sneeze coming on. He scrabbled desperately in his pocket for a handkerchief, yanking it out and stuffing it onto his face to try to muffle the sound. He was only partially successful. *He had to get out of there.* He dashed over to his room, fumbled with the door and leaped inside.

∽⟳⟲

"What was that?" Dad dropped his voice low and held up his hand. "Did you hear something?"

"I thought I heard something in the hallway," said Mom.

Dad opened the door carefully and peeked surreptitiously around. There was no-one in sight. He shrugged his shoulders. "I don't see anyone. Maybe it was Mrs. Tremannon?"

"Well whoever it might have been, it doesn't really matter does it? We're not doing anything wrong," said Mom, looking at Dad for some reassurance.

"No, not at all. That is, I guess we're just trying to keep this kind of private right now. We don't know if Mrs. Renton would really like the Tremannon's to know all about it. Oh, and that reminds me. I need to take this off the back to give to her." Dad carefully peeled the envelope off the back of the photo.

Mom looked at the clock on the mantel. "We do really need to get going. We told Mrs. Renton we'd pick her up at ten."

"Right," said Rachel, jumping up. "Come on you guys, let's get the car loaded up."

The others pushed themselves out of the chairs and headed for the door, sharing secret smiles at Rachel's enthusiasm. Rachel, however, didn't get too far. She stopped in the doorway, causing Emily to bump into her with an exclamation.

"Sorry, but look. This was on the floor outside the door." Rachel held up a small card.

"It's a business card," said Emily, scanning it quickly.

"Here, let me see," said Dad. "Please," he added. Rachel handed it over.

"*Kennedy Professional Estate Liquidation*" he read. "*Michael Kennedy, owner.*"

"That's the man from the café. I talked to him this morning," exclaimed Mom. "But he said he was an insurance salesman." She realized her mistake and gasped.

Danny stiffened, and Dad put his hand on his shoulder. This wasn't how he had planned on Danny getting this piece of news. "It's okay," he tried to hurriedly reassure him. "Yes, it was the guy, but you'll be fine. We'll talk about all this later."

157

"But this wasn't here when we went into the room. Was he outside the door?" said Rachel.

"Let's discuss this later, okay everyone? We need to get ready and go and get Mrs. Renton." Dad ushered the kids out and towards the stairs. He glanced back at Mom and grimaced. She gave a worried look. Somehow they were going to have to deal with Danny's fear, and the significant fact that, out of all the places in England he could have ended up, Mr. Michael Kennedy was here staying with them at the Squire Inn.

⊰⊱

Kennedy waited until he heard a bunch of tramping up the stairs, then opened his bedroom door a crack and peered out. There was no-one in sight. He listened carefully. It seemed like the coast was indeed clear, so clutching his phone, he nipped out of the room, scampered briskly through the dining room and out the front door, his mind a whirl with all that he'd heard. There was something significant about a photo and something about a letter too. *How many clues were there, and would the family solve them all and beat him to the inheritance?* There was absolutely no way he was going to let that happen. He needed to call Jennings right now. Together they'd have to decide what to do.

Kennedy ran to the corner of the house and peered around the side, panting from the exertion. There was no sign of the Tremannons. He slipped around the corner and confirmed that he couldn't be seen from the driveway. *Yes, perfect.* He'd call from right there.

⊰⊱

Danny took a surreptitious peek out of his parent's window. He was supposed to just be getting his jacket from their closet, but some sort of morbid curiosity drove him—the same sort of curiosity that had led him to take a look in that scary library book that one time and regret doing it ever since. Something inside told him he was going to regret this too, but he decided he couldn't help it.

And sure enough there it was, right below the inn sign—the yellow sports car. It was absolutely his worst nightmare come true. *What had gone wrong?* He had hoped and prayed this wouldn't happen, but somehow it had anyway. *Why?* He thought God wanted him to be happy—to feel safe. Hadn't he read that somewhere in the Bible? Well, he wasn't feeling either happy or safe. Not at all.

⊰⊱

"What do you mean you can't?" Kennedy wasn't liking what he was hearing, not that that was unusual these days. Jennings was an expert whiner. "Look, how many are you even going to miss? The town's a graveyard until tourist season."

Kennedy switched ears and peered around the corner again. He tried to keep his voice calm. It probably wouldn't help to lose his temper. He needed to win this argument.

"I promised you twenty percent, and I know this thing's worth tens of thousands—at the very least. It will be worth it—I keep telling you."

Kennedy paused, swallowed hard, and then spoke slowly. "I need you." It galled him to admit it, but it was true. "Right now. I can't follow them. They know

158

my car now, and they know me. This family is on to something. They've already solved two things and we've no idea how many more clues there might be. They could even solve everything today!"

The voice at the other end was trying to sound firm. Kennedy smiled to himself. "Okay, okay, twenty-five percent." It was an easy promise to make since he had no intention of keeping it. "Just get over here quickly. Wait by the corner where you can see the entrance. They have a silver mini-van, French number plate. It's the only other car here. Look, I'll call you if they leave, but you need to be here in five minutes!"

He snapped his phone shut and took a careful peek around the corner. *Good.* The van was still there.

✧✦✧

Dad looked at his watch. It was time to get in hustle mode. "Come on kids, chop-chop. Get on in." *Now who was missing?* "Come on, Danny!"

Danny was lingering in the doorway, shooting fearful glances towards the yellow sports car. He just wasn't sure if that mean guy was seated inside, ready to pounce.

"Danny!" Dad's voice had taken on that 'must be obeyed or else' tone, which managed to trump Danny's fear. He focused his eyes on the van door, fairly sprinted across to it and leaped inside.

Dad slid the door shut and started the engine. As the van started up the road out of the little valley, none of the passengers noticed the plain brown sedan that turned out of a side lane behind them and followed at a distance, keeping them just in sight.

✧✦✧

Mom looked back at Danny. He was chatting with Stevie and appeared to be doing much better now that they had left the inn and any possible encounter with the man. She sent up a brief prayer for him and then turned to Mrs. Renton at her side. Emily had been assigned Mom's normal seat up front in the van so Mom could sit next to the old lady.

She touched Mrs. Renton lightly on the arm. "Are you alright? Are you comfortable enough?"

"Oh, yes, no problem. I'm just so grateful to be getting out for the day." Mrs. Renton patted Mom's knee and smiled. "It's so good of you to take me with you. I don't get around so much anymore. That walk I did up to the chapel the other day was probably the furthest I'd gone in days. I was quite blown."

"Does your kitty, Mr. Pickwick, like to go for walks?" said Rachel from the back seat where she was sitting with Danny and Stevie.

"Oh, yes, he would go out every day if he could. He's just like a little dog in that regard."

"Does he mind being home alone?" wondered Emily, turning to look back at the lady.

"Well, he wasn't too happy. When I get home he'll probably ignore me in protest. That is until I get him a treat."

Emily giggled.

"I think he really enjoyed it when you all came over. He loves the attention," Mrs. Renton continued. *And I enjoyed having you over too,* she thought to herself. It was a continuing source of wonder that she was actually spending so much time with this family that were complete strangers only a few days ago, not to mention sharing some of her most intimate struggles with them. "Thank you again for all your help," she added out loud.

"It's our pleasure," said Mom, warmly.

"Yes, and speaking of that, we have some news for you," said Dad glancing into the rearview mirror.

"Well, you mentioned on the phone that you solved the clue about the tile. Did you learn something more about that?"

"Yes, we did. Do you remember the note said there was a clue with a photo? Well Rachel found the photo in the entryway of the inn."

"Good for you, dear," said Mrs. Renton, smiling back at Rachel who swelled with pride.

Mom rummaged in her purse and produced the envelope. "And this was on the back," she said, handing it to the lady.

"Oh my goodness, another letter."

"Yes," said Dad from the front seat. "We must confess, we were wondering how many more there might be."

"Do you have any idea why the Squire made his will so...complicated?" Mom gestured at the letter in the old lady's hand.

Mrs. Renton shook her head sadly. "I'm not sure, though it does seem like he had a plan in mind." She sighed. "Something he wants me to learn apparently. He was so clever, and loved puzzles and mysteries and all those sorts of things. Perhaps he just couldn't resist making this into one."

She carefully opened the envelope and drew out some pieces of paper and several smaller envelopes, spreading her finds out on her lap while the kids in the backseat strained to see.

"Well, it looks like there are several old letters, but the other paper says '*read first*', so I suppose I should do that. Just a minute." She retrieved her glasses from her purse and put them on. "That's better. Now then, let's see." She was trying to sound cheerful, but inside she was feeling that familiar mix of worry and guilt. She made a conscious effort to stuff the feelings down. "Alright. This is from the Squire again. I'll read you what it says.

"Dearest Ruthie, Congratulations on making it this far! I fully intend for you to succeed on my little quest, of course, but I hope you are benefitting from the experience."

The old lady paused. *Benefitting from the experience?* She wasn't sure that she was. She took a quick look around at the family, but they were all smiling and nodding. Feeling somewhat encouraged, took a deep breath and continued.

"You are probably wondering about all the mystery. Do you remember we used to like doing puzzles together? I'm not sure if you still do, but you'll have to trust me. There is a reason. Read the old letters I've included first. Then continue on with this letter from me."

Mrs. Renton paused and looked up. "Well, I suppose I should do what he says."

Mom nodded and tried to give what she hoped was an encouraging smile. She glanced up front and noticed that her husband didn't seem to be paying a huge amount of attention to the road.

"Er, dear. We need to keep our eyes open for where we turn. As soon as we get to Wadebridge, look for the B3314. It should be off to the left once you get into the town."

Dad nodded and made a mental note to pay better attention to his driving, though he didn't want to miss any of the drama from the back seats.

Mrs. Renton set aside the letter from the Squire and looked at the other two envelopes. One was marked with a small number one, and the other with a number two. She picked up the first and held it up so they could all see, Rachel, Danny and Stevie straining to get a good look from the back.

"Alright, first I'll read who this is addressed to. It's a bit hard to decipher with this handwriting. Let's see." She turned towards the light from the window. "It's to Mrs. Elaine Penrow."

"The squire's last name!" cried Danny.

"That's right. And mailed to 190 Cratchit Road, Penrithen, England."

"That's the home again from the last clue—the coffee place," gushed Mom.

"Really?" said the old lady. "But there's no return address. It just says *Duala Kamerun.*"

"I think it's the name of someone—like a spy or something." Stevie could easily picture what Mr. Duala Kamerun looked like, from his eye-patch and hat down to the revolver stuck in his belt.

"Funny name," said Rachel, doubtfully. "Why isn't there a stamp?"

"I don't know," said the old lady. "It's addressed to Mrs. Elaine Penrow— that was Uncle Kenwyn's mother. She died sometime before the war—before I came out here." She paused for a moment and looked off into space. "Uncle talked about her a lot. She had real strength of character, he said." She looked back at the others. "She had to raise the family by herself, you see."

"Had her husband passed away, then?" Dad asked over his shoulder.

"You know, the details escape me now, but yes, he had died—I think he got really sick overseas somewhere. I know the family was in Africa for a time."

"Africa?" said Mom, surprised. "Were they missionaries or something?"

"I can't honestly remember. I was so caught up in myself and my own problems that I didn't pay much attention to anything else." She shook her head sadly.

"Of course!" said Dad suddenly, slapping the steering wheel.

"What, what?" said Mom in surprise.

"The return address. It's Duala, Kamerun. That's got to be the old name of Douala, Cameroon in Africa." He looked over at Mom. "That's where the Johnsons went on that missions trip. Cameroon used to be a German colony, right up until the middle of the First World War.

"Yes, yes, that would make sense." Mrs. Renton was getting a little excited. "The letter was sent from there to Uncle Kenwyn's mother in Penrithen."

"But why weren't the family together? Didn't you say they lived in Africa?" questioned Mom.

"Yes, that's right, but I'm not sure what happened." She looked around at the expectant faces and smiled. "So, I suppose I should read the letter, right children?"

She took it carefully from the envelope and unfolded it. It had yellowed with age and was starting to crack and tear at the seams. "Alrighty then, but just a moment—the writing is rather shaky." Mrs. Renton held the letter out where her glasses could best focus on it.

"Dearest Elaine, I trust our dear Lord has preserved you and the children on the voyage and you have found safe haven in our old home."

"Aha," interrupted Dad. "That's why it was a haven—from the troubles they'd been going through. Oh, I'm sorry, please go on."

"No problem," said Mrs. Renton. "That makes sense. Now, let's see, where was I? *There would be more room at the manor, of course, but that will have to wait until all is finished there. Please be assured that I am safe, praise God, but it appears you left just in time. Our fears were well founded. It was only scarce five days after you left that Jonathan brought us word that the Germans had executed Bell, fearing his alliance with the British. Naturally, any British citizens are now suspect and several have already been arrested including, I am sad to say, your friends the Olivers. Evidently I had only moments to spare, and I just had time to retrieve the mission records and escape out the back door and across the orchard. I wish now, of course, that I had left with you when the first rumblings of unrest reached us, but who would have guessed that the crisis would come upon us so quickly? The Lord is not surprised, however, and we must rest in that assurance."*

The old lady paused for a moment and looked up. "Are you following any of this?"

The kids shook their heads. Dad spoke up from the front seat. "I think this was written during World War One just at the time when the Germans were rounding up any British people living in Cameroon. Germany was at war with Britain, you see. The Squire's family must have made it out just in time—except his dad that is."

"Would you mind continuing," said Mom. "This is interesting."

Mrs. Renton nodded and found her place again. *"I cannot tell you where I am in case this letter is discovered, but I can say that I am safe for the time being. Our friend (you know who I mean) has agreed to smuggle this out on the next ship. There is still some traffic between here and Europe, and he assures me he knows who to give it to so it can make it to you.*

And now, my dearest, can you be brave? I need to tell you that I have had a severe attack of fever and it has left me very weak. My hosts here have confided that they are fearful of my life. I know what you are thinking, but I insisted on writing this in my own hand, though against much protest. Of course, there is almost no hope for medicine, and the Germans are searching ever harder for us in hiding, having been prompted somehow that several escaped their initial round up. I confess that I often think it would be best for them to find me. Then the suspense

162

would be at an end and perhaps I would even receive some medical help—not that I am clinging on to this life, but I do so want to see you all again on this side of glory and want you to be spared 'sorrow upon sorrow.' Either way, we must rest in the assurance that God is in control, sovereign over the affairs of men.

Please give the children each a kiss from me. Tell them to be brave. Trust our Heavenly Father and your faith will suffice. Know that you are constantly in my prayers. I must end now as they are waiting for me. Yours in expectation of a joyful reunion, Jowan."

Mrs. Renton put the note down on her lap and looked around at the others. This letter had certainly touched her deeply, but what did it all mean and how did it relate to the note from Uncle Kenwyn? She smiled apologetically. "Well, yes. That *was* interesting. It must be the Squire's father who wrote the letter." She laughed nervously. "But I'm not sure why he wanted me to read it right now."

She folded it carefully and picked up the second one. "I suppose I'll just go ahead and read the next." She held up the second envelope. "It just says *Mrs. Penrow* on the outside, so it looks like this is also probably for Elaine, Uncle Kenwyn's mother."

She took out the letter. It also looked old and fragile and she carefully unfolded it on her lap.

"So is this one from the same guy hiding in Africa?" piped up Stevie.

"Shhh, dear," said Mom. "We'll find out. Let Mrs. Renton continue."

The old lady adjusted her glasses and began to scan the letter. She found it rather interesting. "It looks like this was written by someone in a hurry, or perhaps they just didn't have very good writing." She looked up at the others. "It's in a language that I don't recognize, but someone has penciled in a translation line by line. It's a bit hard to read, but I'll try." She looked back down. "Here we go. It starts with a greeting to a Mrs. Penrow. I'll keep going. Let's see." She cleared her throat.

"So sorry to bring you very bad news. Your mister was very sick. We tried to help but no medicine. We prayed but God said no, I want him with me. He is gone now to be with God.'"

The old lady was suddenly having trouble speaking. Tears sprung into her eyes. Mom reached over and laid her hand on her arm.

"I'm alright, I'm alright." Mrs. Renton dabbed her eyes with her handkerchief and wiped her nose. "Thank you, dear, but I'll be okay. It doesn't take much to wet my eyes these days. I'll keep going." She shifted a little in her seat and took a fresh hold of the letter, trying to speak clearly so the whole family could hear. "The writer continues, *'So sorry. I want to say that I am very full of thankfulness for his life. I would not be following Jesus if he had not come to speak with me. I was walking in darkness, but now I have light. His sacrifice was very great and I am sad for you, but want to say that I think his life had great value. I will pass on the light to others. I do not fear the Germans. I have Jesus. If Mister Jowan risked everything for me, I can risk everything too. I hope and pray you get this letter from my hand to yours. I am your grateful friend, Samuel Ndika.'"*

Mrs. Renton looked up. "That's it."

The family was silent, each processing what they'd heard. Finally Stevie spoke up. "So I don't understand. What happened?"

"Well, the letter was from a friend of Mr. Penrow, the Squire's father," said Dad, trying to speak loudly from the front while keeping his eyes open for the upcoming turn. "Unfortunately, it seems that he died out there. I guess it was from malaria. There weren't as many medicines available back then like there are now. And it sounded like he was in hiding from the Germans so he couldn't get to a hospital."

Emily had a sudden thought. "Don't you remember that missions book Mom had us read. They used to call Africa the 'white man's graveyard.' There were so many diseases that missionaries could get."

"And didn't some of them pack their belongings in a coffin when they shipped them to Africa," put in Rachel. "I guess so that they had one there if they died."

This was too much for Stevie. "No way! Why did they go if they thought they were going to die?"

Mrs. Renton pricked up her ears. She was interested in hearing the answer too.

Mom tried to choose her words carefully, realizing that this was an opportunity for the lady to learn something as well. "Well, they were obeying God. He loves all the nations of the world and wants them to know about Him, and so He calls people to go as missionaries to tell them the good news about Jesus. When Jesus changes someone's life— when they're forgiven and saved by Him—they want to please Him by giving their lives to Him, and sharing the good news with others. Mr. Penrow loved the African people more than he loved his own life."

"A life worthwhile," murmured Emily, remembering the previous clue.

Mrs. Renton was silent, trying to digest it all. Stevie too was thinking hard, his forehead furrowed in concentration.

Mom was wondering if she should try to say something more when she suddenly noticed something out the window. "We need to turn left, right here at the intersection!"

Dad had been focused on the conversation in the back again, and had almost missed the road. He gave a sheepish grin. "Thanks, dear. So sorry."

The van had just crossed a large concrete bridge over a meandering river, a fair-sized town of slate-grey roofs visible on the far side.

"That's Wadebridge," added Dad. "So, was there anything more in the letter Mrs. Renton?"

The old lady looked down at the sheets in her hand. "That's it for the letter from the man in Africa. I'm really not sure what either of them have to do with the inheritance."

The family looked at each other. They weren't sure either. This was all so strange.

"Was there more to read in the other letter?" said Stevie.

"Maybe there's another clue," added Danny, ready to do some more detective work.

"If you don't mind," said Mom, worried that they might be bothering the lady a bit too much.

164

"No, no. I'm ready, if you are." Mrs. Renton held up the letter from the Squire again and scanned it for a moment. "Alright. Here's where we left off. *'You may not understand right now why I included that story about my father, but I pray you will later. God's Word, the Bible, says "Trust in the Lord and do good, dwell in the land and enjoy safe pasture. Delight yourself in the Lord and He will give you the desires of your heart.' Psalm 37 verses 3 and 4. Take that to heart, Ruthie."*

Rachel stiffened. That was the same verse her Dad had mentioned at the beach the other day. Dad didn't miss the reference either, and grinned to himself.

"Now, are you ready for your next clue?" Mrs. Renton continued reading. *"You might have to do a little sleuthing, but I'm sure you'll enjoy it. Here we go:*

My game is almost over, one move and then the prize.
Find the winning square and then take note of where it lies.
Look through the City of Auckland, Another board you'll spy.
Locate the square, in looking there beneath the clue will lie.'"

Mrs. Renton finished and looked enquiringly round at the others, not knowing what to think. *What was Uncle Kenwyn doing with all this?* And she didn't understand the Bible verse at all. She hadn't read the Bible in years. How could she take it to heart? She forced a light laugh. "Well, well. Another clue. And this one seems even more difficult than the last. Do any of you have any ideas?"

"Would you possibly mind reading it again," said Emily politely. "It's a little long."

The old lady read it again slowly, and there was silence as each person digested what they'd heard.

Finally, Rachel spoke up. "Um, did anyone else notice that he says his game is almost over? Do you think that means that this is the last clue?" To her inward surprise she wasn't feeling as relieved as she thought she would. This was actually really interesting.

"It could be," agreed Mom. "That would be good news, wouldn't it?"

"Yes, I suppose it would," said Mrs. Renton, "but I confess I don't feel like I've learned much in the process. I mean, I'm not sure if I've learned what Uncle Kenwyn wanted me to learn."

Mom pursed her lips. That's was true. Surely God had more in mind than just the lady getting some money or something in the inheritance.

Danny had been thinking hard. "But it says there's a board. That sounds like a real game; you know, a board game. Maybe with squares, like on my chutes and ladders."

"Perhaps," said Rachel doubtfully. "But what about the city of Auckland? We're supposed to look through it. Is that a place in Cornwall?" Even as she said the words, she regretted them. She didn't want to go driving all over some city when they could be at the beach.

"I think the city must be around here somewhere," said Stevie, sounding as authoritative as possible.

"I haven't heard about a city named Auckland in Cornwall," said Dad from up front. "Ooops, this is where we're supposed to turn! There's a sign for Tintagel pointing left."

"That's right," said Mom, relieved that Dad had been paying attention, since she herself had forgotten to. She turned to Mrs. Renton. "Have you heard of an Auckland somewhere around?"

"No, I haven't. The only Auckland I've heard of is in New Zealand, but we're obviously not supposed to look around there are we?"

The kids' eyes grew wide, but Dad quickly put that possibility to rest. "No, no. That can't be the case. We'll just have to think harder."

"And pray," reminded Mom gently. "God's the one who's got this all figured out."

Does He though? Thought the old lady. She wasn't sure of that at all.

Chapter 11 - Followed

"We're almost there," said Dad from up front. "I think we're just going to have to table it for now and give this clue some time to percolate."

For the last ten minutes the family and Mrs. Renton had been having a lively but unprofitable discussion. So far this particular clue, with all its many facets, had quite stumped them.

"Okay, dear," said Mom. "Kids, grab your wind-breakers. Even though it looks warm out there, there's quite a breeze and it's bound to be even stronger on the cliffs."

The van entered the town and turned left onto a wide, tidy street lined with an assortment of white-washed houses under gray slate roofs, some with brightly-colored bunting strung between them. The kids sat up straighter and peered out the windows in interest. Though still not the official tourist season, there was a fair number of people strolling the sidewalks or poking curious noses into the souvenir shops and cafés.

Danny nudged Stevie and pointed at a shop whose window displayed an assortment of swords, axes and armor. Stevie gave a knowing smile. This looked like a cool place to spend some birthday money. He started daydreaming about buying a real sword of his own. That would be really useful, especially if he had to fight a bad guy.

His thoughts were interrupted by the van turning off the main street into a large parking area. No-one noticed the brown sedan that followed them in about thirty seconds later.

Dad pulled into a parking spot about halfway back. He switched off the engine and turned back to look at the others. "Okay, this is Tintagel. We thought we'd explore the castle and then get some lunch and take a stroll through the shops. How does that sound?"

Everyone nodded. That sounded great. They jumped out of the van, Emily remembering to help Mrs. Renton carefully down. The sky was a bright azure blue, dotted with light clouds, but a stiff breeze ruffled their hair, and they were glad to pull on their jackets. Dad led the way to the main street, pointing out the ancient, stone post office building on the far side. The kids looked at it in interest. It seemed to be slumbering under the weight of its age, its old tile roof slumping crazily in numerous places.

"How old is it?" wondered Danny as they crossed the street.

"Fourteenth century," said Dad. "That means about six or seven-hundred years old."

"Wow!" Stevie was impressed. "That's like really old. Like the oldest thing I've ever seen! Like before they had cars and movies and stuff."

"Yes, like, that old," said Mom, rolling her eyes.

The family trooped along, following Dad. Emily walked beside Mrs. Renton, with Mom trying to make sure they weren't going too fast for the old lady. At a bend in the road another street led off steeply down between two low stone walls. A prominent sign informed them that it was the way to Tintagel Castle, and no motor vehicles were allowed, but that there were Land Rover rides down the hill for a fee.

"This way to the castle," announced Dad, steering them to the downhill route. "And no, we're not driving down," he added, noting the kids' hopeful looks. "We're walking. We can use the exercise."

"If that's okay with you," said Mom to Mrs. Renton. The old lady nodded, making up her mind that it would be.

The road narrowed down to a wide footpath lined with waving grasses and as they trooped along Stevie, with his head down, began to wonder if it would ever end. He tugged as his dad's jacket. "Is this really the way to King Arthur's castle?"

"What does that say?" Dad pointed to a signpost they were just passing.

"Er, castle something?"

"Right. It says 'Castle Main Entrance' and what do you see up ahead?"

Stevie looked up and gave a little gasp. The path they were on continued to drop steeply down to where a triangle of cobalt blue flecked with white formed the backdrop to a rocky cove. Rugged slopes swept up from the road on both sides mantled with stunted grass flocked with wildflowers. As Stevie followed the cliff line up to the left he could now see, silhouetted against the glare, the outlines of what looked like fortifications.

"King Arthur's castle! It's really real!" gushed the boy.

Dad gave an apologetic look. "Well, I'm sorry to disappoint you, but they don't actually think this was his castle. He's a bit of a fictional character, you know. That means we don't really know if he existed," he added, noticing the boy's puzzled look.

Stevie face fell, and Dad hastened to explain. "Just because we're not sure doesn't mean it isn't true. Let's explore the castle and then you can let me know whether you think the legend is true or not."

Stevie perked up at that. "Okay. I will!"

"And a ruined castle is really fun to explore," assured Dad, "and you can try and picture what it must have been like when people were living there."

The lad gave a big grin. Maybe they might find some old piece of armor or sword or something. "Okay, let's do it!" he exclaimed, yanking on his dad's arm.

The sunny lane leading down to the sea was now a rough, graveled path, and as they walked along Danny realized that his shoelace had worked its way untied. As he bent down to fix it, he had a sudden thought and glanced nervously behind him, struggling to master the anxiety that kept welling up inside. He kept imagining that the mean guy was tailing them, ready to pop into view at a moment's notice.

He could see several people following them down the trail: a young couple pushing a baby in a stroller, two giggling teenagers, and a bearded man in a cap and raincoat. As he paused for a closer look, the man stopped and fumbled in his pocket for something. After an anxious scrutiny of the man's face, Danny breathed a sigh of relief. It definitely wasn't the guy from the café. He hurriedly tied his shoe and dashed off to catch up with the others.

Kennedy slumped in one of the big armchairs in the sitting room, crunching salted peanuts and thinking hard. Ever since that time many years ago when he had first heard about the estate auction he had been massively intrigued. He had already learned of the Squire's unique collection from Jennings, of course, and knew how valuable it was. The Squire was apparently quite the historian and had been obtaining various artifacts for years. Jennings had overheard him talking about a certain piece that was evidently priceless, though what it was he hadn't been able to catch.

Then, when Jennings had informed him that the Squire had suddenly become ill and much of his collection was going to be auctioned off, he had seen his chance. Surely, with the Squire out of the picture, he could get his hands on some valuable pieces for dirt cheap. Well, not dirt cheap perhaps, but at least quite a bit under their value. And there was the distinct possibility that even the priceless item, whatever it was, might be had for a song.

Then had come his unexpected financial crisis, and with it a choking desperation. The Squire's collection seemed suddenly to be his only hope for economic survival, and from that point on the thought of striking it big with this mystery artifact had gnawed constantly at his mind. He could still recall that hollow feeling of despair when the auction closed and not one bargain had been seized, not to mention the complete absence of anything remotely priceless. Most of the valuable stuff had been given to charity. *Charity!* As if he wasn't a candidate himself. After putting all his hopes there, he had come away with nothing.

And then that moment in the hallway, when he had overheard the Squire's lawyer talking with some friend of his—talking about a priceless artifact that the Squire didn't want to have sold off. He was going to give it to someone as an inheritance. Someone who wouldn't yet know its value, but who he hoped would one day understand what it was worth. That was why the news from Jennings about the inheritance and Mrs. so-and-so had been such a lifeline to him. Surely he could handle one old lady.

But now it was all at risk of collapsing again! *What was that family doing? How did they know Renton? What had they discovered?* He tried to slow down and recall any of the conversation he had overheard in the sitting room. That's right, they were talking about a photo. In fact, they seemed to have found something on the back—a letter or note wasn't it?

Kennedy jumped to his feet. *The dad had said he was going to put the photo back.*

He had to find that photo.

❧❦

The path up to the castle was really just a narrow track zigzagging up the cliff face, the crumbling walls of the fortress looming above. The kids, drawing from an apparently hidden reservoir of energy, tore off ahead, excited to see what lay at the top. The adults followed slowly behind in the warm sunshine, Dad trying to restrain his long strides and keep a pace more measured with that of the ladies.

Mom glanced anxiously at Mrs. Renton, hanging on to her arm at her side. "This is quite a climb. I'm sorry we didn't know it would be this steep. Are you okay?"

"Oh, yes, I really need the exercise," the old lady assured her, but there was a note of uncertainty in her voice. This did look to be more of a challenge than she had thought. The road down to the entrance had been much longer than she had anticipated and she was already quite tired. Her pride was having trouble accepting it, but truly her age had caught up with her. What made it doubly hard to accept was the active lifestyle she had enjoyed for so many years.

"We'll stop at the top and have a good rest," assured Dad, interrupting her thoughts. He was feeling the climb too, and realized rather ruefully that exercise hadn't been much of a priority lately. He managed to extract the crumpled visitor's guide from his jacket pocket as he puffed on. "It looks like there's one part of the castle right at the top here, and then a path and bridge to the rest of the castle further out on the cliff. There's got to be some place to sit up there."

Sure enough it wasn't too much longer before they spied a welcome sight. The path topped out near the summit and turned along the base of a jutting crag lined with broken but still imposing stone battlements. A small building under a sloping, wooden roof was nestled up next to the cliff where a bored-looking man was checking tickets. Lining the path at this point, a low, stone wall seemed positioned perfectly for weary climbers. The adults lurched over to it like stumbling desert travelers sighting an oasis, the kids waving and encouraging them on.

Mrs. Renton and Mom flopped gratefully onto a flattish section and Dad wiped his sweaty forehead with the back of his hand.

"Can we explore?" said Rachel excitedly.

"It looks like there's lots to see," put in Danny. Stevie was bouncing up and down again beside him.

"Well, we need a bit of a rest," said Dad, glancing at his wife who nodded vigorously. Mrs. Renton had gone slower and slower as they approached the top, and Mom had wondered if she was even going to make it all the way.

The kids looked at each other in concern. Rachel elbowed Emily who glared at her, but then stepped forward, a reluctant spokesperson. "Um, may we please explore around here a bit ourselves? We won't go too far." The others nodded vigorously in agreement.

Dad smiled at their eager faces. "Okay, but don't go over the bridge to the island. Stay on this side."

"Island?" queried Rachel. That sounded kind of exciting.

Dad produced the guide again and flattened it out. "Here's where we are. Up above us on that crag is what's called the upper ward. Ahead is the lower ward. On the other side of that is a path down to a bridge. The bit over on the other side is called the island," Dad continued. "It is almost an island of rock." He stuffed the guide back in his pocket and walked over to the booth. They had got their tickets down below and he showed their receipt and called over his shoulder. "Okay, you can go start looking now, and I'll join you in about ten minutes."

"And don't go near the cliff edge!" shouted Mom after the kids rapidly retreating backs. The steep drop-offs round and about had left her rather concerned.

Mrs. Renton was watching the interplay with tired amusement. This was so much better than just being alone at home she had decided, no matter how tired she was. She was still struggling with that gnawing hint of regret that she had spurned the only real chance she'd had of having a family. Somehow this family was touching on that unmet need and soothing it somewhat.

"You can wait here even longer if you like," suggested Dad, plonking down next to the others. "I don't mind taking the kids around for a spell. I'll do it in a few minutes. We can check back with you whenever you like."

"Okay, thanks," said Mom. "That'll give us time to decide what we want to do."

⋙⋘

Jennings paused as he reached the top of the path. He could see the family grouped together just ahead. *This was ridiculous.* How on earth was he supposed to keep tabs on them without being seen? Were they even following a clue, or just having a day out? Maybe Kennedy had been mistaken. He had no idea. This could be a complete waste of time.

He watched as the family discussed something and then groaned inwardly as the kids tore off in a different direction. Now who was he supposed to stick with?

⋙⋘

Dad stretched out his legs, enjoying this moment of peace. Across the valley and up on the hill beyond he could see the bulk of the Camelot Castle Hotel, still there after all these years, and still looking like a miniature castle itself with its crenelated roof line, standing sentinel at the top of the headland. *There is so much history here*, he thought. He would love to just hang around Cornwall and not worry

171

about those dratted magazine articles. With all the clue business he had actually forgotten about them for a bit, yet there they were still, looming in the background, and every day brought him closer to the crisis point. He set his jaw defiantly. No, he wasn't going to think about that. He was on vacation. He shot a brief prayer skywards and forced himself to tune in to the lively conversation going on next to him. Mrs. Renton was apparently telling his wife about her adventures as a journalist in the Middle East. It sounded very interesting, and would be just the ticket to get his mind off of a more painful subject. He checked his watch. He still had a few minutes. He leaned closer to listen in.

❧❦❧

Jennings strolled nonchalantly over, showed his receipt at the booth and took a seat a little further along on the wall. He had seen no other alternative—he couldn't run all over creation trying to keep up with those kids. Besides, the adults were the ones he was interested in. If he was going to learn anything, it would be from them.

❧❦❧

The kids passed between two tall, rough, slate columns that must have formed the main gateway to the castle and found themselves in a wide grassy courtyard, surrounded by an irregular, crumbling wall pierced by small, ragged gaps that must have once been windows. There was a sign on a pedestal just ahead and they decided to check it out. It had an artist's rendition of what the castle may have looked like, along with a short story about the castle. Emily scanned it quickly and tried to summarize it for Stevie.

"So this says that it was built around 1230 AD. That's about 800 years ago."

"Wow," breathed Stevie. He ran his hand along the ragged, slate wall at his side. "I'm touching something 800 years old. Is that as old as Jesus?"

Rachel and Danny giggled.

"What? What did I say?" frowned Stevie.

Emily managed to keep a straight face. "Nothing. Jesus was on the earth about 2000 years ago, but this castle is still really, really old."

They admired the painting on the sign and tried to picture the ruined walls around them in good repair. It was a little hard to do.

Rachel tugged at her sister's arm. "Let's check around a bit."

They ran over to where a few stone steps led up to a stone platform against one of the walls. From the top there was a dramatic view down to the buildings and pathways at the head of a rocky cove where frowning rugged cliffs sliced into the ocean.

"Look," said Rachel, pointing to another sign. "This is the lower courtyard."

"It was the first line of defense I guess," said Emily, looking back behind them.

"Did it ever get captured?" Stevie wanted to know.

"It doesn't say," said Emily. "It would be pretty hard to attack this place though."

172

They were all silent for a moment, picturing what it might have been like if an enemy were assaulting the castle. The sheer cliffs and steep paths must have made it almost impossible.

Stevie could clearly imagine the scene. "The castle guys might have hidden behind the wall until the enemy got really close and then popped on up and thrown stuff at them."

Danny closed his eyes, seeing the castle as it used to be, whole and strong with its bright flags snapping in the wind. He could almost hear the frenzied cries of the defenders lining the walls, launching arrows and hurling rocks down on the advancing foe.

"I wish it was all still here," said Stevie with a sigh, interrupting his thoughts.

"Come on," said Emily, grabbing his hand. "It's still pretty cool. Let's see what's next."

As she climbed back down the steps, Rachel hesitated and glanced towards the ruined gateway. Her dad had said he was coming soon, and all this talk of attacking and ambushing had given her an idea.

"I'll be right there," she yelled towards the others.

Keeping her eyes on her dad, she sprinted back to the gateway and flung herself panting against the ruined wall next to the opening. Her heart pounding in her chest and adrenaline running high, Rachel forced herself to calm down. She found herself smiling. It wasn't every day she got to play a trick on Dad.

❧ ❧

Jennings made a loud impatient noise through his nose, then, realizing what he had done, tried to cover it up with some fake sniffing and coughing. To his disgust that couple and the lady weren't discussing the inheritance, or anything of interest at all. This was such a ridiculous idea.

His morose thoughts were interrupted by a sudden strident rendition of the 1812 Overture again, a bit muffled, but still way too loud, blasting out from the phone in his jacket pocket. He jumped to his feet and scampered further up towards the gateway, trying to get out of hearing of the group on the wall.

❧ ❧

Rachel was getting a little bored. She had finally decided it was worth it risking a peek to see if Dad was coming when a sudden burst of music caused her to duck back down. *What was that? Was it a phone?* There was a bearded guy in a long overcoat trotting up the path towards the gateway. *Would he blow her cover?* Dad might get curious as to what was going on.

Rachel pressed herself back against the wall, her heart beating crazily again. It would be worth it, she assured herself, if she could just give her Dad a shock.

❧ ❧

Jennings clawed at his pocket, berating himself for having forgotten to turn his ringtone down. As he pressed and prodded, the sound was mercifully cut short. Snatching the phone out, he stabbed the call button.

"What is it?" he hissed.

"Where are you? Have you found out anything?"

173

As he opened his mouth to reply he suddenly realized it was getting easier and easier to assert himself. "Tintagel, and no, because you probably blew my cover by calling me!"

❧❧

Emily and the boys had decided to check out the upper courtyard—an airy, grassy enclosure lined with more tumbledown slate walls. The ragged holes in the ruins formed perfect windows to the wild scene beyond, framing the untamed coastline where crying gulls wheeled far below, skimming the sheer, foreboding cliffs and foaming breakers.

Emily had a sudden thought and dragging her eyes from the view looked back over her shoulder. "Hey, where's Rachel?"

"Probably still down below," said Stevie, not bothering to turn around. "What's she doing?"

"I don't know, but maybe we should get her."

"No, no," chorused the boys. They liked it up there—the briskness of the air and the almost menacing aspect of the coastline stirring up a feeling of excitement and adventure.

"Well, okay," said Emily, hoping Rachel wouldn't mind, but not really in the mood herself to go and ask her. "Maybe she'll be up here soon."

❧❧

Rachel had her back against the wall, trying to stay very still despite her aching legs and the uncomfortableness of the rough stones poking into her back. She couldn't see Dad now which meant that, for all she knew, he could be on his way. On the other side of the wall she could hear the man talking on his phone. She tried not to listen, knowing it wasn't very polite, but it was really impossible not to. He was right there. She suddenly stiffened. *What was he saying?*

❧❧

Jennings glanced back at the group chatting on the wall. "Yes. The kids are off somewhere, but I'm keeping the others in sight and in hearing range. At least I was until you called." He paused to listen.

"Look, I've got to go. I'll call you if I find out anything. Got that? I'll call you. You just keep working on figuring out about the next clue."

He snapped his phone shut and stuffed it back in his pocket, a little surprised at his own boldness. Kennedy wouldn't appreciate it, that was certain. He stood there shaking his head; then, with a sudden thought, he yanked out his phone again and made sure that the ringer volume was turned way down. Now how was he supposed to get back within listening range of the group on the wall?

As he looked up, he realized with an awful shock that the dad was almost on top of him, having come up the path without him noticing. He quickly shaded his eyes with his hand and made as if he was looking at the view across the valley.

Dad ignored him. He was on a mission to find the kids. Rachel, behind the wall, was still trying to puzzle out what the man had said. It was certainly weird how he had mentioned a clue and all that, but it couldn't have been anything to do with what they were doing, could it? What would this guy, who she'd never

174

seen before, and who was miles away from the inn, have to do with Mrs. Renton's inheritance? But it was still weird.

Rachel sprang up, letting out a squeal. Her dad had come around the corner, seen her crouching there and had given her a poke in the side.

"Aha," he cried in delight. "Got you! Lying in wait were you?"

"Er, well..." Rachel wasn't sure what to say. She was all befuddled, still wondering about the man.

"Where are the others?" wondered Dad, looking around.

"We're up here!" came a yell from somewhere above.

Rachel and Dad looked up and saw the others waving from up on the crag.

"Let's go up and join them," said Dad, starting off to where a wooden stairway climbed up the side.

Rachel hesitated, wondering if she should mention anything about the man.

"Are you coming?" said Dad over his shoulder.

Well, maybe it was just a silly coincidence, she decided. She thrust the man out of her thoughts and ran to catch up with her dad.

"That's amazing," said Mom, shaking her head in disbelief.

Mrs. Renton had been continuing to tell her of some of the adventures she had had in her travels as a journalist. She had been briefly married to a photographer, but it had been a rocky marriage from the start and he had left her after a couple of months. She heard later he had lost his life on assignment in Africa. She had traveled all over the world, been in two plane crashes, one civil war, and even been captured by rebels and held hostage for a time.

The old lady nodded. "I've certainly had a full life, though it's had more than its fair share of sorrows."

Mom rested her hand on the lady's worn, wrinkled one. "We were so sorry to hear about your parents, and then your husband too, and after such a short time together. Thank you for entrusting that story to me."

Tears came to Mrs. Renton's eyes and she hastily dabbed them with her hankie.

Mom struggled to come up with the words to comfort the old lady. "Your life has been full of so much—so many challenges, difficulties, dangers...and adventure. But God has certainly faithfully taken care of you."

"Well, yes, I suppose." Mrs. Renton had never really looked at it from that perspective.

"And I know He's still going to." Mom looked into Mrs. Renton's eyes and smiled, trying to sound as confident as she could. *Please do it,* she prayed.

Kennedy was thinking really hard. The family had been looking at a photo, and the dad said he was going to put it back somewhere, but where? *How on earth could he remember something like that?* He pursed his lips, and leant back against the sideboard. At least he was alone for a bit. He had carefully noted that Mrs. Tremannon was outside hanging her washing, and her husband was pottering around in the vegetable patch. The house was quiet as a tomb. He scanned around the big dining room. There were a number of old photos on the walls. *Did the dad say he was going to put it back in here?* He didn't think so. And maybe that was the way to figure this out—by process of elimination.

Had he said the sitting room? No, because that's where they had been talking. *The hallway right outside?* No, because he had been hiding there himself, and he would have remembered if the dad had said he was going to return the photo there. Same went for the staircase. *What about the entry hall?* It came back to him in a flash. The dad was worried someone would come out of the kitchen and notice the photo was gone. Kennedy smiled to himself. That was it—and not so impossible after all.

◈◈

Dad and Rachel had a quick look around the upper courtyard with the others, and then they all tromped back down the steps and strolled over to the far side where there was a narrow gap in the low, crumbling wall. Dad pulled out the guide again and pointed. "That, gang, is the Island. Pretty cool, huh?"

The sight was impressive. They were standing at the tip of the peninsular, hundreds of feet above the sea, and right at their feet the cliff fell away down to a mass of tumbled rock with foaming waves breaking against both sides. Beyond rose a massive island of rock, round-topped and crowned with stunted bushes and grasses. The island dropped sheerly away on all sides, forming an impressive and seemingly impregnable natural fortress, and they could see more castle ruins with the remains of buildings, arches and walls. The wind was definitely stronger now, exposed as they were now to its full force. The tall oat grass and broom bushes around the ruins were being tossed vigorously back and forth.

"So when did King Arthur live here?" said Stevie, leaning into the wind and furrowing his brow.

"Well, they're not sure he did," said Dad. "There was a legend that Arthur had a kingdom somewhere around here."

"So maybe he did have a castle here at some time?" Stevie really didn't want to give up on that idea.

"You know, he may have. If I was a king around here, I think I'd build my castle right on this spot too. What a great position. It must have been almost impossible for an enemy to take it."

Stevie nodded. "Can we go and see?"

"Yup, we go down here." Dad gestured at the stairway in front of them. As he did, he noticed out of the corner of his eye that the cloudbank seemed to be approaching fairly rapidly. "Let's be careful, but we might have to hurry a bit on the other side. The weather looks a bit iffy."

Dad led the way down the steep, wooden steps that curved to the bridge spanning the chasm. They had to watch their feet as they went, all having a tendency to gaze at the view ahead instead of where they were walking.

If they had thought to look behind them, they would have seen, silhouetted against the sky at the top of the cliff, a tall figure watching them intently.

Jennings was facing a nail-biting dilemma. The ladies were still chatting, but the dad and kids were disappearing from sight on the far side of the courtyard. If he chose to stay there eavesdropping, the others might find actually find a clue. But did he really want to keep chasing them all over this place, just on the hope of seeing something? Might they just be exploring the castle for fun?

Aye, but there was the rub. He couldn't chance it. He had to follow them.

Jennings snuck carefully over and watched as the family reached the bridge and started trooping up the steep staircase on the other side. It looked like a daunting climb, and not one he relished doing at all. Why, oh why had he ever told Kennedy about that stupid inheritance anyway? What had it got him so far? Just a bunch of wasted time, not to mention getting him involved in criminal activity that could even get him time in prison! Was there even a possibility of them still beating the old lady to the prize?

Jennings looked off into the distance. Maybe, just maybe it was possible. And it could be a nice chunk of money. He was never going to strike it rich running his shop. This could be his one chance to make it big. He could sense himself being swayed and gave himself up to the feeling.

Glancing back, he noticed that the family were well on their way up the stairs. He had a sudden feeling of panic. If there was any chance at all, he couldn't lose them. Vaulting through the opening in the walls, he started down the path to the bridge.

Kennedy could immediately tell which photo it must have been—the one hanging slightly crooked over by the kitchen door. He listened carefully. There didn't seem to be anyone around. He grabbed it and studied it. It was an old photo with two couples standing in front of a fireplace. *So what?*

He turned the picture over and examined the back. There were four clear tape marks where something had obviously been attached. He narrowed his eyes. This was irritating beyond belief. And not just irritating. It was potentially disastrous. The family was definitely involved, and worse still they were keeping ahead of him in the quest. He forced himself to be optimistic. There were still two small things in his favor. They had no reason to suspect that he was on the same trail, and he had some leverage over that red-headed kid. Maybe he could use that to his advantage somehow.

Puffing and panting, Dad and the kids finally made it to the top of the stairs, stepped through an old arched doorway and found themselves in another open area lined with partially ruined walls. This looked much more complete, however, than anything they had encountered on the other side. Most of the walls were in much better shape and there was even an arch with what looked like part of a tower.

With a sudden thought, Dad checked his watch. Even though the ladies had assured him they were doing fine, he didn't want to take too much time over here, and there was the matter of the weather, too. "Okay, I know we want to see as much as possible, but we can't really dilly dally. Are you ready for the lightning tour?"

The kids nodded.

"Okay," said Dad. "Follow me."

❧❦

Feeling like his calf muscles were going to explode, Jennings finally reached the top of the stairs just in time to see the family running off. He couldn't believe it. He was already out of breath, but a break was out of the question. The way they all seemed in a hurry, they might well be on the trail of the next clue. With mounting despair he realized he would have to force himself to keep going.

❧❦

They had scurried past a ruined chapel, a walled garden and a well, and were now admiring a metal statue of a hooded figure with a massive sword, perched on a rocky hillock near the cliffs. As Dad took a picture of the grinning kids, he noted that it was definitely getting very misty--the horizon line had already vanished. It surprised him how quickly the weather seemed to be changing.

A sharp gust of wind ruffled Rachel's jacket and she shivered. "Dad, it looks really foggy out there." She gestured out to sea. "Do you think we should head back?"

Dad considered. "There's just the tunnel—it's really close and then we'll hightail it."

Rachel nodded and the others followed suit. They didn't want to miss the tunnel, whatever it was.

Dad directed them to where the nearby path descended between rough rocky walls to a low, dark opening. There was a strong, cool breeze in their faces and, stooping a little, Dad led the way in.

❧❦

Jennings came cautiously along the trail, trying to keep his wheezing breath under control. He had just been ready to call it quits for the umpteenth time when he had finally spied the family in the distance. They had apparently paused by a small signpost and then—it was hard to tell from where he was--it seemed like they were going down into a narrow chasm. He waited a moment and then scurried over to where he could read the sign. It was evidently a tunnel to some sort of food storage place. What should he do? He couldn't risk going down. They could be coming back out in any minute.

He looked wildly around him. There was a rocky outcropping about ten yards back down the path from where he could safely watch. He dashed over and flung himself down on a rough patch of grass.

Please don't be long, he thought desperately. It was getting colder and he pulled his jacket closer around himself. His eyes fixed on the entrance, he didn't notice the sea mist suddenly swirling up over the edge of the cliff behind him, quickly swallowing up everything in sight.

178

The floor of the tunnel was made up of large slabs of slate, which, though smooth, were rather uneven, and they had to watch their footing. To their surprise, they could already see the other end—another low archway with diffused light filtering in. For some reason they had expected it to be a dead end. The air was quite cold and Emily could understand now how it would have made a good larder. The sea breeze must have made a fairly constant cooling flow.

"Well this is it I guess," said Dad, apologetically. "We should really get going."

As they stepped out of the far opening into the open air they screeched to a halt, looking around in surprise. They seemed to have surfaced into a completely different world. While they had been in the tunnel the sea mist must have swiftly and silently swirled in, almost obscuring everything in sight. The blue sky and sunshine had disappeared, leaving them in a world of muted light and vague shapes. Dad felt a twinge of concern. He hadn't counted on this. He forced himself to sound cheerful. "Okay, kids, don't worry. It's just a little mist. God's in control."

The rocky path ahead sloped steeply upwards and they were suddenly confronted by a metal railing, looming out of the mist. Apparently this wasn't meant to be an exit, but Dad didn't relish making their way back down the way they'd come. The ground looked solid ahead, so he ducked under the railing and beckoned the others to do the same.

❧❧

Jennings looked around him in sudden alarm. His surroundings were rapidly disappearing in the swirling mist. *Where were the family?* Were they still in the tunnel? Had he missed them?

With a desperate, impulsive decision, he threw caution to the wind and dashed over to where the path descended down to the rocky opening. Screeching to a halt, he leaned forward, straining to catch the sound of voices, but all he could hear was his own blood, pumping in his ears. Creeping downwards, he peered into the tunnel. It was too dark to see very far ahead. He took several cautious steps further and caught sight of the other end, confirming his worst fears. The tunnel was empty. He'd lost them.

Chapter 12 - Something Just Isn't Quite Right

"I hope the others are okay." Mom gave a concerned look to Mrs. Renton who was hastily zipping up her jacket. "What a shock! I wasn't expecting this."

They had decided to go look for the others and had stopped short at the wall of fog that had met them at the top of the staircase.

Mrs. Renton nodded. Hopefully they wouldn't be too long. She was getting quite chilly.

"Please, Lord, help them make it back safe and sound, and soon if it's your will." Mom had prayed aloud without thinking, and even as she heard the words come out of her mouth she wondered what the old lady would think. It was a bit of a risk, letting her know she had prayed. She was hoping to show Mrs. Renton that God was indeed real, and cared about her. What if God didn't answer any time soon?

Even as she was digesting that thought, she felt Mrs. Renton gently tapping her arm, and turned to see an amazed look on the old lady's face.

"There they are coming up the path," she said. She gestured down to where, sure enough, five shadows of varying sizes were emerging from the mist below, quickly resolving into the familiar forms of Dad and the kids. Mom shot a brief smile skywards. That must have been the quickest answer to prayer she had ever had. She looked down again at the family laboring up the path and helloed, waving her hand in excitement.

⛬

The kids talking nineteen to the dozen, they walked back through the courtyard and out to the path leading down to the road, trying to maintain a pace that would be okay for Mrs. Renton while propelled somewhat by the stiff, chilly breeze off the sea. As they stepped carefully down, Emily paused and looked back towards the island. It was amazing to compare how clear the sky was ahead with how socked in it was behind them.

A sharp cry made her turn back in alarm. Mrs. Renton had apparently stumbled right at the end of the path and had had to grab hold of Mom to keep from falling.

"Oh my word, are you alright?" asked Mom, anxiously.

Dad hurried over and offered another steadying arm which Mrs. Renton gratefully accepted. She gingerly rotated her ankle. "Yes, I think so. I just sort of turned my ankle on a stone. I think I just need a minute."

The others gathered round, watching with some concern. Dad's mind was whirring as he tried to figure out what they should do.

"We can wait here as long as you like," said Mom, smiling at the lady. "There's no hurry."

Mrs. Renton slowly put her weight on her ankle and then carefully let go of Mom and Dad. "I think it's alright. I'll just take it easy."

Meanwhile Stevie had been examining the road back up to the town. He suddenly remembered how long that trek had been, and groaned out loud.

"What's up?" said Dad a little sharply, guessing the problem even as he said it.

"I'm hungry, and it's such a long way back."

"Don't whine, please," Dad reminded him. "Mom's got some snacks in her purse, and you can make it back. We'll eat up at the village."

Mrs. Renton was thinking fast. She reached over and patted Stevie's head. "Don't worry about the walk back. I'll take care of that."

The others all looked at her, surprised, but she just smiled. "Come along. You'll see."

⤝⤞

Now this was more like it! Mrs. Renton had insisted on paying for the whole family to take a ride in one of the Land Rovers back up the hill and the kids were grinning at each other in delight as they bounced along. Mom and Dad were both secretly very glad themselves. Not only did this mean they didn't have to encourage any potentially complainy kids up the road, but they didn't have to worry about Mrs. Renton either. They had wondered how she would do trekking back up and it was good to see her safely ensconced in the front seat where the ride was a little less jarring.

"Looks like we were just in time," said Dad, gesturing out the back window. The mist was sweeping further inland, seemingly pursuing them up the hill.

Mom nodded. She leaned close and lowered her voice. "What do you think about Mrs. Renton paying for all this? Did you know she's offered to take us out to lunch, too? Is that okay with you?"

"Really? Wow. I don't know," whispered Dad. "I mean, I appreciate it but it's no small thing taking a whole family out. Do you think she can afford it?"

"Well, that's what's really interesting. She told me she had made a lot of money in her life and had plenty put away still. She said she actually didn't need any money from the Squire's inheritance."

"But she still wants to figure it all out—the clues and all?"

"Uh-huh. She's beginning to realize that for some significant reason he put a lot of effort into all this just for her. I think she's scared about the whole process but intrigued at the same time."

"Well, in answer to your lunch question, I think it's fine. Of course, it's a huge blessing to us, but I think it's a blessing to her too. It's a way for her to say thanks, even though we're not helping her for any reward ourselves." He looked towards the old lady up front. "I think I need to make that clear to her."

❧

Jennings was stumbling forward, straining to pick out the path ahead. The soup-like mist swirled around him, chilling him, seeping through his clothes. It didn't help that the path was so uneven and he had already tripped several times on unseen rocks or roots. He had thought it would be a fairly simple matter to retrace his steps, but now he was seriously beginning to doubt it. His initial impassioned running had, by necessity, slowed to a jog and now his pace could barely even be called walking. Even so his chest was beginning to heave with his breath coming in short pants. He suddenly tripped again and this time found himself tumbling sideways with a yell of fear, coming to a painful rest sprawled in the dirt with his head hanging downwards over the edge. He could sense the drop down to the sea far below and thought he could even hear the surf on the rocks.

That did it. He had always prided himself on being even-tempered, but something in him had just snapped. The resentment that had been simmering all day boiled over in a torrent of swearing. He cursed Kennedy, he cursed the crazy scheme he had found himself caught up in, he cursed his own financial situation that made him even have to consider it, he cursed the family and the old lady and finally he roundly cursed the weather and whoever had made this stupid path so close to the cliff edge.

This is the absolute end, he thought, beginning to sob and not caring a whit that he was doing so. He would get out of this place, go back to Penrithen and call Kennedy and tell him he was finished. Let him do his own dirty work. Let *him* traipse all over creation and almost die—*yes, almost die!*

The thought of Kennedy experiencing this same predicament brought some relief to his misery. He pulled himself painfully to his feet, brushed himself off as best as he could and continued carefully up the path. There was no need to hurry now.

❧

With its bright window boxes and quaint exterior, the café had looked like a good possibility. Pleasant and clean inside with fragrant vases of roses at each table and cheerful watercolors lining the walls, it had turned out to be just what they had hoped for. There was a delicious, savory smell filling the air, and most importantly to Dad, it looked like it wouldn't cost the lady an arm and a leg to foot the bill.

182

The group installed themselves at a round table near the window and eagerly perused the menu. The place was filling up quickly, and a lively chatter competed with the random clanging of pots and pans emanating from what was presumably the kitchen. Dad congratulated himself that they had made it just in time. Everyone ordered quickly for once, Mom and Mrs. Renton choosing soup and salad while the kids and Dad all opting for Cornish pasties and chips. Dad thanked God for the meal and their exciting morning, and after the chorus of amens, Danny and Stevie eagerly filled Mom and Mrs. Renton in on all their adventures.

Despite the busy atmosphere, it wasn't very long before the waitress appeared with a huge tray, loaded with plates of food that she proceeded to place expertly at the right spots.

"Mmm, delicious," said Mrs. Renton, taking a sip of her soup. "This is a lovely place." She ran her hand over the embroidered table cloth. "Thank you again so much for taking me out. It's been harder for me to get out by myself lately."

"It's our pleasure," said Dad, and he meant it. It truthfully was fun having someone else along. "And thank you for lunch!" he added.

"Do you think Mr. Pickwick is doing okay at home?" wondered Emily, suddenly remembering the lady's funny cat. She looked over at Rachel, expecting her to be smiling too, but Rachel was popping fries in her mouth absentmindedly and looking off into space. Apparently she didn't seem to have heard.

"Oh, yes," said Mrs. Renton. "He'll be fine. He's probably made a cup of tea and is curled up watching some TV nature special on flightless birds."

Emily giggled. "But he'll be mad at you when you get back, right?"

Mrs. Renton nodded vigorously. "Oh, yes!"

Mom noticed that Rachel was still off in another world. "Are you alright, dear?" she said, giving her daughter a searching look.

"Oh, yes, I'm alright," said Rachel, snapping out of her stupor. "Just thinking…and hungry," she added hoping to throw Mom off the track. In fact she had been doing a lot of pondering that day. Her conscience had been really bothering her. Was she willing to open the door of her heart a crack and listen to what Jesus was trying to tell her? It was so hard to give up her own plans for this vacation. Giving it all over to God seemed a bit like stepping off a cliff. If they really committed to helping the old lady, it could mean giving up all the possible fun times they might have had. And yet the lady had been so nice, and so grateful, and so...what?...vulnerable? Overhearing that guy today and the possibility, remote as it was, that someone might be trying to take advantage of her—well that had stirred up some compassion, and maybe even some indignation as well. Rachel had a firm sense of justice, and it was awakening her to a cause bigger than her own desires.

She suddenly realized Mom was still looking at her. Was she guessing what she was struggling with? Rachel reddened and looked away, focusing on the view of the street through the window sheers. To her surprise it had started to rain. Not a heavy rain, to be sure—more of a light drizzle. Still, that did limit the choices for what to do after lunch. Was she okay with that? She thought she was.

They could still go shopping, which actually sounded kind of fun. She had a little bit of spending money still.

"Oh, no, it's raining!" Stevie had just looked out the window himself.

"Well, we're safe inside aren't we, and we can still look in the shops," said Dad. "Anyway, there's no rush to finish. Maybe it will stop before we're done." Dad realized that he himself had been wolfing down his food like it was his last meal before leaving a sinking ship. He forced himself to slow down.

"And we could try to help some more with the clue," put in Rachel. Mom looked at her in surprise.

Mrs. Renton looked around at them all. "Well, we could, if you really don't mind."

"No, not all," said Mom.

"Would you mind reading the clue again?" asked Emily "I can't remember it."

"Of course," said Mrs. Renton. She dug in her bag and pulled out the paper.

She was about to start reading when there was a burst of laughter from a nearby table. As she paused for the noise to die back down, the door to the cafe opened and a dripping figure lurched in. The family were all looking at Mrs. Renton, waiting for her to begin; they didn't notice the person look over at them and give a start of surprise.

Jennings couldn't believe it. His mind spiraled into a tornado of whirling thoughts. A minute ago he was done with this whole inheritance thing, but was fate now handing him another chance? Was running into the family again a blessing or a curse? He had to make a decision quickly before they all noticed him.

The sign next to him said *please seat yourself* and that was enough to help him make up his mind. He scurried over to a free table right next to the family. If he sat there with his back to them they wouldn't recognize him, but he should be able to hear whatever they talked about. He picked up a menu and pretended to examine it in detail while keeping his ears wide open for anything interesting.

Mrs. Renton figured it was quiet enough again. She looked around the circle of faces. "Okay, that's better. Are you ready for the clue?"

Everyone nodded, and no-one noticed the man at the next table throw his menu down and grab a pen from his pocket and snatch a paper napkin off the table.

Mrs. Renton read the clue twice through, slowly and clearly so they all could hear.

"My game is almost over, one move and then the prize.
Now find the winning square and then take note of where it lies.
Look through the City of Auckland, another board you'll spy.
Locate the square, in looking there beneath the clue will lie."

Jennings scribbled furiously. *This was amazing!* It was exactly what he had hoped to find out. He looked at his shorthand on the napkin. Yes, he thought he had got it all.

He was interrupted by a cough at his side. The waitress had appeared seemingly out of nowhere.

"'Scuse me, sir, but are you ready?" She pushed an errant curl of hair out of her eyes and poised her pen over her notebook. She noted that the man hadn't even opened his menu yet. *Couldn't he see how busy it was around him?*

Jennings avoided her eyes. "No, I'm not. Can you come back?"

The waitress wasn't to be deterred that easily. "I can wait if you just need a minute."

Jennings didn't appreciate that one bit. He couldn't eavesdrop and order at the same time. He raised his voice a notch, hoping it would get his point across. He really wasn't good at confrontations.

"No, I'm not ready. Give me five minutes, or even better, make it ten."

Rachel, trying to ponder the clue with the rest of the family, was startled out of her thoughts by his voice. There was something a bit familiar about it. She glanced over her shoulder. She could see the profile of the guy at the next table as he looked up at the waitress. She did a double-take. It was the guy up at the castle! She watched as the waitress seemed to be struggling with mastering her emotions, only to suddenly turn and stomp back off to the kitchen. The guy seemed to sense Rachel's stare and shot a quick glance at her. She gasped and hurriedly looked away.

"I still think it's some kind of board game." Danny was saying. "We just need to figure out what it is, and then..."

"I think we should talk about this later," interrupted Rachel, her mind a whirl. "I think we need to let it sit some more."

Dad frowned at her. He guessed what she was up to, and it annoyed him. "No, I think we really need to go over this. We want to help Mrs. Renton, don't we?" he added firmly.

Rachel leaned forward and lowered her voice. "But Dad, I really think we should wait for a bit."

Mrs. Renton was watching the interchange closely. The last thing she wanted was to cause any rift in the family. "It's alright. Yes, I think we should leave it alone for now. Let's not spoil the day."

Dad looked at Mom who shrugged her shoulders, then back at Rachel.

"Please," said Rachel fervently. She put her finger to her lips and leaned her head ever so slightly in the direction of the table next to them.

Dad narrowed his eyes and glanced over to where she had indicated. All he saw was the back of a man apparently scanning his menu up close. He looked back at Rachel. She nodded. Dad took a deep breath. Okay, he would go with it, but what on earth was his daughter worried about? He couldn't wait to find out. He looked around at the family. The other three kids were looking very puzzled.

"Alright, let's finish up and then we can go shopping. We can talk about all this later."

⋞⋟

Jennings didn't get what had happened, but suddenly it seemed like the family had dropped the subject of the clue altogether. What was worse, they were ploughing through their lunches and he hadn't even ordered yet. Where was that wretched waitress?

"Now, what was all that about?" Dad pounced on Rachel as soon as they were all back outside, huddled in the cafe's covered entryway. The others crowded around too, raincoats zipped up and hoods pulled tightly around their faces against the drizzle swirling in and around them.

Mrs. Renton put her arm around Rachel's shoulders and gave a little squeeze. She was feeling awful about all this and wished at this moment that she had never shared her concerns about the inheritance.

Rachel received the hug gratefully, but suddenly found that she wasn't so eager to explain now that everyone was looking at her. "The man next to us," she said slowly. "He was listening, and I saw him. I saw him up at the castle!"

"I don't understand," said Mom. "Why does it matter?"

"I heard him on his phone—when I was hiding, waiting to surprise Daddy."

Danny and Stevie listened wide-eyed. *This was so cool!*

"Okay, go on," said Dad, skeptically, still feeling a bit annoyed.

"He was talking to someone about a clue. He said something about watching us."

"Watching us?"

"Well, watching us kids. Or at least *some* kids." Even as she said it Rachel began to wonder if she wasn't just being silly. "And it seemed like he was listening to us in the café," she added in a quiet voice, feeling decidedly embarrassed now and wishing she hadn't said anything. Now that she was having to explain it, it didn't seem like much of an issue at all.

Dad pursed his lips. He felt Mom's gentle pressure on his arm. A quick glance over at Mrs. Renton and his mind was made up. He swallowed down his annoyance.

"Okay, Rachel, I think I understand. Thank you for your concerns. I think we probably don't have to worry about it though. Whoever he was, he's eating lunch and we're off shopping." He looked around at the others and smiled. "So if you want to brainstorm about the clue as we shop, go on ahead."

Mom nodded. Emily gave a sigh of relief. She hated conflict as well.

Rachel was glad to have gotten off so easily. She would just have to try to put her silly concerns out of her mind.

"Okay, ladies," said Dad brightly, addressing Mom and Mrs. Renton. "Let's get out of the wet. Where would you like to go first?"

Jennings had taken a huge bite of his sandwich and was chewing desperately. The family had already finished up and left, and his own meal had only just appeared. His mind was fully made up now. With the sudden opportunity to overhear the clue, he had some hope again. He would follow this thing through with Kennedy, and maybe he'd even get a chance to stiff him at the end and get the goods all to himself. That was a satisfying little thought. He looked at his scribblings on the napkin. So, what to do now? Was the family finding the answer to the riddle while he was sitting here? He pondered that for a second. As far as he could tell, they hadn't found anything at the castle. Maybe they were as much in the dark as he was. *Now that was an interesting possibility.* Could they just be having a day out? Could their trip here be nothing to do with the inheritance at all?

The old lady was with them though, he reminded himself. Why would they have brought her along if they weren't trying to help her solve the clue? Well, either way he'd better keep up with them.

He looked down at his meal. It would take him forever to plough through all that, but he didn't want to abandon it. He was starving. Coming to a sudden decision he grabbed another napkin, wrapped the rest of the sandwich up and stuffed it in his overcoat pocket. Now where was that waitress again?

Danny wasn't sure he could take much more. After the excitement of the castle, this sudden transition to wandering around countless stores had been too much. If the stores had been interesting, it would have been okay, but instead they had been off-the-charts boring. He checked off a mental list: first a pottery place, then a clothes store, then another clothes store, and now this kitchen place. His legs felt like lead. Why didn't they put couches in these places? He looked over at Stevie who was standing by a display of tea-towels, looking glumly out the window at the weather which had progressed to a full-fledged deluge. *Couldn't they go back to the inn?* At least there they had some games to play.

Danny stiffened suddenly. He had just remembered the scary guy. He was at the inn, waiting for them—him and his scary face and scary hair. The thought of going back there had instantly lost all its appeal, replaced by a slumping feeling of misery.

Stevie turned and noticed his brother. "It's raining. Really raining now," he informed Danny with a sigh. "Why can't we go to a toy store? Or how about that place with the swords and stuff we saw on the way in."

"Let's go boys." Stevie felt his Dad's hands on his shoulder. "Pull up your hoods. We're done here."

Dad held open the door as the family bustled out, the boys slowly bringing up the rear.

"Come on." Dad grabbed their hands. "We need to cross the street and we're going to get soaked if we don't hurry. And I think you'll like the next place. King Arthur's Treasure Trove. I can see swords and shields all over the place!"

Danny looked at Stevie who was suddenly all smiles. As he let his Dad speed them across the street, he let out a whoop of joy.

Jennings had put a quick call in to Kennedy which had turned out to be an exercise in frustration as the phone service been pretty spotty. He had finally made sure Kennedy had the clue written down and then started on what turned out to be a fruitless search for the family. After checking a dozen or so places, he had finally given up and headed back to his car, his rollercoaster emotions having done another plunge downwards.

He was just about to turn down the street to the parking lot when he heard a cry behind him. He swung around, squinting in the pelting rain. *It was that family!* They were heading for a shop—*King Arthur's Treasure Trove*. His luck had returned again. Maybe someone up there liked him after all.

⚜⚜

Talk about a treasure trove! The place seemed like a cross between a toy store and a medieval museum. The walls were hung with all sorts of banners, shields, coats of arms and an assortment of lethal-looking weapons. Tall display cases held glittery jewelry and interesting figurines. Stevie noted a whole bunch of ships in bottles that look pretty cool, and there was a section for puzzles, another for books, and several bins of what might be dressing-up clothes. A suit of armor that Danny eyed rather suspiciously stood sentinel by the door. The kids had to take a moment to decide what to look at first.

"Look with your eyes, not your fingers," reminded Dad. The kids nodded. They'd heard that pronouncement before. Rachel and Emily turned to a cylindrical glass display case near the door, full of attractive crystal figurines, while Danny pulled Stevie over to long counter filled with swords, axes and knives. Dad decided to accompany them. Not every shop owner appreciated eager youngsters with their fingerprints and irresistible urge to handle the merchandise. This particular one, a grim, burly guy in shirt sleeves and a bulging apron looked a bit disapproving at the hoard that had suddenly descended on his shop. It didn't take much effort to imagine the guy with a black hood and axe over his shoulder, straight from some medieval execution scene. *Yes*, he thought, *he would definitely stick close.*

⚜⚜

"Look at these!" gushed Emily. She was pointing at an assortment of tiny crystal castles with colored glass turrets. Lights in the display case made the facets of the buildings shimmer with rainbow hues. "Do you think they're expensive?"

But Rachel was lost in thought again, looking over at Mrs. Renton on her chair.

"Hey," said Emily, elbowing her sister. "Hello?"

"What? Oh, yes...I mean no. Er, what was it again?"

"I said do you think these are expensive?"

"I've no idea. Maybe the price is printed on the bottom."

"Hmm," said Emily bending down to look. The shelves were glass so it wasn't too difficult to see under the bases. Yes, there were the prices.

Rachel turned to look at Mrs. Renton who was sitting in a chair near the book section. The lady's ankle must be bothering her again. It was that fact and the possibility that the guy in the café was trying to steal the lady's inheritance that helped Rachel make up her mind. The lady seemed so vulnerable. Yes, she knew what God wanted her to do and she was finally ready to do it.

"God," she prayed silently. "I want to help the lady. Will you take care of me having a fun vacation? Please help me have a good attitude. I want to do what's right. Thanks."

She waited for a second. Was she imagining it or did she sense a sudden excitement that hadn't been there a moment ago. Had God heard her and answered right away? It did seem like something had happened to both her outlook and her attitude. Could helping the lady even turn out to be fun?

"Rachel, are you listening? They're two pound fifty." Emily nudged her sister again.

"Yes, I am now," Rachel said truthfully. "I think they're beautiful. Are you going to get one with your money? I think you should."

⊰⊱

Dad listened in amusement. Danny was taking his responsibility of teaching Stevie pretty seriously.

"So, Stevie, these are long-swords." Danny pointed at some impressive blades with intricate jeweled pommels. Stevie nodded. They looked long to him.

Danny pointed to a wicked-looking spiked ball attached to a wooden handle by a stout chain. "And that's a flail," he added, proud to have remembered the name from the library book on knights he had checked out that time.

Stevie liked the look of that one. "Maybe I can get it with my money?" he wondered out loud, thinking of how much he would have appreciated having it when they saw that beaver in the closet.

Danny shook his head. "I think it might be a real one. They're kind of dangerous and spiky. I don't think the police let people carry them anymore."

"Nor do Mom and Dad," said Dad, breaking in. "I've got an idea though.'

He moved over to where the salesman was dusting a nearby display. "Sir, do you have any children's toy weapons?"

The man nodded to the far side of the shop. "In the bins."

Man of few words, thought Dad. "Okay thanks," he said out loud. "Boys, follow me!"

While the boys pawed through an exciting assortment of plastic axes, swords and shields, Mom was enjoying trying to find just the right gift for her parents back in America. So far she was toying between a beautifully-painted vase and a wall hanging embroidered with a pretty spray of flowers bordering a view of the coast. She had a sudden thought. Her mom collected souvenir spoons. Maybe they had one of Tintagel. She turned to ask Mrs. Renton if she had seen any, but stopped short.

"Are you feeling alright?" she asked. The old lady was not looking so well. She looked very tired and was rubbing her ankle like it was really bothering her.

Mrs. Renton seemed almost embarrassed that Mom had noticed. "Yes, yes, "she said briskly. "I'm just a little sore. Don't worry about me. I'm enjoying sitting here."

Mom looked at her doubtfully. Maybe they needed to wrap things up here fairly soon. Forget the spoons; she'd just go with the vase.

⊰⊱

Emily was having trouble deciding between three of the crystal castles. Rachel was beginning to get impatient and was about to put in her opinion when the

189

shop's doorbell jingled loudly right behind her. She shifted to one side so she was out of the way and glanced over her shoulder. Her eyes widened in amazement. *It was the guy again.* All her suspicions flooded back. First the castle, then the café and now here! It couldn't be just a coincidence could it?

Jennings was a bit startled to find himself face to face with one of the kids. He gave a nervous smile and stepped quickly into the shop, letting the door give a jingly slam behind him. Not sure what to do, he decided he'd at least better look like he was there to buy something. He quickly scanned the surroundings, noting where each of the family members were located. He could spy the ladies at the back in the corner and there was the dad with the boys. He felt suddenly foolish and awkward. It looked like the family were just doing some shopping. He had to go through with his deception, though, and appear that he was interested in buying something. Maybe he could just hang around for a bit and see if there was any useful information to be gleaned.

❧❧

Dad was amazed that the boys had made their choices so quickly. He smiled to himself. This was the kind of store *he* would have loved to go in as a boy. *Check out those chess sets!*

Near the toy section was a large glass cabinet with several shelves of intricate and interesting chessboards, each themed in a different way--each chess piece beautifully rendered and painted.

"Hey, boys. Look at this." He beckoned them over.

"Are they chess sets?" asked Stevie, examining them in interest.

"Uh-huh," replied Danny, proud that he knew. "They're really cool. All different."

They were indeed pretty cool, Dad had to admit. There was a set that seemed to be pirates faced against British troops, another of knights in black armor facing a set in white.

"What's that one?" asked Stevie, pointing at a set near the bottom. The white side looked pretty neat to him, with knights and maybe elves or wizards, but the black pieces looked pretty scary. They looked like goblins or trolls or something and the tall pieces at the back looked like black ghosts.

"That's a set from the '*Lord of the Rings*.' It's a famous book." Dad diverted the boy's eyes to another set. "Look at this one. It's the Civil War. The Union is on one side and the Confederates on the other." He felt someone plucking at his elbow and turned to see Rachel looking earnestly up at him.

"What's the matter, dear?"

"It's him!" she said excitedly while trying to keep her voice low.

"Him who?"

"Him. The guy. The guy from the castle and the café!" She gestured over her shoulder. Dad gave a quick glance. Sure enough it was the man again, bending over the counter and examining the swords.

He took Rachel's hand and led her a little farther away. "Now Rachel, you know he's just a regular guy. He's just visiting Tintagel like we are. Why shouldn't we see him again? We'll probably see him some more times before we leave."

Rachel looked down at her feet. "I really think he's interested in the clue."

Dad smiled. "Look dear. Just don't worry. We're just about finished here anyway, and then I think we'll be heading back to the inn."

Kennedy pursed his lips. He wasn't getting anywhere with the clue Jennings had dictated over the phone. The *'City of Auckland'* was really puzzling him. He had racked his brains but hadn't come up with any connection between Auckland and Penrithen, or the Squire. What he really needed was to search online. He had his tablet with him, but there was no internet connection in this medieval mansion of course. *Could there be a place in town?* he wondered. There didn't used to be, but maybe things had changed. How could he find out? He didn't want to go traipsing all over creation looking for one.

He heard the sound of a vacuum cleaner start up in a nearby room. *It must be Mrs. Tremannon. Would she know?* He gave a wry smile. In his opinion, she wasn't exactly the brightest bulb on the tree, but, seeing as he had no other choice, he might as well try. He grabbed his tablet and his jacket and followed the noise. He soon found Mrs. Tremannon in the dining room, trying to reach as far as she could under the table with the vacuum hose. He positioned himself across the table from her.

"Excuse me." He might as well be polite, he reasoned.

The old lady continued her work without looking up.

"Excuse me!" He didn't exactly shout but it was pretty loud. There was no pause in the vacuuming. Was she deaf or something? He leaned across the table and smacked it with his hand. It hurt like he dickens but it did have the desired effect. Mrs. Tremannon slowly straightened up and looked him in the eye. She didn't turn off the vacuum though. Kennedy motioned for her to flip the switch. Somewhat reluctantly she did so, and suddenly there was silence.

Kennedy took a deep breath, trying to control his temper. "Mrs. Tremannon. I have a question."

The lady put her hand on her hip. "Very well, Mr. Canopy."

"Kennedy." He rolled his eyes in exasperation. "And I need to know if there's any place where I can get on the internet around here."

Mrs. Tremannon was not feeling especially sympathetic to this man's needs. There was something about his manner that really irritated her—she who prided herself in her ability to get along with anyone—and she was about to say no, whatever his request might be, when she stopped herself. There was that word again: *internet.* She had heard that word recently. *Now where was it?* She racked her brain, ignoring the little snorts of exasperation from the other side of the table. Suddenly she had it.

"Oh, yes, the internet." She would show this man that she was up on the latest gizmos. "There is an internet at a cafe in the coffee place in town. The one that just opened up. Captain John's. Down on the other side of the harbor." She was about to continue with her explanation, but Kennedy silenced her with a wave of his hand.

"That's great." He turned on his heels and made for the door.

Mrs. Tremannon stared after his retreating back. *What an unpleasant man!* She shook her head and started up the vacuum again.

Stevie had lost interest in the chess sets and was studying the suit of armor with his hands in his pockets, trying to resist the urge to poke it with a finger. Danny was still at the display, examining an Egyptian-looking set, his brow furrowed. He was thinking really hard, trying to connect the dots in his mind. The board in the clue—could it be a chessboard? Could it? *Yes, it had to be!* The clue mentioned a square. Chessboards had squares! But what did it mean about the winning square?

Danny studied the Egyptian set in front of him, his excitement mounting. How would someone figure out what was the winning square? Pretty much any square on the chessboard could be the winning one. His book on chess had lots of pictures of games in progress, and the moves needed to get the opponent in checkmate. To find the right winning square, you would have to have a picture of the game in play, just one move from checkmate. Danny scrunched up his nose. This was hard. Should he ask his dad for help?

He looked over to where his dad was crouched down, examining the display of knives. No, he really wanted to figure this out by himself. *So what would the Squire mean about the winning square?* Where would the Squire put the picture of a chess game in progress?

Danny's mouth suddenly dropped open. His eyes widened and his mouth turned up in big grin. He had it! *He was a real detective!* He looked wildly around for someone to tell. Dad had left the knives and was chatting with Rachel.

"Dad, Dad!" Danny cried. "I've figured out the clue!"

Dad strode quickly over, Rachel just behind. "Okay, buddy, but keep your voice down a bit. We're in a store remember!"

Danny's mind was full to bursting, but he made a conscious effort to slow down and carefully explain. "The board in the clue. You know the bit about the square and the game. I think it's a chess game. It fits."

Dad nodded, impressed. *Wow! He could be right.*

"And the inn sign. It's got a picture of the Squire on it and he's playing chess! We need to find the winning square on the board where you can get a checkmate!"

Now it was Dad's turn to get excited. "You know, I think you're right! What do you think?" He turned to Rachel at his elbow.

She was nodding vigorously. "I think so. We need to check it out."

"We do, but we can't just tear off this minute. We need to finish up here first. I'll see if Mom's ready."

As Dad and Danny made their way over to the ladies, Rachel had a sudden disconcerting thought. She looked back over to the counter and gave a start of surprise. The man had moved up closer and was looking right at her, a sort of triumphant smile on his face. He quickly turned away and headed for the door. Rachel felt her heart skip a beat. *Had he been listening? Had he heard everything?*

"Okay, are we all here?" Dad quickly counted heads.

The family was gathered under the shop awning, not ready yet to venture out from its shelter now that the rain had started again, even though they were all excited to get back to the inn and see if Danny's theory was correct.

Mom tapped Dad's arm. "Dear, would you mind getting the car? I think it would be best if Mrs. Renton didn't walk very far."

"Oh, I'm alright," the old lady protested, but perhaps a bit half-heartedly.

"Your ankle is swelling and I think you need to be careful," said Mom firmly. "We can go bring the car here so you don't have to walk."

"Well, if you think so." Mrs. Renton gave in, secretly liking the idea that someone was showing some care and interest in her.

Dad took a quick glance at the soaked surroundings. He pulled his hood down, gave them a grin and shot off down the street, jumping to avoid the puddles.

It only seemed like a few minutes before the van rounded the corner and pulled up at the curb, windshields wipers frantically doing their best against the deluge. Dad set the flashers going, turned off the engine and dashed around to the passenger side. He carefully helped Mrs. Renton into the front seat, made sure everyone else was safely in and then dashed back.

As the van pulled away from the curb Rachel leaned forward and rubbed a hole in the steamed up side window. As she peered through, her eyes widened. The bearded guy was standing outside under the shop awning with his phone to his ear. For just a second their eyes met again, and as the van sped off she could have sworn he looked hurriedly away. She plopped back into her seat, her mind full of questions again. *Was that guy really following them? Did he know about the inheritance or was it just a set of coincidences?* She remembered her Dad's skepticism all too well. She definitely didn't want to embarrass herself. Maybe she would just keep her concerns to herself for now, but she was definitely going to keep her eyes open!

Jennings snapped his phone shut. *No answer.* He couldn't believe it. Here he was with the best news he'd gotten in a long time, and that idiot Kennedy wasn't even answering. Well, maybe it was the cell service again, but whatever the reason it was awfully bad timing.

He eyed the pelting rain, driving in gusts up the street. A fair amount had found its way under the awning and his trousers were feeling uncomfortably damp. He shook his head. There was no getting around it. He had to make it back to his car and try to deliver this news in person.

Chapter 13 - The Pace Picks Up

The van was a babble of noise as the family discussed Danny's theory about the chess sign. The only slightly unhappy one was Stevie, who wished fervently he had been the one to figure it out.

As Dad drove down the hill again to the town of Wadebridge, Mom glanced over at Mrs. Renton, just in time to catch her wincing in pain. "Are you okay," she asked worriedly.

The lady tried to quickly compose her features. "Oh, yes, yes. Just a little twinge."

"You know," said Mom, "I really think you ought to get your ankle looked at."

Dad pricked up his ears. "Good idea. Do you have a doctor you go to?"

Mrs. Renton nodded. "Yes, I do. I found one pretty quickly—right in town. I'm not sure though..."

Mom had a sudden thought. "Are you worried about the possibility that you might have to rest up at home for a while?"

"Well..."

"We could definitely help."

Rachel was listening intently to the conversation. She had a clear idea of where it was going—and it would really mean that this vacation would be out of their hands. A couple of days ago that would have been a disaster, but something had definitely changed since then. Now that there was the possibility someone was trying to steal the inheritance from the old lady it had aroused some sort of protective instinct in her. *They could really help Mrs. Renton, yes they could, and it could even be an adventure!*

"Yes, we'll help!" she said out loud, almost surprising herself as she did so. "We can help solve the mystery for you. You don't have to worry!"

Dad glanced back in the mirror at her in surprise.

Rachel looked round at her siblings. "We can do it, right?"

The others nodded vigorously. Mom smiled at the old lady and patted her hand.

Mrs. Renton felt tears coming into her eyes. "Well, if you really…"

"We do," boomed Dad from the front seat, joining in the enthusiasm. "We'll be detectives and we're officially on the job!"

෨෯

Kennedy jogged down the hill to the harbor and across the bridge, panting with the exertion. Of course there weren't any parking spaces down here, he grumbled to himself. There was just the car park on the cliff, and that was even further away than the inn. Now where on earth was this Captain John's?

෨෯

"Okay, kids. Go ahead. We'll be back soon." Dad set the parking brake and unlocked the doors. "See if you can figure out if Danny's right, and Emily, help make sure everyone gets washed up and ready for dinner around six, please."

Emily nodded. "I will."

It had been Mom's suggestion that they drop the kids off first, and Dad had heartily concurred. Getting Mrs. Renton settled might take a bit of time, and he didn't relish trying to corral four excited bodies in the lady's little house with the old lady hobbling around. He pulled up by the entrance gate to the inn and the kids scrambled out.

"Bye, Mrs. Renton!" said Emily, shaking her hand. "We'll pray for you."

"Yes, bye-bye," chorused the three others.

Mrs. Renton couldn't help but smile, even though her ankle was hurting quite a bit now. "Thank you, dearies. I'll see you soon."

"Bye, kids," said Mom. "We should be back before dinner."

As the van drove off, Emily took charge. "Okay." She grabbed Stevie's hand. "Let's go check out the inn sign. Hey, wait you guys!"

Rachel and Danny had already started to charge up the driveway. Stevie yanked his hand out of Emily's and tore off as well.

Emily broke into a run herself. "Wait for me!"

Danny suddenly skidded to a halt, grabbing Rachel's arm. Stevie bumped into him from behind.

"Hey, what gives!" said Rachel.

"Look," wailed Danny, pointing to where the yellow sports car was parked in front of the inn. "The man's there. I don't want to go in without Dad and Mom."

The others felt a wave of frustration. "Come on Danny, it's okay," said Rachel giving his arm a yank.

Emily felt a prick in her conscience. She didn't want to have to deal with this, but she was sure her parents would want her to try. She looked down at her brother. "Wait a minute, guys. Danny is really scared." She squatted down to his size. "What are you afraid of?"

Danny turned away, embarrassed. "I don't know. He's just mean and scary. He shouted at me."

"He's okay," said Rachel somewhat impatiently. "He's just a bit grumpy. Maybe he was having a bad day that time anyway."

"I tell you what," said Emily with a sudden thought. "Let's pray for him."

"I did pray for him the other day," said Danny, turning back to look at her.

"Well, let's do it again. Do you remember Mr. Peterson at the grocery store? He looks pretty grumpy too. I'm praying for him as well. I want him to be more like Auntie Flo at the bakery!"

Danny couldn't resist a smile.

"Okay, shut your eyes. You, too," added Emily, frowning at Rachel and Stevie. They nodded somewhat grudgingly.

Emily took Danny's hand. "Dear Jesus, please help the café man and Mr. Peterson to not be so grumpy. Whatever is making them that way, please help them. Please help them to understand your love, and come to know you personally. And please help Danny not be scared. Give him your courage. Thank you that you are always with us. Amen."

"Amen," said everyone else, opening their eyes.

"Okay," said Emily, straightening back up. "Are you okay to go, Danny?"

The lad gave a small sniff and nodded.

"Well, here, hold my hand and let's go."

❧❧

Kennedy tapped his foot in frustration. He had found the coffee place without too much trouble. There was a new sign posted in the window of the newsagents that had given pretty clear directions. Of course Mrs. Tremannon had got the name wrong. He wondered if she even knew her *own* name. The problem now, though, was that they were having some issues with the wireless network. The owner had been apologetic and was rebooting the router for the second time.

Kennedy scanned the room. It wasn't very busy. There were several couples chatting or sipping on drinks, and a business man sitting with his laptop by the front window. He glanced at Kennedy and shrugged his shoulders. Kennedy returned a suitably exasperated look. He leaned back against the counter, wondering what to do. There were plenty of open tables, but if he sat at one he would feel more obligated to buy something. He wasn't a coffee drinker anyway. He just wanted the internet.

His gaze roamed over to the big fireplace where a low gas fire glowed in the insert. The mantelpiece had several mildly interesting pieces arrayed on it, like the Georgian clock and the brass bookends. His mind automatically calculated what they were probably worth, and what sort of inflated price he would try to get for them if he were selling.

He suddenly noticed the tile inset in the mantelpiece itself. With a start he remembered the photo in the entry way. *Surely this was the same fireplace.* If so, the photo had been taken here! But who cared, now? The family had already found that clue, he reminded himself.

"Okay, I think you're good." The owner called to him from the counter. "Go ahead and try to connect. I think I fixed the problem."

Kennedy nodded. He couldn't bring himself to thank the man, not after the frustrating delay. He activated his tablet and watched the WIFI icon. It was trying to connect. It was trying, trying...yes! He was on. With a grunt of satisfaction he started up his web browser. Now to find out about that Auckland thing, and finally get ahead in the game.

❧❧

The kids gathered by the front door of the inn and looked up at the sign, swinging lightly in the gentle breeze. Whoever had painted it had really done a very good job. The Squire looked very pleasant, with eyes that seemed to twinkle at them from above his impressive moustache. He was sitting in a sunny room that might have been a sort of office, with dark paneling on the walls, a shaded light fixture overhead, a tall bookcase to one side and what looked like a framed stained glass of a sailing ship hung in the window behind. The chess game on the table in front of him was painted in minute detail.

Danny had forgotten about his fears for a moment. "It looks like the Squire was playing the white side," he announced, proud to be able to tell.

Stevie was just about to respond when Emily heard something and put her finger to her lips in warning. They could all hear it now. Someone was humming to herself, and it sounded like whoever it was was coming along the side of the house.

"Mrs. Tremannon?" whispered Rachel.

"Sounds like it," said Danny. He had a sudden thought. "Maybe we can ask her about the café man." He risked a glance at the dining room windows. Thankfully there was no-one there.

"Okay, but don't slip up and mention the inheritance!" warned Emily.

Mrs. Tremannon rounded the corner carrying a large basket of garden tools. She smiled when she saw the children. "Hello there! How are you all doing? Did you have a nice day? Where did you end up going? I hope you didn't go to the beach, what with the rain and all. We had quite a nasty downpour a wee bit ago. It sneaked up and soaked the washing!"

"We went to Tintagel" said Danny, as soon as he could get a word in. "And we saw a ruined castle."

"And it got really misty and we rode in a truck and bought some King Arthur stuff!" put in Stevie, not to be outdone.

"My, my. That does sound like a full day," said Mrs. Tremannon with a smile, patting his head.

"Mrs. Tremannon," said Danny, raising his hand.

The lady's eyes twinkled. She set down her basket. "Yes, dearie."

"Is the man here? The man with that yellow car who's staying here?"

Mrs. Tremannon looked a bit puzzled. "The man? You mean Mr. Keppleby? No, he's out right now. He's out looking for an internet thing at the coffee shop. I know his fancy car's here, but he walked since there's no place to park nearby, though actually if he'd have parked at the car park up on the cliff it'd probably be closer. Why—did you want to talk to him? I suppose he'll be back shortly. Well, maybe not shortly, but before dinner."

Danny relaxed visibly. "No, thank you. I mean thank you for letting me know, but I don't want to talk to him."

Emily suddenly had a brainwave. "Mrs. Tremannon. Would you happen to know where there's a chess set? We wanted to look at one and there's still some time before dinner. My Mom and Dad are helping someone but will be back here in time to eat."

Rachel gave her sister a sharp look, but said nothing.

Mrs. Tremannon pursed her lips. "Well, there's a game cupboard in the dining room—in the sideboard, on the left side. I haven't looked in there for a good bit, but I think there used to be a chess set and some other games. Other guests might have played them so I don't know what state they're in or if all the pieces are there."

Emily nodded, smiling. "Thank you very much," she said politely. "We'll go look."

"Okay, dears. I'll see you at dinner. I've just got a wee bit of time to weed the veggies while the casserole finishes baking. Cheerio!" Mrs. Tremannon plucked up her basket again and limped off towards the vegetable garden.

"Whew!" said Rachel. "I thought you were going to spill the beans, Emily. Okay everyone, we need to find the chess set. Come on." She ran over to the door.

Emily looked down at Danny. "Are you okay to go in now?"

Danny nodded, though inside his thoughts were in a turmoil. Somehow he had to deal with this thing with the man. If he wanted to be a detective, he had to master his fears. After all, even if the man wasn't there right now, he would be coming back.

Emily gave his hand a squeeze. "Come on. We need your help. It'll be okay!"

Danny wasn't so sure.

⥾⥿

Doctor Reggie Morris had never regretted leaving his stressful old medical practice in London and taking a sort of semi-early retirement out here in Penrithen. He still saw patients fairly regularly, but the pace of life was so much slower here that he almost felt he was on a permanent holiday, the ailments he had to treat being only of the most rudimentary type. Take the current case in point. A simple mildly-sprained ankle and a courteous elderly patient. Nothing to raise the old blood pressure, and plenty of time left in the day to go for a stroll along the coast path before dinner.

He stood up and grabbed his black bag off the side table. "Alright. There you are. Keep the ankle wrapped tightly and elevated whenever you can. Ice it three or four times a day. I think it's wise that you said you can sleep down here, so there's no need to use the stairs. If you need to get up, go nice and slowly. No jogging up and down the hill, and especially no skateboarding."

Mrs. Renton giggled and nodded. She was perched on the love seat, her ankle resting on the cushioned stool. Pickwick the cat, sensing something was amiss, had curled up at her side.

198

The doctor looked over at Mom and Dad, who had been hovering in the background. "And you said you'll check in every day?"

"Yes, certainly," said Mom. "We can pick up anything Mrs. Renton needs at the store."

"You'll be okay here though?" wondered Dad, glancing at the old lady. He really didn't have any idea how frail she might be feeling.

"I can get around fine," insisted Mrs. Renton. "I can potter around the house, get to the kitchen, make some tea—everything I need."

Dad turned to the doctor. "Well, we'll make sure and come by each day for sure."

"Good, good. Well Mrs. Renton, I'll check back with you in a few days. Call me if it starts feeling worse." He gave a general wave. "Good day to you all."

Dad closed the door behind him and looked over at Mom who gave a shrug and nodded.

"Are you absolutely sure you'll be okay," Mom asked the old lady.

Mrs. Renton nodded vigorously. "I'll be fine, I'm sure, but I am really, really sorry for all the bother. You have been so kind."

"Nonsense, nonsense," said Dad. "It's really our pleasure." And he meant it. He had no doubt they were doing the right thing.

"But listen, I need to talk to you about something. Please sit down." Mrs. Renton looked at them with a strange intensity. Mom and Dad sat.

"I need you to know that I don't want you to feel obligated to help me anymore. You've already done so much. I don't want to ruin your vacation."

"Now, Mrs. Renton." Dad tried to sound firm. "We'd love to keep on helping. It's actually been very interesting. The kids love a mystery, too. You haven't ruined anything." He looked at Mom who nodded.

Mrs. Renton turned away. She was silent for a moment—then gave a heavy sigh.

"I used to be so active and fit. I loved adventure—I even loved taking risks. I guess it was a way to block out the pain I had been feeling." She looked back at Mom and Dad, her eyes moist. "I think as well that deep down I didn't really care if I died. That guilt was always there. And now I see that it may be too late. Uncle Kenwyn obviously thought I would be able to follow all these clues, wherever they might lead, but now I can't." She suddenly held out her hands. Mom and Dad stood up and came over, each taking one. She gripped them hard with a sudden resolution.

"Will you help? I need you." She realized it even as she said it, and it actually felt freeing to say it out loud. "I can't talk to the Tremannons. I feel that they may still hold some sort of grudge against me for how I treated Uncle Kenwyn. I don't want them to know about this right now."

Mom and Dad nodded silently.

"Uncle went to all this trouble for me. I need to see this through. It's my only hope."

Mom and Dad were smiling now. Mom knelt down and gripped the old lady's hand with both of hers. She spoke with an earnestness that surprised even her.

"We know God planned all this—that we'd be here at this time, meet at the church—your locket—everything. We want to help. We're here to help."

Dad put his arm on Mrs. Renton's shoulder and their eyes met. If they hadn't already passed the point of no return with this commitment, he knew they had passed it now, and it was okay with him. He was sure of it. "Mrs. Renton. With God's help, we will see this thing done."

❧❧

Rachel pulled things out of the sideboard and the others pored through the finds. There were portions of at least four decks of cards, all mixed together, several boxed jigsaw puzzles with a number of loose pieces as well, a Monopoly game in a crushed box, two plastic boxes of dominoes, and a wooden Mancala game that seemed to have lost its pieces.

"I don't see any chess set," frowned Emily. "Are you sure that's all Rachel?"

"That's it in this cupboard. Oh, hang on. What's this?" At the bottom of the cupboard was a slab of wood that had probably been another shelf whose supports had broken. Rachel had seen something poking out from underneath. She pried up the heavy piece and revealed an almost flattened box. She pulled it out and lots of little pieces spilled out of the sides with some cardboard game boards.

"It says 'Compendium of Games.' And look, it has all kinds of games and one's chess!"

The others crowded around. "Help me get the pieces," said Rachel.

"What do they look like?" said Stevie.

"Here's one," said Danny showing him a little white plastic pawn. He did a quick sum in his head. "We need thirty of them. No, thirty-two."

They gathered all the scattered items while Rachel sifted through the game boards. "Here's a chess one!" she said triumphantly. "I guess you can use it for checkers, too."

"Let me have your pieces," said Emily holding out her hand. She counted the total. "Twenty-nine. We're missing some."

"That's okay, they're just pawns" said Danny. "We can make do with what we've got. We only have to set up the game like the one on the sign. The Squire didn't have all the pieces on the board."

"Are you sure?" said Emily doubtfully.

"Sure I'm sure."

"Okay. Let's quickly put this stuff back. Mom and Dad will be here any minute. We can try to figure it out after dinner."

❧❧

Kennedy was getting mighty frustrated. There didn't seem to be any link between Penrithen and Auckland. There was a Cornwall Park in Auckland, but that didn't seem to make any sense. He'd looked at sites for Auckland tourism, Auckland history and the University of Auckland. He'd perused a map of the city of Auckland, and even watched several videos of city tours. Nothing jumped out at him.

With a sudden revelation he added the word 'board' to the search. That turned up Auckland city boards of directors, trustees and a health board. This was going nowhere. He checked his phone. Only one bar. Of all the days for the cell service to be unreliable, or was it his phone? He tried a quick call, but it failed. He gave a frustrated sigh. It looked like he might as well go back to the Inn and try getting a hold of Jennings from there.

The owner was nowhere to be seen. Kennedy debated whether to sneak out without paying but then thought better of it. He might want to come back sometime and use the internet again. He plopped some money in the jar and headed out the door.

As he hurried towards the bridge, he glanced at his watch. He was risking being late for dinner, and then he'd have to deal with a grumpy Mrs. Tremannon again.

A car appeared from the lane above and turned onto the bridge, causing him to have to jump out of the way with a yell of anger. At that exact moment his phone rang. He wrenched it out of his pocket as he jogged on and glanced at the screen. It was Jennings. He must be back in service range again. He thumbed the talk button and held it up to his ear, panting with the exertion. .

"Kennedy here. What is it? What? Okay, okay, hang on."

He slowed to a walk. "Okay, say it again. Uh huh. Are you sure? What's a chess set got to do with Auckland?"

He switched his phone to his other ear. "Okay, alright. You did good. I'm heading back to the inn. Think hard about the clue. I'll see what I can uncover here."

A cold gust of wind swept by and Kennedy glanced out across the harbor. The sun was low and just disappearing behind a wall of fog creeping stealthily in towards the land.

"Look I've got to go. Call me if you think of anything. We've got to get ahead of this family somehow, but we mustn't in any way let them know we're in on this, you hear! "

Kennedy hung up and resumed jogging up the lane, his face fixed and grim.

"Great job finding a chess set, kids!" Dad smiled around the table at the family, tucking into a delicious shepherd's pie with all the fixings, courtesy of Mrs. Tremannon. Everyone was relieved that the man from the café hadn't shown up for dinner. They had been able to chat freely about the mystery. Mom and Dad had filled them in about Mrs. Renton, and then Danny, with many interruptions from the others, had told about the chess set.

"So, we're all in on this, right?" said Mom, looking each person in the eyes, one by one. She got sincere nods in reply.

"It will be a different sort of vacation, but I have a feeling we may be more blessed this way than if we had tried to make the blessing happen ourselves," said Dad, seriously. "I'm going to pray that each of you are really blessed as you serve Mrs. Renton in this way."

Rachel had a sudden thought. "Remember the verse on the first note from the Squire—the one you reminded me of, Dad?"

"Why don't you remind all of us, dear," said Mom, looking at Rachel

"Trust in the Lord and do good. Dwell in the land and enjoy safe pasture. Delight yourself in the Lord and He will give you the desires of your heart."

"You memorized it!" exclaimed Dad. "Great job!"

"Uh-huh—because I needed to. I want to trust God that, as we stay here in Penrithen and do good for Mrs. Renton, He will give me the desires of my heart."

"And that may mean He might change our hearts along the way," added Mom, smiling.

"I don't get it," said Danny.

"Well, having lots of time at the beach is the desire of our heart right now, but God may change our hearts and show us that we will have the most fun and be the most fulfilled serving Mrs. Renton."

"Hmmm." That gave Danny something to think about.

"Anyway," said Dad, swallowing a mouthful. "We need to get organized. We're the Chapman Family Detective Agency,"—he pointed at each of them with his fork—"and each will have to do their part to solve this puzzle, and what's more, we need to do it before we leave at the end of next week."

Rachel, Danny and Stevie grinned at each other. They liked the sound of the detective agency. Emily was more concerned with the timeframe, however. She didn't want to think about the end of the holiday.

"So what do you want us to do," she said, trying not to sound too anxious.

"Well, the two main things we need to solve right now are the mystery of the chess set, and the reference to the 'City of Auckland.' I think we need to divide and conquer."

The kids got a little thrill of excitement.

"Okay," said Emily, "what do you think we should do?"

"Kids, you have the chess set, right?" Nods all around. "So, you need to find out what the winning square is." Dad did a quick mental evaluation of who would be best working with whom. "Danny and Rachel—you work on that. Emily and Stevie, I want you to look for the other board the clue mentions."

The kids all nodded. This seemed pretty cool.

Emily had a sudden thought. "But do we know the other board is a chessboard, and that it's even here at the inn?"

"Well, we don't know," said Dad. "But that's your job to try to figure out. You can at least eliminate some possibilities."

That made sense to Emily. "Alright, Stevie. You and me."

Stevie liked the sound of that. "Yeah, let's do it!"

"But first," reminded Mom, "we need to finish eating and stack the dishes."

"What about you and Mom," said Rachel. "You need something to do."

Dad was about to respond when they heard the front door open and close. He put a finger to his lips, and the family all nodded, seriously. Seconds later Kennedy appeared at the doorway. He stopped dead when he saw the family, but his features immediately rearranged themselves into something like a smile.

"Hello everybody. I'm sorry to disturb you like this. I'm a bit late for dinner, you see.

"Yes, you are." Mrs. Tremannon had popped into view from the hallway behind him like a genie from a lamp.

Kennedy turned to her, cursing inwardly but still forcing a smile. "I'm very sorry, Mrs. Tremannon. It took me longer to walk back here than I thought."

The lady looked him over for a moment, but then her basic good manners got the better of her annoyance. "Well, that's alright. I've got your dinner in the oven and it's nice and hot. Go wash your hands and I'll bring it out in five minutes."

Kennedy appeared to submit meekly to this request and headed for his room. Mrs. Tremannon disappeared again and Dad took the opportunity to whisper to the family. He set his fork down and leaned forward.

"We want to keep this all hush hush. Let's eat up quickly."

"What about dessert?" wondered Stevie, anxiously.

Dad looked at Mom, who shrugged. "We need to stay for dessert. Mrs. Tremannon took the trouble to make it for us."

Dad smiled. "Mark it down, kids. Mom's requiring dessert!"

᪣᪣

Kennedy dried his hands, thinking hard. He had put on his best act back there—nice and apologetic and respectful, and it had worked. At least it had got the old lady off his back. He would have to keep it up, no matter how hard it was. It was the only way he could get results. Now he had to figure out how to get some information from the family, and that meant engaging them in some conversation over dinner.

He took a quick glance in the mirror, tamed his hair a bit with his fingers and forced his features into a smile again.

᪣᪣

Mrs. Tremannon had just finished setting out a dish of fruit salad with cream in front of each of the Chapmans when Kennedy walked in. The kids glanced quickly at each other and then got to work on their desserts, spoons flying. Mom and Dad tried to slow them down with meaningful looks.

Kennedy sat at the place set for him on the other side of Dad. He adjusted his chair and shook out his napkin. Then he turned to Dad. "So, did you have a pleasant day today?"

Dad was immediately on his guard. "Yes, thank you. We had a nice day out." The rest of the family kept eating quickly but eyeing Dad and Mr. Kennedy.

Kennedy decided to keep going. Maybe he could carefully elicit some information.

"I really like this part of the coast. There's so much to see, and so much history."

"Yes, there is."

"Have you been to Boscastle yet, or Tintagel?"

"Not to Boscastle, no. But yes we went to Tintagel today."

203

The kids' eyes widened slightly. *Don't say too much Dad*, they were thinking.

"Oh, really? Did you see anything of interest?"

Dad was beginning to wonder if the guy's questions would ever end. He took a quick bite and swallow of his fruit salad while formulating a response that he hoped wouldn't say too much.

"Well, we saw the old post office, and the castle of course. In the end we didn't explore quite as long as we had first thought."

"Oh, the fog was a bit thick, was it?" Even as he said it, Kennedy realized his awful mistake. "The fog's always bad on that stretch of the coast," he stammered. "Sweeps in at a moment's notice."

He was saved by Mrs. Tremannon's sudden appearance with a loaded tray.

"Here y'are—shepherd's pie. Here's some gravy and here's carrots and Brussel sprouts." She started unloading everything in front of him.

Dad looked at Mom and gave the merest inclination of his head towards the door. She nodded. They weren't quite finished but close enough.

"Alright kids. Let's stack your dishes."

"Oh, don't worry about that," said Mrs. Tremannon brandishing her now empty tray. "I'll clean up. Did you enjoy everything?"

"Oh, yes," said Emily, and she really meant it. "It was all so delicious."

The others nodded vigorously.

"Truly another masterpiece, Mrs. Tremannon," added Dad. The lady swelled with evident pride.

"Well, I do m'best, but I love to cook and always like to do a good job for nice folks like you." She gave a sidelong glance at Kennedy, who didn't miss the point.

"Well, thank you again so much. We'll see you later," said Mom, gesturing to the kids. Like a hen gathering her chicks, she ushered them out to the stairwell, Dad close behind.

Kennedy glanced warily at Mrs. Tremannon as she loaded the tray with dishes and then limped off towards the kitchen. As soon as she was gone, he slumped back in his chair, shaking his head. *What an idiot*, he thought. *I could have given the game away completely. I've got to be more careful.*

⋰⋱

The family gathered in Mom and Dad's room, a little breathless.

"Well, I think we did okay. We didn't give anything away did we?" wondered Mom.

Dad shook his head. Rachel shrugged. "I don't think so. Anyway, we need to get going."

"But Dad, you didn't tell us what you and Mom are going to do," reminded Emily.

"You're right. Our task is the pesky 'City of Auckland.' I think we need some help on that one. Mom and I are going back to Captain Jack's to use the internet."

"And get a coffee?" said Emily, cheekily.

Mom grinned. "If they insist!" She grabbed her coat off the back of the door. "Are you okay, Danny? You and Rachel will be safe up in our room." Danny nodded, glad he would be out of harm's way. He hated the idea of being in the same house as the mean man.

"You and Stevie might want to wait to look around until the coast is clear," Dad added.

"That's right," said Mom. "Remember to try to be discrete."

"We will," said Emily.

"What's discrete?" said Stevie, tugging at Emily's sleeve.

"It means we need to keep it a secret. We mustn't let anyone know that we're looking for the clue."

"Oh, right!" said Stevie. "Don't worry Mom and Dad. And we'll figure this out before you get back."

✍✍

Kennedy sat on the edge of the bed and pulled off his shoes. He tossed them in the corner and threw himself down on the bed. He felt exhausted. He just wanted to sleep.

Should I be doing something, though? he wondered. *Should I be trying to figure out what the family was up to?* He tried to sort things out in his mind. First of all, they were just a family, with young kids. Not exactly serious competition, right? So what if they wanted to help Mrs. Renton? They were on vacation and probably didn't want to spend all their time chasing clues. Unless they knew the old lady... Maybe they were close friends. Maybe she asked them to come and they were here just to solve the mystery. He needed to find that out. And they did seem to be ahead of him so far.

He checked his watch. Eight-thirty. Those kids would probably be going to bed soon, he imagined. There wasn't anything more they would be doing tonight. Maybe he could just get a fresh start tomorrow. Maybe he could try to get some information from them at breakfast. But he would have to be careful. He didn't want them suspecting he was involved. As far as he knew, that was one of his greatest advantages—that they had no clue he was trying to get there first.

✍✍

Dad carefully climbed the spiral staircase with his laptop in one hand and a large white chocolate mocha in the other. He risked a quick glance at his wife who waved cheerily from a small table near the fireplace. The plan was for her to discretely check the antiques and old photos covering the walls, looking for any reference to a game board, while he did a bit of surfing. Geoff the owner had apologized that the WIFI was on the blink, and it would be best to plug in directly using one of the cables from a desktop computer upstairs. He pulled up a chair to one of the small desks and grabbed an Ethernet cable to plug into his laptop. He noted the connection was good and launched his browser. It automatically opened up to the last page he had visited—his webmail program.

Oh, yes, he thought, his stomach doing a little jump. *The last time I was here I was checking my mail from the editor.* Did he want to check again and see if there was an update? No, he didn't really, and anyway he should be searching for the clue.

It was tempting, though, wasn't it? He had a morbid curiosity to know his fate. Almost before he knew it, he had signed in. His inbox displayed twenty new messages. He scanned the senders. Almost all were spam again, but there, sure enough, was one from the editor. His stomach jumped again. Dare he open it? Should he? No, he shouldn't. He wavered. Better to learn his fate rather than worrying about it. He clicked on the message, and quickly scanned the contents.

Dear Mr. Chapman,

This is just a reminder that we need to see some revised articles before the deadline at the end of the month. We are confident you can provide what we need for our next issue.

Sincerely, Brian Stearns

Okay, short and sweet. Well, maybe not that sweet. Yes, Mr. Stearns said they were confident he could do it, but that was just a polite way to insist he do better than last time.

So, it could be worse news, but it could be better. He realized that somehow he had held out a hope that his original submissions might work. He had a sudden surge of frustration. He really needed this break—the family needed it too. Could he really set aside his work for the rest of the holiday, even with a deadline looming beyond? He remembered Mrs. Renton's earnest face earlier that afternoon. Even though she didn't come right out and say it, he knew she was trusting them to get the mystery solved. And he was sure that was God's will, wasn't he? Yes he was. So then, God would take care of the articles and the deadline. He just had to trust.

With a concerted effort to put his concerns out of his mind, he logged out of his mail and pulled up a search engine instead.

❦

Mom had finished downstairs. There didn't seem to be anything remotely related to Auckland, or a game board for that matter. She threaded her way through the tables and carefully climbed the stairs. Her husband was in the corner, pouring over his laptop. He didn't notice her. She crept over and touched him lightly on the back of the neck.

Dad almost fell out of the chair. "Don't do that! One of these days I'm just going to keel over and die and then what would you do?"

"Hmm. You're right." Mom looked thoughtful. "That would be awful. I'd have to do all the driving by myself."

Dad rolled his eyes. "Glad to know you'd miss me."

Mom gave him a quick peck on the cheek. "Of course. Any success, by the way?"

"No, nothing really. At least I don't think so. I've searched under Auckland and Cornwall together, Auckland and Penrithen, and even Auckland and chess. There's a Cornwall Park in Auckland, but that didn't seem to lead anywhere, and there's a company in Auckland that rents giant chess sets."

"Really, what about that?"

Dad brought up the link again in his browser. "Well, look. See, you can rent one, but what's that got to do with the clue?"

"Look through the city of Auckland. Another board you'll see," quoted Mom. "Why does it say to look through the city? Does that mean search through it?"

Dad sat back in his chair and rubbed his chin. "That just doesn't make sense. It's not like Mrs. Renton needs to go to New Zealand."

"Or that the Squire would think that she could search for the meaning online either." Mom plopped down next to him. "So, it's got to be something closer to home."

"But there wasn't any link I could find between Penrithen and Auckland."

"Wait a minute," said Mom, sitting up straight. "Do you have the clue written down? Can I see it?"

Dad pulled the rumpled piece of paper from his pocket and handed it to his wife. "There you go."

Mom pointed at the line. "Did you copy this exactly?"

"I think so. Why?"

"City is capitalized. Normally it wouldn't be."

"So it could be a name? The *'City of Auckland?'*" Dad was getting excited. "It's something else to try." He quickly typed in the words, putting them in quotes so the search engine would look for them in that exact way.

They scanned the results with disappointment. It was just more links to Auckland, New Zealand. "Nothing," sighed Dad.

"How about doing an image search?" suggested Mom. "Maybe that will turn up something."

"Alright," said Dad without much enthusiasm. He clicked on the image button and within a few seconds the screen filled with photo thumbnails.

"They all look like the same thing. Pictures of Auckland—sky-scrapers, harbor views..." Dad waved his hand at the screen.

"Well at least scroll down. There may be something else."

Dad shook his head, but scrolled down obediently. More and more of the same city shots. He kept going.

"There! Stop!" cried Mom, pointing. "Look at that!"

Among all the city shots there was just one picture that was different--an old black and white print of a sailing ship. Underneath was printed in all caps 'The City of Auckland.'

"Wow," said Dad, sitting up straighter. "A ship. That's something different. Have you seen a ship anywhere at the inn?"

Mom looked off into space. "I do feel like I've seen a ship somewhere." She grabbed her favorite lock of hair and started twisting it round, thinking hard. Then her eyes widened. "Oh, I know! There's a painting of a ship right here at Captain Jack's—on the wall downstairs."

"Alright," said Dad, feeling a bit more hopeful. He snapped his laptop shut, unplugged the cable and stood up. "Let's go check it out."

They descended back into the coffee-scented bustle of the main room. The place was about three-quarters full and the noise-level had increased considerably. Dad put the correct money in the internet cash box, and Geoff gave them a wink as he ducked behind the espresso machine.

"Busy guy," said Dad.

They threaded their way over to the far wall where Mom had seen the picture of the ship. It didn't take a second, however, to determine that it wasn't what they were looking for. The picture was of a much smaller vessel, with only two masts.

"Definitely not the one," confirmed Mom. Her shoulders slumped a little.

Dad pursed his lips. "Nope. And no other ship pictures anywhere."

"Well, we do have an idea what to look for now," said Mom, brightening up. "Let's get back to the inn and tell the children."

"Okay," agreed Dad, zipping up his jacket. "I think it's time for a family meeting."

❧❦❧

With Rachel's help, Danny had finally set up the board on the bed again, just like on the inn sign. Danny knelt down carefully by the bedside and Rachel plonked down on the floor next to him.

"So, can you figure it out?"

Danny looked over the board, frowning a little. "It said one move, right? So I need to figure out who is about to be put in checkmate."

"How about if you move the bishop there," said Rachel, pointing.

"Shhh," said Danny. "I'm concentrating."

Rachel sat back on her heels with a sigh of impatience. She wished she was exploring the house with Emily and Stevie. At least they were doing something constructive.

❧❦❧

"Nothing," said Emily with a small sigh. She looked down at her little brother who was frowning in frustration. They had checked the pictures on the staircase again, then the ones in the sitting room, the dining room and the entryway.

"We didn't look there," said Stevie suddenly, pointing to the closed door off the entryway where the Tremannons liked to watch TV in the evening. They could hear muffled sounds from the other side.

There was no way Emily was going to knock on the door and have to deal with the Tremannon's questions, though. She shook her head firmly.

Stevie looked annoyed. "Well what about the kitchen?"

"We can't go in there," said Emily.

"Why not? What's the point of searching if we can't search everywhere?"

Emily weighed that in her mind. What he said made sense, but she really didn't want to risk being caught. It just didn't sound right to go into the kitchen.

Stevie had a sudden marvelous thought. "Hey, I've got it!" He nodded his head vigorously. "It means a cutting board, like Mom used when she was cutting stuff like apples. There's probably one in the kitchen!" He tugged at Emily's hand.

"But we have to look through a city to see it!" said Emily, desperately thinking of an excuse. "The city of Auckland. How can that be in the kitchen? And anyway, what if the Tremannons saw us?"

Stevie was about to respond when they heard a sudden noise behind them. They both froze. Someone was fumbling at the door of the Tremannon's sitting room. For an instant they looked at each other wide-eyed. Then they both turned and fled.

❧❧

"I've got it!" said Danny, leaping to his feet. "If I move the white knight right here, then the black king is in checkmate!"

"Really?" said Rachel. "Are you absolutely sure?"

"Course I'm sure," said Danny, offended.

"Well, then. You should write it down. Draw a map of the board and mark the square."

"Oh, it's much easier than that," said Danny, proud he knew. "There's a code for labeling each square. The knight needs to be on, let's see…" He did a quick calculation. "KB4 on the black side. Can you write it somewhere?"

"Er, okay." She was writing it on a scrap of paper when there was a sudden, terrific pounding up the stairs. A second later and Emily and Stevie flew into the room.

"What's the matter?" said Danny, alarmed.

Emily looked embarrassed. "We, er, thought the Tremannons were going to see us."

"Cause we wanted to go in the kitchen," added Stevie.

Rachel looked puzzled. "Okay, but did you find a board?"

"No, because we didn't go in the kitchen."

"Stevie, that's not true," exclaimed Emily. "I told you, we have to look through the city to find a board, and whatever that means, I'm sure it doesn't mean one of Mrs. Tremannon's cutting boards!"

Stevie stuck out his lower lip. Emily was getting frustrated and glared back at him.

Rachel wasn't normally the one to intervene, but for some reason she felt she should this time. "Okay, Stevie. It was a good idea, but we'll have to see. Emily, did you think the Tremannon's saw or guessed anything?"

Emily felt her emotions settling back down. She even managed a slight smile. "No, and we didn't see the café man, Mr. Whatsiname either."

"Okay, well maybe Mom and Dad will find out something that will help. Anyway, Danny worked out the puzzle!"

Danny gave an expansive grin. Stevie rushed over to look, but Rachel grabbed him by the arm. "Hang on, you might upset the board."

"But Rachel wrote down the square just in case," reminded Danny. "KB4, black side."

"What does that mean? …Oh, never mind," said Emily, in a hurry to move on. "We've got the square, but I think we need to find out about the city of Auckland."

"But how?"

"We'll just have to sit tight and wait for Mom and Dad."

"But that could be ages!" said a voice from the doorway.

"Dad, Mom!" cried everyone at once. There was a sudden cacophony as they poured out their news.

"Hold it, hold!" said Dad raising his hand. The noise shut off like a trap.

"That's better," said Mom, talking off her jacket. "It looks like you've been busy."

"But we need to discuss this all in an organized way. We need an official meeting."

"Of the Chapman Family Detective Agency," said Rachel with a grin.

"That's right. Give us a sec to put our things away and we'll get started."

Chapter 14 - The City of Auckland

Kennedy couldn't sleep. It was still light outside, and even with the heavy curtains drawn across, there was still enough evening light filtering in to keep him restless. Besides, he couldn't stop thinking about the clue. *The city of Auckland. Find the winning square. Another board...* What on earth did it mean? He stared at the ceiling. Maybe, just maybe he was making this harder than it should be. It couldn't be that complicated could it? After all, the Squire left the clue for the old lady. He knew she'd be able to figure it out somehow. That means it would probably be something she would know about—something close to home.

Okay, he needed to think—starting with the chessboard idea. Had he seen one here at the inn? Not just lying about for sure, but could there be one in a drawer or a game cupboard even? Perhaps, but the clue said he had to find the winning square. The only way to find the winning square was to have a board set up with a game already in progress. Some newspapers carried a chessboard setup in their puzzles section—something where you had to figure out the move required to get a checkmate. Could that be the answer? Where else would there be a chess game in progress?

Kennedy sat straight up. He stared at the door, without really seeing it. A slow smile crept over his face. He knew where the chessboard was. *Oh, yes!*

He grabbed his shoes and started lacing them on furiously. He would need a scrap of paper and pen, and he needed to be sure no-one saw what he was going to do.

☙❧

"A ship? Wow! We never thought of that," said Emily, shaking her head in admiration.

"Look through the *City of Auckland*," said Danny, remembering the poem.

"And another board you'll see," finished Rachel. "Through a ship... What can that mean?"

"Okay, so here's what we need to do," said Dad, carefully setting the chessboard on the dresser and then plopping down on the bed. "First, everyone up here."

The family liked that idea and they all jumped up, Stevie being helped by Mom who then plunked down next to Dad.

"First of all, you did great with your tasks; yes, even you and Emily." Dad nodded at Stevie who was looking rather dejected. "We can't always figure everything out first go."

"And you eliminated a bunch of places the board couldn't be," added Mom, smiling.

Stevie perked up at that.

"So, we need to find something with this ship. It could be a painting, a photo..."

"I think we've got to keep in mind that we need to look *through* the ship," said Mom.

"Uh-huh," agreed Dad. "That's a good point. Let's think about that. What kind of things do you look through?"

"A window," said Stevie.

"Anything glass," said Rachel, following Stevie's line of thinking.

"A telescope," put in Danny. "Maybe we need to look through one to see a ship!"

"But we've got to look through the ship, not something else," said Emily, confused.

They all fell silent. It was true.

"I've got it!" said Danny suddenly. "How about a ship in a bottle! You know, one of those things like they had in the shop today."

Dad nodded slowly. "Could be, could be..."

"You just might have got it Danny," agreed Mom, ruffling his hair.

The others looked at each other in excitement, Stevie even managing to ignore his disappointment at not being the one to figure things out.

"So that's what we need to find," said Dad, standing up. "Let's split up and search."

"Remember to keep quiet," warned Mom. "We're still trying to keep this a secret!"

"But we need to plan a bit though, don't we?" said Emily jumping off the bed. "If we're all going everywhere together, the Tremannons or that man will be sure to notice."

"Hmmm. Perhaps you're right," agreed Dad, rubbing his chin.

"But excuse me, wait a minute," said Stevie, waving his hand. "Me and Emily already looked everywhere and we didn't see a ship in a bottle."

"Emily and I," corrected Dad. "But you weren't looking for a ship then."

"It's true, though," said Emily, suddenly feeling rather dejected. "There aren't that many places to look in the inn."

"It could be outside," said Danny, not wanting to give up hope so easily.

"A ship in a bottle *outside*?" said Stevie, rather scornfully. Danny gave him a look.

"We don't even know it is at the inn," said Rachel. "Why would it have to be?"

They had forgotten that. Their shoulders slumped.

"This is impossible," moaned Stevie.

"You know what?" said Dad, breaking in.

"What?" said Mom.

"We need to pray. We're not getting anywhere and we're all getting frustrated." Dad wished he had thought of it earlier, but better late than never.

"That's right," said Mom, realizing it herself. "This isn't about how clever we are or how difficult the clue is."

The kids looked a bit skeptical. Mom kept going. "Do we think it's God's will that we help Mrs. Renton?"

Well, they were all sure of *that* now. They nodded.

"Okay, then God needs to be the center of our search. He knows where the ship is!"

Dad nodded. "So, let's go ahead and pray." He looked around. Everyone bowed their heads.

"Dear Jesus, thank you so much for your mercy and love. We're sorry we didn't ask you about this first, but we believe that you love Mrs. Renton and you want her to know you personally. And we believe that somehow solving this mystery that the Squire made will help her come to you, so please help us. You know we're trying to find a ship in a bottle and another board of some kind. You know what we need, so please guide us. Help us to work together with good attitudes. In Your name."

"Amen," they all said together.

Dad looked around at their faces. They still looked rather glum.

"So, how do we want to do this? We still need to check the inn again. How about Rachel and Danny this time?"

"Er, maybe I can check somewhere else," said Danny, a worried look on his face.

Dad suddenly remembered that he was still concerned about that Kennedy guy.

"Well, how about you and me checking outside the inn. When I was a boy in England, I remember some people's houses had things embedded in their stone walls, like pottery images and glass bottles. Maybe there's something like that."

Danny wandered over to the window. Dusk was definitely coming on. It would be better to be with Dad, for sure. The man's car was parked in front of the inn which meant he was somewhere around. Danny suddenly froze. "He's there--the man's down there!"

With a bit of pushing and shoving the family crowded around the window. Sure enough, it was Mr. Kennedy, standing next to his car and fumbling in his pocket for something. After a moment he produced what looked like a piece of paper and then turned to look up at the inn.

"What's he doing?" said Emily. "Writing something?"

Rachel had a sudden concerned thought. "Get back from the window!"

They froze for a second then jumped back in a jumbled mess, Emily and Danny falling onto the bed.

"There's Mr. Tremannon," announced Mom, peering around the edge of the window. "He's coming over to talk to Mr. Kennedy."

"Mr. Tremannon doesn't talk," said Rachel cheekily. "He only says one word at a time."

"I think it's cute," said Emily. She came and peered under Mom's arm, watching the scene. The two men were apparently having some sort of heated interaction. As they watched, Mr. Kennedy glanced up towards their window. Mom and Emily both gasped and stepped quickly back.

"What happened?" said Dad anxiously.

"I think he saw us," said Emily.

The others looked concerned at that piece of information. Dad took a very careful peek out of the window again and watched for a moment. "Well, it looks like Mr. Kennedy's given up. He just went back in."

Mom took a peek too. Sure enough the man had disappeared and Mr. Tremannon was heading back towards the vegetable garden.

"That was a bit strange. I wonder what our friend was doing," she pondered.

"Maybe he was writing down the name of the inn, from the sign?" suggested Rachel.

"Oh, my goodness!" said Mom suddenly, gripping Dad's arm. "Oh, my word! Oh, Jesus, thank You!"

"What, what?" said Dad in amazement. The others ran over to the window.

"The inn sign. I just realized. Look at the picture. In the window behind the Squire!"

"It's a ship! It's a ship!" squeaked Stevie.

"It's a stained glass window of a ship!" said Dad, breathless. "And I'm sure it's the same ship we saw online—*The City of Auckland*! At least it looks the same."

He looked around. Everyone was grinning from ear to ear.

"And you can look through a stained glass window," said Emily triumphantly.

"But where is it?" said Stevie.

"Well, we need to figure that out," smiled Dad.

But Mom had something to say first. She held up her hand. "I think we should all thank God for the answer to prayer, and then pray about the next step."

Dad nodded slowly. "You know, you're right, dear. We've been trying to do this pretty much on our own strength. Let's do that and ask for His wisdom." He grabbed Mom and Emily's hands. The family got the clue and formed a circle.

"Let's pray," said Dad.

⤺⤻

For the second time that evening Kennedy pulled off his shoes and flung himself down in bed, his thoughts a turmoil. *That wretched Mr. Tremannon.* What a time to make an appearance, before he could jot anything down. And what were that family doing watching him from the window? Were they getting suspicious?

He put his hands behind his head and tried to slow his thoughts down. He was still being too rash, that was evident. He must be more careful—to really think things through. Tomorrow he would get up early, get the info off the sign and start afresh. He needed to somehow get ahead of the family, and there were only two ways he could see to do that. Either solve things more quickly, or steal from them what they had.

He pondered that for a moment. He hadn't profited yet from the red-headed kid's fear of him. Maybe he could exploit that. Maybe he could get the information he needed from him. But he would have to be careful all right. Very, very careful.

࿊࿊

"So guys," said Dad, looking at the expectant faces in front of him. "We need to find that stained glass window. Any ideas?"

Mom glanced at the kids, wanting to give them a chance to have input, but they all looked puzzled. No help there. "Well, it looks like we need to find the room that the Squire was in when the picture was painted," she said finally.

"Do we know he was in a real room? It might just be a background the artist painted," said Emily.

The others pondered that for a bit. "I think it was probably a real room," said Dad at last. "And wouldn't that make sense anyway? Mrs. Renton needed to be able to find it."

"We could call her and see if she knows about the ship window," suggested Emily.

Mom looked at her watch. "It's too late to call now. It's nine-thirty. In fact, we should really be getting you to bed."

"Oh, please no!" chorused the kids. Mom and Dad exchanged smiles.

"Okay, you can stay up for a bit, but we need to decide what to do. Do I have any volunteers to look downstairs for the window?" said Dad.

"We just looked downstairs," frowned Stevie, "and we didn't see anything."

"But you weren't looking for the ship," said Rachel. "You might have missed it."

"No we didn't. I'm sure we would have seen it," said Emily, feeling a bit annoyed.

Dad held up his hand. "Okay, let's think for a minute. Are there any rooms in the inn we haven't seen yet?"

"Of course," said Mom. "We haven't see the Tremannon's room."

"Or the nasty man's room," said Danny with a shudder.

"Hmmm, there is that, yes," said Dad frowning. "Are there any other guest rooms?"

No-one knew the answer to that.

"Alright then. Let's at least figure out what we're dealing with. I know we've the only guest rooms on this floor. Anyone want to pop downstairs and check how many other rooms there are? They'd be back near Mr. Kennedy's room if anywhere." He looked around at the others. No-one looked very eager.

"Okaaay. I guess it's me. I'll be back in a jiffy." He jumped up and trotted out the door.

Rachel looked at Mom. "Mom, are we really sure there weren't any stained glass windows in any of the rooms we've seen?"

"I don't think there were. It's not like we would've missed something like that. What's up Emily?" Mom noticed that Emily was staring out the window again.

"I was just looking at the sign. The window with the ship in it has the same sort of little diamond-shaped window panes as all the other windows here at the inn."

The others came over to see. She was right.

"Well, that does mean it's at least possible that it's here." said Mom. "But where?"

"It's probably in one of the rooms we can't go in," said Rachel gloomily.

"Let's wait till Dad gets back," said Mom, "and think it through."

The kids peered hopefully down the hallway, and it really wasn't very long before they heard Dad trotting up the stairs again. He grinned at them as he reached the top. He put his finger to his lips though, and they had to wait until he was back in the room. He made a show of closing the door very quietly, which seemed to up the suspense level dramatically.

"Okay, so there is only one guest room down below. It's room number 1 hosting Mr. Café Kennedy."

"So what if the ship's in his room?" said Stevie mournfully.

Dad patted his shoulder. "I had an idea about that. Why don't a couple of us go outside and walk around the house. We could discretely check the windows, and should be able to see if there's a ship stained glass in one."

"What does discretely mean again?" asked Stevie.

"Kind of secretly—so no-one who might see us would wonder what we're up to." Dad pantomimed someone doing a sneaky kind of walk.

"Oh, kind of like a spy then," said Stevie.

"Kind of."

"But what if the ship's in the angry man's room," said Danny, looking anxious.

"Or the Tremannon's," added Emily.

"Let's cross that bridge when we come to it," said Mom. "First of all, we need to find the ship! I'll go," she added, feeling suddenly adventurous. "Who'll go with me?"

"I will!" said Rachel before anyone else could. The idea of doing something with just Mom sounded pretty cool.

"Okay, thanks," said Dad. "The rest of us will...well let's see. What will we do?"

"I could look at the sign some more, and try to figure out if there's anything else there that'll help." Danny wanted to assign himself something fairly safe.

"Alright. Stevie, Emily? How about doing one more pass through the rooms we can get in and make triple sure we haven't missed anything. I'll stay with Danny and think some more for now." Dad knew that would please Danny. He still hadn't really addressed the lad's fear of the man. Maybe this would be a good opportunity.

Mom grabbed her jacket. "Okay, everyone. Break!"

Mrs. Renton fluffed up her pillow and settled herself carefully onto the little sofa. She just fit, with her foot elevated slightly as the doctor had recommended. As she lay there, looking up at the ceiling, her thoughts swept back over the past few days. How amazing that the Chapman family were actually helping her! She had been living life alone for so many years, both physically and emotionally. Oh yes, she'd had lots of acquaintances over the years in all the countries she'd visited, but no real friends—no-one she ever felt comfortable confiding in. Even her brief relationship with Jack, her photographer husband, had remained emotionally distant. All of them had come up against the wall of hurt that blocked any possibility of getting close to her. And now this conflicting jumble of emotions as she found herself opening up more than she ever thought she could—perhaps even more than she had intended.

She felt a wave of embarrassment. *What was she thinking?* That nice family was ruining their holiday, and it was all her fault. All of it was her fault, from beginning to end. Why did she have to drag them into it too?

"God, help them please."

Her own words surprised her completely. *Where had that prayer come from?* Well, it wasn't really a prayer was it? Just an overflow of her distressed emotions, expressing itself in a random irrational plea. She shook her head. God wasn't going to hear any prayer of hers, that was certain.

"So, old chum, how are you doing?" Dad put his hand on Danny's shoulder as the lad stood at the window, looking out at the inn sign.

Silence. Dad waited, figuring his son was wrestling with the question. He felt the boy sigh under his hand. It took some effort, but Dad decided to be patient and let Danny do a bit of processing. He looked over the lad's shoulder at the inn sign, swinging in the evening breeze. The sun was very low now, and the sky was getting a tinge of peach over the darkening blue, like a watercolor painting.

He saw his wife and Rachel appear from the front door. He noticed that Rachel had bare feet, and it appeared that Mom had only just noticed that too. There was some gesturing and discussion, but Rachel must have won because they soon stepped back to examine the building, arm in arm. It must be getting a bit chilly, he noted, seeing them cling together and bounce up and down like they were trying to generate some warmth. Rachel must have had a good argument for going out in bare feet.

Danny still hadn't answered. Dad's patience didn't stretch that long, and he opened his mouth to say something when the boy suddenly tensed under his hand and then spun around to face him.

"Dad, Dad! I just thought of something!" The boy's face was lit up with excitement.

"Er, okay." Dad had to snap out of his other mode. "What is it?"

"When I woke up early the first morning I kind of went exploring. You remember when you found me downstairs? I was pretending I was...well, kind of a spy—no, a secret agent. Or was it a spy?"

"Maybe it doesn't matter." Dad's patience was getting a wee bit tested again. "Keep going."

"Well I was checking out things and looking out the window and I remember looking at the doors and there was something kind of weird."

"What do you mean weird?" Dad was getting interested now.

"The numbers on the doors. They didn't seem right." Danny struggled to explain it. "I mean, they weren't in order or something."

"Show me," said Dad, pulling Danny by the hand. Maybe the lad was onto something.

Danny stopped as they went out the bedroom door, tugging back on Dad's hand. "Look right here. Number five, right?"

"Right."

Now it was Danny's turn to lead. He dragged Dad over to his room and pointed. "Number four."

"Okay."

He pulled Dad down the hallway and onto the stairs. "This way. To the girls'."

At that moment Emily and Stevie appeared from the dining room below and started for the stairs, shushing each other.

"Hang on, Danny," said Dad. "Just a second."

They waited until Emily and Stevie joined them on the landing. "What's up?" Dad remembered to lower his voice. "We should be pretty quiet. It's really late."

"We saw a photo by the kitchen door--the Squire in the room again with the ship in the window."

"That's right," said Dad, suddenly remembering. "It was right below the picture with the mantel's tile! Did you find out anything?"

Emily looked a bit guiltily. "Well, I did lift the picture off the wall."

"Really carefully," put in Stevie.

"Really carefully, but there wasn't anything on the back."

"And we couldn't look through the ship. It was just a picture." Stevie looked crestfallen.

"Well, okay. Thanks for checking. I'm glad you were careful." He smiled at Emily, who relaxed again. "Danny's on to something, though. Tell them, Danny."

Danny gave a big grin. He felt pretty important, and made a show of putting his finger to his lips. "There's something weird about the room numbers. Dad and Mom's is number five. Mine is number four."

"And mine," interrupted Stevie, annoyed at being left out.

"And look at yours." Danny pointed for Emily.

"Number two," said Emily.

"And Mr. Kennedy's was number one." Dad was impressed. He asked the question they were all thinking. "Where's room number three?"

Mom held Rachel's arm as they snuck around the back of the house, trying to be as quiet as possible. Rachel was secretly regretting not wearing any shoes, as the path was liberally strewn with little stones, like a miniature minefield. She tried to keep her discomfort to herself.

They passed what must have been the window for the Tremannon's sitting room. The curtains were drawn and the room looked dark. There didn't seem to be anything hanging in the window. There were no other windows at this end of the building except what must belong to the bathroom—too small to be the one they were looking for. They crept up to the back corner. Mom tried to copy Dad's sneaky spy walk, and Rachel had to stifle a giggle.

They peered around the corner to the back of the inn, Mom's head above and Rachel's below. The back garden was deep in shadow. They both listened. A few birds trilled their evening melodies, and far away, carried on the breeze they heard a horse whinny. It was a favorite sound for the two, and seemed to add to the feeling of adventure.

Mom beckoned to Rachel and they stepped around to where the old kitchen door led to the back terrace. The kitchen window was open a crack, and it was easy to see that there was no stained glass hanging there. They backed up a few paces onto the lawn and stared up at what must be the Tremannon's window. A diffused glow filtered through the drawn curtains, but there was evidently nothing there either. Rachel looked at Mom, who shrugged. There weren't many more windows on the back side. Just the girls' bedroom and the guest bathroom if they remembered correctly.

Rachel's optimism was fading fast. Maybe they weren't going to find anything after all.

⋆⋅☽☾⋅⋆

Dad and the kids stood at the top of the stairs staring at the floor to ceiling tapestry.

"It can only be behind here," said Dad. "Do you want to do the honors, Danny? It was your idea."

But that was an honor that Danny was happy to refuse. There was no way he wanted to be first to check for a secret room, when who knows what might be hiding there.

"Er, no, that's okay. Go ahead, Daddy." He forced a smile.

Dad looked around at the others, but no-one seemed too eager. It was up to him. The tapestry was attached at the top, but hung freely. He carefully lifted it away from the wall and peered around the side. *Bingo!*

⋆⋅☽☾⋅⋆

Rachel and Mom picked their way carefully along the patio, trying not to trip over the uneven paving stones. It was getting a bit harder to see and they didn't want to do anything that might make a noise.

Mom pointed and put her finger to her lips. Rachel nodded. Right there was the window belonging to Mr. Kennedy's room, but like the others it was distressingly empty.

219

Mom led Rachel out onto the lawn and away from the back of the house a little way. Rachel immediately appreciated the cool soft grass. Thankfully, there weren't any lights showing from this end of the house.

As they scanned the windows, however, they suddenly came to the same realization. There was one window on the second story at the end that they couldn't account for.

Rachel grabbed Mom's arm. "Whose window is that?" she whispered.

"I don't know," Mom whispered back. "That's your room there, and that's the bathroom. I don't remember another room there."

"It looks like there's something hanging in the window though," said Rachel excitedly.

Mom shushed her again. "I can see something, though it's hard to figure out what—the window's so dark and the thing's on the inside."

Suddenly Rachel gave a barely suppressed squeal. "There's a face there—in the window!"

≪δ≫

"There's a door here! There's no handle though." Dad scanned the door from top to bottom. "Oh, wait, there's a little catch here. Hang on."

He reached up and flipped the catch, and the door moved slightly. He pushed it gently and it swung inwards several inches. A dim light from beyond illuminated dusty wooden floorboards. Dad glanced back over his shoulder. "Anyone coming with?"

Emily pursed her lips, then nodded. Danny and Stevie shook their heads. Dad ducked around the tapestry and stepped into the room, Emily at his heels. The room was almost bare, with just a barren desk and several empty bookcases along one wall. Dad's attention however was completely taken up by something at the far end. A mullioned window, its diamond-shaped panes of glass letting in the last of the evening light, lay directly ahead, and right in the center hung a beautiful stained glass picture of a ship under full sail.

"Kids," he said quietly over his shoulder. "You're going to want to see this."

The others looked at each other in excitement. Emily nodded firmly, grabbed Stevie's hand and led them into the room. They gathered close around Dad, still a little ill at ease about their surroundings. A thick layer of dust covered what little furniture there was, and Stevie gave a huge sneeze.

"Shhh!" warned Danny.

"I can't help it," retorted Stevie. "My nose exploded."

"Okay, keep your voices low everyone," said Dad. "And try to tiptoe. We might be over Mr. Kennedy's room."

That had the desired effect. They stepped as lightly as they could over to the window. The stained glass picture was truly a work of art. It was apparent that each little piece of glass had been carefully selected and shaped and outlined in black leading. A small brass plaque had been screwed onto the bottom of the frame with the name of the vessel written in perfect cursive script: *The City of Auckland.*

"Is it a warship?" whispered Stevie, hopefully.

"Well, I don't think so," said Dad. "There aren't any guns. Maybe a merchant ship of some kind?"

Emily came up to the window and looked down to the back garden. "Look, there's Mom and Rachel!" She noticed Rachel point up to her, looking shocked. There was some hurried discussion between the two. Emily waved frantically and after a slight pause saw the others wave back.

Dad joined Emily and waved too. "Let's get them to come back up here." They both beckoned excitedly to the two below and were rewarded by them turning and hurrying off around the corner of the house.

"So do we look through the ship?" said Danny. "Like, through the stained glass window?"

"I imagine so, but let's wait for Mom and Rachel. We want to do this together."

"But that might take ages," said Stevie.

"Not if I know your Mom and Rachel. Emily, can you go poke your head around the tapestry so they can see where we are?"

Emily nodded and scurried to the door. It seemed like only a minute before she was back with the others in tow.

"Goodness," exclaimed Mom, panting a little. "This is it! The room on the sign."

"And the ship!" squealed Rachel.

"Shhh," warned Dad. He gestured at the floor, and the others nodded seriously. They tiptoed over to the window.

"Danny, how about you looking first. You were the one who figured out about the secret room."

Danny nodded, delighted at the privilege. Dad held him up and he peered at the ship. Most of the glass pieces were opaque, but there was one exception, the mainsail of the vessel was made of a much clearer glass, like a window through the design. Dad positioned Danny so he could see through, the others crowding around.

"What do you see? What do you see?" said Stevie, tugging at Danny's leg and forgetting to keep his voice low.

"Shhh" said everyone else together. Stevie shrunk back, ashamed. Mom took pity on him and hoisted him up in her arms.

"What do you see?" whispered Dad.

"Well, I see some trees and the back hedge, but I don't think I see anything else."

"Can I look?" said Stevie, remembering to be quiet.

Dad made way, and Mom held the boy up to the window. Emily and Rachel looked out of the main window trying to see anything themselves. Stevie scanned the scene below him, but shook his head. "I don't see anything. Is it buried in the grass?"

"I don't know," said Mom. "Here, let me look. I'm about Mrs. Renton's height." She put Stevie down and peered through the window in the sail.

She stared hard, adjusted her position slightly and stared again. *What was that, through the branches of the tree?* Dusk was deepening rapidly and it was getting hard to see. Then, with a sudden realization she knew.

"My secret garden!" she exclaimed. "Ooops, sorry," she added, lowering her voice. "It's my secret garden. I can see the opening through the hedge, right in line with the view!"

The others all wanted to see, and it was a few minutes before Dad could corral everyone's attention again. He kept his voice low. "Okay, everyone. Listen up. We must remember to be quiet. It looks like that's what we were supposed to see for the clue."

"But what about the other board?" said Emily, remembering the rest of the clue.

"Well, we need to go look."

"Now?" said Rachel, suddenly hopeful. Did Dad really mean they didn't have to go to bed and wait till tomorrow?

Dad grinned, guessing her thoughts. "Do you want to go to bed? We can."

All the kids shook their heads, smiling broadly. This was feeling like a real adventure!

"Okay, quietly as possible, back to your rooms and grab something warm. Danny, get your flashlight. It's getting dark outside. Let's meet in our room in five minutes. And remember to tiptoe!"

❧❧

Kennedy stirred again fitfully. He was having a disturbing dream. The Chapman family were all gathered around a huge chest that they had apparently just dug up. The dad was lifting the lid to reveal an amazing treasure. The kids were all yelling, and Kennedy was standing there in front of them, but they apparently did not see him. He tried shouting at them, but they didn't seem to hear.

Kennedy woke with a start. He propped himself up on an elbow trying to think clearly. *What was that all about?* He rubbed his eyes and reached over for the glass of water on his nightstand. What an unpleasant dream. Could it have meant something? Kennedy wasn't big on dream interpretations.

Some slight noise caught his attention. He listened. *Did he hear muffled voices? Was that the floor creaking above his head?* He sat up, his own bed creaking, and tried to be absolutely quiet. Then he listened again.

All was silent. He must have been imagining it. He thumped his pillow angrily, trying to give it some shape. Then he threw himself down again and closed his eyes.

❧❧

The family snuck through the front door, Dad closing it carefully and quietly behind them. There was a stiff, cool breeze blowing from the direction of the sea, and they all had their jackets zipped up to their chins. The kids could barely contain their excitement, the lateness of the hour adding to the overwhelming sense of adventure. Dad led the way around the house, repeatedly looking back with his finger on his lips, but they were all being as quiet as could be, the only noise being a slight crunching of the gravel between the flagstones of the path.

As soon as possible Dad led them onto the lawn at the back of the house. He paused to get his bearings and then headed off diagonally across the grass in the direction of the secret garden, the family trooping along behind with the kids shaking with excitement. They ducked under the trees and came to the entrance. The garden on the other side looked dim and mysterious in the fading light.

"Check for spiders!" whispered Mom from the rear.

"What?" Dad whispered back.

"Check for spiders. In the entryway."

"Really?"

Mom gave him a look. Dad reluctantly waved his arm up and down in the gap. He knew his wife's fear of creepy crawlies, especially spiders. He wasn't afraid of them himself per se, but he didn't like them dropping in unannounced like that one time in the shower.

"All clear," he reported. He stepped through and made room for everyone else. "No deadly arachnids," he announced to Mom as she hurried through.

"Okay, troops. Here we are." Dad shone the flashlight around at the grinning faces before him. He had to shake his head in disbelief. What a weird vacation this was turning out to be. He grinned back. "Do any of you remember the clue?"

Emily was the first to respond. "Look through the *City of Auckland*," she recited. "Another board you'll see. Find the square, in looking there beneath the clue will be."

"But where's the board," said Danny looking around.

"We'll have to look," said Mom. "Is it buried?"

"Well, maybe," said Dad, pursing his lips.

"It's got to be straight ahead from the window, so that means in the hedge at the back," announced Rachel.

Before Mom or Dad could say anything, the other kids all made a sudden rush to check. Stevie tripped over Danny's foot and sprawled head first onto the ground.

"Kids!" Dad gave a fierce whisper. The other three stopped dead in their tracks. Mom bent over to help Stevie who was whimpering.

"Danny, come over here and help."

He came over slowly, his head hanging in shame. "I'm sorry," he whispered. He held out his hand and helped pull Stevie up.

As Stevie's foot dragged across the ground, Mom gasped in surprise.

"Look at the paving stones!"

Danny shone his flashlight at the ground. Stevie's foot had revealed several old paving stones that had been hidden under the leaves, alternating between squares of faded black and dirty white.

"A chessboard," breathed Stevie, his eyes shining, completely forgetting about his fall.

"Quick everyone, let's clear them off." Dad started brushing away the debris and the others quickly joined in. In a few minutes they had uncovered a complete eight by eight set of square stones, almost filling the area. They stood up and surveyed their results with satisfaction.

"Okay, Danny. You're up. Where's the winning square?" Dad gestured at the board.

Danny stepped back, thrust his hands in his pockets and studied the ground critically. The others looked back and forth from him to the stones, waiting with some measure of impatience.

"Well?" said Dad finally.

"Er, I'm not sure which end is which. Like where each side would start."

"Aha. Good question. Anyone?" Dad turned to the others.

There was a momentary silence. Then Emily raised her hand. "Dad, the Squire would have had to make it obvious to Mrs. Renton wouldn't he?"

"Well, yes, go on."

In reply Emily squatted down and examined the edges of the chessboard. She suddenly pointed at a corner stone. "Look. A letter 'B'"

"For 'black'," said Mom, excitedly. She looked carefully at the opposite corner. There was a small letter W engraved on the stone. "And white here. Danny? Is that what you needed?"

Danny nodded seriously. He put his hands on his hips and frowned at the board. The others held their breaths. He walked forward a few steps, made some pointing motions with his finger, then stopped and indicated a square with his foot. He looked up at Dad and nodded firmly.

"Okay, let's look underneath. Anyone?" Dad didn't really expect any takers. None of the family had the habit of looking under stones just for fun—not with the potential creepy-crawlies lurking underneath.

He felt around the square. It was a cement patio tile, about an inch thick. He gave a tug, but it didn't budge. What to do? He didn't have a knife and didn't want to waste time looking for one.

He had a sudden idea. He unbuckled his belt and inserted the end of the buckle under the corner of the tile. He gave a sharp tug and was rewarded by a reluctant squelch as it lifted up slightly from its muddy prison. He dropped the belt and reached under the edge with both hands. One more good tug and the tile was free. Dad sat back on his heels and looked up with a grin. "Take a look!"

The others crowded around and peered into the hole. They could see the top of what looked like a small, rusty metal box protruding from the mud. Several worms curled frantically on top, and the kids had to stifle their reactions. Dad brushed the creatures off and pulled out the box. He held it up. "Let's clean up here and take this inside for a look!"

⤜⤛⤚

Up on their parent's arena-sized bed, the kids looked on with wide eyes as Dad carefully pried open the box and took out a small black bag, tied tightly at the top.

"Waterproof," said Mom, and Dad nodded.

The knot took some working at, but using her nails Mom was finally able to pry it open.

224

"Go ahead, dear," said Dad. "You earned first look."

Mom carefully drew the top of the bag open and pulled out another bag, this one of clear plastic tied with yet another knot. They could see several paper-looking things inside.

Danny gave a knowing smile. "Yup. More letters and stuff. Just like I thought."

"Me too," said Stevie.

The second knot was much easier than the first and Mom soon had the contents spread out for them all to see. There were two letters and a newspaper article. Written boldly across one of the letters were the words "*read first.*"

"So can we read it?" said Stevie. He made a grab for the papers and Mom had to snatch them away.

"Just a minute, mister. These aren't for us, remember? These are for Mrs. Renton."

The kids all groaned. They had forgotten about that. Did that mean they would have to wait until tomorrow?

Dad confirmed it with a firm nod. "These are to her from the Squire. We'll take them first thing."

"But we're the detectives!" cried Stevie. Emily, Rachel and Danny didn't say anything, but they were feeling the same way.

"Shhh," said Dad. He reached over and pulled the boy close. "Yes we are, but it's like she's our chief. We're doing the field work for her, but it's her inheritance, and the Squire had something special he wanted her to learn from it. We don't want to spoil that do we?"

Stevie sniffed, thought for a moment and gave a reluctant little shake of his head.

"Let's try to be thankful for what we can do," said Mom. "We're getting to participate in this adventure with her, and we've had a lot of fun trying to decipher the clues."

"And it's a real privilege to be able to help her," added Dad.

"Yes," said Emily, warming to the idea. "She couldn't do it without us."

"Especially now that she's hurt her ankle," said Danny.

Rachel suddenly remembered the mystery guy who seemed to be following them today. Should she mention it? No, she was sure she shouldn't, but it did add some significance to their role in helping the old lady, didn't it? "Yes, we really do need to help her. Who knows what might happen if we don't," she said, with a faraway look in her eyes.

Mom looked at her in surprise but didn't say anything.

Dad quickly checked his watch. "Okay, everyone. It's really late and we want to be able to get these things to Mrs. Renton right after breakfast."

He glanced over at Stevie who still looked glum. "Hey, bud. I tell you what. We can at least look at the newspaper. Want to read the headline?"

Stevie nodded vigorously. The others squeezed in around as Dad carefully extracted the paper. He indicated the bold type and Stevie sounded out the words.

"*City wrecked on Otaki Beach. All souls saved.*' Wow!" He pointed at the faded picture underneath—a majestic sailing ship evidently aground and listing heavily to one side.

"The *City of Auckland*! It got wrecked!" exclaimed Danny. "How? What does it say?"

"It will have to wait until tomorrow," said Mom firmly. "It's super late. Let's spend a few minutes thanking God for what He's done so far."

Dad nodded. "Yes, let's do that. And then to bed!"

Chapter 15 - A Crushing Blow

"Come in! The door's unlocked!"

They could hear Mrs. Renton's voice clearly from the other side of the door. To Mom and Dad's relief she sounded surprisingly spry.

The whole family were crowded on the front step of her little house, most of them yawning widely. It had been a real chore prying everyone out of bed in time for breakfast, and Dad had ended up leading a short family prayer time and Bible reading rather than having each person doing their own devotions. To all their satisfaction, the café man—Mr. Kennedy—hadn't appeared while they were eating. They had finished up as quickly as the huge breakfast would allow, and hustled out and down the hill to the row of houses overlooking the harbor, Mom suggesting they walk as much as possible with all the eating they were doing. The weather was cooperating for now, with plenty of blue showing between the fluffy masses of grey and white.

Dad opened the front door and ushered the family inside. Mrs. Renton was sitting in an armchair with her foot up on a low stool. Her tabby cat, Mr. Pickwick, was curled up on her lap, but raised up his head and cocked a sleepy eye at the sudden intrusion.

"How are you?" said Mom, anxiously.

"Better, I think," smiled the old lady. "Come and sit down." She gestured at the couch.

Mom and Dad took their seats while the kids plumped down on the floor at their feet, looking at Dad expectantly. Dad made a 'wait' gesture with his hand and addressed Mrs. Renton. "Are you really okay? We can come back later if you want."

"No, no, I'm fine. I'm glad you're here." She smiled broadly. "I can't wait to hear what you found out. But first you need some tea. We can't have a good tale without tea....and scones. I have some in a tin in the cupboard."

She made as if to struggle to her feet causing the cat to meow in protest, but Mom quickly intervened. "I'll do it. Dave can fill you in on what we discovered last night. I'll be back in a jiffy."

She hurried off to the kitchen before the old lady could say anything, and Dad proceeded to relate all of last evening's adventures, helped by the kids who eagerly supplied any details he overlooked. Rachel struggled again as to whether she should mention her theory about the mystery man, but Mom solved her dilemma by returning at that moment with a loaded tray. They paused to distribute the contents, and when everyone was settled again, finished up the tale.

Mrs. Renton sipped her tea and listened in amazement. "I'm sure I couldn't have figured all that out myself," she said when they were done. "Thank you so much."

"It's our pleasure," said Dad, truly meaning it.

Mom reached in her purse and produced the documents. "Here's what we found." She handed them across to Mrs. Renton.

The old lady scanned the papers and put the Squire's letter on top of the others. "Here's where I'm supposed to start it seems." She gave a nervous smile. "I'll read it out loud, if that's alright with you."

The others all nodded. Of course it was alright.

"My dearest Ruthie," the old lady began. *"Congratulations are in order once again. You are doing so well."* Mrs. Renton gave an embarrassed grin. She put her hand to the side of her mouth. "I think it's you all who are doing well," she whispered. "But I'll keep going." Pickwick stirred on her lap and she gave his chin a quick scratch.

"You may feel very confused but I'm praying this will all make a world of sense sometime soon." She raised her eyebrows at that but continued on. *"Read the newspaper article first. Then the letter. Then come back here for the next clue."*

"Another clue!" exclaimed Danny. "How many are there going to be?"

The old lady shook her head, having thought the very same thing. "I don't know, young man." She paused for a moment, then took a quick sip of tea. "Alright, where were we?"

"The newspaper," said Stevie, bouncing up and down.

"Oh, yes." She selected it from the papers on her lap and held it up so the others could see. It was apparently an article cut from an old paper. Mrs. Renton read the headline out loud. *"City wrecked on Otaki Beach. All souls saved."* She turned the paper back to look at it. "There's a date here—October 29th, 1878, and in small letters it says *'Napier Herald.'* I suppose that's the name of the newspaper."

"What does it mean that all souls were saved?" said Rachel. "Does it mean all the people became Christians?"

"Yeah, after being so scared about being wrecked," nodded Danny.

"Well, we can hope they did," said Mom, "but I think it means that nobody lost their lives. Would you mind reading the article?" she said to Mrs. Renton.

"Not at all. Let's see." She adjusted her glasses. *"The immigrant ship City of Auckland was wrecked on Otaki Beach around 9:30 in the evening, October 22nd. The City was 93 days out of London, heading to Napier with 240 immigrants and a cargo of 400 tons of railway iron. Witnesses report that many immigrants panicked and made a rush for the* boats, and Captain George Ralls was forced to stand over the lifeboats with a loaded revolver and enforce that the women and children disembarked first. This was Captain Rall's sixth voyage as master of the City and he has been commended for his actions during the crisis. The ship was the 3rd vessel in recent months to be wrecked in the vicinity, causing concern for many citizens who are calling for the need of a light to be permanently placed on Kapiti Island."

Mrs. Renton put the paper down and sat back. Pickwick gazed up at her in seeming admiration, purring like a motor boat, and the children all started clamoring at once.

"Hey!" yelled Dad above the din. The noise switched off as if by magic. "Thank you. Now how about we let Mrs. Renton continue?"

"Well," she said. "That's it. I've no idea what that has to do with me and the inheritance." She looked thoughtful. "I suppose I should read the letter, shouldn't I?" She pulled out a folded sheet and carefully opened it. Pickwick yawned on her lap, apparently not too interested in the contents. The kids all scooted a bit closer. They didn't want to miss a thing.

"It's a letter sure enough," said Mrs. Renton, turning it slightly towards the window so she could see it better. "It's dated October 27th, 1878 from Otaki."

"Just a few days after the wreck," said Emily.

Mrs. Renton nodded back and continued. "It's from, er..." She glanced at the back side. "From a Perran Trenholm. I wonder what *he's* got to do with the inheritance. Anyway...let's see." She turned to the front again.

"My dear Davy, I wanted to send you word as soon as I could in case details of our voyage reached you earlier. I have grievous news to relate, and that so soon after our arrival. God moves in mysterious ways, thou knowest. Firstly, He preserved us in what might verily have been otherwise tragic circumstances. Our brave vessel, the City of Auckland, and home for us these three months past, ran aground the night of the 22nd. There was shouting and pounding of feet on the deck above and much confusion around us below. Two hundred forty of us immigrants, packed tight enough, with many young ones besides. Such a crying and a wailing, for of course no-one knew aught but that at any moment the sea could come rushing in. Jenna and I clung together and beseeched our Lord for His aid."

Mrs. Renton paused for a moment, took a deep breath and then continued. *"We soon learned that there was no immediate danger, but that was no assurance to many, and a great press of men tried to make their way up the ladder close by. We heard the crew shout that there was no rescue yet and the safest thing for all was to remain quiet below and they battened the hatches for the night. What a night that was. The ship was listing and we could feel the waves pounding her. We prayed for the dawn. Jenna was distressed about the health of the babe within her, not feeling movement as she was accustomed to. When morning finally came we heard a shout from above that boats had put out from shore to rescue us, and to wait until the women and children could be landed first. I helped Jenna up and we made our way towards the ladder but some of the immigrants started shouting to be let up on deck. A wave hit the ship at that moment and she gave a mighty lurch sideways. Anger turned to panic and a press towards the ladder. Jenna was knocked down and for a moment I lost her."*

Mrs. Renton stopped and looked up. Everyone was staring at her, their eyes wide and mouths open. Her eyes misted over and she wiped them with the back of her hand.

"Don't worry, I'll keep going," she said with a slight smile. "I just need a second."

Mom reached over and handed her several tissues which she took gratefully. The cat stretched and yawned on her lap while she set down the letter and wiped her nose. Dad saw the kids beginning to squirm and he leaned forward so they could see the subtle but firm shake of his head.

Mrs. Renton tucked the remaining tissues up the cuff of her sleeve and picked up the letter again. The kids all breathed a sigh of relief and settled down again.

"Alright, I'm ready. Let's see." Her eyes scanned the small, cursive script. *"Jenna was knocked down and for a moment I lost her."* The old lady sighed, and then continued on. *"I heard her cry out and it filled me with a fury that surprised me. I fought my way to her and stood over her. At that moment there was a crashing sound as the hatch gave way and people poured up onto the deck. I heard the captain's voice shouting and then a gunshot. Someone screamed and we clung to each other, praying desperately. Suddenly all became quiet and we could clearly hear Captain Ralls. He said that women and children would go first and he would shoot any man who tried to force his way forward. I helped Jenna up and some ladies took charge of her and helped her to a boat. I was taken off an hour or so later and tried to find her at the Maori college where they were housing us. Someone told me her time was upon her and a doctor was with her. They would not let me in to see her, though I could hear her cries. I prayed and prayed but it was not to be. I did not even get to say goodbye."*

Mrs. Renton paused again and blew her nose. Mom handed round tissues to everyone else, even Dad, and used several herself.

The old lady swallowed deeply and bravely forged on, her voice quavering a little. *"Jenna and the babe were laid to rest together in the local churchyard. Please pray for me. We left home, family and friends to travel half a world away, following our Lord's command to go to those who had never heard. We knew the cost would be great, but I did not think it would so dear. I waver between giving it all up and sailing home or going on to Napier and beyond to try to fulfill the commission that God entrusted to us. I don't understand the ways of the Almighty. What is the purpose of this path of suffering? If you have any insight, please enlighten me. Is this a sign of God closing the door or saying walk through it? Please forgive the despairing tone of this letter. My grief is so near. I anxiously await your reply,*

Your affectionate brother, Perran."

She set the letter down and closed her eyes. Yes, the man's questions echoed her own when her parents died. Those questions had never left her over the years—had never been far away. What a strange coincidence that this person should have the same hurt, the same struggle with trust in a supposedly good God who allowed such heartache and loss. Yet was it a coincidence? What was Uncle Kenwyn up to?

❧❧

Kennedy gazed through the stained glass to the garden beyond, noting the opening in the hedge with the arbor. After waking up late and missing breakfast, it had taken him a good chunk of the morning to figure out the chess clue and find the hidden room, but instead of a sense of victory, he had a brooding sense of foreboding. He had noted with alarm the tracks and scuffs in the dusty floor.

Someone had been here recently—a number of someones by the look of things—and they had stood right where he was standing now.

He closed up the room and stomped down the stairs, doing some furious thinking. Was it even worth going out back to see if there was anything there? He cursed his luck. He had overslept this morning and missed the family leaving, missed breakfast, and he wouldn't be surprised if he missed the clue as well.

The kettle whistled and Mom hurried to answer its impatient summons. Mrs. Renton had expended quite a bit of emotional energy and needed another pick-me-up from what she called the traditional British restorative. For the others, one cup of tea was plenty—Stevie and Danny didn't like tea at all—but Mrs. Renton didn't seem to have a limit.

They had moved camp to the compact back garden where the calm bulk of Tregarth Watch sloped up above them. The sun had appeared again and the broad swath of uncluttered blue seemed to betoken warmth and sunshine, at least for the time being. There were several comfortable outdoor chairs and Mrs. Renton was ensconced in one--her foot propped up on an upturned flower pot with a comfy cushion on top. Mom set her tea on the glass-topped table at her elbow. Mr. Pickwick was stalking across the small patch of grass, eying the brazen sparrows that flitted around the bushes.

The boys were still inside trying to make Sweedlepipe the budgie say their names while the girls were perusing Mrs. Renton's book collection, but as Mom returned again with the teapot, Dad whistled and gestured for them to come out and perch on the back wall.

When they were all settled, Mrs. Renton smiled around at everyone. "All ready? Then let's continue." She looked at the papers in her lap. "I suppose we are back to the letter from Uncle Kenwyn. Let's see. Here we are." She held the squire's letter up, adjusted her glasses again and read out loud.

"Perran Trenholm chose to stay in New Zealand. It took many months, but with the support of some local Christians and the prayers of many back home he was able to find healing to the point where he could continue his ministry. From his letters it was clear that he did not blame God for his suffering, even though he never understood why God chose to take his wife and child. Several years later he met a young widow named Lilias Cardew and they ended up getting married. Life was not easy for them and they lost their first two children soon after birth, but they ended up raising four healthy children—two boys and two girls. One of the boys became a very significant person in my life.

Even though it was difficult, with many disappointments and hardships, God blessed their ministry and they ended up planting four churches on the North Island. Many lives were redeemed because Perran Trenholm, by God's grace, did not surrender his trust and love for God. He was certain that God would somehow bring good out of his suffering and sacrifice. He clung to the promises in God's Word. Romans 8:28 says 'And we know that in all things God works for the good of those who love Him, who have been called according to His purpose.'

As Mr. Trenholm was able to seek and trust God in his hurt, God worked for good, both within Mr. Trenholm's own heart and also in the lives of those he ministered to.

In all things, the Bible says, Ruthie. Remember that."

Mrs. Renton frowned. She was trying to understand all this, trying to apply it to herself, but it was too difficult right now. She just didn't want to go there. She wasn't sure she even believed the Bible. No, she would just have to set it aside and deal with it later. She glanced down at the letter and read the last line out loud. *"And now we must move on to the next clue."*

She raised her eyebrows. The family exchanged significant looks. *The next clue!* The old lady cleared her throat, took a quick sip from her cup and then continued.

"A squire's lord in days of old stands guard upon a hidden hold.
A box within a box to see, within you'll find my book, and key."

She turned the paper over and continued reading on the back.

"Page 63 recounts the tale, a fateful day, a fearful gale,
Evil confronted, Chynalls fray, A paneled door, a secret way.
Ill-gotten gains made passage thru, but there you too will find the clue.
May God continue to guide you on this quest.
Your loving Uncle Kenwyn."

Mrs. Renton put down the letter. "Goodness." She sighed. "Will this never end?"

"Don't worry. We'll help you," said Mom hastily. "Won't we family?" There was a chorus of affirmatives and vigorous nodding from the wall.

"We're serious, Mrs. Renton, we are ready to keep going," added Dad. "We're in this to the end." But even as he said it, Dad felt a stab of concern again. Their vacation wouldn't last forever. Could they solve this before time ran out?

≼⬥⬦≽

Kennedy sat back on his heels and shook his head in disgust. Sure enough, the space under the paving stone was empty. The family had beat him to it. Right now they could be in possession of the prize and he had nothing.

He stood up rather painfully and pulled a handkerchief carefully from his pocket to wipe off his muddy hands. What were his options? Either the family had solved the clue and had already given the treasure—whatever it was—to the old lady—which meant he was done for—or they had it in their possession and would get it to her soon—which didn't leave him much hope either. Or...or maybe whatever had been under the stone wasn't the final goal and there was more to do. The family would have found another clue, perhaps, and were trying to solve it.

That puzzled Kennedy. Would they really be going to all that trouble for someone they apparently didn't even know? They were on holiday, weren't they? Surely they would be doing some holiday things as well, like the other day when they went to Tintagel.

Kennedy ducked back under the arbor, his mind made up. His only hope was to figure out what the family were doing. Their van was still parked out front so they couldn't be too far away. He would call Jennings to remind him to keep an eye out for them in the village, and then do a bit of scouting himself. It seemed a bit futile, but it was the only thing he could think of to do.

The Chapmans said goodbye to Mrs. Renton, promising to keep her abreast of any new developments. On her part she promised to think over the clue and call them if she came up with any ideas. They left the papers with her after Dad carefully took a picture of both sides of the Squire's letter.

"What do you think?" said Dad as they tromped back up the road to the inn. The sun was hidden again and overall the weather looked very unsettled. A brisk wind rippled the waters of the harbor behind them and caused the hedges along the road to shift and sway. "Are you okay to concentrate on this clue today? I know we all agreed we wanted to help, but I'm just checking you're all still doing okay."

"Oh, yes," said Rachel, and the others nodded vigorously. "This is getting exciting."

"And it looks like it might rain so we wouldn't be missing a day at the beach or anything," added Emily, glancing around.

"I want to solve this next clue all by myself," said Stevie, dancing about and almost tripping.

"No way," said Danny, offended. "I want to help."

"We'll all help," said Mom. "We need each of you." She turned to Dad. "If you don't mind, dear, we need to go quickly to the store again first, and then we can plan out the rest of the day. I left my purse and list in the room."

"But can we assign tasks, like last time?" said Rachel. "I like having something specific to do, and then we can think about it while we shop."

"Okay, sure," said Dad as they turned in through the gate. "How about breaking up the clue into chunks and you can each take a bit to work on?"

"Great," said Emily. "Do you remember it all?"

"Well, no," Dad admitted, "but I'll get it off the camera as soon as we get back to the room, and I can write down a copy for each of you."

Kennedy had finished scraping the mud off his shoes and was just closing the front door when he thought he heard voices. A quick glance through the little window confirmed it, and he couldn't believe his luck. There they were and heading this way!

He dashed to his room, forgetting all about his intention of calling Jennings. First he needed to hide, and then carefully figure out what that annoying family was up to.

"Is the man here?" said Danny, noticing the yellow car parked to one side of the parking area, all his excitement about the clue instantly evaporating.

"Well, it looks like it, perhaps," said Dad, a bit impatient at Danny's continued fears. "But don't worry. Maybe he's gone for a walk"

Mom put her hand on his shoulder. "God's in control, remember Danny? He knows your fears. Anyway, the man's okay—just a guy staying here on holiday like us."

Rachel wasn't so sure. "We should be really quiet though, just in case." She looked around at the others. "Okay?"

"Okay," said Dad, surprised at her earnestness. He heaved open the front door and ushered them inside. "Let's grab what we need for the store and I'll copy off the clue."

⊱☙⊰

Kennedy listened carefully at his door as the family tromped upstairs. He stepped through quietly and tiptoed to the bottom of the stairwell. Could he risk going up to listen? What if they came out and saw him. *But wait--he could hide behind the tapestry!*

He climbed the stairs quickly and quietly, two at a time, checked the coast was clear and ducked behind the tapestry. With the door open he could stand behind and be completely hidden, but still have a chance of hearing what was going on. At least he hoped so.

⊱☙⊰

"Okay, I've got the list," said Mom coming into the girls' room. "Grab your hats—it definitely looks like it could rain. Do you know where the umbrella is, Emily?"

"Uh-huh," she said. "Should we bring water bottles?"

"Good idea, yes," said Mom. She noticed the boys standing in the doorway. "Danny, Stevie, go get yours from your room."

"Can I bring my camera?" said Rachel, looking up from where she had been rummaging around under her bed.

"Sure," said Dad, popping into view in the hallway. "But then I won't take mine. I've copied off the clue from the photos and made a sheet for each of you. That way everyone can work on it and we can get it solved as soon as possible."

⊱☙⊰

Kennedy smiled in satisfaction. He had been frustrated at hearing almost nothing coming from the bedrooms, but he heard that last comment loud and clear. There was another clue and the family didn't seem to have figured it out. And better yet, apparently there was some pictures of the clue on Mr. Chapman's camera, and it was staying here at the inn. *Perfect, perfect, perfect!* Things were looking up again.

⊱☙⊰

A few spots of rain hit the family as they crossed the bridge and began the steep climb up the street towards the grocery store. The sky was a mass of clouds layered one on top of the other—everything from dark, threatening gray to dazzling white piled high above to where patches of blue sky were visible between the puffy columns. Dad pointed out several seagulls seemingly hovering above them as they rode the wind coming in from the sea. He led the family past the fish and chip shop and across the street to the far side where he paused under the awning of the newsagents.

"Tell you what," he said, looking thoughtfully at the sky. "Why don't we head to the bakery first. We can shelter there and divvy up the clue."

"The bakery?" said Mom. "I wonder why?"

"Nice and warm, tables to sit at...you know," grinned Dad. The children exchanged delighted looks.

"Yes, I know," said Mom. "Alright. But let's hurry. Looks like it's going to really come down any minute now."

❧❧

Chippy Twiston sighed and turned from the window. It had just been that family again—the *chips-but-no-fish*' one. And evidently today it was no chips either. With the weather and all, there probably wouldn't be anyone else out and about, so it was another big zero for fish sales at lunchtime. Why didn't he just admit it was a failure and not open for lunch anymore until the real tourist season hit?

He peered through the fish tank glass. "Ahab. You were right, I admit it. Tomorrow I'm sleeping in."

❧❧

Kennedy froze, his hand reaching for the camera on the nightstand. He had heard a door close somewhere down below. Could it be the family were back? Quick, what should he do?

With sudden resolution he snatched up the camera and found the play button on the back. An image of a piece of paper appeared on the screen. He fumbled for the zoom settings and scaled up the image so he could read it. Quick, quick, where was the clue?

He scrolled down, scanning the writing. There, right at the bottom. There it was. He scribbled the two lines down in his notebook, switched off the screen and set the camera back where he found it, his heart pounding furiously. Scurrying to the door, he listened intently. He heard someone having a coughing fit, apparently in the dining room. *Mrs. Tremannon!* His sudden relief was just as quickly replaced with anxiety. What if she found him up here? How would he explain it? There was only one thing to do. He dashed down the hallway and jumped back behind the tapestry. Shutting the door as quietly as possible, he leaned back against the wall, trying to make his breathing return to normal.

❧❧

"Well, dears, what can I get for you?" Flo smiled, her pen poised over her notepad.

"Well, we would love something hot to drink," said Mom. "I'd love a cup of tea. Tea in a tea room would be perfect. How about the rest of you?"

"Tea for me," said Dad. To him, hot drinks and rainy days went together like bacon and eggs. "How about hot chocolates for the rest of you?"

The kids all nodded eagerly except Emily. "I'd like some tea again if that's alright?" she asked a little shyly. Tea sounded a bit more grown-up and she really did need to feel more grown-up these days.

"Righty-ho," said Flo. "I'll make a big pot." She bustled off behind the counter again.

They gazed contentedly out the window at the pelting rain as a passing squall swept across the town. Tea shops were made for days like these.

"May I have my clue?" said Stevie, kneeling on his chair with his elbows on the table.

Dad distributed the copies he had written out and they all looked at the lines. Rachel scooted closer to Stevie and read them to him out loud. Mom smiled in approval.

"A hidden hold," said Danny when Rachel finished, a faraway look in his eye. "Maybe a place where pirates stashed a treasure!"

"A secret way sounds exciting," said Rachel, her eyes shining. "I want to find that!"

"What's Chynalls?" asked Stevie, struggling with the pronunciation.

"I've no idea," said Dad. "We'll have to find that out. And a 'fray' is a sort of battle or skirmish."

The boys seemed to like that idea.

"So how should we divide this up?" said Emily. She was about to say something more when Rachel reached over and tapped her arm, gesturing with the merest nod of her head. Auntie Flo was rounding the counter and heading their way.

"Here y'are dears," she said, balancing the corner of the tray on the table and distributing the drinks. "And I have some extras for you." She set down a plate of her Chocolate-Toffee Brownie Cakes. Dad glanced somewhat guiltily over at his wife who was looking at him with a raised eyebrow.

"There's one for each of you—oh, go on, it's just a bite," said Flo, seeing Mom's hesitation.

Mom gave in and took one, choosing to ignore Dad's grin. "Well, thank you so much, but we really should pay for these."

"Not these," said Flo with a friendly firmness. "But I'll charge you an arm and a leg for the drinks." She burst into laughter, and the others couldn't help but join in. There were a chorus of 'thank-yous' and Flo smiled in appreciation. "Now, how about some cream horns for later?" she went on. "Harry made them fresh. I could make up a box for you."

The kids looked at their parents. Dad seemed to be wrestling with what to say.

"That's very kind," said Mom stepping in, "but we've had a lot of treats lately. I'm sure we'll be back again another day."

"Alrighty then." Flo looked a bit surprised at someone turning down pastries, but gave a smile before hurrying off again.

"Well, someone had to say something," said Mom, looking at Dad.

"You're right, you're right," he admitted reluctantly. "She's definitely generous, isn't she?"

"Yes, but we don't want her generosity being transferred to my waistline," said Mom. "Or yours!" she added with a grin. "Okay, let's get back to the clue." She took a sip of her tea. "Where were we?"

Kennedy rubbed his chin. He was sitting on the edge of his bed, trying to figure out what on earth the clue meant. Mrs. Tremannon had apparently finished whatever she had been doing and he had finally made it back to his room unobserved.

He had puzzled and puzzled over what it meant by the *squire's lord*. A village squire didn't have a lord—no-one in direct authority over him, except maybe the king himself, but that didn't make much sense. Maybe it was an indirect reference to something. Could the squire's lord be his wife—a tongue-in-cheek indication of who really wore the trousers in the family? But what about the standing guard part? And it was something from days of old—something historical.

Kennedy stood up suddenly. He knew what he needed to do. He needed to call Jennings. Jennings knew stuff about history. He grabbed his cigarettes and a lighter off the night stand and headed out. The stone walls of the inn seemed to pretty effectively block cell service, but it worked fine outside the building as he had noted the other day. He took a quick furtive peek around the corner into the shadowy dining room. The coast looked clear as far as he could tell. A sudden dash of rain flung itself against the windows—there must be quite the downpour outside. He'd have to just stand in the porch to call Jennings.

As he edged into the room keeping a sharp look out, he had a sudden shock. Was that someone standing over there in the corner? Then he relaxed, berating himself for his stupidity. It was just that suit of armor standing guard. He was about to go on when a lightbulb went off in his head. A slow smile spread across his face. *Of course!* The squire in the clue didn't mean a squire like *the* Squire—one of the gentry, a lord of the manor. There was another meaning to the word. In *days of old*, back in medieval times, a squire was a knight's assistant—the one who served him, took care of his armor and horse and carried his shield. A squire's lord was a knight, and here was a knight in front of him standing guard. He couldn't resist a satisfied chuckle. Finally, *finally*, he was ahead of the game.

Was there a hidden hold, though? The armor was set up on a square wooden plinth about eight inches high. Kennedy scurried over and felt around the sides, searching unsuccessfully for a catch of some kind. He rapped on the wood with his knuckles. It definitely could be hollow by the sound of it.

He sat back on his heels and tried to think critically. Too bad it was so dim in there, but he didn't want to risk turning on the lights. He felt again around the base. The clue said the hold was hidden, so it may not be easy to get into. He had a sudden thought and pushed hard on each side, hoping one would slide back, but to no avail. What else could he try?

Well, how about pushing down? He tried the front, then the left and right sides but they wouldn't budge. Reaching around, he pushed down hard on the back edge. With a grunt of satisfaction he felt it give way under his fingers. It was obviously attached to some sort of spring, and took some force to move. He adjusted his position and pushed down again with his left hand, feeling with his right. A space had opened up and he could just force his hand inside. His groping fingers touched the edge of something hard and with an extra effort he reached in and grasped it and drew it out. It was a flat wooden box with a small clasp on one side. He smiled. The *box within a box.*

He quickly undid the clasp and lifted the lid. Inside was something wrapped in brown paper secured by some knotted twine. His heart racing, he pulled it out and quickly cut the twine with his penknife. As he unwrapped the paper, something heavy fell to the floor with a dull metallic clunk. It was a small, brass key with a metal tag attached. He lifted it up to the light and saw that that the tag was stamped with the word *Chynalls*. He had no idea what that meant, but at least he had finally found something!

He stuffed the key in his pocket and continued unwrapping, uncovering a fairly large hardcover book. Almost shaking with excitement, he turned it the right way up and read the title: *Penrithin: its People and Times,* by Kenwyn Penrow. *Aha! Very interesting.* He flipped through the book. It was apparently a history of the village, with lots of illustrations and photographs.

A sudden sound caused him to freeze. Was that the kitchen door? He needed to get out of there. He grabbed up the paper and twine and dashed back to his room.

⚬⚬⚬

The family sat staring disconsolately at their empty cups. Despite Dad's suggestion to divvy up the clue, it had become quickly apparent that it was impossible. It seemed to be divided into two main parts. They evidently couldn't solve the rest of the puzzle until they first found the book and the key.

"So we have to figure out this bit about the squire," said Emily sitting back in frustration. "Otherwise we can't find the book and go to the right page."

"It's not fair!" wailed Stevie.

"Shhh," said Mom, glancing nervously over towards the counter. Fortunately, Flo seemed to have disappeared into the back room.

"It's not a question of being fair," said Dad, frowning at Stevie. "The Squire wanted Mrs. Renton to have to puzzle this out. At least we know it *must* be solvable."

He glanced at Danny who was sitting quietly, his nose scrunched up as it always was when he was thinking hard. "Got an idea, son?"

Danny shook his head, then seemed to reconsider. "You know, I've been trying to think like a detective would."

"Uh-huh," said Mom. "And?"

"Well, I was just thinking that the Squire must have thought that Mrs. Renton could find the thing that was standing guard pretty easily."

"Go on."

"Because it was the thing it's guarding that's hidden, not the guard itself."

The others had to puzzle that out for a moment. "Okay," said Rachel. "I think I understand. So whoever or whatever the Squire's lord was should be easy to find."

"Either around the town or maybe at the Inn," continued Dad.

"And did you notice," said Mom, getting excited, "that it's not *the* Squire's lord? It's not capitalized. It's *a* squire, not Squire Penrow."

"So what was a squire's lord?" wondered Emily. "I remember reading that book about that squire who lived in the 1700s. Do you remember? There was those hidden jewels, and the highwayman and everything."

"Uh-huh," said Rachel impatiently, "but he didn't have a lord. A village squire was the main guy."

"*Le grand fromage*," agreed Dad. "The big kahuna. Excepting the king of course."

"Could it be a king?" asked Mom. "Is there a statue of a king somewhere about?" She looked out the window for inspiration. The rain had stopped, but looked like it could start again any moment. Low, charcoal-grey clouds scudded across the harbor.

"We haven't seen one," said Emily. "What about a pub?"

"There's the *White Whale* near the bridge," said Dad, pointing out the window. "I'm not sure if there's another one."

"So can I ask Auntie Flo?" pleaded Stevie, eager to have something to do.

Dad tried to picture Flo's response if a seven-year-old asked her if there was another pub somewhere around. "No, son. Sorry. I'd better do it."

Flo chose just that moment to reappear from the back. She saw them looking her way and scurried over with a tray and dish rag.

"All finished? Everything alright?" She started picking up the cups and mugs.

"Wonderful, thank you," said Dad. He faltered. Here he was again trying to get information out of someone without sounding weird or giving away too much. "Er, we're interested in some of the things in the town."

"Village," corrected Flo. "We're just a village. A town sounds too big and busy."

"Ok, er, a village then. We're wondering if you had any information on..." He paused again, unsure of what to say. His wife looked at him in consternation.

Flo looked puzzled. "On...?"

"On interesting places to visit or take pictures of." There, at least that didn't sound too strange, he surmised.

"Oh, aye." Flo paused and looked off into space, pursing her lips. "Well, there's Capstan Wiggle, up to yonder headland. And Dubbock's Scoop, but that's up the coast a way, and you wanted things near here, right?"

"Right," said Dad, "but I was thinking more of buildings and such."

Flo set her tray down and considered for a moment. "Well, there's the Book Nook—it's in one of the oldest houses in the village. It's worth a visit, and the old church on the hill of course—Saint Piran's Chapel. Then there's Gobbler's Nob—it's mostly a ruin now, but you can still see some of the walls, oh and the old Lock Up, back behind the village, and the Fish Cellars, and the Warren—with all the narrow, twisting lanes."

The kids' eyes were getting wider and wider. What a lot of cool-sounding places!

"That's great," said Dad, impressed, "and how about any old pubs and such?" He hoped that just slipping it in like that wouldn't sound like he was wanted to get a drink.

"Oh, yes, there's the White Whale. It's the only pub in the village. It's pretty old and interesting."

"Well, thank you," said Dad, feeling quite let down. "That's plenty—quite a list." He glanced at the rest of the family, who all looked rather glum. It was a dead end after all.

"Do you need me to write them down?" Flo patted her apron as if looking for a pen.

"No, no, that's alright," said Dad. He paused, not quite sure what else to say. He didn't want to have to answer any difficult questions.

A sudden loud crash from somewhere in the back of the shop caused them all to jump.

Flo quickly recovered her composure. "That's just Harry and his baking pans," she said by way of explanation.

"Is he okay?" wondered Mom, somewhat alarmed.

Flo cocked an ear and listened for a moment. "Yes, he's okay," she said with conviction. "If he weren't, he'd be yellin'."

"Well, alright then," said Dad, thankful that something had proved a distraction from the prior subject. "We actually should be going." He looked at Mom, who nodded. "Can we have the bill?"

"Oh, yes, no problem," said Flo, picking up the tray again. "I'll go ring you up."

Kennedy sat on his bed, puzzling over the book in his hands. He had flipped through it several times, examining the pictures—even holding pages up to the light. He couldn't figure out anything at all. But there had to be something--a link between the book and key.

He was suddenly distracted by a loud grumbling from his stomach. He looked at his watch. Time had flown by and it was definitely lunchtime.

He needed to talk to Jennings, but Jennings was probably out to lunch himself now. He considered his options for a moment, then stood up in decision. He would go grab some cheap lunch at the *White Whale*, have another good look at the book, and then get a hold of Jennings. He might as well walk, he decided—the car park on the other side was a fair step from the Mole Hole, let alone the pub. Anyway, it might throw off the family to leave his car at the inn. Maybe it would be harder to determine where he'd gone. He grabbed up his coat and wallet and headed for the door.

Elton the postman pulled his collar up against the brisk wind and trudged up the hill, barely sparing a glance at the family across the road, huddled under the flapping awning of Peterson's Grocers.

Despite his protestations, Mom zipped Stevie's jacket up under his chin. "Hush up. I know the rain's stopped for now but I don't want you catching cold." She looked up at her husband. "We need to come up with something for lunch.

I was thinking of getting some more deli meat—we could do sandwiches again. We still have some bread left over. Unless you can think of anything else."

"That sounds great," said Dad, pulling some bank notes out of his pocket and handing them over. "But if you don't mind I might just trot down to the fish and chip shop and see if I can get some more chips. They would go great with sandwiches. In fact, I might buy a couple of pieces of fish as well, just to try it out. I haven't had fish and chips in ages—not since I was a boy."

"Alright," said Mom, amused at his eagerness. "Why don't you take the boys? If you get done before us, we'll meet you here."

Kennedy was ensconced again at the back table of the *White Whale*, a steaming bowl of chicken soup in front of him and the Squire's history book propped up against the salt and pepper shakers. He had finally succeeded in reaching Jennings on his phone, who had apparently not appreciated being interrupted at lunch time but had finally promised to look at the book that afternoon.

Kennedy took another look through the chapter index. There just had to be something in this blasted book that would tell what the dickens that key was for!

Chippy Twiston closed the back door of the shop and was about to turn the key when he paused. Had he heard something? He cocked an ear and listened for a moment, but the noise wasn't repeated. He shrugged his shoulders and locked the door. Pocketing the key, he turned and made his way up the sloping path along the back, stepping over an old bucket that had blown over in the wind. As he rounded the corner of the shop, he froze in surprise and alarm. A man with two small boys in tow had just closed the gate and were starting to hurry back up the road.

He couldn't believe it. *No, no, no, no, no!* Paying customers finally, and he had closed early. This was all Ahab's fault. *That's the last time he'd take advice from a fish.*

Emily edged her way along the aisle and took a quick peek around the end. Mr. Peterson had his back to her, standing on a small stool and vigorously polishing the shop windows with a cloth. Even from behind he looked *oh so intimidating*, she thought. Once again her determination seemed to have fled, replaced by a nauseating feeling of fear.

She looked back down the aisle to where her mother and Rachel were examining the various snack choices on the shelves. It would be so much easier to flee back there with them and try again another day.

She threw up a quick desperate prayer. *Jesus, please help me. I know you want to show your love to Mr. Peterson. Please do it through me, and help him be nice. I mean, well, help him to appreciate it.*

The verse from the last clue came suddenly to mind. It was one she had memorized several years ago as part of her Bible lessons. *"In all things God works for the good of those who love Him, who are called according to His purpose."*

It seemed pretty appropriate. She was trying to do something in obedience to God, for His purpose, and God promised He would work it for good. Screwing up her courage, she stepped around the corner. At that exact moment, the shop owner, leaning out to try to reach the corner of the window, slipped partially off the stool. As he flailed wildly, trying to maintain his balance, he knocked over a rack of postcards which crashed to the ground, spilling cards all over the floor.

Without thinking, Emily rushed over and started picking up the postcards. She glanced up at Mr. Peterson who had recovered his balance and was staring down at her in disbelief. Emily stuffed down her fears and tried to give him her most winning smile. "I thought you might need some help."

The shop owner stepped down off his stool and started picking up cards himself. He looked over at Emily as he did it, obviously searching for the right words.

"Er, thank you, young lady," he finally managed to say. He lapsed back into silence and they continued working together until all the postcards had been retrieved and stacked in matching piles, including several that had slid under the counter.

Mr. Peterson straightened himself painfully up and set the postcard rack back in position. Emily handed him the sets of cards one by one and he put them in their holders. She was still amazed to be actually doing something with the feared Mr. Peterson.

The shop-owner put the last set of cards in place and turned to Emily. "Thank you, young lady," he said again gruffly, obviously embarrassed and unused to pleasantries.

"Oh, you're very welcome," smiled Emily. "And I'll take two of these," she said pulling out a couple of postcards of Tintagel with a picture of the castle in the background and a knight on horseback in front. "I need to write to my Grandma and Grandpas."

As he rang up the purchase on the till, the shop owner glanced up at her. "And what is your name, young lady?"

"Emily Chapman," said Emily, surprised that he had asked. She held out her money with a smile.

Mr. Peterson met her eyes. Was there the merest hint of a smile in return? He shut the till drawer firmly. "Well, Miss Emily Chapman, for all your help I believe the least I can do is give you those postcards for free."

Emily couldn't believe it. "Thank you very much! Well, I'd best go find my Mom and help her," she managed to say. "Bye." She scurried back up the aisle with a surge of joy.

Mr. Peterson stood looking after her for a moment, then turned and resumed his cleaning.

☙☙

"And he even smiled at me," gushed Emily, her eyes shining. "Well, kind of."

"Great," said Dad. He couldn't picture Mr. Peterson smiling, *no sir*, but he was willing to believe it happened.

The family were walking briskly down the hill towards the bridge. The rain was holding off for a moment, though they could feel random drops every now and then chased in on the wind.

"Sorry about the fish and chips—it's really weird that he was closed at lunchtime," said Dad as they drew level with the fish and chip shop. He gave his wife's hand a squeeze. "Thanks for getting lunch stuff anyway."

"No problem," said Mom. "I got some more postcards too. Maybe while you all puzzle over the clue I can write one to my brother and sister."

"I got one for Grandpa and Grandma," said Emily, skipping over and waving a small paper bag. She pulled out the postcard and showed it to him. "It's of Tintagel, and there's even the castle. I'm going to write to them about it."

"Can I see?" said Danny, speeding up to catch up with them.

Emily complied, turning it around so he could see it.

"Cool," said Danny, impressed. "And it's even got a knight in armor with a battle axe. Is it King Arthur?"

"I don't know," said Emily. "Maybe. It might not be the King, but all knights were important." Her eyes suddenly widened. "Oh, wait, oh my goodness!" She started jumping up and down, waving the card.

"What? What is it?" said Danny. The others all stopped and gathered around.

"A knight, a knight," squeaked Emily. "Don't you see? A squire was the person who served a knight. The knight would be his lord."

"In days of old," said Dad. "Yes! But where would we find a knight?"

Danny knew that. "In the dining room—at the inn. The suit of armor in the corner—the kind of scary one." He nodded with sure authority.

"What did the clue say?" put in Stevie.

Dad whipped out his copy. "A squire's lord in days of old, stands guard upon a hidden hold."

"So we need to look around the armor," said Emily. "It's got to be right there."

"This is easy!" said Danny. "We're going to solve another clue!"

They all looked at each other for a second.

"Well, what are we waiting for?" said Dad. "Let's go!"

⋙⋘

Kennedy paid his bill and exited the *White Whale*, yanking the heavy door shut behind him. The building was perched on a rocky knoll high above the stream, at the end of a narrow lane that zigzagged up from the bridge. As he zipped up his jacket Kennedy took in the scene around him. There was a fine view across the bridge to the compact harbor, where the fishing boats bobbed and dipped uncertainly in the choppy waters. Water and sky were painted in a palette of grey and the wind flew full in his face. A series of wooden steps led down towards the stream from the side yard of the building, and Kennedy was pondering whether it would be quicker to go that way or back down the winding lane when his attention was arrested by the sight of a family, bundled up against the weather, emerging from behind a building and hurrying on to the bridge itself. He squinted his eyes, and then nodded to himself in satisfaction. It was the Chapman family all right. *Out shopping perhaps?* he thought with a smirk. *They definitely couldn't be working on the clue. He had it!*

Seeing them helped him make up his mind, though. Rather than risk being seen, he would take the longer way down.

❧❧

"There's nothing there!" exclaimed Stevie, peering under Emily's arm.

The family had hurried back to the dining room, checked the coast was clear and then searched around the suit of armor. To their delight, it hadn't taken long to find the compartment and Emily had been designated to examine it, but to their shock her search had been in vain. She felt around one more time, but Stevie was right. It was empty.

"But this has to be the place, right?" said Rachel. "It's a secret spot under the knight."

"I think you're right," said Dad from over at the doorway where he had agreed to be posted as guard. "It can't be a coincidence."

"So what does it mean?" said Mom looking across at him worriedly.

"Well," said Dad coming over, an anxious feeling stealing over his heart. "I guess either the Squire forgot to put the things there, or maybe the Tremannons found them and took them out."

"Or someone else found them first," said Rachel. "I'm just saying it could be possible," she added, noting their disbelieving looks.

"But this was supposed to be easy," put in Danny. "We were doing great! And we're trying to help."

They looked at each other in silence. This was truly a crushing blow. Hadn't they all expected that, if they decided to help Mrs. Renton, God would reward them with a trouble-free experience—that the giving up of their vacation would be the most difficult part?

Mom had a sudden thought. "Is it supposed to be easy though?"

"What do you mean?" asked Emily, puzzled.

"The clues—they're not for us, remember," said Dad, his mind clearing somewhat. "They're for Mrs. Renton. The Squire wanted her to puzzle things out."

"So should we be helping her?"

"Yes, I'm sure we should, but there must be something in the process that's important. That's why the Squire did so many clues."

"But that doesn't explain why this one's missing," said Emily, standing back up. "Did the Squire lead us to this spot on purpose, or did we get the clue wrong?"

"Or maybe someone took it before us," put in Rachel. Emily rolled her eyes.

"Actually, what I was going to say was that maybe this is God's way of telling us that it's not all about us and our ability," said Mom still thinking hard. "Perhaps we're getting a bit too confident in ourselves."

That made them all think.

"So maybe this missing clue is God's way of making us remember we need Him?" said Danny, remembering his own rather prideful thoughts.

"Maybe," said Mom. She looked over at Dad and raised her eyebrows slightly.

He got the message. "Okay, kids. Why don't we stop and talk to God about this. We obviously need His help. Anyone who wants to pray can do it, and then I'll finish up." He grabbed Rachel's hand. "Here, let's hold hands."

The family made a circle and shut their eyes.

"Dear Jesus," said Emily, leading off. "We need your help. Please show us what to do. Help us find the next clue, please."

"Yes, Jesus," said Danny. "We want to trust in you. Help us be good detectives and help Mrs. Renton."

"Please help us find the treasure," said Stevie. "Help us find all the clues."

"Dear Jesus," said Rachel. "Show us what to do. If someone stole the clue, please help us get it back and stop them from being able to get Mrs. Renton's inheritance."

Dad opened one eye and peered at Rachel. She had her eyes screwed up tight and a determined set to her chin. *She must really believe that*, he thought with some wonder. But Mom had started praying and he hurriedly shut his eyes again.

"Thank you dear Heavenly Father, for all your help so far. You have helped us do a lot, and we know you want us to help Mrs. Renton. We can't do anything without you, and we're sorry about thinking we could. Please give us your wisdom and your direction. Show us what to do about this clue. We want to glorify you in all our attitudes and actions. "

"Yes, Lord," finished Dad. "Please show us what to do next. We do want to trust in you and not ourselves." He suddenly remembered what King Jehoshaphat had said in the Bible passage he had read them that morning. "*We don't know what to do, but our eyes are on you*," he quoted. "Amen."

"Amen," they chorused together. They opened their eyes and looked at each other. Somehow they all felt encouraged. Even Dad could already sense a new hope.

"You know," he said. "I feel that this is where God wants us to be—trusting in Him."

"That's right," agreed Mom. "As we go on we have to remember that this is His quest. We're doing it for Him."

"I thought we were doing it for Mrs. Renton," said Stevie, puzzled.

"We are," said Mom. "But in the big picture we're doing it for God. We're trying to obey Him in helping Mrs. Renton, and we want God to be glorified in her life. The real goal is for her to come to know Jesus—to have Him as her savior."

Emily had a sudden thought. "Don't you think that's what the Squire wanted too? I mean, from what we've learned about him, he wanted Mrs. Renton to know God's love. Maybe that's what the whole inheritance thing is about."

Dad nodded. "I think you're right. So what do you think the treasure at the end is?"

"Won't it be a treasure chest of gold and stuff?" asked Stevie, looking disappointed.

"Well, we don't know,' said Mom, giving him a quick squeeze. "But I think the Squire really meant the process to be just as important as the end goal." She had a sudden inspiration. "Yes, that's it! Each person he's talked about has had some lesson to give. He wants them to be an example to Mrs. Renton—showing her what life is like with Jesus."

"But why are the stories all so sad," put in Rachel, confused. "Everyone so far has had some difficulty. How will that help her want to be a Christian?"

That set them all thinking hard. Dad pursed his lips. "Well..." He wasn't quite sure what to say. "Well, we may have to think about that some more."

"But at least we have confidence that God knows what He's doing," continued Mom. "We really need to pray that He will reveal Himself to Mrs. Renton through all this."

They all nodded, inwardly deciding that they would definitely pray for the old lady. Even little Stevie knew he could do that.

"But what about the clue?" said Danny, suddenly. "We still don't know what to do. The book and key weren't there."

"What exactly did it say again?" said Emily.

Dad pulled out his scrap of paper and read aloud. "*A box within a box you'll see, within you'll find my book, and key.*"

Emily peered over his arm and pointed at the line. "What does it mean by 'my book'? Why not just 'a book'? Did the Squire have a special book?"

"That's a good question." Dad looked around at the others, but they all had blank stares.

"Help us please, Jesus," prayed Mom out loud.

"Could the Squire possibly have written a book?" said Emily suddenly. "If he had, that would make sense that he said 'my book'."

Dad nodded, impressed. "I think you may be right. But how can we find out?"

He was suddenly interrupted by a door slamming. The family looked around at each other in alarm. Dad made signs and ushered them quickly to the other side of the room.

"Look," he whispered. "Try to act casual. Kids, go ahead and look through the games cupboard there." He pointed to the sideboard.

Emily got the idea immediately and opened the cupboard door, pulling Stevie down next to her. He was about to voice an objection when Mrs. Tremannon appeared in the entryway. She noticed the family and smiled.

"Well hello all," she called across the room. "Looking for the chess set? Can I help? There are some other games in there, or if you want to play outside there's a few balls in the cupboard under the stairs." She ambled over, smoothing down her rather wrinkled apron as she came. "Did you have a nice morning? Bit wet isn't it? You just never know with our weather in May. Sunny one minute and pouring the next. Makes it really hard to get things dry on the line."

Once again her one-sided conversation seemed to flow effortlessly. Dad was thinking hard. Somehow he had to be able to get the information without her becoming too inquisitive.

"I was wondering if you had any ideas of what to do on a rainy day," he interjected suddenly. The rest of the family looked up in curiosity. Where was Dad going with this?

Mrs. Tremannon loved to be asked her opinion and seemed to expand visibly. "Well now, there's all sorts of things. You could go up to the chapel on the hill, but then again it's a bit of a soggy walk if the weather's iffy, or you could go around the shops, but I think you already did that. Or there's some other places to visit nearby like Boscastle, or Padstow—that's got a lovely harbor front with lots of shops—or you could go to Pencarrow House. It's a nice stately home."

She took a breath and Dad saw his chance. "Is there a library or something like that in the village?" he asked innocently.

Mrs. Tremannon considered for a second. "No, no, not a library." She had lost her train of thought, and that gave Dad another opportunity.

"We really like reading." That was definitely true. Everyone in the family could lose themselves in a book—even little Stevie. "We've seen some books around the inn. Were they the Squire's? I wondered if he liked to read, too."

Now the family understood where Dad was going. They waited in expectation while Mrs. Tremannon adjusted her thoughts, her hands on her ample hips.

"Well," she considered. "Yes, he did love to read and yes, the books you see around here belonged to him. He loved old books especially. Well, he loved history you know. What he didn't know about the history of the village, wasn't worth knowing. He wrote a book about it, he did. Pages and pages of stuff—lots of pictures."

Bingo! The Squire had written a book. Dad couldn't resist grinning—that bit of information had come without even having to dig any further. He glanced at the family and wiggled his eyebrows. The kids were a bit slow on the uptake, but Mom got it right away. She hushed the kids and turned to Mrs. Tremannon.

"That sounds really interesting. Do you have a copy we can look at?"

Mrs. Tremannon studied the ceiling beams for a minute. "I thought I remember seeing one, but that was ages ago. I'm sure a guest wouldn't have taken it, though."

Perhaps, thought Rachel.

"Well, no matter," said Mom, kindly. "Maybe we can find a copy somewhere else. Do you think it might be available in the village? I think someone mentioned a book shop."

"A book shop. Yes there is one definitely, I think. That is, I've heard of one, though I've never seen it." Mrs. Tremannon furrowed her brow. "Now, then. Let me think." The family looked on in silent amusement. She leaned back against the dining table and cocked her head to one side.

"Well," she said finally. "I'm definitely sure that there may be one...."

"But you don't know where it is," finished Dad. "That's quite alright. We've taken way too much of your time. Thank you for your help."

Mrs. Tremannon stood upright and nodded. "My pleasure, dearies. Now I'm off to change the sheets. I hope you find something to do." She ambled out of the room again.

"Oh, yes," said Dad quietly after her retreating back. "We have something to do!"

Chapter 16 - A Curious Place

Bundled against the wind and rain, the family hustled down the lane from the inn. Lunch had been rushed through, but they had paused to ask God for wisdom as to how to find a copy of the book. They really did want to make sure they were fully depending on Him now. Feeling more confident they had donned hats, coats and boots, and plunged back outside into the unsettled elements.

They had all voted to walk again, not for the exercise but since is seemed more adventurous than driving. Indeed, their sense of adventure seemed magnified by the blustery conditions. A search for a mystery book shop on a stormy afternoon...*how exciting!*

Dad did have a few misgivings about the iffy weather, though. *What they really needed,* he mused, *was someone to ask for directions.* They could go back to the Crusty Muffin, but he rightly guessed that his wife might not be too hot on that idea. Too much temptation. Trouble was, on a day like this there wasn't a whole boatload of people wandering around waiting to be asked. And now it was beginning to rain again. He was just trying to decide which other shop they might go in to ask when he noticed some movement off to his left. They had reached the end of the hedgerows and had a clear view of the harbor from above the bridge. A man in bright yellow oilskins and a floppy shapeless rain hat was stomping up the boat ramp hefting a bell-shaped lobster pot. He was heading for a line of low sheds along the top edge of the harbor, and Dad quickly made his mind up to intercept him, trusting the family to follow. Not that he was too keen on stopping this guy, but it was the lesser of two evils. He pulled back his hood and called out. "Excuse me! Sir!"

Jack Carrick stopped and looked around in annoyance, trying to figure out where the voice was coming from. He spotted Dad, approaching with a big smile, followed by a whole parcel of dripping individuals of various sizes. The sight of the little ones caused his gaze to soften somewhat. He clunked down the lobster pot and awaited Dad's approach.

"So sorry to disturb you. We just had a question. We're visiting and don't know our way around."

Jack harrumphed. Just as he thought. *Touristys*. The Cornish word seemed more appropriate than the English one. "Aye, aye, what d'yer want?"

Dad was a little taken aback by his grumpiness. "Er, I am really sorry, but we're looking for the book shop. Is there one in the village?"

"Aye," said the old man, peering from under his wide hat at each of the family in turn.

Dad kept smiling, though a feeling of dismay crept over him. This apparently wasn't going to be easy. Standing here in the rain didn't help either.

"Er, can you tell us where it is?"

Jack pursed his lips. It went completely against his grain to be helping tourists find their way. He wished heartily they'd find their way to another corner of Cornwall, or better yet, have a holiday across the Channel. Let the French deal with them.

"Please, sir," said Danny, sounding, in Dad's opinion, remarkably like Oliver Twist asking for some more gruel. The boy walked over and peered up at the old fisherman, his eyes almost completely hidden by his rain hood.

Jack Carrick's heart softened a touch again. This lad reminded him a bit of his grandson Bobby, who lived down the coast at St. Ives.

"Well," he considered. "Alright. Look here." Firmly but not unkindly he turned Danny to face across the bridge to the other side of the harbor. He squatted down and pointed to the memorial. "Go by yonder cenotaph. Take the left lane on t'other side. Go straight—*kompes* you know."

"Kompes?" said Dad.

"Straight, straight!" replied the fisherman, testily, gesturing with one hand. "*Kledh. Arwodh kurun.* The crown, you know. Sign of the crown. Go left."

Danny was standing stock still, not wanting to upset the old man any more.

"Go down. Right at the post office. *Lytherva, dhow!*" The man gestured to the right.

Dad suddenly realized he wished he'd been writing this down.

"Then right, right, then left, then right. Right? Dhow, dhow, kledh, dhow." The fisherman stood back up. He grabbed his lobster pot, nodded at them all, patted Danny's rain hat and strode off before the surprised family could say anything.

"Er, thank you!" Dad called after his retreating back. The man gave a brusque wave of his hand in reply without turning around.

"Okay," said Mom. "That was a little weird. It was like we had stepped back in time or something. What were all the strange words he kept saying?"

"I think they were in code!" said Stevie, nodding his head. "He was a spy or something."

"Hmmm, well, maybe," said Dad, squatting down to fix Stevie's coat and adjust his rain hat. "But I think it may just be that the old man was speaking Cornish."

"What, do they really have another language here in Cornwall?" said Emily, surprised. "We haven't heard anyone speaking it—I mean until the fisherman guy."

"It's an old language—I think Celtic—related to Welsh maybe…oh, I forget, but I think some older people may speak it here. Like Welsh it might be having a sort of revival—you know, more people learning it again. And some like that man never stopped."

"Fun," said Rachel. "I'd like to learn it."

"Well, run after that guy and tell him. Maybe he'll teach you," said Danny with a grin.

Rachel rolled her eyes.

"But the important thing is," Mom interrupted. "Did we get the directions?"

"Well, I think we know where to start," said Dad, standing back up again and shaking the kinks out of his legs. "We need to go straight past the memorial—he called it a cenotaph, but that's the same thing—then look for some kind of sign where we go left."

"A crown," put in Emily. "He said left at the crown sign."

"And then right at the post office," said Dad. "But then it got really confusing."

"Well, how about if we find the post office and I can buy some stamps? We can ask for directions from there," said Mom.

"Perfect," said Dad. He looked around at his soggy tribe. Yes, they were all still smiling, even Stevie. Rosy cheeked, dripping hair, but smiling. "Okay, gang!" He pointed across the bridge. "Onward!"

🙿🙾

So far so good. The crown sign had been easy to spot, creaking in the wind as it hung over the little shop selling tobacco and cigars. From there it was simple to find the post office a little way down the twisting, narrow lane, where the clerk had been very helpful, dispensing stamps and directions with equal enthusiasm. Dad had scribbled down a map on the back of a mailing label and they consulted it again as they clustered under the dripping red post office awning. The rain had started and stopped several times on their way, and had now been replaced by a light mist, sweeping in from the direction of the sea.

"Straight ahead and then first right. All ready?" Dad received nods from everyone and he led them forward. The lanes in this part of the village had no sidewalks and the family tried to keep to one side or the other, depending on how they needed to avoid the many large puddles. The way was becoming progressively steeper and narrower as the town straggled up the side of the valley. As they stumped along, the buildings they passed were really interesting, all with their own individual character and jammed together into a ragged procession lining both sides. Some were brick, some white-washed stone, some plain, and some decorated with shells or colored glass embedded in the walls. Most seemed to be private homes, but some had "To Let" signs and were apparently holiday rentals. Many had upper stories that leaned out precariously above them, almost within reach of those on the opposite side, and all had brightly-colored doors and painted window boxes, overflowing with dripping geraniums, lobelia, petunias and silver fern.

Mom noticed a sign on the wall as they turned the corner. She pointed at it. "Look. 'The Warren.' I guess it's the name of this neighborhood. No wonder we had a bit of trouble with the directions."

"Didn't Auntie Flo mention a warren?" said Rachel. "What is it again?"

"It's a system of burrows—like for rabbits. A kind of confusing jumble of passages," said Dad, gesturing with his hands. "These narrow streets are confusing. None of them are straight. They just curve any which way."

The family trudged on, beginning to feel a little depressed at the constant light drizzle.

"There aren't many shops back here," noted Mom with a frown. "I've seen a little flower shop and a place selling used clothing. That's all. I hope we're going the right way."

"We are," assured Dad. "The post office lady seemed very confident. Look, here's the next turn. We're supposed to go right again." He led them down another narrow lane which curved tightly away to their left, climbing steeply.

A few minutes walking took them to another intersection. "Left here," he said, trying to sound cheerful, but from the looks of the soggy clan behind him, they were beginning to doubt his ability. An unsettling feeling of doubt welled up in him. *Please Lord*, he prayed silently. *Help us find this place.*

About three houses down on the right, another street branched off. This lane was even narrower and steeper than the others, impossible as that seemed. Dad pulled out the crumpled label with the directions and had a quick look.

"Last turn," he said, with more conviction than he felt. Either this was the place, or they were hopelessly lost.

The family took the corner and started scanning the buildings. To their despair, none of them seemed to be shops. The lane was only about four houses long and ended in a T-junction. Danny gasped suddenly and pulled on Dad's sleeve. "Look! Look!" He pointed straight ahead.

On the far side of the intersecting lane, squeezed in-between a tall, white-washed holiday home and a three-story half-timbered house was the thinnest building they had ever seen. It was only barely wide enough for the arched wooden door. A small square window above peeked out from under a tiny slate section of roof. Above the door was a small curved wooden sign saying '*The Book Nook.*'

"Good spotting, Tiger," said Dad, with an immense feeling of relief.

"But what a tiny place!" exclaimed Emily in dismay. "It doesn't look big enough to hold even one book, let alone a whole book store."

"Well, let's just see." Dad made an effort to sound positive. He ushered the family over to the entrance and tried the door. It opened easily into a narrow hallway and the family squeezed inside, glad to be finally out of the wet. There was a general unzipping of coats and removing of rain hats, little puddles forming at their feet. Rachel edged her way to the front and took stock of their surroundings. The hallway ended about three yards ahead in a wall with another door to the right. On the cement floor at her feet were painted the words '*This way*' and an arrow pointing forward. Painted across the end wall ahead was another sign saying '*Now to your right.*' The lettering was rather clumsily done, as if the author had either been in a hurry or just a bit unskilled.

Rachel giggled and pointed. "I guess we follow the directions."

She went up to the door and saw a small notice pinned in the center which read '*Now through here.*'

"This way," she said gaily, opening the door. This was pretty fun, she considered, adding another little air of mystery to their quest.

The others followed behind chattering in amusement, all their gloomy thoughts forgotten. This door led to a very short hallway which ended in a staircase going up. A sign on the wall said '*Don't give up!*' and pointed up the stairs.

"Amazing," said Mom. "How far away is this place?"

"I think it's cool," said Rachel. The other kids agreed.

The family clumped up the stairs, which were brightly lit by several bare bulbs. Rachel counted fifteen steps before the stairway ended in yet another door, this one with frosted glass panes. A rough wooden sign nailed to the door gave the welcome assurance: '*You're finally here! Come on in.*' From one of the nails hung another little sign saying '*Open.*'

Dad pointed at the sign. "Well, thank goodness after all that the place is open!"

Rachel turned the handle and the door opened with a loud creak. Ahead of her was a large room, lit by a rather cluttered window at the back, and her eyes widened in surprise. Her first impression was that she'd entered some forgotten attic that was in desperate need of a thorough cleaning out.

Most of the wall space was taken up by what looked like an impressive assortment of book cases. A second glance, however, proved that a number of these were actually dressers, side tables or hutches, devoid of their drawers and pressed into service. Not only was every bit of shelf space crammed with books, but there were books stacked to the ceiling on top of each piece, as well as distributed in seemingly random piles on the floor. There were even precarious-looking towers of paperbacks in the corners, with several step-ladders giving necessary access.

Hanging from the ceiling was a collection of objects that seemed to be discards from some forsaken museum. There were a number of taxidermied creatures including a fox, a badger, several birds, and something that looked like a cross between a beaver and a monkey. To their amazement, and Danny's delight, an entire life-sized crocodile ran almost the length of the wooden-beamed ceiling, its eyes closed and legs hanging down limply as if it were having a quick snooze among the rafters.

The family crowded into the room, each enthralled by the unexpected menagerie. Besides the animals and birds, the room was festooned with an improbable selection of oddities peering out from behind the piles of books. Rachel noticed several kites, a penny-farthing bicycle, three or four African drums, a spinning wheel, and a number of fishing rods, their lines impossibly tangled. At the end of the room ran a long wooden counter, its glass top covered with even more items, most notably a globe, a menorah, and a beautiful model of a fully-rigged ship, sailing in a sea of clutter.

"What a place!" said Dad out loud.

"I'll take that as a compliment," said a nasally-sounding voice. They all jumped, Dad turning beet red.

A grinning face with a bald head and bushy brown beard popped up from behind the counter, its chin just barely clearing the top. "It was a compliment, wasn't it?"

"Er, yes, of course," Dad stammered, staring in astonishment at the man who was evidently the owner of the establishment. Was he kneeling? He couldn't be that short.

He evidently was, for the man clambered up onto a stool and they could see that he was the shortest, roundest person they had ever laid eyes on. He gave a wide smile and cracked his knuckles, leaning forward to rest both elbows on the counter. "Welcome to the Book Nook. The nook...er...of books! It's got lots of nooks. And crannies. Lots of crannies. Glad you're here!"

"Thank you," said Dad, recovering his composure. He looked round at the others who were tentatively working their way closer.

"That your family?" said the man. "They're a nice-looking group. Hello!"

"Hello," said Mom. "How are you?"

"Oh, champion, champion. It's a rainy day, I'm in my little kingdom of books, and I have customers. Do you like books?" He addressed this question to the kids who were gathering closer, trying not to stare at the curious man with the funny voice.

"Oh, yes!" said Rachel with such enthusiasm that the man jumped off his stool in delight, almost disappearing from sight again.

"You do! You do!" He reached down for a moment and retrieved an old green hardcover book that he plopped down on the counter in front of his chin. "I do too! I *love* books. I devour books. Like this one. I started it after breakfast and I'm almost done. It's called "Castaway Cove" and it's about a young man who gets shipwrecked and has to survive by eating his own shoes. In fact..." The man paused to clamber back up onto his stool. "In fact, every day is a good day in the Book Nook, because even if I don't have a customer, I can always find a book to read." He reached forward and took a quick sip from one of several mugs that had been almost hidden in the mess on the counter. Rachel noticed with amusement that the one he grabbed said in red lettering *"I'm sorry, I'm all booked up"*.

The man set the mug down again and waved his hand around at the room. "I've no idea how many books I have now, but it's a lot. A lot! You can never have too many books."

Rachel giggled. "I really like books too."

"Wonderful! So wonderful!" The man clapped his hands and jumped down again. He disappeared for a moment and then popped up again with several paperbacks in his hand. "Have you read these? Perfect for young ladies with adventurous spirits. *'Five go to Smuggler's Top,* and *'The Mystery of the Burnt Cottage.'* Both by Enid Blyton. Have you heard of her?"

"Oh, yes!" exclaimed Rachel. "My dad had some of her books growing up and I got to read them."

"Your dad, eh?" said the man, turning to appraise Mr. Chapman. "Well, now. These books are also good for young *men* with adventurous spirits. Do you have an adventurous spirit, sir?"

Dad was rather taken aback by this direct question. "Well...er...I'm not exactly adventurous, or young for that matter, but I do love a good mystery."

"We all do!" piped up Stevie. "In fact we are..."

"In fact we would love to look around the shop if that's okay," interrupted Rachel, glaring at Stevie.

"Of course! I've got books on every subject—we'll almost every one. I was looking for a book on electrified commuter railway lines in the Austro-Hungarian Empire yesterday, but couldn't find one." The man looked crestfallen for a moment, as if this confession weighed heavily on his heart.

"Why do you have so many animals?" said Danny suddenly. He hadn't been tracking with the conversation, being too taken up with the crocodile lurking above his head.

"Good question, good question. They were here when I bought the place. That was back in '86 I think, or maybe '87. I liked the look of them then, and like the look of them now, though they're getting a bit dusty." The man pointed up to the crocodile. "That's Moriarty—up there plotting some dastardly scheme. And Trufflehunter, of course." He pointed to the stuffed badger peering at them with a bright eye from the top of a bookcase. "And over there is Atticus—he's a mockingbird—and then Gandalf, the grey fox. In fact I've named all of them."

Dad raised an eyebrow, then thought better of it and tried to assume a nonchalant air. "Well, that's great Mr...er...sorry. I'm Dave Chapman, and this is my family. We're here on holiday."

"Butterick. Rodney Butterick, Book Nook proprietor, at your service." Mr. Butterick shook Dad's hand vigorously. "Now how can I help you?"

"Nice to meet you," said Dad, retrieving his throbbing hand. "Er, we're actually looking for a particular book. It's a history of Penrithen, written by Mr. Penrow, the Squire."

"If you're looking for a *particular* book, then you've come to the right place. I know that book—*'Penrithen, its People and Times'*—and I do believe I have a copy— perhaps two. We did have quite a number, but many of the locals bought them up. I think I have one left. I *think* so. And then I have a used copy. I have new *and* used here of course." He waved his hand around.

"Are they in here, Mr. Butterick?" asked Mom, a little overwhelmed at the numerous titles surrounding her.

"Nope," said the man. "In here are Fantasy and Science Fiction…oh, and Government. I think those topics fit rather well together, don't you? Now, see that doorway there?" He pointed to a narrow space between two large wardrobes, each stuffed with books.

The family looked. They hadn't noticed the doorway, almost hidden as it was.

"Uh-huh?" said Dad after a few seconds.

"Right. Well, go through there and you can turn right for the Blue Room." Mr. Butterick gestured with his hand. "I call it the Blue Room because its floor is painted blue. It's got the romance and classic literature sections. Go through and on the far side you can get into the Star room. It's called the Star Room because it's got lots of glow-in-the-dark stars on the ceiling. You should turn the light off for the full effect. It's superb! Anyway, the Star Room has the history books. It's mostly alphabetical by author, but some books are grouped by theme—like World War II or the Kingdom of Waalo. The new copy should be there, if I still have one."

"And if you don't?" said Dad, wondering what on earth the *Kingdom of Waalo* was.

"Well, then you can look for the used one. Used are in the Shakespeare room. It's called the Shakespeare room because I like Shakespeare and I wanted one of the rooms to be named after him. It's my favorite room. I love used books! I love the feel of them and the smell of them! And who knows who might have held that book before you did, and where it might have traveled! Ever think of that, hey?" Mr. Butterick grinned at the family.

"Er, well, thank you very much," said Mom, thinking the poor man needed to get out a bit more. "Okay, let's go everyone."

The kids made a bee-line for the doorway, but screeched to a halt as Mr. Butterick called out to them. "But wait. To get to the Shakespeare room you have to go to the left, across from the door to the Blue room. Through the slanted room, past the children's nook and out the far side. Oh, and one more thing that I almost forgot."

"Yes," said Dad, rather overwhelmed and a bit annoyed with all this information.

"I like cats." The owner jumped off his stool again as if in emphasis. "No bookstore worth its salt is cat-less. Anyway, there's Cleopatra, the Siamese. She's a bit aloof, but she might let you woo her. She likes the ancient history section in the Star Room. Then there's Beatrice the silver tabby—she's mostly friendly but a bit unpredictable. She likes to hide out in Romance. And there's Hamlet the black and white. He's nice but seems a bit languid and depressed most days. You normally find him in the clock room, around the Self Help and Psychology sections. Then there's…hang on."

He disappeared under the counter and, from all they could see of his bald head, seemed to be tugging at something, his voice rather muffled. "Come on, out you come. Let go of that, that's right. No, I said let go. Oof."

First a couple of paws appeared, and then with an apparently mighty effort the man hefted a truly monstrously fat Persian into view.

"And this is Falstaff. He's rather large, and doesn't like to do much except eat and sleep to be honest."

The kids ran over to take a closer look, and even Dad had to smile. Rachel and Emily scratched the cat's head which it seemed to enjoy.

"Your cats sound nice," said Mom, a bit puzzled why they had to have such a rundown of his pets.

"All except one. Excuse me." With a mighty effort that must have involved standing on tiptoe, Mr. Butterick hefted the Persian onto the counter where he sprawled like a deflated furry balloon. "Yes, there's one more. Macbeth. He's pure black and a bit of a feral mix. He likes to lurk in several places, but I never know quite where he'll be. Sometimes in the mystery section, sometimes in warfare, sometimes in true crime... When it's close to dinner time he usually hangs out in the bird book section. Or cooking with poultry. He's rather...relationally-challenged. I wouldn't touch him if I were you. But don't worry," he added hastily, seeing Mom's alarmed look. "If you leave him alone, he'll leave you alone."

"O-kay," said Dad, slowly. "Thanks for the tip. Er, let's go kids."

He hurried them all through the narrow doorway between the book cases and took the right turn. As soon as they were out of sight of the proprietor, the family gathered around him, chattering like sparrows.

"What a place! So many books!"

"Did you see that crocodile? Cool!"

"Wasn't that the fattest cat ever?"

"Is that mean cat in here?" That was from Stevie, who grabbed hold of Dad's hand and looked around in consternation.

"This is the blue room, right?" said Mom, looking at the painted wooden floor. She glanced at a couple of the titles on the overstuffed bookshelves. "Looks like *arts and crafts*. I don't think that cat was supposed to be in here."

"Macbeth," said Rachel. "Its name's Macbeth. Isn't that a Shakespeare bad guy?"

"Yes," said Dad. "In fact, all his cats were named after characters from Shakespeare." He glanced at his wife and gave a slight smile. "No, I'm not going to do a 'trivia time'. We need to keep going." He had a sudden thought. "Hey, do you kids want to go to the children's section? Mom and I can check the Star Room and then meet you there."

The kids glanced at each other. Rachel looked excited, Emily doubtful, and the boys rather worried. Stevie spoke out first. "But what about the Mac-Kitty?"

"Sounds like a fast-food thing. Tastes just like chicken," grinned Dad.

"Dad! Gross!" said Rachel. "Anyway, I want to go. The man said the cat would be fine if we just let it alone. And I wouldn't mind seeing the other kitties."

Emily perked up at that. "Yes, come on boys." She grabbed Stevie's hand.

"Dad and I will be right there anyway," said Mom.

"Okay, see you soon!" Rachel confidently led the way back across the hallway to the room beyond.

"Alright," said Dad. He turned to Mom. "The star room, right?"

"Yes," said Mom. "And that's straight through here if I remember correctly. What a strange place! All these different rooms. It must stretch around and behind the other houses."

"I guess so. Pretty amazing." Dad grabbed her hand "Let's go look for that book! First one to find it wins a Chocolate Toffee Brownie whatsit."

The kids were having a great time. True to its name, the slanted room had proved to have a floor that sloped downwards from the entrance towards the door at the far end. It was lined with bookcases and had several armchairs and a couple of small tables, one with a fringed lamp that gave a rosy glow to the surroundings. Danny noticed that all the furniture had little blocks of wood propping up the bases in an attempt to keep everything somewhat on the level. Rachel spotted the small lettered sign saying 'Romance section' and reminded them that this was supposed to be the hangout of one of the man's cats—a nice one if she remembered correctly.

It was Emily who spotted the silver tabby, curled up on top of a rack of paperback books on a shelf by the door. Danny and Stevie still weren't all that happy about the cat situation, but Emily and Rachel didn't have any qualms about giving the animal lots of stroking and scratching which it seemed to appreciate immensely.

"It's purring as loud as Pickwick," said Emily in delight. "Do you remember its name?"

"No, just some sort of Shakespeare lady character," said Rachel, giving the cat a good scratch under the chin.

"Come on please!" said Stevie, tugging at Rachel's sleeve. "I want to go to the children's section. There aren't supposed to be any bad cats there."

"But this isn't a bad cat," said Rachel. "Oh, alright," she added, remembering that she herself wanted to see if there were any Enid Blyton mysteries.

The girls said goodbye to the tabby, who responded with a loud meow as soon as they stopped their petting.

"We'll be back," said Emily over her shoulder as they walked down the slight slope to the far door.

The opening led to a short corridor with another book-lined room at the end, but Rachel spotted a short, arched doorway halfway down. It had been painted to look like an old castle entrance, and Rachel ran ahead and ducked through into the room beyond. She immediately let out a cry of delight and stuck her head back out. "Come on you guys! This is totally cool! I found the kid's area!"

Dad and Mom had worked their way around their respective sides of the room and met together at the back. On the way they had spotted a slender Siamese, looking rather regal as she gazed down on them from her perch on a grandfather clock.

"Cleopatra, no doubt," said Mom. "She apparently likes ancient history."

"Hello Cleo," said Dad. The cat looked down at him imperiously, curling her tail tightly around herself. He reached out towards her, but something in her expression made him pause. He quickly withdrew his hand and continued on perusing the bookshelves.

"Nothing?" said Mom finally, already knowing what the answer would be.

"Nada," said Dad. "And I didn't do a 'guy look' either. I looked for anything by Kenwyn Penrow, and even just 'The Squire.'" He felt anxiety welling up in him again, but then had a sudden inspiration. "You know what. Let's pray. We need God's help."

"Great idea," said his wife, pleased that he remembered. "Let's do it."

They clasped hands and bowed their heads.

Rachel had decided that if she ever built her own house, she would have a room like this one. The floor had a thick, plush, green carpet, and there were all sorts of comfortable chairs and stools, cushions and pillows. A skylight at the end of a long, narrow opening above let in a slanting shaft of light, and the wall-space around the book shelves was covered in paintings of tropical trees, flowers and birds. The trees even arched over onto the ceiling, and the kids felt like they had been transported to the Amazon jungle. Scattered around the room were all sorts of jungle-themed hand puppets. Rachel's favorite was a beautiful macaw parrot, but Emily liked the funny monkey with Velcro on its paws so it could be attached to her arm.

It had taken quite a bit of time to convince the boys that there was no mean cat hiding in the corners, but they were finally satisfied and were now each ensconced in bean bag chairs and engrossed in their particular finds. Stevie was halfway through a colorful picture book about space flight, and Danny was studying a children's Bible that was full of really interesting pictures that brought the stories to life in a way he'd never seen before.

"Hey, kids! What a neat place!" Mom and Dad's faces suddenly appeared in the doorway.

"Hi," said Rachel. "Isn't this great! I've found a ton of Enid Blytons. Can I get a couple?"

"May I get a couple," correct Dad. "Sure, you've still got some money. What did you find Emily? I like your monkey."

Emily gave a big smile. "He's great, isn't he?" She held up the book in her hand, the puppet dangling from her arm. "I found a copy of Treasure Island."

"And I'm reading about rockets and stuff," put in Stevie, his nose in his picture book.

"How about you, Danny?" said Mom. Danny didn't respond.

"Danny?" said Mom, louder. The boy snapped out of his thoughts and looked up.

"Oh, hi. Sorry. This is really interesting. Look, it's Joshua and the walls of Jericho." He turned the book so they could see. There was a lively picture of the priests blowing trumpets, the warriors shouting and the walls of the city in the act of tumbling down. "Did you know that God told Joshua to be strong and courageous? I thought Joshua was really brave, but maybe he was sort of afraid to attack Jericho. Look at what happened though!"

Dad smiled to himself. The lad had obviously been doing a lot of thinking. "That's right. Be strong and courageous." *Wasn't that what Danny struggled with the most?* A good teachable moment if there ever was one. "God does amazing things when we trust Him, even if we feel a bit scared of what might happen. And don't forget it's His own strength that He gives us."

"Did you find the book?" said Emily, suddenly remembering what they had come for.

Mom's face fell. "No," she said with a sigh.

"But there's still the possibility it's in the used books. The guy did sound a bit more confident about that," added Dad.

"Do you want to come with us?" said Mom, realizing that as she said it that it was probably a silly question. To her surprise, Rachel nodded eagerly and Emily set down her book and jumped up too.

"I'll come. We really need to find the book."

"But what about us?" said Stevie. "What if the mean cat comes in here?"

Dad was about to respond when Danny spoke up. "It'll be okay. I'll make sure it doesn't hurt you."

The others all gasped in surprise. This wasn't like Danny at all.

"Do you mean it?" said Dad, smiling at the lad.

"Well, um, I was just reading about Joshua and how he was afraid and God had to tell him to be strong and courageous, and he was and God helped him defeat the whole city. So he can help me be brave and defeat a cat." It was a big speech for Danny, and he had to catch his breath at the end of it.

"Well, that's great Tiger. Okay, we'll hopefully be back really soon."

Rachel and Emily ducked out of the room leaving Danny thinking hard and Stevie feeling decidedly anxious.

✥

Kennedy was trying his best not to say anything, but he was reaching the limits of his patience. Jennings had been dealing with this customer for hours—at least it seemed that way. She was a middle-aged lady, apparently from out of town, who absolutely, positively had to look through every old postcard in the shop. What she was looking for, he couldn't imagine. There wasn't any money in old postcards—at least any that Jennings might have in his inventory. He stared out the window, watching the driving rain sweeping down the road, and several miserable-looking pedestrians hurrying by with their coats up over their heads. As far as he could tell, he was at a dead end. So what if he had the key and the book. He had no clue what to do with them!

"Alright, I'll take these, though I'm terribly disappointed you don't have any better ones." The lady's comment caused Kennedy to freeze. *That sounded promising.* He continued looking out the window, but with his ears cocked to the conversation behind him. Jennings mumbled something to the lady in return and rang up the total. Kennedy heard the till open and close, and Jennings wish her, rather half-heartedly, a good day. Out of the corner of his eye he saw the lady leave the store, and he turned to Jennings with a mixture of relief and exasperation.

"Well, that took forever. Couldn't you have got rid of her? You could see I was standing here like a…a cabbage, or whatever."

"Alright, alright," said Jennings, sulkily. "But I still have a business to run. I can't just chase away paying customers because you suddenly need to chat."

"Paying customers?" snorted Kennedy. "How much did you get for half-an-hours running around? A couple of pounds?"

"Yes, a couple of pounds. And I need every bit I can get. You know how bad my business has been." *And that's the only reason I'm dealing with you,* he added to himself.

"Yeah, yeah, okay, whatever. Listen. I need to figure out this next clue—and before that family beats me to it."

Jennings felt a stab of anxiety. Much as he hated having to deal with Kennedy—and basically be blackmailed by him—he couldn't face the possibility of losing this lifeline that had been thrown to him. Surely Kennedy knew what he was talking about, right? He was the expert, and he was risking everything himself, betting it all on the fact that, whatever this inheritance might be, it was both incredibly valuable *and* retrievable before the old lady found it herself. As far as he, Anthony Jennings, could figure out, he had no other choice than to play along with Kennedy's wild schemes.

"Alright," he said out loud resignedly. "What do you need?"

"Right." Kennedy unfolded a scrap of paper and placed it on the counter between them. "Here's what I copied off their camera. They had taken a picture of the clue, but I can't figure out what it means." He set the book and key down as well. "And this is what I found with the last clue."

Jennings picked up the book and flipped through it. "Oh, yeah, I remember this. It was pretty interesting reading." He set it down again and looked at the tag on the key. "Chynalls, eh? Sounds Cornish. 'Chy' means house, right?"

"Really?" said Kennedy, seeing a ray of hope. "Look, the clue only mentions the book and key. What's the relationship?"

Jennings flipped to the book's index, but Kennedy laid his hand on the page. "I already checked that out. There's nothing in the index about Chynalls."

Jennings thought for a moment. "So I suppose you haven't read through the whole book yet?"

Kennedy gestured at the book's size. "What do you think?"

"Well, okay, that's our plan 'B'. Plan 'A' is to figure out what 'Chynalls' means. Here." He rummaged in his desk drawer and pulled out a slim volume. "My Cornish - English dictionary. Okay." He thumbed through the pages. "Here we are. 'Nalls' means 'cliff'. So Chynalls means 'house on the cliff.' "

"House on the cliff? But most of Penrithen is built on the cliffs."

Jennings gave a reluctant nod. They both stared off into space for a minute or two. Jennings was the first to break the silence. "Look, we aren't getting anywhere. We need to find out which house it's referring to. Once we find it, it's got to be obvious what the link with the book is. The Squire couldn't have made it too hard. If the old lady could figure it out, we've got to be able to. Here, wait a minute."

He went over to a rack of posters and dug through them, finally finding the one he was looking for. He pulled it out and set it on the counter. Kennedy bent over to examine it. It was an old map mounted in a frame, and evidently of Penrithen. At least the outline of the cliffs and harbor looked like the same, but there were nowhere near as many buildings.

"This is from the 1800s," said Jennings. He searched for a moment and then jabbed a finger at some small writing. "There, Samuel McMillian. 1834."

"But I don't see any reference to a Chynalls. Look, there's several houses along the cliffs, but only a couple are named. That one there is named 'Westwind'." Kennedy pointed to a building on the far side of the harbor. "And that one's 'Harbour Cottage' up on the cliff on this side."

Jennings studied the map for a minute. "This doesn't have what we need. Hang on." He grabbed up the map and slotted it back into place, then searched further through the stack. "Okay, here's one from…let's see…1788." He pulled out another framed map and set it on the counter. "It's a copy, but valid enough. And look!" he added excitedly. "That house named Westwind on the other map—it's marked here as Chynalls. *The house on the cliff*. There aren't any other houses along the cliffs on this map."

Kennedy grabbed up the map and spun around to the shop window from where he could see across the low roof of the village hall to the far side of the harbor. He jabbed a finger at the large white house perched on the farthest end of the cliff. "That's it—that's the place. I'm going over right now." He grabbed the book and key, stuffed them back in the bag, and yanked open the door. A gust of wind blew in, scattering receipts and papers across the counter. He dashed out, Jennings hurrying over to pull the door shut behind him. Through the window he could just see Kennedy's back disappearing down the hill.

He shook his head. "You're welcome," he muttered. "Don't mention it."

The so-called Shakespeare room was absolutely stuffed with used books, but unfortunately they didn't seem to be quite so well organized as in the other areas. Dad assigned places, and he, Mom and the girls started a careful, thorough search. Rachel secretly hoped they might run into Macbeth, the infamous kitty, but Emily was hoping the opposite.

"What was the title again, Dad?" called out Rachel from where she was scanning a pile of paperbacks.

"*Penrithen: Its Times and Peoples*", said Dad.

"*People's and Times*, I think dear," corrected Mom.

"*People's and Times*, yes. But I don't think it would be a paperback you know. At least, not one of those small ones."

"I just want to make sure," said Rachel over her shoulder.

"Okay," said Dad, returning to examine the shelf in front of him. '*Beginning Stained Glass*,' '*Low-salt Camping Recipes*,' a biography of George Alfred Henty—were these books ever mixed up! He sighed inwardly and kept on looking.

"Did you hear something?" said Stevie, looking up suddenly from his book.

"No, what? What did you hear?" Danny was suddenly alert, his heart beating quickly.

"I don't know, like a cat or something."

"Where was it?"

Stevie threw his book down and rolled out of the beanbag chair onto his knees. He scuttled backwards and pointed towards the door. "Out there. It sounded like a cat. Maybe a big cat. Maybe black, with big teeth. Like it was about to eat something."

Now it was Danny's turn to jump up. He joined Stevie behind the bean bag chairs and looked around desperately for some sort of weapon. The only things he could see were books. *Well, they might work*, he thought. He grabbed up a children's picture dictionary that seemed pretty sturdy and stood warily watching the doorway. Nothing appeared. He tried to relax and think clearly. *How could Stevie know that it was a black cat with big teeth?*

"How do you know it was a black cat with big teeth?"

Stevie took a quick glance at his brother. He looked a little sheepish. "I don't know, it just sounded like it."

"What did you hear?"

Stevie considered that question for a moment. "Well, maybe like a…well, I'm not sure."

The story of Joshua came suddenly to Danny's mind again. *Be strong and courageous.* Could he do it? This was the testing time. He screwed his eyes shut and prayed. "Jesus, please help me be strong and courageous. Please give me Your strength. Amen." He opened them again and looked across at his brother who was staring at the doorway. "I'm going to go and look. Stay here."

Stevie nodded, wide-eyed. Danny stepped carefully towards the door. "Be strong and courageous, be strong and courageous," he muttered to himself. Reaching the doorway he peered carefully around the corner, and almost jumped out of his skin. A cat, the silver tabby—was right there, about a foot away, looking up at him. He was about to dash back to the comparative safety of the bean-bag chair barricade, but something stopped him. He took a deep breath. He had to think this through.

It wasn't a black cat, so it couldn't be the evil one, right? Right. Wasn't it the one the girls were petting earlier? He peered around the corner again. The cat was still there, looking at him.

He crouched down and stretched out his hand like he had seen his sisters do. He beckoned with his finger. "Here kitty, kitty. Here kitty, kitty."

The cat seemed to become mesmerized by his finger. It took a step forward, then another. Danny stretched his hand out and gave it a scratch under the chin. A loud purring broke out.

Danny relaxed. "Hey Stevie," he said softly. "Stevie. Come here. It's okay. Being strong and courageous worked!"

"Nothing." Dad looked over at the others. "Anything?"

They shook their heads and Dad felt a stab of anxiety again. What were they going to do? Were they at a dead end? What would they tell Mrs. Renton?

Rachel interrupted his jumbled thoughts. "What about that box over there? We haven't looked in that. It says 'Misc. Mysteries.' We're trying to solve a mystery!"

"I don't think that means our mystery book will be in there," smiled Mom. "But go ahead and look."

Rachel reached over to open the folded top of the box when she was startled by a very loud hiss. She snatched her hand away and looked at the others in alarm. "Er, I think there's something in there!"

"What?" said Mom and Emily together backing away, visions of hairy spiders jumping into their minds.

"Aha," said Dad, striding over. "Maybe we've found our Mac-Kitty friend."

He peered at the box. There was a small slot where the intersecting flaps forming the top came together. He looked closer. Did he see something gleaming in there?

"I think it is the cat." He pursed his lips.

"Where? Can I see?" said Rachel, regaining confidence. She peeked over his shoulder. "I can see eyes! Can we open the lid?"

"I'll try," said Dad.

"Be careful dear," said Mom, edging closer.

"I will," assured Dad, carefully reaching out for one of the flaps. "I'll just carefully—yow!" He snatched his hand back. A lightning-fast black paw had shot out, struck viciously and then withdrawn to the depths inside.

"That hurt!" Dad looked around ruefully, sucking the end of his finger.

"Good thing you were careful. Need a plan B?" said Mom.

"Ha, ha," said Dad. "I'm open to ideas."

Emily and Rachel looked at each other and shrugged.

"Tell you what," said Dad. "I'll try to push the box over to the doorway and tip it over. You guys get back behind me."

The others didn't need much persuasion. They scurried over behind him as he reached out a foot and gingerly gave the box a push. He was rewarded with a loud, angry hiss from within.

"It's okay kitty," said Rachel with concern. "It's okay. We won't hurt you."

"But will you hurt us?" muttered Dad. "Okay, here goes." He slid the box along with his foot. The hissing broke out again, morphing into the most appalling angry cat sound they had ever heard. The box began to shake and an ear, then a paw and then a furious pair of eyes appeared, pushing up on the flaps.

"He's coming out!" yelled Mom.

Dad abandoned all caution and kicked the box onto its side just in time. A black blur shot out and tore up the nearest bookcase in a frantic scrabble. The cat spun around at the top and glared down at them, hissing and spitting.

"Whew!" said Dad, taking a step back and mopping his brow. "Small chance of that one winning 'pet of the month!'"

"Let's get the box outside," suggested Mom, keeping a wary eye on the angry animal.

Everyone liked that idea. Dad pushed it out the doorway, and Emily eagerly opened it up. "It's got to be in here. Please, Jesus!"

She didn't have to dig far before she gave a shout of triumph. "It's here! I found it!" She spied Danny down the hallway. "Hey, Danny! We found it!" She didn't see the silver tabby behind him bounding off and out of sight.

Danny looked after it for a second with some regret, but then he shook himself. There were more important things to do. He popped his head back into the children's section. "Hey, Stevie, they found it! Come on!"

Chapter 17 - A Surprise Encounter

Dad lowered himself carefully into a bean-bag chair. The family gathered around him. "So what was the next part of the clue?" asked Emily.

Dad leaned back and dug in his pocket. "Here we go." He produced a very crumpled piece of paper. *"Page 63 recounts the tale, a fateful day, a fearful gale,"* he read aloud. *"Evil confronted, Chynalls fray, a paneled door, a secret way.* I think that will do for now. So I'll turn to page 63." He flipped through the book and the others crowded in closer, straining to see.

"Wreckers in Penrithen: The Fate of the Exeter Rose." Dad read the title aloud. "And there's a picture of the ship. Let's see…she was wrecked off the coast near here on October 11th, 1788."

Dad read the article aloud, the rest of the family hanging on to his every word. According to the book, the Exeter Rose was off the west coast of Cornwall when she was caught in a storm. The rocky Cornish coast, with its prevailing onshore winds, was already treacherous for shipping, but with the strength of the storm the ship had no chance. As she was being driven in to shore, the captain would have been desperately looking for the beacon light marking Wolf Rocks, just outside the small cove at the approaches to Penrithen harbor, hoping to claw past them and find a refuge in the large bay just north of the village. At that time in her history, however, the area around the village was notorious as a haunt of wreckers—men who profited from the cargo swept ashore from doomed vessels. Some even deliberately lured ships onto rocks by shining false lights. The law stated that if there were no survivors of a wreck, the cargo was freely available for salvage. What that meant in practice, though, was that any survivors were virtually doomed to be murdered by those intent on plunder. Dad had to pause and explain that to the children.

"But why would people do that?" said Stevie, incredulous.

Dad sighed. "A good question, Stevie. You know how the Bible says that mankind is sinful—that we're born with a tendency to do bad things? Well, if people turn away from God, and follow those sinful desires, they can become more and more wicked. That's why we need Jesus."

"Oh," said Stevie, considering that thoughtfully.

"Keep going," urged Danny. "I want to hear what happened."

So Dad continued on. The wreckers were led by a man named Peter Dunster, a blacksmith from the village of Penarven, just down the coast. He and his band of some twenty men moved the beacon light from the headland above Wolf Rocks and placed it on the cliffs further to the south. Evidently the captain of the Exeter Rose skirted the beacon, believing he had passed the rocks, and was headed in towards the bay. But he was deceived by the false light and turned too early. The ship struck and broke in two almost immediately.

There were more than just the wreckers watching that night, however. Squire Merwyn Trevithick was determined that the wreckers needed to be stopped. Not only did he feel it was his duty as Squire, he had written in his diary that he had also been convicted by God's command in Proverbs 24 verse 11: '*Deliver them that are drawn unto death.*' With the storm raging, he realized that the band of wreckers might probably be at work that night, and as a local magistrate and respected landowner he was able to gather together a force of concerned citizens including his best friend, Jowan Kernow.

Dad paused for a second. "So Squire Trevithick must have been an actual squire—a landowner who owned Penrithen village."

"Amazing," said Mom. "But keep going."

Dad shifted his position slightly and continued on, pausing every now and then to explain things to the kids.

According to the article, it took over an hour for the squire's group to get ready and armed in case of trouble. It was a wild night, and the men split into two groups, the one led by the squire heading south of the village harbor, and the other led by Kernow heading north. Their goal was to look for any sign of a ship in trouble and make sure the beacon was still in position on the cliff. The squire's group on the south soon found to their dismay that, not only had the beacon been moved, but there was already a ship foundering on the rocks. The Squire knew that every second counted for any survivors of the wreck and quickly sent off two of his men to retrieve Kernow's group. He and his remaining men then carefully descended the cliff, cutlasses and pistols at the ready. It didn't take them long to discover that they were already too late. The wreck had rapidly disintegrated under the pounding of the massive waves and there were no sign of survivors except the bodies of two sailors, both with their throats cut. A number of crates and barrels had washed into the cove, but they were already broken open and empty. The wreckers must have already done their diabolical work. But where were they and where had they taken the goods?

The Squire and his men ascended the steep cliff path again, and as they reached the top they heard shouting, pistol shots, and the sound of steel clashing against steel. Kernow and his men must have run into the band of wreckers. The sounds led them to Chynalls, the old, empty house above the harbor.

Dad paused, and everyone began talking at once. He held up his hand. "Yes, yes, it's the word in the clue. It's the name of a house!"

"Now we're getting somewhere," said Mom, excited.

"Where's the secret way?" gushed Danny, scooting forward to the edge of the bean bag chair. "Did the squire man take it to surprise the wreckers?"

"We'll find out," assured his dad. "Let me keep reading. Now where was I?"

Dad found his place again and kept going with the tale. With a righteous wrath the squire led the charge through the front door and found himself face to face with Peter Dunster. Dunster and the squire fought a furious battle with their cutlasses, and the squire was finally gaining the upper hand when he was struck down by a pistol shot from another of the wrecker band. His friends stood over him and fought stoutly until all the wreckers were dead or disabled, Dunster himself receiving a mortal wound from Kernow's pistol. A surgeon was sent for, but it was already too late. The squire's last words were to Kernow, asking him to help and comfort his family, and particularly to keep watch over the squire's young son, Peter. With his dying breath, the squire prayed for his family and the families of those who had lost loved-ones in the wreck.

Dad set the book down, took a deep breath and let it out slowly. The others were quiet, digesting it all until Danny finally broke the silence. "Why did the squire die? I thought he was doing the right thing, trying to protect the shipwrecked people and stop the bad guys."

"He was," said Mom, gently. "But even when people do what's right, even when they are doing exactly what God wants them to, it still doesn't mean they won't get hurt."

"Like Jesus on the cross, right Mom?" said Emily. "He suffered for doing good."

"Yes," said Dad. "That's the ultimate example of God using something bad to accomplish something good."

"But what was good about the squire's death?" wondered Rachel.

"Well, it was his brave actions that finally put a stop to the wreckers. That may have saved many lives."

"And we don't even know what impact his death had on the community, or on his family—even Squire Penrow—our Squire—himself," added Mom. "There has to be a reason he included it. In fact, it may still have an impact on Mrs. Renton when we tell her."

"That's right," said Dad. "We can't figure out all the meanings, but we can trust that God will bring good out of it. Remember Romans eight twenty-eight?"

"But in all things God works for the good of those who love Him, who have been called according to His purpose," quoted Emily.

"But what about the clue?" said Stevie. "Have we figured out what's next?"

"Well, it seems that the secret way must be in this house called Chynalls." He picked up the book again and scanned the article. "Hey, I didn't see this little note. It says to see the map in the appendix—page 145." He flipped eagerly to the back of the book, but gave a groan of disappointment. "Oh, no! Look at this. The spine is broken and several of the pages at the back are missing, including the map."

Everyone was silent for a moment, digesting the news.

"It isn't fair!" cried Stevie suddenly. "First the book and now the map is missing!"

"Shhh. There, there," said Mom, pulling him close.

"But what are we going to do?" said Emily. "We're really stuck!"

Dad looked from face to face, each one drawn and anxious. At that very moment his article deadline popped into his mind again. He shook his head vigorously, trying to shake out the depressing thoughts, and looked again at the disappointed faces in front of him. He was the head of this family and it was up to him to try to be positive, but he for sure couldn't do it by himself. *Jesus,* he prayed. *I really need you. Help me lead this family.*

He took a deep breath. "Okay, gang. You're right. This is bad, and frustrating. But we're forgetting something. It's not just up to us. This is another test, like the missing book, and didn't God just help us find a copy of the book even though we thought we were done for?" He was seeing slow nods all around. "And are we sure God wants us to help Mrs. Renton?" More nods. "And do you think God wants to change her life—to bring her to Him?" There were nods once again, and Dad realized he was inspiring himself as he said it. "So I imagine that Satan doesn't want us to help her. He doesn't want her to come to know God's love. So we're in a spiritual battle. We should expect opposition."

"Yes," agreed Mom, catching on. "You're right! But we don't need to fear it either. Remember the verse—*'greater is He that is in us than he that is in the world.'*"

"So what do we do?" said Emily.

"*Trust in the Lord and do good,*" quoted Rachel with a grin. She turned to her dad. "See, Dad, I remembered it!"

Dad was impressed. Yes, it fit this situation perfectly. "You're right. We need to trust in God, and continue to do what He has directed us to do."

"Which means we need to pray and put our heads together and see what's next," finished Mom.

"Danny, would you pray for us?" Dad put his hand on the boy's shoulder. It seemed like another good opportunity to give him some responsibility.

Danny looked surprised and then pleased. He shut his eyes and the others followed suit. "Dear Jesus. Thank you for protecting us from any bad cats, and thank you for helping us get this far. We're stuck, Jesus. We couldn't find the book in the armor, and now we can't figure out where the house is, so please help us. Help us figure it out so we can help Mrs. Renton. Thank you. Amen."

"Amen" said everyone together. Then all eyes turned expectantly to Dad.

"Well, let's think for a moment and maybe God will lead our thoughts. We know there was a house named Chynalls here in Penrithen, and we know it was probably on the map in the book. So either we need to find another one of the Squire's books, or find another way to figure out about the house."

"I don't think there are any more book shops in the town," said Rachel with a frown. "I suppose we could try another town."

"Or we could ask Mrs. Renton or the Tremannons," put in Emily.

"Um, not the Tremannons," said Mom. "Unless we can be really discrete. Mrs. Renton isn't comfortable about them being involved."

"Well, how about this," offered Dad. "Let's just make double sure with the owner here that there aren't any more books. If there aren't, we can ask him for a suggestion for somewhere else to look, and if that doesn't work we can go and ask Mrs. Renton. We need to check with her today anyway."

Everyone nodded. At least that gave them some things to try.

Dad heaved himself up and gave Mom a hand up too. "Okay, gang. Let's do it."

"Can we go to the star room and see the stars first?" said Stevie.

"Okay, a quick visit to the star room and then let's do it."

"*Five on a Treasure Island!* That's one of my favorites!" Mr. Butterick waved the paperback that Rachel had handed to him. "That will be 50p."

Rachel dug in her pocket and came up with the exact change. She handed it to the man and looked over expectantly at her dad. Was he going to ask the questions now?"

Dad noticed the look and nodded. "Er, Mr. Butterick. We were able to find the book on Penrithen…" He held up the copy they had found.

"Oh, fabulous. I thought I had a used copy. Couldn't find a new one, eh? I didn't have much hope you would."

"No, no, we couldn't," said Dad. "And you see we have a bit of a problem. We really need the map in the back of the book but this copy is missing several pages."

The shop owner's face fell. "Oh, I see. So you won't be wanting it then? What with its having its appendix removed and all. And probably without an anesthetic even!" He gave a wink at the kids, who didn't understand the pun but smiled back anyway.

"Well, we would still," said Dad, smiling himself, "but we just wanted to make sure that you don't have any more copies."

The man pursed his lips and shook his head. "No, no, I'm sure. I remembered while you were off looking that I had sold my last new copy. So sorry about that."

"But we need the map so we can find the house!" blurted out Stevie. The other kids glared at him fiercely, and he realized what he had said. He turned bright red and hid himself behind Mom.

"Can't find the house?" said Mr. Butterick, puzzled. "Do you need a map of the village? Or maybe I can help you."

Dad looked at him for a moment, weighing the pros and cons. "There's a house called Chynalls mentioned in the book. It was in the story about some wreckers, back in the 1700s. It was a really interesting story and we were wondering if the house was still here, in the village." *There, that was all true, but didn't give away too much.*

The others held their breath as Mr. Butterick took a sip from his mug and looked off into space. "Hmm. Well, I don't know of any house named Chynalls—lots of the houses around here have names you know—but I haven't heard of that one. Hang on a minute."

He dug under the counter and popped up again with a small book. "This is a dictionary of Cornish words. I bet the house name is Cornish—sounds like it anyway. Let's do a quick check." He thumbed through the book while the others gathered around.

"Ah, here's the word 'chy'—it means 'house.' That makes sense. Now for the 'nalls' bit." He searched a little further. "Okay, here it is. 'Nalls' means 'cliff.'"

"Cliff house. A house on a cliff," said Rachel. "That's what we're looking for."

"You're right," said the man, "but unfortunately most of Penrithen is built on and around the cliffs. It doesn't narrow things down much."

Their faces fell.

"But you know what you could do," he continued. "There are a couple of antique shops in town. I would bet a stuffed monkey that one of them has an old map or two of the village. If the house is that old, it may be marked on it. At the very least there'd be less houses to choose from. Why don't you try that?"

Now that was something they hadn't thought of. Dad gave the others a hopeful look.

Mom suddenly remembered the other question they were going to ask. "We also wondered if there might be any other place that sells the Squire's book."

Mr. Butterick shook his head decisively. "No, I'm afraid not. It was a limited print run and mostly folk in the village were interested in it. It's very hard to find now."

Well, that settles it, thought Dad. He looked at the others. Mom shrugged her shoulders. She addressed the shop owner. "Would you mind letting us know where the antique shops are? We're still not too familiar with the village."

"Oh, no problem." The man jumped down from his stool again and grabbed a scrap of paper. He sketched out a very rough map of the harbor and made an x on one side. "Right here is 'Rare Finds.' It's pretty much your standard antiques shop—old photos, china, clocks, furniture… It's across from the war memorial in a little row of shops. Next to the Penrithen Pottery, and Joe's Kung Fu and Karate."

That fact seemed intriguing to Dad. "Seems like a bad idea having Joe's Karate next door to the Penrithen pottery. A little too tempting for the students," he said with a grin.

Mr. Butterick gave a funny snort. "You're right! Never thought of that. Like having the skydiving school next to the clay pigeon shooting club."

Dad and the man shared a hearty laugh, until Mom cleared her throat causing them both to stop and look her way a little sheepishly. She gave a slight smile. "And the other shop. Where is that?"

The shop owner became business-like again. "Oh, yes. That would be the 'Mole Hole'. On the other side of the war memorial up the road a bit and right after the woolen shop."

"Hey, we know that one," said Danny. "It looked like a really neat place."

"Okay," said Dad. "We'll finish up here and then head that way." He turned and addressed the shop owner. "Thank you for all your help. And how much for the book?"

Mr. Butterick took it and thumbed through the pages. "Well, since it's incomplete I'd term it 'well used' and 'well used' books are only 50p. How's that?"

"Perfect." Dad handed over the money.

"And you must come back and visit again sometime!"

Dad looked around at his family's smiling faces. "Oh, yes. You can count on it."

❧❧❧

Kennedy threw an anxious glance at the sky. Right now it was between showers, but judging by the ominous look out towards the sea, he could be hit with another one any time. He tried to increase his speed walking, but he realized he was already going about as fast as he could. He didn't dare jog. Smoking and lack of exercise were already causing him to gasp and pant. He glanced behind him. The family was nowhere in sight. Surely he could take it a bit easier, couldn't he?

He stopped for a minute, rested his hands on his knees and got his breathing back under control; then he started off again at a more moderate pace. As he passed Mrs. Renton's house he stole a sideways glance to see if she was anywhere in sight. She wasn't. Not that it really mattered, he reminded himself. She didn't know him from Adam.

He passed the row of houses, crossed the gravel turnaround and arrived at the gate of the big white house. He gave it a good looking-over. It was an imposing two-story structure with a weathered slate tile roof and several impressive stone chimneys. It was clearly untenanted—its windows were boarded up and the house was surrounded by a stone wall that had almost disappeared beneath a mixed assault of ivy and blackberry canes. A wooden sign saying *Westwind* hung crookedly on the gate.

"Would have been easier if they'd left the name the same," grunted Kennedy, but he was too pleased to stay in a bad mood. He was finally, finally ahead of the game, and that blasted family.

The gate was held closed by a rusty spring, and took a bit of effort to force it open and nip through before it crashed shut behind him. The front door may have been painted black at one time, but it had now faded to a dull, flaking grey. He dug for the key and fumbled it into the lock as the rain began in earnest. It turned easily—which surprised him at that moment—and he pushed open the door and leaped inside.

A sudden gust slammed the door shut behind him, and he was immediately aware of an oppressive stillness. He looked nervously around in the dim light filtering in through the boarded windows. Ahead of him was a wide empty

271

entryway with a bannistered staircase heading up to the landing above. A fine layer of dust covered everything in sight and it smelled decidedly musty. It was obvious no-one had been there for a long time. He relaxed a little and put his hands on his hips. So he was in, but now what was he supposed to do? The clue was pretty worthless if it wasn't obvious beyond this point. He pondered that for a moment. The Squire would have thought that the old lady could find the next clue without too much trouble. It *had* to be something obvious then.

He had a sudden disturbing thought. This house couldn't be the inheritance itself could it? But no—that was ridiculous. He distinctly recalled the inheritance being called priceless, and judging by what he could see around him, this house wasn't priceless by a long shot. And if it were the house, there would be some big bow on it or something. He smiled grimly to himself. No, there was something better. Maybe it was here, in the house. He'd just check it carefully, room by room.

ৰ্তৡ

"Look, the post office," said Emily triumphantly. The Warren had lived up to its name and they were beginning to think they would never find their way back out.

"Thank you, Jesus," said Mom. "I was getting a bit nervous."

"No kidding," agreed Dad, having had to apologize for a wrong turn several streets back.

"Hats and hoods up," announced Mom, noticing the sky. "We might get dumped on."

Dad quickly pulled up his hood and helped Stevie with his own. Danny wasn't paying attention—his eyes had a far off look.

"You okay, Danny?" said his Dad.

"Yeah, I was just thinking of that bookstore. It was bigger on the inside than the outside. Like the stable in the last Narnia book."

"That's so right," smiled Dad, "it was one of the wackiest places I've ever been. I liked the guy's sense of humor though. Anyway Tiger, we need to batten down the hatches. Get zipped, and get your hood up." Dad turned to Mom. "How about you and the girls checking out that 'Rare Finds' shop by the pottery, and I'll take the boys to the Mole Hole? Whoever finishes first can make their way to the other place. Sound good?"

"Sounds good." Mom grabbed the girls' hands. "Come on ladies. Let's hurry!"

A sudden gust seemed to grab them and push them down the street. Mom looked over her shoulder. "Bye dear. See you soon! Stay dry!"

ৰ্তৡ

Dad and the boys were soaked. As Dad yanked the door of the Mole Hole closed behind them, the transition to the warm, cluttered interior seemed incredibly abrupt and he immediately felt self-conscious, realizing they had interrupted the cozy quietness of the surroundings with the sudden appearance of three streaming creatures, sniffling, coughing and creating puddles on the floor at their feet.

"Okay, boys?" He peered into their faces. To his surprise, they were both grinning widely, their dripping faces bright red under sodden strands of hair.

He was suddenly aware of the bearded shop-owner, pipe in hand, studying them open mouthed from behind the counter. Dad decided the only thing to do was to squash his embarrassment and greet him properly.

"Hello," he said, offering his hand. "I'm very sorry about just bursting in like that. Quite the rain shower outside!"

With an apparent effort the man seemed to master his surprise, set his pipe down and shake the proffered hand somewhat mechanically. He opened his mouth but seemed to be having trouble finding what to say. There was a sudden, strident blaring of the 1812 overture coming from somewhere at the back of the shop and the man jumped in surprise.

"Er…I'll be right back," he blurted out, a certain relief showing in his face. He turned and scurried behind a set of large shelves holding assorted chinaware.

Dad looked after him in astonishment. Something about the man seemed familiar. His ponderings were cut short, however, by a noise at his side. Stevie was very close to poking a stuffed penguin in the front window display. "Don't touch, please. Look with your eyes, not your fingers," Dad warned.

Stevie nodded without turning.

"Yes, Daddy?" Dad prompted. Sometimes it seemed Stevie could answer without the message actually passing through his brain.

"We're looking for an old map, right Daddy?" said Danny, looking around.

"Yes, that's right. But they might not be easy to spot, if they're even here at all." Dad suddenly felt very skeptical this would actually succeed.

"Look at that sword," gushed Stevie, pointing to a large, impressive specimen hung above a display case filled with brass candlesticks and horse brasses.

"It's great," said Dad, rather distracted, "but we're looking for maps."

"Like these right here?" said Danny, pointing to the rack of pictures. "There's an old map right in front. Isn't it the harbor?"

"Really?" said Dad, striding over. "It couldn't be."

"But we prayed, right?"

Dad felt a twinge of guilt. *Childlike faith wins again*, he thought. "Okay, let's see," he said out loud, hefting the framed map up and onto the counter. Danny peered at it on tiptoe, and Dad felt a tugging at his elbow.

"I can't see!" said Stevie.

"Okay, here you go," Dad lifted him up so he was half leaning on the counter, then stuck his knee under the boy to keep him in position.

The three of them scanned the map, Dad still a little skeptical. What were the odds that this map would even be the right timeframe, let alone have the name of the house on it?

"There it is!" said Danny, suddenly.

"No way!" said Dad, "where?"

"Right there!" Danny pointed to the spot.

Dad leaned over and shook his head in amazement. "You're right. *Chynalls!* That was so easy!"

"So where's the house," wondered Stevie, straining to see out the window from his perch on Dad's knee. Dad slid him down to the ground and took another quick look at the map to get his bearings.

"It's across the harbor by itself at the edge of the cliff," he said coming over. "It's got to be that big white house over there. The one right next to the path we took down to the cove. Do you remember the windows were all boarded up?" He pointed to the spot. "Thank you, Jesus." *And I'm really sorry for not trusting you*, he added under his breath.

⋙⋘

"So are you sure you checked all the rooms?" Jennings was fed up. His ear was beginning to ache and he'd been listening to a running commentary of Kennedy's failed exploration for the last ten minutes. Kennedy didn't like that question at all, and let Jennings know it.

Jennings was about to respond in kind when he had a sudden, awful thought. "Wait, listen! I totally forgot that family are still in my shop. They might be looking for the house too—and I left that map right where they could find it. I've got to go! Just keep looking. Check the fireplaces. That's a possible spot." He snapped his phone shut, took a deep breath and moved surreptitiously towards the front of the store, listening carefully. He could hear voices. What were they talking about?

He heard the front door open and close and the sound of a women's voice. *It must be the mother*, he thought. He snuck up to the back of the shelves behind the counter and strained to hear.

⋙⋘

Kennedy didn't care to follow Jennings' advice. He'd checked the fireplaces and there wasn't anything there. He threw himself down on the staircase and yanked out the book again. *Somewhere in this book must be the clue*, he mused. *I must be missing something obvious.*

⋙⋘

"Amen." With Dad's reminder, the family had taken some time to thank God for Danny's miraculous discovery of the house on the map. Mom and the girls had been thrilled, especially after striking out themselves at the antiques place.

"It's still pouring," announced Stevie as they opened their eyes. Sure enough it was pelting down so hard the raindrops were bouncing off the road.

"That's not good," said Mom. She looked around at the others. "I know we want to get going, but perhaps it's better to wait a bit until it eases up."

There were a few groans.

"Maybe we can figure out the next part of the clue," suggested Emily helpfully. "Or at least try."

Dad nodded. "That's a good idea." He retrieved the piece of paper again. It was looking decidedly the worst for wear. The others strained to see.

Dad held the clue up high. "Hey, stand back a bit. I'll read it to you."

Behind the shelves, Jennings dug desperately in his pocket for a pen and piece of paper. He couldn't miss this amazing chance to hear a clue again.

274

Dad cleared his throat and read. *"Page 63 recounts the tale, a fateful day, a fearful gale,*

Evil confronted, Chynalls fray, a paneled door, a secret way.

Ill-gotten gains made passage thru, but there you too will find the clue."

"So somewhere in the house is a hidden panel that leads to a secret passage that maybe the wreckers used!" said Rachel, her eyes shining.

"Oh, hurry up and stop raining," said Danny, jumping up and down in frustration. "We want to go!"

⊰⊱

Jennings backed slowly away from the shelves, and then made a bee-line for his little office at the back of the store. He shut the door quietly and called Kennedy's number.

"Hey, yes, it's me. Incredible news. That family were right here and they just read the next clue. There was more to it than you thought. Yes, yes. Give me a second. Okay, here it is." He read off the clue, and listened for Kennedy to repeat it back to him. "That's it. Now get going! I'm going to keep an eye on them." He hung up and peered around the office door. Good. They must still all be at the window.

He tried to assume a nonchalant air and was striding purposely towards the front of the store when he stopped suddenly in dismay. *What was he thinking?* That girl had seen him at Tintagel. They all had. They might recognize him and figure out he was helping Kennedy.

He turned to retrace his steps, but it was already too late.

"Er, excuse me." Rachel had decided she was going to pass the time seeing if they had any old books and had headed further back in the shop to find the owner. "Would you have…?" She stopped short. For a split second her eyes met the shop owner's. He gave a start of surprise and then spun around to hurry back the way he'd come, leaving Rachel staring after him in shock.

⊰⊱

Kennedy dropped his phone and grabbed up the book again. He flipped to page sixty-three and scanned the article, firing glances at his scribbled copy of the clue. Yes, yes, it was all making sense now. The wreckers, the fight, this house…this must have been some sort of hideout. Perhaps there were a number of places where the men could hide if pursued, or perhaps secrete the salvaged goods until the hue and cry had died down and they could sell them off. They were probably into smuggling as well.

"*Ill-gotten gains made passage though,*" he read out loud. Yes, that was it. This was a place where the goods were stashed until they could journey on to wherever they could be sold. Kennedy nodded in satisfaction. *Right, then,* he thought. *Let's find it--before that meddling family does.* He jumped to his feet. Where had he seen paneled walls? The dining room?

He scurried though the front parlor and into the room beyond. To his immense satisfaction, he saw that the walls were paneled in dark wood on three sides—floor to ceiling. Between each row of panels ran a raised carved wooden casing. He started thumping the lower rows of panels one by one, listening for any sign of hollowness, working his way around the room but with a mounting frustration. They all sounded the same—and very solid. He decided to try the upper rows, but with much misgiving. If there was a secret door, it wouldn't make sense that it would be up so high. He worked his way around again, thumping vigorously. The last panel he hit so hard in his exasperation that he yelled in pain.

He stepped back and tried to force himself to calm down, nursing his hand. Getting angry obviously wouldn't help at all. He made a concerted attempt to think objectively. The panel had to be here in the house, but where?

❧❦

Dad tried to calm Rachel down enough so they could understand her. He finally convinced her to stop talking, take a deep breath and start over, reminding her to keep her voice low.

"When we were at Tintagel, I told you about a man—the man we saw at the castle and then later in the café," she gushed. "It seemed like he was interested in the clue—like he was following us. And then he was in the store and heard Danny talk about the chess set. I saw the look on his face—like he was so glad he overheard that."

Dad pursed his lips. He didn't want to go over all this again—Rachel and her silly conspiracy theory. Mom noticed his look and laid a hand on his arm.

"Let's let Rachel continue. Maybe she's really on to something."

Rachel gave Mom a grateful smile and kept going. "Well, you know we were just going over the clue again and guess who was in the back of this shop, listening to us." She paused for effect. "The man again. The same man from Tintagel."

Danny and Stevie gasped. Emily furrowed her brow. Dad looked at Mom skeptically, and she shrugged her shoulders. Could Rachel be right? It would be so bizarre if the guy was really on their tail. She turned to Rachel before Dad could say anything. "Well, dear, it is an amazing coincidence, but don't you think that's all it is? I mean, it was us who chose to look in this shop today, and if he's the owner there's no way he could have known we'd be here."

"But what if he is after the clue?" said Rachel desperately, forgetting to keep her voice low. "The book and key were missing from the suit or armor. What if he took them?"

"Shhh," reminded Dad. He looked at his wife who gave the merest shake of her head. He got the message and tried to soften his response. "Well, sweetheart, it is strange to run into him again, but we can't do much about that now. I can't just accuse him without really any evidence. Tell you what. Let's all keep our eyes open and see if we run into him again outside of the shop." Dad glanced out the window. "It's stopped raining. We can go check out the house."

Rachel nodded glumly. She was sure the man was a bad guy, but had to agree that there wasn't anything they could do about it right now. She made up her mind, though, that there was no way he was going to learn anything more from them. She would make sure of it.

Dad noticed her determined look and gave her a squeeze. "I'm really glad you're concerned about Mrs. Renton getting her inheritance. Now, everyone, got your coats and hats ready? Let's go!"

"But we don't have the key!" said Danny suddenly.

Dad frowned. He had forgotten all about that. He looked around at the others, but it seemed like no-one had anything to offer except glum looks.

"Well," he said at last. "There's not much else we can do. We at least know which house it is. Hopefully we'll be able to figure something out." He paused, and looked off into space. "And you know, God can do a miracle." He turned back to the group and smiled. "So let's pray for one."

⊷⊶

Kennedy had done a lightning scan of the other rooms, both upstairs and down, then hurried back into the dining room, his chest heaving.

The panel *had* to be in here, so that meant he had to look a little closer. He started again at the leftmost lower panel and examined it closely. There didn't seem to be any markings on the wood. He took another look at the casing above. There were little shields carved every few inches or so, each one divided into quarters and encircled by a smooth carved line. He moved to the right, and stopped abruptly.

The second panel along looked just like the others, but one of the carved shields in the casing above it had some tiny etchings. Kennedy peered at them closely. They were hard to make out, but they did mark this panel as different from the others. With a sudden inspiration he pushed hard on the shield and it depressed easily causing a deep rumbling and a metallic scraping noise. The panel dropped downwards revealing a dark gaping hole just big enough for a person.

Kennedy gave a yell of triumph. As he crouched down to peer inside, a cold breeze ruffled his hair and there was an unpleasant, musty smell. He squatted down and stepped cautiously over the sill into the space behind. It was a cubby hole about four feet square and just tall enough that he could stand upright. He stepped aside a little to allow the dim light from the dining room to illuminate the inner walls. Right away he spotted a large rectangular hole about a foot off the ground to his right. The cold air seemed to be streaming in from there. He gave a satisfied smirk.

⊷⊶

Jennings heard the door slam and peered carefully around the shelves. *Thank heaven*, the family had finally gone. But that wasn't really good news, was it? He was sure that the one girl suspected him, and now the family was evidently on their way to the house. He had to call Kennedy, and fast.

⊷⊶

Kennedy was too far away from where he'd left his phone to hear it ringing. He was kneeling down and feeling around the edges of the hole, trying to figure out if there was anything hidden there. The hole itself seemed to be the top of a large, irregular shaft carved out of the solid rock—a shaft that disappeared down into blackness. His searching hands had almost made a complete circuit of the edge when he finally felt something. An iron peg was driven into the rock with what felt like a chain attached at the bottom. He reached forward and felt down the links; it kept going as far as he could reach. Adjusting his position slightly he grabbed it with both hands and pulled. He could feel it move slightly but there seemed to be some resistance. He pulled harder. Nothing. Now it wouldn't even budge.

He sat back on his heels, thinking furiously. There had to be something very heavy at the end of that chain. Something big perhaps? A box? A chest? Yes, that would be very good—very good indeed! *This could be it.*

He stood up, stretched his arm muscles, spat in his hands and rubbed them together, then took a firm, fresh grip on the chain. There was just enough room for him to get both hands around it. He mentally counted to three and gave it a huge heave.

Eyes popping and muscles stretched to the limit he gave it his all, but to no avail. Nothing—not even the slightest movement. Whatever it was it was stuck and stuck fast.

∾📖∾

"I'm scared of the house. It's creepy," Stevie whispered in Mom's ear, not wanting the others to hear.

Mom glanced up to the house at the end of the road. It did look rather ominous, especially all boarded up, and looming against the backdrop of the glowering sky. She looked back at Stevie, his eyes red and his nose runny, and came to an abrupt conclusion.

"Dear," she said to Dad. "I'm going to take Stevie to Mrs. Renton's. You guys go on up to the house and check it out. I'll fill her in on what we've found out."

Dad absorbed that for a second, then nodded.

Mom ruffled Stevie's hair, gave Dad a quick peck on the cheek and led the boy through the gate and up the path to the old lady's door. She glanced back and saw Dad standing there still, the others a little further up the road.

"Go ahead dear. This is best. Go find the clue and come back as soon as you can. We'll be praying for you." She sighed inwardly as she said it. She really did wish she could go on with them, but knew in her heart of hearts that she needed to stay with the boy.

"Alright. Thanks so much. See you soon hopefully." Dad turned and hurried off.

Mom smiled down at Stevie and then knocked firmly on the door.

∾📖∾

Kennedy had been racking his brains. It was infinitely annoying to be so close and yet so far. One thing was certain, though, he couldn't pull on that chain any more. He had pretty much scraped the skin off both palms. He needed something else—some sort of lever perhaps?

He rummaged through the drawers and cupboards in the kitchen, but without success. He noticed the back door and threw back the bolt and hauled it open. The house was partially built right against the cliff, but there was a small yard at

278

this end that stretched around the side of the house. A stained, trellised arbor slouched at the end of a dank, neglected garden scattered with old building supplies. Kennedy grunted in satisfaction. There had to be something there he could use. It didn't take him long to find it—a thick metal rod about two feet long. He snatched it up and rushed back to the opening.

It took him several tries before he could jam the rod under the chain in a way that gave it some purchase. Turning his body this way and that, he finally settled on a position that gave him the most leverage. Taking a deep breath and scrunching up his face he yanked down on the rod. *Nothing.*

Shifting his grip, he put his full weight into it and then disaster struck. He felt something give and he shot painfully backwards to the ground, bashing his head again the wall. There was a sliding, grating sound from the hole that quickly faded away into nothing.

Kennedy sat there, panting, trying to process what had happened. Then with a howl of dismay he leapt up and thrust his hand down the hole. The chain was now only about six inches long with the end link bent and broken. He reached as far as he could but felt nothing except the cold wall of rock. Whatever had been attached to the chain was gone.

Jennings stood in his shop window anxiously watching the proceedings across the harbor through his binoculars. The family had split up, the mom and youngest boy going to the old lady's house, and the others continuing up the road. He tried Kennedy's phone once again. Why, oh why wasn't he answering? *He was going to get caught!*

If only I had a flashlight! Kennedy was almost beside himself with frustration. Then a sudden thought struck him. *His phone. It had a flashlight function.* He ducked back out of the secret room and tore back to the staircase. As he did, he heard something getting louder and louder. *Was that…? Yes, it was!* He rounded the corner and snatched up his phone.

"Yes, yes, it's me. What do you want? And be quick." Kennedy ran back to the dining room, trying to listen on the way. What he heard made him screech to a halt. "What? Here?"

At that very moment he heard the squeak of the front gate and the sound of voices. *Impossible!* He looked around frantically, his mind a whirl. He saw the open secret door at the far side of the room and his eyes widened in horror. Dashing over he pushed hard on the little button. The door slid slowly back up into place. Not waiting to see, he tore into the kitchen, skidding around the kitchen table to the back door. Yanking it open, he leapt through, trying to force himself to calm down enough to shut it quietly behind him.

He looked around wildly. There was nowhere to hide in the yard. Where could he go?

Mrs. Renton's eyes got wider and wider as Mom, with enthusiastic interruptions by Stevie, summarized what had taken place that day. She shook her head in amazement. This family was doing so much for her—she still couldn't understand it.

"Dearie me," she said out loud. "And the inheritance might be in the old house just up the street?" She felt a sudden thrill. Could they be that close to the end?

"We don't know. But Mrs. Renton—if you don't mind—I really want to pray about that—that God's will would be done."

Mrs. Renton didn't really like the sound of that. What if it wasn't God's will for them to find it?

"And," added Mom, "I'd really like to pray for the rest of the family." She paused for a second, with a conviction she hadn't realized until just now. "I've just a funny feeling. Rachel seems to think there's someone interested in the inheritance too."

"What do you mean?"

"Well, we're not sure. She says the man from the antique shop across the way—The Mole Hole—that he was there at Tintagel and seemed to be following us."

"And listening to the clues," put in Stevie dramatically. Though he hadn't really understood all of Rachel's concerns, it did make him feel important to impress Mrs. Renton.

The old lady was dumbfounded. The thought that someone else could be after her inheritance was something she had never even considered. What did that mean? Was that another sign that God was punishing her?

"So you see, I'd like to pray. Do you mind if we do right now?" Mom touched her lightly on the arm.

Mrs. Renton didn't know what to say. Here she was wrestling about whether God was interested in her at all, whether He was interested but actively working against her, or whether, like the family claimed, He actually cared about her.

Mom could clearly see the struggle in the lady's face, but felt in her spirit that she should go ahead and pray. She closed her eyes and Stevie, watching her closely, followed suit.

"Dear Lord, thank you for your help so far. Thank you that you are a loving Father, and you care for Your children. Thank you for Mrs. Renton and giving us the privilege of meeting her. We want to say again that we can't do this without You. Will you please help us with this clue? Please protect Dave and the kids as they look for it. Please help us all to be patient and trust You in the process. And," and here she paused for a moment. "And if there's anyone else trying to steal the inheritance from Mrs. Renton, please frustrate their plans. Please stop them from succeeding. That's what we would desire, but in all this we ask for Your will to be done, and that You would be glorified. Thank you, Father. Amen."

"Amen," echoed Stevie.

Mrs. Renton just looked down at her lap, not knowing what to think. Was God possibly on their side? She could imagine He was on the family's side, but was He on *her* side? How could He be after how she'd rejected Him, and hurt the Penrows too? No, she wasn't sure He was on her side at all.

Chapter 18 - The Secret Way

Dad, Emily, Rachel and Danny stood under the dripping porch, looking at the front door of the old house.

"Okay, kids. We need a miracle. Let's pray." Dad grabbed Emily's hand and the others formed a circle with them and closed their eyes.

"Dear Jesus," he began. "You know we're trying to help Mrs. Renton. And you know we couldn't find the key. We need Your help. If it's truly Your will that we get in this house and find the clue, then please help us get in without a key."

He paused, and Emily jumped in. "Yes, Jesus. Please give us a miracle."

"Help us help Mrs. Renton, dear Jesus," added Rachel earnestly.

"Yes, God. We need Your help. Please help us get in the house," said Danny in turn.

Dad waited for a second or two, then said "Amen." Why was he feeling nervous? He knew his own faith in God wouldn't be shaken if the door was locked. The problem was explaining it to the kids. But surely God was big enough to take care of the kids own walk of faith. He felt a sudden settled conviction that everything would be okay, and he reached out and grabbed the handle. It turned easily and the door swung open.

The kids all gave exclamations of surprise and delight. Dad was amazed. Did that really just happen? *Yes, and it was indeed a miracle.* He felt a wonderful thrill inside. Their heavenly Father had responded to their cry, and the kids had all seen it.

"Let's thank Jesus," said Emily, her eyes shining.

"Great idea, honey." Dad grabbed her hand again. "Let's do it!"

Kennedy was halfway down the slippery steps to the cove, hanging on and trying to decide what to do. If he stayed put, he'd never know what happened. But if he went up again, he risked running into them.

He glanced over his shoulder. The tide was quite a way out but the breakers still seemed to run towards the cove with surprising force. The rain was tapering off, but grey clouds lined the sky to the horizon. He looked back up the stairway. *At least the family wouldn't find anything in the shaft*, he mused. But that was small consolation. If the inheritance treasure really was stuck somewhere in there, he couldn't get to it either. So that brought him back again to his present predicament. Should he go up or down?

The house felt big and echoey, and there wasn't a scrap of furniture to be seen in the dim light seeping in around the boarded up windows. As their eyes slowly adjusted, they noticed with puzzlement the number of scuff marks and trails in the dust on the floor apparently heading all over the house.

"It looks like someone has been here," said Rachel pointing.

"Do you think they still are?" said Danny, scooting behind Dad and grabbing hold of his leg. Dad frowned. He hadn't considered that.

"But it couldn't be the man in the shop. We just left him," said Emily, trying to forestall any panic in her brother, and needing the assurance herself. Rachel gave a puzzled look.

"Maybe it was the Squire," said Danny, feeling a little more hopeful. "When he put the clue here."

"Maybe," said Dad, but inside he doubted that that were possible. Didn't the Squire get sick back in the eighties? It was just too long ago. "Hello?" He said loudly, making the kids jump. "Anyone here?"

They all listened intently. The only slight sound was the distant muffled roar of the surf.

"Do you want me to quickly check the place out, or all go together?" said Dad finally.

"Oh, let's stay together," said Emily. Rachel and Danny nodded.

"Alright. So, we're looking for a secret way, right?"

"Behind a paneled door, I think," said Rachel, peering into the next room.

"Okay, we don't see any panels around here or on the landing, so I'm thinking we need to start in the living room. Pity we can't follow the trail in the dust, but it looks like it goes everywhere in the house."

Dad led the way into the room on the left side of the entryway, which had apparently been a spacious parlor with a large fireplace. The crooked, cobwebbed light fixture looked like the sort that might have once held candles but had been adapted for electric light. There was nothing else in the room except an old mirror that made Emily jump slightly as she caught sight of her own dim reflection.

"Nothing in here," whispered Danny, still keeping as close to Dad as possible.

"Let's go this way," said Rachel in a much louder voice, pointing towards the room beyond. She grabbed Dad's hand and pulled him towards the doorway, feeling a bit more confident now that it seemed fairly certain they were alone. Her sense of adventure was welling up inside her again, and she was remembering all the mystery stories she'd read. There always seemed to be some sort of secret place in them and here she was, searching for the very same thing!

The next room seemed to be the dining room, with a large, low light fixture that must have once been over the table. To their joy, three of the walls were paneled from floor to ceiling.

"It's got to be here," gushed Rachel.

Even Danny forgot his fears, letting go of Dad's hand and looking around in delight.

"In the books I've read, the secret panel sometimes sounds hollow when you tap on it," said Rachel authoritatively. "We need to carefully check each one."

"I already know which one it is," said Danny surprisingly. The others looked at him with raised eyebrows.

"Which one?" said Dad, feeling no small sense of skepticism.

"Follow me," said the lad, with some importance. He felt like a true detective. Wasn't it Sherlock Holmes' powers of observation that always won the day? He led the way to the back wall and pointed at the ground. There was no doubt about it. The floor in front of this particular panel had almost all the dust scuffed away. Someone must have spent some time standing right there.

Dad nodded, impressed. "Great job, Tiger. I think you're right."

Emily gave her brother a squeeze, his face turning bright red with surprise and pleasure. Rachel, however, stood stock still, her mouth open.

Dad looked over at her. "What's up, Rachel? Are you alright?"

She suddenly snapped out of her stupor. "Oh, sorry, what? Yes. Well, sort of. I was just thinking—all these scuff marks. I was wondering if possibly someone got here first."

Dad considered that for a moment. Then he shrugged his shoulders. "There's only one way to find out." He peered closely at the panel and knocked across the wood, listening intently. There didn't seem to be any variation in the sound. He knocked a few times on the adjacent panels, but still didn't hear much difference.

"Can I try?" said Rachel. She was sure she knew how secret panels opened in the stories.

"May I?" reminded Dad, never too focused not to correct bad grammar. "Go ahead."

He stepped aside and Rachel started pushing hard on each of the corners. She then pushed down and tried to slide the wood sideways at the same time. The panel refused to move. She scrunched her nose up in disappointment. *Why hadn't that worked?*

Emily was just about to ask for a turn when Danny gave a sudden yelp of surprise. "Look, look!" He pointed at the little carved shield in the casing.

"What's the matter?" said Dad, squinting at the carved image.

Emily stuck her head in and peered at it under his arm. "That shield. It's different from the others. And those marks—they're kind of like the shield on the mantel's tile!" she exclaimed.

"Push it in!" cried Danny.

Dad was just about to try when Rachel suddenly stopped him with a hand on his arm. "Wait, Dad. Can we let Danny do it? He saw it first."

Dad looked at her in surprise and approval. "You know, dear, that's a great idea and very unselfish of you. Go ahead, Danny."

Rachel smiled. It felt really good to do the right thing. Danny was so surprised he could hardly speak. He flashed Rachel a grateful smile and reached out and pushed hard on the shield, then jumped back as the panel slid downwards.

"It's a secret room," squeaked Rachel. "I can't believe it!"

She and Emily poked their heads through the opening, almost clunking them together.

"Steady on, ladies," said Dad. He looked down at Danny who was eyeing the opening suspiciously. "Do you want to have a peek?"

Danny shook his head, thought for a moment, then nodded slowly. He shuffled a bit closer and the girls made way for him. Taking a firm grip of one side of the opening, he stuck his head through. The first thing he noticed was the cold draught blowing in his face and the next was a strange, slightly disagreeable smell. He looked around, his eyes slowly adjusting to the dim interior. The sides of the room were lined with boards and he could just make out a sort of darker patch on the wall to the right.

"It's pretty small," commented Danny, feeling a bit less nervous. "It's kind of more like a cupboard. There's a bit of room around the side, though."

"Can we get in? I think there's space for all of us," said Rachel, peering past Danny.

"Sure, but first let me test it." Dad thrust a leg through the opening and stomped hard on the floor. Crouching down, he stepped fully in and stood up as best as he could. He jumped tentatively up and down a few times before he bonked his head on the low ceiling and stopped abruptly.

"Oof," he exclaimed, rubbing his head. "But I guess it's strong enough. Come on in."

The girls stepped in and helped a slightly reluctant Danny in behind them.

"Let's spread apart a bit if we can," suggested Emily, "so we can let in a bit more light."

There wasn't much room, but by squeezing away from the opening they could make out a hole a little way up the side wall.

"What's that?" said Danny, still rather ill at ease. "Is that where the treasure is?"

"I don't know—I'll check it out." Dad felt around the hole somewhat gingerly and his hand soon found the broken chain.

"What's this?" he said, pulling it out of the hole. There were only about five links left in the chain and the last one was twisted and broken.

"Oh, no!" exclaimed Emily. "It's snapped."

"What do you mean?" said Danny. "Do you mean the treasure has broken off the end?"

"Or someone broke it off," said Rachel ominously.

"Well, we don't know anything yet, guys," said Dad. "Hang on and let's think."

"What did the clue say again?" asked Emily.

Dad had it memorized now. *"Evil confronted, Chynalls fray, a paneled door, a secret way.*

Ill-gotten gains made passage thru, but there you too will find the clue," he recited.

"This was definitely the secret way behind the paneled door," said Emily.

"And the wreckers' goods were stored here," added Rachel. "And so was the next clue."

"So it must have been on the chain and now it's gone!" exclaimed Danny.

Dad had a sudden thought. "Hey, Danny. Don't you have your little flashlight? I know all good detectives should have one, but I don't seem to have been well-enough prepared."

Danny's face lit up. He dug in one pocket and produced a marble, a one euro coin, a bouncy ball and several small rocks. The others looked at the stash in amusement. Stuffing them back in, he searched the other side. This time he found a paper clip, a plastic spider, two seashells that had seen better days and, finally, his mini LED flashlight. He held it up triumphantly. "Here it is!"

"Great," said Dad. "And I'll remember you have a plastic spider in there in case we need to freak out your mother. Okay, come over here." Dad ushered him into a position where the lad could rest his elbows on the edge. The girls crammed in closely.

"Careful, girls. We don't want Danny to drop the light! Hold it tightly, Danny. What do you see?"

Danny shone the flashlight around in the hole. It was evidently carved out of solid rock.

"The chain's broken for sure, and I don't see any more of it. Hang on."

He knelt down so that his stomach was resting on the edge of the hole and shone his light straight down. "It's a long tunnel going down. It's pretty wide—I think a treasure chest would fit." He adjusted his position and looked again. "Okay, I can see something way down there blocking the tunnel. I can't tell what it is."

"How far down?" demanded Rachel, trying unsuccessfully to get a view down the shaft.

"Really far," said Danny, proud to be the one with all the information.

Dad couldn't see a thing with Danny filling most of the opening. "Hey bud, can I take a peek?"

"Sure," said Danny, offering him the light and actually relieved to be able to get out of his rather uncomfortable position.

"Me too?" said Rachel and Emily at the same time.

"Ok, in just a sec," said Dad, blinking to try and get his vision back after Danny shone the light right in his eyes. He knelt by the hole and held the light as far down as he could reach. Sure enough far below at the limit of the flashlight's beam was what looked like something blocking the shaft. Could it possibly be a box, or was it a chunk of rock? It was hard to tell. He shimmied back out and handed the light to Emily, and while she and Rachel took their turns he stepped back out the cubby hole into the dining room. Danny followed him out, a serious look on the lad's face.

"So, Daddy, what are we going to do?"

It was a good question. Several images flashed through Dad's mind—trying to fish down the hole with a rope and hook, trying one of those snake things they use for unclogging drains… Nothing seemed to offer much chance of success.

The girls rejoined them in the room, dusting themselves off. They looked expectantly at Dad. He shrugged his shoulders. "I don't know, kiddos. I'm stumped. Whatever is down there is a long way down."

"But we can't give up," said Danny.

"No, no, we can't," agreed Dad, ruffling the lad's hair.

"We can pray," suggested Emily suddenly. She was beginning to realize it really made a difference.

Dad smiled to himself. He gave Emily a quick squeeze. "You know, you're right sweetheart. Would you like to do it?"

Emily nodded and they all shut their eyes. "Dear Jesus," she prayed. "We don't want to ever forget that you are here and can help us. You know our needs. We really want to solve this clue so we can help Mrs. Renton. If it's Your will—if that's the best way to help her come to know you, then please help us. Thank you, Jesus. We love you. Amen."

"Amen!" said Dad, feeling suddenly much more positive. Shouldn't they always pray? "Okay, let's put our heads together and see how the Lord leads."

"I have a thought," said Rachel looking serious. "The mark's right there in front of the opening—it looks like someone was here—and not too long ago."

"How d'you mean?" said Danny, getting a bit concerned again.

"I just mean that it wasn't ages ago, like when the Squire put the clue here. The dust would have settled again over the marks—and it probably wouldn't have been dusty when he did it anyway."

"Go on," said Dad, intrigued.

"So if someone did get to the correct panel, they probably figured out how to open it. I mean, we did without much trouble."

"Right," agreed Emily. "And the Squire wouldn't have made that too hard or Mrs. Renton wouldn't have been able to solve it."

"So you're saying we should assume someone got into the secret room and got the clue before us?" said Dad. *Could Rachel have been right after all?* he wondered.

"Well, I think they got in, but I'm actually not sure they got the clue," said Rachel.

"Why not?" said Danny.

"Well, the chain is broken. If the Squire wanted Mrs. Renton to get the clue, I don't think he would have expected her to break the chain to get it."

Now Dad was catching on. "Aha. I see what you're saying. So if someone was here, either they broke the chain getting the clue, or broke it and didn't get the clue after all."

"So it might really be stuck down there?" said Danny, remembering what he saw with his flashlight.

"It could be," said Dad. "But that still leaves us with the problem of how to get it out."

Emily had a sudden thought. "Daddy, what was that bit about ill-gotten gains."

"Ill-gotten gains made passage thru, but there you too will find the clue." recited Dad again.

"Yes, that's it!" said Emily excitedly. "Don't you see? The goods made passage through the shaft. They weren't just hidden there. They came through it."

"I don't get it," said Danny, confused.

"The wreckers must have used the tunnel thing to secretly bring the goods up to the house. That means there must be an opening at the other end."

"I think you've nailed it," said Dad, his hopes rising dramatically. He looked critically around. "So let's see, where would the other end be? In the cove? This house is built right up against the cliff."

"Hey, Daddy. You remember getting spit out of the cave? How about there?" said Danny, jumping up and down in excitement.

"Well, that's very possible. Yes, why not? It would be a great hiding place for the opening, and didn't Stevie say there was a ring or something there?"

"Can we go check it out? Like, right now?"

"Can we?" said Rachel, grabbing hold of Dad's arm.

"Okay, we can, but we should go get Stevie. He would be so disappointed to miss this."

The others looked rather crestfallen at this possible delay, but Emily pulled herself together and nodded. "Yes, let's. He would be so sad."

"Can we go down to the cove and wait for you?" pleaded Rachel. She imagined there might be quite the delay at Mrs. Renton's house. "We'll be really careful and won't go in the cave until you come! We promise. It will be fun to see the cove again."

Danny nodded vigorously, and Emily, after a moment's thought, joined in too.

Dad tried to sort this out in his mind. It *would* be easier than trotting everyone down to the lady's house and back, and he did want to allow the kids to have some fun as well as a bit of responsibility. The kids waited expectantly, hopeful expressions on their faces.

"Ok, I guess I don't mind. Just be really careful on the stairs. I don't know if they're slippery. Danny, stick between Rachel and Emily. Girls—careful and slow, stay away from the cave and the surf!"

The others nodded vigorously. Dad eyed them with amusement. "Alright, let's go." He had a sudden thought. "Wait a sec!" He grabbed Danny's arm as he shot past. "Let's first ask God for wisdom and safety, and then let's go."

Kennedy had finally chosen an uncomfortable perch at the top of the steps, just peering over the ridge where he had a view of the old house. The staircase was hard on his knees as he leaned forward, and his hands were aching from gripping the cold metal. The crash of the waves below and the frequent cries of the gulls chasing each other over the cliffs seemed to emphasize the misery and precariousness of his position—a depressing situation that matched the nature of his thoughts. This wasn't the first time—and probably wouldn't be the last—when he felt like throwing in the towel completely. To his consternation, a sudden image had flashed into his mind several minutes ago—the dusty floor and the trails he had made running all over the house, especially in front of the secret room. The family wouldn't have any problem finding out where he'd been spending his time.

A gust of wind seemed to shake the stairway and he forced himself to take a tighter grip, despite the cold. At least the rain was keeping off, but one slip down the steps and all his problems would be over, one way or another. That wasn't what he wanted though—not at all. There was still a tiny ray of hope that he'd pull this thing off, and he didn't want to let go of it.

He snapped out of his stupor at the sound of voices and automatically ducked down. Then raising himself up ever so carefully, he peered again over the ridge. He spied the dad and three of the kids going out the front gate. He watched a brief consultation in which the Dad seemed to be saying something serious, and then saw with horror that the kids were heading his way.

He ducked down again and shot down the stairway as fast as he safely could.

As Emily, Rachel and Danny reached the top of the metal stairway, they paused and surveyed the scene below them.

"Looks like the tide is pretty far out," said Emily with satisfaction. She had taken very seriously Dad's commands to be careful. "It'll be safer now."

"Uh-huh," agreed Rachel," and it means we can probably get into the cave."

Emily nodded. "Come on, let's go down, but we have to be really careful, don't forget. I'll go first, then you Danny, then Rachel."

"Who's that?" said Rachel suddenly, pointing to the far side of the cove. The others strained to see and could just make out somebody near the bottom of the cliff, apparently looking up at them. As they stared, the figure turned and made off towards the tide pools at the far side of the cove.

"Someone else exploring, I guess," said Emily. "There might be even more people, now that the rain has stopped. Come on."

She led the way carefully down, trying to keep enough ahead of Danny that she didn't get a shoe in her face. The steps were a bit wet and the metal hand rails very cold, and they were all glad when they finally reached the bottom.

"Can we go explore the tide-pools?" asked Rachel. She wanted to get a closer view of the guy over there, just to make sure he wasn't the shop owner.

Emily considered that for a moment. The pools were close to where the waves were breaking. It would have been stretching her promise to Dad that they'd stay safe.

"I don't think we should. Let's look for shells and stuff along the high-tide line."

That pleased Danny, who loved beach-combing. Rachel decided she'd go along with it too for now. She could still keep an eye on the guy.

Mrs. Renton stood at the door and waved goodbye to the family. It was good timing actually—the doctor was due any minute to check on her ankle. She watched as the Chapmans with little Stevie hurried off up the lane towards the cove. It had been quite the visit, finding out all that the family had been doing. She shook her head. She still felt so guilty. It should be her doing all the leg work, but all she was doing was sitting at home waiting for the next clue to arrive. She had never been a sitter or a waiter—she had been a doer. She had gone halfway around the world pursing adventure, trying to stuff her painful past into some dark corner and fill her life so full that there was no room for contemplating regrets. And yet it hadn't worked that way. Regret had pursued her relentlessly, taking the joy out of achievements, sucking the life out of her desperate bids for happiness.

She closed the door and turned back to where Pickwick was sitting patiently by her chair. Her eyes surveyed the room. It was cozy, warm and nicely decorated…downright homey—anyone would have said so. But it didn't feel like a home at that moment. It felt like…yes, like a prison right now.

The old lady shuffled carefully over to her chair and sat down, the cat jumping up almost before she was seated. She put her ankle up on her little stool, scratched the cat's head absentmindedly and reached over for the stack of papers on the table at her elbow. She read them through slowly, one by one. There was a definite pattern. Each person in the clues was in some kind of difficult situation—life-threatening even. In fact, each individual story involved the loss of someone dear. There was death, there was grief.

She looked off into space. Oh, yes, she knew about death and grief. She pictured the faces of her parents—it was so long ago now that the grief truly had dulled through time. It was the same with her husband—just a vague memory of the sorrow she had felt. Then she thought of the Squire and his wife—Uncle and Auntie as they had insisted she call them. That grief hadn't dulled at all.

She gave a heavy sigh and looked back at the papers. Why had Uncle Kenwyn highlighted so many stories of grief and loss? Was he trying to make her feel guilty for the grief and loss she herself had caused? That didn't seem right, though. The notes clearly insisted that he loved her—that they both had just kept on loving her.

And what about the Bible verses he included in each clue? She hadn't looked at any Bible in years and she'd even lost the one they gave her. She looked over the verses, trying to make sense of them. They were all different to some extent, but they all implied one very clear thing: God was real and wanted a relationship with individuals.

A relationship with God. What would that look like? If she had carried any picture of God with her through life, it was of a stern, disapproving task-master—never happy, always angry, always judging, always punishing. But what if God was truly loving? What would a relationship with God look like then?

She thought through the experiences of her life, trying to understand them in light of the possibility of a loving God. It was true she had experienced many close shaves—many times when by all odds she should have died. Her life had honestly been characterized by loneliness rather than relationship, always with that lurking background of guilt and regret.

She looked down at the cat on her lap. "Oh, Pickwick, I just don't understand. And what about the Chapmans? Why are they helping me?"

The cat looked up at her, its features scrunched in the nearest thing possible to a smile. Its purring seemed to fill the room. Something in the cat's expression soothed her somewhat. She stroked its back and sighed again. *Well, whatever the reason, the Chapman's were helping her and they seemed to enjoy doing so.*

A thought struck her. *Could it possibly be that God was motivating them, showing His love to her through them?* A sudden warmth touched her heart as she thought of the family. Yes, there was no denying it, she had felt loved and cared for by them. She remembered Mrs. Chapman's prayer. Was there really the possibility that someone was trying to steal her inheritance? If there was, who would it be? She remembered Rachel's insistence at the café in Tintagel—that there was someone following them.

She stopped stroking the cat and looked straight ahead, a wave of concern coming over her. Could the family actually be in danger of some kind? What could she do? She couldn't go chasing around town—that was for sure. The only thing she could do was pray for them.

Goodness me, she thought. *Where had that come from? Pray for them?* Who was she to think that God would listen to her prayers? And yet…and yet might he? Maybe she could. Maybe she would do it. She would try and pray for them right now.

She closed her eyes and was searching for the right words when at that very moment there was a knock at the door. Her eyes snapped open and she looked over at the clock. It must be the doctor. Well, she would try and pray later. Yes, perhaps later.

❧❦

Kennedy was trying to do his best imitation of a casual beach-goer, examining tide-pools, picking up shells every now and then and attempting to appear relaxed while inside he was fighting a fierce battle with anxiety. He felt absolutely trapped. He didn't want the family to know it was him—he didn't want them putting two and two together.

He squatted down on a low rock by a pool and stared into the water, not seeing the miniature world of anemones, seaweed and shells—just the reflection of someone who looked like his blood pressure was going through the roof. He tried to breathe deeply and slowly—*in, out, in, out.* He had to think clearly. What were his options? Hanging out here for goodness knows how long, trying to avoid the kids recognizing him? Run like a maniac across the beach to the stairs with his jacket over his head as if he was afraid of the rain or seagulls or something? *Ha ha.*

The only other option he could think of was walking casually by, greeting them, and explaining he was enjoying some beach time. He pondered that for a minute. They were only kids after all; surely he could get away with it. They didn't know he had been up at the house, looking for the clue. Maybe he could even get some information out of them, especially that red-headed kid who was scared of him. This might be a blessing in disguise.

He made a sudden decision, stood back up and glanced over his shoulder. There they were, over at the line of flotsam and jetsam marking the high-tide line. He smoothed down his hair a bit and practiced what he hoped was a friendly smile. Then squaring his shoulders he turned and stepped back down onto the sand. He strode purposefully towards the little group and as he drew near he smiled and helloed a greeting. The three kids looked up, startled, and he immediately tried to take advantage of the situation.

"Well, fancy seeing you here. It's a great cove isn't it? I love coming down here. It's so relaxing." Kennedy's years of practice lying were definitely being put to good use. "Are you having fun? Finding any pretty shells?"

The kids looked at each other, too surprised to speak. This was a shocking turn of events—and just when they were hoping that Mom and Dad would show up to help check out the cave.

Kennedy pressed on with his agenda. He wasn't interested in their responses anyway. "So are you having a nice holiday? Seen some more of the places around here?" He kept giving what he hoped was a pleasant smile.

Finally Emily was able to speak. "Er, yes, a few."

"Really? But it's been a bit rainy lately hasn't it? Not the best days for going to the beach. At least it's nice that you have a friend here that you can spend time with?"

"A friend?" said Emily, puzzled.

Kennedy gave a rather patronizing smile. "Yes, Mrs. Renton, the elderly lady who lives just up there in the cottages." He gestured towards the top of the stairway.

If she wasn't already on her guard, this mention of Mrs. Renton made Rachel immediately suspicious. She wasn't sure what Emily was going to say next, but she decided she wasn't going to wait to find out. "Oh, we've found lots of things to do on rainy days. Visit the town, read, play a game—lots of things."

Emily caught on to Rachel's diversion. "Oh, yes. We've visited a castle and went shopping."

"Really? A castle? Which one?" said Kennedy, sensing an opportunity for some more information.

"Oh, Tintagel. It was pretty neat."

"Is that where you went shopping?"

Rachel remembered the man in the toy store and the chess set clue, and decided that this line of questioning had gone too far. She tried to change the subject.

"We're just looking for shells today." She held up a handful. "See what I've found?"

Kennedy wasn't deterred. He quickly switched his strategy. Perhaps this was just the moment he had been waiting for. He would risk exposing his interest in the inheritance, but the pros could outweigh the cons. Turning to Danny he gave what he hoped was a fearsome grimace. Danny looked startled, which was exactly what Kennedy wanted.

"Well, young man. Have you been having fun? Is it hard to be indoors visiting an old lady when you'd rather be out playing?"

Danny just looked up at him, frozen.

"Come on, you can answer me young man. I've noticed your van parked at her house a few times. I suppose you had to sit around while your Mum and Dad chatted about the weather, or whatever it was they chatted about. Mrs. Renton and I go way back actually. We're pretty good friends and I've been helping her with her inheritance. You may have seen that in the local newspaper. The whole town knows about it. It's quite the mystery."

Rachel and Emily seemed frozen too. *What was this man saying?*

Kennedy leaned in a little closer and put his hand on Danny's shoulder. "So, have you been able to help her too? Where is she in the process?"

Danny's lower lip was starting to tremble. The girls suddenly noticed and a wave of indignation swept over them.

"Come on Danny, time to go," said Rachel firmly. She grabbed Danny's hand and pulled him away, not able to resist glaring at Kennedy as she did so. Even Emily was offended but couldn't think of anything to say. She looked over towards Rachel and Danny and suddenly saw the most welcome sight in the world. Mom, Dad and Stevie had appeared at the top of the stairway and were starting to make their way down.

Kennedy followed her gaze and gasped. He looked around wildly. There was no escape.

⋙⋘

Mom, Dad and Stevie had seen the other children talking to someone down on the sand, and wondered who it might be. As they made their way carefully down the stairway, Dad glanced over his shoulder to see what was going on below. This was definitely not good timing for someone else to decide to visit the cove. How could they look for the other end of shaft with someone else lurking around?

To his relief he saw that the kids were headed their way, and the person, whoever it was, was heading to the far side of the cove. Stevie's backside hitting him in the head reminded him that he needed to stop looking and get going on down.

It wasn't long before all three were safely to the bottom where Emily, Rachel and Danny were waiting. All three started talking at once, and he had to raise his voice to be heard. "Hey, quiet down all of you. We can't understand if you're all talking at once. Emily, why don't you start?"

Emily took a deep breath. "Mom, Dad—that was Mr. Whatshisname from the Inn—the café man."

"Mr. Kennedy?" said Dad.

"Yes, and he was asking us all sorts of questions."

"What kind of questions?"

"He asked us what we had been doing."

"Uh-huh, go on. That doesn't sound too surprising."

"But he knew about our helping Mrs. Renton," blurted out Rachel.

"Really?" said Mom. "What did he say?"

"He'd seen our van at her house, and knew about the inheritance and that it was a mystery."

"He wanted to know where she was in the process," added Emily.

"Did he now?" said Dad, frowning.

"And he scared me," said Danny. "He looked at me with his fierce eyes and hair and kept asking me stuff. He kind of kept smiling with his mouth, but not with his eyes."

"Yes, and it was weird," said Emily. "He was really grilling Danny, even though he must have seen that Danny was afraid."

"And what did you do?" said Mom, feeling a rising anger at the man's insensitivity.

"Rachel rescued Danny," said Emily. "She just got him out of there."

"Good job, Rachel!" said Dad.

Rachel blushed. Danny gave her big smile, which made her feel great. "Thanks," she said, "but I really think this Mr. Kennedy knows about what we're doing."

"I thought you were worried about that other guy—the shop owner," said Dad.

"I'm worried about them both. This guy is creepy, and he just kept asking questions."

"Did he seem to know about any of the clues?" wondered Mom, giving Danny a comforting squeeze.

"He didn't mention any specifically. He said he knew Mrs. Renton pretty well, and that the whole town knew about the inheritance."

"He said it was in the newspaper," added Emily.

"That's right, it was, but knowing Mrs. Renton well…? That's weird. She's never mentioned him, or knowing anyone else here for that matter." Dad looked across to where he could spy Kennedy up on some rocks at the far edge of the cove.

"Oh, and he said he had been helping Mrs. Renton with the inheritance," remembered Rachel suddenly. "That can't be true, can it? She would have mentioned it."

"This is all sounding pretty fishy," said Mom. "I wonder what he's really up to?"

"He wants to steal Mrs. Renton's inheritance! Him and that other guy," said Rachel, narrowing her eyes and scrunching up her nose as she did when she was really miffed.

"But we don't know that for sure," said Dad. "I know, I know, you've been keeping your eyes open dear." He patted Rachel who looked like she was about to explode.

"So what can we do?" said Emily. "How can we figure this out, and how can we check the cave if he's lurking around."

They looked at each other. The adventure was definitely taking on a new level of seriousness.

"I have an idea," said Mom at last. "How about you, Dave, and Danny go check out the cave. Emily and Stevie, you keep watch at the cave entrance. Let Dad know if anyone else comes down the stairway. I'm going to take Rachel and go and talk to Mr. Kennedy."

"Really?" said Dad, very surprised. He would have suspected that was the last thing his wife would want to do, considering her feelings for the man.

"Yup, I can handle him." she nodded. She put her arm around Rachel's shoulder. "I think between the two of us and Jesus we can turn the tables and get some information out of Mr. Kennedy!"

❧ ❧

Kennedy was taking sideways glances, checking out what the family was up to. There had obviously been a long discussion, but now what was going on? The dad and several of the kids were heading off towards the cave at the far edge of the cove, but it looked like the mum and a daughter were heading in his direction. Kennedy watched for a moment. Yes, they were definitely heading his way. Was it possible to get some information out of them—like why the others were going to the cave, for instance?

He had a sudden, horrified thought. *How could he have been so stupid?* The shaft might have another opening. Could they have figured that out and be looking for it in the cave? Somehow he had to get the information out of the mum and daughter. But carefully!

The two were striding purposefully towards him across the sand. There was something in the mom's fixed expression that made him suddenly nervous. Why were they headed his way? *Maybe this wasn't such a good idea after all.*

❧ ❧

Dad led Emily, Danny and Stevie towards the cave, glancing back every now and then to check on Mom and Rachel. They hadn't reached the guy yet, but it looked like a confrontation was unavoidable. Dad sent up a quick prayer for help for his wife.

As they reached the cave, they peered anxiously inside. To their relief, there didn't seem to be any water, and the tide seemed to be far enough out to not pose a problem.

Dad addressed Emily and Stevie as they took off their shoes and socks. "Okay, guys, you're on sentry duty. Keep an eye on Mr. Kennedy over there, and on the stairs. We don't want to be surprised by anyone coming over. Yell if you see anything suspicious." He turned to Danny. "Ready?"

Danny gave a nervous nod. Dad looked at him closely. "You sure you're up for this?"

Danny paused, his mind whirring. Here he was again, with something frightening looming large—just like with the cat in the bookstore. *But that had turned out okay, hadn't it?* He had been strong and courageous with God's help. He

295

looked up at his dad. "Yes. I will be strong and courageous." *Help me Jesus*, he added under his breath.

Dad smiled and grabbed his hand. He led the way through the ragged opening and into the darkness beyond. They both noticed that the smell hadn't improved with time. It was a dank, slightly rotten, sea-weedy smell that echoed the rather unpleasant surroundings. The clammy sand felt freezing to their toes and they broke into a trot in an attempt to minimize contact.

↊↋

Mom was praying out loud as they strode towards the tide-pools, asking for God's wisdom and strength. Rachel kept shooting admiring glances at her. She knew Mom was pretty brave and adventurous, but she wouldn't have thought she would want to confront Mr. Kennedy. Rachel was excited *and* nervous. How would God answer Mom's prayers?

Chapter 19 – What's in the Box?

Danny gave a shout. "It's here! I found it. Stevie's ring. Just to the right."

Dad was not relishing his position--his face pressed against the cave wall, Danny's weight on his shoulders. He tried to ignore the dank, sea-weedy smell and speak without letting his lips touch the slimy walls. "Okay, shine your light straight up. What do you see?"

There was silence for a moment and Dad could feel the lad's weight shifting. "I can see the opening. It goes straight up, but there are some rocks and stuff blocking it."

"Okay, be careful. Can you see a box or anything?"

More silence and more shifting of weight. "Maybe. It's hard to see. If I was a bit thinner I think I could squeeze up enough to see."

"Here, let me try to lift you." Dad grabbed the boy's feet and worked his hands under the soles. Then with a mighty effort he pushed the boy up the side of the cave.

"Stop!" yelled Danny suddenly.

Dad stopped, trying to hold his position. "What's the matter?" he gasped.

"There's no room. I'm too big. I can't reach it."

"Reach what?"

"I can see something—a box or something stuck up there, but I can't reach it."

Dad's strength was giving out. He slowly lowered Danny back down, his arms shaking with the effort. "Okay, there." He set Danny back on the sand. "Are you okay?"

"Uh-huh, but I don't think I can get it."

"So what can we do?" wondered Dad out loud.

"We need someone smaller." Danny thought for a moment. He had so wanted to be the hero and get the box, but that was impossible. He took a deep breath and nodded to himself, knowing he was choosing the right thing. "I'm too big. We need Stevie."

⤜❧⤛

Kennedy had given up trying to escape, resolving that he wouldn't be intimidated and would turn this situation to his own advantage. He carefully made his way down off the rocks and approached Mom and Rachel with a wave of greeting.

"Well hello. How nice to see you here! It's a lovely place isn't it?"

Mom and Rachel drew to a stop, and Mom smiled and nodded. "Yes, it is. We've been here a couple of times, and it's lovely. There's lots for the kids to do. It's funny meeting you here. Isn't your work keeping you busy?"

Kennedy was a little taken aback by that question. In a way, trying to solve the inheritance clues was his current work, but he couldn't explain that.

"Er, yes." It was all he could manage to say.

"You're in the—insurance business aren't you?" said Mom, nodding as if she was already sure of his response.

"Insurance?" said Kennedy, genuinely surprised and then just as quickly aghast as he realized his mistake. "Yes, yes, insurance."

Rachel grinned secretly, appreciating seeing Mr. Kennedy being the one to sweat for once.

"What sort of insurance do you sell, Mr. Kennedy? Car? Fire?"

"Er. Well, all sorts," stammered a flustered Kennedy, desperately trying to think of a way to terminate this line of inquiry and seize control of the conversation.

"Really," said Mom, still smiling, but with a little edge to her voice. "If I can give you some free advice, it would help you sell more insurance if you get yourself some new business cards.

That really threw Kennedy for a loop. "New business cards?" he said faintly.

"Yes, instead of ones that say 'Professional Estate Liquidation.'"

This shock was even greater. *How on earth did she know about that?* "Oh, yes, well of course," he blurted out. "I do that…as well. I mean I do need to get some business cards for my insurance work."

"Yes, you should," said Mom. "But estate liquidation must be very interesting. Have you done any of it around here?"

Kennedy wracked his brains to see whether either a yes or no answer would land him in the most trouble. "Er, no…not around here."

"Do you live around here, Mr. Kennedy?" put in Rachel, warming to the game.

"Does it matter?" said Kennedy, edging around to give himself a clear avenue of escape.

"Oh, no, not at all," said Mom with a light laugh, edging over just a tad to cut Kennedy off. "But we just wondered if you had been involved in Squire Penrow's estate sale, or anything to do with Mrs. Renton and her inheritance mystery. The kids said you knew her and had been helping her. How well do you know her, and how have you been helping her, Mr. Kennedy?"

298

Kennedy made a big show of looking at his watch and expressing surprise. "Oh, so sorry. I'd love to stay and chat, but I didn't realize the time. I've really got to be going. Perhaps we can chat later." He sidled over again in an effort to head towards the stairway.

Mom stepped out of his way and motioned Rachel to do the same. "Of course, Mr. Kennedy. You probably need to go visit your brother. Wasn't he seriously ill, you said?" Mom had to call after his rapidly retreating back. "Send our regards, Mr. Kennedy. We, hope he gets better—and Mr. Kennedy…I would highly recommend that the next time you feel like grilling our kids about something, you come and ask my husband and me first."

⋖⋗

"We need you Stevie." Dad squatted down in front of the boy and looked at him seriously. "We think the clue is stuck in the shaft."

"And I can't get it," put in Danny, shaking his head vigorously. "I'm too big."

Dad put his hand on Stevie's shoulder. "You know how you often try to be like the other kids. You don't like being the smallest and often life doesn't seem fair to you."

Stevie nodded. Dad was right.

"And you try to be different. You wish you were bigger and you try to prove you're as capable as the bigger kids. But here we are, trying to help Mrs. Renton and we're stuck. We can't get the clue because we need someone small enough to reach up the shaft. I can't do it, Emily can't do it, Danny can't do it, and Mrs. Renton surely can't do it."

A slow smile spread across Stevie's face. He was getting the point.

"God made you exactly the way you are for a reason. You're the youngest child for a reason. He loves you and when you obey Him He can really use you. Everyone in our family is important, including you, and we need you now. Mrs. Renton needs you."

"Don't be afraid of the cave," assured Danny. "It's really okay. You can have my flashlight." He held it out to Stevie, who accepted it solemnly.

"I'll take care of it," he said, "and I'll do my best, even if the cave does smell yucky."

"That's right," said Dad, standing back up and wincing as his joints protested. "Emily and Danny—I need you to stand guard. Yell if Mr. Kennedy heads this way."

"Yes, sir," said Emily, standing to attention and saluting, a big grin on her face.

Dad took a quick look to see what the man was up to. He was heading towards the stairway, and Dad gestured towards the rapidly moving figure. "Okay Emily, keep an eye on you-know-who. Mom and Rachel are coming. Hopefully we'll be back in a jiffy."

Dad grabbed Stevie's hand and led him back into the cave. Stevie sniffed the unpleasant smell, but chose not to say anything. He was on a mission that no-one else could do.

"You okay?" said Dad, looking down at the boy. "The tide's far out and we won't have any problem with the waves."

"Yeah, that was so cold last time," said Stevie. "But it helped me find the ring."

"That's right," said Dad, trying to ignore the feeling that his toes were getting frostbitten in the chilly puddles. "And here we are." He stopped by the bottom of the shaft. "Are you ready? Got the flashlight?"

Stevie turned it on and waved it around.

"Okay, I'm going to hoist you up. Ready?" Dad carefully lifted Stevie up and set him standing on his shoulders. It was the second time he'd had a pair of soggy feet on his shirt, but he tried to concentrate on the task at hand. "Shine the light upwards. Can you see the shaft? It looks like a narrow tunnel heading straight up."

"Yeah, I see it." Stevie stood on his tiptoes. "There's some stuff in it. Can you lift me higher?"

"Sure," said Dad, with just a slight hesitation. He worked his hands under Stevie's feet, braced himself and pushed the lad up, scraping his elbow rather painfully on the rocky wall.

"Okay, stop," came Stevie's muffled voice from above. There was a moment's shuffling and then a small cascade of stones fell around Dad's head. Dad winced, and spat out some bits of debris.

"Can you push me up some more?"

"Oof," said Dad out loud, but he gathered his strength and pushed himself up on tiptoe, lifting the boy another three inches or so.

There was another sound of scrabbling, a few more showers of stones and Stevie gave a sudden cry. "I've got it, it's loose, I've got it!"

"What have you got?"

"A box. A metal box, on a chain. It's coming!"

There was a metallic scraping sound that got rapidly louder and then box, chain and boy slid down on to Dad's head. He let out a yell, lost his balance and he and the whole mess fell backwards into a chilly pool of seawater.

On her way into the cave, Mom heard what sounded suspiciously like muffled laughter. She came suddenly upon the others, and what she saw in the gloom made her burst out into laughter too. Dad was lying on his back in a pool of seawater doing his best beached whale impersonation. Stevie was sprawled over Dad, his face in Dad's chest, shaking with laughter. A long length of chain was flung in random coils around and over Dad's legs.

"What on earth happened here," Mom finally managed to say.

"Success!" grinned Dad, trying to sit up and help Stevie slide off. Mom gave the boy a hand up and Dad clambered to his feet. He looked quite the sight, with seaweed strands in his hair and his back soaked from top to bottom.

At one end of the chain, now visible, was attached a small metal box. Stevie held it up. "Look what I found! It was stuck and I got it unstuck and then it fell with the chain, and it all slid down and fell on us and we fell down in the puddle."

"That's a lot of 'ands,' "said Dad, shaking his trouser legs in an effort to get rid of some of the seawater. "But Stevie's right. Let's get out in the open."

He led the way, walking somewhat awkwardly and uncomfortably while Mom helped Stevie carry the box, the chain dragging along behind them. As soon as they were back in the open they could see that the box was clipped to the chain by a sort of carabiner. Rachel and Emily clapped their hands as Stevie held up the box in triumph. It was about the size of a small tissue box and made of dark, rusty metal. The top was etched with wavy designs, and a small catch at the front kept the lid firmly closed.

Dad did a quick scan of the cove. "Rachel, will you sneak along the edge of the cliff until you can see the stairs? Let us know if the coast's still clear."

Rachel appreciated that assignment. She flattened herself against the cliff and sidled along to where she could spy the staircase. She scanned it for a few moments and then gave a thumbs up. Dad beckoned to her and she came running over.

"All clear," she said brightly.

"We had a very interesting talk with Mr. Kennedy," said Mom. Rachel giggled.

Mom filled them in on their rather one-sided conversation, and the other kids nodded in appreciation.

Dad narrowed his eyes. "It does sound very suspicious. Maybe he and the Mole Hole guy are in cahoots.

"Great," said Dad. "Now, I don't think we should open the box right now." There were groans of disappointment but Dad held up his hand. "Remember, this is for Mrs. Renton. We'll give it to her and then she can let us know what's next."

"When can we do that?" said Stevie. "It might be the treasure!"

"We don't know the inheritance is a treasure—do we? Not like gold and jewels," said Rachel. Stevie's face fell. "Though it might be," she added hastily.

"Anyway, the poem said they'll be another clue," said Danny.

If it were possible, Stevie's face fell even more. "Is that right?"

"*But there you too will find the clue,*" quoted Rachel. "But don't worry Stevie. There will be an end sometime, and another clue will be exciting. Who knows where it may lead?"

Dad gave Stevie a hug. "That's right. Don't forget you found this one! Great job!"

That made Stevie perk up again. "So what's inside?"

"Well, we'll let Mrs. Renton open it and see. This is what I propose. I'll go first with Rachel and Danny. If Mr. Kennedy is watching somewhere, he's welcome to follow us back to the inn. He won't see anything." He turned to his wife. "And Sweetheart, if you don't mind waiting ten minutes or so and following us. Stay out of sight until the times up. You could drop the box off with Mrs. Renton and see if she'd be open to us coming over after dinner. That way we won't have to wait until tomorrow."

The kids all cheered up at that, and Mom nodded in agreement.

"What do we do with the chain?" she added, looking at it snaking back into the cave.

"I don't fancy bringing it with us," frowned Dad. "What would I do? Wrap it around me? I'd look like Jacob Marley having a day out."

"Who's Jacob Marley?" wondered Stevie.

"Never mind," said Mom, not wanting to have to deal with a little boy's imagination.

"Let's leave it back in the cave," suggested Danny. "You could put it through the ring."

"Good idea," said Dad. "But before I do that, I just want to say something to Stevie, and I want everyone to hear."

Stevie looked suddenly downcast, wondering what sort of trouble he was in. The others guessed what Dad was up to and flashed knowing smiles at each other.

"Stevie," said Dad seriously. "I want you to remember this day. We were stuck. No-one could fit up the shaft to get the box. No-one except you. What would have happened if you were much bigger?"

Stevie's face broke out into a smile. "I wouldn't have been able to do it?"

"Right. God used the littlest one in the family to do the biggest job today. You were the perfect size—the perfect one for the job. Wait until Mrs. Renton hears about it!"

The other kids patted him on the back, and Mom gave him a hug.

"And you know," she added. "We're a family, and each one of you is important. God can and will use each of you."

"The Chapman Family Detective Agency," said Danny, saluting. "At your service."

"No job too big," said Emily, getting into the spirit of the thing.

"No clue too tough," added Rachel.

"No meal too filling," said Dad, looking at his watch.

"What?" said Mom.

"Just a hint that we should be going. Mrs. Tremannon's probably got some culinary creation underway and we don't want to be late."

"But what about Mr. Café man?" said Danny.

Dad patted him on the shoulder. "You, Emily and I will stick together. I'll go up first, and I'll signal you if I see anything. Dear, can you carry the box up the steps?" He looked at Mom, who nodded. "You'll have to hide it under your coat or something at the top. Don't forget to wait about ten minutes. Oh, and one more thing."

They all looked at him expectantly.

"Rachel, this time I want to congratulate you. You get the award for being the master sleuth. You were definitely right about there being someone else involved. I'm sorry for doubting you." Rachel smiled shyly, while the others patted her on the back.

Dad looked around at them all. "Family, from now on we need to assume that we're not the only one's after this clue. That means eyes and ears open. We need the Lord's wisdom, but with His help, and us all working together, we can see this thing through."

Kennedy was fuming. How could he have let himself be manipulated by that woman, and how could he have been so idiotic? He must have dropped a business card or something somewhere. And what about that lie about his sick brother? He was just making one mistake after another. Finding the secret room ahead of the family had been a major coup, but now he had lost the advantage. Somehow, some way he had to gain it back.

He peered through a crack in one of the boarded-up windows of the old house where he had taken refuge. He could see the top of the stairs and a fair way down the street. There was no sign of the family.

Okay, he thought. *I don't want to make any mistakes or miss any detail.* What were the family doing in the cove? And they had been in the house. Had they found the secret room?

He glanced over to the panel. There was a bunch of scuff marks in the dust— more than he himself could have made. Yes, he had to assume that they got in. That means they assuredly would have found the broken chain. Kennedy wracked his brains. If they found the broken chain they would have realized the clue was down the shaft. And where did they go next? *The cove.* While the mom and girl had grilled him, the others had gone in the cave. *Had they found the other opening he had worried about?* He didn't know. So now he had two options. Either they had— and he needed to follow them and get a glimpse of what they had found—or they hadn't, and he needed to wait until they left and have a try himself.

He stared back through the crack and saw a flash of movement. It was the dad, the red-headed kid and the oldest girl. *Were they coming here?* No, thank goodness, it looked like they were headed down the hill. The dad was walking kind of funny. He seemed to be holding something under his coat. The clue, perhaps? But what about the others—the mom and the other two kids?

Kennedy was confused. *What should he do? Follow the one group or wait for the others?* He stared desperately after the group going down the hill. If the dad had the clue, he needed to know where he was going. Yes, that was definitely the best choice. He ran to the front door and slipped cautiously through. Another quick peek assured him that they were still on their way. He glanced over at the top of the cove stairway. There was no sign of the others. He dashed over to the stone steps and listened carefully. He couldn't hear anyone coming up, so he risked a glance over. There was no sign of the rest of the family. *What on earth were they up to?* But no matter. He had to follow the dad. He ran back to where he could see down the hill. They were almost past the line of cottages, so they obviously weren't going to the old lady's. He watched a minute more. It looked like they were heading back up the hill to the inn, so that was his destination, too. Trying to keep as far back as possible, Kennedy slipped around the corner and started tailing them.

Rachel had seen Kennedy poke his head over the ridge from her vantage point at the bottom of the cliff. She had made frantic signs to Mom and Stevie to stay back and they had dutifully obeyed, waiting until she sprinted over to rejoin them.

"I saw him," said Rachel, breathlessly. "He was looking down here."

"Did he see you?" asked Stevie, anxiously. He was shivering, and Mom helped him zip up his coat.

"I don't think so. Do you think he would have seen Dad and the others?"

Mom thought for a second. "Yes, I would imagine so. Maybe he was wondering where the rest of us were. Hopefully he would have followed Dad as we planned."

"How long has it been?" said Rachel. "Should we get going?"

Mom checked her watch. "It's been over ten minutes—maybe we should. Anyway the wind's getting up and it's getting cold."

"But what about the man?" said Stevie, tugging at her sleeve.

"I think it's okay. He'll be confused as to who to follow, and Dad looks like the more likely target. We'll be careful though. It would be best if he didn't see us go to Mrs. Renton's." The others felt a little thrill. This was getting pretty exciting.

She smiled at them. "Are you ready? Rachel, will you help Stevie? I've got the box hidden in my coat. Let's go carefully."

She led them off across the sand, checking carefully for the man as they went, but the ridge at the top of the stairway remained empty.

✦✦✦

Dad, Emily and Danny rounded the corner by the gate and started up the driveway to the inn. On Dad's instructions, Emily and Danny had taken turns surreptitiously checking behind them and at one point Emily had been certain she had seen someone duck out of sight, quite a way down the lane. Since then, though, neither of them had seen anything.

Dad had thought it best to keep looking straight ahead, pretending to carry something wrapped up in his coat—the bait that would keep Kennedy on their tail. He wanted to go slowly enough that the man would be tempted to follow, but not so slow that he had to spend one minute more than necessary in his soaked clothes. The wind was getting up again, and without his coat he felt chilled to the bone, not to mention distressingly uncomfortable in certain areas.

Their goal in sight, Dad sped up the pace, only to suddenly screech to a halt. The inn's front door had opened and Mr. Tremannon had appeared carrying a short step-ladder and some hedge trimmers. He paused and surveyed the group in the driveway and Dad gave an inward groan. How could he explain his wet clothes and fake burden? He tried to paste on a cheerful smile.

"Well, hello Mr. Tremannon. Looks like you're busy."

Mr. Tremannon nodded, looking Dad up and down and taking in the sodden clothes and disheveled hair. He frowned as he fixed his gaze somewhere around Dad's left ear.

Dad felt himself turning red. Obviously there was a piece of seaweed there he'd missed. He swatted at the spot. "I got a bit wet," he said, feeling he had to explain his looks somehow. "I fell in some water—at the cove."

"Right." The old man nodded slowly.

Emily and Danny just smiled politely, realizing that Dad would want this conversation over quickly. Mr. Tremannon switched his gaze to them and his china blue eyes seemed to give the merest twinkle. "Afternoon," he drawled.

"Good afternoon," said Emily. She looked over at Dad who had a rather fixed smile.

"Er, well, we won't keep you," he stammered. "Bye for now." He gave a nod to the old man, grabbed Danny's hand and hurried off without looking back.

"Bye," said Mr. Tremannon, looking somewhat amused. Emily gave him a quick smile, and ran to catch up with her dad.

Kennedy walked carefully up the lane to the inn gate, brushing the hedges with his shoulder as he tried to keep as low a profile as possible. As he got closer he could hear the snip, snip, snip of someone cutting the hedge. That was all he needed. But what could he do? He had to follow the others.

The noise stopped, and he heard something being dragged through the gravel. Mr. Tremannon's head suddenly popped into view above the hedge by the gate. The old man caught sight of Kennedy and froze, his clippers in the air. For a moment the two looked at each other, and then Mr. Tremannon's head disappeared again. Kennedy racked his brains for the best thing to do. Should he go ahead and just go in? *Well, why not?* Why was he afraid of the old man? He squared his shoulders and marched up to the open gate and was about to pass through when Mr. Tremannon suddenly stepped out into his path.

"Er, hello," he said nervously, avoiding the old man's piercing eyes. "How are you?"

"Fine," said Mr. Tremannon, leaning over and peering into Kennedy's face. Kennedy took a step backwards, not anticipating this at all.

"Do you need something?" he squeaked. He started edging out of the old man's way, but just like Mrs. Chapman had done earlier, Mr. Tremannon stepped in front of him. The old man bent over until he was only inches away from Kennedy's spluttering face. He narrowed his eyes and tapped the end of his hedge trimmers against Kennedy's chest.

"Careful," he said with just a hint of steel in his voice. He gazed at Kennedy who turned bright red. Then the old man stood straight up and stepped out of the way. "Go," he said, nodding in the direction of the inn.

Kennedy was completely flustered now. The only thing he could think to do was nod and scurry off towards the haven of the front door. Mr. Tremannon looked after him for a good long moment, then turned and climbed slowly back up his stepladder.

Dad was a bit disappointed that Kennedy didn't show for dinner. He had a few pointed questions for him, but the rest of the family were glad he wasn't around. They had had quite enough of Mr. Kennedy for one day. Besides, if he was trying to figure out the clues himself, the farther away he was the better.

Mrs. Tremannon had prepared a huge exquisite beef and onion pie, with three different sorts of vegetables, potatoes and gravy. She had seemed quite put out that Kennedy wasn't there, and shook her head in disgust before ambling back out to the kitchen to get the forgotten mustard.

Between mouthfuls, Mom filled Dad, Emily and Danny in on the visits with Mrs. Renton. "She was really grateful to Stevie. She hugged him and even gave him a kiss on the cheek!" Mom grinned.

Stevie colored slightly. It had been very embarrassing but sort of wonderful at the same time. "She was so surprised that we found the box," he added, swallowing a piece of pie. "I think she even cried."

Dad raised his eyebrows and looked at Mom who nodded. She set her fork down and addressed the whole family. "Mrs. Renton is…well, she's very emotional right now. This quest of the Squire's is touching her heart in all kinds of ways, but she doesn't understand what to make of it. She's really confused. It's causing her to evaluate her own life and some of the choices she's made."

"But we don't want her to be sad," said Emily, concerned.

"No, we don't," said Dad. "At least, in a way we don't. We don't like knowing people are sad, but often it's in times of sadness that people are most open to God."

"And maybe that's what the Squire intended," added Mom. "Whatever this inheritance is, I'm sure the goal is for Mrs. Renton to truly find healing."

"So we need to keep praying for God to use all this to help her come to know Him personally—to find forgiveness and hope in Jesus." Dad gestured upwards with his fork.

"That reminds me," said Mom. "If Mr. Kennedy and that other man really are trying to get the clues and find the inheritance, then we need to pray that God would stop them. Satan must be involved in motivating them. He doesn't want Mrs. Renton to be saved—to receive Jesus."

The others absorbed that as they chewed and swallowed.

"I guess we should also pray for the men," said Emily suddenly.

"Pray *for* them?" frowned Rachel. "Don't you mean pray *against* them?"

"No, I mean for them. If Satan is using them, they must be pretty miserable. I mean, they don't know God's love themselves."

Dad nodded, impressed. "You're right honey, though I admit I haven't thought about it that way. Well, when we pray, let's include praying for them as well."

Danny nodded too, remembering his earlier prayers.

"Okay," said Mom. "Let's finish up here so we can go and see Mrs. Renton. We don't want to keep her up too late."

This cheered them all up. *What was in the mystery box? What would the next clue be about?* They couldn't wait to find out.

Kennedy wasn't sure if it was hunger or a nauseating worry that was twisting his stomach. He was closeted in his room, mentally reviewing the events of the day. First the confusion of the morning, then the elation at finding the book and key, the interminable wait for Jennings, then the thrill of finding the secret room followed by the agony of being so close yet so far from the clue. To top it all off there was the disastrous encounter with the family at the cove. He should have just kept his mouth shut. He should have just greeted them in passing and got out of there. Now, instead of benefiting from the conversations, he had pretty much revealed his hand. They had to guess he was after the inheritance now.

He dug for a cigarette from the box in his shirt pocket. Smoking wasn't allowed here, and this blatant disregard of the rules made him feel better. His thoughts went back to his tailing the family to the inn. The dad looked like he was trying to hide something in his coat. There was no other reason he would be carrying his coat on a rainy day like today.

He lit the cigarette and drew a long puff, then exhaled slowly. So what did the man have? What had they found? Had there been something in the cave?

He took another drag of his cigarette and stared into space. The shaft must have had an opening down in the cave. The wreckers must have pulled stuff up to the house. They probably used it for smuggling more than salvage, but whatever. The point was, the family must have found whatever was in there. Was it the inheritance—the big payoff? Kennedy pondered that anxiously for a moment. No, it couldn't have been. The family would have taken it straight to the old lady. So it must be just another clue. *Good grief! How many of them were there going to be?* The Squire must have been nuts—*raving bonkers.* Why not just give her the goods right away?

Kennedy mulled that over while a cloud of smoke formed around his head. Why the whole mystery thing? It just didn't make sense. *Well,* he thought philosophically. *At least it gives me a better chance to intercept things—to throw a spanner in the works.*

And there was the rub. The good news was that all he had to do was intercept one clue—to break the chain, leaving the family with no way to go forward. The bad news was, he still hadn't been able to do that, even after his temporary victory today. *What incredible back luck!* It was almost as if fate was working against him— that there was some power or something that was deliberately messing him up.

His mind swept back over his life. It wasn't the first time he'd experienced this. He had left home at sixteen, saying good riddance to his alcoholic father and shrinking mother who would never stand up for herself. With no inclination to keep on with school, and no money to do anything interesting, he drifted from one odd job to the next, living in a series of disgusting, miserable places, with landlords and employers taking advantage of his youth and naivety. Finally, after years of just getting by it had seemed that his luck had begun to change. He had gotten a pretty good job at an auction house and things had been looking up, but then the whole place had gotten investigated by the police for fraud and shut down.

It had given him the one idea, though, that finally brought him a bit of stable income. He had learned a bit about antiques over the years, and knew that most people had no idea of the worth of some of the old stuff they had lying around in attics and old sheds. Through a combination of sheer hard work, tact, and a large helping of outright deception he had got a business going handling estate sales. It was perfect really—dealing with people at a point of emotional fragility, grieving their loss of a loved one and being overwhelmed with trying to handle their affairs. It was a fairly simple matter to misrepresent the value of certain items and make quite a financial haul. He had done quite well for a number of years.

But then his luck had seemed to turn. Someone had put the law onto him and he'd only narrowly escaped going to prison. He had finally managed to settle out of court, but the damages all but ruined him. That was when the desperation had set in. He had taken some risky moves, involving some very questionable behavior that definitely would have landed him in prison if he'd been caught. He'd had one or two encouraging prospects, like when he heard about Squire Penrow's collection being up for grabs—a collection with many valuable pieces and many opportunities for some creative deception on his part. There was that one particular piece that he had heard about—it was rated as 'priceless.' That had clinched his interest and his desire to take advantage of the situation. He'd even landed the deal, but then someone had tipped off the Squire, barely conscious as he was from his illness, and that wretch had backed out leaving him high and dry. That was partly the reason that nabbing this inheritance would be so sweet. Not only was it guaranteed to be a financial windfall, it had the added satisfying savor of revenge.

Kennedy searched around for somewhere to stick the remains of his cigarette, finally selecting a decorated china bowl on the nightstand. He stubbed it out and pulled another one from the pack and lit it up. Yes, he was thinking a bit more clearly now. He couldn't see any way around it—he would have to leave the inn. He couldn't stick around now that the family might have guessed what he was up to.

He sent another cloud of smoke up towards the rafters and narrowed his eyes. Moving out posed several problems, though. He was dirt broke, and couldn't pay for other lodgings. Plus it meant that he wouldn't be close to the action—he wouldn't be able to keep a watchful eye on the family. *So should he stay? Eat his meals in his room?* No, that wouldn't swing with Mrs. T. That meant finding a place to stay for next to nothing, and finding a way to keep watch on the family.

He stared off into space. *What would work?* He had a sudden inspiration. *Jennings.* Of course. His shop was directly across the harbor from the old lady's. The family would be dealing with her a lot wouldn't they? He could stay for free and keep watch on her place at the same time. It was perfect. Yes, Jennings probably wouldn't like the idea, but he wouldn't have a choice. Kennedy still had a hold over him. He couldn't say no.

Kennedy gave a thin smile. Ok. That problem was solved. He'd spend the night here and leave after getting some sort of breakfast out of Mrs. T. Surely he could do that one more time. And then he'd turn up on Jennings' doorstep with suitcase in hand. Now, what about the clue? What had the family found in the shaft and how could he get it?

Kennedy got up and paced back and forth, puffing out smoke like a railway engine. He strode over to the window and looked out. The shadow of the inn stretched out across the grass to just touch the old ramshackle stables, with the setting sun reflecting from their broken windows. He stared at the scene without seeing it.

The clue had to be here, at the inn. It must be a box, or chest or waterproof packet or something and it was probably up in one of the family's rooms. They would be eating right now. *Did he dare go and try to find it?* He pondered that for a moment. *No, that was crazy.* They could be done any time, or one of those blasted kids would have to go use the toilet in the middle of dinner or something.

Okay. He needed to slow down and think this through again. Either they would look at the clue here, which might give him the opportunity to eavesdrop, or they might go see the old lady and take the clue with them. He couldn't follow them to the lady's house—that would be fruitless. So what would he do in that case? He wasn't sure, but he'd better figure it out pretty soon. First things first, though. He had to subtly find out if the family were still eating, and what they would be doing next.

❧❧

Dad dug out his keys and tossed them to Mom. "Let's take the van so we don't have to walk back if it's raining. Do you mind opening it up? I've had a sudden thought and need to run upstairs for a minute."

"Okay," said Mom looking puzzled. "Come on kids."

They were still putting on seat-belts when Dad appeared at the driver's side door, grinning mischievously.

"What have you been up to?" said Mom, pulling her door shut.

"Oh, nothing much," smirked Dad. "Just following a hunch."

The others looked at one another with raised eyebrows, but Dad wasn't giving anything away. He started the engine.

"I'll tell you later." He gestured out his window at the yellow sports car parked alongside. "At least we know Mr. Kennedy is still at the inn. Let's go find out what we're up against with the next clue."

❧❧

Kennedy shaded his eyes from the lowering sun. None of the family seemed to be carrying anything. That meant they must have left whatever they'd found up in their rooms somewhere. *Perfect!* He would check that out as soon as he got a quick bite to eat.

He kept watching out the window until he was sure the family weren't coming back. Then he trotted into the dining room where Mrs. Tremannon was stacking dishes on a tray. He tried to put on his best fake good manners.

"Excuse me, Mrs. Tremannon. I am so sorry. I had a call from my sick brother and he needed some advice. I had to talk, and I'm a bit late for dinner."

"I wouldn't say a 'bit' late, Mr. Canopy. I would say 'very' late. I've already served dessert and I'm cleaning up as you can see." Mrs. Tremannon made as if to pick up the tray.

Kennedy cleared his throat, trying to push down his annoyance and maintain an ingratiating smile. "I'm so terribly sorry. It must be very hard for you, going to all the trouble to serve a wonderful dinner and then having me not turn up. I can't imagine how difficult it must be. Please forgive me."

Mrs. Tremannon took a deep breath, only slightly mollified by Kennedy's apology. "Well, you see, I can't just serve dinner whenever the guests feel like it. It just won't work, and when would I feed my own husband?"

"I know, I'm just so terribly sorry. I promise it won't happen again." Kennedy mentally crossed his fingers. He was planning on it happening again tomorrow morning.

Mrs. Tremannon sighed. She was too good-natured to maintain her annoyance indefinitely. She hefted up the tray and looked back over her shoulder. "Alright. I'll warm you up some pie and veg. Get yourself a knife and fork from the drawer over there."

"Certainly," said Kennedy after her retreating back. "Thank you so much."

"And it's *Kennedy*," he muttered to himself. *Whatever*. At least he had a few minutes. He could run upstairs and have a quick look around.

❧❧

"The old lady, lowering herself carefully into her chair, her cat jumping up immediately, purring furiously. She patted its head and smiled around at the family. "The doctor came by this afternoon and says my ankle looks all better. It wasn't really such a bad thing after all. I'm just getting old and things just don't hold together as well as they used to."

"I'm so glad," said Mom. "And now, can we get you anything?"

"Well, I just had a cup of tea, so I'm fine. Would you like one?"

"No thank you, but we would like to help you with the next clue, if that's alright."

"Yes, yes," said the old lady. "I would really appreciate that, but actually I have something different to propose. I've been cooped up in this house for several days and feel like I just have to get out. Would you be open to going somewhere else? Not the inn," she added hastily. "But maybe a place where we could get a hot drink?"

Does a cow go moo, thought Mom, waiting for Dad to jump on that request.

"I know just the place," said Dad, realizing a White Chocolate Mocha might suddenly be in his near future. "Captain Jack's Coffee House. It's great!"

The kids looked at each other in delight at this unexpected outing, but then Rachel had a sudden thought. "Er, um, excuse me, but do you, er, think it's okay to open the box and look at the clues in such a public place. What if someone is watching?"

They mulled that over for a second. She was right.

"Well, how about this then?" said Dad, not wanting to abandon the idea altogether. "How about we open the box right now, and have a quick look and

310

then go over to the coffee place to talk. Surely we can find a place where we can't be overheard, and then no-one would be able to see anything either."

"Are you up for a walk across the harbor?" said Mom to Mrs. Renton. "It's a bit of a pull up the other side from the bridge."

"I know," said Emily before the old lady could answer. "How about Dad drives us over and drops us off, and then you won't have to walk so far?"

Mrs. Renton looked at Dad who smiled and nodded, fully convinced that dropping people off was one of the primary things in his job description.

"Alright then," said Mrs. Renton. "And it's my treat by the way. There's no stopping me," she said to Mom who was about to protest. "It's the least I can do. Now how about that box?"

The kids plonked themselves down around the lady's feet, while Mom and Dad took their usual spots on the sofa.

"So, let's see." Mrs. Renton pulled out the box from under the little table at her side and held it up. It looked definitely old and rusty, and the designs etched into the top formed an interesting pattern.

"I haven't opened it yet," she added. "I wanted to wait for you all to see it." The truth was she also felt she needed the support of the family to make it through another clue. She didn't know how she could have done this on her own now.

"It looks almost Celtic, doesn't it?" said Emily. She loved Celtic patterns, and had once bought a coloring book full of nothing but Celtic designs.

"It does a bit," said Dad. "Something of the Squire's I suppose."

Mrs. Renton clasped the box to her chest. She gave a huge sigh, and the others looked at her, concerned. "I'm alright," she said. "It's just that I suddenly realized that Uncle Kenwyn actually held this box and put whatever's inside there for me—so many years ago." She gave an apologetic smile. "I know, you're all waiting to see what's inside."

"Could it be the end?" said Stevie, concerned. "It looks a bit small to be filled with jewels and gold and stuff."

"Do you hope it's the end?" said Mrs. Renton, looking at them seriously. "Then you could get back to your holiday."

They all thought that over. Did they want it all to be done? It *was* an exciting adventure.

"I don't think so," said Rachel. "I've never been in a real adventure before." The others nodded.

"But what about you, Mrs. Renton? Surely you would want it to be over," said Mom. "This hasn't been easy on you."

The old lady looked down, absentmindedly giving Pickwick a scratch around the ears.

"Well," she said finally. "This has been so hard. I mean, I never expected Uncle Kenwyn would leave me anything—I didn't think I deserved anything— but to have it be so complicated... Yes, I know he said in his letter that I've something to learn along the way, but I'm still not sure what it is." She looked up with what appeared to be a new determination. "So, I suppose in a way I'm glad it's not over yet. I do want to learn it, whatever it is." She took a deep breath. "Will you pray for me? Will you pray I'll be able to figure it out?" She sensed she was going to cry again and scrabbled for her hanky. Mom quickly handed her a tissue from her purse and put her arm around the old lady. She motioned for the others to come closer.

"We have been praying for you Mrs. Renton, and we definitely will continue."

"Let's pray right now," said Dad. Mom gave him a grateful look.

"Dearest Heavenly Father. Thank you so much for Mrs. Renton. We know you love her. Thank you for protecting her all her life and that we can be with her now." Dad felt a sudden boldness, and laid his hand on the old lady's shoulder. "You know this has been difficult for her, but we believe you have a purpose for it all. *Show us Your ways. Teach us Your paths,* as Your Word says. Please help us find the inheritance, yes, but even more importantly, help Mrs. Renton understand what You want her to learn from this. Help her understand Your love and forgiveness. Thank you that, in Jesus, we can have a relationship with You. You say you'll adopt us into Your family and we'll become Your beloved children. Mrs. Renton needs to know that." Dad felt the old lady stir under his hand. He gave a quick look. Tears were forming in her closed eyes. He closed his eyes again. "Dear Father. Please help us, and protect us from the evil one and anyone else trying to steal Mrs. Renton's inheritance. Thank You. We pray in Jesus' name, Amen."

Mom quickly gave Mrs. Renton another tissue. The old lady wiped her eyes and blew her nose. "Oh, my. I'm probably a sight. I'm so sorry."

Mom gave her another hug, and Emily did the same from the other side.

"Don't worry, Mrs. Renton," she said. "It's okay—you're with friends."

"I am," said the old lady, looking into Emily's eyes. She looked around at the other concerned faces. "I am with friends. I know that." She turned to Dad. "Did you really mean what you prayed? Is that true—that God wants to adopt us as His children?"

"Oh, yes," said Dad, smiling. "It says it explicitly in the book of Ephesians, but it says it in other ways throughout the Bible. God really does desire us to be a part of His family."

Mrs. Renton sniffed and blew her nose again as Mom handed her another tissue. "I need to think about that. It seems too good to be true." She became suddenly business-like and sat up straight. "But for now you've all waited too long. Let's see what's in the box."

She tried to lift the latch but it seemed stuck. Dad gave her a hand, and the box suddenly popped open with a rusty squeak. She reached in and carefully drew out a clear plastic bag with several papers inside. The others craned forward to see.

"It looks like everything's nice and dry," she commented as she undid the bag. "It doesn't look like it's the end of the quest. Let's see. Normally there's a letter from Uncle."

"It really is another clue," said Emily. "That's amazing."

"How many more?" said Mrs. Renton. *And how many more will I need?* she wondered.

She sifted through the papers and pulled one out. "It says '*read this first.*' I'll read just the first bit and then we'll go." She put on her glasses and adjusted them on the end of her nose. It gave her a moment to gather her courage. *What would this note say?* Would it finally shed some light on why the Squire had made this such a mystery? Would it further expose her guilt feelings? She cleared her throat uneasily and held up the letter. Mom sent up a quick prayer again for strength for the old lady.

"*Hello dear Ruthie.*" Mrs. Renton tried to steady her voice. "*You have made amazing progress. It's sort of like those jigsaw puzzles we used to do together. Each piece put in place made the whole picture clearer. Are things getting any clearer for you?*"

No, they're not, she thought. *At least not everything.* It was clear to her that she was guilty and didn't deserve an easy path to follow. It was clear she needed help. It was clear all the people in the clues had had difficult lives. It was just beginning to be clear that perhaps God really did want a relationship with her. But it wasn't clear what exactly she was supposed to get from all this.

She suddenly realized the others were all waiting. "I'm sorry—I was lost in thought. Now where was I? Oh, yes. '*Are things getting clearer for you? I'm praying they will. So firstly I would like you to read the letter in the brown envelope. It will finish the tale of Squire Trevithick and the wreckers. Then come back here for the next clue.*'"

Mrs. Renton set the letter down and pulled out the envelope. Inside was a yellowed piece of paper, carefully preserved in a thin plastic sheath. Paper-clipped to it was a single typed sheet. She held them up so they could all see.

"That looks really old," said Rachel, pointing to the letter. "It's all cracked at the edges."

"It IS old," said Mrs. Renton. "There's a date at the top. December 3rd, 1788. But we need to leave it for now." She gave a mischievous smile. "Let's go get some hot drinks, and then we can see if we can decipher the clue."

❧

Kennedy had thoroughly searched the girls' and the boys' rooms without success. He looked at his watch. It had been almost twenty minutes, but he *had* to check the parents' room. He realized now he should have checked it first, but the other rooms were first in line up the stairs.

The parents' door was shut. He hesitated for a moment. *Could there be someone inside?* No, he was sure he'd seen the whole family leave. He eased open the door and took in the surroundings. There was no-one there, thank goodness, and everything looked pretty tidy, which surprised him at the moment. He stepped into the room. The dressing table had a few items on it, but nothing interesting. There were a couple of suitcases against the wall—he might check them in a minute. The bed was nicely made, but what was that on the pillow? It was a box— an old-looking box, decorated with a border of emerald-looking jewels. Could it be the clue? He snatched it up and shook it. There was something inside. Okay, it was time to get back to the safety of this own room.

He tip-toed out the door, shutting it quietly behind him. He peered down the stairs. The coast was clear. He sneaked downstairs and peered into the dining room. *Good, good.* The old lady had set out his meal. He tucked the box under his arm, grabbed up the plate and silverware and trotted back to his room. Shutting the door behind him, he set the meal on the nightstand and sat on the bed, the box on his lap. He smiled grimly. Finally, he could wreck the family's plans. He carefully lifted the lid.

Jewels! But wait a second! He took a closer look. It was full of cheap, costume jewelry! And there was a scrap of paper at the bottom. He snatched it out and scanned it. "*If a man digs a pit, he will fall into it; if a man rolls a stone, it will roll back on him.* Have a care, Mr. Kennedy."

Kennedy's eyes widened in rage and horror. They had fooled him! And they were mocking him! He flung the box against the wall, scattering its contents. He stared at the mess for a moment and then jumped up and paced back and forth, thinking furiously. They had planted that for him. That meant they definitely knew what he was up to, and even worse, they had the real box—maybe the inheritance itself!

He dashed out to the sitting room and peered out the French doors. The van was definitely still gone. But where were they? At the old lady's probably. *What to do, what to do?*

He charged back to his room, stuffed the jewelry and note back into the box and ran up the stairs. He placed it back on the pillow in as near the same place as he could remember. Then shutting the door behind him, he tore back down the stairs, grabbed his keys off the nightstand, and with an afterthought the plate of food as well. He would have to eat on the run.

Chapter 20 – Figuring Things Out

"Are you ready?" Mrs. Renton looked around at the eager faces, each leaning forward over a steaming cup. They all nodded in unison, and the old lady laughed.

They had found the perfect spot by the front window and had arranged the wingback chairs in a rough circle around a table, just finishing as Dad appeared, puffing a little from his speed-walking trip back from dropping off the car. The curly-haired owner had been amused to see the whole family crowd up to the counter, and to Mom's astonishment had waited very patiently while the kids made up their minds. He had even made a special pot of Mrs. Renton's favorite brand of tea, which had surprised and delighted the old lady.

Rachel took one more quick look around the room. There were only six or seven other customers—seven, she counted carefully—and none of them looked suspicious. With the murmur of conversation punctuated by the espresso machine it seemed very unlikely they would be overheard.

Mrs. Renton lifted a large, brown envelope from her purse and carefully extracted the old letter in its plastic sheath with the paper-clipped sheet. She held them up.

"It's an old letter, rather hard to read, but rewritten clearly on this sheet. Let's see, it says the letter's to someone named Peter, and…" She turned over the paper and looked at the back. "It's from Jowan Kernow. Now where have I heard that name before?"

"I know, " said Emily. "Jowan Kernow was the friend of the squire—Squire Trevithick. I wonder if Peter was the squire's brother."

"Or son," said Dad. "But let's let Mrs. Renton read."

Mrs. Renton turned back to the beginning again. "Alright, now, here we go. *Dear Master Peter. I trust you are well and your time in London has been profitable. When your father sent you to the school there, he had high hopes of you coming back as a young man ready to take up the responsibility of managing the estate at his side. As his only son and heir,*

315

it was your privilege and your responsibility. We won't go back over that ground of which much has been said before, but I am happy to see that you seem to have taken seriously your commitment that you made at the graveside, and are truly seeking to change your ways, by the grace of God. I can undoubtedly say that your father would have been proud of the way you have now been handling yourself and your responsibilities. May I say that I am proud of you too? The legal proceedings are concluded and everything is in order. Your mother is provided for and eagerly awaits your return, as do I. The tenants are somewhat anxious at what the change of master will bring, but I have assured them that you will take up where your father left off and they will have nothing to fear.

Your father was a good man, Master Peter, trying to obey God's Holy Word in all he did. He never lorded his position over his tenants. He always tried to make sure that the village was well managed, that the men were not given to much drinking and would take good care of their families. When anyone in the village was sick, he and your mother would go and visit them and bring them things to help. He invested the rents well, putting the profits back into the village."

Mrs. Renton paused and turned the sheet over. *"He left quite a legacy, but I am confident, with God's help, you can fill his shoes. I will help you as much as I can. I know you are grieving. There are many things you wish you could have done and said that are now too late. We all feel that way, to be honest.*

But here is where you must decide what to do. You can live with regret forever, or find forgiveness and healing with God. He understands pain. He understands loss. Can you imagine His suffering as He had to turn away from His Son—as Christ Jesus took on himself the sins of the world? He can help you live now with purpose and even joy, living in a way that would make your father proud. Your mother needs you. The village needs you. I write in confident expectation of your return within the near future.

Commending you to the grace of Almighty God,
Sincerely, Jowan Kernow."

Mrs. Renton set the letter down and looked around at everyone. "So that's the rest of the story."

She appeared somewhat troubled and Dad and Mom glanced at one another. They each knew what the other was thinking. The end of the letter might as well have been written just for Mrs. Renton. Was this what the Squire was doing then? Trying to lead her on a path of personal healing? It did make sense.

Mrs. Renton took a quick sip of her tea and set the cup carefully back down. "Alright, let's leave that for now," she said with some effort. She pulled out the Squire's note. "Let's continue on. Here we are. *'Peter Trevithick had experienced a great loss. He hadn't realized how much his father meant to him until it was too late. Now he had to decide what to do in his grief. I am glad to say that the letter from Mr. Kernow had the desired effect. Peter returned to Penrithen and took up his role as the village squire. He recommitted his life to God and vowed to follow His Word. He did a great job and the village thrived.*

'You, too, suffered great loss. Having lost my own father, I can understand much of what you went through with the death of your parents. There are deep hurts, deep wounds, and so many questions whose answers lie hidden within the deep things of God. We may never understand why tragedies happen, but this we do know: Our Heavenly Father understands grief and loss. The Bible says He gave His One and Only Son to die in our place. He gave His only

son—His beloved. And He did this knowing many would reject the gift of forgiveness and eternal life offered through Christ. How that must grieve Him! But how that shows His love for us! Look what the Bible says: "But God demonstrates His own love for us in this: while we were still sinners, Christ died for us." Romans 5:8

'Think on these things, Ruthie. The Bible is true. The peace you seek is there. And now for the next clue. Each step in the quest is a step closer to your inheritance.'"

Mrs. Renton put down the letter. She stared at her teacup in front of her, confused by what she had read. After so many years living with her own picture of a distant, arbitrary God, it was so difficult to picture Him as understanding her own suffering. And what had the note said? He had felt the same grief?

She looked up at the others. Seeing the concern in their eyes, she decided to risk asking them a question that touched the depths of her heart. "Do you believe this?" she said. "Do you think God understands my grief—not just for my parents, but for the hurt I caused Uncle Kenwyn and Auntie Rosie?"

Mom and Dad nodded vigorously. "Oh, yes," said Mom. "The Bible says He is close to the brokenhearted."

"I...I need to think about all this," stammered the old lady. "I want to understand it—to believe it—but I've spent a lot of time believing something else. Despite what Uncle says, I'm not sure that the Bible is even trustworthy."

"We understand," said Dad kindly. "We'll pray for you, won't we kids."

Emily, Rachel, Danny and even little Stevie nodded seriously.

Mrs. Renton smiled suddenly. "You are all so wonderful—so patient with an old lady and her troubles."

"We're not being patient. We like you," said Stevie earnestly.

Mrs. Renton laughed out loud. She reached over and patted Stevie's cheek. "And I like you, too. I'm so thankful for your help. But we must keep going." She picked up the note again, took a deep breath and scanned it for a moment. "Here we go again—the next clue.

'A winding way to lofty height, some change will help increase your sight.
St. Piran's cross lines up with where the trail will head up hidden stair.
His life was one that finished well, again the book a tale will tell.
The signs reveal the way when you will put together two and two.'"

Mrs. Renton set the note down. She was feeling overwhelmed again. Mom noticed the look and hastened to set the old lady's mind at ease.

"Don't worry, we'll figure it out. We've got this far haven't we? And we believe that God wants us to solve this."

"Yes," said Dad. "We'll just take it a step at a time."

"We're the Chapman Family Detective Agency," said Danny proudly.

"The what?" said Mrs. Renton with a little laugh.

"The Chapman Family Detective Agency. We solve things as a family."

"No job is too hard," said Stevie, not wanting to be outdone.

"What they mean," said Mom "is that we're enjoying working together as a family on this. The kids like being detectives. And with God's help, we can figure it out together."

"Can you read the clue again?" said Emily. "It was kind of long."

"Yes, certainly." Mrs. Renton read it through again slowly and carefully while the others all sipped their drinks. She set the paper down in the middle of the table so they could all see it fairly well.

"That's a lot of different things," said Mom, frowning. "And not a lot of specifics."

"Maybe we should try and break it down into pieces," suggested Dad. "What was the first bit again? I can't read it very well upside down."

"*A winding way to lofty height, some change will help increase your sight*," quoted Mrs. Renton. "I do know the highest point around here is just south of the village. When you look from the harbor up past the church on the headland, you can see a hill beyond. There's a sort of marker up there."

"I think we saw that when we were up at the church," said Emily. The others nodded.

"Well that's a good start," said Mom. "Is there a winding way that leads there?"

"I don't know," said Mrs. Renton, "but I suppose we can find out. What about that second line, though? *Some change will help increase your sight.*"

"Does it mean that the change in where you are will help you see farther?" said Rachel. "That kind of makes sense if we have to go to the top of the hill."

"But we have to know what we're looking for up there, right?" put in Danny.

Emily leaned forward to look at the clue again. "We have to look for St. Piran's cross."

"And that will show us a hidden staircase!" said Rachel excitedly.

"So the first part seems to be somewhat straightforward," said Mrs. Renton. "At least we need to go up to the height and look for the cross that marks the hidden staircase."

"Do you think it means the church? You must be able to see the church from the top of the hill," said Danny, excitedly. Stevie nodded vigorously. The same idea had occurred to him.

"Is the church named St. Piran's?" Mom asked Mrs. Renton.

"I don't know," admitted the old lady. "I think it may be. I know that St. Piran is the patron saint of Cornwall. There might be a number of churches named after him."

"So what about the rest of the verse," said Rachel, pointing at it. "It suddenly starts talking about a guy and the book again, but it doesn't give a page number this time."

"Do you think there will be a sign at the hidden stairway? Maybe there's a house or something there," said Mrs. Renton.

"That's what I think," said Dad. "It says there are signs, so we'll have to see if we can find them."

"What about putting together two and two?" said Danny. "What does that mean?"

"Well, putting two and two together is another way of saying solving a sort of puzzle and coming up with a conclusion. The signs must have some clues that we figure out to show the way."

"The way to the staircase or from the staircase to somewhere else?" wondered Emily.

"We don't know yet," smiled Dad. "But that's the exciting part." He turned to Mrs. Renton. "The Squire must have been an amazing man. He sure loved all this mystery stuff!"

The old lady gave a wry smile. "Oh, yes, he did, though I confess I didn't realize quite how much until now. He must have really thought this all through."

"But one thing I don't understand is how he was able to make sure all the clues stayed in the right place, even though he set this up years ago," said Rachel.

"That's a good question," said Mom. "I guess some of the things like the shaft in the house and the box under the paving stone were pretty well hidden."

"But the poetry book, and the photo?" said Emily. "I wonder if…"

"Shhh," hissed Rachel suddenly. She gestured with her head towards the counter. The owner was heading their way with a tray.

Mrs. Renton casually picked up the letter and slipped it out of sight. They all looked up expectantly.

"Excuse me folks. I don't mean to interrupt you—well, actually I do, if that's okay." The owner smiled and held out the tray. "It's just nice to see a whole family here together enjoying themselves." He looked around at them all seated in a circle. "I wanted to give you all a little something to say 'thanks for choosing our coffee place to hang out in.'"

On the tray were a stack of small plates and a pile of familiar-looking individually-wrapped brown squares. Dad looked at them in shock. *No way!*

"Chocolate-Toffee Brownie Cakes," said the owner, gesturing with the tray. "Go ahead and take one each. They're free," he added, noting the family's hesitation. They were all looking at Dad, who shrugged his shoulders and took one. The other's followed suit—even Mom and Mrs. Renton—and there were a chorus of thank-yous.

"You're very welcome," said the owner, handing round the plates. "And if you don't mind, I'm going to lower the blinds a bit—it's getting late and I like to get things snug."

❧❦

Jennings was entirely at a loss for what to do. Kennedy's rude, peremptory phone call as he was eating his dinner had taken him completely by surprise. He had put up a feeble resistance, but Kennedy's threats had swept that away, and he had ended up tearing out of his shop and down the hill in an effort to trail Mr. Chapman.

He had just managed to catch a glimpse of the dad turning into the coffee shop, and had now been standing there across the street for at least twenty minutes with an awkward attempt at nonchalance, trying to see what was going on. It had seemed an incredible stroke of luck that the family had seated themselves by the window, but now his enthusiasm had evaporated. With the high backs of the chairs, he couldn't see what they were up to and now someone was lowering the blinds. It was just so useless standing there, but what else could he do? He couldn't abandon them—*Kennedy would kill him.*

The coffee shop owner turned back to the family perched around the table. "You're the Chapman's, right?" he said, beginning to gather up the empty mugs.

"That's right," said Dad, surprised that the man had remembered, "and this is Mrs. Ruth Renton." He wracked his brains for the guy's name again, and then suddenly had it. "And Mrs. Renton, this is Geoff Ketchum. He owns this place."

"With my wife," said Geoff with a smile, shaking hands. "She's the brains of the outfit. I don't know how she does it all, what with all her volunteer work as well. And there she is!" He looked towards the counter, where a young curly-haired lady had just appeared carrying a tray of mugs. "Maggie!" he called out, causing a few heads to turn at the other tables. The lady looked up and he beckoned her over. She set down the tray and wove through the tables to his side. She was about the same age as the man, with similar curly brown hair, laughing eyes and a tiny diamond stud in the side of her nose. The family liked the look of her at once.

"Hello everyone! Has Geoff been boring you all with coffee trivia? Oh, I see, he's been trying to get rid of some of Auntie Flo's goodies. She brings cartloads by and they always sell well. I'm Maggie Ketchum, by the way." She shook hands with everyone in turn including the kids.

Dad introduced Mom, Mrs. Renton and the rest of the family.

"Your husband said you were volunteering somewhere," said Mom politely. "What sort of things do you do?"

Maggie grinned at her husband, who shook his head resignedly. "Well, Geoff thinks I do too much, but I like to keep busy doing something for others. My major project right now is with the chapel."

The whole family pricked up their ears at this. "Do you mean the chapel on the hill?" said Mom.

"Yes, that's the one. After the Squire had his stroke the place fell into disrepair. You see, he was the one who took a lot of interest in it and had a whole crew of people helping him out. When he got sick, well, little by little the volunteering fell off and the place got really run down. The brambles grew up and the roof sprung a leak. I used to love going up there as a girl and couldn't stand seeing it get just so. I've been cleaning it up and trying to get it to the point where it could be used. I only get to go up there every now and then, but I would love to see the church in use again."

Geoff put his arm around her shoulders. "Yes, it's sad to see it empty."

"Are there any other churches in the village?" asked Dad.

Geoff shook his head. "No, there aren't. Maggie grew up here but her family moved away when she was eleven. We met down in St. Ives and we only just moved back here late last year. We were looking for a place to worship, but found out that the chapel was basically closed up." He glanced quickly at his wife who smiled in encouragement. "You see, we're Christians, and felt like God was calling us back here. I don't suppose that makes much sense to you."

"Oh yes it does," said Dad smiling broadly. "We're Christians too." He hesitated suddenly, wondering if he should explain that Mrs. Renton wasn't included in that comment. No, best not to.

"Really?" said Maggie. "Well that's great. God is so good, isn't He? Are you here on holiday? From your accent you sound American, but with maybe a hint of something else."

Dad filled them in with a quick history of his background and the family's past few months. Rachel was concerned he might mention the inheritance, but Dad avoided the subject completely.

The couple listened with interest. "It sounds like you're having quite an adventure," said Geoff when Dad had finished.

You have no idea, thought Dad.

"And thanks again for coming to visit us here at the coffee place. You've come quite a few times in just the short time you've been here."

"We should let them go," said his wife, tugging at his arm. "They didn't come just to chat with us."

"Oh, it's been great meeting you," said Dad, meaning it. He felt Rachel poking him in the arm.

"The church's name," she whispered.

Dad nodded. "Oh, by the way, what's the name of the chapel on the hill?"

"St. Piran's," said Geoff, picking up the last of the mugs. "Have you been up there?"

"Oh, yes," said Mrs. Renton, suddenly realizing how significant her decision to go up there had been. "Thank you for opening it up."

"Well, it's only open four days a week," said Maggie, "But you're welcome. Let me know if there's anything we can do for you while you're here."

"God bless," said her husband, hefting up his tray. He led the way back to the counter and they both disappeared again into the back room.

"Nice couple," said Dad. "And Christians. Rats, I forgot to ask them if they found a place to go to church anywhere around here."

"We can ask them later," said Mom. "But they did give us a big help on the clue. Now we know the church is St. Piran's. There's got to be something about its cross."

"Did it have a cross?" said Rachel, frowning. "I remember looking at the steeple 'cause it was kind of leaning. I don't remember seeing a cross on it."

"Really?" said Dad. "I don't remember either. Did any of you others see a cross?"

The rest of them shook their heads.

"That's funny," said Emily. "What other cross would it be? Maybe a cross on a gravestone?"

"Well, it depends on what the Squire meant," said Mom "Are we supposed to go up on the height and look at a cross and that will somehow mark the secret stair? Or are those parts of the clue unrelated?"

Mrs. Renton put the clue back on the table and they leaned forward to look at it again.

"I think the cross marks the spot where the staircase is, like 'x' marking the spot on a treasure map," said Danny, nodding knowingly.

"Yes, like for pirates and stuff," put in Stevie, liking his brother's train of thought. He gave a chocolatey grin.

"What do you think, Mrs. Renton?" said Emily, wanting to include the old lady as much as possible.

Mrs. Renton looked surprised and then thoughtful. "Well, I'm not sure. It does seem to make sense that we need to go up on the hill and from there the cross will somehow point out the staircase. Otherwise why would we go up on the hill?"

"You're right," said Mom smiling.

"That sounds like the next step then," said Dad. "We could go first thing tomorrow."

"Like, before breakfast?" said Stevie. That sounded pretty exciting to him.

"Like, first thing after breakfast," said Dad with a grin. "But we'll have to figure out how to get there. It looks way too far to walk from here, so we'll have to take the van."

"I would love to come with you—I really want to help—but I'm just not sure I can make the climb," said Mrs. Renton. "Is there anything else I can do?"

Dad considered for a moment. "Well, when we find out where the cross points to we can definitely let you know, and then we can find the stair."

Stevie had been thinking hard. He raised his hand politely and Mom smiled at him. "Yes, Stevie. Do you have a suggestion?"

"Uh-huh. Mrs. Renton could keep watch for the bad guys—so they don't follow us or anything."

The other children laughed, but Dad stopped them with a frown. "We do actually need to remember to be careful." He turned to Mrs. Renton. "You could keep an eye open if you like."

The old lady gave a mischievous grin. "You know what I could do. I could take Pickwick and a thermos of tea and find a place to sit near the bridge. I think there's a bench on the quay nearby. I would have a pretty good view of the harbor, and I could watch the Mole Hole shop."

"The bad guy has a yellow sports car," said Danny. "You could watch for that."

"Yes, I could," said the old lady, feeling relieved and a little excited that there was something practical she could do. "If it's a fine day I would like sitting outside for a spell."

"We'll have to give him the slip at the inn after breakfast. We don't want him following us," said Dad. "And yes, if the other guy's involved, it would be good to watch his shop."

"This is quite the adventure," said Mrs. Renton. "In a way. I mean I wish there wasn't anyone trying to steal the clues."

"Do you have any idea why they might be? Do you know either of the men?" wondered Mom.

"I don't," said Mrs. Renton. "I didn't really get a look at the man at Tintagel, and I don't remember anything about the other man—what's his name?"

"Mr. Kennedy," said Danny. "He's not very nice."

"How would they have found out about the inheritance? I know there was a bit about it in the paper, but it seems like they must know something more," wondered Mom.

"Let's think about that for a moment," said Dad. "What do we know about these guys?"

"Mr. Kennedy has scary hair and scary eyes and is mean," said Danny.

Mom reached over and patted his shoulder. "I know, dear, he has been rather nasty, but I think Dad meant more about where he came from." She turned to the others. "We know that he is some sort of estate seller. Maybe that's why he's interested in the inheritance."

"What's an estate seller again?" asked Rachel.

"When someone dies and leaves a bunch of things behind, sometimes the family doesn't know what to do with them and needs some help selling things. An estate seller—or liquidator as they're sometimes called—will try to sell or auction all the things and keep a percentage of the profits," explained Dad. "Or I suppose some might charge a flat fee—a certain amount of money—to sell the things."

"So this Mr. Kennedy must have found out about the Squire—that he had some valuable things and maybe had left them to me, and now wants to get his hands on them," said Mrs. Renton, shaking her head in wonderment.

"But the interesting thing is that we know he isn't from here. We actually ran into him on the way down—at a motorway café. He must have been on his way here," said Dad.

"Did it say where he was from on that business card we found?" said Mom. "Do you still have it?"

"I don't know. Let me check." Dad fished around in his pockets and gave a grunt of satisfaction. "Here it is. And it says his address is in Canterbury. That makes sense that we ran into him on the way then. We came through Canterbury."

"So he probably wouldn't have seen the newspaper with the article about the inheritance then," said Emily. "Someone must have told him."

"It must have been the other guy—Mr. Mole Hole," said Rachel confidently.

"So what do we know about him?" said Dad. "Apart from the fact that he has a shop here in town."

They all puzzled over that for a bit.

"Well," said Mom finally. "We know his shop sells antiques, so in a sense that links him with Mr. Kennedy. I'm sure Kennedy would know quite a bit about antiques if he's in the estate sales business."

"Good point," said Dad. "There must be a connection there. I bet he was the one to tell Mr. Kennedy."

"But I still don't really understand how the Mole Hole man found out all the details. Somehow he or the Kennedy man got a hold of one of the clues," said

Mrs. Renton. She took a quick, nervous sip of her tea, discovering it was unpleasantly cold.

"Do you ever remember sharing anything about the inheritance?" said Dad.

The old lady set her cup down, looked off into space and then closed her eyes. The others waited patiently. She finally opened them again, nodding her head.

"I think I have it. When I first got the news, I had gone to the lawyers' office just down the road from here. They explained to me some of the legal details, and handed me an envelope. I didn't want to wait until I got home and so I popped into the bakery, ordered a cup of tea and a scone, and I sat by the window to read it. I hadn't thought about it until now, but a man came in soon after. I remember because the shop lady, Mrs. Cribbins, had gone into the back room and he rang the bell twice before she appeared. It kind of annoyed me at the moment. When Mrs. Cribbins came out again, she happened to call across to me to see if I needed anything. She knew my name since I'd been there a number of times, and she's so good with names. Well, when she called to me, I noticed the man sort of take notice and stare at me. I saw him look down at the envelope I had on the table, then back at me. Then Mrs. Cribbins got his attention and that was that. I didn't think much of it at the time—it was just a little bit weird—and the strange clue in the letter drove everything else from my mind."

Dad pursed his lips. "Hmm, so if he heard your name and had read about the inheritance he might have put two and two together. Was it the Mole Hole man? The guy we saw at Tintagel?"

Mrs. Renton looked a bit embarrassed. "To tell you the truth, I don't know. I just wasn't paying attention when we were eating at the café, or in the shop. I don't really know what he looks like."

"He has a beard," said Rachel. "And brownish hair."

"It might have been him. I'm sorry, I just can't remember exactly."

"No worries," said Mom. "At least we have a good possibility that the man at the bakery is our Mole Hole man. The bakery's practically right next door to his shop."

"And if it is," said Dad leaning forward, "we can pretty much guess that he was the one who called Mr. Kennedy."

"So how much do they know, I wonder?" said Mom.

They looked at each other. No-one seemed to have any ideas.

The espresso machine suddenly gave out its steaming roar like an agitated dragon, and Dad waited until it died down again. "Well, either way we need to be extra vigilant. We'll have to help each other to be careful what we talk about and where."

"But to do it kindly," put in Mom with a smile. "We all make mistakes and any one of us could accidentally say something."

The kids nodded, several of them feeling a bit guilty about how they had responded to their siblings' slips of the tongue. Rachel was just about to say something when Emily suddenly put her finger to her lips. She gave the merest nod towards the counter. The owner was heading their way expertly balancing a loaded tray. Mrs. Renton nodded and slipped the letter back down out of sight. They all smiled as Geoff approached the table.

"Excuse me everyone, but I thought you might be thirsty after Auntie Flo's chocolate toffee things." He set the tray down and began serving out glasses of water.

"Thank you," said Mom. "That's really nice of you."

"Best service of any coffee place I've ever been to," added Dad. "And I'm not kidding."

"Well, I feel honored and privileged to hear it!" smiled Geoff. "God has been good to us and we enjoy serving people as best as we can. You sound like you love coffee."

Mom gave a barely-suppressed snort of laughter.

"I have been known to love a cup now and then," admitted Dad with a grin.

"And coffee places," added Mom. "I think he'd own one if he could."

"Well, I could sell you this one if you like," said the owner, beginning to gather up their plates. "I wouldn't mind the break!"

They all laughed.

Dad had a sudden thought. "Hey, would you happen to know how to get up to the monument thing on the hill above the town? We were thinking of going there tomorrow."

"Up Capstan Wiggle?" said Geoff.

"Capstan What-tle?" said Dad in surprise.

"Capstan Wiggle," repeated Geoff with a grin. "The capstan part is because there's the capstan from an old ship up there as part of the monument."

"And the wiggle?" said Rachel, thinking it a very funny name.

"And the wiggle is the path you have to take up to the point. It goes back and forth across the face of the hill. In fact, it's a bit of climb…" He looked doubtfully at Mrs. Renton, who noted the look and smiled.

"Don't worry. I'll probably just stay home and look at the photos afterwards."

Geoff laughed. "Well, maybe that would be just as well. Anyway, it's not hard to get to. Just take the road across the bridge and up past the Squire Inn. Take the first lane to your right after the inn. Follow it along for about a mile and look for a little lane to the right again. There's a small gravel car park and a sign for the footpath up the hill."

"So take the right after the inn and then the next right after about a mile?" confirmed Dad.

"Yep. Right then right. You can't miss it. I hope you have a nice time. I'd best get back before Maggie comes to hunt me down. It's my turn to do the washing up." He hefted up the tray, gave a parting grin and took off back towards the counter.

"Did you catch that?" said Rachel as soon as he was out of hearing. "The trail wiggles—it's the winding way in the clue—it's got to be!" She looked at the others in satisfaction.

"I think you're right," said Dad. "And the directions don't sound too difficult." He took a big gulp of his water. "But if you excuse me, I need to head back and use the facilities." He gave an apologetic grin and scooted back his chair. "I'll be right back."

Dad disappeared towards the back. Mom turned to Mrs. Renton. "How are you holding up? Do you want us to head home?"

Mrs. Renton was just about to answer when the front door behind her opened suddenly to the frantic ringing of the little bell. Rachel's chair was facing the door and she glanced up automatically, her eyes widening in surprise and shock. Mom and Emily followed her gaze and they too reacted in surprise. *No way!* It was the man again—the man from the Mole Hole—and he was right there!

Mom made frantic signs to Mrs. Renton who looked puzzled but then nodded as the man in and headed for the counter at the back. Rachel whispered to Danny and Stevie, explaining who it was and they both froze in their seats. This could be disastrous.

⋘⋙

Jennings' plan was to pretend he hadn't seen the family and just go up to the counter and order something. It wasn't much of a plan, he admitted to himself. He had no idea what he would do then.

It took quite a bit of self-control but he made it to the counter without looking around, and then stood there trying to calm himself down and look at the menu board. He had to order something, that was for sure, but he didn't like coffee at all.

Maggie suddenly popped into view with some clean coffee cups that she set on top of the espresso machine. She smiled at Jennings. "Good evening. And what can I get you?"

Jennings had no idea. "Er, well, I'm not sure. I need a bit of time."

"No problem," said Maggie breezily. "Take all you need." She headed over with a cloth towards where she had spied a table that needed wiping.

Jennings felt himself beginning to sweat. *Was his face turning red?* It probably was. Somehow he needed to pick something to order and then make an exit, checking on the family on the way out. Surely he would at least be able to see what they were doing. Were they all even there? That was kind of crucial to know. Could he carefully check?

He leaned on the counter and casually looked around as if just appreciating the décor. He turned slightly and looked towards the front of the room, past where Maggie was just finishing up with one table and was starting on another. Yes, there they were, and they were looking at him! He snapped his head back around and pretended to be examining the board again. *Why were they looking at him?* They must suspect him surely. *And were they all there?* He tried to replay the brief mental snapshot he had taken. Yes, he thought so. *Wait, no! Where was the dad?*

⋘⋙

Dad had just finished washing his hands and had stepped back out into the main room, enjoying the wave of coffee-flavored warmth that flooded over him. As he passed the counter he glanced sideways at the man studying the list of drinks and stiffened immediately, stopping mid-stride. He studied the man's profile. It was definitely the guy from the Mole Hole. *Where on earth had he sprung from?*

Dad looked towards the family. Rachel was peering around the wing of her armchair and he could tell even from here that she had a frantic look on her face. His wife poked her head out as well and he thought he could see a concerned expression there too. What was going on? Was this guy just getting a coffee or was he here to spy on them? Was that just a ridiculous notion, or could it actually be true? *Help, Lord, what should I do?*

The man seemed to sense Dad standing there and turned his way. There was a momentary spark of recognition and he turned hurriedly back. Dad felt a sudden, strong impulse to head back to his seat. That was the easiest thing to do, but was it the best thing? *No.* A still, small voice said this was not an accident. He needed to say something.

He stepped over to the man's side and spoke clearly and slowly. "Excuse me, but don't I recognize you from somewhere?"

Jennings felt his stomach lurch. He had desperately hoped that the dad would just ignore him. He kept his gaze on the menu board. "Er, no, I don't think so."

"Aren't you the owner of the Mole Hole? We were in your shop earlier today."

Jennings was silent for a moment. He couldn't deny that could he? "Er, yes," he said hesitatingly, without looking round.

"And didn't we see you at Tintagel the other day as well?"

That arrow shot right home. Jennings' heart started beating faster. He couldn't find anything to say.

Maggie had finished wiping the tables and came back behind the counter. She looked questioningly back and forth between Dad and Jennings.

Dad suddenly felt extremely awkward, but went for broke anyway. He leaned in closer. "Didn't we see you at the castle, and then at the café? And didn't you show up in the shop, and here you are again?"

Jennings looked at him suddenly. "No! I mean maybe, but so what?"

Dad decided a smile would be in order. "Maybe it's just a coincidence, but it is kind of funny running into you so much. I just wanted to let you know we'll be looking out for you. Chances are we might just run into you again."

Jennings didn't care any more about his mission. He just wanted out of there. "Yes, maybe," he mumbled. "I've got to go."

He turned and made a beeline for the door, Dad watching closely. The family all quickly turned away as Jennings hurried past them, yanked open the door causing the bell to jangle wildly in protest, and disappeared into the street.

Dad turned back to where Maggie was standing stock still behind the counter, her eyebrows raised in surprise. Geoff had joined her, drying a plate with a tea towel and trying to take in what had happened. He turned a questioning look to Dad who gave a light laugh.

"You're probably wondering about all that."

"Well, yes, it was a little strange," admitted Maggie with a slight smile. "Was he upset?"

Dad looked at them both, weighing whether he should say anything. There was something about the two of them that invited opening up a little—perhaps an outflow of their relationship with God that seemed to make them trustworthy. He decided to risk it.

"Yes, he was a bit upset and I think I know why." Dad took a deep breath. "You see, we've been trying to help the old lady, Mrs. Renton. She's the one with the mystery inheritance in the newspaper."

"The one left by Squire Penrow?" said Geoff. He set the plate down and slung the tea-towel over his shoulder.

"That's right. It's quite a puzzle and we've…well, we've honestly felt led by the Lord to help her. We feel that God is really pursuing her—getting her attention through all this."

"And the man?" wondered Maggie.

"Ah, yes. My daughter was the first to notice, but we're convinced that he and another man are trying to get the inheritance before the lady does. It's…a long story." Dad shrugged. "We're just trying to listen to the Lord and follow His leading. It's all a bit weird, like the plot from some old cheesy B-Movie mystery."

"So did you confront him just now?" said Geoff, getting pretty interested.

Dad gave an apologetic grin. "Sort of. I just mentioned how many times we've seen him and let him draw his own conclusions. I think I lost you a coffee sale though. I'm sorry about that."

"Hey, no problem," said Geoff, smiling. "We're glad you're helping Mrs. Renton."

"I think it's wonderful," said Maggie. "Can we help at all?"

Dad considered that for a moment. "I can't think of anything right now, but of course we would appreciate your prayers."

"Absolutely," said Geoff, putting his arm around his wife. He looked at her and she nodded vigorously.

"Thanks very much," said Dad, pleased that they obviously intended to do it. "And now I think I should get back to the gang. They'll be wondering what's up."

"Oh, certainly," said Geoff. "And God's grace in your quest." Maggie nodded in agreement.

Dad smiled and made his way back over to the family circle. There were lots of questioning looks and he plopped down in his chair and gave them a short summary of his confrontation and his subsequent chat with the Ketchums. He looked at Mrs. Renton. "I really hope you don't mind me sharing a bit with them. I really believe we can trust them. They're Christians and seem like really caring people. They said they'd be praying for us."

"Well, that's nice," said Mrs. Renton, trying to sort out in her mind if this was all good news or not.

"Was that the man you saw in the bakery?" said Rachel.

Mrs. Renton furrowed her brow. "You know, I think it was. Yes, I'm pretty sure."

"I thought so," said Rachel sitting back in satisfaction.

"Should we call the police?" said Stevie. "They could arrest him and put him in jail—him and the man with the yellow car."

Dad pursed his lips. "You know, bud, it's a good idea but I don't think the police would do it. You see we don't have any real evidence."

"But we're sure they're trying to do it!" said Rachel in surprise.

"We are, we are," admitted Dad, "but it's really only circumstantial evidence—we can't prove they've actually done anything wrong."

Rachel sat back and folded her arms, a determined expression on her face. "Then we'll get the evidence." The other kids nodded seriously.

Mom smiled. "We'll try, but for now we'll assume they're up to no good and try to solve this before they do."

"How are you doing with all this?" said Dad, turning to Mrs. Renton.

She looked at him for a moment. Then she set her jaw firmly and leaned forward. "I'm ready to help. I won't let someone take away what Uncle Kenwyn took so much trouble to give me."

The family exchanged surprised looks. This was the first time they'd seen the old lady look this determined. *It's a good sign*, thought Mom.

"Here's my cellphone number and Kathie's too," said Dad, pushing a piece of paper over to the old lady. "Can we get your home phone number? And would you mind copying down the clue for us? Here, you can write it on this." He pushed another scrap of paper over to the old lady. She nodded and dug for a pen in her purse.

"Do you think we're all set then for tomorrow?" said Mom, looking at everyone. There were nods all around.

"Alright then!" said Dad. "I'll go get the car."

As he stepped outside, he was struck by the glare of the peach-colored evening sun reflecting off the dormer windows along the crooked line of roofs. He shielded his eyes to take a quick look up and down the street. It was deserted. With a parting grin to the family, he closed the door and took off at a jog.

Kennedy peered around the wall of the last cottage in the line—the one he had stayed in earlier. From his vantage point he could observe most of the harbor. He noticed a flash of movement down disappearing behind the fish and chip shop. A person appeared from the other side, striding briskly and then breaking into a jog. It wasn't Jennings—he could tell that even from this distance. Could it be the dad? And where was Jennings? *That did it.* He grabbed his phone from his jacket pocket and speed-dialed Jennings. He was just about to give up in frustration when a voice finally came on the line.

"Yes, who's there?"

"It's me, you idiot—who do you think it is?" Kennedy barked into the phone, his face turning red. There was silence on the other end.

"Where are you? I think I see the dad coming towards the bridge. What was he doing? Did you see anything?" Kennedy tapped his foot impatiently. There was a long pause and he was about to really unload when Jennings spoke up, an unusual firmness in his voice.

"No, I didn't and I'm not going to. I'm done. This is never going to work. They know I'm involved and there's no way I'm going any further."

Kennedy couldn't believe his ears. "*What?* Why you...you..." He couldn't think of a description bad enough. "I'm not going to let you get away with this. I've got dirt on you and you know it. I know what you've been selling. I can tell the police—and they'll take care of you and your so-called shop."

There was silence. "Go ahead," Jennings suddenly blurted out. "Call the police. I don't care." He had to get this all out before he lost his nerve. "I've got a lot I could tell them too. So go ahead."

"What could you tell them?"

Jennings let him know. Kennedy listened with increasing horror. He was right.

Even in his fear, Kennedy was livid. "You won't do that, you hear," he blurted out. "I'll..I'll..." Why did he have such a hard time coming up with adequate threats? He heard a soft click and the dial tone. Jennings had hung up.

Kennedy stabbed at the speed dial and then jammed the phone back against his ear. The ringing went on and on and he gritted his teeth until he couldn't stand it anymore. He snapped his phone shut, his chest heaving up and down with emotion. With a sudden thought he whirled around and focused in on where the dad was just coming off the bridge and heading towards the bottom of the lane. He ducked back down behind the wall, his thoughts a seething mess. So Jennings was bailing out was he? And threatening him to boot? *Well, he was going to be very sorry for doing that—very sorry indeed.*

Kennedy's anger was suddenly swamped by a wave of panic. How was he going to do this alone? How could he intercept the clues and still get to the treasure first? He stared into space Something would have to change, and it looked like it might have to involve drastic measures.

Drastic measures. Something had suddenly popped into his mind—a way to absolutely ensure he'd win. The audacity of the thought had surprised even him. He mulled it over. It was a huge risk, and he wasn't sure it was worth it. He'd file the idea away for now, but hopefully he wouldn't need to go that far. Yes, he needed to do something drastic, but not quite that drastic.

❧❦

"Why are you acting so mysterious?" questioned Mom as Dad led with exaggerated stealth up the staircase towards their bedrooms. "Mr. Kennedy's not even here."

"I'll show you," said Dad. He stopped in front of the closed door to their room and pointed to the top. "Do you see anything?"

"No," said Mom, puzzled.

"Exactly," said Dad, with a mischievous grin. He opened the door and examined the carpet just inside the room. "There, look at that."

The family crowded around as Dad pointed to a length of black thread on the floor.

"See that? I left that in the top of the door when I closed it. I wanted to see if someone had been in our room when we were gone. And they have!"

The kids all felt a little thrill of excitement with a little hint of concern, too—at least on the boys' part.

"What do you mean?" said Danny, fearfully.

"It was just a hunch. Mr. Kennedy followed us back here from the cove. If he really was after the inheritance I figured he would be interested in whatever we might have found. Knowing we were out this evening, I thought it might be a temptation for him to see if he could find anything. So I left him something to find."

"What do you mean? What did you leave?" said Mom.

Dad turned and pointed to the box on the pillow in triumph. "A treasure chest."

"Where did you get that?" said Mom, amazed. The kids looked at him wide-eyed—all except Rachel who suddenly giggled.

"What's so funny," said Danny, a bit annoyed a Rachel's seeming lack of awe.

"That box. It was on my nightstand. It's a jewelry box, right Daddy?"

Dad grinned and went over to the box. He examined it closely for a second and then picked it up to show everyone. "I set it on the bed lined up with a small piece of fluff, just to mark its position. Someone has moved it and then set it back in a slightly different spot. That means whoever it was probably opened it and if they opened it they must have seen my note." He lifted the lid and proudly showed them the piece of paper. The family read it and looked at each other impressed. *Good job, Dad!*

"So what does that mean? If Mr. Kennedy came in here should we call the police?" wondered Emily.

"No, I still don't think they would have enough evidence to do anything," said Dad. "But we're all convinced Mr. so-and-so's up to no good. We'll keep our eyes peeled and see if we can thwart him and his friend."

"It's in God's hands, right dear?" reminded Mom.

"That's right," agreed Dad. "So let's pray about that. In fact, it's time for brushing teeth and saying prayers, right?"

"Right," agreed Mom. "We need our rest for tomorrow."

"And our next adventure," said Rachel, wiggling her eyebrows.

"Our next adventure," echoed Stevie. That sounded pretty exciting. Maybe he'd even dream about it.

⊰⊱

Mom and Dad sat propped up on pillows on their aircraft carrier-sized bed. It was a miracle but all the kids had gone down quickly—even Stevie who usually seemed to want to delay the inevitable.

Mom patted Dad's hand. "How are you dear? What are you making of all this?"

Dad shook his head with a tired smile. "I honestly don't know. I think we've kind of stepped on board a train and God is the engineer up front. I'm not sure where we'll end up, but I think we're just going to have to take it a day at a time."

331

Mom looked up at the ceiling. She nodded. "A day at a time. I think that's how God wants us to live anyway. My Bible reading was in Matthew six this morning."

Dad looked over at her. "Do not worry about tomorrow," he quoted. "Was that it?"

Mom nodded. "But seek first His kingdom and His righteousness, and all these things will be added to you as well."

"And you know what?" said Dad. "I'm going to try to apply that to everything."

"You mean the articles you have to write," guessed Mom. "I didn't want to mention them—you've been so stressed about them."

"Uh-huh. I realized that this evening. It's the only thing I can do—leave them in God's hands and trust He'll give me the inspiration when the time comes."

"So in all things to seek His kingdom and His righteousness. Isn't that what we're doing with Mrs. Renton? We want her to come to know Him."

"Yes, I think it is," assured Dad. "As long as we keep putting it in His hands."

"So let's do it," said Mom, grabbing his hand. They both closed their eyes and prayed.

Chapter 21 – Red Herrings

It was six thirty-seven a.m. and Kennedy closed the big front door as quietly as possible, snuck over to his car, and cursed under his breath. That old man had left his wheelbarrow right behind it. Good thing he'd seen the thing or it would have made a right racket backing into it. Tiptoeing over, he seized the handles and tried to push it out of the way. It gave a loud, protesting squeak and the wheel promptly fell off. He grimaced and with sudden desperation heaved it up, tottered forward a few yards, and dropped it down onto its side.

Muttering imprecations against Mr. Tremannon, he climbed into his car, left the door open and released the hand brake. Pushing with his foot he gradually eased the car backwards, grateful that the driveway was on a slight incline. The car picked up speed and he popped his leg back in, pulling the door closed. Steering slightly he guided it down to the gate, braked to a stop and then turned on the ignition. Backing carefully out into the lane, he kept a careful watch out his rear view mirror—in his anxiety he could quite imagine a flock of sheep parachuting in out of nowhere.

The coast was thankfully clear and he shifted from reverse into drive, taking the lane down to the harbor and across the bridge. He yawned widely. He hadn't exactly had the best night's sleep—his mind just wouldn't shut down. All his options, all the possibilities—he had scrutinized them, sorted them, sifted them and finally settled on the only thing that he considered had any chance. Notwithstanding the family's outing to Tintagel, it seemed clear that all the clues so far had centered on Penrithen. Chances were that's where the next clue would lead, and probably even where the treasure would be found. *It had to be.* He couldn't chase them all over Cornwall. He would stash the car out of sight in the parking area on the back side of the village, and then find somewhere central where he could hang out and keep an eye on the harbor and particularly the old

333

lady's house. Tonight he would show up at Jennings' place and demand a bed. All things considered, the day didn't seem to have much hope, but he wouldn't let himself dwell on that. He couldn't.

❧❧

Rachel stirred and turned over. The rising sunlight was doing its level best to stream into the room despite the heavy curtains and she squinted at her watch. It was ten till seven. Breakfast would be at eight so she had over an hour. For a moment she fought the overwhelming urge to just turn over and snooze for a while longer, but then suddenly, with a determination that even surprised herself, she threw back the covers and jumped out of bed. Pulling aside the curtain she looked out to where the sun was cresting the farm buildings, a rosy glow highlighting the clouds straggling across the expanse of sky.

Emily gave a groan of protest. "What are you doing? Put it down."

Rachel dropped the curtain back into place. "Sorry," she whispered, "but it's a lovely sunrise. I'm going to go pray downstairs. We're on a mission and I want to be ready. We need Jesus' help."

Emily's eyes popped open. *That wasn't like her sister at all.* She watched incredulous from her nest of covers as Rachel dressed hurriedly, grabbed her Bible and headed out the door. Emily lay there for a minute, pondering what Rachel had said. Then throwing back her own covers, she jumped out of bed.

❧❧

Grabbing his Bible off the nightstand, Danny opened it carefully at his bookmark—the one he had made in Sunday School back in 2nd grade with the laminated picture of a lion. Finding the place, he read out loud the verses from Joshua 1:9. *"Have I not commanded you? Be strong and courageous. Do not be afraid; do not be discouraged, for the LORD your God will be with you wherever you go."* He pondered that for a minute and then had a sudden thought. *Where was that other verse?* It had to be in the Gospels—he knew that much since it was Jesus speaking. He started with Matthew, flipping quickly past the genealogy, the Christmas story and Jesus' baptism. And there it was! All those words in red meant it was Jesus talking, and there was the section heading he was looking for: 'Love for Enemies.' Matthew chapter five verse forty-four said *'But I say: Love your enemies and pray for those that persecute you.'*

He had heard that verse many times but had always pictured enemies as people like the Teachers-of-the-Law guys that Jesus had to deal with, or pirates or aliens or something. He'd never really had an enemy himself—not until now. He was sure now that the sneaky Mr. Kennedy qualified as one—he was mean, nasty, and wanted to steal Mrs. Renton's inheritance. Danny pursed his lips, thinking hard. It was clear enough what the Bible said, and what Jesus wanted him to do—but he just didn't want to do it.

But what was it now that Mom always said when he needed to do something he didn't want to? *Act in obedience, with Jesus' strength, and your feelings will catch up with your actions.* And it was true—it always seemed to work.

334

So Jesus, he prayed. *I don't feel like praying for the man but you say I should so I'm going to. Please help him to come to know you. Help me somehow to show him your love. And help me to be strong and courageous. Thank you that you've promised me that you'll be with me wherever I go. Amen.*

He opened his eyes and did a quick self-examination. Did he feel better? Yes, as a matter of fact he did. He was still nervous about the man, but along with the nervousness was a real sense that Jesus was going to help him do the right thing.

❧❧

With her travel mug of hot coffee as a companion, Mom had had a wonderful time with the Lord in her secret garden spot. She had continued her practice of writing down items of thanksgiving in her journal, and this time there had been so many that she had filled an entire page. God was doing something, she was sure of it. Not just in Mrs. Renton's life, though that was wonderful enough, but she could tell He was working in her husband and the kids too. Hadn't she seen Rachel praying earnestly in the little sitting room as she passed, not to mention Emily and Danny pouring over their Bibles in their rooms? It was such a blessing that they seemed to be motivated to meet with the Lord all by themselves. That had been one of her prayer requests for them since they were babies.

And what would this inheritance mystery quest thing bring across their paths today? She had no idea. It was kind of scary, but kind of thrilling too. *What was God up to and how would He unfold the day?* Well, they would all find out soon enough.

❧❧

"How was your time with Jesus this morning?" asked Mom, pouring tea into her husband's cup. He was just finished putting chunky marmalade on a slice of buttered toast and had eagerly accepted her offer to pour. There was something about tea, toast and marmalade…they just went together so well.

"You know," he said pausing in his spreading. "It was really great. I mean, I felt like I was able to concentrate so much better this morning than I had for days. I really have a peace about this whole thing, and yes, I'm still not thinking about my articles. And if I don't think about them, I don't worry."

Mom smiled in satisfaction. That was exactly what she had prayed for her husband. "That's great, dear. I'm so glad."

"So what are our plans then?" said Rachel, chasing a piece of sausage around her plate. "Who's going where?"

"Going out are you?" Mrs. Tremannon had seemingly materialized out of nowhere. "I hope you have a good day--a really fruitful day. But I do want to tell you that the weather looks a bit iffy."

"Iffy?" said Dad.

"My bones tell me there's a change in the air. Could be a storm." She picked up an empty platter and balanced it on her arm. "My bones warned me the other day before we had that downpour. At least I thought it was because of that. Maybe it was because I had vacuumed all over creation. Well, either way I've still learned to trust my bones. They're right most of the time. Well, about half the time. Anyway, don't forget your coats. I'll make sure and make a hearty dinner." She picked up a couple more dishes and bustled out. The family watched her go.

"Okay, she's gone," said Rachel, relieved. "So what are our plans?"

"Well, for starters we thought you, Emily and Mom would go up to the point on the hill and see if you can figure out about the cross." Dad looked at his wife. "Do you have your phone dear?"

"Yup, already in my purse and charged up."

"What about us?" said Stevie, concerned. "I don't want to miss the clue?"

"Don't worry," assured Dad. "You, Danny and I have a very important assignment. I told you that Mr. Kennedy seems to have left already this morning. Chances are he or the Mole Hole man are going to want to keep an eye on us and Mrs. Renton."

"You see as far as we know they don't know what the next clue is, so they're going to have to see what we're up to," added Mom. "They can't follow all of us, so you and Dad and Mrs. Renton are going to try to create a diversion."

"How?" said Danny, puzzled.

Dad quickly swallowed a bite of toast. "Well, that's the fun part. We want to see if we can get him a bit confused, so we'll try and make it seem that we've found a clue and are following it."

"Yes," said Danny. "We can pretend we have a clue and are looking for the treasure."

"Right, like in the cove or around the harbor. It would be best if we knew for sure that Mr. Kennedy or the other guy were watching us. Mrs. Renton's going to try to help with that. She'll be down at the harbor keeping an eye on things."

Stevie looked at Danny with a big smile on his face. This sounded like some serious detective work!

"Okay," said Dad. "Let's finish up and get going."

"Don't forget we're going to pray first," reminded Mom gently.

Dad nodded. "Oh, yes—of course. Mom and I agreed that we need to commit this day to the Lord together as a family." He checked his watch. "Let's meet down here in fifteen. Grab your water bottles and a hat, and sun-screen—and use the bathroom. And I guess make sure you have your raincoats too. We need to be ready for anything!"

❦❧

Kennedy found a seat at a window overlooking the harbor and pulled the menu from its slot between the salt and pepper shakers. The Pilchard Café was about the only place open this early, but it was perfect for him, what with having to miss breakfast and needing a place to keep an eye on things. From where he sat he had a clear view from the fish and chip shop on his left across the bridge and a little way up the lane to the inn, and also straight across the water to the line of cottages and the house on the cliff. The only problem was how to hang out there as long as possible on his very limited budget. He scanned the menu and decided on the least expensive items: *toast and tea*. Hopefully he could spin those out for an hour or so and then decide what to do next.

The van pulled to a stop at the end of the narrow lane where a line of hawthorn hedges surrounded a little parking area. A small wooden sign pointed towards a narrow gap where a path evidently led up the hill beyond. Mom and the girls grabbed their jackets, a couple of water bottles and the backpack that Mom had packed with essentials back at the inn including some snacks, a notepad, first-aid kit, and Dad's binoculars. Rachel had remembered her sketchbook and she stuffed it in her drawstring bag. *For clues*, she said to herself. Mom carefully locked the doors and they headed over to the path. Rachel checked back down the lane several times, but to her relief no-one seemed to have followed them.

The beginning of the trail led through a cool and shady copse, but it wasn't long before it broke out into the open. The sun had lifted above the low line of clouds and the landscape was lit up around them—a rather sparse, treeless vista of stunted grass, patches of heather and clumps of vibrant yellow scotch broom, waving in the light breeze. In front of them the ground rose steeply up to the lofty point with its needle-like marker, the ocean beyond a deep blue-green speckled with white.

Mom took a deep breath. The scotch broom had a pleasant, citrusy smell, mixed with numerous other indefinable scents lifting from the landscape around them. She loved hiking and the current sensation of openness, the feel of a backpack on her back and the prospect of a challenging climb with a rewarding view felt delightful. It was a special treasure to share this with her daughters. It wasn't too often it was just her and them alone. She breathed a prayer of thanks for this special moment. *Another thing to write in her journal.*

They followed the path as it took the first of a long series of switch-backs up the face of the hill. "The first wiggle," said Rachel. "And what's this?" A small wooden sign in a patch of scotch broom pointed down a meandering track leading off to the right. She paused to examine it. "There's a picture of an acorn on this. What does it mean?"

"Oh, yes," said Mom, coming alongside. "There's something called the South-West Coast Path that leads all the way around Devon and Cornwall—over 600 miles. That must be the way."

Rachel gave a big sigh, and Mom looked at her, surprised. "What's up, dear?"

"Oh, I don't know. There's just so much to explore. I wish we could stay here longer."

Mom put her arm around her daughter. "I know—I feel the same way, and maybe sometime in your life you'll have the opportunity to do more exploring. You never know with God!" She gave Rachel a squeeze and they started up the trail again.

Emily followed, head down and thinking hard. *More time. Yes, she so wished they had more time.* Rachel had hit on something that had been lurking in the back of her mind again. She wished she could just pause at this moment in life—a time with all the family around her, the security of Mom and Dad taking care of her…

What would it be like, to have to go off on her own? It was only a few years and she'd be facing that, and right now it just seem too scary to contemplate.

She stumbled a little and glanced up. Mom and Rachel were getting further ahead. She picked up her pace and looked up again to the top of the hill. As she did, a verse popped into her head, and she realized it was one they had memorized as part of their home schooling Bible lesson. "*I lift up my eyes to the hills. Where does my help come from? My help comes from the Lord, the maker of heaven and earth.*" How funny. It seemed a perfect fit to her feelings right now. She gazed up at the marker on the hill. *Could it be that God had heard her secret thoughts and sent her this reminder that He would be there for her?* That was worth thinking through. She took a deep breath and ran to catch up with the others.

❧❦

Mrs. Renton wasn't feeling quite as brave as she had the night before.

"Alright, so just to make sure I understand, you and the boys are going to go up to the old house on the cliff. Your wife and the girls will try to figure out the clue on the hill. I'll go and sit by the harbor and keep an eye out for the man from the Mole Hole and the other man—that Mr. Kennedy person. We'll let each other know if we see him, and then you'll try to make it look as if you're searching for something."

"That's right," said Dad with a smile. "Hopefully that will distract and confuse him!"

"And what does he look like?"

"He's tall, and kind of mean and has a lot of grey hair," said Danny helpfully.

"Not like yours," added Stevie, "but really kind of wild and spiky and messed up all over the place."

"Oh my," said Mrs. Renton, putting her hand over her heart. "That would be hard to miss."

"And he drives a yellow sports car," put in Dad.

"Alright, a yellow sports car," said Mrs. Renton, making a mental note and hoping it didn't get misplaced.

"You've still got our numbers, right?" said Dad.

The old lady waved a piece of paper. "I'll have to call from the house though. I don't have one of those new-fangled cellphone whatsits, though I suppose now I wish I did."

"That's alright, just be careful. If you think he's approaching you, go back to the house."

"Alright," she nodded, feeling rather apprehensive again.

Dad had a sudden thought. "Say, when we first came to your house didn't you say you used to do a lot of bird-watching? Would you happen to have any binoculars? Kathie has my pair."

"Well, yes I do. Let me see…" She went over to the dresser and rummaged through its drawers and cupboards while the others looked on.

"Here they are!" she said finally, "in the last place I looked." She held up a cracked leather case.

"Great!" said Dad. "Those will help you." He looked over to the boys. "Okay, let's pray boys and we'll be off."

Praying again? thought Mrs. Renton. Well, it couldn't hurt she supposed, and if God truly was real, she could use all the help she could get.

The waitress at the *Pilchard Café* plunked the toast and tea in front of Kennedy and left in a hurry. She had already experienced a taste of his unpleasant demeanor and didn't want another dose. She wasn't getting paid enough to put up with customers like that. *Toast and tea, and now toast and tea again!*

Kennedy pawed through the selection of jams, finally settling on a little container of blackberry this time. He had been there for going on two hours and was getting fed up. By the time he was done he probably would have had to pay more for toast and tea than if he had just settled on some fried eggs and bacon in the first place. He checked out the window again as he spread the jam on his toast. There were a few fishermen moving about near the water's edge and a small boat throwing off its moorings by the pier. There had been no sign of anyone coming out of the lady's cottage. It had been about twenty minutes since he'd seen the Dad and two boys go inside. What were they up to in there? And where were the Mom and the girls? Had they taken the van somewhere? *Probably just out shopping or something*, he reassured himself. Mrs. Renton and the dad were definitely the bigger fish. If only that idiot Jennings hadn't thrown in the towel they could have covered all the possibilities.

Keeping a watch out the windows, he reached over for the pot of tea and then froze. There was someone coming out of the cottage—no, someones, he corrected himself. He stared transfixed. What a frustrating shame he was so far away. It was hard to tell but it looked like the dad had a big bag of some sort in his hand. He watched as they shut the gate and headed off with the boys up the road towards the old house on the cliff. *What were they doing and where were they going?*

Jennings leaned on the counter, staring morosely out across the harbor. He so desperately needed the money Kennedy was promising, but he just couldn't stand working with him anymore. Kennedy was manipulating him—using him—it was crystal clear now. He so regretted the day he agreed to deal with him, but he had been desperate then, too.

He drummed his fingers on the counter. And that family now--what were they up to? Why were they helping the old lady? *Too many questions and too few answers.*

The bench was slightly damp and Mrs. Renton wiped it off carefully with her hanky. It was still in shadow and the air rather chilly, and she congratulated herself on her decision to bring a thermos of tea. Taking a good sip, she set it down and dug in her purse for her binoculars. It took a while for her to adjust them, and with a wry smile she realized that the last time she had used them her eyesight was a lot better than it was now.

She took a careful look around the near side of the harbor, across the bridge and up to the White Whale pub. There were several fishermen moving about on the quay, but most of the boats seemed to still be out for the early-morning catch. The harbor entrance was empty—the only movement being the black and white flag on the pole at the point of the breakwater as it jumped about in the fitful breeze.

She took a quick sip of tea and then continued her survey on the far side. The fish and chip shop and the village hall almost blocked the view of the road as it climbed, but she could just see the Mole Hole up to the left. To her relief there was no sign of life at the broad front window.

The houses built up on the cliff directly over-looking the harbor blocked the rest of the view. Several were evidently holiday homes, but there was also a café comprised of several levels extending down the cliff. There were a number of figures seated at tables, and she adjusted the focus slightly to examine them. On the left was a young lady, looking like she was reading and eating at the same time. To her right was a man with grey hair, and as she looked he actually seemed to turn and stare right at her. She tried to steady her hand. *Could it be him? It definitely could be.* He was still staring. It had to be him.

❧❧

Kennedy was at a loss as to what to do. The dad and boys had gone up to the house on the cliff and had gone inside carrying a big sack of some kind and he had just decided he'd best go follow them when he'd had another surprise. The old lady had left her house and made her way to a seat halfway down the cliff path, though he couldn't make out what she was doing. And where were the female members of the family? He gnawed his fingernails in frustration.

If only Jennings was willing to help. Could he go and ask him to reconsider? Jennings probably wouldn't give him the time of day. There was apparently only one thing he could do, but it was so painful he didn't even want to consider it. *He could apologize to Jennings.* He could try to go humbly and say he was sorry and ask for help. The very idea galled him.

❧❧

Mrs. Renton paused to get her breath back before crossing the street to her cottage. She unlocked the door and let herself in, smiling as she saw her cat stalking sulkily into the kitchen. "I'm sorry, Pickwick," she called after him. "I'll take you next time."

She found the number and quickly dialed from the phone on the table by her armchair. It only took a second before Dad answered and she quickly filled him in.

❧❧

Dad snapped the phone shut and peered across to the café, but it was too far away to tell if anyone was seated at the windows.

He turned to the boys. "Mrs. Renton says that Mr. Kennedy is watching from across the harbor. Hopefully he's been wondering what we're up to. Let's start our little act."

Kennedy threw some money down on the table, grabbed his jacket and took one more quick look over to the house on the cliff. He froze. There they were! What the dickens were they up to now?

∽⌒∾

Dad and the boys were having fun. It was exciting knowing that Mr. Kennedy was most likely watching them. Danny had found an old spade lying in the bushes and had encouraged Dad to do some pretend digging. Stevie could barely stop himself snorting with laughter.

∽⌒∾

Kennedy was desperate now. Abandoning the café, he tore across the road to Jennings' shop and yanked open the door, causing the door sign to fall to the floor.

Jennings looked up annoyed from where he had been examining an old watch with a jeweler's magnifying glass. When he saw who it was his expression turned to dismay, but then his face suddenly hardened. He wasn't used to being firm but he was getting better at it with practice. He glared at Kennedy. "What do you want? I told you I don't want to be involved anymore."

Kennedy stared at him, breathing heavily. He was trying to calm down, but it wasn't easy. That family could be doing anything right now. He took a deep breath. He had to try to butter Jennings up. *First things first.* He bent down, picked up the sign and set it carefully back in place. "I'm sorry for bursting in on you. I'm in a bit of a hurry."

Jennings looked at him warily. This was Kennedy's conversation—let him carry it.

Kennedy tried his best to look contrite. If he'd had a hat, he would have held it in his hands. "Look, I know what you said yesterday, and you were right."

That was a shocker. Jennings raised his eyebrows in surprise.

"Neither of our hands are clean. That's why we need to work together. The family knows that we're both involved, so we have to be extra careful, but we can still do it. You know we need this. It can solve all our problems."

Jennings looked down, turning the magnifying glass over and over in his hands. It was true he needed this payoff if he was going to have any hope of saving his business.

"They're out there right now," continued Kennedy, gesturing behind him. "The old lady was out by the harbor and the dad and boys are back up at the house on the cliff, digging for something. I don't even know where the ladies are. It's too much for me to do by myself." This was a record for Kennedy. He'd never acted so humble for so long.

Jennings looked up again. He stared at Kennedy, trying to figure him out. *Could he even trust the guy at all? Did he really have a choice?*

"Okay," he said quietly after a long pause. "I'll help you. What do you need me to do?"

Exposed as they were at the top of the hill, there was nothing between them and the brisk wind sweeping in from the open ocean. It was exhilarating, and Emily thought she only had to spread her arms and she would soar up into the air like a seagull.

The view was truly breathtaking. From their lofty point they could see the whole of Penrithen laid out below them. It was easy to see now how the bulk of the village lay on the far side of the harbor, straggling the cliffs and extending up the folds of the landscape.

The top of the hill where they stood was formed by a flattened, grassy area, in the center of which towered a tall, white obelisk. The lower part was a large, wooden capstan—apparently a refugee from some old sailing ship—set at the top of some circular steps. A rusty, metal, coin-operated telescope stood in one corner of the hilltop, pointing expectantly out to sea.

There was a small plaque on one side of the obelisk and Rachel ran over and read it out loud. It explained that the capstan was from the sailing ship *Morningstar*, believed sunk by a Spanish vessel several miles down the coast in 1601. The ship had been transporting families who were fleeing from Holland, and was lost with all hands.

"How sad," said Emily. "The people never made it to safety."

"Why did they need to escape Holland?" wondered Rachel, reading the plaque again to herself. "And what's a capstan anyway?"

"I don't know," frowned Mom. "You'll have to ask Dad. Oh, hang on. I just got a text." She pulled out her phone, stared at it for a minute and then rapidly typed a message. "He wants to know how we're doing. I told him *nothing found yet.*"

"Anyway," continued Rachel. "We need to find the cross. Do you have the binoculars?"

Mom swung down the backpack and dug inside. "Here you go." She handed them over and Rachel scampered across to the edge of the gravel where there was a clear view down to the village.

"Can you see the church?" said Emily, hovering just behind Rachel and hoping for a look.

"Hang on, I'm just focusing." Rachel adjusted the view and after a moment's searching pinpointed the steeple. She looked carefully, and then lowered the binoculars in disappointment. "I don't see anything. There's no cross on the steeple, and I don't even see one in the graveyard."

"Can I see?" said Emily, not waiting for an answer and grabbing the binoculars out of Rachel's hand.

"May I see?" corrected Mom, who like Dad was always in grammar mode. "Go ahead and then I'll have a go."

Emily found the church and reluctantly had to agree with Rachel's assessment. There was no sign of a cross. What were they going to do now? She held the binoculars back behind her for Mom, but nothing happened. Turning, Emily saw that her mother was standing looking at the obelisk, a puzzled expression on her face.

"Mom, do you want a go?"

"Hmmm? Oh, thanks but just a sec. I'm thinking. This doesn't make sense. I mean, how can we line up a point from here if we don't know exactly where to look from?"

"I don't understand," said Rachel. "Aren't we supposed to stand up here and look for a cross?"

"Yes, but don't you see? We have to know exactly where to stand. If we're lining something up, we need to be in the right position, or things won't line up correctly."

The girls processed that for a moment. It did sort of make sense.

"So what do we do?" said Emily. "Is there anything else in the clue to help?"

"That's a good question," said Mom. She shuffled around in the front pocket of the backpack for a few seconds, and produced a folded scrap of paper. She smoothed it out. "Okay, here—I'll read it to you. '*A winding way to lofty height, Some change will help increase your sight. St. Piran's cross lines up with where the trail will head up hidden stair.* What do you think? Is there anything there to help?"

Emily and Rachel both crowded in so they could read it themselves. There had to be something.

Dad set the shovel down and turned to the boys. "Hopefully Mr. Kennedy's been really wondering what we're up to. I think our plan is working."

Danny and Stevie smiled at each other in satisfaction.

"And for our next little act," said Dad. He pulled a pen and paper from his pocket.

"Something else to really make him confused?" said Stevie. "This is fun!"

"Okay, we've gone up the winding way to the lofty height," said Rachel. "What's next?"

"*Some change will help increase your sight,*" said Emily. "We thought that meant that we needed the change from being down in the village to be able to see, didn't we?"

"Yes, but now I don't know," frowned Mom.

"Why?" said Rachel. "What are you thinking?"

Mom shrugged her shoulders. "I'm not really sure, but I'm thinking that in the other clues each line is important. Why did the Squire put this one in? It wasn't necessary if all he wanted us to do was go up the top of the hill."

"So you think this might explain something about how we line up the cross?" said Rachel, a bit confused. "I don't see anything in it to help."

"I know—I don't see anything obvious. Can there be a hidden meaning?"

They puzzled over it for a couple of minutes, but no-one had any inspiration.

"I tell you what," said Mom finally. "Let's go about this a different way. If we need to be standing somewhere specific, how would we know where? There would have to be a marker or something."

"Like the pillar thing?" said Rachel, excited. "Like if we stood with our back to it?" She ran over, jumped up on the first step and looked around. Then her face fell. "But that still doesn't make sense. I can't see over the edge of the hill from here, unless I got up high."

Mom and Emily came over and looked. Even Mom couldn't see the village.

"Mrs. Renton's shorter than me," said Emily. "And wouldn't you have to know exactly how high to be if you needed to line up with the cross? We don't even know which step to stand on."

"Right," said Mom. "Good thinking. So it can't mean the pillar." She looked around for a moment, and then a slow smile spread over her face. "You know what girls? I think I've got it!"

"What, what?" they exclaimed together.

"Come with me." She led the way over to the telescope and rested her hand on the top. "How about this? You have to stand here to use it, and everyone has to be at the same height."

The girls looked at each other in delight. *That must be it!*

"Go ahead and look, Mom," said Emily. Rachel nodded eagerly.

Mom smiled, and with some effort pivoted the heavy telescope around so it was pointing at the village. She bent down and peered through the eyepiece, only to stand up again, puzzled. "I can't see anything. Oh, wait a minute." She examined the large metal base and found what she was looking for.

"See this? It takes a coin to operate it. Ten pence. Do any of you have any change?"

Rachel started to dig in her pockets, but stopped as Emily grabbed Mom's arm. "Change!" she squealed. "Change! Don't you get it? *Some change will help increase your sight.* The telescope increases our sight, but it needs change to work it."

"Wow," said Rachel impressed, wishing she had thought of it herself.

"That's my clever girl," praised Mom, giving Emily a pat on the shoulder. "That clinches it. This is where we're supposed to look."

"So who's got change?" said Rachel, digging again in her pocket which was a little hard to do as she was bouncing up and down in excitement.

"I don't," said Emily. She looked at Mom expectantly. "You've got to have some Mom, don't you? Dad says you always carry something for every emergency."

"He does, does he?" said Mom with a grin. She unzipped the pocket of the backpack again and pulled out a little coin purse. Unsnapping it she reached in and pulled out a shiny ten pence piece. She held it up and winked at the girls, then pushed it in the coin slot and turned the knob. There was a satisfying clink as the coin dropped home and Mom bent down to look through.

"Do you see anything?" said Rachel, crowding close.

"Hang on," said Mom. "I just started." She slowly rotated the scope, tilting it slightly up and down until she had made a pass across the whole village to the fields beyond. Then she slowly retraced her path, frowning hard. The girls watched with baited breath.

Mom was just about to straighten up in disappointment when she saw something that made her pause. She peered at it hard, and then looked at the girls with a frown.

"What is it?" said Emily. "Do you see something?"

"Come and look," beckoned Mom, standing up straight. "What do you think?"

Emily was almost exactly the right height to look through the eyepiece. It took her a second to focus, and what she saw puzzled her. She turned to her Mom. "A flag?"

"Can I see?" said Rachel, hopping from one foot to the other in her eagerness. Emily graciously stepped aside and Rachel stood on tiptoe to look. She had to close one eye, but after a moment she was able to see clearly. In the center of the view piece was the flag they had seen down at the harbor, flying on its pole at the end of the breakwater.

"The flag?" she said, puzzled. Then her eyes widened in understanding. "Ohhh, it's got a cross—a white cross on a black background. Do you think that's it?"

"I don't know," said Mom. "It's the Cornish flag, but the clue says we need Saint Piran's cross, and Saint Piran's is the name of the church."

"Call Dad," said Emily. "He might know."

"Ok, I will." Mom speed-dialed Dad on her phone. It seemed like it had only barely begun to ring when he answered.

"Hi dear, it's me," said Mom, pushing her hair out of her eyes. She turned away from the wind. "I've got a quick question. Uh-huh. We can't see an actual cross anywhere from up here, but we did see the cross on the flag in the harbor. It's the white cross on the black background. Yes. Oh, so it is definitely the Cornish flag. Could it be the cross of Saint Piran on it? He was the patron saint of Cornwall, right?" She paused for a moment to listen.

Rachel and Emily smiled at each other. It looked like they were getting somewhere!

"Oh, wonderful! Thanks. Love you!"

She ended the call and the girls looked at her expectantly. She gave a huge smile. "Dad said it's St. Piran's cross, sure enough. Now to find the hidden stair!"

"Oh, really?" said Dad into his phone. "Where do you see him? Okay, we'll be careful!"

He listened for a moment, and then nodded. "Okay, that's great! Thank you so much. I'll call you as soon as I can. Bye-bye."

He shut his phone and turned to the boys. "Okay, we don't have much time. Mrs. Renton was looking out her window and saw Mr. Kennedy coming down the hill and heading towards the bridge. He might be coming this way."

The boys' eyes widened. "What do we do?" said Danny with a sudden stab of fear.

"Don't worry", reassured Dad. "We're going to confuse him so we can buy the girls some time. I'm going to put this paper in the house." He waved the sheet he had been writing on a few minutes earlier. "You boys go to the back of the garden. I'll be right there."

He ran off up to the front door, trying to keep as low as possible. Danny looked at Stevie. He swallowed a lump in his throat and grabbed his little brother's hand. "Come on—we need to do what Dad said."

He pulled Stevie with him to the far side of the garden, close to where it met the face of the cliff. They had barely reached it when Dad burst out of the back door, causing them both to jump in surprise.

"Quick boys, over the wall." He helped them over and then swung over himself.

"What are we going to do, Daddy?" said Danny anxiously.

"Follow me." Dad led them at a run over to the stone steps leading to the cove and bounded up. He paused to let the boys catch up. "Okay, we're just going over the top here to hide. I'm pretty sure that Mr. Kennedy is going to check out the house. As soon as he goes in, we'll make it back down to Mrs. Renton's. Okay?"

The boys nodded, their hearts beating fast. *Talk about an adventure!*

❧☙

Mrs. Renton peered carefully through the side of the window sheers, watching the road in front of her house. It was only a moment before she saw Mr. Kennedy walking quickly past. As he got level with her house he looked her way and she instinctively ducked back. She held her breath. Would he come up to the door?

She waited for what seemed an age, her heart pounding. When she couldn't stand it anymore she carefully checked through the sheers again. There was no sign of him. Keeping well back from the window she moved to where she could see the path up to her door. To her immense relief it was empty.

❧☙

Kennedy paused at the end of the line of cottages and took a quick survey of his surroundings. Where had the dad and boys got to? He didn't want to run into them, but he desperately needed to check out what they had been doing at the house. Had Jennings been keeping an eye on things? He had promised he would, with one of those old telescopes he had in the front window display. It was apparently the maximum effort he was willing to give, and Kennedy had had to accept it.

As if in answer to his question, his phone gave a low tone and vibrated in his pocket. He snatched it out and checked out the screen. It was hard to see in the light, but it looked like he'd received a text. He hit a button and scanned the message.

'*All gone over steps to cove.*' Aha. That was what he needed to know. At least for this moment, the coast was clear.

Mom adjusted the telescope's position slightly and then held still and stared, producing several oohs and ahhs that made the girls fidget with excitement.

Rachel grabbed at Mom's sleeve. "What do you see? Can you see something?"

Mom straightened up, smiling broadly. "Praise God, I think we've found it! Go ahead Emily. Look just above the top of the flag. Don't say anything, though. Let Rachel have a turn and then we can talk."

Emily stepped up, stared through the lens for a minute and then nodded her head. She turned to Rachel and beckoned her forward. Rachel stood on tiptoe again and focused in on the top of the flag. Then she looked beyond it to where the cliff face rose steeply above the harbor. Right in a line with the flag pole could just be seen a sort of narrow cleft in the cliff, with what might be a section of rough-hewn steps leading up and around a projecting point. Rachel moved the telescope slightly to the left. Beyond the point she could just make out the top of what may have been a small tower, encircled by windows.

"It's right there, isn't it? Almost at the end of the cliff above the harbor," said Mom, pointing. "Do you see? The clue doesn't say anything else about a place to go to—just the hidden stair—but I wouldn't be surprised if we have to get to that place with the tower."

"How can we get to it?" said Emily. "Do we go along the harbor side?"

"I'm pretty sure," said Rachel, staring hard. "We would go along the quay and the staircase must start somewhere along the cliff. Do you remember we took a staircase the first day we were here?"

"Right," said Emily, "but I don't remember going that far near the edge of the cliff. We went straight up and there weren't any turns."

"But there was another path, leading out along the cliff," said Rachel excitedly. "I just remembered it. Mommy, can we go and check it out?"

"Yes, I think we're done here. Good job everyone!" Mom hoisted the backpack onto her shoulder. "I'll just text Dad the good news and we'll be off."

Dad watched carefully until he saw Kennedy appear from the end of the cottages, then snatched his head back out of sight. The boys looked at him wide-eyed and he put his finger to his lips.

His phone vibrated in his pocket and he quickly pulled it out and checked the display. "Mom texted," he whispered. "They've found the hidden stair!"

The boys nodded and exchanged grins of delight

Dad waited a minute or so and then ever so slowly inched his head upwards and sideways until one eye could see over the rocks. He let out a sigh of relief. Kennedy was no-where in sight, so he must have gone into the house. This wasn't a moment to waver in indecision. "Quick boys," he said, grasping Stevie's hand. "Let's go."

Almost dragging Stevie up and over the rocky ridge he led the way back down the short flight of steps to the parking area, Danny close behind.

"Keep going—to Mrs. Renton's house." Dad set a pace that the others could keep up with and the three of them quickly made their way back down the road.

❧❧

They were all gathered around Mrs. Renton's kitchen table, munching slices of Victoria sandwich cake while Mom and the girls shared the details of their trip up the hill. Then Dad related their own adventure, punctuated by enthusiastic comments from Stevie and Danny.

"So what was on the note you left in the house?" wondered Rachel, setting her empty plate down on the table and reaching for her teacup.

"I made up a clue for Mr. Kennedy to follow," grinned Dad. "It wasn't the best rhyme in the world, but it was all I could do on the spur of the moment. Hopefully it will get him out of the way for a bit. If he takes the bait, he'll be spending some time in the cave down in the cove."

The others were impressed. "So what do we do now?" wondered Danny. "Can we go and look for the hidden staircase?"

"Yes, we should do that right away," said Dad, "while Mr. Kennedy is indisposed."

"But we mustn't forget the Mole Hole man," Mom reminded them. "He might be watching for us."

"How can we get over there without being seen?" asked Emily, concerned.

"If we could get to the top of that path we took up from the harbor—you know, the one that brought us out across from the bakery—then we could go down that path and then take the other one we saw that goes along the cliff," said Dad.

"But we would have to go right past the Mole Hole to get to it," frowned Mom.

Mrs. Renton cleared her throat and they all looked over at her. She gave an embarrassed smile. "I just had an idea. There's another car park up on the cliffs behind the village, on the far side of the harbor. If we drive out past the inn where you're staying, there's a narrow road leading off to the left that circles around the back side of the village and we can get to the car park without being seen. Then we should be able to go down the hill to that path without passing the Mole Hole."

"That's it," said Dad. "That's perfect!"

The others all nodded their approval. Mrs. Renton was so pleased to have been a help that she actually blushed. Mom gave her a hug.

Danny had been thinking hard and put up his hand. "Excuse me, but what if the Mole Hole man sees us, or Mr. Kennedy comes back from the cove? Shouldn't we split up again? That way they wouldn't know who to follow?"

Dad looked at Danny thoughtfully. "That's not a bad idea. What would be best?"

Mrs. Renton set her cup down. "I'm not sure I'm the one to be going up and down secret stairs. How about if I go down the hill past the man's shop. I'll make sure he sees me. Then I'll find somewhere to wait near the memorial. Hopefully that will get him confused and keep his attention off of you."

"That's a great idea. I'll go with you," said Mom. "I've had an adventure already this morning. Anyone else willing to come?"

"I'll go," said Emily after a moment's reflection. She was really trying to listen to the still, small voice of the Holy Spirit, and it seemed that He wanted her to be an encouragement to Mrs. Renton. It wasn't easy though. She definitely didn't want to miss out on any of the mystery. "Will you come get us though as soon as you find something?"

"Of course," said Dad. "I really appreciate your willingness to go sweetheart. It's a really important part of the process. We have to keep those guys confused."

Chapter 22 – The Hidden House

Kennedy snatched up the note lying near the secret panel and scanned it quickly. He gave a cry of triumph. It was amazingly careless of the family, but a veritable coup for him—the next clue--in his very hands! He read it slowly.

'Back to the cove and through the cave. Do not fear but go be brave.
A hidden hole behind a rock. And there the clue you will unlock.'

So it was back to the cove again, was it? He wasn't too happy about that. The dad and boys had gone down there. The cove only had one way in and out, and felt like a trap. Was there any better way? He couldn't think of anything. Following the clue was his only hope.

He sighed. Though it seemed pretty reckless, he would just have to go down there and be as careful as possible.

❧❧

The cliff-top car park was a large, graveled area bordered by stunted grass, a few random benches and a number of garbage cans. Beyond spread an impressive panoramic view of the ocean with a backdrop of somber grey clouds.

As Dad pulled the van to a stop Danny gave a sudden cry, pointing out the window in alarm. "Look, over there! Isn't that the man's car?"

Sure enough the yellow sports car was parked slightly askew in the corner of the lot.

"Well," said Dad after a moment. "I guess that's not a surprise. He's in the village and had to park somewhere, just like us. Let's go ahead and keep on with our plan."

"But we'll keep our eyes open," added Danny anxiously. "Just in case, right?"

There was a sudden burst of activity, and soon everyone was bundled up in jackets and hoods and waiting for orders. Mom managed to stuff the already bulging backpack with some extra items she thought might prove useful including some biscuits from Mrs. Renton and several water bottles, knowing from experience that someone was going to be hungry in the not-too-distant future.

Dad carefully led the way, scanning ahead as the road curved down the hill towards the harbor. Emily and Mom stayed close to Mrs. Renton, making sure she was doing okay. The other kids kept their eyes peeled for the men, with a mixture of anxiety and excitement. They passed the Penrithen Grocery on their left, and the café and a couple of holiday homes on their right with snatches of the view of the harbor between them.

Dad slowed down suddenly and raised a warning hand. "Okay, everyone. We're getting close to the Mole Hole. The alley to the stairway is right here, so this is where we split up."

"Can we quickly pray?" suggested Mom. "We definitely need God's help."

"Great idea," said Dad. "Gather in close everyone. That's right. Okay." He closed his eyes. "Dear Heavenly Father, thank you that you've brought us this far. Please keep leading us and helping us. Protect us from evil and please confuse the guys who are trying to steal the inheritance. May Your will be done. In Christ's name, Amen."

"Amen," said everyone, even Mrs. Renton.

"So where do you think you'll be?" said Dad, looking at Mom.

"I've been thinking it over and I guess we'll start at the memorial. We can appear to be looking for something and then move on and hang out somewhere else interesting—at least interesting for our audience—to keep them guessing." Mom gave a smirk.

"That sounds great. We'll see you in a bit. I'll text you how we're doing."

"Okay, dear. We'll keep in touch." Mom put her arm through the old lady's. "Are you ready?"

Mrs. Renton nodded in reply, a look of determination on her face. She grabbed Emily's arm as well. "Alright girls. Let us go and be the best decoys we can be!

⚬⚭⚬

Kennedy was both surprised and perplexed. Jennings hadn't texted him again, yet there was no sign of the dad and his boys in the cove or, it seemed, in the cave. He had entered the disagreeable, smelly place as far as he dared, listening carefully and trying not to inhale too deeply. Apart from the muffled roar of the distant surf, the place was quiet as a tomb. Had he beat them to it, or had they been and gone? He pondered that for a moment. Surely there hadn't been time for them to come down here, solve the clue and make it back up and out without him seeing them.

The moist sand sucked at his shoes and he put a hand against the cave wall to steady himself, hurriedly snatching it away again as he touched something squishy and cold. He shuddered and tried to focus back on his task. The clue had mentioned a hidden hole behind a rock, but that could almost be anywhere. The dim light made it almost impossible to find any holes. He took several careful steps forward, but then paused and frowned. *What was that sound?*

He had only a second of wild, panicked realization before a splashing, sweeping mass of water tore around the bend and soaked him to his knees. He stumbled backwards, tried to steady himself again and suddenly found himself on his back with cold seawater swirling around and over him. He gasped and clambered back to his feet as the water disappeared back around the corner, leaving him drenched, dripping and mad as a hornet.

He gave full vent to his feelings with a string of profanity as he stumbled back out of the cave. Several sharp gusts of wind knifed right through his shivering body

That did it. There was no way he was going back in that cave like this. With a sudden fierce determination he sprinted off across the sand towards the staircase. He needed to get a hot drink and a change of clothes before he died of hypothermia. Then, and only then, he'd figure out what to do next.

✺✺✺

Jennings had completely forgotten about Kennedy. A van had just left a delivery, and Jennings knelt down, slit the box open with his pocket knife and folded back the flaps. He shook his head in frustration. This particular supplier was getting worse and worse at getting things out in a reasonable time. He'd have to give them a call, worst luck. He hated confrontations and he'd had too many of those lately.

He dug through the peanut packing and extracted a large, ornately-bound book, accented in gold. He sniffed it and nodded in approval. Hopefully the buyer he'd got lined up would be happy. He could use some more satisfied customers. He turned to set the book on the counter, but suddenly froze. Someone…no, several someones had passed by the window, and out of the corner of his eye he thought he had recognized them.

He dropped the book and leaped to his feet. Hurrying to the door, he yanked it open, causing the bell to jingle frantically in alarm. A quick glance showed him what he needed to see. It was the old lady flanked by what looked like the mother and the oldest girl. As he watched they stopped outside the newsagents, and he jumped back out of sight. Were they going to turn around?

He carefully leaned forward until he could just see around the doorframe. They were huddled together, evidently talking about something. The mom patted the old lady on the arm, and then gestured over towards the harbor. Jennings glanced that way, too. *What were they looking at?* He looked back at the group. Now the girl was pointing too—a sweeping gesture that took in the whole harbor. She turned back to the others and starting jumping and gesturing excitedly. Jennings stared as the group huddled together again, looking like they were discussing something important.

Jennings tried to think. Were they on the trail of another clue, or just doing something innocuous? He had no idea. *What a fiasco.* He suddenly remembered Kennedy. He'd better call him. For better or for worse, that's what he'd promised to do. He dug out his phone while watching the group.

But what was up with the call? It had connected and was ringing, but there was no answer. He let it ring until the service gave up and dropped the call. Then he shrugged his shoulders. He had done his part. If Kennedy didn't answer his phone, that was his own fault. He had a business to run. He turned into the shop and went back to his package.

❦

Dad and the kids had cautiously descended the rocky staircase and then turned and taken the uneven path that led out along the cliff. Here and there the rock surface glistened where water seeped out from above, and the family had to step carefully despite their hurry. Rachel was almost beside herself with excitement. The trek along this secret path was so exactly like the plot of one of her favorite adventure stories that she almost wanted to pinch herself to make sure it was real. Dad had to keep on reminding her to watch her steps.

"We're getting close to where that hidden staircase must lead up," she announced, and Dad was just about to respond when Stevie, deciding to dash on ahead to see, tripped and fell sprawling on the path. There was a couple of seconds of silence and then Stevie broke out into anguished cries. The family gathered anxiously around.

With a little coaxing, Stevie allowed himself to be examined amidst his tears, displaying a scraped knee and a scraped shin. The sight of blood caused the lad to break out again into loud cries. Dad wasn't the greatest at dealing with medical emergencies. He tried to shush the boy and racked his brain what to do. What he really needed was some antibiotic cream and a Band-Aid, but here he was without so much as a tissue, and his wife with her bottomless bag of supplies too far away to help.

Rachel grasped the situation and leaned over to whisper in his ear. "Let's pray for Stevie. Maybe that would help."

Dad nodded. That was something they could do.

❦

Kennedy squished up and over the ridge of rock and down the few steps to the parking area, leaving a trail of wet footprints. A seagull, perched on the chimney of the end cottage, eyed him warily and then launched into the air, crying in annoyance at this intrusion.

Kennedy stopped, glared at the bird and tried to shake some excess water from his trousers. What a miserably uncomfortable feeling. He felt like just grabbing his car and driving off somewhere—anywhere—where he could do something less risky than this ridiculous quest. He looked across the harbor, thinking of Jennings, safe in his warm shop, probably sipping a cup of tea or something. There was no doubt about it—he had to put the screws on Jennings somehow. This thing was slipping from his grasp—almost like fate had made up its mind to oppose him at every step.

His fatalistic thoughts were interrupted by a faint yelling coming across the narrow harbor. He searched for the source of the noise and located a small group of persons on a barely discernible path halfway along the cliff. He rubbed his eyes and stared hard.

353

Glory be, it was the family—it had to be. He counted the dad, a girl and two boys—and yes, even from here he could definitely tell that the bigger boy had red hair. The littlest boy seemed to be sitting down. It was apparently he who had been doing the yelling. *Aha—it looked like he had hurt himself.* But why were they going along that cliff path? And where were the others?

Abandoning his despondency, Kennedy made a snap decision. He needed to get over there and follow them. *Could he catch up? Did he have time?* It was a long way around the harbor, and they could spot him at any moment. Well, maybe the curve of the cliff might partially shield him from their view, but they could see him if they looked his way. *No matter what, he had to do it.* This wasn't the time for pondering worst-case scenarios.

With a sense of desperation, he launched into a squelching sprint down the lane.

✂︎❧

With a strong reluctance, Jennings tried calling Kennedy again and this time was rewarded with an answer. The voice at the other end seemed to be struggling for air, and mad as all get out. "Yes…what is it?" Kennedy managed to growl in-between gasps.

"I saw the mother and the old lady and one of the girls. They went past my shop and down to the monument. They were looking around and discussing things."

Kennedy switched hands as he reached the stairway down to the harbor—the one Mrs. Renton had taken earlier. He paused for a second and scanned the cliff path across the way, his chest heaving. It looked like the little group were all still there.

"Okay, so keep an eye on them. I'm following the others."

"But I can't keep an eye on them—I need to watch my…"

Kennedy didn't wait to hear any more but snapped his phone shut and started down the steps. Jennings just stood there, staring at his phone. This was turning into an absolute nightmare. He had no control over his own life anymore. He ran his hand through his hair. *What on earth could he do?*

He jumped as the bell on the door rang suddenly. Looking up, he froze in recognition. It was the owner of the coffee shop. Apparently, the man recognized him too. There was an awkward pause. The man finally extended his hand. Jennings took it gingerly and received a firm handshake in return.

"Hello there, I think we've met before. My name's Geoff—Geoff Ketchum—from the coffee shop."

Jennings had trouble meeting the other man's eyes. "Anthony Jennings," he mumbled wishing he was somewhere—anywhere—else.

Geoff sized him up for a moment, and then came to a sudden decision.

"Mr. Jennings. I know this seems a bit forward, but I think you've got something on your mind."

Jennings didn't move, but inside he felt a rush of alarm. *What did this guy know?*

"I know a bit about what's going on--about the inheritance." The man now had a steely edge to his voice.

Now Jennings had a real reason to feel alarmed. *This was the end. It was prison for certain.*

Even though he couldn't see the man's face, Geoff could sense the emotions he was struggling with. He tried to soften his voice somewhat. "I think you're struggling with what to do—with what's right and what's wrong."

Jennings still wouldn't look up. *Why was this chap toying with him like this?*

Geoff reached into his pocket and put a business card down on the counter. "Mr. Jennings. If you need to talk, anytime, just call me. Seriously. I want to help." He put a hand on Jennings' shoulder. Jennings stiffened, but didn't move away.

"I'm going now," said Geoff, turning for the door. "I'll come back on a better day. I'm looking for some things for the coffee shop, but they can wait." He opened the door and paused for a second. "I mean it. Give me a call." With that he was gone.

Jennings couldn't move. He just stood there, looking down at the card in front of him.

๛

"Do you think you can make it?" Dad looked anxiously at Stevie, whose cries had settled down to an occasional sniff. The boy nodded somewhat reluctantly.

"Thanks, Rachel," said Dad with a grateful look. It had been she who had found an unused tissue in her pocket and suggested bathing the cut in water from one of their bottles.

"Can you walk?" said Danny, anxious to get going again.

Stevie nodded again and Dad set him back on his feet.

"Go ahead and lead the way again Rachel, but let's go easy—we don't want any more tumbles." Dad had a sudden, anxious thought and scanned the harbor. He had forgotten about Kennedy. There was no sign of him as far as he could see, but that could change any moment. "Let's be careful, but we mustn't dally. We don't want to be seen."

Rachel nodded. "Okay, follow me." She started off again down the path and it wasn't long before she paused and looked back with a triumphant grin. "This is about where we saw the stairway through the telescope—at least we saw part of it. Come and see."

The others made their way up to where she was standing. The path widened there slightly at a scoop in the cliff. A large boulder partially blocked the way with several stunted bushes grouped behind it.

Rachel pointed to a cleft in the cliff that reached up from the boulder. "That must be where the stairway goes. Let's have a look." She fearlessly pushed aside the bushes and gave a cry of joy. "Look, right here—the stairway!"

Sure enough a narrow way led behind the boulder and into the cleft where a series of worn, even steps had been carved in the rock.

"Great job!" praised Dad.

Danny and Stevie got a thrill of excitement. *This really was a hidden way!* It must have been used by pirates or smugglers or something.

Rachel started up the stairs, the others close behind, Dad with a quick check over his shoulder. *Still no sign of Mr. Kennedy.*

355

The way twisted and turned a little, following the line of the cleft. At one point Rachel paused and looked behind. "Do you see here? The steps must be visible here from the top of the headland where we were this morning. Look, you can see the marker on the hill."

The others crowded up and checked out the view, but Rachel was already off again. Her excited voice soon came down. "I'm here, and there's a house. Come on!"

Dad and the boys hurried up, Dad holding on to Stevie's hand and helping over some of the uneven places. The steps took one last turn and the passage widened out to a large shelf of rock, sheltered from the stiff ocean breeze by a border of windblown bushes. Straight ahead was a slate wall with an arched wrought-iron gate. A small sign was attached to the gate and Rachel was studying what it said.

"This place is called the Lonsdale house," she announced over her shoulder. "We can go into the garden during daylight hours, but the house is currently closed."

Dad tried the gate and it opened easily. It led to a broad paved patio, its rocky walls almost obscured by a profusion of plants including several exotic fan palms swaying almost imperceptibly in the light snatches of breeze that managed to sneak their way in. As they stared, the sun suddenly broke through the clouds and lit up the house—a large, white-washed, two-story dwelling with cheerful blue trim and an attractive sunroom overlooking the patio. At the far side another gate apparently led back to the cliffs, and above it loomed a square tower, its peaked top story having windows on all four sides.

It must have a magnificent view, thought Rachel. *A great place to sit and read and watch a storm.*

Several seagulls perched along the peak of the roof seemed to have the same idea, staring out to sea where once again a bank of dark clouds was forming.

"What a lovely house," exclaimed Rachel, summing up what they were all thinking.

"I want to live here," announced Stevie, decidedly. "I think it's an old pirate house with a tower so they could watch the ships go by."

Danny nodded, thinking hard. It looked great to him too—full of mystery. "Or maybe a smuggler's house," he added. "It's probably got a secret tunnel down to the sea, kind of like the other house but with a secret staircase they could all sneak down."

Dad chuckled. "You guys have great imaginations. It is a lovely spot though, I must agree. Even though it's got a great view, it's really sheltered here on the patio. It looks like someone's been taking good care of the place too."

"It's beautiful," said Rachel, spinning round with her arms outstretched.

"Are you going to burst into song?" said Dad, amused at her antics.

She slowed down and stopped, allowing herself a moment to get back her balance. "I almost forgot, we're looking for a clue." She ran over to the sunroom and peeked inside, then took a closer look at something by the door. "Did you see over here, Daddy," she called. "There's a plaque on the wall right here—and another one by the front door."

They all crowded over. Dad read the first one out loud. *The Lonsdale House. Home of the Lonsdale Family from 1551 – 1732."*

Rachel pointed to the one by the door and read it out loud as well. "*In memory of William Lonsdale, 1542 – 1601. He gave his life so that others would have a chance of freedom."*

"Wow!" said Danny. "I bet the clue's about him. What's it say again?"

Dad pulled out the piece of paper on which Mrs. Renton had written out the clue in her careful, flowing script. *"His life was one that finished well, again the book a tale will tell. The signs reveal the way when you will put together two and two,"* he quoted.

"The book!" exclaimed Rachel. "I bet that's the Squire's history book! Do we have it?"

Dad displayed his empty hands. "Sorry, I didn't think we'd need it. It's back at the Inn."

The others looked at each other in alarm and disappointment.

"So we won't know how he finished well," said Rachel, dejectedly.

"We can later on, but let's at least try to figure out what we can right now," said Dad, trying to make the best of things. He had a sudden idea. "So what would Sherlock Holmes do? We can't just give up. We need to have something to tell the others."

Danny grabbed a hold of that thought at once. It was a chance again to be a detective. "He would look all around and check out everything."

"Okay," said Dad. "Let's do that. Remember the clue says we have to put two and two together. That means there might be a puzzle to solve."

"What sort of puzzle?" said Stevie, peering into one of the many large stone plant pots as if the answer might be found in the earthy depths.

"I know," said Rachel suddenly. "You said something about signs, right?"

"That's right," said Dad. "The signs reveal the way."

"So somewhere around here must be some signs that point to where we are to go next."

"I hope it's up in that tower," said Stevie looking up at it rather wistfully.

"Well, maybe," said Dad. "Let's split up and look carefully."

They each took a corner of the patio and started a careful examination. Rachel rattled the other iron gate but it was padlocked shut. Danny looked into the sunroom. It had several comfortable-looking armchairs, quite a few potted plants and an empty book shelf. "I wonder who lives here," he said out loud. "The plants look good—someone must water them—but there aren't any books or stuff."

"Maybe it's a holiday home," said Dad. "You know, a rental or someplace where the family only lives during the summer."

"Do you think it belonged to the Squire's family?" wondered Rachel over her shoulder, from where she had been examining the cracks in the stone wall.

"I think so," said Danny. "Otherwise he wouldn't have put it in the clue to come here."

"Good point," said Dad, nodding. "So let's keep looking."

⊷⊶

Kennedy paused and listened carefully. The rattling of some rigging, a few gulls crying in the distance and the lap of water against the pilings—there was nothing out of the ordinary. He had jogged along the cliff path to the point where he had seen the family stop and from there on had continued much more cautiously. The wind was a bit fresher up here and he shivered in his dripping clothes. It was too cold just standing there—he had to keep moving.

With one hand on the rocky wall, he stepped carefully forward, his ears cocked to any sound of the family. Coming to where the path widened slightly he stopped again. Did he hear something? He strained to listen. There it was again from somewhere above—the faint sound of voices. He looked around. There was a cleft in the rock at this point. Could there be a way up through there? He frowned and started a careful examination around the boulder, pushing aside the bushes. *Aha. There it was—a hidden stairway.* Now he was getting somewhere. With a quick glance behind him to make sure no-one was watching, he thrust his way through the branches and crept stealthily upwards.

⊷⊶

"Shhh", warned Dad, causing Danny to abruptly halt his celebration. The lad had experienced a sudden inspiration, calling out to the others in his excitement. Dad put his hand on the boy's shoulder. "I'm glad you figured something out, but we need to be careful—just in case."

The boys looked around in alarm. Dad smiled. "I think we're okay. Tell us what you're thinking."

Danny took a deep breath and pointed to the plaque by the front door. "Do you see that? There's some funny raised bits of metal around the words. Kind of like bits of a frame that isn't all there."

The others looked at where he was pointing. Rachel made a skeptical noise, but Dad silenced it with a frown. "Go on Danny. What do you mean? Couldn't it just be that bits have been worn away?"

"I think it just wasn't made very well," said Rachel.

Danny was getting frustrated. "No, but don't you see? Look over on the other one." He pointed to the second plaque by the patio door. "See how it's got the same sort of thing—but not quite the same. The clue said the signs will reveal the way. These are two signs and maybe—well, I thought that maybe there's a sort of code here."

Dad furrowed his brow. "Hmm. You might have something. I didn't think about the signs being actual, physical signs—I was thinking of something a bit less obvious."

Rachel was quiet, a bit ashamed at her reaction to Danny's discovery. She looked at the weird marks on the signs. They were like little raised lines and curves, seemingly randomly distributed across the surfaces. "Danny may be right," she said finally. "Do you think they're in a sort of language or something like Morse code?"

"Not Morse code," said Dad, looking closer. "Those would be dots and dashes. These are much more uneven."

Stevie traced the lines on the plaque by the patio door. He wished he could come up with a suggestion himself, but he had no idea—no idea at all.

Mom, Emily and Mrs. Renton were now on the harbor slipway. The tide was heading out, leaving a number of stranded fishing boats leaning forlornly at odd angles. Emily was feeling a little forlorn herself, wishing now she could have been with the others.

"How about going over to those sheds?" suggested Mrs. Renton, pointing across the bridge to a line of low buildings at the edge of the little harbor. "I think they used to be what they called fish cellars—for storing the day's catch. We could be seen quite easily."

"We could look in the windows and act like we see something," said Emily, warming to the idea. Perhaps this could be more interesting than she had thought. She looked carefully over her shoulder.

"Do you see anyone?" said Mom without turning.

"There's a couple of people over by the memorial, but they don't look too suspicious."

"Where's that Mr. Kennedy?" said Mrs. Renton. "Do you think he's finished down in the cove?"

"I hope not," said Emily, looking anxiously in that direction.

"He may be soon though," said Mom. "And it's important that he sees us down here. Come on."

She led the way along the edge of the sand and up a few steps onto the low concrete path that bordered the harbor. Emily helped Mrs. Renton up and held her hand as they made their way over to the line of sheds. The fishy, harbor smell was even stronger here and Emily wrinkled her nose.

"Thank you for the help, dear." The old lady gave Emily a grateful smile. "This wouldn't be a great time to hurt my ankle again."

Mom waited for the others to catch up, and then pointed to the first of the sheds. "Okay, I know this sounds silly but I think we just need to assume someone might be watching. Let's put on a bit of a pantomime."

"Like we think the treasure is in there!" said Emily, catching on. "That would be fun!"

"I'm game," said Mrs. Renton with a grin. "Let's hope Mr. Kennedy is watching."

"Or the Mole Hole man," added Emily.

Mom had a sudden disquieting thought. She gazed across the harbor to where the hidden staircase must start. *Could Mr. Kennedy have already left the cove without them seeing him? It was just possible, and if so where was he now? Would he spot the others?* She looked back. "You know, I feel a real need to stop for a sec and pray. Let's pray that the others can solve the clue and then get out of there as quickly as they can."

Kennedy inched slowly up a few more steps, straining to hear. He had almost forgotten the disagreeable dampness of his clothing. Something was going on up there for sure. He could hear the dad's voice, and the kids' too, but they were all too muffled to make out any words. He reached the top and peered round the edge of a straggling bush. *Yes!* There they all were, inside a walled garden area.

He sidled nearer to the arched gate where he could see them through the fronds of a drooping palm. A gull chose that moment to swoop down and land on the top of the arch, from where it fixed him suspiciously with one shiny black eye. He tried to shoo it off with a discrete wave of his hand, but the gull was unimpressed. Kennedy abandoned his efforts and focused in on the little group over by the house. They were having an intense discussion about something. *What on earth were they up to?*

✀❧✀

"There's got to be something more in the clue," said Dad, beginning to feel pretty frustrated. This was taking way too long. Kennedy wasn't that stupid—he'd figure out sometime that he had been duped.

"Maybe we need the book," said Rachel. "Maybe that's why we can't figure it out."

"What does it mean again to put together two and two?" wondered Danny out loud.

"It's a poetic way of saying using your brain to solve a puzzle—putting two and two together to make four." Dad took another look at the plaques. "We need to puzzle out something on these signs."

"If these are the ones," said Rachel gloomily, "and not some others—maybe even in the book."

Dad noticed Stevie standing by himself and frowning, and went over to him, feeling a bit guilty for not taking notice of the lad's struggle. "Hey, Stevie. We need your help over here. We need to puzzle this out about the signs."

Stevie turned and looked at Dad, still frowning. He suddenly realized that Dad was talking to him. "What? Sorry, Daddy, what did you say?"

"We need your help to puzzle this thing out."

"Putting two and two together," said Stevie, furrowing his brow again.

"That's right."

"Well I was just thinking about a Tintin book."

"You mean those ones you and Danny liked checking out from the library?"

Danny pricked up his ears. Tintin books had lots of puzzles to solve.

"Uh-huh," nodded Stevie. "In the one about the treasure ship, there were three maps."

"*The Secret of the Unicorn*," said Danny, coming over.

"Uh-huh. You had to put them together and hold them up to the light to read the message."

Dad was puzzled. "So what does that have to do with the clue?"

A lightbulb went off in Rachel's head, but before she could blurt out anything, Stevie ran over to the first plaque and pointed at the strange marks.

"What if we can put these marks together with the other ones? Maybe they'd make a message."

"That's what I was thinking!" said Rachel.

Dad looked back and forth at the two plaques. "But how can we do that?"

Rachel slipped her bag off of her shoulders and dug around inside. "With this," she said proudly, extracting her sketchbook. "I've got pencils too. We can make a rubbing. Here you are." She carefully ripped out two of the perforated pages. "It fits," she said, holding one up to the first plaque. She grabbed a pencil and was about to start rubbing when she noticed Stevie's lower lip protruding. She felt another stab of conscience. Maybe she needed to slow down a little. She did really want to do what was right.

"Hey, Stevie, do you want to do it? I'll hold the paper?"

The boy's eyes lit up and he nodded eagerly.

"Can I do one?" said Danny anxiously.

"You can do the other one," said Dad, "if it's okay with Rachel."

Rachel nodded. It felt good to be unselfish. She held the paper carefully while Stevie tried his best to rub over the paper. He wasn't succeeding very well. Dad reached over and helped guide his hand and soon they had a fairly good representation of the plaque. Next Rachel held the paper for Danny, who didn't have any trouble making a legible rubbing.

"Okay, Stevie," smiled Dad, handing him the sheets. "Let's see if there's a hidden message."

Stevie took them gratefully and was about to figure out how best to hold them when he froze. That sounded like a sneeze—and super close by! The gull on the gate rose up in alarm, screaming out a warning. The other gulls took up the cry and launched themselves off the roof. Dad and the kids looked around wildly. They must not be alone after all!

❧❧

Kennedy stumbled down the stairs, cursing his luck and wiping his nose with the back of his hand. Of all the moments to have an uncontrollable need to let loose a whopping great sneeze—he had been seconds away from hearing the answer to the clue—with a good chance of beating them to the next place!

His wet shoe slipped sideways on the slate steps and he almost missed his footing, just managing to save himself from a nasty fall. Moderating his pace a fraction, he continued quickly down and pushed his way through the bushes at the bottom. He took a frantic glance behind him. *Now what to do?* They'd be down in a second. He made a snap decision and took the path to the right that continued around the cliff.

❧❧

"Alright, and thank you for coming in." Jennings smiled at the departing customer—a customer who had actually bought something! Those bronze candlesticks had been up on that shelf since the first day he opened the shop and he'd long ago given up any hope of selling them. And yet there they went, and at a nice profit too.

361

With a momentary pang of conscience he remembered that those candlesticks had been one of those transactions he'd made with Kennedy way back when—a transaction about which it had been better not to ask too many questions.

Kennedy—that's right, he was still supposed to be keeping an eye out for that family for him. *What an absolute pain! And yet did he have a choice?* He checked his watch. It had been a while since he'd seen the ladies at the memorial. Maybe he could just step outside to check again. He threw his coat on, yanked open the door and stepped out into the street. The temperature was definitely dropping and the wind was getting up again—probably signs that a storm was on its way.

He looked up and down the street. There was the postman, up beyond the grocers, and a young couple down by the newsagents, but no-one he was looking for. He moved a few steps down the hill to where he could see between the village hall and the house next to it. There was some activity down there in the harbor, but it was a bit far away to tell who it was. For a moment he debated going back in and grabbing one of the telescopes, but then thought better of it. The young couple were headed up the hill his way. *Maybe they were potential customers. Maybe he'd even get another sale.*

He dashed back inside, ripped off his coat and tried to look as welcoming as possible.

∾∾

Dad returned from carefully checking the stairs and informed them that the coast seemed clear.

"Are you sure?" said Danny.

"Well, I went all the way to bottom and there wasn't anyone in sight."

"But do you think there was someone there—listening to us?" wondered Rachel, peering down.

"I actually do," said Dad. He pointed to a damp spot beside the gate, and some faint marks leading away. "Those are wet footprints—and they weren't there when we came up—I'm sure of it."

Danny felt a shiver come over him. The others felt rather queer themselves. It was a very unpleasant thought that someone had been right there, watching them without them realizing it.

"Do you think it was the Mr. Kennedy guy?" said Danny, struggling again with that sickening feeling of fear that seemed to pounce on him whenever he pictured the man in the café.

Dad examined the lad's face. What he saw troubled him, and he tried to push aside his own concerns. He knelt down and looked into Danny's eyes. "Yes, I do think it was him—maybe damp from being in the cave—but we needn't be surprised. He's really trying to get to the inheritance before we do. He wants it for himself."

"But why?"

"Well, because he thinks it must be some treasure or something. Maybe he's just plain greedy for money, or perhaps even desperate to get a hold of it for some other reason."

"Like what" wondered Rachel, puzzled.

"Oh I don't know—why do people try to steal things? Maybe he needs the money for something—like to pay off a debt or something." Dad looked back at Danny. "But whatever the reason, it's the wrong thing to do, and that means we need to stop him."

"But I'm scared of him." *There*, Danny had said it out loud.

"Right, I understand, but that's where we really need to keep trusting Jesus. He's the King of kings, and He's absolutely in control of all this. He sees everything and knows everything." Even as Dad said it, he realized that he himself needed to hear it as well. He went on with renewed assurance. "There's nothing those guys can do that can get by Jesus. In fact, one way or another, they are sure to fail."

Danny brightened a little. "You mean we know we're going to get the inheritance first!"

Dad had to process that for a second. "Well, we don't know that for sure. We think that would be the best thing of course, but God has a much bigger picture in mind. He wants Mrs. Renton to come to know Him and He knows the best way for that to happen."

"Does he want the café man to come to know Him too?" said Stevie, trying to make sense of the conversation.

Dad pursed his lips, and then nodded slowly. "Yes He does—the Bible says clearly that God wants all people to be saved. I just haven't really been thinking about that. We've been concentrating on Mrs. Renton's need for Jesus, but boy oh boy, Mr. Kennedy sure needs Jesus as well."

"And the Mole Hole man," added Rachel.

"And the Mole Hole man," agreed Dad. He looked around at the others. Danny dropped his eyes. What Dad had said made sense, but it was really difficult to accept.

"So, what do we do?" asked Rachel. "They might still be hanging around nearby."

Danny and Stevie looked around anxiously. Dad frowned. "Okay, I tell you what. Let's take the clues and high-tail it back down to meet the others. We'll keep an eye out for you-know-who and find a place where we can look at the sheets undisturbed."

❧❧

Chippy had no idea what to do, and Ahab hadn't been any help whatsoever. The fish seemed content to just lurk behind his plastic fern, looking bored. The unsettled weather didn't help either. If it was raining, there was almost no chance that people would be wandering around town, getting hungry. Yes, so far the rain had held off, but for how long?

What a dilemma. The new Star Trek DVDs he had ordered had finally arrived and were tugging him home like a tractor beam. He could be back in his flat right now, a big bowl of Frosted Sugar Balls in his lap, his favorite Spock pillow at his side. Trouble was, to pay off those DVDs on his credit card, he desperately needed to sell some fish.

Chippy checked his watch. It was pretty much lunch time. He might as well hold on here for another hour. If nothing showed up, that would be his sign to pack it in. The fryer was on, the batter was mixed and he had a dozen cod fillets ready and waiting. Now all he needed were customers.

He glanced automatically at the door and what he saw made his mouth drop open. He rubbed his eyes to make sure he wasn't dreaming. Yes, there were five, six…no, seven people coming up the path! *Well, beam me up, Scotty! It's fish time!*

❧❦

Mom was amazed. Fish was for sure and certain the last thing she would dream of ordering, but this was different--moist, flaky, steaming and covered in the best batter she had ever tasted. Most importantly, it didn't taste remotely fishy. She looked over at her husband who winked at her, guessing her thoughts.

The family were seated around one of the two Formica tables in the corner of the fish and chip shop, the kids digging in like their lives depended on it while the adults were eating at a more leisurely pace.

Mom wiped her mouth with a napkin and leaned over to Mrs. Renton. "Thank you so much. You really shouldn't have."

"Nonsense," said the old lady firmly. "You have done so much for me—I love being able to do something in return."

"So can we see the rubbings you did?" said Emily with her hand over her mouth, hiding the bite of fish she'd just taken.

Dad wiped his hands. "Sure. Rachel, may I have your bag?"

Rachel slid it over and Dad carefully extracted the two sheets of paper. "It was Stevie who had the idea of putting them together," he said proudly, smiling at the lad. "Here Stevie. Wipe your hands and see if you can hold them up together at the window."

Stevie smiled broadly, wiped his hands and took the sheet, trying to look as important as he felt. It took him a moment to get them lined up just right, one on top of the other, and he held them up to the window with a little help from Mom. The others craned their necks to look. It was certainly easy to see the strange markings on both pieces despite the greasy spots from Stevie's fingers, but they still didn't seem to make any sense.

"Try one sheet up the other way," suggested Dad. Mom helped Stevie rotate a sheet, but it was immediately clear that it didn't help.

"Oh, bother," said Mrs. Renton, expressing what everyone else was feeling. "I was certain you had the right idea young man." She patted Stevie on the shoulder.

"But I was sure the Tintin book was right!" he blurted out.

"Don't give up so soon," said Mom. "We may be closer than we think. It definitely does seem as if those marks are a piece of the puzzle. They really look like lines and curves that should make a word or words."

Help us please Jesus, whispered Emily.

"Can you read the clue again?" said Rachel. "There might be something there to help."

Dad knew it by heart by now. "'*His life was one that finished well, Again the book a tale will tell. The signs reveal the way when you will put together two and two.*'"

"The book!" said Rachel. "Maybe there's a clue there!"

"But it's back at the inn," groaned Stevie.

"No it isn't," grinned Mom. "She dug down into the backpack at her feet and, like a rabbit from a hat, dramatically produced the Squire's history book and dropped it on the table in front of them causing cries of appreciation from the family.

"Shhh," reminded Dad. He turned to his wife. "You amaze me, dear." He shook his head in admiration. "You're sure you don't have the inheritance stashed away in there?"

Mom wiggled her eyebrows, adding a mischievous grin. "Maybe I do, maybe I don't. Anyway, let's look up the man on the sign—Mr. Lonsdale wasn't it? Would you do the honors please Mrs. Renton? Yes, Stevie, you can put the signs down for now." The lad was gamely trying to keep them in place while straining to see the book.

Mrs. Renton took the book and turned to the back. With one hand she extracted her reading glasses from her purse, expertly flipped them open and stuck them on her nose. "Let's see…J, K, L…Lonsdale. William R. Page 24."

She thumbed through the pages and found the right one. There was a general scraping of chairs as the family tried to see the pages, Stevie actually climbing onto the table itself.

"Whoa Nellie," said Dad. "Back off everyone. Let Mrs. Renton read. Then we can pass it around."

The kids shrunk back into their seats looking a little ashamed. Mrs. Renton smiled round at everyone, cleared her throat and started reading, the others trying to take it all in as the story unfolded.

The Lonsdale family had apparently moved to Penrithen from the city of Exeter back in 1550. The city had been besieged during the so-called Prayer Book Rebellion and a number of citizens had decided to up and leave. John Lonsdale was one of these, quitting the city with his wife and three-year-old son. He owned several merchant vessels and moved these to Padstow on the west coast of Cornwall. He had a house built there and also one at Penrithen. He and his wife Mary had both been raised Catholic, but had secretly converted to Protestantism sometime after their marriage. As the Spanish tightened their grip on the Netherlands, persecuting the Protestants there, John became involved with a group of merchants secretly trying to help fund the Protestant cause. His wife's family were Dutch and had many relatives who had suffered persecution. John evidently kept this a secret from his son William, who by all accounts was a bit of a rebellious lad as he got older, fond of food and ale and good company.

When William reached thirty-four years of age, he married a cousin—Anna Winthrop--whose family were also Protestant. Their marriage couldn't be deemed a happy one though, as William's reckless living kept them only a step above financial ruin and it was only his wife's thriftiness and hard work as a seamstress that allowed them to survive. Then John Lonsdale suddenly passed away after contracting pneumonia, and William inherited his father's merchant business. By then it had increased in size and profit, but the son had no capacity for managing it. John's former merchant friends approached William, beseeching him to continue to help the Protestants as his father had done. William refused, and by his continued wild living and poor business skills managed to lose most of the assets until there was just a single merchant vessel left to his name.

Mrs. Renton paused in her relating of the events and looked around at the eager listeners. "Are you all following this?" She looked particularly at Stevie who had a decidedly furrowed brow.

"I'm not getting it," he admitted. "Is the William guy a bad guy? And who died?"

Dad stepped in and explained the main points so the lad could get the gist of it all.

"So the son was pretty bad then," said Stevie, nodding. That much made sense to him.

"Yes," said Mrs. Renton. "Let's see what happens next."

She adjusted her glasses and continued on, simplifying some of the text as she read it so that the younger ones could better understand.

William and Anna had four children, though it was Anna who practically raised them by herself. There were no Protestant services nearby, so she taught the children herself from the Bible—William refusing to have any part in their religious education. He did finally agree to the hiring of a tutor—a Mr. Nicholas Carpenter—who was a strong believer, and this man did much to help Anna and the children in their relationship with God.

However, disaster struck the family in the spring of 1591. England had experienced outbreaks of the Bubonic Plague, and it made its way to Penrithen. Anna and three of the children succumbed.

"That means that they died," explained Mrs. Renton. "The poor family."

Emily sighed. She really didn't like sad stories, and there seemed to be so many of them on this quest. Her thoughts were interrupted by Mrs. Renton as she continued on reading.

"It seems, however, that this tragedy shocked William into a dramatic change of heart. He sought out the help of Nicholas Carpenter who gladly took the opportunity of befriending the man and comforting him in his loss. It was through Carpenter's influence that William finally understood God's love for him and made a profession of faith in Christ in early 1592." Mrs. Renton stopped for a moment with a thoughtful, faraway look in her eyes. The others were quiet, expecting her to make some sort of observation, but without further comment she turned back to the book.

"William was a changed man," she read. "He started keeping a diary, most of which has survived to this day. In it he states how he regretted having wasted his life, selfishly neglecting his family. He committed all his resources to helping the plight of the Dutch Protestants who were still resisting the Spanish Empire. His last diary entry states his complete devotion to Christ, and his desire to finish his life well. Taking command himself of his remaining ship, the *Morningstar*, he made a voyage to the Netherlands, successfully rescuing several Dutch families who were trying to escape to England." Mrs. Renton noticed Emily out of the corner of her eye, nudging Rachel and whispering in her ear. "Did you have something you wanted to say, dear?" she questioned.

"Oh, yes, please, if you don't mind." Emily's eyes were shining and she nodded at Rachel who was looking pretty excited herself. Mom gave a knowing smile, guessing what they were thinking.

"When we went up to the memorial on the hill," explained Emily, "there was a sign explaining that it was in memory of a ship that was sunk with everyone on board."

"The *Morningstar*," put in Rachel, unable to let Emily tell the whole story. "And there was a piece of ship there—what was it called?"

"The capstan," said Mom. "Sort of like a wheel." She glanced over at Dad with raised eyebrows.

"It was used for hauling in ropes, like for raising an anchor," said Dad. He turned to Mrs. Renton. "Do you mind finishing the story? This is really interesting."

"Of course. Let's see." Mrs. Renton scanned the article and found the place. "Okay, yes, the Dutch families were fleeing to England. On the way home, however, the ship was sighted by a Spanish vessel and pursued up the English Channel. After a long chase the Spaniard overhauled the *Morningstar* and opened fire within sight of the Cornish coast. According to eyewitnesses on the cliffs, there was a tremendous explosion and the *Morningstar* seemingly vanished. There were no survivors. Pieces of the ship washed up along the coast, including one of the ship's capstans. It was preserved in the vaults of a chapel until finally being installed as part of a memorial on Tregarth Watch, locally known now as Capstan Wiggle. Several bodies were later recovered, including that of William Lonsdale. He was laid to rest in the churchyard of St. Piran's above Penrithen, overlooking his old home. He had indeed finished well." The old lady set the book down. "That's it for that chapter. Yet another tragic story, but what does it all mean?" She looked questioningly at the others. "Is there anything there to help us with the clue?"

Dad leaned back in his chair and puts his hands behind his head. He furrowed his brow. "Well, detectives. What do you think?"

Chapter 23 – Up to the Graveyard

Kennedy kept glancing over his shoulder as he tried to quickly get a rubbing of the signs. He had performed a hurried and challenging change of clothes back at his car, grabbed paper and a pencil from his briefcase and carefully made his way back to the stairway, keeping his eyes and ears wide open. He couldn't believe his luck when he made it up to the house without any sight or sound of the family. He considered it the first lucky thing that had happened in a long time.

He was so nervous though, it took him several tries to make a good rubbing of the first sign without ripping the paper. He did better with the second one, his confidence building as he began to accept the fact that the family really weren't coming back. Finally finished, he put the two pieces of paper together and held them up to where the sun was struggling to make its presence known through the clouds. Frowning hard, he tried them several different ways, but the weird markings didn't make any sense at all. *Was there a hidden message or wasn't there?* The family had apparently thought so, hadn't they?

His arms aching, he dropped them back to his side. *Nothing.* What should he do? Use Jennings? He was good at this sort of thing, wasn't he?--deciphering old documents and maps--and this was sort of in the same category. Kennedy shook his head in dejection. He hated relying on that chap, but it had to be done. He carefully folded the rubbings, slipped them inside his jacket and stole back down the stairs.

⚓⚓

Chippy was almost beside himself with joy. That big family had ordered a full meal of fish and chips, and now he'd had five other customers besides. He might make enough today to pay off those DVDs—maybe even order a couple more.

He looked over to where the family were all hunched over a book in the middle of their table and wondered what could be so interesting as to distract them from fish and chips. The bell ringing above the door grabbed his attention and he thought no more about it. More business was heading his way. *What a day!* He gave a discreet thumbs up to Ahab who was watching the action from his tank.

Over at the table, the discussion had been spirited and creative, but so far no-one had come up with any solution. They had begun to wonder if they were completely on the wrong track. Mom, Dad, and Emily were all studying the book, hoping to find some clue in the account of William Lonsdale. Mrs. Renton was looking off into space, thinking about the man's life and trying to make sense of it and how it related to everything else. Rachel was sifting through her memories of every mystery book she'd ever read, trying to find some inspiration. Danny was holding up the two pieces of paper, twisting them this way and that, hoping to figure out a secret message. Stevie, having given up completely, was quietly trying to finish up all the leftover French fries.

"How are you doing?" said Mom suddenly, noticing the old lady's faraway look.

Mrs. Renton didn't really feel like sharing all her worries right now. She glanced down. "Oh, alright, I suppose. I'm still trying to process all this. It just keeps going on."

Dad looked up. "It is amazing. The Squire went to a lot of trouble. This is, what, clue number four?"

"I think so," said Mrs. Renton. "All similar in some ways. Do you think that would help us—to look at the big picture? Could that be what it means to put two and two together?"

"And two and two make four and there have been four clues, haven't there?" said Emily getting excited.

"Now there's a thought," said Dad, impressed. "That might be the answer. Two and two make four clues and there's something in them all that will help us with this one."

"Have there been four clues?" said Mom. "I thought there had been more than that?"

"Well, let's count," said Dad. "The first one was the note in the letter from the lawyers."

The old lady nodded. "It was about the birds and the book of verse."

"That led us to the second clue—in the book in the cabinet thing," remembered Emily.

"That clue was about the tile and photo," said Rachel. "It talked about the Squire's father. But I don't remember what the next one was—the one behind the photo."

"It was the chess one!" exclaimed Emily. "The inn sign and the *City of Auckland*. Number three."

"And that was about that guy in the shipwreck—whose wife and baby died," added Rachel.

Dad took a quick furtive glance over his shoulder. "This is great, but let's try to keep our voices down—just in case." They got the point and leaned in a little closer.

"Okay," said Mom quietly. "So the box in the garden had clue number four then."

"That one had the other squire and the wreckers. It led to the suit of armor and the box down the shaft," said Emily.

"That's right," said Mrs. Renton. "And the clue we found there is the one we're following now with Mr. Lonsdale."

"That makes five," said Rachel, disappointed. They mulled that over for a moment.

"But only four individuals in the clues," said Mrs. Renton slowly. "Could that be the two and two we have to put together?"

"Maybe," said Dad. "Let's think about that."

"Well, to tell you the truth, I've been really trying to understand why Uncle Kenwyn put in all these stories about the different people." The old lady shook her head. "I just don't know. Is there a connection between them? Am I supposed to learn something from each of them?"

Dad touched his wife on the arm. "Do you have a piece of paper dear? We had to use some from Rachel's sketchbook for the rubbings."

"I've got something in here," said Mom, rummaging in the backpack.

"Of course you do," said Dad with a grin.

Mom pulled out a small notebook with a pen stuck through the spiral binding and handed them over, unable to restrain a certain smugness in her expression.

"Perfect, sweetheart." Dad gave her a wink. "Okay, let's see." He drew a table with three columns and four rows. The others looked on, intrigued—all except Danny who was still working on trying to match up the rubbings—oblivious to everything else.

Dad pointed to the first column. "We'll put the guys' names in here. *Squire's Dad, NZ missionary, wrecker guy, shipwreck guy*." He listed them one by one. "There. I can't remember all their exact names but that will do. Now what other stuff is pertinent?"

"How about what happened to them?" said Rachel, brushing the hair back from her face. "Didn't they all die?" She shook her head. "No wait, the one guy lost his wife and baby but didn't die."

"But it's true that they all experienced death," said Mom. "At least—there was a significant tragedy for each of them." They were all quiet for a moment. Yes, of course—all the stories had been sad ones.

"I do remember that there was some good that happened though in each story," said Emily quietly. "When the Squire's dad died, he left behind a group of Christians that found strength from his sacrifice. And then the man who lost his wife managed to heal up and stay a missionary."

"And the squire who fought the wreckers—his son came back to the Lord through the example of his father," remembered Dad.

"We don't know about this one yet—Mr. Lonsdale. But then we haven't got the rest of the story." Mom sat back and stretched out her legs.

"I've just thought of something interesting," said Mrs. Renton suddenly. She smiled at Dad. "And it was your drawing that helped. How about if you put in the next column the date when each person lived? Not the exact date, but the time period."

Dad nodded slowly. "Alright, so what was it? The early 1900s for the Squire's dad?"

"Yes," said Mrs. Renton. "Around World War I. And the missionary to New Zealand was in the 1800s—at the time when people were emigrating there."

"The 1700s for the squire with the wreckers," said Dad, excitedly scribbling down the dates.

"And this man we're working on is in the 1600s," finished Mrs. Renton. "Do you see? Each one is in a different century."

"We're working our way back in time!" said Rachel. "Cool!"

"But what does it mean?" said Emily.

"Well, if there's another clue it might be about someone in the 1500s," said Mom.

"But I hope we're not going to just keep on going forever," said Stevie with a mouthful of French fries that he had found on Emily's plate.

Dad reached over and hid the sight with a napkin. "Here, don't talk with your mouthful. Don't worry. We've got to stop somewhere." He sounded more confident than he felt, though. Their vacation would run out someday soon.

"What was Uncle Kenwyn thinking?" Mrs. Renton wondered out loud. She studied Dad's chart again. Then with a sudden thought she looked over at Danny whose mouth had just dropped open. "Danny, you've been very quiet. What do you think? You look like you've got something to say."

"Have you any ideas about all the clues? We're trying to put two and two together," added Dad, amused that Danny apparently hadn't heard anything they'd been saying.

Danny looked around the table and grinned. Every eye seemed to be on him. He sat up a bit straighter and picked up the rubbings. "I do have an idea Daddy. I've put two and two together. Look!" He held the two signs up to the window, one overlapping the other. Then he adjusted the top one up and over to the left a little. The others gasped. The mysterious markings had lined up to form three words.

"*Tend…the…grave*," read Mom aloud. "That's amazing!"

There was a sudden outburst of questions and comments, and Dad had to quickly gesture with his hand. "Keep it low please everybody. Remember?"

With some difficulty they all quieted back down. Dad's chart was forgotten.

"How did you do it young man?" asked Mrs. Renton, looking at Danny.

Danny's grin widened. "I put two and two together!" He set the papers back on the table. "See? There's a two on the date there…" He indicated the year 1732 on the first rubbing. "And a two on this sign as well—when the man was born."

He pointed to the year 1542 on the second rubbing. "I lined them both up and there it was!"

Dad tousled his hair. "Fantastic, Tiger, fantastic! I would never have thought of that. You're an ace detective—putting together two and two!"

Danny's chest swelled with pride. Then he had a sudden thought. "You know, it was probably Jesus who did it—He showed me what to do."

Mom nodded. "You're right Danny, and we don't want to forget it. God is answering our prayers for help, but he used you to do it!"

"So what does it mean--*tend the grave*?" said Rachel, putting the papers back up to the window and trying to line them up like Danny had done.

"To tend means to take care of," said Mrs. Renton. "I suppose that means we're supposed to take care of the man's grave—the man in the story I suppose— William Lonsdale. What that means I've no idea. Maybe his grave is overgrown and if we clean it up we'll see something. But where is his grave?"

"Up at the churchyard, perhaps?" said Dad.

Mrs. Renton shrugged her shoulders. "I suppose so. I don't know of where else to look. I imagine he was buried near here." She picked up the book and quickly scanned the article. "Oh, yes, I completely forgot! It says he was buried at St. Piran's, here in Penrithen."

"Well, that's our next stop," said Dad, feeling a sudden excitement. He pushed his chair back. "We're all done. Let's clean all this up and head out."

The family sprang into action. There was a sudden clattering of chairs and a general gathering up of napkins and boxes while Mrs. Renton looked on in bemusement. This family had a lot of energy—a lot more than she felt she had.

Emily offered her an arm and she gratefully accepted it. "Thank you, sweetheart. I would appreciate the help." At the touch of Emily's arm, a wave of emotion swept over her and tears sprang into her eyes. *Now where had they come from?* She used her free hand to wipe them away. Had Emily noticed? No, she didn't think she had.

She had to pull herself together—such a mix of emotions swirling around. Confusion and frustration, yes…excitement, sadness, fear perhaps? And then the other ones that she was almost afraid to enunciate in case they vanished as she voiced them: that elusive feeling of hope and now, with the family taking such an interest in her, the definite, astounding impression that she was actually loved.

⟅⟆

"Thank you for staying with me," said Stevie earnestly. He looked up from where he was sitting on the sofa with a pile of stamps in his lap, the cat curled up at his side where it cast an occasional thoughtful look at what he was doing, purring contentedly. Stevie had been very nervous about going looking for graves, and was so glad when Mrs. Renton offered to let him stay at her house.

The old lady smiled. "Oh, you're so welcome dear. I wasn't up for a climb up the hill and so this is perfect. Are you sure you don't want anything to eat or drink?"

"No thank you. My tummy's full of fish and fries." Stevie looked down at it ruefully. That was another reason not to go—he was feeling a bit uncomfortable down there.

The rest of the family had decided to walk up to the churchyard rather than going all the way back for the car, and the old lady had declared she needed a bit of a rest and would wait with Stevie for them to come back with the news. Mrs. Renton had given them her trimming shears, and a bag with some cut roses from a vase in her kitchen window—*to tend the grave*, she had explained.

"Righty-ho. Well then, I think I'll just make myself a cup of tea." Mrs. Renton heaved an inward sigh of relief. With the little boy taken care of, she could concentrate on what was really bothering her. The discussion in the fish and chip shop had brought to the forefront of her mind what she had been consciously burying. In all of this quest—for want of a better word—Uncle Kenwyn must have had a definite purpose, and somehow these stories of historical persons were a part of that. She needed time to think—time to step back again and look at the whole. Yes, the stories had individually touched her heart, but what was the overall message? How far was he taking her back in time? She knew Uncle Kenwyn had something to say to her, and with all her heart she didn't want to miss it.

❦

Kennedy pulled the collar of the raincoat up around his ears, both to keep out the wind and to make an attempt at hiding his face. Jenkins had proved no help at all in deciphering the papers, but had at least lent him a coat and hat, albeit very reluctantly.

He peered out from behind the monument and watched the rest of the family disappear up the lane. *Where were they going? The Inn? Up to the church?* He narrowed his eyes. This chasing after the family was so ridiculous. If only he could solve a clue ahead of them and thwart them completely. Of course to do that he had to stay close enough to find out what they were doing.

He gave a racking cough. Just from a cold, he assured himself—not from all the smoking he had been doing lately. Either way he wished he could tail them in the car, rather than having to haul himself on foot all over creation.

There, he had waited long enough. He couldn't let them get too far ahead or he wouldn't know which way they'd gone. Ducking out from the shelter of the monument, he slipped into a sort of lumbering jog along the road towards the bridge, coughing as he went.

❦

"Steady on lass," said Dad, reaching out a helping hand to Rachel who had tripped over a bump in the path. "We're not in that much of a hurry."

Rachel gave him a concerned look. "But what about the café man? Isn't he on our tail?"

Mom, Emily and Danny caught up to them and overheard the last comment. Danny and Emily looked anxiously behind them, but the road was empty. The sun had managed to briefly break through the clouds again and was reflecting off

373

the puddles along the line of hedges. The breeze was somewhat blocked and the air felt close in the sheltered lane, heavy with the scent of damp earth and wildflowers.

Mom adjusted the backpack, glad for a pause. "I really don't think he could have solved that last clue. He wouldn't know to come up to the graveyard."

Even as she said it though, she had a twinge of doubt. He had proved several times that he was adept at keeping on their trail.

Emily must have been thinking the same thing. "Are we sure though?"

Dad pursed his lips. "We don't really know," he admitted. "All we can do is keep our eyes open."

"And pray," added Mom. "Let's all keep praying as we go."

Danny nodded. He hadn't shared it with the others—especially Stevie—but the idea of searching the graveyard was already out of his comfort zone. Searching the graveyard with Mr. Nasty somewhere out there trying to sneak up on them— well that was off the charts scary. He would definitely be praying.

They started off again, Dad at the front this time, Mom in the rear and all of them checking over their shoulders and praying for protection. The hill seemed steeper than they remembered and as they trudged on, they began feeling a few prickings of sweat as the sun seemed to be making up for lost time. Truly the English weather was living up to its reputation for changeability. They were all relieved when they rounded the bend and saw the old chapel resting peacefully in its little hollow, seemingly enjoying the fleeting sunshine. The surrounding graveyard seemed almost pleasant with the vibrant grass and scattered flowers, and their spirits rose. Even as they looked, however, the scene transformed before them as the sun was smothered by a towering ashen cloud. The chapel seemed to shrink back within itself and the graveyard became instantly a gloomy and lifeless place. They felt a sudden chill, which wasn't only due to the change in temperature.

Dad voiced everyone's feelings. "It's okay. The sun's just gone in for a while." He gestured upwards where layers of massive grey and white cumulus clouds filled the sky, with small patches of blue between. He tried to sound as cheerful as possible. "It will come out again. Don't forget God's with us. Let's find the man's gravestone!"

He led the way through the gate and along the path, the others following rather reluctantly behind. There were two stone steps up to the graveyard proper, and Dad paused there to address the others. He shifted the bag with the things Mrs. Renton had given them over to his other hand and pointed to the right side of the graveyard. "How about Emily and Rachel go with Mom and start over there, and you Danny come with me on this side?"

The others nodded, the kids rather unenthusiastically. Mom gave a concerned look to Dad who nodded. "Let's remember who's in control and why we're doing this. It's a challenge but we're doing this for Jesus and to help Mrs. Renton come to know him."

"Let's ask Him for help," added Mom. They joined hands and Mom prayed. "Dear Jesus, here we are. Please help us find the grave and whatever's there. If it's the inheritance, we'll be so glad, but if it's another clue please help us solve it and find what we need to for Mrs. Renton. Please protect her and Stevie, and help her understand what you're trying to teach her through this. And please confuse Mr. Kennedy so he isn't able to get the inheritance first. In Jesus name I pray, Amen."

"Amen," said everyone else, feeling slightly better.

"And gravestones are actually really interesting," said Dad, trying to be positive. "They each tell a story—you'll find out what I mean. Come on, let's go." He grabbed Danny's hand and led him over to where the first granite slab rested askew under the twisted branches of a rambling shore pine.

Mom smiled encouragingly at the girls and led them off the other side of the path. There were a few crumbling steps up to a grassy sward and they surveyed the scene from the top. Most of the gravestones were simple slabs, crumbling slightly, dotted with lichen and leaning this way and that. A few were more elaborate, set on square plinths and topped with crosses.

"Let's not all look at the same ones—it will take too long," suggested Mom. "Emily, why don't you go along the edge of the church, Rachel take a section next to her, and I'll go along next to you."

The girls nodded. At least they would be close to one another. Emily started near the big front doors and scanned the ground in front of her. A few of the graves were marked with long flat stones sunk a few inches into the grass. She bent over the first of these and tried to read the inscription. *In loving memory of…Jane Winthrop, perhaps?* It was hard to make out. *Died October 14th? 24th?* Anyway, it wasn't William Lonsdale—that was for sure. She moved on to the next one.

❧❧

Kennedy shifted his head ever so slowly sideways until he could just see around the hedge and up the path to the church. He spied the girls over in the graveyard to his right—and there was the mother too. What were they doing? They appeared to be searching.

Aha. They must be looking for a clue on one of the graves. He nodded in satisfaction. Now he just needed to get close enough to overhear them. There had to be a way to make it up there without being seen. The path wouldn't do at all. He started scanning his surroundings for a safer route.

❧❧

"Mom, come and look at this," beckoned Rachel. As her mom came over she pointed down at the inscription on a small stone, almost hidden in the grass. "I think it says *'sleep sound in Jesus' arms'*."

Mom squatted down and pushed aside the grass. "You're right. *Mary Woods, age five months.*"

"Five months?" said Rachel, distressed. "She was just a baby."

Mom nodded and gave her a hug. "It's true, sweetheart. Childhood deaths were much more common back then. What's the date here?" She pressed down the grass with both hands. "I think it says 1737. That's quite a while ago!"

375

Emily stopped to listen for a moment, and then continued on in her search. She was feeling quite melancholy. It had suddenly struck her that all these people were…well…real people with real lives and had been missed by those they left behind. She sighed. A gust of wind blew from the direction of the sea and she imagined for a second that she could hear the waves beating against the base of the headland.

But what was that? Had she heard someone singing? It was a woman's voice, she was sure of it. She stood up straight and looked around her. Mom and Rachel were close by, but it hadn't been either of them, she was sure. She turned towards the church and listened, pulling her hair back behind her ears. Yes, there it was faintly again. It must be coming from inside. She couldn't make out the words but it sounded pleasant enough—definitely not scary.

Her curiosity getting the better of her, she ran lightly back down to the path and trotted up to the church door. It was ever so slightly ajar. She opened it a bit wider and slipped inside. Even though she had been in there before, the abrupt feeling of peace and quiet surprised her. She inhaled deeply. Yes, that same musty smell mixed with a hint of furniture polish or something. The doors to the nave were wide open and she stepped carefully over to where she could see up the aisle. There was a lady over there, sitting on the third or fourth pew back, head bent down and seemingly rubbing something vigorously while singing to herself. The woman must have sensed something, for she suddenly stopped and looked up. Emily recognized the face of the lady from the coffee shop—*what was her name?*

"Well, hello," said the lady. "Where did you spring from? I remember you. You're with that family who are helping the old lady. I'm Maggie Ketchum, from the coffee shop."

Emily stepped fully into view and nodded. "Yes, that's right. I'm Emily."

"Hello there, Emily," smiled Maggie, standing up. She wiped the back of her hand across her forehead. "I'm polishing up the old pews here. I'm trying to get the chapel back into shape so it can be used again. It's been a while." She beckoned Emily over, who came timidly up the aisle.

Maggie gestured up towards the ceiling where some discoloration of the roof could be clearly seen. "There was quite a bit of water damage from a big storm a few years ago. The roof's not in the best of shape. In fact, the whole place has had its problems with damp. The Squire did so much for it—fixing it up, replacing the broken stained glass windows. He put a lot of money into restoring it."

"The Squire?" said Emily, surprised.

"Yes, but when he got sick the place gradually fell into disrepair. It was almost buried in brambles when I first started working here—you could barely squeeze in the door." Maggie put her hands on her hips and looked around. "But it's coming along. I put in a wee bit of work every moment I can."

"I think it's lovely," said Emily. "You've done an amazing job."

"Well, God is good, and it's getting better and better. Are you here visiting the chapel?"

Emily suddenly wasn't sure what to say, but she was saved by a voice calling her name from somewhere outside. "That's my Mom. She's probably wondering where I am."

"I'll come along and say hello," said Maggie, stretching out her back. "I could use a break."

Emily wasn't sure if this was good news or not. This lady was a Christian if she remembered rightly, but she didn't remember if her Mom and Dad had shared with her about the missing inheritance or not. She didn't have much time to worry about it, however, because her mom suddenly appeared at the entrance to the nave, Rachel just behind. She smiled when she saw Maggie.

"Oh, hello again. You're…oh, I'm sorry. I've forgotten your name."

"Maggie," said Maggie. "And you're Mrs. Chapman aren't you?"

"Call me Kathie, please. And this is Emily and Rachel. It looks like Emily has been checking out what you've been doing. I hope we haven't been a bother."

"Oh, no. Quite the opposite. I needed a break. I've been up here for a couple of hours, polishing away. I'm going to lock up the chapel again around four-thirty, so if you want to look around it'll be open till then. I like to keep it open as long as possible for folk."

"Thank you," said Mom. "We're actually all outside, checking out the gravestones."

Rachel and Emily both gave her a look. *Was she saying too much?* But Mom had remembered that the couple from the coffee place already knew what they were doing.

Maggie was intrigued. "Were you looking for a relation or someone? I know a lot of people have been researching their family trees."

"No, it's actually to help the elderly lady you saw us with—another clue towards her inheritance. We're supposed to find the grave of a man who died in the 1600s—William Lonsdale." Mom smiled reassuringly at the girls who were listening wide-eyed as she gave this information away.

Maggie led the way back outside where the sun had briefly appeared again. "The oldest graves are actually on the far side." She waved a hand towards the back of the church. "Unfortunately, it's where the brambles are the thickest." She smiled ruefully. "I haven't got to that part yet."

This was a bit of a letdown, but Mom tried to be optimistic. "Well, at least you've narrowed down where to look." She waved at Dad and Danny and beckoned them over.

"We found the Squire's grave," announced Dad as he came up. "No clues there though." He smiled at Maggie and shook her hand. "Good to see you again."

Mom got Dad quickly up to speed. He grimaced as he took in the brambles reaching around and over the back of the church.

"I tell you what though," said Maggie. "I've got several clippers in the narthex. Would you like to use them?"

"I've got some," said Dad, pulling out the ones Mrs. Renton had loaned him.

Maggie looked at them and grinned. "Those are okay, but hang on just a sec…" She disappeared back into the church and quickly reappeared holding two industrial-sized sets of tree clippers. "Now these will be a wee bit better suited to the job."

They all laughed. Dad took one of the clippers and Mom took the other. Maggie reached around inside the door and produced two sets of heavy gardening gloves. "Here's some armor. Thanks for taking care of some of those thorny beasties for me! I hope you find the grave back there!"

"We'll give it a go," said Dad, wondering just what they were getting themselves in for. "If we're not back in an hour, the brambles have got us!"

❧ ❧

Kennedy had needed to go quite a long way around, but he had finally—using hillocks and clumps of bushes as cover—made it close to the side of the church farthest from the path. From where he crouched behind a prickly gorse bush, breathless and sore, he could see most of the graveyard in front of the building. The back side seemed enveloped in an impenetrable nest of brambles.

He had watched with interest the family examining the gravestones. Obviously that had to be part of the clue—finding a particular one. It shouldn't be too hard to note the one they found.

It was with some dismay, then, that he suddenly saw the family all move towards the front of the church and out of his direct view. *What were they doing?*

He waited, getting more and more uncomfortable, shifting his body as various parts protested at his cramped position. His mood, already foul from the setbacks of the previous few days, was rapidly worsening into a malignant concoction of anger and depression as the family failed to reappear. *Were they now searching for something in the church? What if they had found the inheritance? But wait--wasn't Mrs. Renton back at her house? Would they have left her there knowing that they were about to solve the whole puzzle?*

He gritted his teeth. That was the problem. He had no idea. And he couldn't spend one moment more crouching behind that bush with his joints popping and calves burning. He jumped up and massaged his legs vigorously. Forget the risks—he would have to get closer.

❧ ❧

Maggie had showed them the little door at the back side of the vestry that led to the area behind the church. The old wooden door had been stiff, and when it finally opened they had been confronted with a formidable wall of brambles, twisting and curling like snakes. The sun seemed to be permanently hidden now and the grey light added an ominous aura to the scene.

After a moment to take in the situation, Dad and Mom, with the kids' encouragement, had attacked the mass with their clippers, snipping, tugging, pushing and whacking to form a pathway forward. The brambles formed a literal canopy, and within its shadow they could just make out a number of gravestones, glowing dimly in the half light. Dad had given one glove to each of the girls and they were trying to help, gingerly pulling at severed sections and giving little yelps as the thorns made frequent inroads to their skin. Danny hung back, rather overawed by the task at hand and content to just offer exclamations and encouragement from the doorway.

Dad paused for a second to wipe the sweat from his brow. He glanced at his wife who was gamely attacking a patch so dense that it seemed to be as thick as a tree. He gave a wry smile. This wasn't exactly what he had pictured their holiday in Cornwall to be like. *It was for a good cause, though, wasn't it?* he reminded himself. He just needed to keep intentionally putting it all in the Lord's hands. God would take care of the consequences.

He consciously thrust his concerns out of his mind. Taking a fresh grip of the clippers, he selected a particularly intimidating-looking patch and attacked it with vigor.

❧❧

Maggie smiled to herself as she polished. She could hear snatches of sound from the family as they worked out the back. *What a blessing to have some help,* she thought. They were trying to serve the old lady, but would be helping her as well. God really did work out things wonderfully.

She stopped for a minute and examined her cloth. It was getting pretty dirty—definitely time to get a new one. There were several out in the foyer--in a bucket behind the door if she remembered correctly. As she hurried up the aisle, she glanced around, taking mental note of all the jobs to do. She had made progress, but there was still a long way to go. Would this place ever be able to be used again for its intended purpose?

With her mind elsewhere she had a huge shock as she stepped into the foyer. A tall man was silhouetted in the outside doorway. He had his hand on the door knob and he seemed to jump in surprise at the exact same time she did.

Maggie recovered first. "Oh, my goodness, you did give me quite a turn." She moved over slightly. "Come on in. You're here to visit the chapel, right?"

Kennedy's mind was racing as furiously as his heartbeat. *What could he safely come up with to say?* "Er, yes. I'm looking for something...I mean someone. Some friends...a family with children." What was their last name again? It wasn't coming to him. That scatterbrained Mrs. Tremannon had ruined whatever remembrance he may have had.

Maggie furrowed her brow. There seemed to be something about this chap that didn't ring true, though she couldn't really nail down her suspicions. She decided to play it safe. "A family? You said they're friends of yours?"

Kennedy formed his features into a smile. "Yes, yes. Good friends. I found out they were coming up here and wanted to surprise them. You won't give it away will you? You can just point me in the right direction so I can see them."

A clanging alarm bell seemed to be going off in Maggie's brain. This fellow didn't strike her as the friendly type, let alone a friend of the Chapmans. She managed a pleasant smile in return. "I'm sorry, what were your friends' names again?"

Kennedy froze. "Er, they're the..." What was it? He frantically wracked his brain for even the smallest hint. "Well, isn't that silly," he managed to stammer.

He consciously tried to slow down. "That happens to me sometimes—complete mental block." He gave a nervous laugh. "It will come to me in a second. It always does. Anyway, have you seen the family—mother, father, four children…"

Maggie was fully on the alert now. This gent was definitely not on the up-and-up. Hadn't the Chapmans mentioned someone possibly trying to steal the old lady's inheritance? What could she do? She didn't want to lie—that would be stooping to his level if he was the bad guy. He must know the family was up here somewhere. Maybe he had seen them on the road, or even out front. She had to say something.

"Oh, yes, I did see a family. They were here in the chapel, but they went out again. They're definitely not in here anymore." There, that was truthful without anything away.

Kennedy peered over Maggie's shoulder and took in the obviously empty nave. Maggie prayed silently that the Chapmans would be quiet enough and not choose that moment to come back into the building. The thick stone walls definitely cut down on the noise—and the vestry door was almost shut. It had a habit of swinging closed by itself, thank heaven.

Kennedy narrowed his eyes. She was obviously telling the truth. *Where could they be?*

Fortunately neither of them had seen Danny's eye glued to the crack in the vestry door. He had gotten bored and had come back inside to see what Maggie was up to. Then he had heard voices.

Maggie was trying desperately to come up with a plan to get rid of this bothersome guy. She glanced at her watch. *Hmm. That might work.* It *was* getting late. "Look, I have to close up here fairly soon. If your friends were here they would probably take the path over on the far side of the graveyard, through the hedge. It goes down around the side of the fields and comes along the back side of the Squire Inn. You should hurry, though."

Kennedy absorbed that piece of information, trying to keep the frustration off his face. Had they really left and gone that way?

Maggie decided she had to be a bit more forceful. "I'm sorry I'm going to have to shoo you out," she said brightly. She turned and closed the doors to the nave to emphasize her point. Kennedy got the message and reluctantly quitted the foyer. He glanced nonchalantly around the graveyard, but it was empty under the lowering sky. Maggie moved to the front door and stood watching him.

"Well, thanks for the help." He unsuccessfully tried to keep the sarcasm from his voice. "I'll go see if I can find them."

He strode off in the direction of the gap in the hedge where the other path supposedly took off. He scanned around him as he went, but saw no sign of the family. He kept half an eye on Maggie and as soon as she went back inside, he broke into a run, doubled back and positioned himself once more behind the wall near the gate at the top end of the lane. He settled himself down to wait. That family had to be up here somewhere and he wasn't going to lose them again.

380

Mom and Dad were carving two separate paths through the brambles towards where they could see gravestones through the tangled mess. They had already uncovered several, but discovered they weren't the one they were looking for and had sought out fresh targets. Mom reached hers first. She snipped away the brambles covering the face of the slab and bent down to examine it. It was so old it wouldn't have been easy to read in the best of conditions, but in the half-light it was next to impossible. Tracing with her finger, she finally made out one of the dates—1688. *What a disappointment.* "I got to one," she called out. "But it isn't the one we want." She looked over to where Dad was going like a machine. "Anything there?"

"Almost got to one," Dad grunted. Rachel and Emily moved closer to try and see, while attempting to avoid getting caught on the thorny sections strewn across the ground.

His eyes popping, Dad cut through a particularly monstrous stalk and exposed a tall marble stone. It was in very good condition, compared to the others they'd seen. *It couldn't be that old then, could it?* he thought. *But hang on…*

"That's it!" Rachel's voice exploded in his left ear. "That's the one!" She had moved in and was peering over his shoulder.

"Okay, okay," said Dad, a little annoyed. He waggled his finger in his ear to emphasize.

"Sorry," said Rachel, her voice much softer, "but it is the one, right? William Lonsdale, Captain of the *Morningstar.*"

"*1542 to 1601,*" read Emily from Dad's other side. "*In loving memory.* And look at the bottom. *He finished well.*"

"Why is it so new-looking?" wondered Mom, who had abandoned her own area at Rachel's cry. "It should be four-hundred years old."

"It's possible the Squire had it replaced," said Dad, considering. "Maybe because it was too hard to read, or maybe because he wanted to honor the man or something."

"Will you go get Danny?" said Mom to Rachel, suddenly realizing he had disappeared. Rachel tore off, not wanting to miss anything, and soon returned with the boy at her side.

"Look Danny, we found it," said Dad pointing at the grave, but surprisingly Danny didn't seem to be that interested. Instead he looked rather worried.

"That lady in the church was talking to someone. I think it was the man!" he gushed.

"Really?" said Mom, immediately concerned. "Are you sure?"

"Pretty sure. He was in the lobby thing but I could hear him."

Dad pursed his lips. With Danny's fears, it was possible the lad could have been mistaken, but on the other hand, it was possible the guy was still on their tail. *What to do?*

"Okay, how about I go and stand guard at the door." He looked around at the brambles that still enveloped most of the back of the church. "We should keep our voices down. See if you four can figure out what it means to tend the grave."

The others nodded. Dad disappeared back inside and Mom finished up snipping away the last of the brambles covering the grave. She carefully scooted the cut sections away with the side of her foot. The girls gave her some help with their gloved hands while Danny peered nervously through the tangled canes, looking for any sign of movement.

"There now." Mom stood aside so the others had a clear view.

"What's that," said Danny, pointing at a small circle of plastic embedded in the earth just in front of the marble slab.

"I think it's one of those places where you can put flowers." Mom pried at the edges of the plastic piece and it suddenly popped out revealing a narrow receptacle.

"We should put the flowers in there that Mrs. Renton gave us," said Emily, looking up.

"They're in here," said Rachel, carefully extracting them from the plastic bag. "A little squished, but not too bad."

"Hang on just a minute," said Mom excitedly, putting her hand on Rachel's arm. "We're supposed to tend the grave, and that's what we've been doing right? We've cleared away the brambles and are putting in some flowers. Maybe there's something we can find now."

"You mean a clue in what's written on the gravestone?" said Emily.

"Maybe," said Mom doubtfully, "but there doesn't seem much there to go on."

"How about in the plastic hole thing?" said Danny.

They all looked at each other. No-one relished the idea of sticking a hand into the hole. Finally Mom spoke up. "Okay, I'll look."

The light was too dim to see the bottom of the receptacle, however. Mom had a sudden mental picture of worms and spiders eagerly congregating in the dark. She turned to Rachel. "Um…may I borrow your glove?"

Rachel nodded vigorously, totally understanding. The glove was rather bulky, but Mom felt much safer now. There was just enough room to thread her hand down and feel around at the bottom.

Her eyes widened suddenly. "There's something here," she gushed.

Rachel clapped her hands in delight. "We found it!"

"Thank you, Jesus," Emily said, nodding in satisfaction.

Mom carefully extracted a very dirty, folded-up plastic bag, zipped closed at the top. She held it up so the others could see and then carefully pried it open. Inside was another similar bag, but slightly smaller. This one was clean and they could clearly see some paper inside. There was a note positioned so it could be clearly read through the bag.

"Look," said Mom excitedly. "It says 'Congratulations! You're getting very close.' That's wonderful!" She turned to Emily. "Would you run and get Dad?"

Emily nodded eagerly and trotted off.

Rachel grabbed Danny's hand and shook it hard, to the lad's amusement. "We're getting close, Danny! We're almost done!"

Stevie set the stamp down and looked over at the old lady. He was sure he had heard something funny—like a little sob or something. She had a pile of papers in her lap. Were they the clues? It looked like it. Was she crying about them? Maybe she was sad because they were so difficult, or maybe because there was a lot of them.

As he watched, Mrs. Renton looked up and met his gaze. She started a little and dug for her hankie. She blew her nose, and then gave a forced smile. Quickly gathering up the papers she put them back in the table drawer by her side.

"Er, would you like something more to drink?" The old lady addressed Stevie, trying to sound as cheerful as possible.

"No thank you," the boy replied politely. "I'm okay." He bent his head back down, a little puzzled at the lady's behavior. He kind of wished now he'd gone with the others.

❧❧

"And then I showed him the other path to get him out of your way. He went off in that direction." Maggie finished relating her tale and looked at the family, hoping she'd done the right thing.

"Did he now?" said Dad. He didn't know whether to feel relieved or more anxious than before. That guy was really persistent. *Had he really gone?*

"Thank you so much," said Mom, noticing Maggie's anxious look and correctly guessing the reason. "It sounds like you handled him perfectly."

Maggie relaxed visibly. "Well, I'll be keeping an eye out for him. He's a real shifty character. Have you thought about calling the police?

"We did consider it," said Dad, "but we really don't have any proof they'd accept."

Rachel nodded. In all the mystery stories she'd read, the kids tried to solve everything themselves and only called in the police as a last resort.

"Well, I'll be praying for you." Maggie waved a large rusty key. "I'm going to lock up now and get down in time for the late afternoon rush. Being optimistic!" she grinned.

"We're heading down too. We can go together if you like," said Mom smiling.

"That would be lovely," said Maggie. "I'll just get my things and we can be off."

❧❧

With a gasp, Kennedy suddenly realized the oversight in his plan. Here came the family down the path, and he had nowhere to go. He looked desperately around for a hiding place.

❧❧

"Can we look at the horses?" asked Rachel suddenly as the family and Maggie descended the lane back towards the harbor.

Mom considered for a moment. "Okay, have a quick look, but you'll have to catch up."

"Come on, Emily." Rachel grabbed her sister's hand and pulled. Emily nodded somewhat reluctantly. She wasn't as obsessive of horses as Rachel was.

383

They sped over to the gate leading to the horses' field, jumped up on the lowest wooden rail and looked across the grass.

"There they are," said Rachel excitedly. "A bay, a roan and a chestnut. I wish I could ride them!"

Emily nodded. "They do look pretty."

They watched in silence for a minute or two. Then Emily stepped down and patted her sister on the shoulder. "We should get going. They'll be at Mrs. Renton's before we can catch up."

"Just a minute." Rachel made clucking noises, hoping to lure one of the horses over.

"We really need to go now," said Emily, getting impatient. "They're going to look at the clue and I want to hear what it says. And remember—it said we're almost done."

Rachel sighed. She hated leaving, but she did want to hear the clue. "Okay, I'll come."

Crouched painfully behind the hedge a few feet away, Kennedy smiled thinly. He hadn't expected to hear anything from his emergency hiding place and now he knew where the family was heading, and that, amazingly, after so many setbacks, he was finally getting close to the prize. The smile left his face and he narrowed his eyes. He was going to make sure nothing else went wrong, no matter what it took.

✖✖

"So was it scary?" whispered Stevie in Danny's ear. He kind of hoped it had been. Then he wouldn't feel bad for staying with the lady.

"No...I mean sort of. I saw the man!"

"No way!"

"*Way*. He was in the church and I was hiding in a room and saw him. He was talking to the lady we met at the coffee place."

Stevie's eyes got really wide. "He was? Is she a traitor? I thought she was nice."

"No, she's okay. She..." Danny was interrupted by Dad calling everyone to sit down in the front room. Mrs. Renton had just finished making tea, and getting some orange squash for the children.

Stevie and Danny took their usual seats on the floor in front of Mrs. Renton's armchair. Pickwick the cat brushed between them, tickling Stevie's nose with its tail. Stevie gave a sudden sneeze and the cat looked round in mild surprise.

"Bless you," said the old lady, settling into her chair, the cat immediately jumping up onto her lap. She looked around at the family, amazed again that they were all there, eager to help. She honestly had no idea what she would have done without them.

"Here it is," said Mom, handing over the plastic bag. They had already related to Mrs. Renton how they had found it.

"We cleaned it up a bit with some tissues," said Emily. "It was kind of muddy."

"Well, thank you!" said the old lady. She opened the bag and took out the papers. She immediately noticed the little note. "Oh my, it says we're getting very close."

"Yes," said Dad. "Can you believe it?"

Mrs. Renton tried to absorb that piece of information. Yes, it was good news…in a way. Of course she wanted this to be over—it had been such an emotional upheaval for her—but it also meant that whatever the Squire had intended her to learn needed to be learned very soon. She had an idea she knew what it was now, but the idea was downright scary. She wished she could put off thinking about it indefinitely, but the end of the quest seemed like the time of reckoning. If she didn't take hold of it right now, would the opportunity be lost forever?

She suddenly became aware of everyone's eyes on her. Smiling apologetically, she pulled the rest of the papers from the bag. "Alright, here we go again. Let's see." She held a folded piece of paper up where they could all see. "This one says 'read first,' so being the obedient old lady that I am…" Here she winked at the kids. "…I'll read it first."

She set her reading glasses in place and unfolded the paper. "Here we go. 'Dearest Ruthie, I am so proud of you. I knew you were an adventurous type, and loved a good mystery, and here you are successfully nearing the end. Not far to go now. I hope you are beginning to see a pattern in what I have been showing you. I'm praying that God will make it clear and reveal to you what He wants you to understand.'" Mrs. Renton looked up again, sensing she needed to say something in response.

"Well, I am trying to understand, but I think Uncle Kenwyn had a higher opinion of my abilities than perhaps is the reality. I wouldn't even be reading this if it wasn't for you."

"We're in this together," said Mom quickly. "It's a blessing to help."

"Thank you for letting us be part of a real adventure," added Rachel, smiling broadly.

"Oh, you're so very welcome," said Mrs. Renton, suddenly feeling quite a bit better. "Well, I'd better keep going. Let's see… 'William Lonsdale's grave was in sad repair when I first saw it. The stone had all but crumbled away, and I only knew which one it was because of records I found in the chapel. I thought he deserved a better memorial so I had a new headstone put in place.'"

"So that's why it looked so new," blurted out Danny.

"Yes, but shhh," warned Mom. "Let's let Mrs. Renton continue."

She looked over at the old lady who smiled and kept going. "'As you read in the book, Mr. Lonsdale was quite an interesting character. One might say he wasted most of his life, and it's true he had many regrets, but what's most important is how he finished. I was amazed and delighted to find his diary in an old chest in his attic. Stop for a moment and read the photocopy of one of his diary pages that I included. Then come back here.'"

Mrs. Renton set the letter down and pulled out the second folded sheet. She unfolded it and held it up. "The writing's really hard to read but Uncle Kenwyn wrote in a translation under each line."

"Isn't it in English, then?" wondered Emily.

"It's in old English," smiled Mrs. Renton, "which has some different words, but I think Uncle Kenwyn rewrote it mainly because the hand-writing is so hard to decipher. Here we go: *'Wednesday, October 8th. Praise God that he opened my eyes before it was too late. I am redeemed, dead and buried with Christ and raised to new life in Him. How I regret the wasted years when I kicked against the goads, as did Saint Paul, but all thanks be now to God for rescuing me on my own Damascus road. What remains of my life I dedicate to Him. I yearn to finish well. The war between the Spanish and the Dutch continues—not just a war between two nations but a battle between religious bigotry and religious freedom, between works and faith. The bright light of Protestantism must not be extinguished in the Low Countries. Where Spanish cruelty sunders families, and many seek to flee, what more can I do but offer myself, my livelihood, my very life to Him for this great cause. I start tonight and hope and pray for a successful and speedy return. My child will be in God's hands."*

Mrs. Renton paused, impacted deeply by what she'd read. *To finish well. Was that still an option for her?* As she mentally gazed back on her life, it did seem like such a waste in so many ways, living in selfishness and bitterness. Was it not too late? Or could she be like this man—William Lonsdale? She tried to thrust aside the thought for now. The family was waiting for her to continue.

"That's the end of the diary page," she announced to her audience, carefully folding up the paper. The others were quiet for a moment, taking it all in. The sound of the budgie exploring his food dish could be clearly heard from over by the kitchen.

"So did he come back safely?" wondered Stevie finally.

Dad shook his head sadly, still processing that fact himself. The man evidently had given his life for God's service.

"Was that his last diary entry then?" said Emily.

Mrs. Renton checked the Squire's note again. "It looks like it. Here, I'll keep going with the Squire's letter." She shifted in her seat a little. Pickwick stood up for a moment, stretched and then settled down again, nestling himself into her lap.

"William Lonsdale never returned from that voyage, but he had got his wish. He did indeed finish well. A life lived in service to God is a precious, fragrant offering, but there is something imminently important according to Scripture, of a life that finishes well—that doesn't give up but builds to a roaring crescendo of faith. In the mystery of God's economy, the worker who is hired last and works energetically in the time he has left, is just as valuable as the one who is hired first. In that way, it is never too late in life to decide to give all one has left in grateful service to God. We can lay our regrets, our misguided choices, our selfish decisions before him and say 'Lord what I have left I give to you.' The Apostle Paul wanted his life to be like this— he wanted his future to be marked by a passionate desire to know Jesus. He himself had many reasons to live in regret, but instead he looked to the future—to what Jesus could do in him and through him—to take hold of all that Jesus wanted for him. In the Bible, in his letter to the Philippians, chapter 3 verses 13 and 14, he said 'Forgetting what is behind and straining toward what is ahead, I press on toward the goal to win the prize for which God has called me heavenward in Christ Jesus.' Seek this prize with all your heart, Ruthie. Your life is not summed up by the past, but by your future with God in Christ."

Mom and Dad were listening intently, watching Mrs. Renton's countenance as she read, knowing the Squire had written this to speak directly to her need. They both noticed a slight mistiness in her eyes, and prayed silently, urging God to open her heart. They watched her struggle to master her emotions, both sensing that this wasn't the time to say anything. God was at work, and they didn't want to interfere.

The old lady didn't look up, but took a deep breath and continued on, managing to successfully steady her voice. "*And here we are, dear Ruthie, at the next clue. This one should be fairly short I hope, and then you'll be on the home stretch. Don't give up. God will help you.*

The kelly an crows, a sacred place, A faithful soul there soared to grace.

His life a service for the word, its end a testimony sure.

The marker hides another clue, the key for what you need to do."

"Short and sweet," said Dad. "Well maybe not that sweet," he added, frowning."

"I'll read it again," said Mrs. Renton with a sigh. *How could Uncle Kenwyn have thought she could figure all this out?* She read it slowly and clearly while the others listened carefully, trying to grasp onto any part that made sense.

"It seems to be about another guy," said Rachel, "and it sounds like he died doing something."

"From the 1500s, no doubt," said Mom, "if the pattern holds true and we're going back in time."

"What was the first line again?" said Danny. "It didn't seem to make sense."

"The kelly an crows, a sacred place," read Mrs. Renton, pronouncing it carefully.

"That sounds like a pub," said Danny. "The kelly and crows."

"No it doesn't," contradicted Stevie. "What's a kelly?"

"I don't think it's the name of a pub," said Mrs. Renton gently. "It's not capitalized like a name, and besides it says 'an' not 'and.'"

"Oh," said Danny, abashed.

"Let's stop and pray," said Emily, remembering what they had discussed earlier. "God knows the answer."

"That's my girl," said Mom, reaching over and rubbing her back.

"May I do the honors?" said Dad. The others nodded. The old lady closed her eyes and clasped her hands. For the first time she felt absolutely sure they needed to do this.

"Dear Heavenly Father, thank you again for all you've done for us. Thank you for the privilege of helping Mrs. Renton, and for all the clues you've helped us solve. Please help us figure this one out. Give us strength and wisdom to carry on to the end. Help dear Mrs. Renton as this is hard for her. And please protect us from anyone trying to stop us. Confuse their thinking. We want you to be glorified in it all, so Your will be done. In Jesus' name."

"Amen," chorused everyone, Mrs. Renton included. After all, she considered, it may help, since it was Mr. Chapman who was doing the praying.

"So, we have a strange phrase that isn't a pub," said Mom. "It must be a place name though, right? A sacred place."

"What's a sacred place?" said Stevie.

"It's a place that has a special significance—something that makes it special."

"Like a church?"

"That's right," said Dad. "Or a shrine, or someplace where something important happened that was meaningful."

"And I think Rachel was right about the next line—that it was a place someone died," said Mrs. Renton, glad to be able to contribute. "A faithful soul there soared to grace. That sounds like someone going to heaven."

"That's right," said Dad. "Do you remember the memorial at Omaha beach in Normandy? There was a statue there that looked like a soldier's soul ascending to heaven."

Mom and the kids nodded. That had surely been a sacred place.

"But that doesn't leave us much to go on," said Mom. "Where is this place?"

That was a puzzle. They looked at each other confused.

"We know it has a marker," said Mrs. Renton, studying the clue again. "We're supposed to look behind it for the next clue."

"I can only think that the weird phrase at the beginning must be what we need to find the place," said Dad. "What was it again?"

"Kelly an crows," replied Mrs. Renton. "It sounds a little bit like Irish."

"Are we supposed to look for Irish crows?" said Stevie, seriously. Danny looked really puzzled at that.

"Why would the Squire put something in Irish?" wondered Emily. "We're in Cornwall."

"Right," said Dad, his mental wheels turning. "How about if it's in Cornish then."

"The bookstore guy had a book on Cornish," squeaked Rachel. "We could ask him."

"We could," said Dad doubtfully. "But it was a bit of a trick finding that bookstore. Do you think we can find it again quickly?"

"The afternoon is getting along," agreed Mom with a slight frown.

"Let's do it!" said Dad, throwing caution to the wind and jumping to his feet.

"I'll come too," said Mrs. Renton, giving Pickwick a gentle push off her lap.

The others stared at her in surprise. She saw their looks and smiled. "If we really are getting close, I want to help out any way I can. I've done enough sitting."

"Well, okay then," said Dad with just a tinge of concern. It felt like they should be in a hurry, and he wasn't sure the old lady could keep up the pace. He tried to squash his concerns, and gave her a smile. It was her quest, after all. "Let's go find the last clue," he added, trying to sound as positive as possible.

Chapter 24 - Trapped

Kennedy huddled miserably on the bench in front of the White Whale pub, nervously drawing on his cigarette through clenched teeth. He fumbled for the half pint of ale at his side, keeping his eyes fixed on the old lady's cottage over on the lane above the harbor. The tide was almost all the way in, and with it most of Penrithen's little fishing fleet, urged into the harbor by a sharp wind from the west—a wind that had nothing in the way to prevent it from piercing directly through to Kennedy's shivering flesh. As he took a quick sip, he realized his thoughts were as dark as the line of threatening clouds hovering over the sea. It was ridiculous having to sit out here in this arctic blast when he could hear the people in the pub behind him enjoying the warmth and camaraderie. He couldn't watch the lady's house from inside, and couldn't afford anything more to drink anyway, let alone eat, so he was stuck here out in this frigid weather. *It just wasn't fair*. In fact, this pretty much summed up his life right now—excluded from the comfortable life he considered his right, with nothing on the horizon but an ominous expectation of what was soon to come.

His dark musings were interrupted by his phone buzzing in his pocket. After a brief struggle he managed to extract it, and he threw an annoyed glance at the number. It wasn't one he recognized. "Kennedy here," he snapped.

He listened to the reply with a growing sense of alarm. He recognized that voice, and it wasn't one he ever cared to hear again.

"Look here," he broke in as the caller stopped to draw a breath. He desperately tried to gather his nerves and sound forthright. "You don't know what you're talking about. They were the genuine article, certified and everything. How do I know you haven't done a switch and you're trying to stiff me?"

Kennedy put as much dignified affront into his voice as he could considering the circumstances—and the fact that he knew full well they weren't the genuine article at all but cleverly contrived fakes. The voice on the other end rose to fever pitch and Kennedy resisted flinging his phone into the bushes across the path.

He weathered the storm with the phone several inches from his ear and then took the opportunity to do some yelling back. "You can't threaten me. You're the one who needs to watch his back. I've got connections and they'll make your life too hot to survive. Never call me again!"

He snapped his phone shut, effectively disconnecting the call. His heart hammering in his chest, he stared at his shoes, trying to process what had just happened. If there was ever a time he would have a heart attack this was it—he was certain. He had thought things couldn't be any worse, and now this. A sudden dread seized him. What if that guy followed through on his threats? He was a mobster if ever there was one. He probably had connections—someone who could even hunt him down. Maybe he shouldn't have threatened him back. No, that had not been a wise move.

He remembered all the other shady deals he had made over the years. *How many times had he swindled someone?* He had lost count. He had been an expert at it. But where had it got him? He was same as penniless, and perhaps even in danger now of some serious repercussions. He had to get out of here—out of the country—disappear for a while. But disappearing took money, and that was definitely one thing he didn't have.

His throat tightened in panic. He must, *must* steal the old lady's inheritance. There was no other option, no other way, especially with that guy on his tail now. He knew it was something valuable—either some priceless antique or some collection of rare coins or jewels or something--that would fit what Penrow would have stashed away for her. *And it had seemed so easy to do*, he thought, bitterly. Steal the letter, find the goods. But that was before he'd found out about this mystery quest thing, and that he wasn't just dealing with the old lady but this stupid family as well. Now it seemed ridiculous to think he could get ahead of them and beat them to the prize--it was all slipping from his grasp.

His fear was replaced by a boiling rage. This had to work—it *had* to. This treasure—whatever it was—was his. He should have had it years ago, and he deserved it now anyway after all he had been through. *And by George he would have it.* Nobody was going to stop him.

He jumped to his feet knocking over his glass. That idea had popped into his mind again—something that might help ensure he would get the prize—and there was no feeble resistance from his conscience this time. Ignoring the biting wind he made a quick assessment. Yes, he could make it to Jennings' shop while keeping the lady's house in sight almost all of the way. *Perfect. That family had better watch out.*

❧❧

The weather was looking mighty iffy again—it was amazing how changeable it was—and the going had been pretty slow, trying to keep at the old lady's pace. Dad so hoped they wouldn't be caught in a downpour—the afternoon was getting along and they had to be back at the inn for dinner.

They had all just crossed the bridge and were passing the slipway ramp down into the harbor. The tide was in and the wind was causing a lively chatter from the rigging of the fishing boats bobbing and swaying in the dark waters. There was a strong fishy smell, and the kids noticed a few fisherman in hats and oilskins stacking lobster pots on the quay. They looked up as the group passed and Danny gave a gasp and tugged at his dad's sleeve.

"Dad, Dad, it's that guy again!"

"Who? Where?" Dad looked wildly around, thinking Danny meant Kennedy or the Mole Hole man.

"No, no." Danny guided Dad's gaze to the men on the quay. "There. The fisherman who spoke Cornish. He could help."

Dad nodded slowly, weighing his worries about the long trek to the bookstore against having to talk to the somewhat grumpy fisherman. He hadn't been exactly easy to follow the last time.

Mom had secretly been sharing Dad's concerns about the weather, the distance and Mrs. Renton's staying power. She nodded, vigorously. "That's a good idea. Why don't you ask him, Dave?"

Dad knew exactly why he didn't want to ask him, but realized he'd better keep his thoughts to himself. "Okay." He squared his shoulders. "Danny, come along too. He seemed to like you."

Danny wasn't expecting that. "Er, but..." The verse from Joshua popped into his mind again. *Be strong and courageous.* He looked up at his Dad who smiled and grabbed his hand.

"It'll be okay," said Dad, sounding more confident than he felt. "We'll go together."

❧❧

Kennedy peered out from behind the memorial. He had spotted the family coming down from the old lady's house and had ducked behind the pillar. He could continue on his quest in a minute, he mused, after he figured out where they were going. That was more important right now.

❧❧

"That's about it, Jasper. Time for a pint." Jack Carrick hefted the last lobster pot onto the quay and stretched his aching back.

His colleague nodded and spat into the water. "Aye, I'm ready as I've ever been. Wind's been a right devil today. Won't be many minutes afore it'll be sommat to reckon with."

Jack was about to reply when he noticed two figures coming tentatively towards them hand in hand—one tall, the other short. He muttered under his breath. Those *havysi* again. Summer visitors, interfering with life—probably want to take a photo of a real Cornish fisherman or something. He noticed that Jasper had suddenly made himself scarce. *Nice friend he was.*

As they got closer he recognized the young boy. So it was him and his dad again. *Probably lost*, he grunted to himself. Well, he supposed he'd give them the time of day, if just for the boy's sake, but he didn't have to be happy about it.

"Hello. Excuse me." Dad approached the fisherman with his hand outstretched. Jack was unzipping his oilskins and glanced at the hand but made no move to shake it.

391

Dad withdrew his hand and took a deep breath. "Er, I'm very sorry to bother you…"

The man nodded, evidently in agreement that he was indeed being bothered.

"But," Dad continued, "we need a little help again with some directions."

"Aye." That monosyllable was so tonelessly delivered that Dad was strongly tempted to abandon ship and go find someone else.

Danny looked at his dad and then at the fisherman. *Why was the man being so grumpy?* Had he had a bad day fishing or something? The memories of some of the books he'd read about fisherman and sailing ships came back to him. They always seemed to have a storm and a shipwreck in them. He suddenly felt some compassion and his fear melted away.

"Did your fishing boat get shipwrecked?" he blurted out.

Both Dad and the fisherman looked startled at the question. Jack glanced over his shoulder and then gestured to where his boat rocked lazily next to the quay.

"That's ma boat, and she's doing fine." A slightly amused look came into his eyes. "Why d'ya think it was wrecked? There's a storm on its way for sure, but we're safely in."

Danny had run out of words to say. The fisherman wrestled himself out of his jacket and looked closely at the lad. He did remind him of his grandson, Seth. He reached over and patted the boy's head.

"D'you need me for summat?" He addressed his question to Danny who nodded brightly, finding his voice again.

"Yes please, sir. We have some directions in Cornish and we didn't understand you last time and thought you were maybe speaking Cornish so we thought you could help this time."

Jack actually felt a smile coming over his face. "Alright, alright, I'll do it. What have ya got." He set his jacket down on the top of a stack of lobster pots.

"Kelly an crows," said Dad, as clearly as possible.

Jack nodded. "Aye, kelly. It's…what d'ya call it? It's trees—like a bunch of trees."

"Aha," said Dad. "A forest?"

"Nah. Smaller."

"A copse? A grove?"

The fisherman grunted appreciatively. "That's it. That'll do. Grove. Grove of trees."

"And crows?"

Jack shook his head. Wasn't it obvious? "Crows. Aye, crows you know."

"Crows," repeated Dad, puzzled.

"Aye, crows. You know what a crows is don't ya?"

"Er, some birds?"

Jack shook his head in disgust. "Crows! Eglos!" He pointed up towards the headland.

Suddenly Danny had it. "It's a cross!" he exclaimed.

Jack smiled at the lad in approval. "Exactly. Crows."

"So…kelly an crows. Is it a grove of crosses?" said Dad, wondering how long this guessing game might take.

"Nah, nah. T'other way round."

"A cross in a grove?"

"Aye." The fisherman took Danny firmly by the shoulders again and turned him towards the memorial. He leaned over and pointed. "Back there. Kelly an crows."

"Beyond the memorial?" said Dad, trying to understand which direction was being indicated.

"Roight. Skochfordh." Satisfied with his explanation, the man gave Danny a quick pat on the head and then stumped off in the direction of his boat. He would find Jasper and give him what for—leaving him to deal with all this by himself.

"Okay…," said Dad after his retreating back. "That was…ah…difficult enough." He smiled suddenly and gave Danny a hug. "Thanks for your help. I couldn't have done it without you. I think we have the general direction. Let's go tell the others."

⋘⋙

They were heading his way! For a moment Kennedy stood frozen. Then he shook himself and looked quickly around him. Okay, he had a plan. He backed slowly down the steps, keeping the memorial between him and the family. Then he turned and scampered over to the florists shop at the far side of the intersection. Yanking open the door he jumped inside.

⋘⋙

Dad glanced at his watch. Almost three-twenty. The afternoon was motoring by, but at least they seemed to be getting somewhere. He waited till everyone had gathered at the base of the memorial.

"Okay, according to Mr. Fisherman person, somewhere near here is a grove of trees."

The others nodded and looked around. The valley in which the village lay was fairly steep and narrow until it reached the head of the harbor, at which point it suddenly widened out. The bulk of the town sat ahead of them and off to the left, following the line of the cliff. Straight ahead was the road that led into the maze of streets that steeply climbed the valley side. They knew the coffee place was ahead and to the right and the bookstore somewhere up in the jumble of buildings above them. To their immediate right was the pottery and the other shops facing the harbor.

"Which way, Daddy?" Rachel came and stood at Dad's side.

"Good question, honey. Do any of you see some trees?"

"Not many," said Mom, frowning. "Just one or two—nothing like a grove."

"Could it be further up the valley?" wondered Mrs. Renton. "There may be more trees up there."

"But didn't the fisherman guy say it was near the memorial?" said Danny.

"He did, he did," admitted Dad. "At least I think so. I don't see anything obvious around here though, but let's split up and look around. Don't go too

393

far—stay where you can see each other." He had a sudden vision of kids disappearing permanently into the nooks and crannies.

The kids needed no further encouragement and tore off. Rachel and Emily headed straight ahead, and the boys took off towards the shops on the right.

"I can stay here with Mrs. Renton," offered Mom. "We can keep an eye on everyone."

"And keep an eye out for the nasty men," added the old lady.

"That's right." Dad had forgotten about them for the moment. "That would be great. I'll check the road up towards the pub." He had barely started when he heard an excited hail from Danny.

"Over here! Over here!"

The family converged on the spot where Danny and Stevie were pointing triumphantly to a small gap between two of the shops. It was a shadowy, cobblestone alleyway, so small and narrow that it was really only visible from the spot where they were standing.

"What do you think?" said Danny, smiling broadly.

"Can we try up here?" said Stevie, proudly. Hadn't he found it with his brother?

Dad looked at Mom who nodded. "Okay," she said, "but let's go together."

"Another secret passage," said Rachel with delight.

"Yes, sort of," said Dad, smiling. "But it does lead up the valley."

"Will you come with us?" Emily asked Mrs. Renton.

The old lady nodded, still determined to be a help in some way. "If you don't mind."

"Of course," said Mom, hoping it would be okay. "We're in this together."

∞∾

Bettie Cadgewell, owner of *Bettie's Blooms,* was not amused. "Sir, if you are not here to buy anything or even consider buying anything, then I'm going to have to ask you to leave."

"It's a shop, for heaven's sake." Kennedy was peering furtively between two large flower arrangements where he could see the goings on outside. He spun his head around and glared at the shop owner. "As long as you're open, I can be here," he snapped.

"Well, I can fix that," retorted Hattie. Her lips pinched into a look of haughty disgust. She eased her ample self around the edge of the counter and marched over to the door, her high heels tapping their irritation on the tile floor. Seizing the "open" sign hanging on the glass she flipped it decisively over.

"There. Closed. Now if you don't leave, I'm going to call the police." She knew full well she would never have the gumption to do it, but it sounded like a dire enough warning.

Kennedy was about to spew an angry reply when he noticed something out the window. The family were disappearing in-between two of the shops over to the left. With a yelp of dismay he yanked open the door and dashed outside.

Bettie smiled smugly to herself. Oh, yes, she still had what it took. *What a tale for the girls at Bingo!*

394

The narrow, cobbled passage made a few steep turns and mounted several flights of stone steps, snaking between colorful, crooked cottages and on up the hillside. Rachel was in front with the boys just behind. Emily and Mom hovered around Mrs. Renton, making sure she didn't trip and helping her up the steps. The old lady was already having second thoughts about coming along.

Dad brought up the rear, sensing a strange feeling of disquiet. He kept checking over his shoulder, but the passage behind remained empty. He felt slightly silly—surely those guys couldn't possibly know where they were. He stopped and strained his ears to listen. It was cold in the passage and he caught the whistling of the wind across the roofs above. There didn't seem to be any other sound, except the footsteps of the group further on. He shook his head and hurried to catch up.

Rachel was already out of sight. She loved this sort of thing, feeling like she was truly living an adventure story. She came upon another flight of steps and trotted up, the boys trying to keep close behind her. The slate stone wall of a house rose up right in front, but to its left was a gap between the buildings. She took the turn without hesitating and what she saw caused her to give a cry of delight. They were finally at the upper limits of the village. The path opened up into a round paved area surrounded by an old crumbling stone wall and overhung by a number of wizened trees, their straggling leafy branches forming a somber canopy. Straight ahead the valley side formed a sharp cliff—a rocky backdrop visible through the trees and dotted with stunted bushes and small clumps of wildflowers. A narrow path led off through gaps in the wall in both directions along the bottom of the cliff. In the center of the cleared space stood an ancient stone pedestal topped with what appeared to be a cross set in a circle. Weeds and grass had sprung up through the paving stones and the whole place had a sad, lonely feeling.

Rachel turned and was about to yell to the others about her discovery, but something stopped her. She looked back at the stone cross. It was dark under the trees and the place looked very solemn. She heard the boys arrive and turned with her finger to her lips. "Shhh," she warned.

The boys managed to catch their exclamations just in time and took in the scene, wondering what Rachel was worried about. Emily, Mom and Mrs. Renton appeared, the old lady breathing heavily. They looked around in amazement.

"What is this place?" whispered Emily.

"I'm not sure," said Mom in an equally low voice, "but it does look promising."

Mrs. Renton gave a rasping cough and Mom looked at her concerned.

The old lady gave a slight smile. "I'm alright…really I am. It's just the most walking I've done in a while."

"How's your ankle?" asked Emily softly.

"Not too shabby. Holding up."

"Why are we whispering?" said Stevie.

"Because this is a sacred place," said Dad near his ear, making the lad jump. He had come up without anyone noticing.

"Do you think so?" said Rachel. "Like in the clue?"

"It's a grove—*the grove of the cross*. It must be it," said Mom, looking around.

"Can you read the clue again, please?" said Danny.

Mrs. Renton dug in her purse and pulled out the letter, glad to be of some help. *"The kelly an crows, a sacred place, a faithful soul there soared to grace. His life a service for the word, its end a testimony sure. The marker hides another clue, the key for what you need to do."*

"Thank you," said Mom. "So where is the marker it mentions?"

That was the sign for the kids to start searching around the pillar, and it was only a matter of seconds before there was a cry of success, hastily stifled.

"Here it is! We found it." Emily beckoned everyone over.

"Here, at the bottom," added Stevie. The others crowded around as Emily and Stevie held the weeds and grass out of the way. Attached to the base of the pillar was a small brass marker, discolored with age but still clearly readable.

Emily read it aloud. *"On this sacred spot on the 30th of July in the Year of Our Lord 1515, Cadan Nancarrow, servant of the Word, surrendered his body to the flames. His light still shines brightly."*

"Aha," said Dad.

"Aha what?" Mom turned to look at him.

"This must be where someone was burned at the stake. He gave his life on this spot."

"But why?" said Emily, shuddering. "Was he a Christian?"

Dad nodded soberly. "That time of English history was a very difficult one for true followers of Jesus. The established church was powerful, but unfortunately wasn't too interested in really obeying the Bible—they were religious in practice, but didn't necessarily have a relationship with Jesus. Many didn't even want the everyday person to have access to the Scriptures. It's significant that it says here Nancarrow was a '*servant of the Word*.' He must have somehow been able to read and obey it."

"We need the next clue!" put in Stevie impatiently. "Where is it supposed to be again?"

"Behind the marker," said Mrs. Renton. She shivered involuntarily—was it the chilly air, or was it with excitement? Or was it the thought that someone had been executed on this spot? She wasn't sure.

✧❧✧

Kennedy crept up to the corner and tried to position himself so he could peer around with the minimum amount of exposure. *And there they were!* He snatched his head back. They were gathered around a sort of pillar thing. Was this where the next clue was hidden? He would have to wait and see.

✧❧✧

Emily had taken a closer look at the little brass sign. "If this is the marker, it's screwed on. Does anyone have a screwdriver?"

There was a pause, Dad shook his head and then all eyes turned on Mom.

"What, me? Why would I have a screwdriver?"

"You always have everything," said Rachel. "Can you check in the backpack?"

Mom's eyes widened for a moment. Then she shrugged her shoulders. "Okay, I'll look."

"I told you so," said Rachel to Emily. Emily wasn't so sure.

"Let's see," said Mom, peering inside and rummaging around. "An adjustable wrench, a hacksaw, a stud finder…"

"A Geiger counter," added Dad, peering over her shoulder. He winked at the kids.

"A Geiger counter," echoed Mom. "A coffee grinder…and I think I can feel a small toaster oven, but…no screwdriver."

Mrs. Renton was looking very surprised at all these revelations.

"It's a long story," said Dad.

"But I do have these," said Mom, presenting with some flair a small pair of tweezers.

"Are you going to try to pluck it off?" grinned Dad.

"No, but I think you could use the flat end to turn the screws." Mom nodded in satisfaction.

"Not a bad idea," Dad nodded, impressed. "Why don't you do the honors?"

Mom flashed Dad a smile and knelt down by the pillar. She examined the metal sign and then inserted the end of the tweezers in one of the screws.

"It's working," exclaimed Stevie, who was peering under Mom's arm.

It was. In a very short time all the screws were out and Mom carefully set the metal sign down and pulled out a plastic-wrapped package from the small cavity behind. She held it up in triumph. Rachel and Emily clapped their hands in excitement, and Danny and Stevie did a sort of war dance, chanting "We got the next clue, we got the next clue!"

Dad held up his hand. "Okay kids, I'm really happy too, but we should keep our voices down. Not only is this a special place, but we also need to remember that Mr. Kennedy may be on our trail."

This had the desired effect. They quietened down at once and looked around in consternation.

"I tell you what. I'll go and check and make sure he hasn't followed us." Even as he said it, Dad felt a stab of concern. He had no desire to have a confrontation with Mr. Kennedy. Hopefully he was nowhere to be found.

Though it was hard to catch all the discussion, Kennedy had no problem hearing Mr. Chapman's last announcement. He dashed back down the alley and jumped into the first doorway he could find. Pressing himself against the door, he tried to flatten himself out of sight in the alcove.

Dad thought he caught a flash of movement somewhere down the alley. He stopped and took a good look. No, he must have been mistaken. It looked completely deserted. With a sigh of relief he turned and went back to join the others. Mom was putting the brass sign back in place and the rest were anxiously watching for him. He gave them a quick thumbs up. "No-one out there. Did you look at the clue yet?"

"No, we were waiting for you," said Mom. "Would you mind, Mrs. Renton?"

"Not at all. Here it is." With a concerted effort she kept her hand from shaking and unwrapped the plastic. *Could this even be the end of their quest?*

Inside was another sealed plastic bag, and she opened that too and pulled out several sheets. As she did, something fell to the ground with a bright, metallic tinkling sound. It was a small brass key. Dad picked it up. "This doesn't look hundreds of years old. Strange."

"Maybe the letter explains," said the old lady. She cleared her throat and tried to steady her voice, then looked at the papers. "This one says read first of course, so here we go. *'Congratulations, Ruthie. You're getting really close! God has answered my prayers. There's just a bit more sleuthing to do and then you'll be at the end—the inheritance you've been working so hard to find.'"*

Mrs. Renton stopped to let that sink in. To her surprise she realized she didn't even really care what was at the end now. This whole process had been teaching her so much—she wasn't sure she was ready for it to stop. She wasn't waiting for a big financial payoff, she just wanted her mind and heart to be at peace. She suddenly noticed that the others were watching her, and she colored slightly. "Dear me, I was off in another world again."

"That's no problem," said Mom, kindly. "We understand."

"So, Uncle Kenwyn says to read the letter. Let's see…" Mrs. Renton examined the papers and selected a photocopied sheet. "This looks like something similar to last time. It's a copy of a very old letter, and Uncle has written in the explanation. Here we go.

"My time is short. I expect any moment to be denounced and imprisoned. What follows from that we all know will not be easy, but it will be light and momentary compared to eternity. It has always been a risk, but I know you, as do I, count our appointment worth it all. Though I miss her dearly, I know now it is best that Kathryn went to be with the Lord before me. Little Henry is with my cousin who will I trust raise him in the true Way. I entrust the treasure to you. You know where it is hidden. Share it as God allows. Be wise as a serpent, innocent as a dove. Hold all earthly things loosely. You will likely not see me again this side of heaven save at the stake. Go in God's grace and strength. Cadan."

Mrs. Renton stopped, her eyes downcast. Mom and Dad looked at each other, both visibly moved. Emily and Rachel were silent, trying to understand the sacrifice the man had made right there where they were standing. Danny and Stevie just looked puzzled.

Finally Danny spoke up. "So, I guess I don't understand. What happened to the guy?"

"Well," said Dad, trying to figure out what to say. "The man must have angered the authorities somehow—it seems by preaching the Gospel so that people understood the true message about Jesus."

"But why would that make people mad?"

Dad sighed. "It's hard to explain, but throughout history there have been people really against Christianity, and also many people who said they were Christians but weren't really following Jesus."

"They tried to use the church as a way to get power and riches," added Mom. "They wanted the everyday people to have to depend on them—to believe that the only way they could possibly get to heaven was to obey the leaders and give money to the church."

"But why would people believe that?" wondered Stevie.

"Because of fear," said Dad. "Fear that they wouldn't go to heaven if they weren't good enough, and fear of punishment if they didn't obey."

"God would punish them?" Danny asked, trying hard to understand.

"No, God wants people to follow Jesus. He accepts anyone who gives their life to Him. But the bad church leaders would actually kill people who tried to follow Jesus and do what the Bible teaches."

"I get it," said Rachel. "I remember reading about this in history. The church had become really powerful and said that the only way to get to heaven was to be a church member and obey its rules."

"Exactly," said Dad. "Good summary, Rachel."

"So the man didn't obey the church and so they killed him?" said Stevie, still not really sure he could believe what he was hearing.

"I'm afraid so," said Mom.

"But our church back home didn't seem like a bad place. Did Pastor Bill ever punish someone for not going to church?"

The others laughed and even Mrs. Renton had to smile. "No, no, buddy," said Dad. Our church is a Bible-believing, Jesus-following group of people. The church we're talking about was like a big powerful organization in history. Most people couldn't read, and didn't even have the Bible in English, so they just believed what the bad church leaders told them."

"Didn't have it in English?" said Stevie, incredulous.

"The Bible wasn't written in English, Stevie. It was first written in Hebrew, Greek and Aramaic. It was translated into English about 500 years ago"

"Wow, am I glad!" said the boy, shaking his head. "I already know English."

The others giggled.

"Didn't the letter mention a treasure?" said Danny. "Would that be Mrs. Renton's inheritance?"

"Maybe." Dad hadn't thought of that.

"Could the key be to a treasure chest then?" said Danny excitedly. He could picture that clearly—just like a pirate chest with gold and jewels and crowns and things.

"Well, I guess we need to find out," said Mom brightly. "Would you mind continuing?"

"Not at all dear," replied the old lady, amused at all the interchange again. It was funny, but it actually had made a few things clearer for herself. She looked at the papers and found the place. "Alright, we're back with Uncle Kenwyn. *Cadan Nancarrow was indeed arrested and imprisoned, but he had hidden the treasure in time. Until the day of his execution he was held in a place not far from here. Follow the symbols to the place and use the key to gain entrance."*

"So it's not a treasure chest key," said Danny, disappointed.

"Let's not interrupt," said Mom. She smiled at Mrs. Renton "Please go on."

The old lady nodded and continued. *"Cadan Nancarrow died with a full assurance that he would go to be with Jesus, not because of anything good he had done, or that he finished well, but because he believed God's Word to be true. He believed and accepted that Jesus paid for his sins on the cross—a free gift. His assurance of heaven was not based on his own character and merit, but on the character and merit of Jesus—the perfect holy sacrifice, accepted by God as the Bible says. Nancarrow was longing to meet Jesus and his hope was steady to the end despite his suffering. Psalm 119:81 sums up his firm conviction: 'My soul faints with longing for Your salvation, but I have put my hope in Your word.'*

Will you put your hope in His Word, Ruthie? It says that you can find salvation in Christ, freely offered by a loving Father who knows all about suffering. I am praying you will grasp this.

Now here's the final part of the clue:

27 in 66. Count 3 in 27.

15 in 3, and for the lines, now count the days in prison.

'Upon this rock', is built the place, the stories there displayed.

The man of mercy points the way to where the treasure's laid.

Up, and left then down and right, the hidden hold revealed.

The greatest treasure man has held, for ages there concealed.

Its riches will provide for you all that you're seeking for.

The answer to your hopes and needs, both now and evermore.

I commit you into God's hand again for this last stage of the journey, Ruthie. I have prayed that you will find your way and that God will provide all you need. All my love, Uncle Kenwyn."

"Wow!" said Mom. "What a clue!"

"Impossible," said Mrs. Renton, shaking her head. What had her uncle been thinking? There was no way she could figure this out.

"Can you read it again, please," said Emily. "If you don't mind."

"Of course, dear," said the old lady, trying to swallow down the panicky feeling rising within her. She steadied her voice and read it again, slowly and carefully.

"There's so much in there!" exclaimed Rachel.

"But it's the way to the treasure!" said Stevie. "Finally!"

"Yes, finally," agreed Dad. "But I must admit it does appear a daunting task." He felt that gnawing sense of worry again, but this time another thought came quick on its heels. There was only one way to respond to worry. "Let's pray, before we get too overwhelmed," he said out loud.

"Great idea, honey," said Mom. "Let's join hands."

The family stood in a circle and held hands, Mrs. Renton feeling less awkward and embarrassed than she had feared as she stood between Emily and Mrs. Chapman.

"Dear Father," said Dad. "Thank you so much for getting us this far. You are truly good. Thank you for the answers to prayer. It's amazing that we're so close to the end. You know we need your help again. This clue is hard. Please show us the meaning. Show us your way, give us wisdom and please protect us. Help dear Mrs. Renton understand what the Squire has been trying to communicate."

Oh, yes, thought the old lady.

"And help her understand what You are wanting to tell her too," Dad continued.

Why not? Yes, God, she agreed silently.

"And please confuse our enemies," added Dad. He paused for a moment, wondering what those men had been up to since they'd last run into them.

"And please bring them to you," added Danny, taking advantage of the pause.

Dad looked at him, pleased. "Yes, and please bring them to you, for your glory, Amen."

"Amen," they all said in unison.

"Thanks, dear," said Mom, feeling a lot more optimistic. She loved this praying together as a family.

"But where to start?" said Stevie.

"How about at the very beginning?" said Mom.

"A very good place to start," sang Rachel with a grin at Dad.

"Oh, no," said her father, shaking his head. "We're not singing anything from *The Sound of Music!*"

Mom frowned. "I meant at the part before the clue. Didn't the The Squire's note say something about following some symbols?"

"Oh, yes," said Mrs. Renton, suddenly feeling a hint of hope. "I forgot to mention that there's a little drawing here next to that line. Here…" She showed the letter to the others. Sure enough there was a hand-drawn picture of a cross within a circle.

"It looks like the top of the pillar thing," said Rachel, studying it again.

"You're right," said Mom. "Let's see if we can find a symbol like it somewhere."

The kids immediately tore off in different directions. Mrs. Renton stood looking bemused and Mom slipped her arm through the old lady's. "Are you alright?"

"I think so," Mrs. Renton replied. "I'm just amazed. You just keep asking God for help and then it seems like you get an idea right away-- like He really wants us to get to the end!"

"I think He does," said Mom with a laugh. "God doesn't always just say 'yes' when we pray—He knows that sometimes it's better for us to wait and deepen our trust in Him, but I have a feeling He wants you to figure everything out on this quest." She paused. "He loves you, you know?"

"Well, I am open to the idea now," agreed the old lady with a shy smile, realizing as she said it that it was indeed the truth.

Dad was about to say something, when he was interrupted by a cry from Emily.

"I found one! Over here."

They joined Emily at the gap in the wall to their right, where an uneven path led off between the trees. She pointed at the wall. "See—a symbol. That didn't take long!"

Sure enough there was a small circle with a cross etched into the stone by the gap.

"It must mean we go this way." Emily pointed along the path.

"Great! Alright then." Dad started directing traffic. "Let's keep together, and Emily, you can lead. I'll bring up the rear. Everyone keep your eyes open."

"Mom, you and Mrs. Renton can follow me." Emily beckoned to them both. "I'll go slowly."

Mom looked questioningly at Mrs. Renton and got a determined nod in reply. She took the old lady's arm and they all set off up the path. The way was rocky and a bit slippery with mud, and Mom kept a firm grip and a close eye on Mrs. Renton. She would let the others look for the signs—she wanted to make sure the old lady was absolutely secure.

The trees rapidly thinned out and the cliff to their left receded into a gentler, grassy slope. Danny was examining the rocks scattered on either side of the path and suddenly spied something. He took a second look, Stevie bumping into him from behind.

"Here's another one!" He pointed to where another symbol was etched in a dark-grey rock embedded in the ground beside the path.

"We must be on the right track," said Mom. "Let's keep going."

They started off again, Stevie trying to scan in all directions at once, hoping to be the next to find one. His efforts were rewarded as he spotted another symbol on a rock, almost hidden behind a screen of oat grass. "I found one!" he yelled, and it was Danny's turn to feel a bit jealous.

"Well done," said Dad from behind, wondering how long this might go on. He was struggling with an increasing feeling of uneasiness, not just about how Mrs. Renton was holding up, but he kept getting an eerie sensation they weren't alone. He quickly checked behind them again, but the way was empty.

"The path splits up ahead," announced Emily. "Which way should we go?"

"There's got to be a marker," said Rachel. "Can I come up front and look?"

"I tell you what," said Mom. "Why don't all you kids go ahead and look. Just don't go out of sight."

The kids tore off and it wasn't long before there was a shout of triumph from Rachel a little way up the left fork. The path here climbed steadily up the side of the valley until it disappeared behind a large rocky outcropping about twenty yards ahead. With Rachel in the lead, the four kids ran up the path and skidded to a halt at the rocks. The others watched in amusement as they peered around the corner and then started waving enthusiastically.

"We found it! Right here!" Rachel yelled.

Dad gave her a thumbs up, and Mom turned to Mrs. Renton. "Do you want to go up there? The path's a bit steep."

Mrs. Renton nodded vigorously. "Oh, yes. It's not so far, and I do feel I should be helping."

Dad surreptitiously checked his watch as they started up the path. They were doing okay for time, though he wasn't too sure about the weather. The sky ahead of them had a low ceiling of light grey cloud, but behind them in the direction of the sea the color was a much darker slate. Every now and then a gust blew in from that direction, causing waves to ripple across the grassy hillside and the merest sensation of misty rain on his cheek. Normally Dad would have liked the invigorating feeling, but right now, with the family and the lady as his responsibility, it was just one more thing to be concerned about.

"Please help us, Lord," he murmured.

It wasn't long before they caught up with the kids who were staring at the outcrop of rocks. The path here took a turn along the bottom of the outcropping before continuing on a ragged climb up the valley. Right at the turn, at the bottom of a sharp, natural cleft in the rock was the narrow entrance to a cave, completely closed off by a barred metal gate, padlocked shut.

There was a small plaque set into the rock by the entrance and Emily read it aloud. "*Penrithen Gaol. This site was used for holding prisoners awaiting trial or execution and was in use from the 1400s up until the mid-1800s. A guardhouse stood nearby but was demolished in the early 1900s.*"

"So this must have been where the man was held," said Mrs. Renton, breathing heavily from her exertions. "And we have the way in!" She produced the key and handed it to Emily. "Here you go, dear."

Emily held the padlock steady and inserted the key. It turned easily and the lock dropped open. "The padlock looks pretty new," she said as she unhooked it from the latch. "I wonder if the Squire was the one to lock it up."

"That's a thought," said Mom. "It is really amazing all the trouble he went to."

"And amazing that all these clues and things are still in place, undisturbed," said Dad thoughtfully.

"Well, in any case, we can get in," said Mom. "Go ahead Emily."

Emily pulled on the bars and the gate swung in easily, with just the merest creak. She peered inside. It was pitch black, and she felt a strong aversion to being the first to go in.

Dad guessed her thoughts. "I don't mind going in first. Let's see…" He dug in his pocket for his phone and turned it on. It gave out a dim glow that didn't make much impression on the darkness.

"How about this?" said Mom. She reached into the top pocket of the backpack and pulled out a small LED light.

"You are a treasure, dear." Dad shook his head in amazement. "Okay, follow me."

Dad went in, followed by the others. Emily was last in line and as she went through the gate, she hung the open padlock back on the latch, the key still in the lock.

⋙⋘

Kennedy watched from the trees as the adults made their way up the path and disappeared around the outcrop of rocks. He could clearly see the rest of the trail up the hill and he waited for them to appear again. As the seconds passed, the frown deepened on his face. A minute…two minutes… Surely they'd pop into view again.

They didn't. *What on earth should he do? Could they have found something up there?* It might be possible to make it to the rocks and try to find out, but he would be exposed the whole way. It would be risky, but he couldn't afford to wait and contemplate it. *Who knows what they could be doing up there?*

Without a further thought, Kennedy jumped from the shelter of the trees and tore up the path.

❧☙

The cave was actually not very deep, with a narrow entrance several yards long that turned and widened out into a small round room, the rocky ceiling brushing the hair on the top of Dad's head. They crowded in and Dad shone the light around. It felt cold and damp inside, and obviously must have been an unpleasant place to spend any amount of time.

"Is this a prison then?" said Stevie, holding on to Dad's leg. He wasn't too sure about this place. *Didn't prisons have skeletons in them? Or was that a dungeon? Well, wasn't this a dungeon?*

"Well, it used to be," said Dad. "It must have been a pretty secure place."

"But what are we supposed to be looking for in here?" said Danny.

"I've got the clue," said Mrs. Renton, barely visible in the gloom.

Dad aimed the light and she recited the first stanza of the poem again for them.

"So we've got to count the days in prison," said Emily. "How will we know how many it was?"

Dad shone the light more closely at the walls. After a brief search, he gave a grunt of satisfaction. "See those marks." He pointed to a series of vertical lines scratched into the wall. "I think those are tallies—one per day I suppose. The prisoners made them to keep track of how long they'd been there. And look there's some more." He shone the light onto another set—rather uneven but still very clear.

"And here too," exclaimed Rachel. She had noticed some just at the edge of the flashlight's glare.

"How can we tell who did the marks?" said Emily. "Would they all have been his?"

Dad shone the light on each set again.

"There's some other marks there," said Mom, crouching down to get a better view. "I think they're letters, but they're very faint. Perhaps an 'F', an 'A' and a 'W'."

"Initials maybe?" said Dad. "Here, let's look at the others."

They examined both other sets of marks. Only one had some letters near it.

"That's got to be a 'C' and an 'N'," said Dad. "Cadan Nancarrow. That's the one!"

"Can I count the marks?" said Stevie. "Please?"

"Go ahead." Dad held the light steady while Stevie tapped each mark with his finger.

"Twenty," he announced a moment later.

"Are you sure?" said Rachel skeptically. She knew math wasn't one of her brother's strong points.

"Yes," retorted Stevie, offended. "Look." He tapped them as he counted again.

"So what does that mean?" said Emily.

"Well, that he spent twenty days in here," said Mom.

"No, I mean what about with the clue?"

"May I have the light again?" said Mrs. Renton. Dad shone it on the paper in her hand.

"*27 in 66. Count 3 in 27. 15 in 3, and for the spot, now count the days in prison,*" quoted Mrs. Renton. "Now pardon me, but isn't that just really confusing? What are all those numbers?"

"27 in 66," said Mom. "That sounds kind of like a fraction. But sixty-six what?" Even as she said it, she realized what it was.

"Books of the Bible!" said four voices in unison. In the glow from the flashlight, there were four grinning faces.

"We learned that in our Awana Bible club," said Rachel. The others nodded vigorously.

"I remember that too," said Mrs. Renton, astonished at herself. "I learned that in Sunday School. *Ages* ago! But what about the twenty-seven?"

Mom and Dad knew the answer to that too, but enjoyed letting the kids have a chance.

"Twenty-seven books in the New Testament," said Stevie proudly before anyone else could speak.

"That's right," said Mom. "Now what's next?"

"Count three in twenty-seven," said Mrs. Renton. "That's a bit harder."

"Matthew, Mark, Luke," said Emily. "One, two, three. It must be a code for the book of the Bible."

"I think you're right," said Dad impressed. "What's the next bit?"

"Fifteen in three," said Mrs. Renton. "Would that be the fifteenth chapter of Luke?"

"It's got to be," said Dad. He touched his wife on the arm. "Do you have your little backpacking Bible with you dear?"

"I do, but I'll have to dig. Can you shine the light here?" Mom set the backpack down and unzipped the main compartment. She pulled out the water bottles, Mrs. Renton's cookies, the first aid kit, the Squire's book and a number of other items until there was quite a pile on the floor.

"Here it is," she said finally. "Now all we need is the verse number. What was it Stevie?"

"Twenty," said Stevie decidedly. He grinned. "We're getting good at this!"

"Remember, Stevie," corrected Dad. "It's God who's helping us. We couldn't do it without him."

Stevie looked down. "Uh-huh. I just meant he's helping us get good."

Mom patted him on the back absentmindedly. "Right, dear. Now—Luke fifteen twenty." She thumbed through her Bible. Dad adjusted the position of the flashlight to help her. "*So he got up and went to his father,*" Mom read. "*But while he was still a long way off, his father saw him and was filled with compassion for him; he ran to his son, threw his arms around him and kissed him.*"

"I know that Bible story," cried Stevie. "It's the parable of the...the...what was it?"

"Prodigal son," said Mom. "The parable of the prodigal son."

"So that's the key to the treasure. The parable of the prodigal son," said Dad excitedly.

"There's got to be something in it that's important," said Emily.

"Can we go back outside?" said Mom. "I think we're done and I'm getting chilled."

Dad was about to reply when there was a terrific crash from the direction of the gate.

"What was that?" said Rachel with a start.

"I don't know, I'll go look," said Dad, concerned. He turned back up the short passage, the others at his heels. What he saw made him stop short in his tracks.

"What's the matter?" said Mom, right behind him.

"The gate," said Dad gesturing in dismay. "It's closed, and the padlock's back in place."

"No! Who has the key?" said Mom. "Emily?"

"I left it in the lock," said Emily miserably. "I'm so sorry."

"It wouldn't have mattered," said Dad, his heart sinking. "There's a metal plate in the way. We couldn't have unlocked it. We'll have to face it. We're locked in."

Chapter 25 – The Race to the Finish

Clutching at his chest, Kennedy skidded to a halt by the cross and almost collapsed in a paroxysm of coughing. He shook his head. His body surely wasn't up to all this. Hopefully it would be over soon.

He took a hurried, nervous glance back up the path. There was no-one there. Had he really done it? Had he managed to put that meddling family out of action? With a growing feeling of amazement and satisfaction he realized that it was true.

His decision to lock them in had been a spur of the moment one. After hiding behind the rock for several minutes, he had finally got up his courage and sidled up to the gate. He could hear voices but they were too muffled to understand, so in desperation he had taken several steps into the cave, straining to hear. He had caught the mention of several numbers, none of which made sense to him, but then he had heard the youngest boy's exclamation. The clue was a story from the Bible—something called the *prodigal son*. What that was, he had no idea, but he had heard the Dad saying it was the key to the treasure. Then when the mom mentioned going back outside he had panicked. Without thinking, he had slammed the door, snapped the padlock shut, pocketed the key and sprinted back down the trail.

He pulled out his cigarettes and quickly lit one, leaning against the pillar. Taking a long drag he exhaled slowly, chewing over the situation. *Did he have enough to go on?* In retrospect it would have been better to have gleaned some more information, but that hadn't been possible, of course. The dad had said this Bible story thing was the key, so that must surely be all he needed. He had to act quickly. He had no illusions that the family would be out of the way forever--someone would find them. This was his last chance—he had to solve this thing right now, and for that he needed a Bible.

A Bible. He'd never even touched one, let alone owned one. *Where on earth would he get a Bible? A book shop?* He knew there was supposedly one in Penrithen, but he'd never seen it.

He had a sudden inspiration. *Jennings' shop.* He'd seen a huge old Bible there, ornately decorated. His rising hopes suddenly plunged again. He'd have to deal with Jennings. He detested the guy and imagined the feeling was probably mutual. *Could he really go back?*

A low rumble echoed from the direction of the sea. *Thunder?* Kennedy hurried over to where he had a clearer view. It was getting dark. A storm must be on its way. He didn't want to get caught out in it. He mashed out his cigarette on the wall. There was no time to figure out anything else--that family could get out any time. He glanced back up the hill and felt a surge of angry frustration again. Maybe it was a stupid idea to have locked them in. Now he'd be forced to figure this out alone, and he didn't have that much to go on. Jennings surely wouldn't be disposed to help. But what else could he do? He would just have to go to the man and deal with whatever attitude he was presented with.

Jennings better cooperate, though. He wasn't in the mood to put up with any nonsense—none at all.

❧

Mom put her arm around Mrs. Renton's shoulders. "It's okay, it's not your fault. It was our choice to help you. God led us to you, remember."

The old lady pulled out her handkerchief and dabbed her eyes.

"He'll take care of us," added Emily, anxious to help. "We really are glad to do this."

"But we're stuck here!" Mrs. Renton's voice quavered. "What are we going to do?"

Danny was grabbing at Dad's hand and Stevie was beginning to whimper. Dad realized he'd better step in quickly. "It will be okay. We won't be in here forever." He sounded more assured than he felt though. *How on earth were they going to get out of this mess?*

"Who locked us in?" said Rachel. "The café man, or the Mole Hole guy?"

"It must have been one of them," said Danny. He had no problem picturing Mr. Kennedy doing something like that. "And now he'll get the treasure. We'll lose everything!"

"Oh, no!" wailed Stevie.

"Hush," said Mom. "Let's not forget that someone much bigger and stronger than us is in control."

"That's right," said Dad, catching on quickly. "Look, we know there's a God in heaven, right, and we're convinced He's more powerful than anyone or anything in the universe, and we know that He loves us." The kids nodded.

"And so He's not only able to help," continued Dad, feeling suddenly inspired, "he wants to help."

That made sense. The kids felt a surge of hope.

"So why don't we ask Him?"

"And let's start by trying to thank Him," said Mom, remembering her journaling goal.

"Thanking Him?" said Mrs. Renton, astonished. *What on earth could they thank Him for?*

"There's something I read this morning in the Bible. *Do not be anxious about anything, but in everything, by prayer and petition, with thanksgiving, present your requests to God.*"

"*And the peace of God, which passes all understanding, will guard your hearts and your minds in Christ Jesus,*" finished Emily. "I memorized that one too, from Philippians."

"That's so great," said Dad, appreciating the reminder. "This is a battle, and God's Word and prayer are our weapons! So let's pray. If any of you want to thank God out loud for something, go ahead, and when you're done I'll go ahead and pray for our situation."

The family grabbed for each other's hands in the dim light. Stevie shyly put his hand in Mrs. Renton's. She gave it a squeeze and accepted Emily's hand on the other side.

"Thank you, Lord, for helping us get this far and find all the clues," began Mom.

"Thank you, Jesus, for protecting us from the bad guys, and that we won't get wet in here if it rains," added Stevie. The others couldn't help but smile at that.

"Dear Jesus, thank you for Mrs. Renton—that we can get to know her better—and for the Squire and all his clever clues and how he wants Mrs. Renton to learn something from it all," said Emily.

"Thank you that we can stay at the inn and for Mrs. Tremannon and her amazing food," said Danny, suddenly realizing he was getting hungry.

"And Jesus, thank you for giving us such an exciting holiday, with clues, and secret passages and hidden staircases and all kinds of cool things," said Rachel fervently.

There was a pause, and Mrs. Renton suddenly felt very uncomfortable. Were they waiting for her to pray? She wasn't sure she could.

Dad was trying to figure out if he should wait for her or not. After several seconds he decided he should just go ahead and finish. "Dear Father, thank you for all your kindness and for helping us all this way. We believe you led us and Mrs. Renton together, and that You have something special you want her to learn. We don't know if it's Your will that we find the inheritance, but we do know that You love us all so much that You sent Jesus to die for us. Please show us how to get out of this place. We need Your help. If you want us to find the inheritance then please keep those two guys from stealing it and confuse their thinking." He suddenly remembered Danny's prayer from earlier that day. "And please bring those guys to You somehow. Thank you that You see us here and know our needs. Your Word says that our hope is in You all day long. Amen."

"Amen," they said together. They stood there for a moment holding hands. Mrs. Renton was intrigued by their prayers and actually did feel a bit better. *Maybe God really was listening.* It was true that what she needed most wasn't a material inheritance—it was peace of mind, freedom from regret and a feeling of hope for the future. *Could she have all that?*

They finally dropped each other's hands and looked expectantly at Dad. He lowered his eyes, still not sure what to do. *Call the police?* That sounded a bit drastic, but who else could they call? Not the Tremannons—they'd never hear the phone. *Auntie Flo?* He didn't know her number. *Who else?*

Danny ran over to the door and examined the lock. "But it's still closed!" he cried. "I prayed inside for another miracle like at the house on the cliff."

Dad sighed. He gave the lad a hug, searching for the right words. "It's good to pray for miracles, Danny…." He paused. "But if they don't happen it must be because God has a better plan in mind."

"Like what."

"Well, I…wait a minute!" Dad dug in his pocket and triumphantly produced a crumpled business card. He waved it at the others. "I've got the phone number of the guy at the coffee place—Geoff Ketchum. I'll call him. Maybe there's your miracle, Danny."

Everyone heaved a sigh of relief. Dad pulled out his phone, double-checked the number and, with everyone's eyes fixed on him, tried a call. He immediately got a message saying the call had failed.

"Er…it says it couldn't go through. No signal. I'll try over here." He moved over to the gate and checked the phone again. There was still no signal.

"I think this cave is blocking the cell service," he admitted reluctantly. "I'll have to come up with another idea."

Mom looked at him anxiously. She was about to say something but thought better of it. Her husband looked stressed enough. Instead she turned to the kids. "While Dad's figuring things out, why don't we work on the clue? After all, we've got the time to do it!" She gave a slight smile.

Emily thought she understood what Mom was trying to do and tried to force her voice to sound positive. "Okay, that's sounds great, Mom. Mrs. Renton? Would you mind reading the clue again?"

Dad handed over his flashlight, grateful to have some time to think, and Emily held it so Mrs. Renton could see to read. The old lady produced the paper and took a deep breath. She made up her mind to try to put aside her fears and do what Mrs. Chapman had asked.

She scanned the clue for a second. "Okay, we've solved the first part. How about the next? *'Upon this rock' is built the place, The stories there displayed. The man of mercy points the way, To where the treasure's laid.'* What does that all mean? Which rock was Uncle talking about?"

The kids gathered round and stared at the clue, glad to have a distraction.

"Could it mean this rock here?" said Rachel. "This prison thing is in a rock."

The others nodded, excited. *That had to be it.*

All except Mom. She was looking closely at the paper in Mrs. Renton's hands. "I'm not sure, but I don't think that's the answer."

"Why?" said Rachel, her euphoria vanishing. "It fits, doesn't it?"

"It is a good guess," admitted Mom, "but I'm wondering about the quotation marks." She pointed at the first phrase "'*Upon this rock.*' Like it's a title or something—or a saying."

"Something like a book title?" asked Mrs. Renton.

"Oh, oh!" broke in Emily suddenly. "There's a song called '*Upon this rock.*'"

"That's right," said Mom, getting excited. "*Upon this rock*—it's talking about that passage in the Bible when Jesus says '*Upon this rock I'll build my church.*'"

"The church!" exclaimed Rachel. "Oh, do you think that's what it means? Is the treasure hidden up at the church? We were just up there!"

The others felt a thrill of excitement. *Could that be it?*

"It would make sense," said Mom slowly. "The Squire was the one directing its renovation."

"And the '*stories there displayed*'?" wondered Mrs. Renton. "And the '*man of mercy?*'"

"Would it have something to do with the first part?" said Danny, hoping to have something to add. "The story of the prodigal son?" They thought about that for a moment.

"It could be," said Mom slowly. "The man of mercy could be the father in the story, but where would he be at the church?"

"In a Bible up there? Or maybe a painting or something?" wondered Emily.

The others shrugged their shoulders. Their memories of the church weren't that clear.

"It could be anywhere up there." Dad looked around at the faces of the others just visible in the gloomy light. "We need to check it out—before Mr. Kennedy and Co. figure it out ahead of us."

"We've got to get out of here," exclaimed Rachel, bunching her fists.

"Help us Jesus," said Mom fervently.

Dad checked his phone again. Still no service. *How incredibly frustrating!* "If only we could get a signal," he murmured. He looked over at the gate, and shook his head. Then he paused, thinking hard. "Stevie," he said suddenly. "Will you come here?"

"Yes, Daddy," said the boy, coming to his dad's side.

"I've got an idea. Do you know what my phone looks like when it's got a signal?"

"Do you mean the little lines at the top, like when the computer has Wi-Fi?"

"That's right." Dad bent over and picked up the lad. "Okay, here's my phone. Can you fit your hand through the gate?"

Stevie had a try and found he could just squeeze his hand through with the phone.

"Alright!" said Dad, getting a better hold of the boy. "Can you see any lines now?"

Stevie looked hard. "Maybe one? It's a bit hard to see."

"Great! Okay, bring your hand carefully back through. Try not to drop the phone."

Thankfully, Stevie managed the manoeuver without a problem.

"Okay, may I see it?" Dad set Stevie down and took the phone back. The others gathered round.

"Can you do it?" said Mom. "Did you get a signal?"

"I think so," said Dad. "Hang on a second." He tapped away on the phone and then looked up. "Okay, I typed a text to Geoff Ketchum. It will send if it gets a connection. Ready to go, Stevie?" He handed him the phone again.

Dad picked Stevie up and the boy carefully slid his hand between the bars.

"Okay, I see a line again," he exclaimed.

"Hold it there for a second," said Dad. He heard a slight beep. "Okay, now bring it back through."

As soon as Stevie's hand was back through, Dad set him down and took a look at the phone. "Message sent!" he grinned. "Stevie, you did it!"

The boy turned red, then grinned widely.

"Another reason that being the smallest may be the best after all," said Mom, laughing.

"I won't forget," assured Stevie.

Dad patted him on the back. "Okay, now let's thank God and pray that Geoff'll see it."

❦❦

The coffee place was getting busier by the minute, a number of people apparently deciding that a hot drink was just the tonic against the cool, unsettled weather. A buzz of conversation was building and a line forming at the counter. Geoff and Maggie were performing a well-practiced coordinated dance around the espresso machine. Neither of them heard the beeping of Geoff's phone from where he'd set it in the back room, next to an unopened tub of white chocolate mocha mix.

❦❦

Jennings wasn't appreciating this visit at all. If he never laid eyes on Kennedy again, he couldn't have been happier.

"I know we haven't always seen eye to eye," wheedled Kennedy, trying unsuccessfully to lighten the mood, "but we have been business partners for a long time."

Business partners indeed, thought Jennings sarcastically, just managing to hold his tongue.

"I know we can solve this. That meddling family is out of the way."

"What do you mean out of the way?" said Jennings, narrowing his eyes.

"I just mean that they won't be bothering us anymore. This is our chance to get ahead of them."

"Why? What have you done to them?" Jennings felt a growing sense of alarm. This whole thing was getting way out of hand.

"Nothing. They're fine." Kennedy dismissed them with a wave of his hand. "They're just stuck somewhere. They'll get out soon enough, so we've got to hurry. I need that Bible you had. Where is it?"

Jennings hesitated. Did he really want to help Kennedy in any way at all now?

"Where is it?" shouted Kennedy, slamming his hand down on the counter. Jennings took a step back. There was something in Kennedy's eyes that he hadn't seen before—something wild and uncontrolled.

"I'll get it," he stammered, turning and scurrying to the back of the store.

He returned a moment later carrying a large book covered in metal-bound leather. He set it carefully on the counter in front of Kennedy, and then stepped back, eying the other man warily.

Kennedy gave a smirk and wrenched open the volume. Jennings gave a yelp of surprise. "Be careful. It's an antique."

"I know what I'm doing," snarled Kennedy, his anger rising again. He scanned the index. It was apparently a list of the chapters. No, wasn't it individual books? Weren't there books in the Bible? He recognized Genesis—he'd heard of that one. And Exodus. They'd made a movie about that. So where was the one about the—what was it? Prodigal son?

He looked up at Jennings, who was in the act of trying to back away. "Hey, where do you think you're going? I need your help."

Jennings paused, staring like a cornered animal.

"I overheard them talking about a story in the Bible--the prodigal son or something. The dad said it was the key to the treasure." Kennedy gestured angrily at the book. "This thing's huge. Tell me!"

Jennings was feeling decidedly sick inside. Kennedy was getting more and more unstable. *Why, oh why had he ever agreed to work with the man?* If only he could go back and do it over again—he'd choose a very different path.

"Er, I'm not sure." That wasn't entirely true. Jennings still remembered some of those stories from when he was a boy. "I think it's a story that someone told—maybe Jesus, or Moses?"

"So, where do I look?"

"I don't know. You'll have to thumb through. Start at the beginning and look for the section headings." Jennings wasn't going to give any more hints, and definitely wasn't going to mention using the Internet to search for it. Let Kennedy think of that himself.

"Thanks for the help." It was Kennedy's turn to be sarcastic. "Go on, get out of here!"

Jennings nodded silently, and gladly fled the room.

∽⤙⤚∽

"So, how many songs are there in 'The Sound of Music'?" Emily had taken charge of entertainment and was sitting with her sister and brothers with their backs against the wall of the corridor. Every now and then Dad would summon Stevie and they would see if there had been any reply to the text. So far there hadn't been; in fact, they hadn't even seen a signal, and everyone was beginning to get nervous.

"Eight," said Danny authoritatively. "I'm positive."

"Nope. There's more than that." Emily shook her head. "Keep trying. Count them off."

"But I can't count when I'm hungry," complained Danny, rubbing his stomach.

It must have been catching, because Stevie realized he was hungry too. He gave a groan.

A little way further in Mom was sitting next to Mrs. Renton. Dad had gallantly taken off his coat to provide them with something to sit on. Mom heard the complaints and dug into the backpack. She pulled out the biscuits and passed them over. "Here you go, kids. Take one each and pass them back." She turned to the old lady. "Thank you for these. God must have known we'd need them."

Mrs. Renton gave a little smile, but her mind was too preoccupied to really focus on what Mom was saying. She was feeling so embarrassed, so awkward, she could barely stand to look at the others. Wasn't it all her fault, no matter what they said or how they tried to say it was God's will?

Mom prayed silently for wisdom. Somehow she needed God to show her how to reach the old lady. She felt a tap on her shoulder. It was Stevie, looking forlorn.

"Can I sit with you? I don't want to play Trivia Time. Emily's questions are too hard."

"Sure, honey." Mom scooted over a bit but Stevie plunked down on her lap. "Wow!" Mom gasped. "You're getting heavy. Did you and Daddy see a signal?"

Stevie gave a huge sigh. "No. Why isn't God answering our prayer? It's been half an hour."

Mom thought for a moment. She wanted to make sure she gave a wise response, especially as Mrs. Renton was right there listening too.

The old lady tried not to look too interested, but she definitely wanted to know the answer.

"Well, you know how we've told you before that when we ask God for something sometimes the answer is 'yes', sometimes 'no', and sometimes 'not yet.'"

Stevie remembered. He nodded. "So is this a 'no' or a 'not yet?'"

Mom smiled. "We don't know, but we do know God loves us. When you ask me for something, do I always say yes?"

Stevie had to think about that for a second. "No, I guess not. Sometimes I want dessert but I haven't finished my peas yet."

"That's right," smiled Mom. "And remember the last time you had to get a shot."

Stevie's eyes grew wide. He definitely remembered that.

"And you pleaded with me not to have it." Mom gave him a tight squeeze.

"Uh-huh."

"I honestly didn't want you to. In fact, I would have rather the doctor had given it to me than you."

"Really?" Stevie was amazed. "Why?"

"Because I love you, I don't like to see you afraid, or in pain. But I knew it was better for you to have the shot. You know why we get shots, right?"

"Um…to protect us from bad diseases."

"Right." Mom sent up a quick prayer, knowing this was a crucial point for Mrs. Renton as well. "I've been learning a lot about thankfulness, even in difficult situations. It really helps me see the good things God is doing, even in the midst of trials. So when bad things happen, I'm trying to learn to trust there's a reason, and that God loves us, even when we don't understand why bad things are happening."

Mrs. Renton couldn't keep quiet any longer. "But when it's something awful—I mean really awful like the…like someone you love dying..."

Mom turned and looked at her, her eyes moist. "That's when we just have to cling to our Daddy in heaven and trust that He feels the same pain we do."

Mrs. Renton leaned her head back against the wall. "If God really is powerful, and really is loving, why didn't He save them? We could have had a whole lifetime of happiness together."

Dad's voice broke in. He had approached without them realizing it and had heard the last part of the conversation. "I guess that depends on how you see life. Are we supposed to always be happy, to have a life of ease and then all die peacefully in our sleep? That's what I always thought growing up." He squatted down beside them. "But that's not what the Bible says. God is in the business of renewing us, making us like Him. Unfortunately, because we are all messed up and this is a broken world, the only way we learn and grow is through difficulties. We don't grow when everything goes our way."

Mom nodded. "If we always had everything we needed, we wouldn't ever think about God. When we are needy we learn to put our trust in Him. And He is always faithful. We are blessed and God is glorified."

"But it's not easy," Dad admitted. "Not at all. I've been a Christian for nearly twenty years, and I'm still struggling with trust. Like right now! I really want to be out of here, but for some reason God is wanting us to wait and trust." He shrugged. "It's always easier to tell someone else to do it than to do it yourself." He clearly remembered his ongoing struggle with the articles.

"It is so hard to trust Him," said Mrs. Renton, wiping her nose with her hanky.

"It shouldn't be, but it is," agreed Mom. "We all struggle. What helps me the most is to remember all the ways He's been faithful in the past, and to remember that in Jesus, God proved once and for all His love for us. He did the impossible for us—finding a way to pay for our sin. And he still can do the impossible for us, even when things look really dark."

"It depends a lot on how you see Him," added Dad. "Is it as a stern God in the sky looking down on us in disapproval, or a loving Father walking at our side, holding our hand, leading us on like a shepherd? All sheep have to do is trust and follow."

Mrs. Renton was quiet for a moment. Then, to their surprise, she turned and grabbed Stevie's hand. "Young man, do you have trouble trusting God?"

Stevie was so shocked he couldn't speak for a moment. Then he nodded seriously. "Uh-huh. Sometimes, like when I have to get a shot or something, but I guess it always turns out okay in the end."

"So do you know that He loves you?"

That question was a lot easier for him. "Oh, yes."

"How?" Mrs. Renton wanted to know.

Mom and Dad listened with baited breath. *What would he say?*

"Well, He sent Jesus to die for me. Jesus didn't have to come but He chose to do it. I know I've done bad things, but Jesus died for me anyway."

Mrs. Renton looked full into his eyes. "Thank you young man. I just needed to hear it from you."

"You're welcome," said Stevie, not understanding what was going on at all.

Mrs. Renton sat back and closed her eyes. Mom and Dad waited, unsure if they should say anything.

"Well," said the old lady finally. "I'm going to try to believe that He loves me too."

Dad and Mom exchanged glances. Something was happening in the lady's heart for sure.

Stevie looked up at his Dad, who smiled at him and tousled his hair.

"Dad?"

"Yes son."

"Can we check the phone again? Just in case God says 'yes' this time."

Dad smiled. "Sure thing. Let's go do it."

❧❧

"A caramel macchiato, vanilla soy latté, and a decaf white chocolate mocha—all larges," said Maggie Ketchum over her shoulder as her husband sped past with two carafes of the house blend. *What was it with today?* The place was usually getting quieter at this time, but it seemed like everyone and their uncle had decided they needed a coffee before dinner. *Weird, but a blessing, too!*

"Coming right up," said Geoff. He thumped the carafes onto the counter and grabbed the empties. Threading past his wife he ducked into the back room to drop them off by the sink. He glanced over at the tub of white mocha mix. He would need to get that—they had just finished one a few minutes ago. And there was his phone, for goodness sake. He had wondered where he had left it.

He snatched it up and was about to drop it in his apron pocket when something on the screen caught his eye. A text message—but he didn't have time to look at it right now.

He was stuffing it in his pocket when something stopped him. *Maybe he should just check who it was from.* He pushed the button and quickly scanned the message. What he read made his eyes widen in surprise. He dashed back to the counter and thrust the phone into his wife's surprised face.

"Mags, Mags, can you hold the fort?"

"What? What do you mean?" Maggie couldn't believe her ears.

"It's that family—the Chapmans. And the lady too. They're stuck in the old prison. Someone locked them in." He started madly tapping a message back.

Maggie had to let that sink in. "Oh my! The poor dears. I'll try. But hurry back! Please!"

Geoff hit 'send' and gave her a kiss on the cheek. As he headed for the door, he threw a look over his shoulder. "You're an angel. I'll pray for you!"

"Okay, here we go again," said Dad, hefting Stevie up. "Oof. How many biscuits did you have?"

"Just one," said Stevie. "I'm not that heavy. I'm only little." He didn't feel ashamed saying it this time, though. He was realizing it was okay to be little.

"You're just right," said Dad. "Here's the phone. I've sent the message again. Hold it out, just like last time."

"Should I check if the signal bar is there?" Stevie threaded his hand through the gate.

"I suppose so," said Dad, feeling his spirits droop again. Surely this wasn't going to work.

But Stevie suddenly gave a cry of surprise. "Daddy, did you hear that?"

Dad certainly had. "I got a text. Quick, let's look."

Stevie carefully extracted his hand and handed the phone to Dad. Dad pushed the button, scrutinized the display and his face broke into a huge smile.

"It's from Geoff!" He let Stevie slide down his leg and then ran to the others. "He said don't worry. He'll be right here. Did you hear that everyone? He said he'd be right here!"

Kennedy ran his hand through his wild hair. This was going absolutely nowhere. He was…*how far through this thing?* About a quarter of the way, and it had taken him half an hour. He was having the increasingly horrible realization that he would never find what he was looking for, and the miserable regret that he'd ever locked the family in. So what if they couldn't get any further—neither could he. At least when he was following them he had a chance, remote as it had seemed, of getting ahead of them at the last minute and snatching the prize. *This was ridiculous. And where was Jennings?* Kennedy had a sneaking suspicion that Jennings knew more than he was letting on. He sure had disappeared in a hurry.

"Jennings, get out here!" Kennedy yelled, banging on the counter in emphasis.

There was no answer. Kennedy tried one more time, trying to put as much authority into his voice as he could, but there was still no response. He could feel his blood pressure rising. This anger had been simmering for weeks and, since that cursed family had come on the scene, was now coming in ever-increasing waves that built up suddenly and threatened to overwhelm him.

He looked down again at the Bible in front of him and could easily picture himself throwing it at Jennings' face. He gripped the edge of the counter in an effort to calm himself down. He had to control himself, breathe, focus on the task. The family could possibly be rescued by someone. Either he had to go back and trail them again—which seemed impossible right now—or keep going with what he was doing and find that passage. There was only one choice.

He grabbed up the book and started flipping through as quickly as he possibly could.

The family were gathered at the gate, straining their ears. It had been about fifteen minutes since they got the text and they were getting concerned. *But what was that?* Was that a distant shout?

"I think it's him!" said Dad. "Thank you, Lord!"

"Yes, thank you, Jesus," breathed Mom, giving Mrs. Renton a squeeze.

The voice was getting nearer. They could all hear it clearly now. "I'm coming!"

A few seconds later Geoff Ketchum appeared, red-faced and breathing hard. He produced a key and grinned at them through the bars as he unlocked the padlock. "Hello there! Looks like someone threw the lot of you in jail. Well, we obtained a royal pardon and the Queen says you can go free."

As soon as the gate was opened the family poured out, grateful to be back in the open air. Dad shook Geoff's hand heartily. "Thanks so much. We were well and truly stuck."

"No problem at all. Are you all okay? What happened?"

Dad quickly filled him in on the details. Geoff nodded seriously. "So, the quest continues and it looks like you really do have someone trying to trip you up."

"It does look that way, but we can't be a hundred percent sure it was him who locked us in. How did you find a key, by the way?"

Geoff smiled. "Fortunately I knew who had another copy." He gestured at the cave. "This place is maintained by the Penrithen Historical Society—an organization that the Squire set up, funnily enough. The current president of the society has the extra keys. It wasn't hard to get them."

"Anyone we know?" said Mom, brushing down her jeans. "We should tell them thank you."

"I don't know—have you been to the supermarket up the hill? It's the owner—Mr. Peterson."

The family looked at each other in amazement. "Er, we have met him, yes," said Dad.

Geoff laughed. "I know what you're thinking. He's an interesting character, but really a nice person when you get to know him. He grumbled a bit when I dashed into his shop with my request, but when I mentioned who it was for he was eager to help. Which one of you is Emily?" Emily raised an embarrassed hand.

"He mentioned how nice you were to him. So there you go!"

"Great job, Emily," said Mom, rubbing her daughter's back. "A little kindness goes a long way."

"Well, I'd best be heading back to rescue poor Maggie. The shop is crowded today—can't complain though! It's an answer to prayer."

"You're an answer to prayer," said Dad. "Please tell her thank you."

"I will." Geoff grinned, but then suddenly turned serious. "Be careful. You're doing a wonderful thing, but it definitely seems like there's some opposition. We'll be praying for you, and I mean it. Let me know if you need any more help. You'd best hurry right along, though. I think we're going to have quite the storm. The weather forecast looked pretty grim." He gestured at the sky, which had taken on a truly ominous appearance—a solid wall of dark slate grey with ragged lighter grey clouds driving in before it. A rumble of thunder accentuated the sinister aspect.

"We'll be right behind you," said Dad, feeling a stab of concern. "We're off to the church. We think we're getting close!"

"Good for you, but don't forget you'll need the key. Maggie's got it at the shop. You could come in and have a hot drink—on the house!"

For a second Dad was tempted—a white chocolate mocha sounded heavenly—but there was a growing foreboding in his mind—something more than just the weather.

"We would love to, but I'm concerned about the possibility of those men figuring things out ahead of us. If it was one of them who locked us in, we've no idea if they heard us discussing the clue. We'll get the key if you don't mind, but we'll come and celebrate at the coffee shop when we're all finished."

"Sounds like a plan," said Geoff with a grin. "I'll be off then. Got to get back to Mags." He waved cheerily and dashed off down the path.

"Such a nice man," said Mrs. Renton, watching his retreating back.

"Definitely," said Dad. "Now, in light of the weather I think I should get the car. Do you mind if I run on ahead? I can meet you at the memorial." He sprinted off down the trail, calling over his shoulder. "Get a copy of the clue!"

"Okay," yelled Mom, digging for her pen.

"Rachel and I can get the key," said Emily. Rachel nodded vigorously.

"Thank you, girls," said Mom. She turned to Mrs. Renton. "Do you think you'll want to come up to the church with us?"

The old lady shook her head. "I'd really love to, but I'm quite exhausted and I know I'd slow you down. If you could drop me off home, I'd really appreciate it, and so would Pickwick. He's probably digging through the cupboards for a can opener this minute. Would you mind calling me to let me know what you find?"

"Of course," said Mom, a might relieved. It would be a challenge just to get her home before the heavens opened.

∽❧⟨

Kennedy was seething, flipping the pages with ever-increasing exasperation. Everything was falling apart. He had no money, no future, no hope. This inheritance chase had been a ridiculous idea. *Did he really think he could just muscle his way in and grab it?* And since that family had showed up it felt like there was this power, this active *presence* working against him. He gritted his teeth. No, he would not let them beat him, whatever it took.

He took a frantic glance out the shop window, noticing how dark it was becoming. Was the family still in the prison or had someone released them? Either way he was in dire straits if he didn't find the clue soon. His eye fixed on the old pistol in the front window display. *Was that the answer? It would sure solve his problems—to end it all that way.* He shook his head angrily. No, he wasn't ready to give up yet. He had to keep going. There was no other way.

If his gaze had rested outside just a moment more, he would have recognized, to his horror, the muffled figure hurrying up the hill towards the car park on the cliff.

⊰⊱

The first drops fell on the heaving deck of the crabber 'Maid Marion' as she barely outpaced the storm, racing into the haven of the harbor. A sudden brief squall dumped a shower of rain across the village, the accompanying wind banging the shutters on the White Whale pub and sending the weathervane on the chimney spinning wildly. A bold gust spattered spray on the windshields of the cars up on the cliff as Dad fumbled for his keys beside the van. Several gulls, flecks of white against a leaden canvas, soared past him, riding effortlessly on the wind. He glanced up, taking in the awe-inspiring sight. Sea and sky were one, broken only by the heaving lines of foam and driving scud. It was like something alive, something menacing steadily approaching, eating up the ocean towards him.

Out of the corner of his eye he noticed Kennedy's car, still parked over in the corner. *Was that good news or bad?* He wasn't sure, and there wasn't time to worry about it. He just needed to rescue his family before this thing hit.

⊰⊱

Mom pulled Danny and Stevie close to her and turned her face away as a sodden gust swept down the lane, rattling the awning above her head. An assortment of leaves and flower petals blew past, along with a water bottle that bounced and rolled down the road. Mrs. Renton produced a clear plastic rain hat from her purse and tied it under her chin.

They had decided to shelter in front of the Newsagents while the girls dashed off to retrieve the church key from Maggie in the coffee shop, but it wasn't turning out to be much of a shelter after all. The proprietor had already hurried all his goods inside again, and Mom wondered if they might come up with an excuse to follow him in. She looked over her shoulder again at the sky beyond the harbor. She didn't remember ever seeing such a threatening prospect. It didn't in any way look like the time to be chasing another clue, but did they have a choice? Mr. Kennedy could be ahead of them.

She suddenly felt Danny tugging at her sleeve and looked down at his face, just visible from within his hood. "What do you want, dear?"

"Look, Mommy." Danny pointed towards the bridge. An old lorry was just cresting the top and coming towards them. "Isn't that Mr. Tremannon's truck?"

It was. It rumbled noisily up to them and screeched to a halt. Mrs. Renton gasped and turned away—not ready for this surprise encounter. The driver's side window rolled slowly down exposing Mr. Tremannon's concerned face, his blue eyes seeming to shine in the gathering darkness.

"Alroight?" he questioned, looking them over and then out at the approaching storm.

"Yes, we're fine," said Mom. "My husband's getting the car."

"Roight," said the old man, nodding. He looked hard at Mrs. Renton who stood with her back to him as if studying the contents of the shop window.

Mom had a sudden thought. "Have you, er, seen Mr. Kennedy? We saw his car up at the car park, but haven't seen him today. We just wondered…"

Mr. Tremannon's eyes were like two headlights piercing the gloom. "Nope," he said finally, a slight frown creasing his forehead.

Mom checked her watch and had another thought. "Mr. Tremannon? I know dinner is usually at six. We're heading up to the church to look for…er, something. We shouldn't be late but with the weather…"

He gave a strange look. "Church?"

"Yes, the church," repeated Mom, puzzled.

"Roight," said the old man. "Roight." He gave a half smile, then nodded again. He wound up the window and the truck lurched off up the hill.

Mom shrugged her shoulders. "A man of few words," she murmured to herself. "I hope I didn't say too much. And I hope Dave hurries."

As she looked up the street again she saw a line of thrashing rain speeding down towards them. A second later and they were enveloped in a massive downpour.

❧❧❧

Geoff Ketchum watched the two girls go back out and turned to his wife who was expertly putting her signature touch on the top of a hazelnut mocha. "Thanks again, Mags. I'm sorry I had to leave you when everything was going bonkers but you should have seen those poor things locked in up there."

Maggie flashed him a smile as she set the mug up on the counter. "No probs, love. And God helped me. It really slowed down for a bit there."

"And you feel alright about them going up to the church?" added Geoff, grabbing a rag off the counter and wiping the steam wand on the espresso machine.

Maggie nodded, frowning a little as she tried to decipher her own writing on the next order ticket. "Oh, yes. I've got another key, and the girls promised they'd lock up. I can check on that after closing."

Geoff paused in his cleaning. "No, I didn't mean about the key. I'm just—it's hard to explain but I feel concerned about them all going up there. You know they mentioned someone else might be trying to steal the lady's inheritance, and then they got locked in. I just hope they don't run into any trouble. And it looks like a massive storm's coming in—worse than last autumn's."

His wife looked up, surprised at how serious he sounded. "Well, we can be sure and pray. Oh my, that was silly!" She suddenly shook her head in exasperation.

"What was?"

They were interrupted by a crash of thunder. Maggie looked concerned. "There's no electricity up there. There are some candles, but I ran out of matches last time and forgot to get more. With the weather like it is they'll be in the dark. Please help them, God!"

Jennings peered around the bookcase and his shoulders drooped. Kennedy was still there flipping through the Bible on the counter. How could he get rid of that bloke? How he wished he could just close the shop and go escape somewhere—until all this mess went away.

He could hear Kennedy muttering and cursing, and the angry outbursts were getting louder. To his horror he saw Kennedy suddenly pick the book up and fling it across the room. It hit a display case whose arrangement of brassware exploded in a bouncing, clanging, overpowering cacophony of noise.

Jennings froze in stupefaction. Then a tidal wave of anger overwhelmed him. "Hey! What do you think you're doing? How dare you throw that! That's an antique and it's...it's a Bible for heaven's sake!

Kennedy turned his rage on Jennings. "So there you are, are you? Where've you been? This is all your fault." He waved a hand at the destruction. "And are you getting religious on me now? Really?" he sneered. "When have you ever cared about the Bible?"

"I don't know," stammered Jennings, his confidence evaporating. "It's just...I don't want any more bad luck. We're in enough trouble as it is."

"Trouble?" Kennedy yelled. "I tell you why we're in trouble. It's *you*. You're weak and you're soft and now that cursed family is going to get that cursed inheritance before me. *Before me!*" He voice rose to a scream and Jennings backed hurriedly away. There was something in Kennedy's eyes—a wild desperation he'd never seen before. He suddenly didn't feel safe. This chap was going off his rocker.

"But they're locked up," he managed to stammer. "You told me yourself."

"Do you think they're going to stay locked up forever you idiot," Kennedy yelled. He pointed out the shop window. "They could be solving the whole thing right..."

To Jennings infinite surprise Kennedy suddenly stopped short and with a cry of alarm dashed outside, the wind slamming the door behind him.

The wind whipped mercilessly around Kennedy and within seconds he was drenched. It was as dark as dusk outside and thunder rumbled in the distance. Ignoring it, he watched incredulously as the family's van swept down the street and braked hard at the bottom. It paused for a moment, the red lights reflecting off the streams of water rushing down the glistening road. Then it was off again over the bridge, its headlights carving a path through the downpour, and up the steep turn to the cottages. Kennedy couldn't move, feeling like his whole future hung in the balance. *What would they do?*

The van pulled up in front of the lady's house as a flash of lighting lit up the clouds behind the headland. Kennedy held his breath. *Had they solved the puzzle?* But no, the headlights were still on. Great Scott, they were going on up and turning around!

The headlights flashed momentarily across the harbor as the van turned and then lit up the lane again down past the cottages. Despite the knifing wind and sheets of rain, Kennedy felt rooted to the spot. He had to see where they were going. The van reached the bottom, paused, then turned to the right. *They were going up the road to the church.* Kennedy's mouth dropped open. *Of course. The clue in the Bible—it must have pointed to the church.* How more stupid could he have been? *He had to get up there.* He needed his car. Without a second thought he turned and dashed up the lane, head down into the storm.

Chapter 26 – The Final Confrontation

The old lady straightened up rather painfully. "There you are dear Pickwick. A special treat for you—your favorite. I'm sorry I've been gone so long."

The cat ignored her comment, hunching down for some serious business with the pile of tuna in its bowl. She could tell he was pleased though, by the way his tail curled and snapped back and forth. After all the upheaval of the day, there would normally have been a simple pleasure in seeing her pet enjoying his dinner, the house still and silent except for the quiet ticking of the clock above the sink. Yes, she should have felt more at ease than she did considering the comfort and familiarity of the surroundings, but there was something nagging at her, a strong disquieting feeling that seemed to be growing rather than diminishing since she entered the house.

The kettle whistled and she mechanically made herself a cup of tea. She turned on the lamp and lowered herself stiffly into her armchair, setting her tea on the table at her side. Rain dashed against the windows and the wind moaned somewhere up in the rafters. Thunder rumbled again in the distance—*perhaps a little louder this time?*

Was that what was bothering her? The Chapmans were out in that storm, heading up to the church. Wouldn't they rather have been inside like she was, sheltering comfortably from the weather? They were doing all this for her. *Shouldn't she be out there with them?* It was her task, her responsibility. What would Uncle Kenwyn have thought?

Uncle Kenwyn. The thought of him brought tears to her eyes. For the first time in her life she really understood his love for her. *What had she done to him and Auntie Rosie?* She had been so focused on her own grief that she had never spared a moment to think of how they must have hurt when she rejected them—not just once, but over and over again. She had shut them out—even punishing them in a perverse attempt to mask her own culpability. And what had she gained? Her life had been nothing more than a prolonged attempt to bury her pain—to escape from God's perceived disapproval and rejection. She clearly understood now that her rejection of them was just a symptom of her rejection of God.

Waves of guilt and regret washed over her. The tears came readily now and she let them fall untouched. The discomfort felt appropriate somehow—to wipe them away would have masked the guilt she felt—the guilt she must allow herself to feel.

That was what was really bothering her—her guilt, her shame. She deserved punishment—she understood that clearly. Her grief at her parent's death was real and necessary, but how did it compare to her lifelong rejection of her uncle and aunt, and of God Himself for that matter?

With a sudden clarity she realized that the love Uncle Kenwyn had been communicating was God's own love for her. She saw the quest in a new light. *Of course it shouldn't have been easy. It had to be difficult because it had to produce change.* God himself wanted her to understand something. Her heart gave a leap. There was hope there and she was desperate for it.

She dug through the drawer where she had stashed all the other clues and pulled them out onto her lap. Then she retrieved from her purse the ones they had found that day. Pickwick stalked gracefully into the room and, seeing her lap was occupied, jumped up on the sofa where he proceeded to wash himself with focused dedication. For once the old lady barely noticed his presence. She felt like she was in a desert, desperate for a way to quench her thirst, and that these precious letters were the oasis. She would read them all through again—and this time she would truly try and open her heart to their message.

Mr. Tremannon set the bulging shopping bags on the passenger seat, shaking his head as the rain soaked the upholstery. He slammed the door shut and made his way over to the driver's side, carefully stepping over the rushing torrent running along the gutter in front of Penrithen Grocers. Clambering in and closing the door, he was about to start the engine when his attention was caught by a gangly, sodden figure lumbering past the window, head down against the wind. The old man frowned. *Could that be who he thought it was?*

He started the engine and pulled away from the curb, the headlights illuminating the hurrying figure through a shining stream of raindrops. Moderating his speed he brought the truck level with the man and took a second quick glance. It was definitely him.

Accelerating quickly, Mr. Tremannon pulled ahead and sped up the hill.

"Are you ready?" Mom looked around at the kids, bundled up in raincoats and hats in the back. They had all had another snack, chattering like magpies, exclaiming each time the van was buffeted by wind and rain at its exposed spot at the top of the lane.

They nodded, the girls looking flushed and excited, the boys suddenly somber and quiet.

"This could be it," said Dad looking at them in the rearview mirror. "This could be the last step!" He felt a rush of excitement and nervousness as he said it. Here he was again, stepping into the great unknown. Hopefully there would be no more nasty surprises.

"Are you sure we'll be okay?" said Stevie. He wasn't big on storms at the best of times, and the thought of a storm and a graveyard together was a bit much.

Dad actually wasn't sure what to say. True, Kennedy's car was back in the town, but that didn't mean he or the other guy weren't lurking around.

"Yes," said Mom decidedly, wondering why Dad hadn't answered. "Remember how we were able to get a message to Mr. Ketchum when we were stuck? That was a miracle wasn't it?"

Stevie nodded. It was a miracle he had participated in!

"So we can trust God to help us now," finished Mom.

"Be strong and courageous," said Danny suddenly. "Like Joshua."

"Right," said Dad, realizing what a timely reminder that was again. Boy, he needed that on a T-shirt or something. "Because the Lord your God is with you wherever you go," he finished. He craned his head to look at them all. "It's a bit wild out there, so stay together. It'll be better in the church." Dad looked at his wife, who nodded. "So let's commit our way to the Lord--that God's will be done."

As the van shook under a powerful gust, the family bowed their heads and prayed.

❧❧

Kennedy struggled up the street, fighting the power of a wind which threatened to pluck him up and send him tumbling back the way he'd come. He finally reached the top and turned towards the car park, drenched to the skin. As he jogged wearily through the entrance, he couldn't believe his eyes. Apart from his own car, the parking lot was empty...except for one important exception— an antique-looking lorry parked obliquely behind his back bumper, effectively blocking him in.

❧❧

"I've got the umbrella," shouted Dad to Mom, trying to be heard over the storm as the family struggled out of the van. "I'll be right around to you."

"Thank you," yelled Mom in return. As she slammed the car door something flew past her head, brushing across her hair. "What was that?"

"That," yelled Dad, "was the umbrella. It's probably in Devon by now. Sorry!"

They hurried up the path and through the lych-gate, trying to shield their faces from the driving rain. A canopy of wicked-looking clouds hung low over them, dark tendrils reaching out for them as they ran. Thunder rumbled again in the distance. The path was littered with twigs and branches, but Danny and Stevie kept their eyes fixed straight ahead as they scuttled through the graveyard, not wanting to even think about their surroundings. It seemed like an eternity before they were all crowded up against the massive doors, bobbing up and down in shivering eagerness to escape the weather.

For a frantic moment Dad couldn't find the key and they all breathed a sigh of relief when he finally found it in his inside coat pocket. He quickly unlocked the doors and heaved them open, the family fairly leaping inside. Dad pulled the doors to behind them and the transition was almost overwhelming. The wind and rain were suddenly cut off, and the quiet solemnness of the chapel descended on them, driving out the confusing voices of the storm.

"It's dark in here," whimpered Stevie. This was distressingly like a bad dream he had once had.

Mom produced the flashlight and shone it around, lighting up the circle of dripping faces. She gave Stevie a hug. "We're here. We made it! And you know what Stevie, God is here with us. This is a church. It's His house. You don't have to be afraid."

Stevie nodded, brightening up a bit. He liked the idea that this was God's house.

"So," said Dad, looking round. "Is there a light switch or something?"

Mom shone the flashlight on the walls, and they found a switch by the doors leading into the nave. Emily flipped it back and forth several times, but there was no answering flood of light.

"No electricity. That's unfortunate," murmured Dad, concerned. He definitely didn't want to delay their search very long.

"Maybe there are some candles," said Danny helpfully.

"Or maybe an old lantern," said Rachel. "In the adventure stories I read, they always had to explore with an old lantern.

"Well, we'll look," smiled Mom. She shone the flashlight carefully around the foyer.

"There's something, up on the shelf," said Rachel suddenly. Sure enough, next to a tall can of fly spray sat several brass candleholders, each with a slightly drooping candle.

"Now we just need matches," said Dad, lifting them down. "They should be close by."

They weren't though. After a thorough search in the foyer they stepped into the nave, Danny and Stevie staying very close to Mom and Dad. The stillness was even more apparent there—their footsteps on the stone floor sounding very noticeable. Stevie didn't like the fact that they could only see a small piece of the area at a time, with their shadows chasing the beam of the flashlight as Mom directed it around. The air felt very cool and Emily shivered. Dad gave a sudden sneeze that made them all jump.

"Sorry," he said. "Okay, let's try and find some light as quick as possible, just in case."

"Just in case?" said Emily.

"Yes," said Dad, regretting he'd said anything. "Just in case."

Kennedy beat on the door of the truck with his hand. He couldn't see inside because the windows were fogged up, but there was no response anyway. Whoever had parked the vehicle seemed to have disappeared.

Leaning into the wind, Kennedy struggled over to the front of his own car. Was there enough room to move forward a bit and then back around the truck? No, curse it. He had parked too close to the concrete bollards. *What could he do?* He was fairly exploding with frustration.

An extra strong gust almost bowled him over and he clung to the side mirror until its force subsided somewhat. *That did it.* He yanked open his car door and leaped inside. At least here he was out of the elements. He caught a glimpse of himself in the rearview mirror and almost jumped at the wild eyes staring back at him. He would be surprised if he made it through this without a nervous breakdown.

Where was that stupid driver? He hit the steering wheel in frustration, causing the car horn to squawk in protest. *Hey, that was an idea.* He leaned forward onto the horn, bellowing out a long, blaring blast, holding it until he couldn't stand it anymore. He paused some seconds, then did it again. *Maybe that would bring whatever idiotic imbecile had left his truck there back to set him free.*

In the truck, Mr. Tremannon grimaced at the noise as he lay back with the seat reclining as far as it would go. How long would he have to put up with that racket? He checked his watch. His wife was counting on the shopping for making dinner and he was already late. Despite the cacophony he wished he could delay a little longer, but there was nothing for it—he had to go now.

Kennedy gave the horn a rest for a second and was just preparing for another blast when he almost jumped out of his skin. The inside of the car was suddenly illuminated by an intense, searing glare that pierced the back window, reflecting into his eyes. At the same moment there was a frightening feral roar that drowned out even the sounds of the storm.

Kennedy couldn't immediately process what was going on. He shrank down in terror as if assaulted by some raging monster. Whatever the thing was it gave a final mighty roar and leaped backwards, the noise and light diminishing rapidly. There was a squealing sound and Kennedy spun around in the seat, just in time to catch a glimpse of the truck barreling out of the car park.

He sat there, his heart beating like a jackhammer in his chest, his shock rapidly being replaced by a surging rage. With a violent twist of the key he cranked the engine into life, shifted into reverse and shot backwards. Wipers on high and his face almost pressed against the windshield, he spun around with a spray of gravel and shot like a comet into the lane.

❦❦

Mrs. Renton sat with the pile of papers on her lap and her old photo album balanced on the arm of the chair, tears running down her cheeks. She looked again at the photo of her and the Squire. She could even remember when it was taken. It had been his birthday, and Auntie Rosie had made him his favorite dessert—apple crumble and custard. They had just finished a crossword puzzle together; well, Uncle Kenwyn always said she was an invaluable help, but it was really him who knew all the answers. He just said that because he loved her.

428

The old lady traced the man's face with her finger. "Dear Uncle," she murmured. "I'm so sorry…so sorry." She wept freely now, sobbing unrestrainedly.

The cat jumped down from the sofa and rubbed back and forth across her leg as if trying to console her. "Oh, Pickwick," she whispered. She reached down and stroked his back and he arched up in pleasure. She smiled through her tears. "There, there, I'm alright."

She took a deep breath. "Yes, I'm alright." She wiped her eyes and blew her nose with her hanky, then sat up straight in her seat and leafed through the papers again.

"So Uncle," she said aloud, looking down at his picture. "What did you want me to understand from all these? That you loved me and forgave me? I really do believe that now. But what were you trying to teach me with these stories? God, please help me understand."

With a shock she realized that she had just uttered a prayer. She considered that fact for a moment. Well, why not? "Yes, God. Please help me. If you're real and you're there and you love me, please help me understand."

She sat there for a second. Had he heard her? Had he answered? She had no idea.

She looked at the first letter from the Squire—the one that came with the second clue. He had said that the quest itself was important. And the Bible verse, Proverbs 20:21, seemed to emphasize that. She could well believe that now.

The second clue led to the photo with the note about the Squire's missionary dad and his sickness and subsequent death in Africa. It was such a sad story. What was she supposed to take from it? Was it something in the Bible verse Uncle Kenwyn had written at the end? What was it again? She found the spot. *Trust in the Lord and do good; dwell in the land and enjoy safe pasture. Delight yourself in the Lord and He will give you the desires of your heart.'*

She sat back. Yes, Uncle Kenwyn himself must have struggled with trusting God at the news of his father's death, just like she had struggled when her parents died.

'Dwell in the land and enjoy safe pasture.'

What had that meant to Uncle Kenwyn? To accept that God would take care of him here in Penrithen perhaps? And what was her own safe pasture? Was it here, too? Could this become a real home for her?

'Delight yourself in the Lord and He will give you the desires of your heart.'

The desires of her heart. To be loved, to belong, to have hope, to be forgiven. Was this the answer—to put her delight in God? Were these desires things that God wanted to fulfill as a loving father? Could it really be true? When she thought God was coldly distant, was he really close and compassionate?

She felt a tiny surge of hope. Was she beginning to understand? She snatched up the fourth clue. Perhaps it would make it clearer.

Hands gripping the wheel, Kennedy tore around the corner by the monument, filled with a mix of fury and misery. Everything felt like it was collapsing around him. Despair was enveloping him in a choking, boiling cloud. He struggled to rip himself free. He wasn't going to succumb, *no way*. He couldn't. In the dark turmoil of his thoughts one thing suddenly stood out clear. This was his absolute last chance. Whatever it took, he had to get the treasure. *Whatever it took.*

He stomped on the brakes and the car slewed sideways, coming to a sliding stop at the top of the slipway. He knew what he needed now—something that would ensure he would get the prize. Something very persuasive.

Tires spinning and squealing he muscled the car around and tore back the way he'd come.

⊰⊱

Mrs. Renton took several sips of her tea while she scanned the clue, refreshing her memory. Oh, yes, the man on his way to New Zealand. He lost his wife and child.

She skimmed down to the end. Yes, there was another Bible verse: Romans 8 verse 28. *'And we know that in all things God works for the good of those who love Him, who have been called according to His purpose.'*

In all things. Uncle Kenwyn had emphasized that fact. *In all things God worked for the good of those who loved him.* That certainly applied to—what was his name?— *Perran Trenholm?* He clearly loved God, but what about her? Did she love God? Was it too late, or was it a promise that if she did give her love to him even now, God would still work all things for good—even her past? *That would be amazing!*

She set the letter down and grabbed the ones from the fifth clue. She felt like she was gulping great drafts of living water, but instead of quenching her thirst it was increasing it.

She scanned the sheets and refreshed her memory of the contents. It was the tale of the old village Squire and his confrontation with the wreckers. Then the letter written to his son, urging him to come back and take his rightful place, and the note from Uncle Kenwyn explaining how God understands grief and loss because of the death of His only Son, Jesus. The Bible verse that time was Romans 5:8. *"But God demonstrates His own love for us in this: while we were still sinners, Christ died for us."*

She tried to absorb that for a moment. Jesus had been put to death almost two thousand years ago—she remembered that from Sunday School. So when he died, she herself hadn't committed any sins, obviously. But she *was* going to. *Did God know that back then?* Of course He did. So all her sins were still there in the future, and Jesus died for them. All of them—even the sins of rejecting God and hurting the Penrows. The verse said that was how God demonstrates His love for her. Okay, that was a bit harder to grasp. It sounded good, but she had a hard time applying it to herself. Maybe the next clue would help.

As she pulled out the papers there was a violent gust outside that rattled the windows, and a distant banging like somebody's shutter had come loose. Pickwick glanced up from where he was washing himself on the sofa.

"There, there," she soothed. "It's alright." She thought of the family. *Were they okay out there?* Maybe they would give her a ring on the phone fairly soon—they were really good at solving clues. She still felt guilty for not being up there with

430

them, but she wouldn't deceive herself that she would be of any help. No, with her tiredness and muddle-headedness she would probably slow them down. Besides, she really felt that the process she was undergoing right now was crucial to her understanding of Uncle Kenwyn's purpose, and that the family knew this was what she needed to do. Yes, she somehow felt sure that they would understand.

⛣⛣⛣

"We don't need candles," said Rachel confidently. "We can use the flashlight. It's more mysterious."

"I don't really like mysterious," said Stevie.

Danny silently agreed. Being a detective and strong and courageous was all well and good out in the light, but in a darkened church it was another thing entirely.

"Help me, please Jesus," he whispered.

"Alright," said Mom. "I guess this will have to do. But where do we start?" She waved the flashlight around the nave.

"We were going to look for the *man of mercy* in the clue, right?" said Emily.

"The guy in the Prodigal Son," added Danny. "Maybe the dad?"

"Okay," said Dad, trying to sound upbeat. "Lead the way, dear. The Chapman Family Detective Agency are on the job. As long as they don't kill their shins on a pew."

⛣⛣⛣

Kennedy screeched to a halt in front of the Mole Hole and jumped out leaving the engine running. He yanked open the door, the bell jangling frantically in protest, and sprang into the room. Jennings, still tidying things up in the display case, jumped in surprise at this sudden bestial apparition. Kennedy truly looked like a wild man.

"What...? What...?" Jennings couldn't get the words to come out.

Kennedy didn't care. He knew what he needed. In two strides he was at the display case, knocking Jennings out of the way. Reaching above it he wrenched down the sword, swinging it towards Jennings who ducked instinctively, throwing up his hand to ward off the expected blow.

Kennedy stopped the blade a few inches from Jennings' neck. He glared down at the man cowering beneath him. "You're lucky I don't just finish you off like I've a mind to, but you're not worth the effort. I've got an appointment with that family, and they're the ones who are going to need to look out. I'm going to settle this thing once and for all."

So saying he shoved Jennings to the ground and turned for the door. As he did he spotted the pistol lying there in the window. With a sudden, ruthless determination he grabbed that up too and stuffed it in his pocket. Then snatching open the door he disappeared back out into the storm.

Jennings lay their stunned. *This was worse than he ever could have imagined.* The man was a maniac, and he was going to do someone some serious harm.

431

He had to do something. Should he call the police? He felt a stab of fear. No, he didn't want to go there—he didn't know where that might end up. He didn't need them looking into his association with Kennedy. *So what could he do? Who could he call?*

Something made him look over at the cash register. He had set the business card right on top. He remembered the man's compassionate offer. *Was it sincere?* He surely hoped so.

⤜⧉⤛

Mrs. Renton drained her cup as she examined the next clue. That's right, this one was about the ship captain—the man who had lived a wasted life for so many years, and yet in the end had finished so well. That had really resonated with her. After realizing in many ways she had wasted her own life, she was desperate for some hope, and this story had given her some. The verse Uncle included was part of that. *'Forgetting what is behind and straining toward what is ahead, I press on to take hold of that for which Christ Jesus took hold of me.'* She didn't have to let her past define her. Could that really be true? Would God accept her now and still do something wonderful in her life? How could she do that though? She still didn't understand. Would the last clue help?

She turned to the note from Uncle Kenwyn that they had found in the base of the cross. Another sad story. And yet, and yet... As she thought it over she realized something for the first time. Yes, it was true—all the people in the clues had suffered loss in one way or another, and yet there was still something good that came out of the struggle—some way in which God worked through them for good.

But what about this last man—Cadan Nancarrow? He was martyred for his faith. What good came out of that?

She scanned Uncle Kenwyn's note. What was the verse this time? *'My soul faints with longing for Your salvation, but I have put my hope in Your Word.'* And then there was Uncle's comment right after: *'Will you put your hope in His Word, Ruthie? His Word says that you can find salvation in Christ, freely offered by a loving Father who knows all about suffering. I am praying you will grasp this.'*

Longing and suffering. Oh yes, that summed up her life. Not just her own suffering in losing her parents she now realized, but the suffering she herself had caused in rejecting her uncle and aunt's love. *Had their suffering been even greater than her own?* That was an awful reality to consider.

And her longing for healing from hurt—that things could have been different somehow. That longing had truly characterized her life, but she was only now realizing that her longing had been misplaced. Her real heart longing, down deep where even she hadn't realized it lived, was to be loved and accepted by God— to know that He cared about her and could give her hope.

Hope...that word describing a concept utterly foreign in her life until these past few days. Now it had suddenly risen like a star before her, shining with increasing radiance. She had felt it—those sudden surges of joy that marked its presence.

'*I have put my hope in Your Word.*' Yes, her hope wasn't based on circumstances, but on the truth she was discovering—truth from these verses Uncle Kenwyn had given her. Surely the Bible was true after all.

Suddenly she knew that she wanted this more than anything. She wanted that assurance that she'd go to heaven, that God was her heavenly Father and would help her finish well—to finally start living for Him instead of herself. But how did one do that? Who could help her take that step?

Out of the blue came a picture in her mind's eye—the image of a compassionate face looking directly at her, caring for her, sharing her grief. Mrs. Chapman—in fact, the whole family—yes, they could help her. *Hadn't God sent them to her?* Yes, she was absolutely sure of it. Would they call her soon? She was desperate to settle this as soon as possible.

Her thoughts were interrupted by a terrific crash from just outside the window. Pickwick leaped out of the sofa and shot into the kitchen in a furry blur. Mrs. Renton quickly set the papers aside and struggled to her feet. She went over to the window and lifted aside the sheers. No, with the darkness outside and the reflection from the lamp-lit room it was impossible to see anything.

She quickly donned her coat and cautiously opened the front door. A gust of wind almost yanked it out of her hand as it swept into the room, scattering the papers around her armchair. She took a cautious step outside, shielding her eyes from the stinging rain. Lights were on all over the village even though it was still fairly early, the darkness of the storm casting the whole scene into a surreal light. She could just make out the boats in the harbor being tossed every which way, but what had caused the crash?

She wrestled her way to the front gate. No, she couldn't see anything amiss. *Wait a minute?* What was that over at her neighbor's? The large metal plant stand they had by the wall had blown completely over, the clay pots smashed to pieces and their contents strewn across the paving stones. Her neighbors didn't seem to be home. All their lights were off. Would they be back soon? Should she try to clean up the mess?

Her attention was suddenly grabbed by a vehicle speeding down the lane across the harbor, taking the corner at the memorial at high speed and tearing across the bridge. Even in the dim light she recognized it clearly. There was only one car like that in the village. It was that yellow sports car—the one belonging to that Mr. Kennedy fellow. *Where was he going in such a hurry?*

A feeling of dread came over her. *What if he was heading up to the church?* The family were all up there. Could he have figured out the clue? If he had been the one who had locked them in, it was possible he had overheard something. The children had been rather scared of him. How desperate was he? Would he do something to hurt them? What should she do? Call the police? Yes, that would be best.

She scurried back inside, forced the door shut again and tried the phone. There was no dial tone. The storm of course—the land lines must be down. And she didn't have a cellphone. What else could she do?

Before she knew it she was praying desperately. "God, please help me. Please show me what to do. Please protect the Chapmans. What should I do? What should I do, God? Where can I go for help?"

A thought suddenly came into her mind. That man at the coffee place—Mr. Geoff someone. He would help, she was sure of it. But could she make it down there? The rain, the wind... She gave a shudder. It was a long enough walk on a good day, but today... No, she couldn't even imagine it.

And yet what other choice did she have? She pictured the Chapmans again. They had done so much for her. Couldn't she now do this one thing for them?

"Oh, God, I don't know how I'm going to do this, but please help me do it for the Chapmans."

With a sudden resolve she zipped her coat up to her chin, tied on her rain hood, waved at Pickwick, took one last look around the room, and struggled out into the tempest.

Maggie couldn't understand it. That was the second order Geoff had got wrong and he was usually so careful. She took a quick glance at him as she closed the till. Yes, he definitely looked like he had something on his mind. And his lips were moving like he was muttering something under his breath—or was he praying?

His phone suddenly rang and he snatched it from his apron pocket. "Hello, this is Geoff. Uh-huh...yes, I remember you. Uh-huh...what? No! When? Really? Okay, I'll do it. Right. Okay. Bye."

He turned to Maggie, a look of concern on his face. "That was the chap at the Mole Hole antiques shop. He said that Kennedy fellow—the one the Chapmans thought was trying to get the inheritance from the old lady—he said he was just in his shop, absolutely crazy. Kennedy is obsessed with getting the treasure and he's right now headed up to the church to try and stop the Chapman's from getting it first, and he's armed!"

Maggie couldn't believe what she was hearing. "What do we do?"

"Well, first thing is to call the police, but listen—can you hold the fort again?"

His wife looked quickly around. There were only two people left. She nodded.

"Then I'm going to grab the car and go up there myself. I just feel I need to...I can't explain. Listen, I'll call you as soon as I find out something."

"Okay, sweetheart." She held his face in her hands and gave him a concerned look, then a quick kiss. "I'll be praying."

"That's what we need," said Geoff, snatching the apron off his head. "I'm off. Oh, will you call the police? Explain the situation. Tell them we think the fellow's dangerous."

Maggie nodded again. "Okay, I'll do it. Be careful. I love you!"

"I love you too," called her husband over his shoulder. He waved a hand and was gone.

"Oh, Lord," breathed Maggie, pulling her cell phone out. "Please help!"

"What was that?" said Stevie, his anxious face just visible in the glow from the flashlight. The family were examining the pews one by one, looking for anything that might help them with the clue.

"It was just the front door banging in the wind," said Dad quickly. He was a bit on edge himself.

"Will you go check," said Mom anxiously.

"Er, sure," said Dad a little reluctantly, not relishing the thought at all. He definitely didn't want a confrontation with those guys. *Oh, please don't let there be anyone there,* he prayed. "Can you give me some light?" he added out loud.

Mom directed the flashlight so he could make it out the end of the pew and down the aisle to the foyer. She held it there while he disappeared through the doors. They waited a second. Then a second more. Then he reappeared and gave an enthusiastic thumbs up. They all breathed a sigh of relief.

"Door unlatched," explained Dad hurrying back. "Man, it's wild out there. Where were we?"

"I don't know, maybe we're completely on the wrong track," said Rachel. "I mean with the book thing. How about a picture or something?"

"I don't remember any pictures," said Mom swinging the flashlight around, making shadows dance along the walls. "Wait a minute, though!" She directed the beam up onto the stained glass window above her. "What about the windows? Each one has a different story from the Bible, remember? This one's the Parable of the Lost Sheep. Do you remember seeing the Prodigal Son?"

"Oh, yes," said Rachel eagerly. "Let's go one by one." She grabbed at Mom's arm.

Chattering excitedly in the gloom, the family worked their way from window to window, and as Mom shone the light on the fourth one, they gave a collective gasp.

"That's it," said Emily. "That's the one!"

The flashlight illuminated a beautiful stained glass rendition of the Biblical parable with the prodigal son, dressed in rags, kneeling before his father who was reaching out to him.

"It's the *man of mercy* in the clue," squeaked Emily in excitement. "Look, he's reaching out his hand. Aren't we supposed to follow the way it's pointing?"

"Yes, yes!" said Mom, feeling her stomach jump in excitement. "Let's stand back and look."

They moved back into the pews and Mom traced the flashlight in a line from the man's arm to the direction he was pointing towards.

"It's just the wall," said Danny in disappointment.

"Let's move back some more," suggested Mom. "Maybe we're too close."

They all shuffled backwards and Mom once again found the man's arm and traced it across the wall with the flashlight. Right at the corner of the transept they noticed something this time—a thin shadow that moved back and forth with the moving light.

"What is that thing?" said Dad. "Let's get a closer look."

They hurried over to the spot and Mom held the flashlight up. "It's some sort of iron post or bracket or something." She quickly shone the light back around the walls. Look, there's more of them."

"Maybe they're for holding candles or something," said Rachel.

"Could be," said Dad. "Anyway, this is the one we want! Can you believe it? I think this is the spot!"

"This is so cool," breathed Danny with a rush of excitement. Even Stevie had to agree. He was warming up to this exploration in the dark, especially if it meant finding the treasure!

"What do we do with it?" said Emily. "What did the clue say?"

Dad pulled out the paper and held it up to the light. "*Up, and left, then down and right, the hidden hold revealed,*" he read. "Okay then, let's have a try." He thrust the paper into his pocket and gripped the bar. "Up and left," he repeated, exerting some pressure. For a second it didn't seem like it would move, but then with a dull groan the bar tilted upwards.

"It's moving!" squealed Stevie.

"Yes it is!" said Dad, smiling broadly. "Now left."

Again it took a bit of effort but the bar swung to the left.

"Now down," said Dad. "I feel like I'm driving a stick-shift!"

Mom laughed but the others were too intent on what was going on. The bar swung straight down and then Dad pulled it back towards him. "And right. I wonder if…" He stopped suddenly. They could hear a grinding noise and then a sort of rusty clanking. To their amazement and delight, one of the large stones in the wall nearby ground slowly backwards revealing a dark hole.

"We did it!" shouted Danny, unable to contain himself. "We found the treasure!"

"For which I am heartily grateful," came a sneering voice from the end of the nave.

They gasped in horror. Mom swung the flashlight around, revealing the last person in the world they wanted to see.

Dad's eyes went wide at the sight of the wild figure—crazy hair, rumpled sodden clothes, and a creepy, triumphant expression on his face. *And what on earth was that in his hand?*

"Get behind me everyone," ordered Dad in a quiet voice. "Quickly."

"Yes, listen to your father." Kennedy gave a mocking laugh. He brandished the sword. "If you don't want to get hurt." With his other hand he pulled out a flashlight. He turned it on and shone it in their eyes.

Dad felt a surge of anger rising within him. *How dare this guy threaten them? How dare he…?*

He took half a step forward but felt a gentle hand on his arm. He turned to see the concerned face of his wife. She gave the merest shake of her head. Dad nodded slowly, realizing he needed to calm down and not do anything rash. This guy was clearly unstable. *He was waving a sword, for crying out loud!*

"All of you move back—away from the wall," commanded Kennedy. He walked slowly towards them, holding the sword out in front.

They obeyed, Mom and Dad ushering the kids together until they were all standing by the vestry door. In the glow from Mom's flashlight their faces looked wide-eyed with fear.

"It'll be okay," whispered Dad, fervently hoping it would be. "Pray!"

The kids nodded.

"No talking," yelled Kennedy. "Not a word. Stay exactly where you are and keep your hands where I can see them."

"Listen," said Dad. "Why don't you let us go? At least let my wife and the kids go. They won't do you any harm."

"I said no talking," screamed Kennedy.

Dad nodded, holding up his hands. They should just do what he said. That was advised if you were mugged, wasn't it? *Don't resist—your wallet isn't worth your life.* This inheritance wasn't worth his family's life. *God, please give us wisdom*, he prayed silently. *And send help.*

She couldn't do it. She couldn't go on.

The wind was tremendous, roaring in off the sea, flinging rain at her as she hobbled across the bridge, head down and footsteps faltering. Even worse, her ankle was giving her major problems again. She had slipped coming down the lane from her cottage and had almost fallen, twisting her foot slightly in the process. There was a dull pain at every step.

She gritted her teeth and struggled forward, trying to focus her thoughts. She was so concerned about the family. *What might that man be capable of?* If he was wicked enough to lock them all in and leave them, what else might he be driven to do? *Dear God*, she murmured. *Please help me.*

Her mind suddenly swept back to the words she had read in the Squire's letter. That last verse she had read—she couldn't remember it all but she knew it talked about putting her hope in God's Word. And God's Word, the Bible, said that God loved her, that He was a God of compassion, that He could bring good out of everything. She stopped in surprise at the thought. Could it be God truly was her Heavenly Father and really did love her? Yes, somehow she knew it in her spirit for the first time.

She closed her eyes. "Dear Father. I need you. Show me the way. And please come and help me."

Somehow, in the midst of that raging tempest she was suddenly flooded with peace. She knew her prayer had been heard. She felt herself shaking with joy. "Thank you," she whispered. "Thank you."

She took a deep breath of wonder. It was truly amazing. She actually felt she had new strength to keep going, knowing that God was going with her. Ignoring the pain she bent her head and took a faltering step forward again.

Kennedy sidled over to where the space had opened in the wall, keeping his face towards the family. He set his flashlight down and felt into the hole. A smile of satisfaction crossed his face. Turning slightly he reached all the way in and pulled out a large, heavy, reinforced wooden box, held shut by a metal clasp secured with a huge combination lock. Kennedy set it down on the pew in front of him, picked up the flashlight and shone it at the family so they had to shield their eyes from its glare.

"What do you think of that? I found the treasure before you did. *Finders keepers* I always say." He smiled smugly.

Shining his light down on the box he examined the combination lock. It was of a strange design with six dials set with letters instead of numbers. Kennedy frowned. He hadn't expected this. The box looked really solid and he didn't want to damage whatever was inside by trying to force it open.

He had a sudden thought and swung the light back over at the family. "What's with this lock? It's got letters on it. Where's the combination? Was it in the clue? Tell me!"

Stevie whimpered and Mom pulled him close.

"Listen, Mr. Kennedy. We don't have any idea." Dad tried to sound as conciliatory as possible. "The clue only said how to find the box, not how to open it."

"I don't believe it," said Kennedy. He took a step towards them, holding the sword out threateningly.

Dad had always hoped he'd be able to defend his family in a crisis, but he never thought he'd actually have to do it. What was the best thing to do? Keep calm and pray seemed like a smart choice. He knew his family was praying, and he sent up a quick cry for help again himself. "Mr. Kennedy, you don't need to threaten us." Dad forced a smile, trying to reduce the tension as much as he could. "We're not trying to deceive you. We've just been trying to help Mrs. Renton because she needed it. Can we help you? Are you in trouble?"

A puzzled look crossed Kennedy's face. "What do you care about my trouble? You have no idea. My only trouble is that the Squire stole from me what was rightfully mine, and now I'm taking it back."

"Stole from you? I don't understand." Dad thought it best to keep him talking.

"He gave me the rights to sell off most of his estate, and then suddenly reneged on the deal. I was left holding the bag. He almost ruined me." None of this was strictly true, but Kennedy had said it so many times, he had begun to think it was.

Dad didn't know what to think. "Well, I'm sorry that happened to you."

"Yes, we're sorry," said Emily, hoping to help. The others all nodded as well.

Kennedy wasn't prepared for that. What were these people up to? Were they trying to butter him up? "That's enough," he snarled, waving the sword. "Give me the combination!"

⤙⤚

Mrs. Renton held desperately on to her rain hat, expecting any minute that the wind would whip it away. She battled forward another step but then glanced up in surprise. The headlights of a car had appeared again, swinging around from behind the memorial. It must have been traveling fast for it was only a second or two before it pulled up beside her—one of those tiny microcars with its wipers swooshing frantically. The driver reached over to open the door. She bent down and saw the anxious face of the coffee shop owner, Geoff whatever-his-name-was.

"Mrs. Renton isn't it? You look about all in."

She nodded, not quite believing what she was seeing. It was really him, and he had found her!

Geoff set the hand brake and leapt out of the door, running around to her side. "Let me help you."

As soon as she was safely seated he dashed around again and jumped back in. "Are you okay?" he asked, concerned, wiping the rain out of his eyes. "Where were you headed in this awful weather?"

"To find you!" Mrs. Renton's story gushed out. "The Chapman's need help—up at the church…"

"And that crazy Kennedy chap is up there, too!" finished Geoff. He was about to elaborate when a glare appeared in his rear-view mirror. A police car sped by them, lights whirling furiously.

"Thank heaven," he breathed in relief.

"You called the police?" said Mrs. Renton. "What a miracle!"

Geoff thought of Jennings's frantic confession. "Yes, it was. But look, I was headed up there to help in any way I could. Do you want me to drop you off home?"

"No thank you," said the old lady fervently. "Let's go up there. I need to see this thing through."

Danny had been staring at Kennedy the whole time, almost mesmerized that he, their arch-enemy, was there in front of them, and with a sword no less. He should have been terrified—this was his worst nightmare—and yet he didn't feel as scared as he expected. Instead, for some strange reason he was beginning to feel sorry for the man himself. Maybe this was what it felt like to be strong and courageous!

"We've been praying for you," said Danny suddenly.

"What?" said Kennedy, astounded. He shook his head. "I don't believe it. Look, I don't want to hear any more of this nonsense. Give me the combination."

"We honestly don't have it," said Dad, with a sick feeling. This wasn't getting anywhere.

"And I honestly don't believe you," mocked Kennedy sarcastically. "Look, I'm done playing games." He threw the sword down and pulled the pistol out of his pocket. "Give it to me now."

The family gave a collective gasp. Mom grabbed on to the boys and held them close. The girls clung to each other. Dad raised his hands, trying to keep between Kennedy and the family.

"We'll give you everything we have, Mr. Kennedy. You don't need the gun."

Kennedy pointed the pistol at Dad. "You're right you'll give me everything. Hand it all over."

"Freeze!" The voice was so loud and unexpected that everyone jumped including Kennedy. A flood of light illuminated everything in a blazing, unnatural glare. "This is the police. We've got an AEP pointed at your back. Put the weapon down slowly or we'll fire."

Kennedy froze, then slowly lowered the pistol. There was a rush of feet and he felt strong hands grab his arms and pull them roughly behind him—then the cold metal of handcuffs snapping around his wrists.

The Chapmans had a hard time processing what had happened. The sight of Mr. Kennedy in handcuffs, and two strong, unsmiling police officers holding on to his arms finally convinced them, however. They looked at one another for a second and then rushed to smother each other with hugs. Mum was crying with relief. Emily felt like collapsing from the sudden release of tension. Danny and Stevie thought it was the coolest thing in the world to see an actual police raid first hand. Rachel was overjoyed that she had actually experienced a real-life scary adventure—just like in the storybooks—and everything had turned out okay—just like it did in the books too.

"Thank you, Jesus!" said Mom and Dad at the same time. They laughed. Dad gripped Mom's hand and squeezed it. Mom leaned forward and kissed him tenderly.

One of the police officers came over to the family, and cleared his throat. He gave a slight smile. "Looks like we got here just in time. Are you all alright?"

"I think so," said Dad, looking at the others. Their smiling faces convinced him. He let out a huge sigh. "Yes, we are, thank the Lord, yes we are."

Chapter 27– The Greatest Treasure

Everyone seemed to be talking at once. The kids had never imagined so much excitement. Mom just couldn't stop thanking God. Dad felt like he'd never before experienced such a feeling of relief, such a sudden release of stress. He was doing his best to focus and answer the policemen's seemingly endless questions.

"But how did you know to come here?" said Mom, breaking into the conversation.

"Maggie called them," said a voice from the aisle. "It was quite the turn of events." It was Geoff, hurrying up the aisle, a huge smile on his face. Behind him was someone they knew very well indeed.

"Mrs. Renton!" cried Emily. "You're here!" She rushed over and gave her a huge hug, followed by Rachel and then Mom.

The old lady seemed quite embarrassed at this display of affection, but she beamed around at them all. "I am here, but it looks like I missed the adventure." She turned to Kennedy who was standing with his head hung in despair. "You should be ashamed of yourself, threatening this nice family."

"He'll get what's coming to him," said the policeman, nodding grimly. "You know his pistol wasn't loaded, by the way."

They all absorbed that piece of news. "Well, it was a good thing, but he sure fooled us," said Dad. "He had that sword too. We didn't know what he was going to do."

"Well, we heard the last part of your conversation. It sounded like you were doing the right thing. You can't be too careful with nutters like him."

"Did you actually have a gun on him?" said Dad. "I thought the British police didn't carry guns."

"Some do," said the policeman, "but I was talking about this." He showed them a stocky pistol with a wide barrel. "It fires a big plastic bullet. Non-lethal, but would have put a stop to his shenanigans pretty effectively.

"Wow!" said Danny and Stevie together.

"We're going to get this chap back to the station. Will you come by tomorrow and give a report?"

"We will," Dad promised.

"Thank you," chorused the kids. The policemen gave them a friendly wave and started to pull Kennedy down the aisle.

Danny had a sudden, brave thought. "I'll keep praying for you, Mr. Kennedy," he called after him. "God will help you if you ask him!"

Kennedy threw him a last, puzzled glance as he was led out by the two burly policeman.

Dad gave Danny a squeeze. "You're so good. If you remind us we'll all try to keep praying for Mr. Kennedy. He needs it!"

"I need to go, too," said Geoff with a smile. "Maggie's having to keep things going by herself at the shop. I'm so glad you're all safe."

"Do you have to go?" said Dad. "We'd love to share the end of the quest with you."

Geoff hesitated, but his thoughts were interrupted by a cheery voice from the entryway. "Hello everyone. I came as soon as I could. I closed up early—there wasn't anyone left."

It was Maggie, followed by, of all people, Mr. Tremannon. He gave a slow smile and held up his hand in greeting.

Mrs. Renton gasped. She looked away, unsure of what to do, but Mr. Tremannon strode deliberately over to her. "Ruthie," he said fondly, holding out his hand.

"It's been a long time," said Mrs. Renton shyly shaking it.

"Mr. Tremannon met me down at the corner, soaking wet and wondering if I'd make it" said Maggie with a grin. "He was kind enough to give me a lift."

Mr. Tremannon looked round at everyone, his china-blue eyes shining. "Dinner?"

That wasn't what they were expecting. Dad looked at his watch. "Oh my, it's past dinner time. Mrs. Tremannon must be wondering where on earth we are. Is anyone else famished?"

There were impassioned nods all round. Dad wasn't sure what to do. How could he please poor Mrs. Tremannon, but not abandon the others at this emotional moment? And the treasure had been found too!

Mr. Tremannon solved Dad's dilemma. He beckoned to Mrs. Renton and the Ketchums. "Come."

Geoff and Maggie looked at each other and nodded eagerly in agreement. Mrs. Renton took a second more, but then gratefully accepted the invitation. Surely God would take care of her awkwardness.

Dad was thrilled. *Problem solved.*

"But what about the treasure?" said Rachel in consternation. "Mrs. Renton, we found the secret hiding place! And there was a box inside! We think this is the real inheritance!"

She ran over to the pew and pointed to the box. Mrs. Renton gasped and clasped her hands together. "You found it!"

"It was in that hole in the wall," said Danny, pointing.

"I can't believe that was there this whole time," said Maggie, shaking her head in astonishment. "And me cleaning all around it. The Squire was an amazing man."

Mom suddenly remembered that Mr. Tremannon must be quite shocked by all this. They had done their best to keep this whole thing under wraps. To her surprise, though, he didn't look shocked at all.

"We could bring the box with us and fill you in on all the details," said Dad, still anxious that Mrs. Tremannon was waiting for them.

The others nodded. They could enjoy one of Mrs. Tremannon's incredible meals and then have the excitement of finding out what the treasure was. That sounded good to everyone. Everyone except Stevie, who couldn't believe they weren't going to open the box then and there. He ran his hand over the lid.

Mom guessed what he was thinking. "Mrs. Renton can open it right after dinner, dear."

Stevie frowned, then raised his eyebrows in surprise. He had thought of something. "But how do we open the lock? We don't know the code. Where's the note from the Squire? There's always been one."

Mrs. Renton realized he was right. If this really was the end of the journey, surely there had to be something from the Squire—something to explain the whole quest. She wasn't worried about what he might say anymore, though. After her experience in the storm, she actually felt a rush of excitement, like she was on the verge of something wonderful—something that might seal all that she was beginning to understand. She came over and put her hand on Stevie's shoulder. "I think you must be correct, young man. Would you like to come and see?"

Stevie nodded eagerly. The others gathered round and Dad lifted him up so he could reach the hole. He gingerly put in his hand and felt around, a bit concerned about spiders, but a smile soon spread across his face. "Look, I found it! It was right at the back."

He pulled out a plastic-wrapped package with what looked like some folded papers sealed inside.

"Young man," said Mrs. Renton as Dad lowered the grinning boy to the ground. "You are quite the detective. You all are," she added smiling round at them. "Let's go and eat supper and then we can figure out the end of this adventure."

❧❦❧

It was quite the procession turning into the driveway of the Squire Inn. First came Mr. Tremannon in his rattling old truck, then the Chapman's van, packed with the family and Mrs. Renton talking nineteen to the dozen, and finally the Ketchum's microcar, its wipers frantically trying to keep up with the rain. They parked in a line in the gravel and crowded up to the front door. Mrs. Tremannon must have been watching for them, for she opened the door before Mr. Tremannon could get to it. She didn't seem at all fazed by the crowd in front of her, and dismissed Mom and Dad's apologies with a wave of her hand.

"Oh shush, now, and come in out of the rain. Mr. Tremannon, I've set you out some dry things in the back room. Chipfords, I've set out fresh towels in the bathrooms. Go ahead and get dried off and come down for your supper. I've kept it warming on the hob. It's a simple beef stew but it should warm you up and fill you up at the same time. I'll get some towels for the rest of you, too."

The Chapmans squeezed past her, all except Dad who paused to make the introductions. "Er, Mrs. Tremannon, this is Geoff and Maggie Ketchum—they run the coffee shop in town. They've been, er, helping us." Dad still wasn't sure what he should share about the whole inheritance thing.

The Ketchums shook Mrs. Tremannon's hand. "Mrs. Tremannon," said Geoff with a beaming smile. "It's good to see you. How has your week been going?"

"You know them?" said Dad, surprised.

"Of course," said Mrs. Tremannon. "Why I've known Maggie since she was a little-un. Her Mum used to help on the farm—back when we had the dairy going. And Geoff here—he's no stranger either. You'll stay for supper, won't you? There's plenty enough for the whole village—I used my biggest pot. Big storm, big stew."

Geoff and Maggie laughed. "Thank you, we'd love to. Your husband actually invited us already."

"He did, did he?" Mrs. Tremannon turned her ample bulk and fixed a stare at her husband who looked somewhat sheepish. "Mr. Tremannon, you dropped my shopping off in the kitchen like it was a load of dirt from your tractor, disappeared with barely a word— not that you ever speak more than a word—and then made free with your invitations to supper?"

The others felt a bit uncomfortable for a moment, not sure if she was really upset. Mr. Tremannon solved their dilemma by striding over to his wife and planting a big kiss on her cheek. "Surprise!" he said, his eyes twinkling.

Mrs. Tremannon started giggling, then laughing, her body shaking with mirth. "Oh sorry everyone," she managed to gasp. "It's a standing joke with my husband. He knows I've always said the more the merrier. It's been too long since we've had Geoff and Maggie over, but who's that still outside?"

Mrs. Renton had purposefully hung back in the entryway. She was feeling very nervous. Mr. Tremannon was one thing, but how would Mrs. Tremannon treat her—after so many years without any contact, and then her basically hiding out in the village and avoiding them both. They knew her history with the Penrows, and how she had abandoned them. What must Mrs. Tremannon think of her?

Mrs. Tremannon was having none of that though. She scurried through the door, grabbed Mrs. Renton's hand and pulled her inside. Then she enveloped her in a massive hug. "Little Ruthie, oh my, I can't believe it! After all these years. Why you look almost as old as me!"

Mrs. Renton started laughing, and it felt so good to release all that tension. Then she started crying, and Mrs. Tremannon held on to her, patting her back. "There now, ducky, let go of the past. You're here now." She stepped back, grabbing both her hands. "You go get washed up and come and eat with us. We'll join you too. This is a special occasion and we want to hear all about your exciting adventure."

"My adventure?" said Mrs. Renton, wondering how much Mrs. Tremannon actually knew. "You mean up at the church?"

"Up at the church, hither and yon, following clues all over creation. Oh yes," she added, looking at their shocked faces. "I know about the inheritance mystery. Go get washed up and we'll talk all about it."

✥✥

"This isn't just a stew, Mrs. Tremannon. This is the pinnacle of culinary perfection." Dad shook his head in disbelief. "And you said it wasn't much! Mushrooms, carrots, parsnips, potatoes…you've got everything in here. I think the Queen herself would fire her chefs and hire you on the spot!"

There were confirming exclamations all around. Mrs. Tremannon blushed— for once speechless.

"But what I don't understand is you said you knew all about the inheritance," said Mom, leaning forward. "What did you know?"

Mrs. Tremannon put down her fork. "Well, dear, it's really quite simple. You see, the Squire had planned all this out knowing that he wouldn't always be able to make sure all the clues stayed in place, so he took us into his confidence. When he got sick he arranged for us to move here to the inn so we could keep an eye on the things. He owned the house on the cliff, and the Lonsdale house, so those were fairly easy. Mr. Tremannon made sure everything stayed accessible. If I remember rightly, there was the flag on the quay and some others things that he had to make sure stayed where they needed to be."

"Roight", nodded her husband, listening intently from the head of the table.

"Aha. We did wonder about that," said Dad. "This all makes a lot more sense now."

"And the key to the case with the birds," Emily suddenly remembered. She gestured to the corner of the room. "It wasn't there and then it suddenly showed up. Was that you?"

"Roight," nodded Mr. Tremannon again with a smile.

"So you see," his wife went on, "we were a bit puzzled at first, but then figured out you were helping Ruthie, so we thought we'd better help you too. Mr. Tremannon tried to get in the way of Mr. Kennedy, once we learned he was trying to steal the inheritance. I helped by trying to keep you well fed!"

"Well, you both did wonderfully well," said Mom.

"What an incredible tale," said Geoff, shaking his head in amazement.

"I don't know how I can thank you," said Mrs. Renton. She felt like she was literally in a dream. This feeling of love and acceptance from those around her almost took her breath away. All that she had been dreading had dissolved to nothing, left by a genuine, pure sense of peace.

Mrs. Tremannon patted the lady's hand. "You don't have to. It's been what we've wanted to see, ever since you had such a hard time as a youngster. I was twenty-five when you came to stay with the Squire and Mrs. Penrow. I can remember it plain as day. Mr. Tremannon was just my sweetheart back then…"

She paused and smiled at her husband who winked back. The kids thought that was really cute.

"And," she went on, "the two of us were broken-hearted when everything seemed to fall apart. We've waited a long time to see you come back. But now, speaking of keeping you well fed, if you're finished with the stew I have a little something warming in the oven. Do you have room for a bit of apple crumble and custard? Or cream? Whichever you like, or have it with both."

"It sounds marvelous, but I think we might need to go on another adventure to lose the extra pounds," said Dad, patting his stomach.

"But what about the box!" said Stevie, unable to keep quiet any longer. Dinner had been great and all, but it was agony having to wait to open the treasure box. It was worse than waiting for his parents to wake up on Christmas morning.

"It can wait a few more minutes, Stevie," said Mom, frowning a little.

"I tell you what, young man," said Mrs. Renton, coming to his rescue. "I could not possibly eat another bite, so why don't I read the last letter while you all eat dessert?"

That sounded great to everyone. With Mom's gentle prodding the kids all quickly helped clear the table while Mrs. Tremannon retrieved the crumble. Then, when they were all comfortably seated again and oohing and aahing in appreciation of the dessert, Mrs. Renton unwrapped the papers and started reading the one that said 'Open me first.'

"*My dearest Ruthie, I am writing this in full confidence that you will get this far. I feel sure that God will answer my prayers and protect all the clues, using each one to better explain what is on my heart. I love you so much, Ruthie. Even though we never had the opportunity to really adopt you, we've always considered you to be part of our family.*" Mrs. Renton stopped and nodded, her eyes misting over. She dabbed them with her hanky and read on. "*But before I go any further, you must be wondering how to open the box.*"

"Yes," shouted Stevie, jumping up. Everyone laughed and he flopped down again, turning bright red.

"We'll find out, young man," assured Mrs. Renton. "Here we go…" She continued reading. "*A family tree upon a wall, five names are there that you'll recall.*

Each name will help you set a wheel, but one remains beneath the seal.

This name must take its rightful place, its heritage to now embrace.'

That's it—that's all he wrote."

"I thought there weren't any more clues!" exclaimed Rachel. "We have to find a family tree now?"

Everyone looked puzzled—except the Tremannons, and Danny who looked strangely smug.

"Alright Tiger," said Dad, noticing his son's face. "What do you know that we don't?"

Danny grinned. "Look behind you, Daddy. Do you remember?"

They all turned. "The family tree!" gasped Mrs. Renton. "Oh, my! Well, that was easy after all."

Mr. Tremannon got up and walked over to the wall. He lifted off the picture and held it up.

"Let's clear a spot," said Mrs. Tremannon. They all helped and Mr. Tremannon set the picture down in front of Mrs. Renton.

"Well, thank you," said Mrs. Renton. "So what are the names we're supposed to find?"

"I've no idea. The clue says that we'll recall them," said Mom. "Do you see any you recognize?" The others moved to where they could see the picture and studied it closely.

"I do," said Danny. "Look, William Lonsdale. He was the guy with the ship."

"That's right," said Dad. "So these must be the people in the clues!"

"There's Merwyn Trevithick," said Emily, pointing. "He was in a clue. Who was he again?"

"The other Squire," said Mrs. Renton. "He was the one who fought the wreckers. There were five people in the clues; we need three more."

This was exciting. The others eagerly scanned the names on the little cards. "There's Jowan and Elaine Penrow, near the bottom," said Mom in triumph. "That's the Squire's parents."

"And the Squire too," said Emily. "Right below. Kenwyn Penrow—but he doesn't really count because he wasn't one of the clue guys."

"There's the last guy—the one we just found," said Rachel, pointing up towards the top of the picture. "Look, Cadan Nancarrow."

"I'm having trouble remembering the other one," said Dad. The others nodded.

"I think I know it," said Mrs. Renton, looking up. "I went over all the clues this afternoon. It was quite the experience. It was…well, I'll tell you about it in a minute." She studied the picture for a moment, then reached over and indicated a name on the tree. "There's the last one. Perran Trenholm—the man who went to New Zealand."

"That's it then," said Dad, sitting back in satisfaction. "What are you supposed to do? Use the first letter of their last names?"

"That's an idea," said Mrs. Renton. She reached for the box, Stevie holding his breath in anticipation, but then she stopped suddenly. "Oh, my goodness!"

"What?" said Mom. "What's the matter?"

"I can't believe I only just realized. Those names are all on the Penrow's family tree. That means all the people in the clues were relatives of Uncle Kenwyn and Auntie Rosie!"

They looked at each other in astonishment. *Why hadn't they thought of that?* They would have to let that sink in for a minute.

"No wonder the Squire wrote about them. They weren't random people—they were his family," said Mom.

"I knew he loved history," said Mrs. Renton, shaking her head in wonder. "He must have found all this out as he researched his family tree." She suddenly noticed Stevie hovering at her elbow and turned to him with a smile. "I know, Master Stevie—you are wondering why we can't open the box!"

Stevie looked embarrassed, but glad at the same time. "Well, I wondered if…like, yes!"

"Very well. Why not?" The old lady pulled the box towards her with some difficulty. "My, it's heavy. Okay, let's try the combination. First would be…what?"

"Try a 'P' for Penrow," suggested Dad. "He was first. Is there a 'P' on the first dial?"

Mrs. Renton turned it all the way around. "No, there isn't. There are only about ten different letters."

"How about an 'N' then?" said Mom. "'Nancarrow is the last guy's name. Perhaps it starts at the oldest and goes the other way."

"There is an 'N'," said Mrs. Renton. She turned the dial to the correct spot. "What's next then?"

"'L' I think," said Emily. "For Lonsdale."

"Then 'T' for Trevithick, and another 'T' for Trenholm," said Rachel, watching closely as Mrs. Renton set the dials. "And 'P' for Penrow."

"Hmm," frowned the old lady, "there's one dial left. There's six of them and only five names."

"What did the clue say again?" said Emily, peering at the note. "*One remains beneath the seal.*"

"Oh, no," said Stevie in agony. "Do we have to go find a seal in the harbor or something?"

Everyone roared with laughter. "No, no," smiled Dad. "There's more than one type of seal. I think we're looking for some sealing wax—the kind of stuff used to close an official document."

"And here it is," announced Mrs. Renton. "It was in the package." She held up a piece of paper, carefully folded into a square with a red seal holding it closed. She peeled it open and gasped, her eyes filling with tears again. Nestled within was a small rectangular card—an exact match of the ones on the family tree. Neatly written across its face was the name *Ruth Anne Renton*. She read aloud the words written on the inside of the paper. "*Put this in its rightful place on the family tree.*"

With trembling hands she placed it in the little slot provided for it on the family tree, just below the names Kenwyn and Rose Penrow. There was loud cheering, Mr. and Mrs. Tremannon clapping with delight.

"There now," said Mrs. Tremannon. "That look's so right. The family tree's complete now. The Squire and Rosie wanted so much for you to be a member of the family; in fact, they always considered you one, always talked of you as 'their little girl' even when…" The old lady stopped, looked stricken and put her hand over her mouth.

"Even when I went away and left them," finished Mrs. Renton through her tears, amazed at this further proof of their love. "It's alright. I have no doubt of how much they cared for me."

"But you can see," said Mrs. Tremannon, recovering her composure, "that they wanted you to know that they always held that love for you. That's why the Squire came up with this entire quest thing. He knew you would need to be convinced of their love and, even more, of God's love." She gestured at the box. "Go ahead and open it—you know the last letter now."

Mrs. Renton nodded and adjusted the last dial to the 'R' for Renton. There was a little click, clearly heard as everyone held their breaths, Stevie's eyes as big as frying pans. The old lady slowly lifted the lid, enjoying the drama of it all. Ten heads craned to see the contents. She lifted a large package out, wrapped in blue plastic, with a smaller one underneath.

Stevie frowned in disappointment. Where were the jewels? Where were the coins?

Danny shared his concerns exactly. This didn't look like a pirate treasure or anything. Besides, pirates didn't wrap their treasure, did they?

"This one says to open first," said Mrs. Renton, examining the smaller package. "I wonder what it can be?" She carefully unwrapped it and gave a cry of delight. "I don't believe it! I don't believe it!"

"What is it?" asked several voices at once.

Mrs. Renton held up an old, black, gilt-edged Bible. "It's my Bible! The one I got from the Penrows for my birthday. Do you remember? I told you I thought I lost it forever after I ran away from them. They must have kept it all these years! I can't believe it. This just keeps getting more and more surprising!"

"There's a note in it," pointed out Mom. "Is it from the Squire?"

The old lady pulled out a folded sheet of notepaper and spread it open to read. *"Dearest Ruthie, Were you surprised? We've kept this for you, hoping and praying that one day you would want it. Truly, it contains riches beyond price. In it is found the wonderful message of grace that God gave to mankind—His gift of the Lord Jesus Christ 'in whom are found all the treasures of wisdom and knowledge,' and in it are found God's wonderful precepts that show us how to live in gratitude for all He's done. 'They are more precious than gold, than much pure gold.' Read it, Ruthie. Drink it in. It is water to a thirsty soul. I pray you will find Him in its pages."*

Mrs. Renton didn't know what to think. This wasn't exactly what she was expecting. And yet, if she really considered what she most needed in the world, it wasn't riches, or homes, or jewels, or money. It was assurance—assurance that she was loved, that God had forgiven her, and that she had a future of hope. Yes, this was by far a greater treasure. She saw it all clearly now. Hadn't the verses in the clues seemed written just for her? With her recent revelations and this message from the Squire, she felt like she was on the edge of something marvelous.

Stevie and Danny were shocked though. *Mrs. Renton's old Bible? That was the inheritance?* The Bible was great and all, but it seemed like a lot of work—and expectation—for something so simple.

Dad must have been reading their thoughts. "You know boys, when you think about it, the Bible is worth more than all earthly riches."

Mom nodded vigorously. Wasn't this exactly what she had hoped the family would learn?

The girls still had to let it sink in, however. They had truly been expecting something very different.

Mrs. Renton snapped back to reality and smiled at the children. "Well, youngsters, perhaps I should open the other package. This one says 'open very carefully.' What more could there be though?"

Once again everyone held their breath. With great care Mrs. Renton unwrapped the second package. It was another book, much larger and much older, with a beautifully decorated leather cover with metal clasps. A piece of paper with a lengthy note was laid on top and the old lady picked it up to read.

"Hello again, dear Ruthie. This is it—my final note. I hope it will answer all your questions."

Mrs. Renton looked quizzically round at the others. They were all watching her. Mom and Dad were praying hard.

The old lady turned back to the note. *"I never gave you the rest of the story about my ancestor, Cadan Nancarrow. I found reference to him in some old documents I unearthed when I was renovating the chapel. They referred to Penrithen's history and its status as home for a group of Lollards—followers of John Wycliffe. If you remember your English history, Wycliffe translated the Bible from Latin into English. He wanted everyone to be able to read the Scriptures – not just the clergy. Of course back in the late 1300s there were no printing presses so books were hand copied. The church declared that it was illegal to translate the Bible, however, or read any Bible other than the Latin Vulgate version. The religious leaders were threatened by what Wycliffe had done. If the common people could read the Scriptures for themselves, they would figure out that the leaders were not living the life Christ would have wanted them to live. The Lollards secretly carried copies of the Bible to share with those who were hungry for the truth. The church tried to unmask them and make sure they would no longer spread what they considered heresies. Cadan Nancarrow was born here in Penrithen, but his parents died at an early age. Incidentally, it was that fact that made me think of you and inspired me to come up with this quest. Nancarrow was adopted by the blacksmith and his wife who were secret followers of Wycliffe. He grew up hearing the scriptures read in English and they transformed his life. As an adult he decided he wanted to share that treasure with others. He was entrusted with a copy of the Bible, but he was discovered, denounced and then went through the mockery of a trial. He was burned at the stake on July 30th, 1515, praising Jesus, according to eyewitnesses, until he succumbed to the flames."*

Mrs. Renton looked up for a moment. Every eye was fixed on her. You could have heard a pin drop. She swallowed hard and continued on. *"Normally, another of the group would have taken the Bible and continued the mission, but Nancarrow's arrest sparked an intense outbreak of persecution. Every member of the Lollards in the area were captured and executed. Somehow Nancarrow must have sensed the danger ahead of time—or rather God's Spirit must have warned him—for he was able to hide the copy in the hidden vault at the chapel. In my research I found several vague clues which narrowed down the location, but in the end I stumbled on the hiding place almost by accident—though there are no accidents in God's kingdom purposes of course. I couldn't believe the treasure I had found. Yes, an original Wycliffite Bible might be valued at well over a million pounds…"*

Here there was a gasp from several of the listeners. Mrs. Renton shook her head at the wonder of it all and kept reading. *"But what it represents is worth so much more. Do you understand, Ruthie? Cadan Nancarrow considered this book to be worth more than life itself, as did all my godly relations who suffered much to see the treasure of its message brought to others. Through the ages my family have valued it above all things, and that is the heritage I pass on to you. I was not able to adopt you, but that does not mean I can't treat you as my own child. Even more than that, God's precious Word says that those who believe that Jesus died for them and rose again, and who repent of their sins and receive the gift of Jesus as their Saviour and Lord, to them God will grant adoption into His family, forever and ever, inheriting all spiritual blessings in Christ. He invites you into a relationship with Him, 'an inheritance that can never perish, spoil or fade, kept in heaven for you.' This inheritance is, indeed, THE greatest treasure: to be adopted into God's family. It's what you've been truly longing for all your life. God's Word says 'Yet to all who received Him, to those who believed in His name He gave the right to become children of God.' Will you receive the gift? He offers it freely, arms outstretched to you."*

The old lady's voice had been faltering and it finally gave out altogether. She sat there, staring at the words the Squire had written. She felt naked and exposed, seeing herself and her rebellion against God completely for the first time. But incredibly, along with that understanding of her guilt, was a sudden surge of hope and joy greater than any she had ever experienced before. She finally knew—she knew it without a shadow of a doubt. God did love her and accept her—even in her messed up state. He wanted a relationship with her—for her to truly be His child. She finally understood what she had to do.

She looked around at the others with tear-stained eyes. "I need to do something." Her voice cracked. Mom quickly poured her some water and she gulped it down. It took her a moment to master her emotions. "I need to do something I should have done a long time ago. I need to pray. Will you stay here with me while I do? It seems so right that you're here with me. You, too," she added, looking at Geoff and Maggie. They nodded seriously.

"Alright. I'm going to do it." She took a deep breath and closed her eyes. "Dear God. It's me, Ruth. Little Ruthie, who ran away from you so long ago. I don't understand why my parents had to die, but I understand now that you didn't abandon me then." She paused and gulped back some tears. "You sent me another couple to love me and take care of me. I'm so sorry for rejecting that gift, and the gift of Jesus that you gave to me. I'm sorry for all my years of anger and rebellion—all my sins. Thank you so much for giving Uncle Kenwyn the idea to put together this quest. It truly did lead me to you. I believe you sent Jesus to die for me. I accept that gift. Please make me your child. I want to follow you the rest of my life. I want to finish well like those who went before me. Thank you, dear God. Er…Amen."

She looked up with shining eyes. There was a moment's pause and then suddenly everyone was surrounding her, crying, laughing, hugging her, kissing her on the cheek. The kids jumped for joy, even Stevie, who had finally figured out that this was more important even than bags of treasure. Mom and Dad hugged each other, too joyful to speak. Even Mr. Tremannon looked like he was misty eyed. As for Mrs. Tremannon, she unashamedly wept for joy.

Finally everyone quietened down again. Mrs. Renton held up her hand and they all fell silent. "Thank you—all of you. I can't express my gratitude enough. I wish there was a way to truly show you how much you mean to me."

"You already have," assured Dad.

"But I took up all your holiday."

Dad looked around at the rest of the family and they all nodded, smiling, guessing what he was going to say. "You know," he said smiling broadly himself. "I can't think of a better way to spend a holiday."

"And I know why the Bible is a better gift than treasure and gold," announced Danny to all their surprise.

"Why, sweetheart?" said Mom, feeling a thrill of joy.

"Because it lasts forever."

"You are so right," said Mom. "And it changes lives."

"Amen to that," said Geoff. "We've seen that today." Mrs. Renton nodded vigorously.

"And so I want to do something," said Danny, suddenly serious.

"What Tiger?" said Dad, wondering what it could possibly be.

"I want to send Mr. Kennedy my Bible. I think he needs it."

"What a fantastic idea," said Mom, delighted. "We'll make sure it happens."

"But can I have another one? I want to finish reading about Joshua."

"You sure can," said Dad, ruffling the boy's hair.

"And what about the Mole Hole man?" wondered Stevie.

"Don't worry about him," said Geoff, smiling. "I think his heart is softening. I'll deal with him."

"Wow," said Dad, shaking his head in wonder. "So many good things happening at once."

"Speaking of good things, there's more to the Squire's note," said Mrs. Tremannon, smiling. "You haven't finished it yet."

"So there is," said Mrs. Renton. "What else could there be? I can't imagine anything better than what I've already received. Well, let's see." She found the place and continued. "*Well now, Ruthie, I've explained to you what the greatest treasure is—the wonderful inheritance God has given to us. There are some earthly details to share as well, however. As my sole inheritor there are some things you should know. My hope for the Wycliffe Bible is that you might find a place where many others can benefit from it. I would like you to choose a Christian charity to which you can donate it who would make it accessible to others. I only ask that it is displayed with a note explaining how through its message anyone can partake of the greatest treasure—a relationship with God Himself. I have also left money in a fund for you to administer here in the village—to help those in need. There is a special fund for the repair and upkeep of St. Piran's. My heart is that it would be used as a place of worship once again.*"

Maggie clapped her hands with joy. Geoff gave a whoop of delight and planted a kiss on her cheek.

"*You have also inherited what is left of my family's estate. This includes Chynalls—the house on the cliff that you know so well and the Lonsdale house that you also know. I put those in your name a number of years ago, as I believed that would help you with regards to the taxes. I have put aside money for you to help with that as well. Present this letter to the lawyers and they will explain it all. As to our old family home, the manor house, I already gave it to the*

Tremannon's to whom I also gave a charge to protect the clues until you came to reclaim your inheritance."

The old couple smiled and looked at each other knowingly.

"In the attic of the Lonsdale house are stored carefully away, many precious antiques. You may do with them what you will, though I trust you will seek to bless others as you yourself have been blessed."

Mrs. Renton nodded fervently. Her heart was so full, she felt it would burst.

"So my dearest Ruthie, it is with all my love and fervent prayers that this inheritance will both provide for your earthly needs, and more importantly for your heavenly ones. You are and always will be, my precious little Ruthie. With Christ's love, Your Uncle Kenwyn."

The old lady set the letter down and looked up at the others.

"Truly," she finally managed to say, "I can't imagine a more wonderful ending to this adventure." She looked at the children, paused for a moment, and then gave a coquettish smile. "But there is one last thing that would make it perfect. How long do you have left in your holiday, children?"

"Only four days," said Emily, suddenly realizing that this happy time was soon coming to an end. She thought of what was ahead and a little knot of dread formed in her stomach.

"Only four days and then you have to leave Penrithen?"

They nodded, glumly. Did they really have to think about that now?

"But why do you have to leave?"

"Well," broke in Dad. "Much as we love staying at the Inn, we can't stay forever. You know…"

"But what if you had another place to stay?" smiled the old lady.

"I'm not sure what you mean," said Mom.

"Well, I've just found out that I have inherited a wonderful place to stay. I'm quite comfortable in my cottage, but there's a lovely house at the top of a secret stairway—a house with a dramatic view of the sea from its tower." She paused, her eyes twinkled and she gave a mischievous smile. "A house—that really needs an adventurous family to live in it."

The children gasped and looked at their parents. Hope and longing rose so suddenly in Rachel's throat that it almost choked her. Mom and Dad were speechless. They looked at Mrs. Renton.

"There wouldn't be a charge, of course. It would be lovely knowing there was someone there to help me go through all those antiques in the attic, if that sounds like fun."

The girls squealed and the boys ran over and tugged at their parent's sleeves. "Can we? Oh, please can we? Instead of going to Birmingham—until we go back to Oregon in November."

"May we?" said Dad, grinning. "Well, if Mrs. Renton insists."

"I do insist," said the old lady firmly.

"And we can come and visit you and Pickwick and Sweedlepipe," said Emily.

"And we can really explore the village, and go to the cove whenever we like," gushed Rachel. "And go to that cool bookstore with the cats."

"If we can find it again," chuckled Dad.

"And do our home schooling in the sun room," cried Emily with joy, "rain or shine."

"And watch for pirate ships from the tower," said Danny.

"And look for secret passages," added Rachel, wiggling her eyebrows.

. "And...other really cool stuff," finished Stevie, realizing all the best ideas had already been taken.

"And you can come join our house church...if you like," broke in Geoff. "We meet in the coffee shop every Sunday."

"What a wonderful place to meet!" said Dad. Mom nudged him, laughing.

"And you can come too," Maggie said, putting her hand on Mrs. Renton's shoulder. "We'd love it."

"Of course I'll come," said Mrs. Renton.

"We're a smallish group, but we're growing," said Geoff. "The Tremannons come, of course, and a couple of other people you might know—Flo and her husband Harry from the bakery...they often bring treats to share."

"Oh, my," said Dad.

"And Mr. Peterson from the grocers!" finished Geoff with a grin.

"Aha," said Dad.

"He's so nice when you get to know him," Maggie said with a laugh.

"Well, that sounds wonderful," said Dad, slightly overwhelmed. "We'd love to..." He stopped short.

"What?" said Mom.

"Oh, my goodness! I've suddenly had the most wonderful, amazing thought," said Dad, slapping the table. "I can't believe it!"

"What, what?" said Emily.

"This quest! The Squire's relatives...the persecutions...the victories...how it all fits together. I have something to write my articles about! It's just what I needed!" He started dancing round the room, to everyone's rich amusement.

Mom just looked heavenward, her eyes moistening. She smiled a knowing smile. What an incredible abundance of treasures to record in her journal. "Thank you, Father," she whispered. "Thank you. For doing more than we could ask or imagine."

Made in the USA
Las Vegas, NV
15 May 2021